Praise for M
an
EMPIRE'
se.

M000113427

"With energetic prose, lavish attention to detail and a fantasy world that feels both familiar and foreign, *the Empire's Legacy* series is as impressive as it is triumphant. Not only did it captivate me from the very first sentences, but it also continued to enchant until the very last full stop."

Mary Anne Yarde, author of *The Dulac Chronicles*

"...this whole series has been one of the best I've experienced."

Cover to Cover Book Reviews

"...a series that sucked me in from the start."

Karen Heenan, author of *Songbird*

EMPIRE'S DAUGHTER

"...easily one of the most intriguing books I've read all year..."

Writerlea Book Reviews

"*Empire's Daughter* is a story that enriches the imagination. A compelling tale of survival and strength in unity."

Avril Borthiry, author of *Triskelion*

"...expertly builds an entire world and an entire society..."

Bjørn Larssen, author of *Storytellers*

"Within the first few pages, I realized I'd stumbled upon a truly special story; for Thorpe has created an alternative world that bends gender and sexual norms in brilliant form."

Two Doctors Media Collaborative

EMPIRE'S HOSTAGE

"A bold vision of historical fantasy written beautifully from start to finish; *Empire's Hostage* takes us on an epic journey that is at once intriguing, convincing, and deeply affecting."

Jonathan Ballagh, author of *The Quantum Door*

"*Empire's Hostage* is as immersive as Marian L Thorpe's first book *Empire's Daughter*. Filled with beautiful imagery and well-developed, realistic characters, *Empire's Hostage* surpassed my expectations. "

D.M. Wiltshire, author of the *Prophecy Six* series

"With its multidimensional protagonist and its vivid rendering of her world, Empire's Hostage elevates the genre."

Maria Luisa Lang, author of *The Pharaoh's Cat*

EMPIRE'S EXILE

"*Empire's Exile* should put Thorpe on the map of must-read authors of historical fantasy."

Amazon review

†††††

Visit my website:
marianlthorpe.com
find me on Facebook
https://www.facebook.com/marianthorpe/
Twitter
@marianlthorpe

Marian L Thorpe lives in a small city in Canada with her husband and a varying number of cats.

EMPIRE'S
LEGACY

Marian L Thorpe

Arboretum Press

Empire's Daughter

The swallows gather, summer passes,
The grapes hang dark and sweet;
Heavy are the vines,
Heavy is my heart,
Endless is the road beneath my feet.

The sun is setting, the moon is rising,
The night is long and sweet;
I am gone at dawn.
I am gone at day,
Endless is the road beneath my feet.

The cold is deeper, the winters longer,
Summer is short but sweet;
I will remember,
I'll not forget you,
Endless is the road beneath my feet.

Tice's song

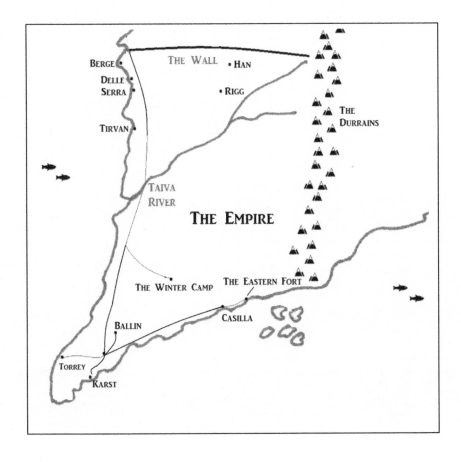

PART I

CHAPTER ONE

I WAS SEVENTEEN THE SPRING CASYN CAME TO TIRVAN. He rode quietly into the village late one morning, a few weeks after Festival, with his tools and a few personal possessions. I—along with my cousin and partner, Maya, and her young brother, Pel—had sailed out in the still dawn that morning to check crab traps around the south side of the rocky headland. In the warmth of the spring sun, we hauled traps, took the catch, and reset the lines.

At my insistence, we sailed a bit further along the headland, into coves we hadn't fished before, setting a few traps to see what these waters might yield. The late sun shone on a golden ocean before we moored back at the harbour, tired but with work still to do. My aunt Tali had come down to the harbour to collect fresh crab for supper. She helped us unload the catch, sort the damaged traps onto the jetty, and sluice down the deck of *Dovekie* before she mentioned the arrival.

"There'll be a meeting tonight, Lena," she said, sorting through the catch for the largest crabs.

I looked up from the trap I was examining. "A meeting? All of us?" I frowned. Only a major event would justify a full meeting outside of the usual schedule. If something minor but urgent needed attention, the council leaders—my mother, our Aunt Sara, and Gille the herdswoman—met to mediate or decide.

"What's happened?" Maya asked.

Tali stood, her basket full of crabs. "Take this, Pel, and go home. I'll be there soon." Pel, tall and strong for his six years, took the heavy basket and started up the hill to the village. Women's business held no interest for him. Tali watched him for a minute before turning back to us.

"What's happened?" Maya repeated.

"We have a prospective tenant for the forge," Tali said.

I looked at her in puzzlement. This was expected. After burying Xani, our metalworker, in the cold of last midwinter, we had heard of a young smith looking for work at Delle village, several day's ride to the north. She had just finished her apprenticeship and their forge had no place for her. We had sent a message north in the saddlebags of a returning soldier; her arrival was expected any day.

"Of course," said Maya. "What's her name?"

"Is there a problem?" I asked.

Tali grinned, her teeth white against her tanned face. "Oh, there's a problem," she said. "Our prospective new metalworker is neither from Delle, nor newly-qualified. As a guess, I'd say our new smith brings thirty years of experience—military experience. And his name is Casyn."

I stared at my aunt, my hands tightening on the crab trap. Maya gasped. All men left the villages at seven to enter the Empire's military schools, spending their adult years serving in the army. In retirement, they raised horses or grew grapes or taught in the schools, finishing out their days with whatever part of their regiment had survived. Twice a year, war and distance allowing, they came to the villages for Festival, to be provisioned, to gather food and cloth and wine, to make love and father children, to give and carry messages. Festival lasted a week, and then they left. This pattern had shaped our lives for generations. I shook my head. "But he can't."

Tali shrugged her narrow shoulders. "That's to be decided at meeting. He was born here: he's Xani's son, actually, so that may give him double claim." She bent to pick up a broken crab trap. "Are these to go to Siane? Let's get the catch into the holding pools and take these up. If we stand here talking much longer, you won't have time to clean up or eat properly before meeting, and I want to get those crabs into boiling water." We finished our work quickly, and together walked up the short hill to the village, leaving the broken traps stacked outside Siane's workshop. The traps carried *Dovekie*'s mark. Siane would notify us when she finished the repairs.

We walked in silence, tired from our long day on the water. At Tali's house, where Maya and I shared the big front room upstairs, we stopped on the porch. Maya leaned into me, her slight form light against mine. Her head just reached my shoulder. I gave my partner a brief hug. "I'll see you at the baths in half an hour," I told her. "I'm going to see my mother for a few minutes."

"Don't let her feed you," Tali said. "In fact, tell her to come here to eat. We'll have more than enough crab chowder."

I turned to go.

"Lena?" Tali called after me. "If Gwen has some extra bread, we could use that at supper."

I nodded. The smell of freshly baked bread always fills my mother's house, except during the twice-yearly periods when the offspring of Festival liaisons are born. My mother is the village midwife.

I stepped off the porch onto the path before I realized my hands were empty. "Maya!" I called. The shutters to our room opened. She leaned out. "Bring my towel and clothes, will you?"

She laughed. "Maybe."

I chuckled, continuing on. I probably hadn't needed to ask. As I walked up the path to my mother's house, I remembered her teaching me how to bake bread when I was eight or nine. I had kneaded the dough with all the strength in my young arms, while Maya, learning with me, did the measuring and supervised the baking. She liked order, even then, never forgetting a step.

The smell of crab rose off my hands and clothes. Daughters sometimes followed their mother's craft, or an aunt's, but just as often they chose to apprentice outside the immediate family. My choice at twelve to go to the boats had met with no argument: I belonged in the open air. When Maya had announced six months earlier that she wanted to fish as well, I hadn't been surprised. For six years, we'd done just about everything together. Breaking with usual practice, the council had let her wait so we could begin our apprenticeships together.

We'd served our five years, and this spring, we'd outfitted *Dovekie* and passed from apprentices into craftswomen. Fully adult now, part of the village council, we addressed all women as equals, could form Festival alliances and bear children, or just slip *Dovekie's* moorings some morning to sail away into adventure. All this could happen in the secure village world we had grown up in and had taken for granted would continue forever. Tali's news had shaken the foundations of my assumptions. Adult or not, I wanted my mother's counsel.

My mother's house stands in the centre of Tirvan village. Like most village houses, it's built of wood, two storeys high, with gabled ends. Salt air is hard on paint, so the wood of the house has weathered to a soft silvery-grey, matching the shingles of the roof. The shutters are painted blue, as is the front door, which stood open to admit the cooling breezes of late afternoon. My sister Kira, three years my junior and apprenticed to my mother, sat outside in deep conversation with a young woman. They looked up as I approached.

"Lena, you stink of crab." Kira looks like my mother, compact and curved, and likes to wear her hair up. With my darker hair and eyes and long limbs, I take after my father. Or so I'm told. His name is Galen. He serves on the northern Wall. I've never met him.

"I know. I'm on my way to the baths." I looked at the other woman. "Hello, Cate." Six months older than I, trained as a weaver by my aunt Sara, Cate had helped make *Dovekie's* sail. Festival had concluded six weeks ago, so I suspected that she had come to confirm pregnancy. But that was for her to tell when she chose. "Is Mother inside?"

"Writing records," Kira answered. The midwives must record all alliances that result in pregnancy, so we know who our fathers are, and our brothers. Inside, the seabreeze had chased out most of the day's heat. My mother sat at her desk in the workroom, her record book open on the long pine surface. Neat lines of her writing covered half the page. She looked up, the fine lines around her blue eyes creasing in pleasure.

"Six babies to be born in the new year, all being well," she said. "How was the catch today, Lena?"

"Good. We found some new coves. Tali's making crab chowder for supper. She asked for you to come and bring bread if there is any." I paused. "Mother, what's going on? Tali says Xani's son has come to take over the forge. We won't let him, will we? Why would he want to live here and not with the men?"

Mother closed her record book, standing. "I'll come to the baths with you," she said. "I'll give you what answers I may when we've soaked out the day. Or at least this half of it. We may be in for a long night." She glanced at me. "Did you bring clean clothes? Or a towel?"

I shook my head absently. "Maya's bringing them."

Mother smiled. "She takes good care of you. Give me a moment to collect my things, and we'll go."

As we climbed up the hill, the forty or so houses that make up Tirvan, clustered together along the paths, came into full view. The village had grown according to need, with no real pattern. The oldest houses surrounded the harbour or sheltered under the hill pastures; newer houses filled the spaces between. Only the forge sat alone, half-way up the hillside, isolated to protect against fire.

At the very top of the village, hot springs bubbled out of the hillside. The very highest, the sacred one, provided us with water for the rituals of birth and fertility and death. The bracken that surrounded it sheltered small offerings brought by women asking the goddess for intervention or bringing thanks. Another group of springs fed the stream that ran down to the harbour on the far side of the village. At the lowest springs, our foremothers built the bathhouse. Here, the channelled water flowed into two large pools, tiled and stepped to allow us to sit partially or completely submerged, sheltered by the walls and roof of the structure. The steaming water rushed in from the springs and out again through pipes to form a stream that then flowed west, tumbling down a cliff to the ocean. After a day on the boats or in the fields, the water—clear, sulphurous, and very hot—felt wonderful.

Maya was waiting for me, clean clothes in hand. The three of us washed quickly, settling into the hot pool to soak. I stretched my legs out, worked my sore shoulders, and sighed.

My mother repinned her knot of greying hair tighter on her head, a sure sign she was thinking out what she wished to say. "Casyn is Xani's son," she said. "He is here as an Emperor's Messenger, but part of his request was that he stay here to take over the forge, to be our metalworker. The Council told him that we alone could not make such a decision. The village must hear his reasons."

"What did he say?" Maya asked. "Was he angry?"

"Not at all. We offered him Xani's cottage to use until we make a decision. He is there now. I took him bread, cheese, and apples this afternoon." She paused. "He is a quiet man, grave, I would say. I don't remember him. The records show that Xani bore him forty-eight years ago."

"Will he be at the meeting tonight?" I asked.

"Yes, at first. He asked for that, too, when Sara and Gille and I spoke with him this morning. He said he knew there would be debate, and that he shouldn't be present for that, but he has something to say that needs to be heard by us all before we make our decision. And that, my dears, is all I can tell you." She sat up. "Enough? This has been a busy day, even with Kira taking most of the new pregnancies off my hands. I'm hungry."

Reluctantly, we dried off. Maya combed out her hair. I kept my own hair short, which was better for working on the boat, but I loved Maya's hair. Most of the time, she wore it braided and tied back. Loose, it reached past her shoulder blades. In our bedroom, later, I would brush it for her.

Walking back from the baths, we passed the forge. A roan horse grazed in the paddock, but other than smoke rising from the chimney, there was no sign of Casyn. At home, the rich smell of crab chowder greeted us. Tali put bread and salad on the table. I followed Maya up to our room. The warm evening sun brightened the braided rug on the floor and the blue of the coverlet. Maya sat on the bed. "I don't like this, Lena."

I looked at her in surprise. Maya was so practical, the organizer and record-keeper of our working partnership. I was the dreamer, the one given to mood swings and doubts. "What don't you like, love?"

"This man. Casyn. Something doesn't feel right." She shrugged. "I'm scared. I feel like I did when I was six and Garth was leaving." Garth, her older brother, following custom, had gone with the men after the Festival after his seventh birthday. Born only fifteen months apart and sharing a father, Garth and Maya looked almost like twins. We had all played together as children. I'd liked him, in the uncomplicated way of small children, but Maya had adored her brother, grieving for months when he left. Maya swore she would bear no children, and I thought this was why.

"I'm scared, too," I said slowly. I wondered if I spoke truly. I sat beside Maya, putting my arms around her. She rested her head on my shoulder. I kissed the top of her head. We sat like that for a few minutes, each lost in her own thoughts, until Tali called us for supper.

Tali had simmered the crab in milk with root vegetables and onions. Freshly churned butter filled another bowl. I spread some on the bread, eating with an appetite honed by a long day on the water. Maya ate very little. I caught my mother and Tali sharing a concerned glance. Tali shook her head, slightly. I said nothing.

After the meal, I washed the dishes while Maya made tea. We spoke only of trivial things: a cracked mug, the need for more firewood. Siane's daughter Lara arrived to stay with Pel; she was eleven, too young to attend the meeting. My mother slipped out, and a few minutes later, the bell rang, calling us to the meeting hall.

The hall sat on a slight rise on the right-hand side of the village, looking up from the harbour. Wooden, like all village buildings, the octagonal shape of the hall allowed us to sit in a circle, more or less. Whoever spoke, stood, to be easily heard by all. The three senior councillors: my mother, my aunt Sara, and Gille, sat last, never together, and always at random. The rest of us sat where we pleased.

Some meeting nights, people straggled in for a good half hour after the bell rang. Not so tonight. Word of Casyn's arrival had spread quickly. Tirvan has an adult population of about eighty, and everyone was seated not ten minutes after the last peal had faded. I looked around. Someone had lit a fire against the cool of the evening. The wood crackled loudly. The faces of the women in the room showed differing emotions: curiosity, anger, worry. I looked for my mother. She stood, speaking to Sara in soft tones. I could not see Gille.

My mother walked across the hall to sit between Siane and Dessa. Maya and I had bought *Dovekie* from Dessa, a soft spoken, level-headed boatbuilder. Sara remained standing but moved into the circle.

"Women of Tirvan." Sara's voice, never loud, commanded immediate attention. "Thank you for coming to this meeting, so promptly and on such short notice. Most of you know why we are here, of today's extraordinary arrival of Xani's son, Casyn. Most of you will have heard of his request to take over the forge, to stay in Tirvan. He would be the first man to live in a woman's village in ten generations." Sara raised her hand to quell the rising murmurs. "This in itself will need much debate. But there is more. Before we say yea or nay to Casyn, he has asked to speak to you as an Emperor's Messenger."

I glanced at my mother, but Sara had her attention. Men came, occasionally, emissaries from the Empire, to ask for more food or more trade goods, but I remembered no talk at Spring Festival, six weeks past, of new or increased trade. If Casyn wanted to stay at Tirvan, how then could he be an Emperor's Messenger?

"Women of Tirvan," Sara spoke again, "will we hear Casyn speak in the name of the Empire?" While we had the right to turn down such a request, in practice they were always granted, making the question essentially a formality. We voted with raised hands, unanimous in our decision to hear Casyn speak.

At once, a middle-aged man, not tall, his dark hair streaked with grey, entered from the north-facing door of the hall. Gille walked beside him. If eighty pairs of women's eyes made him uncomfortable, he did not show it. At the ring of benches, he paused, turning to Gille. She gestured him on. He strode into the centre of the circle, where he turned slowly on his heel, taking us in. His eyes met my mother's. He inclined his head to her, looked around once more, and began to speak.

"Women of Tirvan." His deep voice and measured speech conveyed a sense of authority. My mother had described him as a grave man. Now I could see why.

"I thank you for allowing me to speak. I would ask one further thing: that you hear me out. The message I bring you tonight will not be welcome, and I am afraid your first reaction will be to reject the messenger." Maya inched closer to me. I found her hand and held it briefly.

Casyn hesitated, then turned to Gille. "Forgive me," he said, "but I am unused to speaking in such an arrangement. May I join the circle, so that my back is to no one, or speak from outside it?"

"From outside the circle, I think," Sara said from her seat. "We can turn to face you." He nodded, moving past the benches; we shifted ourselves, and he continued.

"Forty-eight years ago, I was born in this village to Xani, your smith. For seven years, I played in the fields and at the harbour and called Tirvan home. And then I left, as all boys do, and learned another life. This is how things are, and have been, for many generations. For all those generations, there has been peace in the Empire, or if not peace then small wars, wars in which we have been victorious. We have policed our borders and administered our lands, with little disturbing our way of life." His eyes moved over us as he spoke. "But the world changes. In all the women's villages of the Empire, this week or next, a soldier like myself will arrive to ask to live in the village, to take up a trade." Casyn paused, for a breath, a heartbeat. "And to teach you and your daughters to fight."

No one spoke. Casyn watched us in silence. In some small part of my mind, I felt myself measured, judged; the rest of my thoughts scattered like grouse from a harrier. I gripped Maya's hand, looking up. In the firelit room, I could see my own confusion reflected on every face. Teach us to fight? I struggled for clarity, to make the words mean something. I heard Dessa speaking, her voice very low, and strained to hear.

"Do you know what you ask of us?"

Casyn met her eyes. "Yes," he answered. "Are not all boys taught, at our mother's knees, why we must go with the men when we turn seven? Why women's comfort and love and the laughter of our children are ours for but one brief week, twice a year? Why we live apart and die apart? You teach us first, and then the Empire yet again, to remember that decision, made two hundred years ago, to divide our lives." He spoke evenly, but with an undertone of resignation, or regret. His gaze widened to take in the room as his voice rose. "You all know the facts: At that assembly, two centuries past, after a ten-day of passionate debate, our forbearers chose Partition as the compromise, to save an empire divided. For our forefathers wanted a strong army, to war on the frontier against the northern folk, and defend against incursions from the sea. But our foremothers wished only for peace to fish and farm. And so came the assembly, and the vote, and Partition there has been for these long years." His voice softened. "For the most part, it has worked and satisfied both sides, though we both have paid a price." He fell silent.

He knows our history, I thought, but he does not truly understand. All those long years ago, the women's council voted for more than Partition. They voted to turn their backs on war and weapons, to make them only the province of men. Women did not fight. We learned, in our youth, enough hunting skills to protect our herd animals or add to the cooking pot. I could shoot a bow to take down a hare or a deer, and if need required, throw a spear with reasonable force and accuracy, but that was all. More went against our teachings and our skill. How could Casyn, not taught this way, and with forty years of military life behind him, even begin to comprehend? I looked toward Gille and my mother impatiently. Tell him, I thought. Tell him we cannot do this thing. Tell him to go away.

"Why, then, do you ask this of us?"

Casyn met Dessa's gaze. "Because," he said simply, "there is need."

"What need?"

"Great need," he replied. Again, his focus seemed to widen, to encompass the room. "There is, a week's sail to the west and south, another country, Leste— an island both large and rich, warmer than our lands. You will have heard rumours and stories of this land, of their jewelled hands and green eyes, and their boats, each with a leopard's head on the prow. They may even have come here, to trade their spices and fruit for your cloth and grain. But their island grows crowded, and food is short. Trading is no longer enough. We have spies among them who report that in the autumn, just at harvest, Leste will attack us. They will first come here, to Tirvan and Delle and the other villages, to the unprotected source of food."

My mother spoke for the first time. "Could you not send part of the army to all the villages, to lie in wait?"

"We could," Casyn said. "It was, in truth, our first plan. But it would be only a stopgap at the beginning of many years of raids and counter raids. Better, we thought, to finish things once and for all. So, women of Tirvan, women of the Empire, this is what we ask of you. Learn, against your inclinations and beliefs, to fight. Defend your villages against the raiders. And while you do so, the men of the Empire will have sailed to an island depleted of its fighting force. There will be no one to mount a defence against us. We will take the island in a matter of days, and the thing will be done. The choice is yours: fight once and then go back to your peaceful way of life, or live with years of uncertainty and battle."

"Can you not defend us and still send an army to take the island?" Sara asked from the position she had taken beside Gille and my mother.

"No," Casyn said. "There are not enough of us. We cannot leave the northern wall undefended. We can leave you the veterans, and the youngest men, but in the end, they will not be enough. The men of Leste would take the villages, growing strong on our food while we grew weak and hungry in their land. Come spring, they would sail home to defeat us. I think you can imagine what they would do to you over that winter."

Above the sudden din in the room, I heard Gille calling for order. Women stood, clattering benches, speaking urgently to partners or family members. Maya called my name. I turned to her.

"We can't fight," she said. "We can't. We don't. Men fight. They must protect us. They have to. That's what was decided at the Partition assembly. We feed them; they protect us. Isn't that right, Lena?"

"Yes, love," I said slowly. I heard the fear in her voice. Maya needed order and predictability. In our business partnership, her need for stability balanced my impulsiveness. In our personal relationship, it had always cast a small shadow. I searched for words, wanting to reassure her, but knowing in my gut that our world had just changed. I pushed away something else, something I could not let Maya sense. While Casyn answered my mother's last question, I had named what churned inside me: not fear, but excitement.

I took a deep breath. "Maya," I said finally, hugging her close. "They'll protect us. That's why they want to take Leste, to subdue it and protect us. They're just asking us to help."

She pulled away from me. "No," she said, her panicked voice rising. "I won't fight. I won't, Lena."

"Hush, Maya," I said. "Gille wants to speak."

Slowly, the room quieted. Gille waited until the last murmurs died away. "Casyn," she said, her voice clear and strong, "we thank you for your honesty. I will ask you now to leave us, so we can debate this matter with no hesitancy." He bowed his head to her, glanced at my mother and Sara, and left. I heard his footsteps crunching on the path outside. A log cracked in the fire. Someone gasped. Gille waited until the sound of Casyn's steps had faded before she spoke again.

"Women of Tirvan," she said formally. "What we have been asked to do tonight is beyond easy understanding. We are being asked to put aside the decisions made by our foremothers, decisions that have shaped our lives for ten generations. We cannot do this in haste. All of us must give this much thought. We will make no decision tonight. Tomorrow morning, the council leaders will speak again with Casyn, and then we will all meet here, to debate and to decide. We will adjourn this meeting until one o'clock tomorrow. But," she added, her tone changing from formal to her normal way of speaking, "the hall will remain open tonight, as long as the firewood lasts. There is tea in the kettle. Please remember that Gwen and Sara and I know no more than you."

I wanted to talk to my mother, but I felt Maya trembling. I rose to fetch tea from the pot, adding more honey than usual. She drank it in silence, not meeting my eyes. Around us swirled voices—angry, soothing, unbelieving. I sat with my arm around her shoulders, wondering a bit at her shock. No decision had been made; we were only going to talk, to debate. We could vote no.

Eventually she spoke. "I'm going home," she said. "I know how I'll vote, and nothing will make me change my mind. Are you coming?"

"No," I said. "I want to talk to my mother. Maya, don't—"

"Don't what?" she snapped. "Don't make up my mind so soon? I know how I feel, Lena. What Casyn is asking, what the Empire is asking, is wrong. I know that, and so do you. Women don't fight. We don't kill or harm others." Her voice held conviction now, certainty.

"Except in self-defence," I reminded her. She shook her head.

"Maybe that's true, further north, near the wall," she said. "But who have we ever needed to defend ourselves against?" She pulled away from my encircling arm. "You think this is an adventure, Lena?" she said fiercely. "Something new? Something different? You always want to sail a little further, find another cove, even though the ones we know provide us with all the fish we need. But this isn't the same; we can't just sail out into this for a day or two, and then turn around and come back to our safe harbour. If we sail into this storm, Lena, we won't come out."

Tears stood in her hazel eyes. She knew me so well. I put my hand on the cloud of her black hair.

"But if we don't sail into it, Maya," I said gently, "it will find us anyway. It will batter our boats at their moorings until there is nothing left. Our safe harbour will become a prison."

CHAPTER TWO

I SLEPT LITTLE THAT NIGHT. I sat in a chair by our bedroom window, watching the moon set over the boats in the harbour. Maya lay in the bed, sleeping or pretending to. No words passed between us.

I had spoken with my mother as I walked her home from the meeting. Even in the moonlight, I could see the lines of strain around her eyes. I told her what had been said between Maya and myself.

"Maya has always looked for certainties," she said wearily. "But you know that, Lena. When Garth left, she could only find peace by putting her faith in tradition. I warned Tali that to have two so close together, and with the same man, was a mistake. But she loved Mar and didn't listen. Like her mother, Maya can be stubborn when she believes she's right. I think, in this, she is wrong." She stopped on the path to face me. "Until tomorrow, Lena, these words are for you only. I see no choice for us but to accept this."

I shivered in the night air. Somewhere an owl called. "Will the village agree?"

"In the end, I think they will." We resumed walking. "To not fight, but to passively wait for whatever happens, is the greater violation of the spirit of the Partition assembly. Tradition then would have dictated that we support the men in their empire-building."

"But we do support them," I argued. "We feed them, make saddles and stirrups, and weave cloth for them."

My mother smiled tiredly. "You forget your lessons, Lena," she said. "We do now. But not at first, not in the first years following Partition. Then, there was only Festival, and sons for the Empire."

I had forgotten. I had endured my schooling, not enjoyed it. "Then we have changed the rules once, and we can do it again."

"We can," my mother agreed. "And I think we will, but it won't be easy, for any of us." We paused outside her house. "Maya is right. At the end of this, even if we are victorious, the world will have changed." She opened the front door. "I am very tired, Lena. Try to rest."

But I could not. At the first light of dawn, I slipped down to the kitchen, brewed tea, found some bread left over from dinner, and went to the boats. I was scrubbing the hold, brush in hand, when Maya joined me several hours later.

"Did you sleep?" I sat back on my haunches.

"A bit," she said. She re-tied her hair, not looking at me. "Did you?"

"No. I got back fairly late and couldn't stop thinking."

She met my eyes. "Can we just work and not talk about it?"

I sighed. "If you like." I knew from experience that when Maya did not want to talk, insisting on it would just irritate her more. "Can you see if any of the ropes needs splicing? I thought one was fraying yesterday." She nodded, turning away. I held my tongue, channelling my frustrations into my scrubbing.

We worked until the noon bell rang, talking only of the boat and the fishing, calmly but distantly. The routine of the work eased my irritation. Around us, other fisherwomen went about their daily chores. To an outside eye, the life of the village would have appeared to go on as normal. When the bell rang, I gave the hold one last swipe. I dumped the dirty water overside and put the bucket and brush away. Maya, on the dock, coiled the rope in her hands, stowing it neatly. We walked back up the hill with a half-dozen other women and apprentices. The illusion of normalcy had vanished. The tension crackled like summer lightening, and few of us spoke in more than brief murmurs or sharp retorts as we returned to our houses. Tali had put bread, cheese, and fresh radishes on the table. My stomach growled at the sight.

"Maya?" I asked. "Do you want some food?"

"No." She turned away to climb the stairs.

"Tali?"

She leaned against the sink, drinking tea. She shook her head. "I don't think I can eat," she admitted.

I sliced the radishes thinly onto the bread, layered cheese on top, and sat outside on the steps in the noon sun to eat. I wanted space, not walls. Maya came back down the stairs, her footsteps resonating on the pine planks. I ate half the food, and suddenly, I had had enough. I took the remainder back to the kitchen, wrapped it in a cloth, putting it on a shelf. Tali hadn't moved. She had lighted a candle in the small shrine by the hearth, an offering to the goddess. She looked at me, and in her eyes I saw both fear and resolve.

"Time to go," she said quietly. I nodded. Maya emerged from another room. She had pulled her hair back and braided it tightly, accentuating the pale planes of her face. Without a word, she walked past us and out the door.

"Maya," Tali's voice was almost pleading and so quiet I did not think Maya could have heard. I looked at my aunt. Tears gleamed in her eyes.

"Tali?" I said. "What is it?"

She brushed a hand across her eyes. "I'm so afraid for her," she said. "Of what she might do."

"So am I," I said slowly. "But even if we vote to defend Tirvan, she won't need to fight. Someone will have to take care of the babies and cook."

"Maybe," Tali said. "Maybe."

Maya waited for us on the porch, standing apart from the other women who had gathered there. When we entered the hall, she walked beside her mother. We stopped just inside the door, letting our eyes adjust to the dimness. Women sat on the benches or stood in small groups around the walls, talking in low tones. Tali saw my mother across the room and went to join her. Maya slipped onto a bench. When I sat beside her, she slid an inch or so over. I reached over to take her hand. She shot me a cold look, giving a tiny shake of her head. I felt a spurt of anger. We'd had arguments before, of course, but usually she accepted my gestures of reconciliation. I shrugged, and increased the distance between us on the bench, bumping into Kyan. I murmured an apology. Kyan made space for me, sliding closer to her partner, Dari.

Gille rose to speak. "We meet here this afternoon under the rules of the council," she said formally. "You were all here last night. You know what Casyn, in the name of the Emperor, has asked. Gwen and Sara and I have met with Casyn for much of the morning, but there is little I can add to what he told us yesterday. There is good reason to believe that Leste is planning to attack the women's villages in the autumn, after harvest, to take food for their land. We are being asked to defend ourselves, to allow the men to subdue Leste and, at the same time, keep the northern Wall manned. This afternoon, we need to debate and discuss this, and then vote." I heard a few whispers as Gille spoke, but mostly we kept to the rules and did not interrupt. I looked at Maya. Her face was grim, and a muscle worked in her cheek. "That is our task," Gille reiterated. "Who wishes to speak?"

A dozen women stood, scraping benches. Sara scanned the room. In council, we speak from youngest to oldest. Maya did not stand. Sara nodded. "Cate," she acknowledged.

"The men were here so recently." She frowned. "Why did we hear nothing from them? Even rumours? All the talk was of the Wall. How do we know this is true?"

"Aye!" The agreement came from several places in the circle. A good question, I thought. At Festival, the men had many stories, told publicly and, no doubt, I assumed, privately. I knew only the songs and the tales told in the public gatherings, but Cate spoke truly. The Wall loomed large in those. Occasionally stories of Casilla, the only true city of the Empire, down on the Edanan Sea, took centre stage, but I remembered nothing about Leste.

"Casyn spoke as an Emperor's Messenger," Sara reminded us. "They are bound to speak the truth. As to why we heard nothing from the men, it is simply that they did not know. Only the Emperor and some men of rank were fully aware."

"That's what he says, is it?" I turned to see who had spoken out of turn: Minna.

"Mother!" her daughter hissed. Minna muttered something, then subsided. I turned away. Minna's mind wandered, we all knew; she could not be held responsible for the lapse of council etiquette. The murmurs of assent audible in the room, though, told me many shared her doubt. I turned to Maya again, hoping to see some reaction, but she stared at the floorboards, not looking up.

Ranni spoke next. Six months into a difficult pregnancy, she leaned on her partner's shoulder for support. "If it is food they need," she asked, "why can't they just trade for it? Or we could just give it to them." A louder wave of murmurs swept the room. Gille raised her hand, requesting silence. Feet shuffled, bodies shifted. Gille waited for the room to calm.

"They have little to trade, or little that we want," Gille answered. "Even the military needs only so much dried fruit, or spices, or wine. And we have only so much extra without going short ourselves."

Ranni nodded and sat. Her partner put her arm around her. Sweat beaded on my forehead and neck. Again, Gille waited for silence. "Mella," she indicated, nodding to another pregnant woman.

"Does an Emperor's Messenger have the right to ask this of us?" she said simply. "Does even the Emperor have the right to ask us to break the precepts of Partition?" She cradled her unborn child with both hands, looking down at her swollen stomach. "How would I explain that, to her?"

"You can't," someone called.

"Quiet!"

"There's reasons!"

"It's not right!"

The hall resounded with voices. I'd never seen us break order before. Startled, I turned again to Maya, but she seemed unaware, still locked inside herself. When I put my hand on her rigid shoulder, she pulled away again without looking at me. I felt tears threaten, tears of fear and sudden loneliness. I scanned the room, searching for Tali, or my mother, and met the eyes of Tice, our new potter, sitting alone across the circle. Her face showed no emotion, but she cocked her head slightly to acknowledge me. She gazed back at me steadily. I looked away, embarrassed that she might have seen the tears glinting in my eyes.

The clang of the meeting bell reverberated through the room. When the last vibrations had stilled, and with them the voices, my mother spoke, quietly and firmly. "All of you," she reminded, "learned the rules of Partition in your school days. Siane," she addressed a seated woman, "your Lara is still a student. Have you helped her learn the rules, as they were written at the Partition assembly?"

"Yes," Siane replied.

"Would you remind us what it said, regarding food?"

Siane did not rise. She had been a herdswoman before a berserk bull smashed her left leg to pieces, and now stood and walked with difficulty. She kept the village accounts and breeding records, and had a prodigious memory. "Whatever foodstuffs a village produces, whether meat or grain, fruit or vegetable, is theirs to keep and trade among the villages. No tithe will be given to nor expected by the Empire's armies, fleets, or messengers, or by the Emperor himself," she recited. She looked questioningly at my mother, who nodded. "This was superseded some fifty years later, as a benefit to both the villages and the men. Many villages produced much more food than they needed, and the men fighting the northern peoples and building the Wall could not farm as well. But," she paused, "I do not know how that change was made."

Several of the women waiting to speak sat down again, relinquishing their opportunity to be heard. Casse, nearly eighty, leaned on her stick. Once a council leader, her thoughts bore weight among us.

"Casse," my mother said.

"When we move the herds to the hills, in the spring," she began, "we send the apprentices with them, to guard them against the eagles and the wildcats that prey on the newly-born lambs and calves." Casse spoke in a strong voice that belied her years. "We give those apprentices weapons: slings and sometimes staves. Those are enough, even in the hands of a twelve-year-old, to keep those hunters off. But nearly seventy years ago, when I was first apprenticed to the herds and the hunt, they were not enough, because wolves, packs of wolves, still roamed the hills and took even fully-grown sheep and cattle. Shepherding then needed an adult woman, or several, who had skill with spear and knife and bow. We defended our animals, and ourselves, with weapons." She thumped her staff on the floor. "I have killed a wolf or two in my time, and I would again. Why is this any different, except this time the wolves have two legs?" She gave a sharp nod and sat down.

No one else remained standing. My mother looked around. I followed her gaze. Around the room, women leaned forward, tense and focused, or huddled with their eyes downcast. Some grasped hands, others hugged. Some sat alone. I could smell the tang of sweat and fear in the room. "You have questioned Casyn's veracity, and his right to ask this of us," she said. "You have suggested that food be traded, or given, to turn aside the threat of invasion. You have been reminded that the rules of Partition are not fixed but have been changed before when there was benefit perceived for both the villages and the men. And that, sometimes, killing is necessary for survival." Beside me, Maya flinched. I reached for her hand again, and this time, she let me take it. I slid a little closer to her.

"I speak on behalf of your council leaders." She glanced at Sara and Gille. "Our thoughts, as always in a council vote, are only to guide you, not to direct you. We recommend that Tirvan accede to the Emperor's request, that we learn the skills and tactics needed to defend our village against invasion, even though this goes against the precepts of the Partition agreement. If we do not, if we refuse to defend ourselves, and the invaders are victorious, we will have no voice and no choice in what happens to us after that. If the Empire wins, we can write a new agreement. So say I, Gwen of Tirvan, Council Leader," she ended, with the formal words.

"And I, Sara of Tirvan, Council Leader."

"And I, Gille of Tirvan, Council Leader."

The formal recommendation of the council leaders signalled the preparation for the vote. Gille and my mother walked the circle. Gille handed each of us a dark pebble for no, my mother a light one for yes. The stones felt cold against my palms. Sara unlocked the two voting boxes, one for the vote, one for the discarded pebble, showing the room that both were empty. Then she locked them again, standing them on a table. Sixty light pebbles in the voting box meant no further debate, no second vote.

Separating the pebbles meant letting go of Maya's hand. She did look at me then. Her eyes were anguished, but dry. I reached out to hold her, but she shook her head. "No," she said quietly. "Not now."

"Maya," I pleaded. "Don't be angry."

"I'm not angry. Not at you. I just can't—" She broke off, took a breath. We walked toward the boxes, pebbles hidden in our hands. Maya's knuckles were white. Mine were, too. My pebble dropped into the voting box, where it clicked against the others already there. I dropped the dark one into the discard box. I watched Maya flatten her palm against the hole and heard her pebble drop.

We sat again to watch the others vote. Finally, the council leaders opened the boxes, pouring the pebbles onto a cloth. Maya moaned. I could hear my heart beating out the seconds. It took less than a minute of those beats to count, one by one, the sixty-three white pebbles.

Sara stood. "All women of age in Tirvan have witnessed the count. Tirvan votes to accede to the request of the Emperor." The required words spoken, she hesitated. "We have voted to change the rules of Partition, for only the second time in two hundred years," she said. "Whether this was wisdom, or no, only the future will tell us. But it is our choice."

"Not all of us," Siane reminded her. Tears glistened on her cheeks, but she spoke clearly. "Seventeen of us voted no. What of us?"

Gille stepped forward. "Siane, must we do this now?"

"Yes!" Maya said defiantly. "We need to know. I need to know."

Gille sighed, and turned away, speaking softly to Sara and Gwen.

"Maya," I cajoled, "can't this wait? Let's see what Casyn wants us to do."

"No," she said, her voice high. She wrapped her arms around herself, pulling her knees up, rocking slightly on the bench. "It's not what Casyn wants, Lena, it's what the village wants. What the rest of you, who voted to fight, want of me, and Siane, and whoever else said no. That's our choice, not his, not the Emperor's. Ours," she repeated. Her eyes glittered. She looked feverish. At the table, the council leaders' talk ended. They turned towards us.

"Siane," Gille said. "You will lead the group who decides this. For the women of age who voted no, and for the apprentices who hold the same views, what will we ask? Casyn told us last night he believes we should train all girls over the age of thirteen. What you, Siane, and seven more must decide is how we handle this. Do we excuse some from the training, and if so on what grounds? Do we make training compulsory, and if so, what are the consequences for refusing? It will not be easy, nor will whatever you choose be accepted easily by all."

Siane nodded in acceptance. "I will do this," she confirmed. She pushed her stocky body up and bent to hold Dessa, murmuring something. Then she took her stick, limping out to the porch to await, by our customs, the rest of the chosen group. I looked around. In theory, I knew how this worked, how we chose the women who now would decide the question given them. In practice, I'd never seen it happen. Four of the eight walls of the hall had doors. The chosen leader sat outside the north door, away from the village; one council leader standing at each of the others. Which door we exited from depended on where we sat in the hall.

"We go east from here, don't we?" I asked.

"That's right," Kyan said beside me, stretching. "You remember the rest?"

"Two hands," I murmured. Each of us offered a hand to the council leader as we left the hall. If she grasped it with one hand, we continued on. But if both her hands covered the offered hand, we did not leave.

"Right again," Kyan said. She ran a hand through her cropped, fox-red hair. "Difficult one, this." She worked in wood, building boxes or barns with equal skill, and on long winter nights made our hunting bows. Slight, dark-haired Dari worked with her.

In joining the line, Dari had moved forward to speak to Maya, and now both she and Kyan stood between us. I could just see Sara take Maya's hand with her right, touching her gently on the shoulder with her left. Just perceptibly—to me, at least—Maya relaxed. She glanced back at me, but protocol said she could not wait near the porch.

"Maya," I heard Dari call. "Come for tea." Good, I thought. I can catch up with them on the path. Kyan blocked the light for a moment, then went on her way. I held out my hand to Sara. She took it in both of hers. I froze.

"Sara," I said, "I can't do this."

"Yes, you can," she replied quietly. "I know Maya is one of the seventeen. That is, in part, why we chose you." Unexpectedly, she touched my cheek. "You are very much like your mother, Lena. The mix of pragmatism and compassion that makes her both an excellent midwife and an excellent council leader is in you, too. Find Siane and begin what you have to do."

Someone had arranged chairs in a circle on the porch. Six other women were with Siane, Casse and Mella among them. I was the eighth. The porch held the warmth of the day. Someone brought out a jug of water and cups. I poured myself a cup and sat. My mouth was dry.

"You are the last of our group," Siane said. She held her injured leg out in front of her. I could see the twist in it, where the bones had knitted wrongly. Her partner, Dessa, a woman of strong views, would almost certainly have voted to fight. Maya and I were not the only partnership in the village to be divided in this matter. Somehow, that thought made me feel less alone. "You all know our task?" Siane asked, glancing around the group. We nodded. "There are several issues here," she continued. "Casyn expects the attack to come in late September. At that point, we will have three women, Mella among them, with new babies, and several more, I assume, who will be nearly six months pregnant. Lena, do you know how many?"

"Six."

"That many?" Siane said. "Well, those six, barring complications, should be able to participate in the training."

"We always work during pregnancy," someone said. "This should be no different."

"I'm willing to learn what I can for the next five or six weeks," Mella said, "but I can't deny that I am getting clumsy." She smiled ruefully, her blue eyes crinkling, "Of the others who became pregnant last autumn, Ranni's is a first pregnancy, and she nearly lost the baby a few weeks back, and Nessa is carrying twins and is even more awkward than I am. But there must be work in planning and carrying out a defence that isn't dependent on being able to shoot a bow or throw a spear."

"A tactical role, I think Mella means," Casse said, "which is where I think I might be able to help a bit." Casse had led hunting parties for many years and had spent hours out in the fields.

"For you, yes, and I can see Nessa in that role," Mella said. "But for myself and Ranni, I was thinking more of giving support, supplying arrows or new spears. Something like that."

"But," I found myself saying, "you'll still need to defend yourselves, if it comes to that. At the very least, all of us will need to be able to use a knife."

"Lena has a point," Siane said. She shifted, grimacing as she bent her leg. "If we are willing to participate, a role will be found regardless of physical limitations. That isn't really what we're here to decide. But what about those of us who don't wish to fight? I'll assume for the moment that all of us who voted that way did so for the same reason: we find the taking human life abhorrent. What is to be expected of us? You know that I do not hold that belief lightly."

We all knew Siane found the concept of taking life repellent. She ate no meat or fish, and even the man who had fathered her daughter held a medic's post, not a soldier's. Sara had chosen wisely, I realized, in appointing Siane to lead this group. Whatever our decision, it would be respected by all because Siane had led us.

"Perhaps," Casse said gently, her wrinkled face compassionate, "you should tell us what to expect of you."

"A fair request," Siane acknowledged. "I spent most of last night wrestling with this. I don't believe I can kill a man."

"Not even," I asked, "if he were trying to kill you?"

"Not even then."

"What if it meant life or death for Dessa? Or for Lara?" The woman who spoke was my senior by a decade. I did not know her well, but her son had played with Pel until Festival this spring. He had ridden away with the soldiers only six weeks ago.

Siane said nothing. We could see the struggle of her conscience reflected on her face. We waited. When she finally spoke, her voice choked with emotion. "I thought of that, too. Truly, I thought of little else. For Lara," she said, "I would kill."

Casse reached out to squeeze her hand. "Do not judge yourself harshly. We all would, for our children." Her gaze turned to me. "Lena, would you endanger yourself to protect Maya?"

"Of course," I said.

Casse held Siane's eyes. "You see?" she asked softly. Siane nodded.

"Individual convictions must be acknowledged and respected," Casse said firmly, "but not to the point at which they endanger others. I propose this: all able-bodied women in Tirvan must, regardless of how they voted or of personal belief, learn to defend themselves with a knife. More than that will be up to each woman and her conscience."

I thought of Maya, of her passionate conviction that women did not fight, did not kill. I wondered if she would see the necessity of this ruling, or if she would think only that we had betrayed her beliefs.

"What if a woman refuses?" I asked, though I knew the answer. We all did.

Casse, once a council leader, answered anyway. "Then she is free to leave Tirvan," she said. I held her calm gaze for a moment. I saw compassion in her eyes. Compassion and pragmatism, my aunt had said. I tried for pragmatism. Using a knife? Maya could do that. We gutted fish and killed the occasional seal. She could agree to that, for self-defence only.

"I second the proposal," I whispered.

The clang of the meeting bell called the village back. Gille pulled the bellrope steadily as the women filed in. From where our group sat together, as required, I saw Kyan and Dari come in. Maya was not with them, nor did she accompany her mother. Then I spotted her with Dessa. Terror filled me. What had we done? How could we make her fight when she so passionately believed it wrong? Who gave us that power? I leaned forward, gulping air. A cold sweat broke out on my forehead. A hand gripped my shoulder. "Courage," Casse said quietly. "Find it. You have it in you." No, I don't, I thought, but my breathing steadied under her strong fingers. After the last women hurried in, Gille let the bell swing to silence.

My mother spoke in a clear voice. "Women of Tirvan, we have called you to hear a binding decision. Eight women, one tenth of the council, have debated this question. Seventeen of us voted not to fight. What will be asked of those seventeen, in the weeks of preparation to come, and when the fighting begins?" She turned. "Siane, you led the debate. Have you reached a decision?"

"We have," Siane answered.

"Tell us, please, so we may know the ruling."

Siane stood, leaning against a chair to support her bad leg. No one moved. "I was one of the seventeen," she said. "You all know my views. This is our ruling: We will all learn to fight to the point that we can defend ourselves. All of us, without exception."

A buzz of voices rose in the hall. Casse's grip on my shoulder had not lessened. When I saw Maya rise from her seat beside Dessa, I tried to rise, too, but Casse held firm. The voices stilled. When Maya's eyes found mine, they held an expression I could not read. Then she looked straight at Gille. "I dissent," she said, in the ritual words. Even from across the room, I could see she was shaking, but her voice barely wavered. "I know what I say and what I do. I dissent. I will not fight."

Sara and Gwen moved to stand beside Gille. "Maya," my mother began, "do not do this." She turned to me, anguish on her face and in her voice. "Lena, can't you stop her?" But even as Casse released me, and I stood to go to her, Maya spoke again, the third and final and binding time. "I will chance exile," she said. "I dissent."

CHAPTER THREE

I TRIED TO RUN TO HER, BUT HANDS CAUGHT ME. I twisted and kicked helplessly. The bell tolled once. Gille spoke the answering words—words we had all learned, but I had never heard spoken.

"Maya, daughter of Tali," she said with grief coursing through her voice. "You stand against the will of the Tirvan council. Go you now from this hall, and by tomorrow at sunset, go you from Tirvan. All doors and gates and harbours are closed to you, Maya, for three years and a day. You are exiled, and no longer welcome here. Go you now."

I heard Tali sob.

I watched Maya go to her mother. Tali bent to hold her daughter, rocking her. After a minute, Maya pulled away. She said something, very quietly. Tali shook her head, and Maya repeated it. Then she turned. Even from across the room, I could see the determination in her eyes. I was struggling again to pull away from the many arms that held me when I saw Maya mouth the word "No." I stopped. Maya turned back to Gille.

"Tomorrow morning, I will be gone. I go on foot and alone," she said. Her voice echoed in the silent hall. "I will go now, to prepare. I will sleep tonight at my mother's house." She paused. "Alone." She did not look at me again. "Farewell, women of Tirvan." She turned on her heel and walked out.

My aunt Sara held Tali by the upper arms, speaking low and urgently. Dessa still restrained me, but my strength was suddenly gone. I slumped against her. Dessa guided me to a bench. I let her sit me down. Nothing made sense. I heard Dessa speak, but her words had no meaning.

Distantly, I realized others were leaving. Women stopped to speak to me and to Tali, but I heard only noise. Someone brought me tea. I held the cup, registering the warmth. Finally, only my family remained: my mother, Sara and Tali, and Gille, in her role as headwoman.

My mother put the mug of tea to my lips. I swallowed obediently. The warm liquid suffused my throat, and the fog in my head cleared a little. I sipped again, then took the mug from my mother.

"Oh, Lena, I am so sorry," she said, sitting beside me. She put her arm around me. "I didn't think it would come to this."

"She said," Tali said, her voice flat, "she would go to look for Garth."

Sara and my mother exchanged looks. "I'm not surprised," Sara said.

"But," I said, finding my voice, "Maya isn't brave. How could she do this? How could she walk away from Tirvan and all she knows?" And from me. Tears pricked my eyes.

"Lena," my mother said, "this isn't bravery. In Maya's mind, Tirvan is deserting her. There are some things that perhaps you don't know, that Maya has never told you. Did she ever talk of Garth's leaving?"

I shook my head. "She would never speak of it."

"Then I will," my mother said. "Unless, Tali—?"

"No," my aunt said. "Better from you, Gwen. It's not a good memory." My mother straightened, letting me go. She stood, her hands automatically retying her hair.

"You know," my mother said after a moment's thought, "that Maya was just a few months short of her sixth birthday when the time came for Garth to go with his father. What you don't know is that he did not want to go. Most boys are happy to join the men. Pel, as you know, is already talking of little else. Garth was different. He liked the sea and the woods and was happiest herding the sheep and watching the gulls. He threatened to run away, and Maya swore to go with him if he went."

"In the end," Tali interrupted, her voice low, "we had to drug him. Mar took him, a day early, from his bed, so heavily dosed with poppy that he wouldn't wake until they were far from Tirvan. We drugged Maya, too, a lesser dose, but enough to keep her from realizing what was happening." I could see the strain in her face as she spoke.

"And then," Sara sighed, "we convinced her that tradition said Garth had to go, and that tradition ruled us all. We had many long arguments when I would take her with me to gather herbs for dyeing. Somehow, over that long summer, we won her over."

"Now," my mother added, "we are seeing the fruits of what we did all those years ago. She missed Garth so terribly, Lena. You must remember." I nodded, thinking back. I, too, had been only five, but I remembered Maya crying, endlessly, inconsolably. I had tried, even then, to entice her into games, but she would not be distracted. Finally, the tears had stopped, leaving a solemn, quiet child.

"When we apprenticed together," I said, remembering, "she always wanted to know why things were done the way they were. The answer that seemed to satisfy her the most was 'it has always been done that way'."

Tali continued. "That summer, she prayed endlessly. If we couldn't find her, we only had to look at the holy spring. But when her offerings failed and her prayers weren't answered, she turned her back on the goddess and turned to tradition as a source of meaning and consistency."

"Maya would say," my aunt Sara added gently, "that she isn't rebelling. That it's we who have rebelled, gone against tradition. In her mind, she's doing the only thing she can to maintain the old ways."

"Could she find Garth?" I asked.

Tali shrugged. "If Garth is alive, she might find him by asking every patrol she meets. She knows their father's name and the number of his company. But the seventh were posted to the far reaches of the Wall the year after Garth left, and Mar was killed ten months later. When the message finally reached me, it contained no mention of Garth. I did nothing. Garth belonged to the Empire by then, and I was afraid to unbalance Maya again."

"And if she does find him?"

"I don't know," Tali said. "Maybe she thinks they'll run away together, as they promised when they were children. She may think that Garth will honour that oath over his oath to the Empire, if he lived to make it. I do not know, Lena."

I nodded. Regardless of our love for her, there were places in Maya that neither Tali nor I knew. "May I go to her now, to say farewell?" I asked.

"No, Lena," Gille said. I had opened my mouth to protest when she cut me off. "Not because I forbid it, but because she did." I frowned.

"Maya knows the ritual words as well as any of us," Gille reminded me, gently. "She knew exactly what she said when she commanded that you stay with Gwen. It is her right, as an exiled woman, to protect you, her partner, from blame. She will go without seeing you again."

"No," I said, "no," and then the tears started. My mother held me. When nothing remained but desolation, they took me to the baths. The heat of the pool stopped my shivering, and they gave me wine and poppy. They must have carried me to my mother's house, but I do not remember. I slept, dreaming the dreams grief and the poppy bring. In the morning I woke, as Maya had eleven short years before, to an empty world.

I heard the meeting bell through the waning effect of the drug. In my dreams, the bell had rung first as a warning and then become the tolling-bell for a funeral. My head ached when I finally woke. I closed my eyes against the light of the room. Maya would have left at sunrise. I lay on my back, trying to think through the pain and noise in my head. I could tell from the sun's position that perhaps four hours had passed since dawn. Maya would have climbed the track up into the hills to find the military road. If I got up now, packed some food and clothes, I could catch her. But the road ran north to south, and footprints would not show on its cobbles. How would I know which way to go? Maybe she left a sign.

No. I opened my eyes. My head throbbed. We had never spoken of the world beyond Tirvan, never travelled in thought to Berge, or Casilla. I had no idea where she would go. Besides, she had told me to stay, and in that command absolved me of what she knew I would choose. For all my wishing, for adventure, for something new, at the end of the day, I always turned for home. I would not follow her.

Shamed, I wept again, tears of anger and self-loathing, deep, racking sobs. I slid off the bed and wrapped my arms around my knees, my body shaking. When the sobs ended, I sank onto my side and lay still, my mind empty.

Eventually, the need to relieve myself forced me to get up. I used the chamberpot. Then, reluctantly, I washed and dressed and went downstairs. I drank some water, feeling it cold against my raw throat. I stepped outside into the late morning sun, and with nothing else I could think to do, turned towards the meeting hall.

I hesitated at the door, but Siane beckoned me in. The plans for the defence of Tirvan had begun. Casyn had organized us into planning teams—food, supplies, fortifications, secure penning of our herd animals. Every detail mattered. Casyn himself sat with a group of women.

"They're talking about weapons—spears and knives, how many we'll need, and what metal there is at the forge," Siane explained, when she saw me looking their way. I nodded, not really caring. I wondered where to go. My head throbbed dully. I felt as if I moved against a tide.

"Where are the other fisherwomen?" I asked, looking around.

"Over by the south wall," Siane answered. I thanked her, turning to thread my way through the groups to join them.

"Lena," Casyn approached me, his face grave. "I regret I have brought sorrow to you so soon." He touched my shoulder lightly in what seemed a formal gesture. I murmured thanks. Part of my mind registered surprise that he knew my name. He nodded. Not knowing what else to do, I nodded too, and went on to join my group. They made room for me, speaking quiet words of sympathy and concern. Dessa reached over to squeeze my hand.

"We're talking of how we can catch as many fish as possible," she explained. "Casyn thinks we may be besieged, or the fields burned and cattle slaughtered. If either of those happens, we might need to rely on smoked fish over the winter."

I tried to concentrate. I didn't think I really cared, but the planning gave my mind something to do.

"We could start the pilcod fishing early," I suggested. The pilcod were the small, schooling fish of the cold waters to the north.

"Will they be there?" someone asked. "We'd be six weeks early. They won't have moved south yet."

"We can sail further," I said.

"It's rough further north, dangerous."

"They'll be feeding where the waters change," Binne countered. "We can fish just inside the chop line, stay in sight of each other. Should be safe enough." Some fifteen years older than I, Binne fished from *Petrel* with her partner. She had let Maya and me sail *Petrel* a time or two when we were trying to decide what to buy for ourselves. *Dovekie* had been built to the same plans.

"And we'd be out longer."

I shrugged. "I don't mind."

"Is anyone else willing to sail out to catch pilcod?" Dessa asked. "I think there should be at least three boats, maybe five, to be safe. I'll go. Anyone else?"

Several fisherwomen shook their heads. Others conferred with their fishing partners. "We'll go," Binne spoke up, "I won't take my apprentice though," she said. "Can someone else take her on for this?"

"I'll put her on *Curlew*," Dessa said. "I had a mind to send Freya with Lena, anyhow, so that'll make space." Dessa's boat, large and graceful, needed a crew of six. Maya and I had apprenticed on *Curlew*.

"We'll go, too," another pair confirmed.

Everything we spoke of made Maya's absence palpable. These women had trained us and worked alongside us every day. I clenched my jaw against the scream that wanted to burst out. My head started pounding again, and I lost the thread of the talk.

The group planned for another hour. I said very little. Food had been placed on tables against the west wall. We took a break to eat. I nibbled a piece of bread and some cheese without appetite. My mother came over to me, her look questioning. She handed me a mug of sweetened tea. "You need to drink," she said, "and eat a bit. But drinking is more important." She studied me. "I'm glad you're here," she said. She was beginning to say something else when someone interrupted us. I nodded, and she moved away. Others spoke to me, and I answered but did not encourage further talk.

After lunch, Gille asked us to sit again as a large group, so Casyn could address us. We settled, and he began speaking, I noticed, from inside the circle.

"Thank you," he said. "You have worked hard this morning, truly, and I know that your decisions have been made wisely. My job here is only to teach and to advise. I am not here to lead. You already have leaders, and they are admirable." He inclined his head to the council leaders. "You have some skills with the tools of war, with bows, spears, and knives, but they belong to the hunt and to husbandry, not to combat. You must all train for part of every day to learn to use the weapons of war, for war. I will teach you to do that."

Gille raised a hand to still the chatter. "To allow time for this instruction," she said, "you will work only half-days unless the immediacy of a task demands otherwise. Half of you will train in the mornings, half in the afternoons, until there are women among us who are skilled enough to teach. We begin tomorrow."

Before dawn the next morning, I untied *Dovekie's* ropes and began to row away from the dock. I took Freya with me, as Dessa had suggested. Quiet and competent, Freya had eighteen months left in her apprenticeship. We sailed north to the edge of the waters where the pilcod schooled, accompanied by the little boats *Petrel* and *Dunlin*, and Dessa, fishing from her second boat *Avocet*. A light fog hung at the chopline. We maneuvered the boats along the line where the cold waves of the north broke on the warmer southern waters and dropped sail.

Quickly, we moved to the stern and picked up the first of the fine, weighted nets. "We're shallower than *Curlew*," I explained to Freya, "so you'll need to throw upward a bit, so it goes far enough out and doesn't foul." I considered. Freya stood half a head taller than me, and her shoulders carried muscle. With Maya, I held my arms lower, to compensate for our height difference. "Drop your arms a bit," I instructed. She nodded, and we threw. The first net landed and sank, well out from the boat.

"Nicely done," I offered. Freya simply nodded again. We stood in silence on the rolling deck. I noticed her glancing at me a time or two, but she didn't speak. After ten minutes, we drew in the ropes that ran through the metal rings at the edge of the net, pulling it tight. "Tie those off," I said. Freya wrapped the ropes around the cleats with no wasted effort.

When Freya picked up one of the boathooks, I grabbed the other, and we hooked them into the net. "Pull!" I yelled. Together, we hauled the heavy pursenet close to the boat. "Hold it," I said, and Freya kept her boathook in place. I attached the winch rope and untied the rope from the cleats. Immediately Freya dropped her boathook to run to the winch, winding up the rope to bring the dripping catch over the side and onto the deck. "Wait," I called, pushing the net away from the gunwales with my boathook. The little boat rocked, but Freya stood steady, and we brought the catch up without incident.

"Not bad," Freya said, looking at the catch.

"About half of what we would get in another month or two," I estimated. "But I agree, not bad. We'll keep fishing." We dumped the catch into the hold and refolded the net to throw it out again. After that, the routine took over: throw, draw, haul, dump, fold. We had two nets going: hard, slogging work, and not without danger, but the hold filled steadily. The work focused me. A lack of concentration could mean a full net fouling and a boat capsizing. I had long ago learned to ignore physical pain or emotional turmoil. The world shrank to sea and net and fish, the shriek of gulls, and the burning in my muscles.

In early afternoon, we returned from the northern banks, leaving the catch and the care of the boat to women who had spent the morning in training. At the house, I stripped off my scale-smeared fishing gear and found bread and cheese to eat. Then, as instructed, I found my hunting bow and its quiver of arrows and climbed up to meet the others at the flat field behind the meeting hall. No one had washed. Collectively, we smelled of fish and byre and sweat.

Casyn waited with a sword held loosely in one hand. "Welcome," he said. "If you have brought a bow, please put it to one side, then sit. You will be watching for some time and sitting will give you some rest after your morning's work." I lowered myself to the dusty ground and crossed my legs. Across the circle, I saw Tice drop gracefully into a similar position in one move.

"The first thing you must do," Casyn said without preamble, "is hold your sword, or your knife, firmly but not too tightly." He took his sword with both hands, holding it out from his body, pointing down, the tip just brushing the ground. "Look at my hands," he directed, as he turned slowly through the circle. His right hand gripped the sword just below the crosspiece, his left, just below the pommel. "If I hold tightly, if I clench my hand," he demonstrated "there are two results. My wrists and forearms become less supple, which means I have less control of the sword, and, my hands and arms will tire more quickly. You know this," he added, "from the tools you use every day. You must learn to handle a sword the same way."

"Now," he said. "Look how I stand, at the position of my feet and legs." Casyn's left leg extended forward, his knee bent slightly and his left foot directly under his hands; his right leg angled back with the foot turned away from his body. I nodded in recognition: the stance provided balance and stability. I stood the same way, hauling nets on a rocking boat, or rod-fishing for big sea-fish.

"How I stand, and how I hold the sword," Casyn continued, "is called a guard. You protect yourself while judging what your opponent might do. There are five major guard positions and five minor. Additionally, there are five major strikes, which are used to counter the cuts and thrusts from your opponent. Watch."

He held the sword up, in front of his right shoulder. "Eagle's Guard," he called, swinging the sword down and to the front, keeping the point upward. "Scythe strike, into the Horn Guard." The sword thrust forward, twisted upward, "Thrust and cut," Casyn called, pausing with the hilt at his left shoulder and the point slightly down. "Bull's Guard."

He kept going, turning slowly through the circle, calling the guards and strikes. Gradually he swung faster, and faster again, until the swordblade blurred against the sky. I saw the power and control from his years of discipline, but like the stoop of a peregrine or the leap of a wildcat, beauty and grace lived in this lethal dance. I realized I was holding my breath. I'll never be able to do that. Never. And if Leste fights like this, what chance will we have?

When he finally slowed and stopped, sweat matted his hair and stained his shirt. Tice spoke, echoing my earlier thought. "It's a dance," she said. "Just a dance."

Casyn considered. "Not just. Dancing and sword fighting do have many things in common, but your partner may not take your lead. Also," he added drily, "he is trying to kill you. Never forget that." A few women laughed. He wiped the sweat from his eyes with the back of his hand. "Under the tree are the wooden practice swords I made in the past few days. Find one that is the height of your waist and hold it the way I showed you. Try the Snake's Guard—like this." He held his sword out in front of him as he had when he first demonstrated the placement of the hands.

We went to the practice swords, neatly ranged in order of height. I held one beside me: too tall. The second one I tried seemed right, the crown of the pommel reaching to just below my hip. I moved away from the women still testing swords for size, holding it as I thought Casyn had. The sword, with a blade the width of my closed hand, had a cross-piece a bit more than two hands-widths down from the curved pommel. Tightly wrapped leather covered the grip. I hefted it, surprised to find it heavier than I had expected.

He came over to where I stood. "Move your left hand back," he instructed. "Good, now turn your upper hand just a bit. Now grip more with your littlest fingers, and let each finger after relax just a bit, until your forefingers and thumbs are the loosest, but not loose." I tried.

"Like holding a rod," I observed, "when fishing for braidan."

"Is it?" he asked. "I've never sea-fished. Now, let's see how you're standing."

He looked at my legs and feet. "Good. Bring the sword up to the Eagle's Guard." He moved my arms up to the correct position with the sword at shoulder height, pointing slightly down. "Now bring it down like a scythe to the middle of your body, or just beyond, with the point just upward, like a bull with its head down." I tried the move. It had similarities to rod casting, but as I brought the greater weight of the sword down, I stumbled, embedding the point into the ground. I grunted, feeling the shock of impact through my body.

"You bent too far forward," Casyn said calmly. "Stay straight. Keep working on it." He moved away to work with another woman. I walked a bit further away from the group to try again.

I stumbled several more times. On the next stroke, I brought my hips forward and leaned back as I did when playing a sea-fish on the line, and on the scything downstroke I fell backward. I sat for a moment where I had landed, flushed with humiliation. I glanced over at the others. Casyn moved among the women, correcting a stance or a hand hold. I saw Freya stumble, falling forward, and Dessa drop her sword on the sidestroke. Tice, though, turned as she swung and thrust, already graceful, in control of her body and the sword. I set my jaw, wiped the sweat from my hands, and stood to try again.

After an hour, Casyn called a halt. "You've done well," he said. "Wipe the grips, and then oil the blade and pommel and leave them propped up to dry. The oil and cloths are under the tree. After you have had some water, we will start on archery."

I found a rag to wipe the leather, then poured oil on the cloth, rubbing it in into the wood. Dessa came over to work beside me. "I'm sore," she said. "I feel like I've been fighting a king braidan for hours. I'll need the baths, tonight."

I flexed my shoulders. "I'm not too bad."

She snorted. "You're less than half my age."

"Do you think we'll ever learn this?"

"Yes," she replied. "We will. Some of us faster than others, and to different levels of skill. But we must, and so we will." She wiped the pommel, propping the sword against the trunk of the nearest tree. "Let's give Casyn a hand setting up the butts. You won't have much to learn, here."

The butts—the frames that held the targets for archery—belonged to the village. Many of us knew how to use a hunting bow. Herds-and-hunt apprentices, of course, had to, but others of us, me included, had learned for the pleasure of the hunt. We placed the withy-and-straw stands at the eastern end of the field, with the sun behind us, and hung the painted targets, woven of straw, on the butts.

"Who can shoot?" Casyn asked. Several hands went up, mine and Casse's among them. "Show me." Those who had no skill in archery settled down at the edge of the field to watch.

Casse shot first, using a light bird bow. Three arrows, short-shafted and tipped with a fine, single bone point, flew from her bow. All landed in the central ring of the target. Casyn nodded in approval. She walked forward to pull out her arrows. "I can't see to fletch them properly anymore," she said, "but the target is as clear as it has always been."

"Can you handle a hunting bow?" Casyn asked.

"No," Casse admitted. Casyn had excused her from learning the sword, I knew, beyond the basic holds and thrusts. "The big bow is too heavy for me now. But I can teach its use still, as I always have."

"And you will," Casyn said. "Lena?"

I stepped forward. I had strung the bow as Casse and Casyn talked, bending the curved frame back to loop the gut string over the ends. I strapped the quiver on my back and pulled an arrow out. Meant for killing deer, my arrows had a thicker, longer shaft, and a wider point; a groove ran down the shaft to create a blood-trail if an animal did not fall immediately. The deer hunt occurred in the fall, although we would take animals throughout the winter and even later if the food supplies ran low. I hadn't shot for half a year.

I raised the bow and nocked the arrow, feeling my muscles remember the task. I pulled back the bowstring, sighted along the arrow, and released. I felt the arrow speed by my cheek, flying true to the target. With pleasure, I saw it hit the centre. I nocked and released two more in quick succession. The second one hit the target just outside the centre ring. The third landed beside the first.

"Can you use a bird bow as well?" Casyn asked as I retrieved my arrows. I shook my head.

"Not as well," I said, "and better on rabbits than birds."

"We'll need both. Practice with the light bow, but you will teach with the hunting bow."

I watched as several others shot, using a mix of light and heavy bows. Almost all hit the centre at least two times out of three, pleasing me. I wanted Casyn to see our skill with the bow. He spoke briefly to each archer as she finished, and when all had shot, he gave us our instructions.

"As yet we do not have enough bows for everyone, but Kyan tells me she and her apprentice will soon rectify that. For now, each teacher will work with a small group who are close to her in height, so that you can share the bows. Today, you will only string and unstring, and learn the fingering on the bowstring. That will be enough."

Mella joined me along with two others. Mella's breasts had swollen with her pregnancy, and the others too had large breasts. "You'll need to see Kyan to be fitted for breast straps. Otherwise, the breast on your shooting side interferes with the shot. And it hurts, too, I'm told." I held out my bow. "This is a deer bow. It's made of hazel. Kyan made it, of course. Pass it around. Feel its weight."

"It's light," one of the women said.

"To string it," I explained, "you loop the bowstring around the notch at the lower tip, steady the bow with your foot, then push down on the upper limb and loop the bowstring over and into the upper notch." I demonstrated. "Mella, you try."

I unstrung it, handing her the bow and cord. Awkwardly, she looped the string into the lower notch, stood the bow upright, and rested her foot on the curve of the limb. Then she pushed on the bow, hard.

"Stop!" I cried. I took the bow from her to examine it. It appeared undamaged. "Push gently, but steadily," I explained. "Otherwise, you can break the bow."

"You didn't say that," she said angrily. "How was I to know?"

"I'm sorry. Try again?" She took the bow from me, looking unhappy, and repeated the actions, this time pushing much more gently. She nearly had the string into the upper notch when it slipped from under her foot. The rebounding bow hit her hip.

"Ahhh!" she cried, rubbing her hip. "Lena, you didn't warn me that could happen. What if it had hit my belly and hurt the baby?" Her eyes filled with tears of pain and fright.

"I'm sorry," I said again. Why did Casyn think I could teach? Just because I could shoot a bow? "I've never shown anyone how to do this before. Maybe if we do it together?"

She shook her head. "No. Let me watch someone else. I'll try again later, maybe."

I asked another woman. This time, I stood beside her, steadying the bow myself, and guided her in pushing down to loop the string. We strung and unstrung the bow three times in that manner, and when she tried it alone, she got it on the first attempt. By the time the other two had also strung the bow successfully, Mella had overcome her fright, and using the same guided motions, strung the bow without mishap.

Once everyone had strung the bow two or three times, I took it back, holding it in the shooting position. "I'm right-handed, so my left hand grips the bow here." I indicated the grip, the wood shaped for a hand and cross-hatched to make it less slippery. "I use the first two fingers on my right hand to draw the string back." I drew, bringing the bowstring back to just below my ear where I held it for a moment before releasing. "Mella?"

She hesitated, then took the bow.

This time I stood behind her. I helped her discover how to hold the bow, showing her where to put her fingers. Then I stepped back. "Pull now," I said, and she did, the bow wobbling a bit in her inexperienced grip. "Keep pulling," I urged when she stopped with the bowstring still in front of her head.

"It's hard," she said, pulling further and biting her lip in concentration.

"Release," I ordered, once she had got the position right and held it briefly. She let her fingers slip off the string too slowly. Had she nocked an arrow, it would have tumbled harmlessly to the ground a foot or two in front of her.

I asked her to repeat the action several times. By the last attempt, the bow shook noticeably. "You're tired. That's enough."

"Oh, thank you," she said, breathing hard. As she handed me the bow, I considered: Mella spun wool and kept bees, for honey and for candlewax. Neither resulted in the type of strength she needed for the hunting bow, regardless of her pregnancy.

"I think you would be better learning the small bow."

"So do I," she agreed. "But so many went to Casse, and the others with small bows are shorter than I am. So I came to you."

"I'll speak to Casse. Someone can switch." I said, wondering who.

"Thank you," Mella said. "I'm sorry I spoke angrily earlier, Lena. But I thought I would only be learning the knife because I am so clumsy in this pregnancy. Then Gille told me to try all the weapons because I might need to know how to use them. I am trying," she spread her hands, "but I'm not doing very well."

"I fell over my sword at least a half-dozen times, earlier."

"Did you?" she said in surprise. "Really?" I nodded. "That makes me feel better," she said, smiling.

"Stop, now," Casyn called after some time. I unstrung the bow and wiped down the wood, coiling the string to tuck in the quiver. After we stowed the bows, I drank some water, then joined the semicircle of women sitting in the dusty grass. I sat beside Tice, who glanced at me, smiled slightly, but said nothing.

When he had our attention, Casyn bent slightly to pull a short knife from his deerskin boot. He tossed it into the air. It tumbled, point over hilt, shining in the afternoon sun. He caught it effortlessly.

"This is the secca, the throwing knife," he said. "You saw how it spun when I tossed it. It is balanced to do that." He threw the knife at a butt. It turned in the air, flying straight and true to the target, embedding itself to the hilt.

"You will learn to do this," he said bluntly. "The knife is the thing that can save your life, either from a distance, in the throw, or in hand to hand fighting. This is the one weapon that you all, all," he emphasized, "even Casse, even Mella and Ranni, must learn."

I gazed at the secca with bile rising in my throat. A handspan of metal—the size of the knives we used to debone a fish or to cut line—and Maya chose exile over it. Anger rushed through me. I took a deep breath to keep myself from screaming. Tice glanced at me, raising an eyebrow in question. I shook my head, re-focusing on Casyn's lesson.

He sheathed the secca and brought out a wooden knife, banded with metal. "Like the swords," he explained, "these are for practice. They are weighted so as to spin and fly like a secca, but are less dangerous. When we learn close combat, the points will be guarded, but we will first learn to throw them."

He divided us into groups of five. Each group had one practice knife. It was all he had time to make, Casyn explained. "Now," he said, "this is what you will do, for the rest of this hour. Hold the knife with the tip pointing into your palm, grasping the blade from the top, and flick it upward. As it tumbles back down, catch it by the hilt." He tossed the wooden secca and caught it. I saw a hint of a grin on his face. "The first group to have all its members catch the knife correctly five times in succession wins the first lesson at the target tomorrow."

Someone whooped, and suddenly the seriousness of the afternoon disappeared. The lesson had turned into play. We spread out. Laughter and curses rang over the field as we tossed and dropped the knives, scratching ourselves before we began to catch them properly. Groups began to shout their scores. As I threw and caught the knife for the fourth time in a row, my group chanting encouragement, the pain inside me receded, just a bit.

We lost to Dessa's group, but we threw second the next day, and I fell over my sword less. Gradually, as spring gave way to summer and we spent our afternoons with sword and bow and knife, my muscles and nerves learned the skills, and my swordplay went from clumsy to competent. I learned the guards and the strikes; I could hold my own when we moved on to practice fighting. All around me on the field, I could see similar transformations taking place. Mella, her belly huge now, could, with a bird bow, hit the red centre on the target nine times out of ten from a hundred paces. Casse learned to throw the secca with deadly precision, delighting in learning something new at her advanced age. Casyn watched, corrected, sometimes chastised, and with his grave good humour kept us working through the long summer afternoons.

I slept well at night from sheer physical exhaustion, but when Freya and I sailed to and from the fishing grounds, I rarely thought of anything but Maya. In calm seas, I could sail without thinking, while my mind replayed the events of that evening, inventing scenarios in which I stopped her from leaving, or, alternately, went with her. Freya's natural quietness, combined with, I suppose, her reticence to interrupt my reverie, meant that mostly my thoughts had free rein. Inevitably, this led to remembering the insights of that first, terrible morning, but I shied away from too deep a re-examination. When I forced my mind away from that fruitless course, by trying to think about the finer points of swordplay, or teaching archery, it always led me back to Maya, alone somewhere in the outside world, with no skills to defend herself. I feared for her, but more intensely, I missed her. Only the relentless focus of the practice field could distract me from the physical ache of her absence.

†††††

Two weeks after Maya left I had moved back to Tali's house. "Are you sure?" my mother had asked gently. "You know you're welcome to stay."

I shook my head. "Tali is alone, too," I said. "It'll be better for us both. We can be company for each other." I didn't know if that was true. When Tali and I had spoken, she had said little about Maya, but at my mother's, I found myself reverting to the familiar roles of childhood, arguing over little chores, squabbling with Kira. I wanted to grieve as an adult. At my mother's house, I could not acknowledge the emptiness of my arms and my body's need for Maya's warmth. I cried into my pillow, but I needed to howl. My mother considered, twisting her hair.

"I do worry about her," she acknowledged. "But please come here, to eat, or to talk."

"I will," I promised.

Once a week, we had a day with no training after our morning's work. Casyn insisted on this, saying our minds and bodies needed rest. On the next free afternoon, I packed my few clothes, slung the bag over my shoulder, and walked down the path toward the harbour and our house. Empty rooms greeted me. I climbed the wooden stairs to our room, hesitating before the closed door. Then I stepped forward, opening it.

Tali had changed the bedclothes, and an unfamiliar blanket covered the bed. Why? I wondered, then realized Maya must have taken the other one. With that thought, all the grief and anger resurfaced.

I began to cry. Pulling the wardrobe doors open, I dragged a shirt she had left behind out to hold it to my face, smelling her on it. "Maya." I wailed. I collapsed across the bed, sobbing, despairing of comfort. I could find no hope in my mind for Maya, or for me. When I could cry no more, I simply lay on the bed, staring at nothing, hugging the shirt. Tali found me there when she returned from the fields. I blinked up at her.

"I slept with Mar's tunic for a year," she said gently. "I think you were right to come home. Pel misses you, both of you, and it will help him to have you here. Supper's ready. Wash your face and come down."

Pel chattered happily to me, and I made the effort to respond with interest. We ate chicken and dumplings while he told us about shepherding on the hills, where he spent much of his time with the young apprentices guarding the sheep and lambs.

"Is Maya coming home, too?" he asked suddenly.

Tali raised her eyebrows, signalling me to answer him. I swallowed, hoping my voice wouldn't betray me. "Not yet," I answered. "Maya's gone to another village. She won't be home for a long time."

He thought about this. "Will I have gone with the men before she gets back?"

"Yes," Tali said. "You will have. I told you she said goodbye, and told you to be good, too. You remember?"

He nodded. "I remember, but I miss her. Do you miss her, Lena?"

I smiled, blinking rapidly. "I do, Pel. I do."

CHAPTER FOUR

IN HIGH SUMMER, ANOTHER MESSENGER CAME. He arrived in the morning, spending the day with Casyn and the council leaders. None of us expressed surprise the next day when we heard that afternoon training would be replaced by a meeting on the following day. It seemed a luxury to return from the fishing and have time to soak in the baths and eat a leisurely meal twice in one week. Generally, I disliked rest days, as nothing distracted me from thoughts of Maya, but today, with the expectation of something new happening, I welcomed the change.

After a meal of fish and early root vegetables, we walked up the hill to the meeting hall. Heat radiated off the ground, and a fine layer of dust covered everything. The world seemed baked and hard, and around me, the women seemed the same, skin burned brown from the sun, muscles taut in hard bodies. We had been fit before, but not like this. We settled in the circle. I sat with Siane. I had taken to visiting with her when I could find the time.

Casyn and the messenger spoke quietly to my mother and Gille. The new man, slightly built and about my height, appeared not more than some half-dozen years my elder. His hands were callused like mine, or Dessa's, hands that worked with ropes in salt water.

Gille called the meeting to order. "This is Dern," she said simply, after the formal words of opening had been spoken. "He has come to tell us what the Empire requires of us now. We—Casyn, Gwen, Sara, and I—went over the plans with him this afternoon." She paused for a moment, then continued. "In a week or two, a ship will arrive at Tirvan, a fighting vessel from the Empire's navy. The ship is called *Skua*. Dern is her captain, and she has a crew of forty men. While she is here, *Skua* must be provisioned and made ready for the invasion of Leste. Also, and perhaps more importantly, *Skua*'s crew are fighting men, who will test our readiness to defend Tirvan. Over the weeks they are here, they will hone their skills, and ours. They will attack our defences, to find our weak points. And they will help us correct them." Gille paused. "I find this reassuring. We will not go into battle untried."

From the reaction of the women around me, I gathered that most of us felt the same. If nothing else, this new challenge would provide a diversion from the rote practice on the field. Gille called us to order.

"With fair winds, *Skua* should arrive in ten days," Casyn said. "In those ten days, we will continue to practice with sword and spear and bow, but we must also give thought and time to organization. I will not be here when the attack comes. I will be leaving aboard *Skua*."

Several women gasped. We had assumed Casyn would be staying with us. He continued. "Gille will command, with Gwen and Sara as deputies. They know the strategies and the plans. We need now to divide you into cohorts, with one woman designated to command each cohort. I have watched you for ten weeks, on the field and about your work, and I have met with the council leaders. In battle, there can be no democracy, so I—we—have chosen the cohort leaders, and the cohorts." He paused. "I know this is not your usual way of doing things, but these are not usual times. Shall Dern and I leave you for a while, so you may debate this?"

He watched us, grave and courteous as ever. I wondered if the soldiers sent to the other women's villages had the same qualities. I had thought soldiers brusque, rough in manners and speech, from what I had seen at Festival. Casyn's boundless patience, his courtesy towards our customs and traditions, his gentleness seemed at odds with this. Did it have to do with the skills needed to command?

"Do we need time for debate?" Sara asked the assembly.

"I'll abide by your decision," said Kyan, the bowyer, from the other side of the hall. "We've all had ample time to see that Casyn knows his business. If he and the councillors have chosen our leaders, I trust they will have chosen well."

A chorus of "ayes" followed this statement.

"Does any woman here request debate?" Sara asked again. Silence pervaded the hall.

She glanced over at Gwen and Gille. "We will proceed. Casyn, if you would?"

He nodded, stepping forward, a list in his hand. "There will be seven cohorts, twelve women and apprentices each. Your council leaders, and a few of the oldest women, are not included in any cohort. I will address their roles later. Some cohorts will be specialists in one skill; for example, we have put the best archers together. Others will have a mix of skills. Each cohort will be assigned a specific role in the defence of Tirvan. I will tell you, first, who the cohort leaders are and then who is in each cohort."

Women leaned forward in their seats, waiting.

"These are the cohort leaders. Please stay in your seats for now," Casyn said, "but I will want to meet with you briefly, after all the assignments are made. Kyan, Tali, Dessa, Dari, Binne, Lena, and Grainne. Do you all accept?"

Kyan, I thought, would lead the archers, and do it well. Tali had proven herself expert with a sword, endlessly patient in correcting the parries and thrusts of others. But the others... I realized Siane was clapping me on the back. "Lena," she said urgently, "Lena! Casyn is waiting for your answer."

"What?" I said stupidly.

"You have been chosen as a cohort leader. You must formally accept."

"But I'm only just eighteen." My birthday was a few days after midsummer.

"You are an adult and more than competent." Siane said firmly. "Do you doubt Casyn's judgement, and your mother's? Give him your answer."

I thought of Casyn watching me on the field, his rare words of praise. A week ago, we had spoken at the end of training.

"Tell me, Casyn," I remembered saying. "We haven't learned anything new for a week or two. I know we need to keep practicing, but won't there come a point at which we think we know it all, get bored, and start making mistakes?"

He had looked at me gravely. "Complacent, I think you mean."

"Yes," I had agreed. "Complacent. That would be dangerous, wouldn't it?"

"It would be. You have good instincts, Lena. You would make a good soldier. Be patient just a little while longer. Changes will be coming soon."

The changes had come. I met Casyn's gaze. "I accept."

The cohort I would lead consisted of younger women and several apprentices.

"You will need to become highly skilled with the secca," Casyn explained. "I told you once before that it is the knife, above all other weapons, that may be the difference between life and death. Your skill with it may also mean the difference between winning the battle here, or losing."

I glanced around the cohort. Their eyes flicked from Casyn to me, and I realized they were waiting for me, their leader, to respond.

"How so?" I asked, thinking as I spoke that the question lacked insight.

"When the invasion comes," Casyn answered, "this cohort will not fight openly. Your job will be to lay hidden, to be the last line of defence. You will need to know every loft and winter store and stable in the village—all the places you can hide. You must be able to move between them silently in the dark, and to kill, silently, in that dark."

I swallowed. "Why were we chosen?"

"Youth," he answered, "and the speed and reflexes you have all shown in the training. You all handle the secca well, too, but you also have something more: fearlessness, perhaps, although that does not quite describe it. A willingness to take chances, when chances are required."

Take chances? If I took chances, wouldn't I be with Maya now? How could Casyn think me not just fearless, but capable of leading such a group and such a task? To command women older than I, if only by a few years, disconcerted me. I marshalled my thoughts.

"What must we do first?"

"Choose a second-in-command and begin your work together."

The twelve of us sat in a circle at one side of the council hall. Four apprentices, including Freya, and eight women, including myself, under thirty. Looking around the circle, I saw no hostility, no obvious challenge to my leadership. I knew I had to show decisiveness in this, my first task as leader. My eyes travelled round the circle again to rest on Tice. I knew her only slightly better than I had at the beginning of the summer. At spring Festival one night, she had danced in the southern style, graceful and precise and silent. I thought of that, of her grace with the sword, and of her calm, assessing gaze. "Tice, you are cohort-second."

Her dark eyes met mine, and she nodded. The other women said nothing, but I saw Freya nod in approval. I glanced out the window. A good hour of daylight remained. "Fetch your knives," I said, "and meet in the upper corner of the training ground in ten minutes. Tice, stay back, please."

"I need you," I said when we were alone, "to teach the others to move silently. And to teach me, too. I've always envied the way you dance."

Tice chuckled. "What a reason to be chosen cohort-second," she said. "Because of the way I dance!" Her chuckle became a deep, full-throated laugh.

I blinked, spluttered, and then found myself laughing with her. The tension drained out of me. I couldn't remember when I had last laughed.

"Can you think of a better reason?"

Tice shook her head, still laughing. I realized we had piqued the curiosity of other cohorts still in the hall. "We'd better go out to the training ground."

She nodded, solemnly, then burst out into gales of laughter again. "Yes, commander."

"Don't call me that!" I protested. "It makes me feel about six again, playing soldier with the boys in the hills."

She stopped laughing. "Isn't that exactly what we're doing? Except now, the boys have grown up, and the game is deadly serious. I will teach them, and you, silence, as best I can in such a brief time, and you will improve their knife skills and show us all how to think. Casyn did not choose you as cohort-leader because of your skills with secca and bow, Lena. You are good, but so are others. He chose you because you think differently. You see what could happen and plan for it. That's your strength. Teach us to think like that, a bit, and you may keep us alive, more so than silence in the night."

"She's right," a voice said from behind me. I turned to face Dern. His eyes— blue, with fine lines radiating out from the corners—met mine. "Casyn said as much to me, and Casyn is a fine judge of men. Of soldiers," he amended. "He was my cadet-officer, once. I am Dern, captain of *Skua*. You are Lena, and this is—?"

"Tice," I said. "She'll be our cohort-second."

He inclined his head to her. "From Karst?" he asked. She nodded. "I have served with men from Karst. They are like cats, all stealth and grace and silence. You have chosen well, Lena."

"We were just going to watch some knife play." Dern's casual judgement of both myself and Tice annoyed me. How could he know anything about us?

"May I come?" he asked. He must have seen the look on my face, for before I could answer, he spoke again. "I wish only to observe and to hear your recommendations afterwards. I will start to teach tomorrow, but the cohort is yours to lead. I would not usurp that leadership, but I would like to see what your cohort can do. With your permission."

I shrugged. "If you like."

"I will meet you on the field." He turned gracefully, striding across the hall to where Casyn stood with Kyan. Tice looked at me, one eyebrow cocked, but said nothing.

"They're waiting," I said.

On the field, we divided the women into more-or-less evenly matched pairs, based on height and weight. Each woman had her own wooden secca now. Casyn had been hard at work, forging real ones in the evenings. Dern stood back, under the trees, watching.

Freya and Rai had lost the draw. They walked onto the field to face off, each holding her secca close to her body. They circled each other. I watched them, conscious of Dern's gaze, wondering what I should focus on. Freya had strong shoulders and arms from fishing. Rai, ten years her elder, stood half a head shorter but carried more muscle. I judged she outweighed the younger girl by twenty pounds.

Freya feinted first, and Rai stepped sideways, turning her body so that Freya had less of a target, moving backwards at the same time. Freya's cut went wide. She turned quickly, but Rai had swung too and had her knife up, aimed for Freya's unprotected left side. Freya twisted, not away from Rai, but towards her, bringing her secca up to catch Rai's knife arm. The blade struck Rai's forearm. A metal secca would have cut deeply. The wooden practice knife only bruised, but Freya struck with enough strength to force a grimace of pain from Rai. She did not drop the knife, but forced her arm down against the secca to push Freya off-balance. In the same motion, she tossed her knife sideways, caught it with her other hand, and had it up against Freya's throat in an instant.

"Enough," I said. They stepped apart, panting.

Rai rubbed her arm. "That hurt," she said. She shook the arm to loosen the muscles. "But I've had worse from an angry ram," she added, grinning at Freya.

"It would have hurt more had Freya held a real secca," I said. I wanted to glance at Dern, to see what I could read in his face after this first demonstration, but I kept my eyes on Rai. I wondered if he could hear all we said. "You wouldn't have been able to push back against her without driving it deeper into your arm. So while that was a good move now, you shouldn't rely on it. Freya, what did you misjudge?"

"I didn't expect her to push back," she replied, pushing her hair back from her face. "But I suppose if the enemy wear leather, or have arm-guards, they just might. Although then I might not have gone for the arm."

"Right," I said. "Who is next?"

"Wait," Tice said. "I have some things to add."

"Of course," I said hastily.

"Freya, your stance needs work," she said bluntly. "If your left foot had been further back, you could have withstood the pressure without losing your balance so early. We can work on it."

Freya blinked, then glanced at me. I kept my face impassive.

"Yes, all right," she said after a moment, her voice flat. I knew her well enough now to know she took criticism too personally.

"I imagine many of us will need to perfect our stances," I said. "A good observation, Tice. Who is next?"

Aline and Camy, both apprentices, took the field. Slight and wiry, neither had the advantage after three minutes of thrust and parry, and neither had landed a blow. I called a halt. They stopped with some reluctance.

"You're fast," I said, "both with the knife and on your feet. I think you've practiced together quite a bit?"

They looked at each other. "Every day," Camy said.

"So you know what each other will do," Tice said. "Are you practicing, or playing?"

"We're practicing," Aline protested. "Sometimes one of us adds a new move, something we've learned or want to try. We're not children."

"How you will do paired against someone taller or heavier will prove interesting."

"That will be fun!" Aline said. "I bet we're faster." As she turned to leave the field, she made a move towards me with her knife. I jumped back.

"Aline!" I shouted. Tice moved forward, ready to take the secca, but I held up a hand. "Never do that again, to me or anyone," I said, my voice still raised, "or I will take your secca and have you reassigned to another cohort. You say you're not a child. Don't act like one."

She hung her head.

As they walked off the field, deflated, I turned to Tice. "Your comments are accurate," I said very quietly, "but somewhat blunt. Perhaps you could be a bit gentler?"

"Their lives may depend on their knife skills. I see no point in being gentle. And they need to learn that you and I are in command. I would argue that blunt and calm is better than shouting, as you just did."

I bit back an angry retort. Aline had startled me, and I had reacted. I thought of Dern watching. "You may be right. Shall we watch the next pair?" She nodded, turning away from me in a fluid motion, returning her focus to the field where two more women prepared to fight. Solid women, both of them, with the agility required to move up and down rocky hillsides or to maintain balance on a rocking boat. Tice moves so gracefully, I thought. She controls even the tiniest move of her body. Telling a story through dance requires such control. The rest of us have balance, strength, and speed, but our skills come from countering forces—waves or winds or the pull of the earth. Our enemies will have the same skills. Tice can teach us how the move of a thumb, the slightest turn of wrist, can change the odds and the outcome when we fight.

I signalled for the fighters to begin. With my new insight, I saw where a turn of a foot, or the angle of a thrust, needed not correction, but refinement. "Her balance is too far back. She needs to bring it forward, to the balls of her feet," I murmured to Tice, pointing at one of the women.

"You're right," she said, surprised.

"I was thinking about why you move differently." Just then, one woman stumbled backward, and the other had her pinned, knife at her throat, in a second. "Stop now," I said to them. "Tice, tell them what you saw."

We had little light left. I stole a look at Dern but could not read his expression. "We better do two pairs at once," I said when Tice had finished her critique. "Tice, will you watch the next two? I'll take Salle and Kelle."

When we completed the round of pairings, I divided the women again, this time with as much disparity in size as I could find, then we watched and critiqued again. Tice tempered her comments a bit, and I tried to keep my voice calm.

By the end of the day, we had a rough evaluation of each woman's skills. Dern had moved closer as the light faded but had said nothing.

Finally, in the deepening dusk, Tice and I both took a knife. As we circled, I again marvelled at her grace. Dern had likened her people to cats; I thought it an apt comparison.

I focused on Tice's eyes and the muscles in her knife arm. When I saw her tense to strike, I slid sideways. I twisted up, striking at her, but she danced backwards, then pivoted and thrust at me again. Her secca brushed my arm. I stepped away from the thrust, my eyes on her face. For a heartbeat, neither of us moved, then I feinted left. As she turned just slightly, I changed direction, knifing upward towards her left side. She ducked, falling forward onto her hands, then springing up again. She moved so fast that by the time I had rebalanced and turned, she had her knife against my stomach. I held up my hands and dropped my secca, grinning. The cohort applauded.

I glanced over at Dern.

"Well done, both of you," he said. "May I speak with you both, for a while?"

"Tonight?"

"I would prefer it."

"Yes," I said. "We can go to my mother's house. When should we meet in the morning?"

"Three hours after sunrise?"

I nodded then turned to the waiting women. "Meet here two-and-a-half hours after sunrise. Bring your knives. If you're sore now, go soak it out in the baths. Sleep well tonight." The women drifted away in pairs and small groups.

"They'll all go to the baths," I said to Tice. "I hope it doesn't turn into a late evening, with lots of wine, or they'll be useless in the morning."

"You're thinking like a leader already. I was just envying them the baths and the wine."

"There is wine at my mother's," I said, "if you want it."

"I would be glad of some," Dern said.

My mother's door, as usual, stood open to let in the evening breeze off the sea. When we arrived, my mother, Sara, Gille, and Casyn sat around the kitchen table. The lamp glowed softly, attracting moths to its flame.

"Mother," I greeted her, "Dern and Tice and I need somewhere to talk. May we use your workroom? And may we have some wine, and some cheese and bread?"

"Yes, to all of that," she said. "Tice, Dern, you are very welcome. You'll need to bring in a third chair from the porch." Dern went out to get the chair. Tice followed me to the kitchen cupboards. I handed her the wine flask and cups, pointing the way to the workroom. I put bread and cheese on a plate. In the workroom, I opened the shutters to let in the air and lit the lamp. Dern came in with the chair and closed the door. Tice poured wine for all of us. She held up one cup, its deep red glaze reflecting the lamplight. "I made these."

"With great skill," Dern observed. Tice inclined her head, acknowledging the compliment. "You are both women of many skills," he said, looking steadily at me. The comment made me uncomfortable, and the confidence I had felt after he had praised us slipped away. I picked up my cup without meeting his eyes.

We sat sipping wine in silence. Dern leaned forward, helping himself to bread and cheese. In the flicker of the lamp, he looked older than I had first judged him to be, and very tired. Finally, he spoke. "Savour the wine, and remember it. This is Lestian wine. If we are not victorious when the battle comes, you may never taste it again."

"What did you want to talk about?"

"Lena, you were chosen to lead these women for several reasons: for your ability in the practice ring; for your family connections—the women of Tirvan are accustomed to having your mother and your aunts as their leaders; for your depth of thought." He paused. "But we also chose you to lead this cohort because you have shown that you can make a difficult decision, even when it affects you personally." He held up his hand to prevent me from speaking. "You may need to do that again. You may need to send someone from the cohort— Freya, perhaps, or even Tice—into extreme danger, alone and to certain death. A single death might mean the saving of Tirvan, or of the Empire. I am not exaggerating."

A chill ran through me. I stared at the wine-cup in my hands, my mind in turmoil. I thought of all the hours I had spent on *Dovekie*, reliving that evening. On the basis of that day, those decisions, Casyn appointed me to this task? What could he know of the recriminations, the fears that had haunted me since? "What if," I said angrily, "I made that decision from cowardice? What if I did not go with Maya simply because I was too scared? What sort of leader would I be then?"

Dern leaned forward. "Is that true? Look me in the eye, now, here in this room with only the three of us and tell the truth." He spoke gently, but with an undertone of command. I swallowed, looking at the floor. I didn't want to answer him.

"Tell us," he said, firmly.

I looked up and met his eyes. "No," I whispered in a voice barely loudly enough to hear. I cleared my throat to try again. "It is a night thought, or a thought for the empty sea, nothing more."

His gaze did not release me. "Then why did you let Maya go?"

"Because," I hesitated, "all of us, in the village..." How could I say what I knew inside me? "We have been here so long...our history, what our foremothers built here...it matters. It matters more than one person. Or two people."

Dern smiled slightly. I realized I had just passed a test. I could hear Tice breathing in the silent room. "Drink your wine," he said gently. "We did not misjudge you."

Tice put down her cup. "May I go? I understand why you wanted me here, but I think there are things you would say to Lena alone."

I opened my mouth to object, but Dern nodded. "Sleep well, Tice."

"Can we speak, tomorrow, before practice?" I asked, remembering my earlier idea and wanting to delay her departure.

"At the field?" she asked. I nodded. She said goodnight, closing the door carefully behind her.

"A perceptive woman," Dern said, leaning back in his chair. As he reached for his wine cup, the lamplight accentuated the lines of fatigue around his eyes. "I am twenty-six. I chose the sea at twelve. Like you, I am from a fishing village—Serra, in the north. When I was sixteen my captain called me to him and told me he was sending me back to land. He sent me to Casyn, to learn to do what you must learn to do." He took a drink of the wine. "I know what it is to send a friend to die. You can do it, Lena. Even now, when I first told you, your thoughts were not that you could not do this, but only that perhaps you would do it for the wrong reasons. When the doubts begin, come to me, Lena."

Not likely, I thought.

"You need to talk them out, not to your cohort or your cohort-second or even your mother. I am here to teach your cohort, but I am also here to teach you, as Casyn taught me."

As I pondered this, something that had been puzzling me at the edges of my consciousness came into focus. "Casyn doesn't seem to be an average soldier. He taught you this...craft of secrecy...and now you are here to teach us. Why could Casyn not have taught us? Why is there such a concentration of expertise here in Tirvan? Is the Empire spending talent this generously on other villages?"

Dern smiled again. "Always thinking," he said. "You are right, of course. I am primarily here to plan tactics with Casyn. We have learned things about the invasion plan in the past few months, and they need to be considered. Casyn is a master of this craft of secrecy, as you call it. The Emperor was unwilling to let him come to Tirvan, but he argued that he needed to have first-hand experience of what a woman's village was capable of before he could make his final plans against Leste. I'm here to make him privy to our newest information, and to take him back, in a few weeks, to our command post."

"What does he think us capable of, after his months here?"

"He believes you to be physically capable of as much as a group of men would have been, after only a few months training. But he believes you will fight much harder, and with more tenacity, because you'll be defending your houses, your village, and your way of life. You said, a few minutes ago, that you belong here, that Tirvan is something more than the sum of its parts. Almost all of you feel the same way, in different degrees. You will fight for that feeling of place and belonging." In his voice, I heard the same faint echo of regret that I had heard in Casyn's voice, the night he first came to Tirvan.

"For what do you fight, Dern?" I asked softly.

"For the Empire, and for brotherhood, and because it is what we are trained for from the minute we leave our villages." We sat in silence, sipping our wine. The lamp flickered in the night breeze.

I broke the silence. "What happens to boys, to men, who don't make good soldiers? Who just want to farm or fish?"

"They can be medics, or cooks, or teach the little ones. If they insist, we let them go at sixteen. They work with horses or go to the farms and villas of the retired officers, to pick grapes and make hay. But they can't come back to the women's villages."

"Not at all?"

"No. Not that they would likely want to. They pay a price for choosing not to serve the Empire. This village farms as well as fishes. You must know a bit about breeding horses, or cattle. What does your herdswoman do with colts that are weak around the quarters or ewe-necked? The empire needs men to be soldiers, not farmers. We need our sons to be strong, so we make sure that only those who serve the Empire father sons."

Shaken, I drank the dregs of my wine. From our earliest childhood, we knew how our lives were structured and where the duty of both men and women lay. I had not considered, until tonight, that sacrifice underpinned that structure, that each of us paid some inestimable price for our calm and ordered existence. Until tonight, I had thought only of Maya, and of myself.

Dern stared upward at nothing, his lips tight, exhaustion or worry webbing his face. "I said too much." He sounded apologetic. "Blame the wine."

"It's late," I said. "And the Lestian wine is strong. I won't repeat what was said here tonight."

He nodded. "Thank you." He gazed at me steadily for a minute before standing. "I sleep at Casyn's cottage until my ship is in harbour. Would you point the way?" I took the lamp from the wall and opened the door. Darkness shadowed the outer room. We walked out onto the porch. A light still burned at the forge cottage: Casyn, bent over papers and maps, planning. Dern bade me a soft goodnight and set off, silent, on the gravel path. I blew out the lamp, setting it on a bench before turning in the opposite direction, downhill, to Tali's house and bed.

CHAPTER FIVE

THE DAY DAWNED HOT, THE AIR STILL AND HUMID. As I washed in the morning light, at the open window of my room, I could hear Tali in the kitchen below me, talking to Pel. I brushed my hair back off my face, strapped my knife onto my belt, and went down for breakfast.

"Dessa was here last night," Tali said. "She wants to borrow *Dovekie* while you're not fishing. She said she would sail her herself and let her senior apprentices sail *Curlew*."

I poured myself a mug of tea, considering. Both Freya and I now trained all day with Dern, and the village needed all the food it could stockpile. Reasonably, I could not refuse. "Can Pel go down to the harbour to tell her yes?"

Pel looked unhappy. "I wanted to watch the knife play."

"It won't start for another hour," I said. "Go to the harbour now to tell Dessa that I said she may use Dovekie for as long as she needs her. If you're quick and don't linger at the boats, I'll teach you a move or two with the knives before we start practice this morning." Pel brightened and jumped up. He glanced at his mother for permission, running out the door almost before Tali had finished saying "Go." I cut a slice of bread, spreading honey on it.

"Don't let him become a nuisance."

I shrugged. "There's always a gaggle of them about, the small boys and some of the girls. It won't hurt them to learn a bit." I finished my bread and took a sip of my tea. It had cooled, so I drank it down. "Would you send him to the practice field when he gets back? I want to speak with Tice before the others arrive." I rinsed my mug and plate, setting them to drain on the wooden rack over the sink. From a basket on the table, I took an apple and a pear. Tali filled a water bottle. "What are you doing today?" I asked.

"Picking more apples," she said. "They're a bit green, but they should dry well." She grinned. "If a big storm blows up and drowns all the invaders, we're going to be sick of smoked fish and dried apples this winter."

I laughed and went out into the sunlight. From long habit, I turned to look out to sea. A haze hung over the horizon, but the white sails of fishing boats dotted the bay. I walked up the hill to the empty practice field, my sandaled feet kicking up small clouds of dust. I stopped in a shaded corner and began the stretching exercises Casyn had taught us. Methodically, I counted my way through the routine, one-two-three, one-two-three. My skin gleamed with sweat when I sensed rather than heard someone approaching. I looked up.

"Good morning," Tice said.

"And to you. Did you sleep well?"

"Yes," she said. "The wine helped. Did you stay with Dern long?"

"We talked for a while longer," I said. "Tice, I want you to teach us to dance."

"To dance!" she exclaimed.

"Will you?"

"I can try," she said, "but we don't have much time. I don't know if what I can teach in a few weeks can make much difference."

"In a few weeks, we have learned the sword and the secca, and the bow, for some."

"True," she said. "I'll do my best, cohort-leader."

I grinned. She pulled her dark hair back off her face and tied it, then joined me in the stretches. When our muscles felt loose and supple, we switched to knife play, and then to wrestling. When Pel arrived with his friend Salle, we taught them the simpler moves with the wooden knives. They went off to the far corner of the field to practice. Tice and I sat in the shade of the tree. I gave her the pear, and we sat in silence, savouring the crisp tartness of the fruit.

I tossed my apple core aside. "Show me how to move more quietly, before the others get here."

"I can show you some things," she said. "But unless you have danced the dances of Karst since you were a babe newly on your feet, you—or any of the cohort—will never be truly silent."

"Anything would be an improvement. I couldn't sneak up on a hibernating bear."

Tice laughed. "You're quieter than you think," she said. "Your body has learned some grace from the knife-play, and the beginnings a different sort of balance than you needed on the boats. But come," she said, on her feet in one swift move, extending a hand to help me up, "I'll show you what I can."

Patiently, she explained how to roll my weight along my foot and push off lightly from the ball of my feet and from my toes. I practised this for a while. My movements felt exaggerated and artificial, but I did make less noise. We had moved on to the steps of the first dance learned by Karst children when Dern arrived. I stopped, suddenly self-conscious.

"Taran taught me that dance, too, when we served together," he observed. "Come, Lena," he said, grasping my hands. "Dance with me." I stopped myself from stepping back. His hands felt cool and dry against my moist palms. Our heights matched. "To the left, to begin," he said, sliding his left leg sideways in the first move of the simple dance. I looked at my feet and followed.

After two or three steps, I looked up to find Dern also watching his feet. Tice slowly chanted the moves, and I relaxed. We managed a dozen steps or so before our feet collided. Dern stumbled, and I stopped. We looked at each other, his hands still holding mine. For a handful of heartbeats, we stood, his eyes travelling from mine, down to my lips, and back again to meet my gaze. I flushed, pulling my hands away. "I was never a dancer," I said.

"And I am out of practice. Apologies for my awkwardness. Shall we return to the knives, where we know the moves?" He turned away to begin his warm-up exercises. Tice caught my eye, grinning. I felt myself flushing again and busied myself with my knife.

The cohort began to arrive a few minutes later. After the stretching exercises and basic moves, I sent half the women to work with Dern, and Tice and I began the remedial work with the other half. We worked on grip and angles, on wrist actions and on movement. By the end of two hours, I could see a marked improvement in the entire group. Lara arrived with water. We took turns drinking before stretching out in the shade for a well-earned rest.

After the break, Tice took over. As a group, we kicked off our sandals, to learn how to walk in a new fashion. Dern excused himself and went back down the hill towards the forge. The cohort practised silence—foot-silence, anyhow. Laughter and muffled curses punctuated the activity, especially when the time came to judge each woman individually. Freya topped us all.

With about an hour left in the morning's training, I called a halt. The cohort settled into a rough half-circle on the grass.

"You've all worked hard this morning," I said. "But we're going to introduce something new now. I think you've all noticed how graceful Tice is, how smoothly she moves?" Several heads nodded. "I'd like us all to move our bodies like that, and to help us learn, I've asked Tice to teach us to dance."

"To dance?" Aline said, unknowingly echoing Tice's reaction of the previous night. "I'm not going to learn to dance. We were chosen to learn knife skills, not to dance." She sounded disgusted. I almost laughed, remembering how black and white the world seemed at fourteen. "You're not my apprentice-master," she continued. "Casyn chose me, not you."

"As he chose me to lead this cohort," I said quietly. "So you will do as I say, and as Tice says, and you will learn to dance. Not for pleasure, but for the precision of step and balance and movement it teaches. I will be learning right beside you. It is Tice who is the master in this. Do you understand?"

"Yes," she muttered, but she did not meet my eye. Had I misjudged my response? I thought of Casyn's words: In battle, there is no democracy.

"All right," I said. "Let's get started."

I went to my mother's to eat. Neither she nor Kira answered my call. They were out in the village, I surmised, checking on Nessa's newborn or one of the other soon-to-deliver women. I took some cheese and bread and sat on the porch, where breezes from the sea cooled the air a little. I watched the gulls over the sea, and the sails of the boats out on the fishing banks, the blue-and-white of *Dovekie* among them. There was a line of clouds on the horizon, building up from the heat. Rain later, with a bit of luck. Will Maya have shelter, if it rains wherever she is? Does she have food? My chest tightened. I blinked back tears. No, I thought. Think about something else. Think about correcting Gayl's balance.

A while later, I saw my mother walking up the path, looking tired. I got up to bring her water. She sat on the porch, drinking thirstily. "Ranni's labour started. I've left Kira with her for a bit. She's capable of handling the early stages, now."

"Will it be all right?" I asked. Nessa had lost one of her twins at birth a few days earlier, after a long and difficult labour.

"Everything seems normal, but she's scared, with it being her first baby. And with the times. I shouldn't stay away long." She poured herself another drink. "I will be calling meeting tonight, or tomorrow—tonight if the rain comes early."

"Why?"

"*Skua* will arrive soon," she said. "Her crew of men will be going into battle soon, chancing death. We are a village of women facing the same truth for the first time. I won't deny either group comfort, but neither can we risk new pregnancies. All of us, apprentice to elder, who are of childbearing years must begin to drink anash tea as soon as possible."

Anash tea, if drunk before and after Festival for a few days, and each day during, prevented pregnancy. A poor harvest or a bad winter meant general use at Festival, but an individual woman drank it whenever she did not wish a Festival liaison to result in pregnancy. I thought of Dern and forced the thought away.

"Apprentices?" I asked. "But we don't allow apprentices liaisons."

"No," my mother agreed, her voice tired, "in usual times, we do not. But we feel, Gille and Sarah and I, that we cannot deny that these are not usual times. In the coming raids, some of us will die or be raped. These are not Empire's men. Providing the council agrees with us, we won't stop liaisons between *Skua*'s crew and our girls and women, regardless of status. And all of us will drink anash tea until the war is over, both against wanted encounters, and unwanted."

"I see," I said slowly. I did see, but I didn't want to drink anash. I fetched my mother some food, and we sat on the porch and ate and drank cool water. After another half hour, I went back to the practice field.

Dern did not come back in the afternoon. I wondered where he was, and with whom. The cohort worked and danced for another two hours, until the thunderheads building in the western sky rumbled, and the fishing boats ran back into harbour ahead of the storm. I went down to the docks to help unload and prepare the boats.

Lightening flashed, and the first fat drops of rain splashed into the water when we finished. The air smelled of wet dust and the sharp tang that followed lightening. I stood on the dock, holding my face up to the rain. Maya loved thunderstorms, loved the feel of the rain and the play of light and shadow in the clouds. She would sit in the window of our room on summer evenings, watching the storms out over the sea and the seabirds playing on the storm winds, laughing in pure delight. A wave of loneliness poured over me.

I closed my eyes. Behind me, I could hear someone moving around on the boats—Dessa, probably, inspecting for storm-readiness. Work provided the antidote. I opened my eyes and went to help her, checking ropes and hatches while the rain grew stronger.

By the time we finished, my hair and clothes were dripping. I walked up the hill, grabbed a change of clothes and a towel, and went to the baths. Someone had tacked an announcement of meeting tonight to the door. I went in, rinsed my feet and hands, and sank into the hot pool. For a while, I just floated, letting the warmth ease my tired muscles. The gentle movement of the water against my skin comforted me. Maya had excelled at back rubs, working the kinks out of neck and shoulders, aching from hauling nets. I missed her touch, missed not the pleasure but the solace of lovemaking, the basic human need for connection. If I wanted, I knew, Dern would meet that need, both mine and his.

I considered. Maya and I had paired before puberty, her sadness evoking some instinct for protection in me. We had become lovers as adolescents, and in the eyes of the village had partnered in all senses. Liaisons with men had little effect on most partnerships between women, although some women, like my aunt Tali, who had truly and deeply loved the man who fathered her elder children, chose to live partnerless. We'd talked about this: Maya had wanted no children to give up to the Empire. I remained ambivalent, but childbearing had nothing to do with how I felt. Loneliness did. I wanted, simply, arms around me, the scent and warmth and feel of another body against mine.

The sound of the door opening startled me out of my reverie. Dessa, I guessed, correctly, and Siane with her. They joined me in the hot pool, Dessa supporting Siane carefully as she edged into the pool. "Ranni's doing well," Siane said, once she had settled. "We stopped on the way up. Gwen thinks it'll be another five or six hours."

"Good," I said. Dessa moved forward and began to rub Siane's bad leg. Siane sighed, leaning back. I had seen this a hundred times, but in my current state of mind this casual, accepted support of each other rankled. I wanted the same, and Maya had taken it away.

I left the baths, saying goodbye to Dessa and Siane. I dried and dressed, going out into the early evening. I walked along the gravel path, passing the forge and Casyn's cottage. Through open windows, I could hear the murmur of voices: Casyn and Dern, I surmised, planning tactics. The storm had cooled the day and an evening breeze, gentle now, blew off the sea. I felt a sudden urge to be out on the water. Why not?

I readied *Dovekie,* rowing her out beyond the shelter of the harbour, to where the winds would fill her sail. The sun westered in a clear sky, only a few wisps of cloud trailing eastward behind the storm. I shipped the oars and set *Dovekie's* sail, tacking northward along the coast. Seabirds soared and plunged around me, hoping for fish. The breeze blew more stiffly here. I became lost in the familiar, the feel of the tiller under my hand and the smell of the sea around me, the rush of water against *Dovekie's* side and the cries of the gulls overhead. I sailed north, until the land curved out to meet me. Beyond that promontory, the bay gave way to the open Lantanan Sea, wilder and crueller: no place for a lone sailor even on a calm summer's evening. I brought *Dovekie* about, heading home.

"How do we know anash is safe to use for weeks on end?" Kyan asked, after my mother had explained both the council's reasoning and decision on the subject. "Or for young girls?"

"To answer the first," my mother said, "let me tell you that I read what books I have carefully. While I cannot say with certainty that anash is safe for long use, it is clear that, before Partition, most women drank it regularly to space their pregnancies and to limit them. I wish I had more books, but I could find nothing to suggest there was any danger attached to the practice."

"Fair enough," Kyan said. "But for the girls?"

"I truly do not know. It was first used against the Eastern fever, so it would have been given to girls, surely. I gather our foremothers learned of its other properties accidentally. I doubt its use is a greater risk than pregnancy for girls of twelve or fourteen. If a girl is capable of conceiving, she needs to use the means to prevent it."

"But a twelve-year-old?" Siane said, her voice wavering with fear. "Or even younger?" Siane's daughter Lara, only eleven, had remained home tonight, but when she brought water up to the practice field, I had noticed how her shirt pulled against her developing breasts. Her menses could begin at any time.

"Rape," Sara said, "especially in wartime, has little or nothing to do with normal desire. Rather it is an act of domination and aggression. Age will not matter, if it comes to that."

Casse stood to speak. "I doubt anyone here but Gwen knows my mother was not Tirvan-born, but came from Berge to be the smith here a hundred years ago," she said. "I was born when she was thirty, so these memories are very old. When she was a girl in Berge, raids from across the border were not uncommon, and rape happened. Do not think it cannot, here." She sat down again.

Siane buried her face in her hands. I shuddered.

Sara continued. "For girls below apprentice age, the use of anash is a decision for the girl and her mother. The council will not interfere. But for girls of apprentice age, we deem the use necessary."

"What do I say to her?" Siane said, clearly not expecting an answer. Sara chose to answer regardless.

"That is between you and Dessa and Lara, Siane," she said. "You have some time. We see no need for the younger girls to begin drinking anash more than a week or two before the autumn equinox.

"Perhaps," my mother added, "I can be of help." Several women assented eagerly. "We can talk after meeting is done," my mother offered. "But now we need to speak of the older apprentices. We are proposing that those sixteen this year and above be allowed liaisons with *Skua*'s crew, if desired."

Freya's mother, Binne, stood. "I asked my daughter," she said. Freya sat with the other senior apprentices. This age group came to meeting at the invitation of council leaders, to hear debate and to learn the protocols, but they had no right to speak. "Freya would like the right to choose a liaison this summer. If we lose, she knows that may mean no choice at all, and she would prefer her first experience with a man to be something she wants, with a man of her choosing. I cannot find fault with her argument."

"Except," another woman said, "that we could make the same argument for those younger than sixteen."

"How old are the ship's crew?' Marna asked.

"I asked Dern that," Gille said. "There are no cadets; the youngest will be about eighteen."

"Fifteen is just too young," Kelle said. "We structure our apprenticeships so that we have little experience in making decisions until we reach sixteen; we observe, and do what we are told. I couldn't have made a good choice about this at fifteen."

"Nor I," said her sister Salle. "I agree with Kelle."

"Shall we vote?" my mother asked. Hearing agreement from the women of voting age, she continued. "Two votes, then. First, in the red boxes, we vote on the requirement of all apprentices under sixteen to drink anash, beginning shortly before the equinox. Second, in the black boxes, we vote on whether to allow apprentices sixteen this year and older the opportunity for liaisons with men from *Skua*'s crew."

The council leaders distributed the pebbles, and we voted. Both proposals passed, although fewer women voted for the first proposal than the second.

"Now," Sara said, "for practicalities. Does anyone need anash? There is plenty of time yet this summer to harvest and dry it." Every house had an anash bush, or two, in the garden, but they needed to be either harvested or pruned yearly to maintain the growth of the young leaves. The midwife's house, not surprisingly, had several bushes, and I had picked leaves since earliest childhood as one of my chores. I knew my mother would have a lot put by, but I doubted the supply would serve the entire village.

A few hands went up. "See me," my mother said. "Please remember to teach your daughters to steep it for at least three minutes and to drink it at the same time every day."

"And to add honey," Tali said, grimacing. "I can't stand the stuff without honey."

The meeting dispersed. Tice fell into step beside me on the path. "How about some wine? I've got a flask, not from Leste, but good southern stuff, and some food to go with it."

I hadn't eaten, and Tice's invitation meant I would not have to go back to my solitary room. "Thank you," I said. Where the path divided, we went left, uphill to Tice's cottage. I hadn't entered this cottage since old Minna had given up the wheel and kiln entirely to move in with her daughter, some eighteen months before. Tice had whitewashed the walls and softened the wide boards of the floor with intricately woven rugs in bright colours. On shelves, scattered around the room, stood examples of Tice's craft—vases and pots in deep reds and rich cobalt blue. A tortoiseshell cat stretched itself awake from the windowsill, mewing a welcome.

"Have a seat," Tice said.

I sat cross-legged on one of the rugs, holding out a hand to the cat. It approached warily, sniffed my fingertips, and immediately broke into an ecstasy of purring. I scratched its ears. It collapsed on the rug, rolling over. "Don't!" Tice said, as I reached over to rub the cat's stomach. I looked up. She handed me a wine goblet and a flask. "It's a ruse. Rub her belly, and she'll tear your hand to pieces with her hind claws." She picked the cat up before sinking gracefully to the floor a few feet away.

I poured two glasses of wine. The cat curled up on Tice's lap, purring. I held up my wine glass. "Health and luck," I said.

"Health and luck," Tice replied. "Although in the south we have a saying: choice is better than chance. "She sipped her wine. "Hence the anash."

"Tell me about the south. I've never been more than a day's sail from Tirvan." The wine was spicy, tasting of blackberries.

Tice rubbed the cat's ears, reflectively. "The land in the south is flat, with long fields running down to the sea. Karst isn't really a village, not like Tirvan. No one wanted to waste land on a village, so each farm has its house and outbuildings, scattered over the district. There is a hall, at a central crossroads, for meetings. Above the meeting hall is a belfry. In an emergency, the bell is rung. It can be heard for miles across the fields."

"It sounds lonely."

"Do you find it lonely on the sea, in a small boat, all day?"

"No," I answered, "but we come back to the village, and the baths, and the people."

She nodded. "In the south, we reverse this. We tend to work communally, at harvest or in the spring when the grapes need tying. Each farm is slightly different: the grapes grow faster or slower depending on the soils and how close the farm lies to the sea. So, we're together a lot, and there are many dances and celebrations and meals, but we go home to our own farms, and the open space above us, and the long views down to the water."

I thought about this and my need today for space, and the wind and seaspray against my face. "Why did you leave?"

"Karst had no need of another potter, so I saddled my pony and brought my skills north, seeking a village that did."

I hesitated, conscious of the warning in her voice. "Was it hard, on the road?"

"Hard enough," she said. "You're thinking of Maya?" I nodded. "She should be all right, if she thought to take warm clothes, and if she finds a place to stay before winter. The inns always need help. North, south or east, she will be able to find work and food and a roof over her head, if she wants it." I knew very little of the world beyond Tirvan. A single dirt track, dusty or muddy according to the season, lay between Tirvan and a pass in the hills. I had never wondered, until now, what lay beyond those hills, where that track met the broader, paved roads of the Empire.

The cat meowed, a demanding, plaintive sound. "She's hungry," Tice said. "Let's all eat." She stood, holding the cat against one shoulder. I put my wine on a low table. Tice led the way into the small kitchen. She put the cat down on the stone floor, pouring milk from a blue jug into a bowl glazed to match the tortoiseshell of the cat's fur. Tice caught me looking at the bowl. "That way I know it's hers and don't eat my soup out of it," she said. She took a covered crock down from a shelf, handing to me. "Olives," she said. "Put some on a plate. There are pickled onions in the red bowl." I scooped pickles and onions onto a plate while Tice cut a loaf of barley bread. The cat lapped at the milk. Tice handed me the basket of bread. "It's getting dark. Take the food back into the other room. I'll light the lamp."

We sat on the rug again, the lamp on the table and the food between us. The cat jumped onto the windowsill to wash. I bit into a pickle, relishing its tang.

"Has Dern said anything about when *Skua* will arrive?"

I shook my head, my mouth full. "Nothing more than what was said in meeting. Why?"

"Just wondering," she said. "It'll be a bit like Festival, won't it?" The lamp gave enough light to eat by, but I could not read her eyes.

"I suppose," I said. "Are you thinking of a liaison?" I wondered if I presumed too much in asking this, but Tice just smiled.

"No," she said, "no liaisons for me. And you?" She took a piece of bread from the plate.

"I don't know," I said. She cocked an eyebrow in the quizzical expression I was beginning to know well.

"Dern will ask."

"I know." I took a mouthful of the wine. "Tice, have you—?"

"Have I been with a man? Yes. And you haven't?"

"No." I admitted. "I've only been old enough for one Festival, and Maya and I...well, we had each other. But now...I'm confused, Tice." I was suddenly glad of the low light in the room.

"Do you want him?"

"Yes, I do." I had said it.

She smiled, a slow and somehow sad smile. "He is an honourable man, I think," she said, "and you are well matched. But only you can decide, Lena. Choice is better than chance."

Through the open window, I could see stars in the night sky, and the rising full moon, the last of summer. We sat in silence for a while. The lamplight flickered in the night breeze. Tice began to sing, unexpectedly, a slow, sorrowful song.

The swallows gather, summer passes,

The grapes hang dark and sweet;
Heavy are the vines,
Heavy is my heart,
Endless is the road beneath my feet.

The sun is setting, the moon is rising,
The night is long and sweet;
I am gone at dawn,
I am gone with day,
Endless is the road beneath my feet.

The cold is deeper, the winters longer,
Summer is short but sweet,
I will remember,
I'll not forget you,
Endless is the road beneath my feet.

"Is that a song of your people?" I asked, after the last bittersweet note had faded.

"No," she replied. "It is a song from Casilla, which is many miles east of Karst. I learned it from an old soldier, a general, who had his retirement farm half a day from our vineyard. He grew grapes and raised horses and collected songs. Jedd, his name was."

"A general?" I said, surprised. "But, then, there were men around? I mean, not just at Festival?"

Tice laughed. "Not every day, no. But, Lena, the retirement farms have to be somewhere! And Jedd and his household were old, as old, nearly, as Casse. We traded with him, a bit, for new varieties of grapes, or we would buy casks or corks from a trading ship and then he would buy some from us."

"If Jedd was that old, who worked the farm?"

Tice looked uncomfortable. "He mostly hired women from Karst, to prune and tie the grapes in the spring, and for autumn harvest. But there were some men, young men, I mean, who worked with the horses. Some of them were slaves, from the northern peoples." She hesitated. "And some were not. But they never came to Festival."

Nor would they, I thought, remembering what Dern had told me.

"I knew there were retirement farms, but somehow I thought they were far, far away, not near the women's villages at all. Although I suppose there are villages throughout the Empire, too."

Tice nodded in agreement. "Jedd showed me a map, once. Some of the villages are on the coast, but most are inland. But in the far north and east there are none, not near the Wall or the mountains. After all those years serving in the north, the men want warmth and sunshine." She grinned. "And if they live to retirement, they are too old to want anything else, so they are not, shall we say, disruptive, to the villages."

"There's so much I don't know," I said, feeling both frustrated and foolish.

Tice shrugged. "Why would you? I didn't know of the world beyond Karst, either, until I left, except what Jedd told me. And even now I can't claim to know much more, except of the road between here and Karst, and the inns I stayed at."

Tice filled my wine glass. After the lamp flame flickered and guttered, we sat in the moonlight, listening to the night sounds. The cat made a soft sound and jumped off the windowsill, heading out to her night's hunting. I stood, stretching.

"Thank you, Tice. I enjoyed the evening."

I let myself out. I could tell by the stars that it was near midnight. I looked east, into the night, toward the road I knew lay beyond the hills, the road Tice had ridden, the road Maya had chosen to take, and I had not.

CHAPTER SIX

I SPOONED HONEY INTO MY MUG OF ANASH TEA, stirring it vigorously. After eight days, I had nearly grown used to its smoky, slightly bitter taste. I covered the teapot to keep it warm for Tali. I could hear her moving about upstairs. The day had dawned cloudy, with a band of sea fog about half a mile off shore. I could hear voices down at the harbour, but they would wait for the fog to lift before setting out. Already the sun showed weakly through the cloud. When it rose higher, in an hour or two, the day would heat up. The autumn equinox was approaching. Soon the fog would last all morning, and then all day. On many days not fogbound the wind would blow too strongly to safely sail, and the boats would stay in the harbour, sails furled, or be hauled up on the beach for repair.

Last night, Tice and Dern and I had eaten together at Tice's cottage. Tice had cooked a spicy bean stew, and I had begged a loaf of fresh bread from my mother. We did not eat together every night, but I had suggested we needed to review the cohort's progress.

"Little Aline is deadly with that secca," Dern said. "She can throw accurately with either hand when she's standing, and even crouched, she's hitting the target most of the time."

"She's still resentful of me," I said. "Not overtly, but there's just a bit of sullenness there when I give her an order." I sipped my wine.

"She wants you to notice her," Tice said. "She's very young. She needs your praise."

"Which she gets," I pointed out, "when she earns it." The cat appeared from somewhere to wind around my legs. I put a hand down to pet her.

"Praise her privately," Dern said unexpectedly. I raised an eyebrow. "I've worked with cadets like this, too. Praise on the field is good, but impersonal. I agree with Tice."

"I'll try. We need to begin working on the hiding places in the village." I said, changing the subject. "Tice won't know most of them,"

"Or even any," she interjected, "saving the loft and cellar of my own cottage."

"Do we give the cohort a day off, and the three of us investigate where we can hide, and how we can move across the village without being seen? Or do you, Dern, take the cohort, and Tice and I do it together?" I looked from one to the other.

"We don't give them the day off," Tice said immediately. "Aline and probably Camy would only follow us. I'll take the cohort. You and Dern work together."

I saw her logic. Dern had experience and training. I needed him with me to analyse the possibilities. "You're right," I said, after a pause.

"When do you want to do this?" Dern pushed his chair back to stretch his legs. His fingers played with the stem of his wine goblet. I wondered what they would feel like on my skin.

"Tomorrow?" I suggested. He nodded.

"Tomorrow, then, at our usual morning start." He stood. "And now I should find Casyn. Goodnight, Lena. Goodnight, Tice. Thank you for the meal and the wine." He smiled at us both, bent to stroke the cat, and left.

"You should find lots of possibilities, tomorrow," Tice said, when his footsteps had faded. She grinned.

I blushed. "We're working."

"All day?" she inquired, eyebrow cocked. "I see the way you look at him. And the way he looks at you. Probably half the cohort is betting on it. Freya would like to use her secca on you, she's so jealous."

"Really?" I said, startled. "Freya?"

"Freya," she confirmed. "Cohort-leader, you're good with tactics and planning, but you need to think about your cohort as individuals. You've known them all so long, I think you just don't notice things." She shrugged. "I'm still an outsider, so they don't have that gloss of familiarity for me. I'm trying to understand them. Maybe I see more."

"Maybe you do," I said slowly.

Dern was waiting for me at the forge, so I finished my tea, called a goodbye to Tali, and walked up the hill. I walked as Tice had shown me, rolling my weight along my feet. It no longer felt as awkward or as artificial as it had a week ago, and I thought I moved more quietly. Dern stood in the paddock, currying his horse, and I reached the fence before he looked up.

"Lena," he said, surprised. "Did you come up the path?"

I grinned. "Yes. I could have put a knife into you ten paces back."

"You could have," he agreed. "Well done."

"The waterfall masks a lot of sound up here. Are you ready?"

As he removed his horse's headcollar, it nuzzled him, blowing through its nostrils, looking for a carrot or a piece of bread. "Nothing this morning, boy," he said, slapping its shoulder. He took the headcollar and the brush to the stable, pausing to rinse his hands in the water trough. I looked up at the cottage.

"What exactly are we looking for?"

"A few things," Dern said. "Places where a woman can hide, armed with a secca, and take a man by surprise. Ways to move through the village without being seen, to reposition part or all your cohort, or to send a messenger. Secret places, secret routes." He looked up at the forge cottage. "There is a tiny loft above the rooms," Dern said. I followed his gaze. "The door is in the ceiling of the west bedroom. It's not much. You can only crouch. But there are ventilation windows, with sliding panels to cover them in winter."

"Likely, no one would think of it being there," I said. "It's clear there is an attic of some sort over my mother's house, and Tali's, but here, and I think at Tice's, you wouldn't think of it."

He nodded. "Exactly," he said. "They will look for the forge immediately, to repair weapons or to make more. There would be no easy escape for a person hidden in the loft here."

"Down the waterfall," I said, without hesitation. "It's dangerous. Some of the boulders are far apart, and you must jump from one to another. They're also very slippery, and some of them move, but I'd guess almost every eleven or twelve-year-old here can do it. It's strictly forbidden, of course."

"Of course," Dern said, with a hint of a grin. He considered for a moment. "Did you ever climb up it?"

"I did," I said. "It's difficult. You have to jump up. I made it, but I never tried again. Freya has climbed up, too," I remembered. "We talked about it, once, when we were fishing." In unspoken agreement, we walked the short distance uphill to where the stream channelled out from the bathhouse pools to begin its westerly descent down the rocky cliff face. On either side of the watercourse, thick thorn bushes grew. In the spring, the thorn blossom hummed with bees from the hives kept nearby. "Where is the hardest part?" Dern asked. "Climbing up, I mean?"

I paused, remembering. "About two-thirds of the way up, there's a spot where the cliffside has fallen away, leaving a sheer wall with just slight depressions in the wet rock for your hands and feet. Freya and I both made it because we're tall and could reach the handholds, and because we'd already fished for a season and had strong arms."

"If we fastened a knotted rope there, would it help?"

"Yes, I think so. But it would still be a dangerous climb."

"These are dangerous times," Dern said. He walked over to where the water began its descent. Green algae grew on the rocks, and a faint sulphur smell rose from the stream. He squatted to put his hand in the water. "Warm," he said. "Does it freeze?"

"No," I replied, following his train of thought. "But some of the pools form ice at the edges, further down. And the rocks ice over. I wouldn't want to climb it, up or down, past the first snowfall."

"Climb it soon, Lena. You and as many of your cohort as can manage it. Up and down, until you can do it in the night, if need be. If Leste takes the village, or even just the forge, this might be the only way up from the harbour. Add ropes or even ladders where they're needed. Casyn will help you fasten bolts into the rock. Leste is a flat isle. Lestian men have no skill in rock-climbing."

He straightened. "Lena," he said quietly, "what is your father's name?" The first question of courtship.

I flushed. I could tell him he did not need to know, the usual, gentle refusal. "Galen," I said, "of the third regiment, born at Skeld."

Dern nodded. "My father is Valder. He sails on *Albatross*," he said, holding my gaze.

I looked away, up to the hills, confused. The heather made waves of purple between the rocks. Sheep dotted the lower hillsides, and a golden eagle soared far above them. "There are caves, up on the heights. We played in them as children. They're not large. I think streams like this one made them. One or two of them still have a trickle of water running through them. They could hide a woman or two, and weapons."

"Can you find them again?"

I shrugged. "Some of them, yes. The children will know better, the older ones. Lara will remember, or we can ask the shepherd apprentices. They shelter in them, sometimes, when it rains."

"We could send the children there if we have is sufficient warning."

"We could," I said doubtfully. "But food cannot be stored in the caves. Wildcats take it, or the foxes."

Dern grinned. "Not even a fox can take ship's biscuit from inside a metal box, and there is a good supply of such on *Skua*. If there is water, as you remember, then we can equip the caves for survival, if not for comfort. No one," he added ruefully, "would call ship's biscuit comforting."

I laughed. "We can look over the caves," I said. "We'll take Pel. He spends a good deal of time up there with Sarr, whose sister is apprenticed to Gille. The girls stay with the flocks, but the boys wander, playing soldier. Sarr and Pel will know the caves."

"As I did, once," said a voice from behind us. We turned to see Casyn approaching. "Good morning to you both," he added. "I am going to shoe Siannon. Dern, is your horse in need of reshoeing?"

Dern considered. "Yes," he said. "It's been some weeks. My thanks, Casyn."

Casyn nodded. "I heard you speaking of the caves," he said. "If memory serves, there is one, quite large, where a stream runs across the back and into a pool of some size. I remember it as being big enough to live in, comfortably, but those are the memories of a child of six. If you can find it, it should be equipped with food, blankets, and a store of firewood. And weapons. It was a good thought, Lena. I had forgotten the caves."

I flushed again. I found being praised in front of Dern by this man, once his teacher, now his superior officer, discomfiting. I felt Casyn's eyes on my face, but he said nothing, turning instead to Dern. "Does Tasque stand easy to be shod?"

Dern nodded. "He'll give you no trouble." He paused. "Did you ever climb the waterfall, Casyn, up or down?"

Casyn looked surprised. "No," he said. "I was too small. Oh, I clambered on the rocks and in the little pools on a hot day, but no more. I remember falling, once, on a slippery rock at the base and truly scaring myself. We thought, the little boys, I mean—" He glanced at me. "My pardon, Lena, if I trespass here. We thought it a ritual, a rite of womanhood, I suppose, because only the girls who were of an age to be apprenticed climbed down it. I did not know anyone ever climbed up it."

I grinned. "The only rite it was, was one of defiance. When Cate fell and broke her arm, we carried her along the shore until we came to the shellfish pools and then told her mother she had slipped there." I stopped, thinking of what Casyn had said. "I had never considered," I said slowly, "that my mother, and her sisters and their mother before them, had climbed down that waterfall, too. It's never spoken of. I've climbed up it, and Freya too, but no one else that I know." Half to myself, I added, "I will have to ask Tali."

"You are thinking of it as an escape route?" Casyn asked.

"Possibly," Dern said. "But more as a way up to the top of the village, if needed." Casyn cocked his head. "If the fight goes badly," Dern continued, "there could be several reasons to have Lena's cohort able to climb up the waterfall: to coordinate an attack from the heights, to send a messenger out from the village, to reach the caves if we use them. And an equal number of reasons to climb down: to reach their boats, to fire the Lestian ship, to kill."

Casyn nodded. "Sound thinking," he agreed. "But a last resort, I hope. We will talk tonight. Can you eat with us this evening, Lena?"

"Me?" I said.

Casyn laughed. "You are a cohort leader, and you have proven again this morning that you know more about this village than either Dern or myself. We need you there if we are to plan tactics. Bring Tice. You will both need to know the plans and the reasons behind them and be able to explain them to your cohort. Those plans, and your cohort, may be Tirvan's saving." His tone had become serious, with his last words. "And now I am going to heat the forge and shoe horses," he said, cheerful again. He turned away, moving back toward the forge.

I looked at Dern. "We have forty cottages to look at and nearly as many outbuildings."

"Do you know how many might have lofts or cellars?"

I shook my head. "No. Most cottages will have a cellar of some sort, if only to store root vegetables and apples. Both my mother's cottage and Tali's have cellars and lofts. But there is something else, too,"

He cocked his head.

"Some of the older cottages have tunnels between the house and the barn."

"Tunnels," Dern said, thoughtfully. "Yes, Serra had these, too. I can just remember one between my grandmother's house and her barn. She showed me, once. The blackness and the cobwebs scared me." He shook his head in wonder. "I had completely forgotten the tunnels. They were built because of the snows, many generations ago. Is that right?"

"So we were taught," I said. "But they're long unused and may have collapsed. I only remembered them in the night." I had lain sleepless, thinking about Dern. "Perhaps we should start by speaking with Casse."

"The snows," Casse said. "I remember my mother speaking of them from her own mother's memories. But yes, I think I remember where all the tunnels are."

"What about the forge?" I asked.

"No. There is a cellar, of course, where ore and wood are stored, and the unwrought bars of metal, but the stable isn't connected."

"Thank you, Casse," Dern said. "Tirvan is lucky to have you."

She smiled. "You flatter as well as any young man ever did, but I am glad to be useful, and even gladder I still have my mind. Now, go to work. You should start with my loft and cellar."

After we examined Casse's home, we moved on to her neighbours. When women could not be found at home—the case more often than not—we investigated anyway. Our etiquette required knocking, and checking the garden and byre or stable for the owner before entering an apparently empty house during the day. Word of what we did would travel quickly.

After the first five houses, we stopped. All had lofts, and three of the five had cellars. None had tunnels. We stood looking at the village. Casse's house, and the four nearest, lay on the northern, rockier side of the wide, curving bowl of flatter land where Tirvan had grown. The northern side of the valley rose more steeply to the headland and the deep valley of the waterfall. Large boulders embedded in the ground meant suitable building space for only a few houses, with small yards that ran upward to the edge of the cliff. Between these five, and Tali's house below them, a ridge of reddish rock ran parallel to the shore. Above them, a deeply eroded gully blocked easy access to Tice's cottage. "Perhaps," Dern said, turning to look northward, "we could find a route up to the forge behind these houses, along the cliff edge. It might be safer than the waterfall."

"It may look that way," I said, "but it isn't. The rock here is soft and the cliff edge dangerous. And we would have to bridge the gully, somehow."

"It can't be that soft."

"It is. A foot or more of the cliff edge falls into the sea every year, either after heavy rain or after the winter. That's why there are so few houses on this side."

He walked nearer the edge of the cliff. "See?" I said, following. I pointed out the cracks feathering the rock. "And look at the waterfall. It's washed out all the softer rock, leaving only the big grey boulders, like the ones in the ground on this side."

He nodded, turning back to look southward, to the far side of the valley where most of Tirvan's houses stood. Here, the land sloped slowly up to the hillfields and the headland; the stream on this side of the village flowed gently down to meet the ocean behind Siane's workshop and the docks. "Then we need to concentrate on that side."

"I think so," I said. "All the tunnels are over there, at the oldest houses."

We crossed the central common of the village to where three more cottages stood in a loose cluster. I knocked at the first. From inside, a voice bid us enter. The door opened into a large, low-ceiling room, windowed on two sides. Cate sat at her loom. She turned on her stool, her pregnancy just beginning to show in the curve of her belly. "Lena," she said, surprised. "Dern. How can I help you?"

"We're planning defences," I said. "Remind me, Cate, does this cottage have a loft?" She nodded. "Is there a cellar? Or a tunnel to the byre?"

"Why, yes," she said. "There is a tunnel, but no real cellar, only a space dug out under the kitchen floor for vegetables in the winter. No one has used the tunnel in years and years."

"May we see it?" Dern asked. Cate pushed her stool back, indicating we should follow. She walked through the kitchen, out into the lean-to at the back of the cottage. Firewood lined two walls in neat stacks, and a large vat held spun wool soaking in a dye bath.

"We'll have to move the wool," she said. Dern stepped forward and took one handle. I took the other, and we managed to move it without slopping. Behind where the vat had stood a door lay, flush to the floor at the bottom but angled up by stone walls to about my waist at the top, where it abutted the shed wall. Dern pulled its handle. Nothing happened. He tried again, and this time the hinges gave just a bit. A smell of dank and damp rose from behind the door.

"Try this on the hinges," Cate said, taking a crock down from a shelf and handing it to me. I opened it. I knew from the distinctive smell that it was fleecefat, the natural oils that make the fleece of sheep repel water. I dipped my hand in, rubbing the hinges with the oily substance, doing my best to work the fat into the mechanism. Cate handed me a rag for my hands. Dern pulled at the door again, and this time it opened with a shriek of metal.

Stone steps angled downward into cobwebs and darkness. "We'll need a lantern," I said, and Cate disappeared into the kitchen. I looked at Dern. "Shouldn't we see if the door in the byre isn't blocked before we explore the tunnel?"

"A good idea," he agreed. Cate returned with the lantern. "What about the other end?" Dern asked her. "Is the door blocked there, too?"

She shook her head. "No," she said. "We store the turnips there, the ones we feed the goats in winter. So I know the steps and the first part of the tunnel are good. It's empty, now, but the door opens easily."

Dern held the lantern up as we descended the steps. We could just stand upright. In the lantern's glow, I could see the beams and crossbars that supported the earth. White fungus grew on several of them, gleaming damply in the light. Roots curled downward between some of the beams, and cobwebs furred the walls. I shuddered.

"Come," Dern said. When I hesitated, he reached out a hand.

"I'm all right," I said. We moved forward, slowly, Dern holding the lantern up so we could inspect the beams. He took his secca from his boot to pry at a beam where the fungus grew in profusion. The tip penetrated the wood, breaking a chunk off.

"Rot," Dern said.

A short distance further, one of the roof beams had collapsed, partially blocking the tunnel. Enough space remained in the gap between the fallen beam and the roof of the tunnel to allow a slim and agile person to pass.

Dern raised the lantern to light the space beyond the fall. "It looks clear," he said. I eyed the gap.

"Do you want me to try to go through?"

"No," he said. "We can investigate from the other side. If this is all that has collapsed, we should be able to shore it up and dig it out. The rotten beams will need to be replaced."

I nodded. I waited for him to precede me with the lantern, but he didn't move. Slowly he put the lantern on the floor, his eyes, wide and dark in the low light, never left mine. He took a step closer. "Lena," he said, his voice deep. I swallowed. He put out a hand to touch my face, then pulled me to him. He kissed me, gently, tentatively, and then more deeply. I felt the response in my body, low and deep. I pulled away.

"I don't know," I said. "I don't know if I can. I...." I hesitated. "I want to, Dern, but...not yet. I need to think."

"Thinking hasn't got much to do with this," he said. He watched me for a moment. "I won't stop asking, you know."

"I know," I said. "And I will tell you, yes or no, soon."

He smiled. "I'll try to be patient." He picked up the lantern.

The other end of the tunnel proved to be cleaner and drier, probably due to its use as a turnip store. The fall that blocked the passage could be easily cleared. We climbed out, closing. Outside, we breathed fresh air gratefully.

Dern looked around. "This is the only house Casse thought had a tunnel, of this group?" he asked.

"Yes," I answered. I measured the distance from this cluster of cottages to the next with my eyes. "Not a lot of use, if we're trying to move any distance through the village."

"True," he agreed, "but potentially useful as a hiding place. Look," he said, squatting in the swept earth of the yard. He sketched the harbour with his finger, placing small pebbles to represent the houses. I squatted beside him. "If I were commanding this raid, I would divide my men into four. One squadron I would send up the main path, one up the right side of the village, and one up the left." He drew the routes in the dust.

"And the last group?"

"Would stay at the harbour to guard the boat."

I looked at the sketch. "So these cottages could provide shelter for an attack on either the left group, or the centre."

"Exactly. But an attack from archers, maybe swordswomen. One or two of your cohort can hide in this tunnel until need brings them out. If need brings them out," he amended.

I studied the rough map. "Or," I said, "we could fence the common, at least on the harbour side. That would force the left squadron over to the cliff edge. It's rough going through those rocks, and with a bit of luck, the cliff will collapse and take a few with it."

"Very good," Dern said. He grinned. "And a knife or two in the back, thrown from the loft of Tali's house, might encourage them to move closer to the cliff edge." He straightened. "Those tactics we can repeat, from any of the lofts or tunnels throughout the village. But you also need to be able to move about the village, up and down, and maybe across, without being seen. We haven't found those routes, yet."

"The oldest houses are over there," I said, indicating the southern cluster of houses. "They have more tunnels and less space among the houses." We—Maya and Garth, Cate and the other boys and girls under seven—had played hide-and-seek among those houses and barns in the long summer evenings, with bats hunting insects around us and the first stars gleaming in the deepening blue of the sky. I thought I still remembered some of our hiding places and the spots where hedges could be wiggled through. Whether or not they would be useful remained to be seen. "Let's start at the harbour."

Investigating the oldest houses took most of the rest of the day. One or two of the tunnels needed digging out and shoring up, and several lofts needed knotted ropes to provide quick egress. When we finished in mid-afternoon, I poured water for Dern on the porch of my mother's house. Chaff and cobwebs clung to our clothes and hair. I could hear Tali calling the guards with the sword cohort and the clang of metal as they struck and parried. The heat of the day had not yet begun to recede. I glanced at the man beside me, who drank deeply of the water.

"This evening," I said on impulse, "do we have to talk of tactics?"

"What did you have in mind?" Dern asked, putting his empty mug down.

"Practice," I said. "I think I can move from the docks to the forge without Casyn seeing me. At dusk."

"Only unseen by Casyn? Not by me?"

"You know where the routes are."

"True," he agreed. "But perhaps you can prove too evasive for me, too."

"Perhaps. Even better, if I can."

"I think Casyn will agree to this," he said. "I'll leave a lantern at the forge. When you get there, light it. We'll watch from the meeting hall, on the hillside."

Just before moonrise, I crouched in Siane's dockside workshop. I eased open the shutters that covered the storeroom's window, slipping out into the shelter of the bushes. The shutters moved silently; we had greased them earlier. I wore dull green and grey and had darkened my face and hands with ashes. On my feet, I wore soft deerskin boots. From the hedge, I picked a careful route up the hill, keeping behind bushes and boulders, moving slowly. Haste here would be a mistake. I could move faster on the flatter ground of the village. I gained the first building: Kyan's woodshop. The woodshop's big doors, which were tall enough to allow long timbers to be passed up directly to the second floor, opened onto the village street. On the other side, a rough shed abutted the back of the workshop. This shed sheltered oddments and enclosed a privy, with doors at both ends as well as into the workshop. Regardless of the ventilation, it stank. I passed through the shed, holding my breath. The next building, a stable, lay about thirty feet away, and the cottage's goats kept the space between close-cropped.

At the door, I paused, watching the shadows. A bat quartered the goat's field, hunting insects, and then suddenly changed direction to disappear over the cottage roof. I dropped to my stomach to crawl across the space, moving a foot or two and then stopping, keeping my breathing steady and quiet. Goat droppings covered the area, and I could feel them squash beneath my weight. I thought wryly that I might cause less commotion in stable and byre if I smelt like goat and not human. At the stable, I pulled the door open just enough to slip inside. Three goats munching hay looked up at me in the dim light and then went back to their haybags. I edged my way to the corner of the stable to a trapdoor. As I bent to raise it, an animal jumped, snarling. I froze, my arm raised over my face in instinctive defence. The creature crouched and spat. I could hear mewling: the straw-filled corner beyond the trapdoor held a nest of kittens. I moved forward to open the trap. The tabby growled low in her throat but made no move toward me.

Dense blackness filled the tunnel. I pulled a candle from my pocket and lit the wick. This tunnel, I knew from the afternoon's exploration, needed no repair. It led to the pantry of Rette's cottage, where a woven rug covered the other trapdoor. The pantry and kitchen of the cottage stood at the back of the main building to help isolate them in case of fire. Most of the village houses had the same plan, with a separate entrance in the kitchen opening onto the kitchen garden and well. At Ranni's cottage, I knew I could cover the space between the trapdoor and the door to the garden in four paces. With enough stealth, no one in the living areas of the cottage would know I had passed through.

The candlelight showed me the outline of the trapdoor above me. It opened easily, and I held it open with one arm while I licked my thumb and forefinger to douse the wick. Then I waited, letting my eyes adjust again to the dark, listening. I could hear voices in the cottage, but they sounded stationary, as if whoever spoke remained in one place. I pushed the trapdoor open, hearing a faint slither from the rug, and slid out onto the floor. I let the trap down again, easing it closed with only the tiniest sound, and slowly stood. The voices in the cottage did not change. I stepped forward, rolling my weight along my feet as Tice had taught me. The garden door had two halves that opened separately to allow light and air in but to keep the goats out, and the faint light seeping in at the join gave me my bearings.

I had just reached the door when I heard a scrape of a chair on wooden floorboards. I froze, rapidly trying to remember what in the pantry might provide cover for me, but footsteps did not approach. I felt along the lower door to find its latch, slid it upwards, and slipped out.

The rising moon lay low in the east, giving me almost full dark for cover. A fence edged Rette's kitchen garden against the goats, but a stile led into the field beyond. I kept to the fence, pausing once to clean off my shoes as best I could.

Barley had grown in the field until last week. The stubble crunched sharp and noisy underfoot. The breeze brought the spicy smell of thyme to my nostrils. I froze. Someone gathering herbs? I moved to the edge of the field, where a footpath ran beside the south stream. Willows grew between the two bridges used to cross the stream to the fields and fruit trees, and the footpath ran beneath their overhanging branches. I followed the path for about a hundred yards before I turned off the path, jumped to grab an overhead branch, and pulled myself up into the tree.

I waited, tucked up against the trunk behind the screen of leaves. I saw movement at the stile. Slowly, I crept out onto the thick branch overhanging the stream. With relief, I found the half-remembered route, where the limbs of a willow leaning from the other bank intertwined with the tree I had climbed. I slid over into the other tree, and then down its rough trunk to the ground, pausing to catch my breath, grinning with enjoyment of the task.

I used the willows for concealment as I moved. The bubbling of the stream down its rocky bed masked the noise of my movement. At the upper footbridge, I dropped to my hands and knees to crawl across.

Another footpath ran along this bank behind the outbuildings of a half-dozen houses, my mother's among them. I headed upstream for a few hundred yards before turning left across a stile, moving in and out of two byres. At the last byre, I stopped. The meeting hall lay opposite me now, with open ground between where I stood and the forge. I planned to move across the hillfields, where the natural unevenness of the land and the deep heather would provide camouflage, but I had to do that without coming too close to the sheepcote. The herd dogs would raise the alarm if they caught my scent or heard me move. I also had to cross the stream again.

No trees or structures bridged the stream this high up, but generations of children, not wanting to go around by the bridges, had dragged rocks to create stepping stones across the flow. I had added to them myself, carrying chunks of frost-sheared rock down from the hills to repair the crossing after the damage of the first spring spate. I slid down the bank to pick my way along the stream until I found them. I crossed quickly.

I used a stone wall for cover until I reached the first of the rough hillfields. A sheepdog yipped once, but when the other dogs remained silent, she did not bark again. I turned left, from the shelter of the wall, and in a half-crouch moved through the heather, going from boulder to gorsebush to boulder, keeping to the low ground. The moon gave just enough light to keep me from tripping over rocks or splashing in puddles, but even so I had wet feet and scratches on my face and arms from unseen branches when I reached the forge.

In the shelter of some bushes above the forge I paused, listening, for a good five minutes. I could hear Siannon snuffling and moving in his stable, and faint voices from the village. When a passing cloud darkened the moonlight, I crawled the last few yards to the forge, eased open the door, and stepped in.

I listened. Nothing. I lit the lantern, then reached for the bucket and dipper and took a long drink.

"Well done," Dern said as he came in the door. "I saw you once, or rather, I had a sense of movement, for just a moment. If I hadn't been watching for you, I might have thought I had seen a fox, or another night creature. I wasn't expecting you for at least another quarter-hour, or perhaps a half. How were you so quick?"

"I crossed the south stream below my mother's house," I said. He looked at me quizzically. "The willows lean into each other there. I climbed one on the north bank and came down another on the south. I did it all the time as a girl. It's much faster than going up or down stream to the bridges. You can climb and go from branch to branch along the stream, too." I added. I paused. "When did Casyn decide to follow me?"

"You saw him?" Dern exclaimed.

"Only barely," I admitted. "Like you, just movement. I guessed it was one of you, and as you are here and he isn't, it had to be him."

Without answering, Dern moved to the door and whistled, a piercing sound. "Our signal," he explained.

"You thought I might elude him?" I asked, pleased by this thought.

"We debated the possibility," Dern said. I heard footsteps outside. Casyn came in, breathing deeply as if he had run up the hill.

"You did well, Lena," he said, with a brief smile. "You climbed the willows, I assume?"

"I did."

"By the time I made the bridge, I had lost you."

"That's not all you lost," Dern said, chuckling. "You owe me a flask of wine, Casyn."

"You bet on me?"

Dern laughed. "Soldiers wager on almost anything, Lena. It provides diversion. Casyn bet he would catch you. I bet he would not. You should be pleased. We can share the wine."

Casyn spoke before I could. "What was the hardest part, Lena?"

I considered. "The hillfields. On a darker night, I could well have fallen or blundered into a pool. But I don't see an alternative. If I had gone higher, into the rocks, the sheepdogs would certainly have barked."

"There will always be risk," Casyn said. "The higher route might be safer, if time is not of the essence. But you did well tonight. Now, take yourself to the baths. Change your clothes, collect Tice, and join us here for dinner in an hour."

I could smell goat rising from my clothes. Dern put his hand on my shoulder, a comrade's gesture. "You did well."

I smiled and slipped out. Walking down to the baths, I could still feel the touch of his hand, warm and gentle, resting on my back.

I left my clothes soaking in a tub of hot water and soap, bathed myself, and tended to my scratches. Tice met me outside the baths, and we walked up the hill together to the forge cottage. The door stood open to the evening, but I knocked. From inside, Dern called to us to enter. Casyn had a pot of soup simmering on the stove, smelling richly of fish, and bread and greens to go with the chowder. We sat around the plain pine table to eat, talking of what we had learned today, and the work needed with the cohort.

"Do we tell the rest of the village what we are about?" Tice asked.

"I think we have to," I answered. "Many women helped us inspect the lofts and tunnels today. In some cases, we had to ask for furniture to be moved, doors to be unlocked, or to be shown the location of the trapdoors. We were asked if we were looking for hiding places for valuables, for the children, for ambush. Rumour will be rife, and the sooner it's ended the better. Also, if we don't explain our plans, we risk finding a door blocked against us."

"But if the others know our plans, they could reveal them under threat of death or torture," Tice countered.

"That is true of all the plans. I don't want secrets," I finished, more sharply than I had intended.

Casyn nodded, then spoke gently. "I agree with Lena. We cannot afford to divide the village against itself, and things kept secret have a way of doing that. The risk is one we will have to take."

Tice looked thoughtful, but did not argue. We spoke some more of assigning the necessary work, and of how to train our cohort. We agreed that I would show Tice the routes and hiding places tomorrow, and then she and I would take the rest of the cohort through the training. We would practice in the evenings until all of us could move through Tirvan unseen and unheard.

When we left the men an hour or so before midnight, the moon rode high. The breeze, still on-shore, had freshened, holding a hint of dampness.

"Rain tomorrow," Tice said.

"Likely," I agreed. "We'll meet at the training ground after breakfast, rain or no." We came to the point where our paths diverged. Tice took a step up the path to her cottage.

"Goodnight, Lena," she said quietly.

"Goodnight, Tice," I answered, before a thought struck me. "Can you climb trees?"

She stopped, chuckling. "There weren't many in the grape fields, but I can shimmy up a rope and walk the timbers of a barn twenty feet up. Will that do?"

CHAPTER SEVEN

THE NEXT EVENING, I SPOKE TO THE VILLAGE as a whole for the first time. "Women of Tirvan." My voice sounded high to my ears. I cleared my throat, beginning again. "Women of Tirvan. Yesterday, Dern, commander of *Skua*, and I explored your houses and your barns." I saw heads nod. "Many of you have been wondering why." I glanced at my mother, who smiled back. "We were looking for hiding places. Hiding places and routes to allow my cohort to move through the village unseen."

"Why?" someone called.

"My cohort's job is to use our knives, to kill those who get by our swordswomen and our archers," I explained, forgetting my apprehension. "For that, we need surprise and stealth. We need your lofts and cellars, and your tunnels. We need hinges to be greased, and doors unblocked. We'll need to repair tunnels and hang ropes. My cohort will do the work, but we need you to give us access. Are there any objections?"

Heads shook. I looked around the hall. "We'll start in a day or two. I—or Tice—will let you know what exactly we need." I started to step away, then stopped. "Thank you. If you have questions, I'll be glad to answer them."

"Well done, cohort-leader," Tice said, after the few women with questions had dispersed. "You made us proud."

Aline bounced up to me. "Did you find the tunnel from the sheepcote to the big barn?"

"No, I didn't. Casse must have forgotten about it. Will you show me tomorrow?" She grinned and nodded before running off to find Camy. "That could be useful," I said to Tice, "if we can teach the dogs to be silent."

"I wonder what else we might have missed."

Over the next few days, we tested routes in daylight, added ropes, and planed down a door or two. The more difficult work of rebuilding the two collapsed tunnels we left to the women of the village with experience in building. Aline showed us the tunnel, luckily undamaged, between the hillcote and the barn, and contributed the inspired suggestion of making the ropes we hung into swings, so that they would appear to be only children's playthings. I praised her both publicly and privately for this; she blushed and beamed.

A few days later, in the early afternoon, we gathered at the top of the waterfall.

"Has anyone here not climbed down the waterfall?" I asked.

The youngest girls looked up with surprise on their faces as they heard me, an adult, speak casually of something so forbidden.

Tice spoke. "I haven't."

"Why," Salle demanded, "are we climbing down the waterfall?"

"Because we may need to," I said simply. "What if it is the only unguarded route down to the harbour, or by doing so it gives us the chance to fire the catboat?"

"I thought that's what the tunnels were for?"

"In part, yes," I replied, "but what if we can't use them?"

I watched as my cohort glanced at each other. "I suppose," Salle said finally.

"It is dangerous, but it may give us an advantage of surprise or speed, which is why we need to practice. Now, who will show Tice the way?"

"I will," Freya offered. She slipped off her shoes, tying them on her belt, behind her back. Tice did the same. Freya walked to the top of the waterfall and jumped down to the first of the boulders. Tice followed. I could hear Freya instructing Tice for a moment or two, and then the sound of the water drowned their voices. We waited. It took, I remembered, about ten or fifteen minutes to clamber down, and no one else should begin the descent until Tice and Freya reached the bottom. If a climber higher up on the rocks fell, she endangered one immediately below.

One by one, we climbed, jumped, and slid down. I went last. The initial descent was easier than I remembered, but, I reflected, my body had changed since I had last done this, three or four summers back. At one point, the cliff face had broken off, leaving a vertical drop of about seven feet. I hung from the rocks at the top by my fingers, feeling the strain in my arms, then dropped down onto the boulder below, remembering to lean into the rockface. Even so, I fell hard on one knee. I stood on the wet rock, rubbing my knee, looking up. I could see the irregularities that I had used as hand-and-foot holds when climbing up. They looked horribly shallow. I judged it next to impossible for the cohort's shorter members, and absolutely impossible for any of us at night. A ladder, bolted into the rockface, would provide the safest answer, if we had the time. Otherwise, I thought, a rope, looped and knotted, would work.

I finished the descent, joining the others shivering in the cool breeze off the sea. No one had had serious problems in the descent, but we all had scratches and bruises, and wet clothes. "Now," I said to the waiting cohort, "who has climbed up, other than Freya and myself?" Silence. "No one?"

"I tried, once." Salle said. "But there's a place where I couldn't reach anywhere to hold on to. I had to come down again."

No one else had tried the climb. I looked at the cohort. Freya and I had strong arms from hauling nets, and the height needed. Tice, taller than either of us, could not climb with me. As cohort-second, she would need to take command if I fell. "Freya," I said, "you and I will climb up, again. The rest of you, go back to the top of the waterfall to wait for us. Practice knife-play to keep warm. Tice, a moment, please." She waited as the rest of the women began to pick their way along the rocky pools at the edge of the sea, back to the harbour. Freya waited at the base of the waterfall, where the rush of water would obscure our words.

"If I fall—" I began.

Tice shook her head impatiently. "You won't. But, yes, I know. I will be in command. I pray I know the plans by now. But you won't fall. Go, before you get cold and your muscles cramp. I'll see you at the top."

I insisted Freya follow me. If I could reach the handholds, so could she. The first part of the climb passed easily. The cliff sloped gradually and the boulders clustered close together. But as we climbed, the rocks grew further apart, requiring us to pull ourselves up half our height in some cases. Water drenched us. After each particularly difficult piece, we stopped briefly to study the rocks, to determine where ropes or iron bars set into the boulders might help.

At the rockface, we stopped. "Watch where I put my hands and feet. If you see a better choice, call up to me." I stood about eighteen inches out from the wall, bent my knees, and jumped, reaching up to a small ledge. My fingers grabbed the wet rock; at the same time, I brought my right foot up to a knob of protruding rock about half an arm's length above the boulder where I had stood. My left foot swung free for a minute, and then found a crevice about a handspan's above and to the left of the protrusion. I pushed up with my bent knees, reaching my right hand up to another crevice about a foot above the ledge. I pulled my body upward. I could hear my heart pounding. Above me was another small ledge. I brought my left hand up, grabbed it, hanging for a moment, my bare toes searching for grip on the rockface. I looked up. The falling water hit my face. I blinked, shook my head to clear the water from my eyes. I felt my left hand slip slightly. A bolt of fear shot through me. I scrabbled with my feet, seeking purchase.

"Bring your right foot up a bit further," Freya called from below me. "To the left, there," she shouted, as I found the grip. "Now push up. The top of the rockface is an arm's length above you." I heaved myself up, reaching blindly with my right arm. I found the ledge, pulling myself up onto it. I lay panting for a moment. The pounding of my heart slowed. I rolled to my stomach, looked over the edge, and talked Freya up.

"How did either of us do that as kids?" I said to Freya, when both of us rested safely on the ledge. She grinned. "Blind luck," she said, still panting. "And dry summers. The water makes it difficult to see. It's not really that hard a climb."

"We're not done yet," I said, but I knew she was right. The rest of the climb repeated the lower part, jumping upward from boulder to boulder, still dangerous enough but not really difficult. When we reached the top, the cohort gave us a round of applause. Eager to try it for themselves, they moaned, arguing when I vetoed the idea.

"None of you is tall enough except for Tice. We will have to put ropes in place. Then," I said, "you will climb it, up and down, and so often you'll know every rock intimately." I looked at the sun. "Go to the baths. It's early, but we are all wet and starting to chill."

Dern and I explored the caves the next day, leaving Tice with the cohort. Pel and his friend Sarr came with us. We climbed up the hillside through the sheep meadows, crossing stone walls and wading small streams.

Gille's apprentice spent some of her day up on these hillsides, but today there were only the younger girls. They watched the sheep with half an eye each while playing the ring-game on a flattish space, cropped flat by the sheep. They had fallen to the ground, giggling, when one of them spotted us. They sprang up. Dern spoke to the girls—two of them nine, and one eleven—respectfully, and they responded in kind.

"The largest cave would be up there," the older girl said, pointing higher on the hillside, "The big rock, there, in the heather—looks like a lobster pot? The opening's just to the right. Sarr knows," she added. I remembered he was her cousin.

"I'll show you," Sarr said. "Pel hasn't been there." He looked doubtful, suddenly. "I don't think," he added. Pel shook his head.

"Let's go," he said, impatiently, wanting the adventure. We thanked the girls, leaving them to their games and their sheep. There was a faint track climbing up beyond the pastures, into the rougher ground. The boys ran ahead. Far above us, a buzzard screamed. Behind me, I could hear Dern's breathing.

The boys waited for us at the mouth of the cave. From the opening, which was maybe as wide as I was tall, we could see the rock walls and floor sloping down and then turning. The boys hung back. I pulled the lantern from my pack, lit it, and entered.

The floor sloped gently downward. At the sharp left-hand turn, where the natural light ended, a small lantern sat in a niche in the wall along with a metal box of flint and some tinder. I lit the second lantern, giving it to Dern. In the flickering light, we could see where the tunnel turned again, to the right. The air smelled damp. Beyond the second bend, the walls and roof opened up into a room perhaps fifteen feet wide and twice as long. Water seeped down the furthest wall, to collect in a small rock pool before trickling away. The roof curved maybe two feet over our heads. "Is this natural?" Dern asked. I shook my head. I remembered being here, with Maya, and Garth, playing at being borders scouts.

"I don't know," I said. "Enhanced, maybe? Dug out a bit, the seep water captured? If so, it was done before Tirvan kept records, or no one thought to write it down. The shepherds use it, always have. That's all I know." Dern raised his lantern, taking a few steps more into the cave. He looked around.

"Have you gone through there?" he asked, speaking to Sarr, indicating the narrowing fissure where the walls converged again.

"It just peters out," Sarr answered. "Gets too narrow even for me. But," he added, "there's something beyond, because a candle flame gets pulled toward the back, and you can feel a breeze."

"Good lad," Dern said. "That means there's airflow," he said to me, "so if we had to mostly block up the entrance, the air won't go stale. What's in the boxes?" he asked, indicating the two wooden boxes against the closest wall.

"Hay," Sarr answered again, "and some old blankets. In case the shepherds get caught in a storm," he added. "The hay's for sleeping on, and for feeding the lambs."

"The cave's dry," Dern said, "enough to store ship's biscuit and maybe some dried fish in metal boxes to keep out the vermin." Pel, bored by conversation he could take no part in, had wandered off to explore. Suddenly I heard his voice calling me, though the sound was faint. Dern pointed up the entranceway. Urgency made Pel's voice shrill, but the words were clear.

"A boat, Lena!" he cried. "A big boat!" A frisson of fear ran through me. I looked at Dern. He saw the alarm on my face and grinned.

"*Skua.*"

CHAPTER EIGHT

IN THE MORNING, LISE, WHO HAD BEEN WORKING at the forge with Casyn, brought me a dozen knives and the leather belt sheaths to go with them. Neither knives nor sheaths were handsome things, but they were made well, and with care. I held one. It had the weight of our wooden practice knives, but not the feel, or the sound as it passed through air. The handle was wrapped in thin leather and bound tightly. I thanked Lise, gathered the knives into my shoulder bag, and walked up the hill toward the practice field. Light cloud webbed the sky this morning, creating a haze over the sea. Tice joined me where the paths met. She looked tired.

"So they're here."

"Lise brought them this morning," I answered.

She shook her head. "I meant the men."

"Oh," I said, feeling stupid. "Yes. The boat's here. Nobody knows anything else."

"A bit of time will fix that," she said. "Let me see the seccas." I gave her a knife. She feinted with it. "It's different," she said. "It weighs the same, but the blade cuts the air—how? Faster? Everything will happen more quickly."

"I felt the difference," I said, "but I couldn't put words to it."

She shrugged. "It's like clay," she said. "My fingers, hands, know the smallest difference in the clay itself or how wet it is. I'd imagine you can tell, from the play of a line, what fish is on the other end."

"Usually," I admitted. Suddenly I wanted the feel of a line in my hands, the smell of the sea, and the simplicity of wind and tide. I pushed the thought away.

At the practice grounds, the cohort waited. They should have paired off to practice or to wrestle—the morning warm-up exercises. Instead, they stood talking in tight clusters, their voices edged with excitement.

Skua had reached our cove in the early afternoon. Dern had excused himself immediately after Pel brought her to our attention, striding off down the hillside. I had stayed in the hills, investigating other caves, studying the hollows and outcroppings, thinking about cover. When I saw *Skua* anchor in the cove, and the first of the small boats being lowered, I abandoned the task to return to the village. But the small boat had held only one man; it had been sent to ferry Dern and Casyn to *Skua*, where they had remained.

The conversations quieted as Tice and I approached. Aline looked ready to jump out of her skin, and even Freya's eyes shone.

"I don't know anything," I said without preamble, once everyone had moved into the shade of the oak. "Nobody yet does, not even the council leaders. And we won't know anything until Dern and Casyn return."

"When will that be?" Aline asked.

"No one knows. Now, I have the real seccas, but I won't give them to you until I think you are all ready to concentrate. These are dangerous weapons." I held one up, but most of the women looked only briefly before flicking their gazes back to the water. I bit back a sharp command.

"Into the meeting hall," I said firmly. "Clear the benches to the sides, and close the shutters on the seaward walls." The cohort hesitated.

"Do it now!" I snapped. Freya moved first, and the others followed, Aline and Camy trailing after. I stole one last glance at *Skua* before I followed them.

The hall, lit only from the west windows, had just enough light to allow us to practice. The cohort moved the benches against the walls. I handed out the knives and sheaths.

"Space yourselves well apart," Tice instructed, "and try some moves. You'll feel a difference. And be careful!" As she finished speaking, Aline yelped. I looked over to see blood dripping from the first finger of her left hand. She stuck the finger in her mouth, speaking around it.

"I was just feeling the edge," she mumbled. I dug in my bag for a bandage. Even the wooden seccas had drawn blood. I had learned quickly to have supplies available. I smeared the shallow cut with a concoction of fleecefat and herbs and tied a strip of linen around it.

"At least it's your left hand," I said to Aline. "Keep it clean."

The cohort practiced individually for a quarter of an hour with no further injuries. When I thought they had grown used to the different feel, I called a halt. Along with the sheaths, Lise had given me a leather bag with a couple of dozen balls shaped from the corks of wine flasks—Tice's idea. We showed the cohort how to ease one onto the tip of the secca, deeply enough to keep the ball in place, but not so deeply that the knife tip protruded. "We'll use these for a while," I explained. "We can't afford to injure each other. Try not to lose it, and always check it's in place before you begin practice."

The women put the tip guards in place, dividing up to begin one-on-one practice. Their first hesitancy with the real knives had just begun to subside when Freya slipped on the wooden floor and fell. The knife clattered harmlessly away, but everyone stopped.

Freya sat up and rubbed her knee. "I'm fine," she said. She reached for her secca, but I held up a hand.

"I hadn't thought about the floor being slippery. You're all used to being outside, on the field, and I don't want you having to think about both your footing and the new knives. We'd better go back out." Tice nodded.

We trooped back outdoors into dazzling sunlight. A moment passed before I saw the group of six men climbing up the path with Dern leading them. He raised a hand in greeting.

"Cohort-leader, cohort-second, good morning," Dern said formally, when they reached us.

"Captain," I replied, following his lead. I met his eyes. His gaze was direct, business-like, soldierly.

"These are men of *Skua*," he said, "those with the best knife skills. I wondered if we might practice together over the next weeks." I noted how he had worded the request, establishing that he did not command here. I looked at the men. They ranged in age, I guessed, from about eighteen to well into their thirties, perhaps older. The youngest among them looked the most apprehensive.

"We might," I answered, "but not today. My cohort just received their seccas, newly forged, and we haven't yet grown used to them. But let me introduce my cohort, and perhaps we can know who our opponents will be?"

"Of course," Dern said.

I had the cohort give their names, which they did with differing levels of confidence. Camy spoke her name, but stared at the ground. The men seemed surprised when she and Aline stepped forward. They must not have expected girls quite so young.

The oldest of the men spoke first. "Anwyl," he said, in a relaxed manner. He would have been in and out of women's villages for Festival for many years. The other men followed suit, oldest to youngest: Ferhar, Largen, Tiernay, Danel, Satordi. I doubted I would remember who was who, at least at first.

Men and women eyed each other. Aline and Camy giggled. None of us, I realized, knew how to proceed: This was not Festival, and we had no other customs to guide us. I needed to say something, to establish my authority, and set the tone.

"Cohort," I said. "Shall we show the men how we fight? Find your practice knives. We won't use the new seccas for this. Tice, pair them, please." I turned back to Dern. "Captain, would your men be more comfortable watching from the shade of the trees?"

"I want each man to watch one pair, and to do that, we need to be around the edge of the field, if we may, not grouped in the shade," he said. I nodded. "Men," he said, his tone relaxed but unmistakably still that of command, "watch a pair practice, and look for what is different. Not for mistakes, but for moves you would not have used, holds that are unfamiliar. Understood?" The men murmured their assent. As the cohort took their places on the field, the men spread around the periphery. Dern remained beside me.

Tice had paired the women by size for this first round. They fought confidently, used to their partners and their tactics. Camy and Aline showed off a little, but behaved after I took them aside briefly. The men watched, some squatting, others standing, speaking quietly among themselves. The oldest, Anwyl, watched with a sceptical look on his face.

After ten minutes, Tice stopped the demonstration to pair the women again, this time by disparity of size. At the end of this round, Freya had a welt on her arm from a fast strike from Camy, and I had heard much more discussion among the men.

"Our turn," Dern said. He turned to me. "May we borrow your practice knives?" I agreed, and six of the cohort handed their wooden seccas over. As Tice had done, he paired the men by size for their first round.

We watched as they circled on the field. The sun, high in the sky now, could not be used to advantage. The two youngest—Danel and Satordi—moved lightly, their mode of fighting not dissimilar from ours. The two oldest fought quite differently, using their strength and weight of muscle, striking less often but with more force. Tice focused on the youngest pair; I watched the oldest two.

Dern re-divided them after a quarter of an hour, again following Tice's lead to pair them by the greatest difference in size and body weight. This time Satordi fought against Anwyl. The younger man danced around the older, not landing many blows but not being hit, either. About ten minutes into the bout, Satordi landed a blow on Anwyl's upper arm. Anwyl lunged forward, aiming for Satordi's chest, but he stepped back and sideways. Anwyl tried to check his momentum, turning towards the younger man, but he fell, unbalanced. He tried to roll into the fall, but his left shoulder hit the ground hard. He lay still for a moment, then pulled himself up. He put a hand to his shoulder.

"Let me see it," Dern said.

"It's nothing," the soldier said. "Just a bruise."

"Let me see it," Dern said again. Anwyl grimaced but pulled his tunic off. Dern probed the shoulder. I saw Anwyl wince.

"More than a bruise, but not a sprain," Dern concluded. "Keep it moving, but don't overdo it." He looked up at the sun. "Enough for today."

"We're needed in the fields," I said. "Can we eat together this evening, all of us, to talk over the morning?" We made the arrangements, sent the injured to the baths to soak, and went to find food.

Harvest-time would not wait, even for an invasion. Now that *Skua* and her men had joined us, the council leaders had decided that practice and defence work occupied the mornings, the harvest the afternoon, and a review of the morning's work in the evenings. I ate bread and pickled fish quickly, found an apple and my hat, and went back out, this time to the grain fields. I found Tali teaching *Skua*'s crew how to scythe.

"Hold the top handle in your left hand, and grasp the middle grip with your right," she instructed. Each man did as she said, their movements awkward. I was surprised to see Anwyl holding a scythe. Perhaps his shoulder injury had been slighter than Dern had thought. "Now," Tali continued, picking up her own scythe. "Watch."

Holding the mowing tool with her body twisted to the right, she positioned the blade, curved and very sharp, and as long as her arm, less than a handspan above the ground. Then, with a smooth turn to the left, she moved the scythe in an arc, keeping the blade parallel to the ground. The cut wheat fell neatly beside her.

The men did their best to duplicate her movements. One or two made a decent job of it, but others hacked at the cereal, chopping rather than cutting.

"Stop," Tali said. "Watch me again. Hacking at it wastes energy, and it's more dangerous. Dern, you weren't bad, but keep the blade higher: you'll need to sharpen it every stroke if you hit soil and rocks."

They tried again. Inwardly, I grinned. They'd all be needing the baths tonight. Scything, for someone new to it, took a lot of effort, and left the reaper sore and aching, especially on the first day. Anwyl misjudged his sweep, digging his blade into the soil, jarring his already sore shoulder. He dropped the scythe.

"Pah!" he spat. "This is work for women and slaves, not soldiers." Before Tali could speak, Dern had dropped his own scythe to round on Anwyl.

"Pick up that scythe, soldier," he said, his voice calm and low and cold. "You asked to do this, against my recommendation. So now you will do it, until I tell you otherwise." For a moment Anwyl stared at him. A muscle in his cheek twitched. Then he dropped his eyes.

"Yes, Captain," he muttered. He bent to pick up the scythe, turning back to the work.

After ten minutes more of instruction and observation, Tali pulled two of the men—Ferhar and Danel—out of the scythe line. "We don't have time to let you learn," she said matter-of-factly. "Lena, show them how to tie and stook." I looked up from my work to beckon them over.

I straightened, taking the opportunity to press my hands against my lower back. I hated tying and stooking, but I had never learned to scythe well. "This is fairly simple," I said to the two men, "but you have to get it right. First you gather up a cut," I demonstrated, pulling a neat pile of cut wheat up into my left arm, "then wrap the ties around the sheaf, top and bottom, and tie it off firmly. It has to be tight enough to keep the stalks together. Use a reef knot, and tuck the ends under."

They tried it, making sheaves ranging from neat to ragged, but they would do. We bent to the dusty, prickly work, gathering and tying. Every twelve sheaves made a stook, a circle of sheaves leaning into each other, the heads a shaggy ring at the top. This allowed the sun and wind to dry the wheat, and if it rained before we took them into the threshing floor, the grain would not rot.

All the village worked. The children twisted ties or carried water. Lise went from one scythe team to the next, sharpening the hammered leading edge of the blades with a whetstone. Scythe blades dulled easily, needing to be sharpened several times an hour. Other women gleaned, picking up the heads that had broken off. From a perch, a yellowhammer whistled his "oh see-me see-me see-me please" over and over.

Halfway through the afternoon, the women's scythe line began to sing. They had moved faster than the men, and their swath of cut grain was neater, not that the cattle would care. The song had a rhythm that matched the swing of the scythe. Danel stopped, listening.

"I remember that song," he said. "The women sang it at harvest in my home village, too. As a child, I carried water and twisted ties, like these boys." He indicated Pel and Sarr.

"Where is your home village?" I asked.

"Torrey," he said. "In the south."

"Near Karst?"

He considered. "Not too near. North and west of it. Lena," he added shyly, "tell me, if you would, who is the woman in the scythe line, two from the right? I do not remember her name."

I looked up the field to where the scythe line moved rhythmically through the grain. I smiled. "Her name is Freya."

He flashed me a quick smile that lit his face. "Thank you."

When Casse and Siane arrived a bit later with freshly baked cakes and tea, Tali called a halt. We sat or sprawled in the cut swathes and ate and drank. The cakes, dense with dried fruit, renewed my flagging energy, and the tea, sweet with honey, soothed my throat, dry with the dust of the harvest. I surveyed the field. We had eight days until the autumn equinox. Another two afternoons would finish this field, but another two wheat fields, and three of oats, awaited. We had finished the barley harvest before the men arrived.

Casse, I noted, had brought her bow and arrows. As the scythe teams moved closer to the centre of the field, rabbits and hares, and possibly game birds, would break from the diminishing cover. We ate a lot of rabbit during harvest. I finished my tea and had just stood to return the mug to Siane when Dern's voice—his command voice—rang in the warm air.

"Stop scything now, Anwyl," he said. "If you continue, you will damage that shoulder beyond what heat and a night's rest can heal, and you will be useless to us. You have made your point. Go and stook grain." I watched as Anwyl thrust the scythe at Dern and turned away, not looking at his crewmates. He started towards us.

"Soldier," Casse called out. "Yes, you," she added, when Anwyl looked at her questioningly. "Please come here." Anwyl changed course to walk over to Casse, who had her birdbow in her hand. She said something to him I could not hear. He nodded. After a moment or two of further talk, he took his secca out of his bootsheath to show her. They spoke a minute longer. I saw him indicate his left shoulder, shaking his head. "Captain," Casse called. "I am going to try for rabbit and quail for the pot tonight. I would like this man's help. May I borrow him?"

"Certainly," Dern called back. "There is no danger to his left shoulder in hunting rabbits. Throw true, Anwyl," he added. "I like rabbit stew." The two men I was working with glanced at each other. Was that relief on their faces?

The long rays of the westering sun had turned the heather on the hillside a brilliant purple before we stopped, aching and exhausted. Far overhead, a golden eagle cried as it hunted on the last of the warm updrafts over the hills. Smells of stew and fresh bread drifted up from the village.

The scythers stopped first, making their way to the forge to leave their tools. Lise, and Casyn, I supposed, would work into the night, rehammering and sharpening the edges. The rest of us finished stooking the last sheaves before we left the field. For the first part of the evening, only women could use the baths. The men could soak later. Twenty minutes later, I sank into the hot pool with a deep sigh. I soaked for half an hour, letting the heat penetrate, just floating. All around me, women did the same. Almost no one spoke. After some time, I started thinking about the morning, the women and men fighting, how they differed. I sat up. Across the pool, Tice saw me move, and she too sat up, cocking an eyebrow. We climbed out and dried off. "My cohort," I said to the soaking women, "meet us at the council hall in twenty minutes."

During harvest, the oldest women cooked, and we ate communally at the hall. With bowls of stew and chunks of bread in hand, I claimed the west-facing porch for our meeting spot, sitting on the step to eat. The cohort drifted out, followed by Dern and his men. Danel slid into a spot near Freya. When we had eaten the stew, Camy and Aline brought out a tray of fruitcake and tarts.

"I would like to talk about what we saw this morning," I began. "What is different, about the way we use the knives, and how you do. And what that might mean when we fight."

"You're not as strong," Anwyl said bluntly. He sat slightly apart from the others, leaning against one of the posts that supported the roof of the porch. "I could take the knife away from any of you, easily."

"Not easily," another man said. "Satordi is not as strong as you either, but you've never bested him in practice because he's faster. Strength isn't everything, Anwyl."

"There is something else, though," Satordi spoke. He could be no more than eighteen, I thought. "I can't explain it, but you move differently. It's like seeing an animal from a distance: you can tell whether it's a dog or a fox, just by its movement."

"He's right," Tice said. "The men move differently than we do. They carry more muscle on their upper bodies, and their centre is higher. They move from their chests. We have more strength and more movement lower down on the body, from the hips."

Dern reached for a tart. "What does this mean?"

"We tend to aim low, or at arms, not chests or backs," Freya answered. "We can duck away easily and move out of range, but stabbing at the body takes more arm strength. We do it, but not as much as the men."

"So we should expect more attacks directed at our upper bodies," I said. "Think about that and prepare for it. Tomorrow we will pair off with the men, with our practice knives, to begin to learn what it is to fight a man. Is there anything else?" No one spoke. "My cohort, to bed, then." They stood, gathering bowls and mugs. I picked up one of the trays and piled dishes onto it. Danel said something to Freya. She smiled, bidding him good night.

I heard Dern order his men to the baths. He followed me into the meeting hall, carrying one of the trays. We deposited them on a table. "May I walk with you?" he said quietly.

I shook my head. "Go to the baths with your men. I'm tired. I need to sleep."

He nodded. "I suppose you do," he said without inflection. "Good night, then, Lena. I'll see you in the morning."

I called a goodnight to Casse and her helpers and walked out into the night. I didn't want to think about Dern. Watching Freya and Danel tonight, their budding awareness of each other, had changed something. However I felt about Dern, it didn't have the same delight as what I saw between Danel and Freya. I wanted him. But was that enough?

The next morning dawned on another cloudless harvest day. We gathered at the practice field, the men climbing up from harbour and the boats where they slept. I saw another group of men with bows, heading for the butts, and others joining in the work of the cohort building the fences above the tideline that we hoped would funnel the invaders along defended paths. Dern and his men brought their own wooden seccas.

We conferred on how to pair them off, deciding on height to begin with. I named six women. "You six fight first. The rest will watch."

"Go slowly, at first. We want no injuries from carelessness or pride," Dern added.

Wooden knives in hand, the combatants moved out onto the packed dirt of the practice ground. They paired off, and at a nod from me, the practice began. Tice and Dern and I watched the pairs. At first, they hesitated. The men, I supposed, not comfortable with the idea of fighting women; the women unsure of the strength and expertise they faced. In almost all cases, the fighting only began in earnest after a skilful blow from one of my cohort. I moved over to Dern to tell him what I saw. "We can't let this continue, or we will come to expect it, and the advantage it gives. The Lestian men won't hesitate."

"You're right," Dern said, "but neither will they attack with full force. They won't be expecting any sort of skilled resistance." He hesitated. "From what I know of Leste, they won't attack to kill, not at first. They'll attack to overpower, and then use you for their pleasure."

"Casyn warned us," I said, keeping my voice calm. "Can we begin again?"

We stopped the practice, and while Dern spoke to his men, Tice and I talked with the cohort. I told them what I had seen, and what it meant. When we began again, with different pairs, it looked better. It looked real.

We practiced, in different pairs, until late morning. I pulled Tice aside at one point to tell her of the attraction between Freya and Danel, advising her to watch them closely when they paired.

"They're unlikely to be the only ones, but I'll pay attention. If they are too gentle with each other, I'll step in." While she watched, I fought several men, trying to note the differences, predict the moves. Anwyl kept me completely at bay: I could only defend myself. Finally, I turned, ran, and then threw my knife.

I hit his shoulder—the left one—and he roared in pain and surprise. His pride had let him think I had panicked and run, and he had not thrown his own knife. By the end, bruised and dusty, I thought I had the beginnings of an understanding of what fighting against the invaders might entail.

For the next five days, we practiced in the mornings and went to the grain fields in the afternoons. The weather held. No rain soaked the grain or replenished the streams. On the fifth morning, I left the cohort with Tice, and went with Anwyl and Tiernay to build a trail up the waterfall.

Dern and I had spoken of it two nights before, at dinner. I had kept him at arm's length all week, which he had seemed to accept, but we still needed to plan. We sat on the west porch of the meeting hall after the others left. I sipped tea as he outlined what he believed needed to be done at the waterfall.

"I want you to take Anwyl and Tiernay," he said. I started to protest, but he held up a hand. "Casyn has made half a dozen iron rings that can be hammered into the rocks where needed, to tie ropes to. And before you object to Anwyl, hear me out. Anwyl has skills you need. He was born in a tiny village east of Casilla where the mountains come down to the sea. He grew up scrambling up and down cliffs, taking seabird eggs and nestlings even before he was six. A dozen years ago, he was sent into the Durrains as part of a scouting group because of his skill with climbing. He's not the easiest of men to deal with, but there is little about climbing rockfaces safely he doesn't know."

"All right," I answered slowly. "And Tiernay?"

"Tiernay is strong and careful, and Anwyl likes him. And he has a head for heights." Dern said. "Who will you take from the women?"

"I was going to say Freya," I said, "but that's not right. She's as tall as I am. Kelle, I think. She's strong, but she's a lot shorter. If she can climb the trail we build, everyone else should be able to as well."

He nodded, reaching out to cover my hand in his own. I felt the tug of desire, but I turned my hand up to squeeze his, then withdrew it. He looked at me quizzically.

"Dern, I think the answer is no."

"Are you sure?"

I exhaled. I owed him the truth. "Not quite. Part of me wants to—very much. But part of me says whatever I'm feeling—it's not enough. Can you understand that?"

"Not really," he said. "But perhaps the difference is that you have loved someone, and I haven't. But I certainly want you, and perhaps there could be more." Crickets chirped in the night. I looked up at the stars. He shifted slightly. "I'll ask one more time, Lena. But no more."

"I understand," I said. "I don't want to mislead you, Dern."

"I'll survive," he said. "Sleep well."

I stood at the base of the waterfall, with Kelle, Tiernay, and Anwyl, and the tools—picks and shovels, a bag of iron rings, drills and hammers and rope—that we needed.

Anwyl studied the waterfall for some minutes while we waited. I had told Kelle of his expertise, and that I would defer to his advice. "Wait here," he said finally. Taking off his overtunic—the morning had not yet warmed—he began to climb.

Nearly half an hour passed before he returned. "Down is easy," he said briefly. "You climbed up it?"

"I did. Twice. So has Freya." He raised his eyebrows. I thought I saw new respect in his eyes.

"You were lucky not to fall," he said. "She couldn't, though," he indicated Kelle.

"No," I agreed. "Kelle is too short. We need to make it possible for Kelle and the rest of the cohort to climb it. Not easy, but possible."

He nodded. "Let me take Tiernay up, to start getting those rings in place. That's going to take some time, and then we'll start stabilizing some of the rocks that wobble." He handed Tiernay tools, and the bag of rings. "Meanwhile, start looking for flattish rocks, about this big"—he indicated with his hands—"that we can wedge under boulders."

Kelle and I had a fair pile of flattish stones when Anwyl joined us. He nodded with approval at the pile. "We'll need a lot more."

"Kelle, see if you can round up some of the children. If not, get Camy and Aline." She nodded, turning towards the village.

"Get some bags, or baskets, too," Anwyl called. "For carrying them up."

Anwyl showed me how to hammer the flat rocks under a midsized boulder that rocked. Once he saw I understood, he left me to it, scooping up some of the pile, climbing higher to begin on the next unstable rock. I could hear the chink of hammer and chisel on the rocks higher up, where Tiernay worked. Occasionally, a chip bounced down to join the pebbles on the foreshore.

When Kelle returned with Camy, Aline, Lara, and Sarr, we toiled through the morning, wedging and digging, carrying rock higher and higher up the waterfall. As it grew warmer, we welcomed the splashing water for its cooling qualities. Anwyl came down several times to check our work. "Good," he said briefly. He was not a man of many words.

At midday, Lara left to bring us food. When she returned, we sat at the base of the waterfall to eat. Tiernay had climbed down, reporting that he had one ring in and a second well on its way. "After we eat," Anwyl said, through a mouthful of pickled fish and bread, "Kelle will test our work."

Kelle looked at me. I swallowed my own mouthful. "Anwyl," I said, as calmly as I could muster, "it is up to me to tell Kelle what to do. I appreciate your expertise in rock-climbing, and I'm glad you are here to direct what needs to be done, but my cohort is under my command." I waited. Anwyl stared at me for a moment before dropping his eyes.

"As you say."

"Thank you." I wondered what Dern had said to him. "I'd prefer it if you would show us both and let us practice with you watching. Climbing is your skill, and we'd be glad to learn from you."

He chewed. "When you're ready, cohort-leader."

We finished our food, and after a brief rest, started up the waterfall. The first part of the climb went easily. Anwyl had indicated we should climb ahead of him. Tiernay had gone up first to attach the rope. I climbed first of our group, with Kelle following. From just behind us, Anwyl gave instructions whenever I or Kelle hesitated, sometimes pointing out a better choice of hand or foot placement. After ten minutes, we reached the first place where frost and water had sheared off a section of the cliff. Where Freya and I had hung on with fingertips to the upper ledge while we scrabbled for toeholds, Tiernay had drilled and hammered an iron ring into the cliff-face above the ledge, and chiselled out a smooth half-circle in the rock to let the rope pass through without fraying. The rope itself, a thick mooring line, had been knotted to provide hand and foot grips.

"Not much to it," Anwyl said. "Climb up the rope. When you get to the ledge, put your elbows on it and pull yourself up until you can roll on. Who's going first?"

"I am," I said. I grabbed the rope at a knot to pull myself up, then cursed, dropping down again. I took off my shoes, tied them through my belt at my back, and began again, grasping the rope with my feet. The falling water had soaked it, but the knots provided purchase. Slowly I worked my way up the rope to the ledge, and, tightening my toegrip, slid my elbows up onto the ledge, found places my hands could grip, and pulled myself up. Much easier, I thought, than when I'd climbed it earlier this summer. I sat up. The knotted rope continued for some distance above my head. I swung my body back out onto the rope and descended.

Anwyl nodded. "Good," he said. "You could have been quicker, but that will come with practice. Better to be safe."

"Kelle?" I said. She swallowed hard but nodded. She had already taken off her shoes.

Two thirds of the way up, she froze. I started to speak, but Anwyl stopped me. "Move your right hand up," he instructed. "Just your right hand." Slowly she complied. "Now your left," he said. He gave her firm instructors until she lay on the ledge. He gave her a minute. "Now come down. You saw what Lena did. Grab the knot."

She came down without freezing, to stand, panting slightly, on the boulder. "Well done," Anwyl said.

"Very well done," I echoed.

"You'll do it again in a minute," Anwyl said. He glanced at me. "Providing your cohort leader agrees, of course. First I want to check the rope." He climbed rapidly, reaching the ledge in only a few seconds. There he examined the rope where it brushed against the ledge, looked up at the metal ring, then dropped back down to the boulder faster than he had climbed. "No fraying," he said. "Do you want Kelle to climb again?"

"I do," I said. "Kelle?" She nodded, beginning to climb, not hesitating this time. She rolled onto the ledge and did not pause for breath before coming back down.

"It's not bad," she said, "once you're used to it. Thank you, Anwyl."

We spent another couple of hours stabilizing the last of the boulders, by which time Tiernay had the next ring in place and the rope knotted and hung. With Anwyl guiding us we both climbed to the top, and back down again without mishap. At the bottom, as we gathered our tools, I stopped to speak to him.

"Thank you," I said. "You gave us both confidence. If I embarrassed you earlier, I apologize."

"You didn't." he said after a minute. "I was out of line. Although..." He hesitated.

"Although?"

"You could take it as a compliment, I suppose," he said. "When this was all first told to us, I thought, women, what can they do? I mean," he flushed slightly, "I know you farm, and fish, and do all the things that need doing in a village, without men, but when it comes to fighting, that's men's work. But what I've seen, here, this week—I'm impressed. So when I told Kelle to climb, instead of asking you, it's because I was treating you both like cadets. I did forget you were in command, but I didn't mean to be disrespectful. I was just teaching you like I usually do."

"And will keep doing, I hope. Will you come back with us, when I bring the whole cohort to climb, tomorrow morning?"

"If the Captain says I can," he said.

The next morning, Dern took the rest of the men off to assist elsewhere in the village, and my cohort and Anwyl spent the morning at the waterfall. By noon, we could all climb up and down with reasonable speed and confidence.

The last of the oat fields fell to the scythes that afternoon. From the lower wheat fields, I could hear the shouts to the oxteam as the wagon filled with dried sheaves, heading to the barn for threshing. That night, the temperature fell suddenly. We woke to a thick rime of frost on the grass and clear blue skies. As I stood at my window looking out, I heard the sound I had subconsciously been waiting for: the peal of the hunting horn. The first heavy frost of autumn marked the start of the deer cull. I dressed, took my hunting bow from the corner where I had propped it, and went downstairs.

Tali had made tea, and the smell of bacon frying made my stomach rumble. Eggs sat in a bowl, waiting to be fried in the bacon fat. The pace of a hunt frequently left no time to eat again until late in the day, so we ate well at breakfast. I sliced bread and set the table.

Siane and Lara joined us, Siane eating only the bread and eggs. Too lame for the hunt, Siane oversaw the preparation of the smokehouse and kept the hunt records. Tali and I left the clean-up for later and walked up to the stableyard.

Only a few women would ride. We had, as a village, very few hill ponies. Horses, expensive in terms of feed, served few purposes that could not be met by oxen. The riders, with the help of the dogs which spent most of the year herding sheep and cattle, moved the small, delicate, red-coated deer off the hilltops and down into the lower slopes. There we chose a few young males to cull each year. After last year's mild winter and the fine summer, we might take half-a-dozen this year.

I took my orders from Gille, who acted as hunt leader. For the first half of the day, my job would be to walk the hillsides, flushing deer from small coombs and copses. In a friendly rivalry—soldiers, did, after all, need to be competent hunters of fresh meat—we divided the range of hills between *Skua*'s crew and the villagers. I had Lara with me. At eleven, she was old enough to participate in the first half of the day.

We walked up the path into the hills, skirting the springs and the burial ground, going higher even than the caves. As we walked, a thought occurred to me.

"Lara, does your mother mind you joining in the hunt?"

"No," she said, surprised. "Why would she?"

"She doesn't eat meat, and she disapproves of killing."

"But she didn't always. She was a farmer, remember?"

"Yes. And she still keeps the herd and hunt records, I know."

"Long ago, before I was born, she had a liaison with a soldier who told her all about the soldier's god, the bull they worship. She had forgotten about it, but on the day the bull attacked her, she suddenly remembered. She prayed to it. She promised that if it spared her life, she'd never kill again. She says the bull turned away at the last minute, and its horn only hit her in the leg. So she keeps that promise. She says she owes the soldier's god her life."

"I see," I said slowly.

We had reached the high moorland. The heath shone with dew. "Shhh, now," I whispered. "Feel the breeze. It's coming down over the hills, so we're upwind of the deer." Early frosts always resulted from clear nights and a wind off the hills. Wind from the sea carried too much warmth to allow frost to form. "We need to move very quietly through the heather, down towards groups of boulders, or the little coombs, where the deer spend the night. As we approach, stay quiet, but hold your arms out like this"—I demonstrated—"to make yourself look as big as possible. We want them to move down."

"What if they go up?" she whispered.

"Then the riders and the dogs will force them back down."

As we approached the first group of boulders, I could see the antlers of a seated stag poking up from the heather. I pointed them out to Lara. With hand signals, I indicated she should approach from one side of the boulders, I from the other. She waited while I made my way to the far side of the boulders, and then, arms outstretched, we approached the deer.

When the stag saw us, he bolted up, snorting, to bound down the hillside, followed by three others that I hadn't seen. I gave Lara a signal of approval, and she smiled. We continued to work along the ridge. Slowly, through the morning, we drew the noose of people and dogs tighter, driving the deer down to the lower meadow.

As we approached, I saw Gille conferring with Siane and Gwen. I picked up my bow, and Gille motioned me over. "We will take six," she said, "four for us, one for *Skua*, and one for the Empire's provisions." She paused. "Do you see the young stag with the malformed left antler? The first shot is yours."

I nodded. If I missed, or only wounded, someone else would let a second arrow fly before I could re-nock. This policy kept the kill swift, reducing the time we held the deer.

I positioned myself and waited for the first signal. When it came, I sighted, drew, and on the second signal, released. The arrow hit the stag in the neck, as I had intended. He leapt forward, took three or four steps, and fell.

We killed our six animals with eight arrows—four from the hands of *Skua*'s crew, four from women's bows. It was a good, clean, cull. Cleaning and butchering took the rest of the day. Much of the meat went for smoking, but tonight we feasted.

The smell of fresh liver frying over the fires brought us all to the council hall by early evening. Tice waved to me from across the hall. I worked my way through the bodies to her. She was in high spirits. "A good shot, cohort-leader," she said. "So why the boats and not the herds, then?"

"Simple," I replied, picking up a plate and spearing a slice of liver from the platter of roasted meat. "The hunt is once a year, but herds-and-hunt apprentices—and masters—look after the sheep and cattle, too. And I hate sheep."

Tice laughed. "Fair enough." We added vegetables and bread to our plates, moving outside where the cooking fires, now banked to heat water for tea, acted as focal points for groups of women and men. Freya saw us, waving us over to where she sat with Danel and a group of men and women. Freya and Danel sat close enough that their legs touched. Pastries, fruit, and quite a bit of wine followed the meat, making the meal leisurely and prolonged. Sitting around the fire, the night felt celebratory, a mood, I suddenly realized, of Festival.

"That was a good shot, Lena," Tiernay said suddenly.

"Thanks."

"Do you ever stalk deer in the hills?"

"Yes," I said, "sometimes, in the winter, if food is running low. I've taken one or two like that."

"It's harder, yes?" he said. "The wind can change suddenly, and they smell you, or you misjudge the arrow flight."

"Yes," I agreed. I sipped my wine, listening to Tiernay describe a winter hunt where they had taken three deer in the end, saving the camp from starvation. "And better for the deer, too," he ended. "There was so much snow, they couldn't find food."

"Where was this?" a man from across the fire said.

"Under the Durrains," Tiernay said, "some four or five years back."

"Winters are vicious over there," the man agreed. "Like being north of the Wall."

"By the god, yes," someone else said. "We did a winter sortie a few years back, with dogs, chasing after northerners who had tried to raid a guardpost for food. We had to turn back. I think they go underground."

"I heard they can walk on the snow," Largen said.

"On the snow!" Salle said.

"Yes," Largen answered. "They strap frames of hide and wood to their feet."

"It's true," the man across the fire said. "I've seen these frames. But I don't think you can move very fast."

"Faster than we could," the second man said. "I've never been so cold." The woman beside him—Lise—slipped her arms around him.

"You're warm now," she said. He nuzzled her hair.

"I am," he said.

As the conversations became more private, I sat quietly. Tice had excused herself some time earlier. Freya and Danel slipped away, hand in hand. Casyn and Gille were at the next fire. I watched as he put his hand on her shoulder and she leaned into him. Voices murmured, laughed. String and wind instruments played.

Dern approached, crouching beside me. "Walk with me, Lena," he said. He stood and held out a hand. I took it, letting him pull me up. We walked away from the fire, uphill, towards the sound of the waterfall. Beyond the ring of light from the fires, he stopped. "Last time, Lena," he murmured, putting a hand on the back of my neck, kissing me, hard and insistent. I felt the expected shock of physical desire, and beyond that, a deep regret.

Dern stepped back, running a hand gently down my upper arm.

I shook my head. "I can't. I'm sorry, Dern," I said. Tears pricked my eyes. "But Maya believed—believes—that she had been betrayed by everything she trusted. To go with you, when there is nothing more between us than physical desire, would be to betray that trust one more time."

A half-smile crossed his face. "I guessed as much. But I had to ask one last time." He looked back, toward the music, and the fires.

"Go," I said. "Enjoy the night." He looked at me steadily for a moment, then nodded. Beyond us, in the hills, an owl called. I could see a light in Tice's cottage window. I waited. Dern turned to walk back to the others. He would find comfort somewhere. I watched him for a moment, then took the uphill path to Tice's cottage.

She sat on the doorstep, a flask of wine and a cup beside her, looking out at the night. She must have seen—or heard—me coming but said nothing until I was only a few feet away.

"Said no to Dern, did you?" she said softly.

"I had to. For Maya. I only wanted physical comfort from him, Tice. There is no love between us."

She nodded, a half-smile playing around her lips. "You're still very young, cohort-leader. I hope you can keep to your ideals in what is coming."

I wanted to protest, but what could I say? Tice gestured. "Get a cup from the kitchen and join me." She edged over on the doorstone. I walked past her into the lantern-lit cottage, found a cup, and sat beside her. Tice reached for the wine to fill my cup. We drank in silence.

Tice spoke first. "Have you ever wondered why I left Karst?"

"Yes," I said. "Was it not by choice?"

"No," she said, so quietly I had to strain to hear her. "I was banished, sent away by the council. Do you want to know why?" I heard a challenge in her voice.

"Do you want to tell me?" I answered softly.

"Yes," she said, in a normal tone. "You're my friend, I hope, Lena, and my leader in these strange times. You deserve to know." She paused. "I had a child. A son. Out of season, conceived between festivals by a Lestian trader."

"Why?" I blurted.

"Why?" She laughed. "Because I was young and rebellious, and because the woman I loved had conceived a child the year before, and I was jealous, and angry."

"But, Tice, liaisons produce children."

"I wasn't jealous of the liaison. I am not proud of this, Lena. I was jealous of the child. Once she knew she was pregnant, all her attention was given to the unborn baby. And I was angry because she had gone against my wishes. I didn't want a child in our household, but Tevra did."

"She didn't come with you into exile?"

She shook her head. "She left before that, even before the babe was born. I had made our life together unbearable, so she went to Casilla to live with an aunt."

"Does she know what has happened to you since then?"

"No," she said. "Not even my mother or sisters know where I am."

"And your son? Where is he?"

"Being raised in the slave quarters at Jedd's retirement farm. The council arranged that. What else would there have been for him? No father to claim him, no regiment to house him. He will never know. They let me bear him and name him—Valle, I called him—and then they took him. They sent me away a month later." She fell silent. The cat appeared from somewhere to rub against Tice's legs. She stroked it absentmindedly. After a while, she spoke again. "I had gone to the farm to see the accountsman—something about payment for some grapes. But he was chambered with Jedd and the captain of the Lestian ship, and my errand was not important enough to disturb him. I decided to wait. I wandered around a bit, looked at the horses. And met Kirthan. He was a junior member of the Lestian entourage, bored by all the waiting. He had a flask of wine, and I was just an afternoon's distraction." She shrugged. "He was too young, probably, to even know the taboos we were breaking."

"Does the council know?"

"Yes," she answered. "I was exiled, and so must tell. Maya chose exile: she need not tell her reasons. You know that," she added. I remembered it, vaguely, from schoolgirl lessons. It had seemed very unimportant, then.

"Tice," I said, "what if—"

"Kirthan is aboard this raiding ship? We shared next to nothing, Lena, and I have paid all the price. I and Valle. Kirthan is nothing to me. If my knife finds his heart, I will feel no regret. You need not worry, cohort-leader." Something in her voice told me the moment had passed and the subject was closed. I poured some more wine.

"Tomorrow, will we practice one-on-one combat with the men, or should we test our routes again?"

"Practice, I think."

We spoke of tactics for a while before I bade her goodnight and walked back to my room. The house was dark. I could hear music and laughter. It did not touch me. Too much betrayal, done or revealed, this night. I let the tears come. I wept for the pain Tice had caused and carried, for my own fears for Maya and for myself, and for the comfort I could not give, or take.

CHAPTER NINE

SIX DAYS LATER, ON A FOGGY, WET MORNING, *Skua* sailed on the tide. For the last few days, Dern had not accompanied his men to the practice field but had spent his days with Casyn. I had seen him only from a distance. While he always waved and shouted a greeting, he did not come to me privately. Nor did I go in search of him.

The day before, I had met Casyn at the lower footbridge. I was carrying a basket of carrots and small turnips on my way to Tali's from the fields.

"Lena," he said, in his measured way, "I hoped to find you."

"Casyn," I greeted him, putting my basket down. "Do you need something?"

"No," he said. "Only to tell you we sail tomorrow, on the morning tide."

"Tomorrow! Then you think the invasion is very soon."

"A week, give or take. We need to be well away, out beyond the quickest routes from Leste, so that we are not seen. We will approach the island from the west, as they sail east."

I glanced at the sky. The breeze blew from off the hills, and only a few clouds lined the western horizon: good weather to sail west.

"Are we ready?"

"You are," he said. "Trust your training, Lena, but also your instincts."

"I wish you were staying."

"You have to do this yourselves," he said. "Were I here, you would defer to my experience and not take true leadership. This way, you must." He held out a hand. "Fare you well, Lena. I will see you again."

I too held out my right hand. He took my arm in the soldier's grasp, his hand at my elbow. I returned the grasp, feeling the muscles of his arm, hard against my hand. "Farewell, Casyn. We will have tales to tell, when we meet again."

The entire village came out to see them leave. The men rowed aboard in small boats until only Dern and Casyn stood on the jetty. They saluted us, and we them, and then they boarded the last boat to begin their short, measured trip back to the ship.

We watched, singly and in small groups, until the sea fog obscured the last glimpse of *Skua*. I wished suddenly I had spoken to Dern before they sailed, if only to thank him for what he had taught me. But I had missed my chance.

As women began to walk away, up the hill to the meeting house, cohorts fell in behind their leaders. I saw Freya watching me. I nodded, joining the exodus from the shore. We walked up the hill without much talk. My cohort sat together at the meeting house, Tice taking her usual place beside me. Gille, with Sara and my mother, stood in their familiar place in the centre of the circle. When all had gathered, Gille raised her hand for silence.

"Women of Tirvan," she began, "we are once again a village of women. Four months ago, our lives consisted of farming and fishing, and our thoughts and our skills were given to these pursuits. We are something more now: a military unit, trained to fight. And we have paid a price, both personal and collective."

I listened, puzzled.

"We have changed our traditions. We have learned to fight. We have lived beside men, abandoning the role of Festival in our personal relationships with them. After the invasion, we will resume our normal lives, but we will not be as we were before this summer. But in this time before the invasion, we must maintain the structures of authority in the village. Much of our autumn work awaits completion. In the fields and on the boats, authority still belongs to the masters of those trades, regardless of their position in our defensive cohorts. When this is finished, when the invasion is quashed, and the Empire is safe again, we will need to think about the future, and what it will look like. But not until then. Are there questions?"

No one stood. Tice met my eyes, cocking an eyebrow in her usual unspoken question. I shook my head slightly. Had Gille meant to raise speculation?

Sara stepped forward. She spoke of the tasks still needing to be done, the familiar autumn work: root vegetables to be dug, boats to be cleaned and repaired, cider apples to be pressed. The bulk of the harvest was done, thanks to the work of *Skua*'s crew. We would accomplish these remaining tasks in the afternoons and continue to drill in the mornings.

Gille spoke again. "Casyn and I, with Dessa's help," she nodded toward the cohort-leader and master fisher, seated to her left, "have studied the tides, and the moon. We believe that the most likely time for the attack is between six and eight days from now, at dawn. The tide will be high and the moon set." She paused. "We will use against them what they believe they are using against us: darkness and surprise. We will be waiting, armed and hidden. With luck and skill, they will never get past the beach."

I considered what Dern had told me about the catboats of Leste—keeled longboats, driven by oars and a single sail, that floated in less than three feet of water. At high tide, they could gain our harbour, which meant they would attack at full force. They would have no reason to send an advance party. Lestian catboats had come occasionally to trade with Tirvan, so they would know the harbour and expect no defence. Forty men against eighty women, skilled with bow and knife and with the advantage of surprise. I felt suddenly confident.

Gille continued. "Cohort-leaders and seconds, please remain. The rest are needed in the fields and at the boats, but before you go, I would say one last thing. Women of Tirvan, we have a job to do. We have much at stake. We cannot slacken. The patrols and exercises must continue. We fight for our lives." She paused, then continued in a voice softened by fatigue and sorrow. "You have done well, my friends. We will come through this, but not unscathed. Some of us will die. We will win our lives, but we will pay yet another, grievous price. Be brave, my friends, and strong." She stepped back, her face drawn. I thought of what these weeks must have cost her. She had found brief solace with Casyn, both sharing the strains of leadership, and now he was gone.

The hall emptied of everyone but the leaders and their seconds. I moved forward, to the inner ring of seats, with Tice beside me. When only the cohort-leaders remained, Gille began.

"We have gone through the records for the last twenty years. Leste has sent boats thrice in that time, the last six years ago." Heads nodded among the women. I remembered the boat, the graceful curved sides of the longboat and the carved leopard's head on the prow. At eleven, I had found that of far more interest than the men who had sailed on her. "Casyn believes that it will be that boat's captain who will steer his ship into our harbour, both for his knowledge of our waters and his memories of the village. They were here five days, and we took him and some of his men around the village to see fleeces and cloth and grain stores. Xani did some small repairs for them, so they'll know where the forge is. The men traded freely for small items, pottery and jewellery and the like."

I saw the logic. The Lestians would leave a few men to defend the boat, moving the rest, under cover of darkness, up to the top of the village. They would then drive us down through the village to the harbour at first light, catch us between the invading force and the sea, giving us no choice but to surrender.

"We'll let them get themselves into position above the village," Gille went on. "At that moment, the mounted cohort, who will be hidden and waiting by the shellfish ponds, will attack the men who stayed with the boat. Archers lying in wait in the net sheds will defend the riders. The men above the village will, we believe, rush back toward their boat through the centre of the village. The main path from the baths will be visible and clearly the fastest way to the harbour. We hope they will run that way, to be trapped on the path, with archers and mounted swordswomen below them, and the rest of us above, on foot and in the second floor of houses with bows and knives."

I nodded. Dern and I had spoken of this plan. The wattle fences around the path would not hold them for long, but in the confusion and surprise of those first few minutes, under an unanticipated attack, we would have the advantage. I shivered. I saw my cohort slipping through tunnel and loft, solitary and swift, to kill those who had escaped the battle. Assassins. I looked at Tice. All the laughter had gone from her. She sat still and hard and cold.

"I'm not going to live in a cave!" Minna shouted. "I want my own bed and my chair."

"You must, Mother." Her daughter tried to soothe her. "It's for your safety, and it's only for a few days."

"You must," Gille echoed, her voice firm.

"I won't," Minna said.

Casse stood. "Let me try," she said, looking to Gille for permission. Gille nodded, and Casse moved to stand in front of Minna. "Look at me, Minna," she said. Minna obeyed. "Who am I?" Casse asked.

"Casse," Minna mumbled. "Council Leader."

"When we give the word, Minna, you will go to the caves," Casse repeated calmly. "You are needed there, to help care for the babes and the new mothers. Do you understand?"

Minna dropped her eyes. "Yes, Council Leader."

"You will not argue?"

"I won't," Minna said. "I will go where I'm needed."

"Thank you, Minna."

"Thank you, Casse," Gille murmured as Casse returned to her seat. "As I was saying, there is food aplenty in the caves, and straw and blankets and water. We cannot risk a fire, so you must huddle together for warmth and wrap the little ones well."

"I worry we can't keep the children quiet," Nessa said, jiggling her grizzling baby.

"There is poppy, dissolved in wine. It can be given in sips, or rubbed on the gums for the littlest ones, just enough to keep them sleepy," my mother said. "And Casyn warned the boys that any reports of disobedience would become part of their cadet records. I think they believed him."

"Pel certainly did," Tali said. "Is there any fencing left to do or work on the tunnels?"

"Nothing," I said. The wattle panels already fenced the common and the path. We had dismantled the hunt enclosures, and some of the sheep pens, to do this, so that fresh wattle did not warn of recent change.

"All the boats not fishing daily are anchored in the hidden cove," Dessa reported. "There will only be a few left at the jetty, just enough not to look odd."

The meeting over, I had stood to leave when my mother called my name. Tice was waiting for me on the porch, so I signalled to her to wait before turning to my mother. She looked very tired, and spoke quietly. "Lena, there may be no other time to say this. Much has been asked of you this summer, losing Maya, being called to command so young and in such a role. I am proud of you. But I think you will soon have to make some terrible choices, with no one to advise you. You must always consider what course of action benefits the most. The village comes before the individual."

I found my voice. "Do you think I do not know my job, Mother? When have you had to make such a decision?" I heard my own words with an odd sense of detachment.

"Many times, and your sister is learning, too." Her voice was soft, but I saw a flash of anger in her eyes. "When we had to choose, this summer, between saving both of Nessa's twins and losing Nessa, or letting the second child die to keep Nessa and the first one safe, were we not making the same decision? For the village, a mother who will live to raise her child, and to work and to contribute and to bear more children if she wishes, is worth more than two babies. If the decision had been Nessa's, she would have died to let both twins live."

I flushed. "Forgive me, Mother. I should not have said what I did."

"Kira cried for two days after that birthing, but you won't have that luxury. Nor do I think you have properly grieved for Maya. You will do what you need to do, but when this is over—and it will be over, soon—you need to grieve. For Maya, for our changed life, for the lives you will have taken and lost. If you do not grieve, Lena, you will break."

I could feel the tears threatening. I looked away. "Do your job," my mother said.

"I will," I said softly, turning away.

We rehearsed the attack, pulling two women from each cohort—different women, each day—to be the invaders. We practiced being still and keeping the ponies quiet. We practiced with sword and bow in the half-light of dawn and at dusk. We timed how long it took the mounted cohort to reach the harbour. We perfected signals—night bird calls, the bark of a fox. My cohort hid in lofts and tunnels and crawled and leapt and perfected landing on the balls of our feet, knives out, ready.

On the third morning, just as the sun crested the ridge above the sheep pastures, a shout came from high in the hills. Horses, silhouetted against the sky: two with riders, the rest riderless but saddled and carrying packs. Gille, with her eyesight honed by years of herding and hunting, spoke. "The riders are women."

They clattered into the village, pulling up outside the hall where we had, by habit, gathered. The riders were not much older than I. They wore their long hair tied back, carrying swords in scabbards on the saddles, shields on their backs, and spears in their hands. The horses they sat on were muscled, conditioned, and disciplined. Warriors. I tried not to stare.

Gille stepped forward. "Welcome to Tirvan."

The riders dismounted. The shorter of the two women spoke. "I am Dian, and this is Rasa. We come from Han village, in the grasslands. Four weeks ago, the three grasslands villages met in joint council to determine our role in fighting Leste. We decided that half of us would go to the coastal villages to add to the defence. The others would stay to act as a rearguard against any Lestians who might slip through the coastal defences. We brought what horses we could."

The grasslands villages bred and trained the majority of the horses for the army. The villages raised cattle, too, making, from the tanned hides, the saddles and bridles for the Empire. Horses, beef, and harness. For everything else, they traded.

"Thank you," Gille said. "We welcome your assistance. I am Gille, council leader; Sara and Gwen make the three. And this is Grainne. She leads the mounted cohort. We expect attack within three days."

Dian nodded. "We had hoped to be on time."

"Grainne, your cohort is excused from field duty," Gille said. "For the rest of us, to work!"

As we dug root vegetables that afternoon, the women of the mounted cohort learned to control the warhorses in the lower pasture. Han had sent six horses, plus the two Dian and Rasa rode. That meant we now had ten horses trained to war, as Casyn and Dern had left their horses with us when they sailed. The hunt ponies would now, I surmised, be ridden only by the smallest women.

In the late afternoon, we called a halt to the harvest, ate a quick snack, and, as the evening deepened, took our places once again to rehearse the defence of Tirvan. I slipped into the loft above the forge, sliding open the ventilation window. From here, I had an almost unobstructed view of the village. I settled down on my heels to wait.

The night call of a thrush, repeated twice, sang through the dusk. From the harbour, I could see the group who represented the Lestians moving up to the top of the village. I waited. When they gathered above the houses, I barked twice, and then twice again, the sharp sound of a fox on its evening hunt. The horses erupted from the scrub that hid the shellfish ponds, their riders shouting, spears held high. The group of women above the village drew their weapons as they ran toward the harbour.

All but one. She turned away from the group, beginning to run toward the forge and the waterfall. I dropped silently through the trap door onto the bedroom floor below, creeping out the door to the small porch. As she passed the corner of the cottage, I leapt, knife in hand, and brought her down. I felt the resistance and strength in her muscled body, but when my knife found her throat, she capitulated. Dian.

I squatted beside her as she caught her breath. "Well done," she said, sitting up and pushing her black hair back. "I thought I would test your defences. I wouldn't be sure that all the men will immediately return to the boat. One or two may realize it's a trap and do what I did. You're well prepared," she said ruefully, brushing the dust from her hands. "Now what do you do?"

"Move down through the village, to help where I'm needed."

"Then do it," she said. "I'm dead. Take my knife and go."

I hesitated, then took the knife from her belt, slipping it into mine. I moved away, using bushes and boulders as cover, heading for the stream and the willows.

An hour later, we met in the council hall to discuss the evening over tea. I found Dian and returned her knife. "Would you eat with me?"

"Surely," she said, "after I have seen to the horses and bathed. Rasa has much to talk about with Grainne, so I'll be glad of the company."

I told her how to find Tali's house and left for the baths myself. Twenty minutes later, I walked down to Tali's. I had slept at the forge cottage for the past few nights but didn't bother to cook for myself. Tali had stew simmering, and there was bread on the table.

"I asked Dian to eat with me."

"There's plenty," Tali said. "I've eaten, and I'm going to help Rette string herbs for drying. There's cider if you want it."

I found the cider, poured a small amount, taking it out on the porch to wait for Dian. She came about forty minutes later, her hair newly braided and clean.

"Your baths are wonderful," she said, accepting a mug of cider. "We have nothing like them in Han."

I ladled bowls of stew and cut bread. We sat at the kitchen table to eat. The stew was venison, the last of the fresh meat from the hunt, redolent of herbs, with a rich, thick gravy.

"Dian," I said, "I really could have killed you this afternoon."

She nodded, her mouth full of stew. A moment later, she spoke. "I know. I could see it in your eyes. For a moment, I was actually frightened."

"I didn't realize...the training takes over. It's all reflex, and no thought, except to stay alive. It's so—cold."

"If it wasn't, I doubt we could do it. If one of our horses breaks a leg, we cut its throat immediately, or we will have second thoughts. We would try to save it and just extend its suffering. And that too feels cold. All killing must."

I nodded. "Are your horses all right?" I asked, changing the subject.

"Fine. The barn is clean and airy, and we brought extra grain with us. Tell me, what did you think of Casyn?"

I looked up from my stew, surprised. "How did you know he was here?"

"His horse. We bred him at Han. The mare I ride is from the same dam. Casyn visits Han every few years to buy horses, and he has two daughters there. He wanted to buy my mare last time—she was still a foal then—but she had been promised to me as my coming-of-age gift."

"Casyn was born here," I said. "He was the right man to send to Tirvan." A thought struck me. "Is that what was done, all over?"

"I think so," Dian said. "The man who came to work with us is my uncle, my mother's brother." She looked at me steadily for a minute. "It was easier for us, I think. We are half-trained in warfare already, to prepare the horses."

"You look like warriors. We only hunt," I added, "but we have learned."

"You have," she said. "I am impressed. And your mounted cohort ride well. They have good balance, which isn't surprising, being used to hunting in these hills." She sipped her cider.

"How long did it take you to reach us?"

"Three weeks. But we didn't come directly here. When we left the grasslands, there were eighteen of us and seventy-two horses. We stayed together on the road, with smaller groups breaking off on the byways to the villages. We left the last two, heading north to Delle, four days ago."

"Did you stop at the inns?"

"Sometimes," Dian said. "Although we made camp more often, and picketed the horses. The inns can't cope with large numbers. But we stopped for water or to buy cheese or bread." She looked at me curiously. "Why do you ask?"

I hesitated. "My partner, Maya, chose exile, rather than learn to fight. She is out there, somewhere, alone. I was hoping you had seen her. She's about your height, with long dark hair and hazel eyes."

Dian remained silent for a minute. "Not I," she said finally, "but Rasa is the best bargainer amongst us, so she went most often to the inns. I'll ask her. Maya is unlikely to be alone, Lena. In almost every village, one or two women made that choice. No one did from Han, but from Rigg, the village just to our north, three went. They will find each other on the road." She put down her cup. "Thank you for the food. I sleep at Grainne's cottage."

I said goodnight, watching her walk up the path. *They will find each other on the road.* A certainty settled inside me about what I would do after the invasion. I stayed outside in the warm night for a long time, looking west, up to the hills, and the road that ran beneath the glittering stars.

CHAPTER TEN

THE DEEP PEAL OF THE MEETING BELL REVERBERATED through the village in mid-afternoon. I looked up from the knife I was sharpening, muscles tensing. Dessa stood watch this afternoon. I slipped the knife into its sheath and ran to the meeting hall. Other cohort-leaders did the same as the cohorts gathered in their appointed places.

The council leaders waited. Longsighted, accustomed to searching the sea for the movement of birds or water that told of fish, Dessa spoke with authority. "I saw something on the horizon," she reported. "It could be no more than a flight of seabirds, far out, or a breaching whale, but I think not."

My heart skipped as my mind raced through our preparations. The leaders ordered the children and new mothers to the caves while I counted weapons in my head. No one panicked. No one argued. Freya would be in Ranni's byre, and Camy in a loft.

"Cohort-leaders," Gille said. "Check your weapons and your gear one last time, then command your cohorts to rest." Her voice did not waver. "They will wait till night." Her gaze quartered the room. "Eat lightly, but enough. I doubt there will be another chance for food for some time. Carry water if it will not hinder you." She paused. "We are ready," she continued, her voice gentler. "Remember that."

My cohort had gathered under the trees at the training ground. No one spoke as I approached. They had gathered their weapons.

"Cohort-leader," Tice said formally. "What is the news?"

"Dessa has seen a sail," I said. "Or, something she believes to be a sail. I doubt she is wrong."

"She won't be wrong," Freya confirmed. "They are very far out, then?"

"Yes," I said. "It will be very late when they land. We will review our posts and our tactics and check our weapons. Then you all must try to rest and take some food and water. You should be in your places two hours before midnight. Tice will review with half the cohort, and I'll take the other half." I hoped I sounded calm and in control. The cohort divided. I looked at the girls and women standing in front of me.

"Freya, your orders?"

"Ranni's byre," she said. "I do nothing until I hear the dogfox bark twice. Then I pick off any man who comes within throwing distance or closer. If they do not climb the hill, but attack the buildings, I will use our routes to move up to the hills and wait until our skills are needed." I nodded.

"How many knives do you have?"

"Six."

"Sharp?"

"Yes."

"Good." I had grown to both like and trust her in these last months. I put out a hand to touch her shoulder. "Get some rest. I'll see you at your post." She nodded, moving away, making room for Kelle.

The review took no more than twenty minutes. Each woman knew her orders and posts and answered me calmly. Finally, only Tice remained. She and I would both be high in the village, I at the forge, she at the big barn, places where we thought men might splinter off to, to hide or regroup.

"Aline and Camy are nervous."

"Everyone is nervous. They just can't hide it as well as the older women. Will they hold their posts?"

"I believe so," she said. "But if either thinks the other is in trouble or hurt...I'm not sure."

I nodded. "They are closely bonded." As Maya and I had been at that age. They would be posted in the lofts of adjoining houses on the far side of the village.

"May they be safe," Tice said. "May we all be safe."

Shortly after midnight, I crouched in the loft of the forge. I had done my rounds, checking on each member of my cohort, over the previous hour. A light seafog shrouded the village, and no breeze moved the air. I sat back on my haunches. Listening. An owl called and mice rustled in the roof. Stars wheeled through the sky. I shifted quietly to keep my muscles from cramping. I smelled the sharp musky scent of a fox about its night's hunt. I heard the rhythm of the waves on the shore. Then, above the gentle susurration of the waves, I heard the sweep of oars.

My heart beat faster, and my breathing quickened. I forced myself to relax my grip on my knife. Tired muscles grew clumsy. I waited. I heard them disembark, the noise muffled by the fog. I heard footsteps, and then a thrush called, sleepily, twice. From the barnyard, a cock crowed.

I crouched, staring into darkness as minutes passed. Then I heard them climbing the hill toward the open space above the council hall. We had guessed right. I listened until no more boots sounded on the path. I barked twice, and twice again.

The horses exploded from their hiding place, hooves hitting sharply upon the rocks, riders screaming defiance. The sheepdogs gave tongue from the barns. I heard the scrape of metal on leather as swords came out of scabbards. Voices spoke in surprise. The horses and their shouting riders grew closer. Steel clashed on steel as men and women screamed. Arrows cut the air, whistling. I strained to see through the small window and the dark.

Two shapes broke off, heading towards the barns and the fields. I saw them fall, as Casse calmly rose from behind her sheltering rock to throw a knife, once, twice. Beneath me, in the village, the battle raged in full force. I heard the chop of sword on leather, the whir of bowstrings, screams of pain and challenge. My heart pounded in my ears. A man turned from the melee, running toward the forge. I dropped out of the loft, landing silently, and slipped through the door. He wore no helmet. I grabbed his hair, and his cry of surprise turned to a gurgle as I slit his throat. His hot blood spilled over my hands. I felt my gorge rise. No different than the hunt, I told myself. Don't think about it. I bent, wiped my hands on the grass. I took his knife from his boot.

More followed. I could see at least three pounding up the path. I ran behind the forge and into the longer grasses, working my way toward the barns. I forced myself to stay quiet, to move slowly. I reached Casse. She had taken the knives from the men she had killed and was hefting them in her hands, judging their usefulness for throwing. She looked at me sharply.

"I'm not hurt," I assured her. "I'm going to the barn. Stay here. There are three at the forge, at least."

"None got past me," she said. "Not that I saw." A shout of rage rose from the battle below us. The water of the harbour reflected the flicker and glow of fire: the catboat, burning.

I moved through the field until I reached the barns. I whistled softly, the meadow pipit's call. Tice answered and stepped out from behind a partition.

"They sent two men to burn the barn," she said. "They're both dead, though one killed a sheepdog first."

"Good," I said. "There are three, or more, at the forge. I killed one. Casse remains on guard. Stay here, Tice, and watch this end of the village. I'm going down to assess where we are needed." She nodded, and I moved through the barn and out the far end, into the heather.

I reached the stream and its cover of willows easily. I climbed up, to edge through the branches, keeping parallel to the stream and the footpath. Once I thought I saw movement in the field beyond. I paused to watch, but saw nothing more. A fox, perhaps, or a badger. From the village and the harbour, the sound of battle continued, but women's voices were raised in command more often than men's. The morning grew lighter.

I crossed on the branch, sliding to the ground on the other side of the stream, taking the now-familiar route through byre and tunnel toward the harbour. Freya was gone from her hiding spot in Rette's kitchen, but a dead man lay in the doorway. Fifty feet from Siane's workshop and the net sheds, where the archers had lain in wait, I stopped.

The flames of the burning catboat and the rising sun gave enough light to see well. The fog had lifted with the dawn. A group of six men fought with swords and shields at the base of the dock, surrounded on three sides by the sword cohort. As I watched, one man broke, running along the jetty. I heard the twang of the bowstring, and he fell with an arrow in his back. Further up the hill, a horsewoman swung a sword, and another man dropped.

As the day brightened, I saw the tallest of the fighting men look desperately around. The catboat smouldered, listing on its side in the shallow water at the edge of the jetty. Above, in the village, a few men still fought, but the main path was littered with bodies. He stepped back and dropped his sword. "I surrender," he said, hoarsely, in the accents of Leste.

The men with him did likewise. Tali stepped forward to pick up the swords, passing them back to other cohort members. "Shields," she said. They too, dropped. She bent, taking the knives from the men's boots. "Take off your belts."

They tied the men's hands with their own belts. "Now," Tali said to the leader, her voice calm and deadly. "Call your men to you. Tell them it is over." He stood impassively. She put the point of her sword at his neck. "Tell them." The sun broke over the ridge.

He raised his head and called out, one word, three times.

"How many on the boat? How many men, in total?" Tali demanded.

"Three and forty," he said.

We gathered at the meeting hall. As my eyes adjusted to the dimness, I looked around for my cohort members. I heard quiet sobs from across the room where my mother stood with her hand on Dessa's shoulder. Dessa kneeled beside a covered body. Siane. I approached them, hoping I was wrong. My mother looked up. I saw the flash of relief on her face. Dessa did not move. With a motion of her head, my mother indicated we should move away.

"What happened?" I whispered.

"Her knee gave out," my mother said. I could see the tears in her eyes. Mine remained dry. "She stumbled and fell into a swordstroke meant for someone else. It was quick, at least." She shook her head. "She should have gone to the caves."

"Anyone else?"

"Not yet. But not everyone is back. Is all your cohort here?"

I looked around. Aline and Camy were slumped against a wall with mugs of tea. Freya sat beside them. Kelle spoke to her sister on one of the benches. Casse had gone to Dessa. Everyone but Tice. I had just opened my mouth to tell my mother this when I saw her at the door, her eyes searching the room. She saw my mother, and then me, and beckoned us over.

"Gwen," she said. "You are needed, although I fear it is too late. Lise is near the common with a sword cut to the thigh. She is bleeding badly."

"Is the blood deep red?" my mother asked. "Is it pumping out?"

"No," Tice said. "But she's lost a lot of blood, and she's unconscious."

My mother nodded. "I'll come." She found her basket, following Tice out the door. I was hesitating, wondering if I should go too, when Tali called me.

"Lena! Please join me."

I went to where she stood with Gille and Sara at the side of the hall.

"We can account for thirty-two men—dead, wounded, or surrendered." Tali said. "You said there are three at the forge?"

"That I saw," I said. "Others could have joined them."

"True, but I doubt all eleven are there. We need your cohort, Lena to check everywhere a man could hide. I think we should leave the forge alone for now."

I considered. "Yes," I agreed. "We'll have to plan an attack there. They will have made peepholes in the walls, so we won't be able to take them by surprise. But we should guard it, with horsewomen, perhaps?"

"A good plan," Gille said. "Is your cohort ready?"

"They will do what is needed. But Tice isn't here. She went with my mother to tend Lise, who is badly hurt."

"Send someone down for her," Gille said.

I nodded. "Give us ten minutes." I walked over to Kelle. "We'll need to go out again soon. Can you fetch Tice? She's at the common with my mother."

Kelle nodded and slipped off the bench. I did a circuit of the room, speaking to each of my cohort, ensuring they had eaten and drunk. I had done neither myself, I realized, so I filled a mug with sweet tea and took a hunk of yesterday's bread. I had a mouth full of stale bread when Tice and Kelle came back. I could see the news in their faces.

"We were too late," Tice said.

"I'm sorry. But we have work to do. Mourning must wait." Shock flickered over Kelle's face. Then she nodded, and I saw her body straighten.

"We hunt?"

"We do."

"Good," she said.

I found my first man in Kyan's timber loft. He chose to surrender, eagerly offering up his weapons. I tied his hands and took his boots, and once out in the street, found a member of the sword cohort to take him to the council hall, where the prisoners were being held. As I turned away, I saw Freya slip out of a byre. I whistled. She held up one finger, then drew it across her throat. Thirty-four.

My second man did not surrender. The deep wail of a cat caught my attention; I moved towards the stable behind Ranni's cottage. I heard the tabby growl, then scream in pain. I opened the door. The man sprang up, leaving the bleeding cat on the stable floor, to come at me with his knife out. I sidestepped, but the knife grazed my upper arm. It stung. He turned against his momentum, stumbling. I ducked, letting the knife swing harmlessly above me. I stood, grabbed his arm, and drove my knife up under his ribs.

He did not die easily. In the half-light of the stable, I watched as he moaned and coughed, a froth of blood around his lips. He seemed younger than I, and thin. Blood trickled down his chin, and his eyes held only terror. He tried to speak, but coughed. Blood bubbled up between his lips. He began to choke. I stepped forward, pulled his head back, and cut his throat as if he were a deer at the autumn cull. Then I fell to my knees beside him, vomiting bile until nothing came up. I heaved a few more times, then pushed myself up to a squat, not looking at the body. I found straw, wiped my hands and my mouth, the motions automatic, without thought. I kept my eyes averted, and stepped, shivering, out into the day.

At mid-morning, we gathered at the training ground. Inside the meeting hall, the shackled and bound prisoners sat against the wall. My mother and sister tended the wounded and shocked. Aline had stumbled over the body of Binne, the knife that had killed her still in her chest. We had all heard Aline's screams. Kira gave her wine and poppy, and she slept now

I shook my head to dislodge thoughts of Binne and our other dead. The cohorts reported five men killed or captured. That left six, still, somewhere in the village.

Grainne rode up, on Siannon. "We can find no one in the hills," she reported. "The children and the women with them are fine and have seen nothing. I left Dian and Caryn on patrol."

Similar reports came in from other cohort-leaders. We turned our attention to the forge.

"They have swords and knives, perhaps spears," Gille said.

Kyan knelt to sketch in the sand. "Look," she said. "The forge building has three solid walls. At the front, the large doors are split horizontally to allow the top half to be opened separately from the bottom. At the back, there is a small door meant only for escape from fire."

"What's underneath?" someone asked.

"The metal store, where the ore and charcoal are stored."

"They will have found that, by now." Gille said. "But they have no food, nor a water source."

"There's a little water in the forge, for cooling iron," Kyan said. "But it won't last long."

"Why don't we negotiate surrender?" Sara asked. "Have their captain—Kolmas, his name is—order it, even."

"Do you think he'll do it?" Tali asked.

"We can ask," Sara said.

Gille unlocked the Lestian captain's chains, leaving his hands shackled, bringing him over to where we met.

"We want to negotiate surrender with the men hiding at the forge," she explained. "We need to you to speak to them. Will you do this?"

He grunted. "Do you know names?" he asked, his use of our language passable.

"No," Gille admitted. "Does it matter?"

"Maybe. If Dann is there, he will not listen. But I will try."

We escorted Kolmas to within hailing distance of the forge, under close guard. Tice and I flanked him with knives at the ready. Horsewomen and archers made a semi-circle around us.

Kolmas took a step forward. A tall man, barrel chested and strong, he did not test his shackles. He called to the men inside, in Lestian. I thought I heard his name in the string of sounds.

The doors remained closed, but a voice answered from inside, the derision intelligible, even if the words were not.

Kolmas shrugged. "Dann. He will do as he choose, and others will follow him. I can do no more."

"Does he speak our language?" Gille asked.

"He understands." Kolmas said. "But speak? A few words only."

Gille raised her voice. "I am Gille, headwoman of Tirvan. I give you one more chance: surrender, or die."

Dann laughed. "No, woman," he said, heavily accented, followed by a stream of words, guttural and angry.

"He says that not easy," Kolmas translated. "He is not weak trader, he says, but soldier. If he led battle, you would be dead or in chains. He says he is man, not traitor or coward, like men you breed."

"He has chosen," Gille said calmly.

Later, at the training ground, Gille told us what she had learned from Kolmas. "Leste has a small army. They sent half-a-dozen soldiers with each raiding boat to teach arms and tactics. Dann is the most senior among them, but Kolmas's captaincy, and his knowledge of the village, made him the leader."

"Kolmas is being uncommonly helpful," Tali observed.

"He is hoping for clemency, I suppose," Gille said. "And in the end, he is, as Dann said, only a trader, and half his crew lies dead. He was led to believe this would be a quick and bloodless raid, with glory to those who led the capture. Glory matters to the men of Leste. Their reputations are everything to them."

"Which means," I said, "that Dann would think a glorious death preferable to an ignominious surrender."

"Yes," Gille said.

"So let's give them an inglorious death," I said. "If we burn the forge, they will be forced to choose between death by fire and death at the hands of women."

Gille considered. "The forge won't burn easily. The roof is sod, and the walls are fireproofed with plaster."

"The plastering is on the inside, not the exterior," I said. "If we start the fires on the outside, the boards will catch quickly."

"How will you set the fires?"

"With tinder and kindling, piled along the foundations. Three of us, one for each wall, can do it quickly in the dark of night. When the men run, we will have armed women waiting to pick them off."

"How will you get there without being detected?" Tali asked.

"The waterfall."

"In the dead of night?" my mother exclaimed. "Lena, no. It's too dangerous."

"Gwen," Tali said. "Lena is right. There is no other way."

"There is," my mother said firmly. "We can simply starve them out. They will be forced to surrender, and that will be even more inglorious than death at our hands."

I shook my head slowly. "These men are soldiers. They will be planning tactics, as we are now. They won't wait until they are weakened but will attack soon. I believe we would win, but not without a considerable fight. We have already lost three women. Do we wish to lose more? We can burn the forge tonight."

"I do not want to lose you, Lena," she said sharply.

"Tirvan comes first," I reminded her, as gently as I could. I saw the tears in her eyes, but I could not let them move me. I had a job to do.

"It will work, I think," Gille said, considering. "They may go to the metal store, though."

"Then they'll die of suffocation." Tali said. "The fire will take all the air."

I briefed my cohort on the plan, and we spent some time preparing bundles of fatwood, the resin-soaked interior wood of the pines that made the best kindling. All houses had a supply. We chose the best, shredding the ends well. Then we practiced building and lighting small fires until we could—and did—do it blindfolded.

At mid-afternoon, I called a halt. We finished wrapping our wood in greased leather pouches, with flint and tinder tucked deep inside the packages. We would carry these on our backs to keep them as dry as possible as we climbed. I had chosen Freya and Salle to climb with me. Now I bade them rest, to sleep if possible, and to eat lightly. "We'll meet at the waterfall's base, at dark."

I walked with Tice toward the cottage that Dessa and Siane had shared. My mother and Kira had washed Siane's body, and she lay on the bed. Among several other women gathered there, I found Dessa. As my apprentice-master, she had taught me, disciplined me, and become my friend. She sat at the kitchen table, a cup of tea in her hands. When I put my hand on her shoulder, she reached up to take it. Dessa did not give way to outward expression of emotion, but I could feel her hand trembling. "I will miss her, too," I said.

"I wanted her to go to the caves, but she would not," Dessa said. "She did not want Lara to think her mother a coward."

"Does Lara know?"

"We sent the message with the horsewomen. The children are to stay at the caves until it is completely safe." She looked up at me. "I wish you luck tonight, Lena."

"Thank you."

I stepped away. Tice spoke briefly to Dessa, the formal words of sympathy, and then we left. We made our visits to where the other victims lay. We would bury our dead in the hills tomorrow, or the next day. Outside, women dragged men's bodies down to the rocks beyond the net sheds where we would build their pyre. The tide would take the remains. Blood and vomit dried in the sand of the paths.

We climbed onto the porch of Tali's house. She had guard duty at the meeting hall, so the house stood empty. Inside, I went to the sink to pour water, washing my hands and face and arms. The blood on my tunic had dried, brown and hard.

Tice washed. I found a loaf of day-old bread and some cheese, and gave her half. I poured water. We sat at the table and ate in silence, tasting nothing, the bread dry as ashes. Tice spoke first. "How many did you kill today?"

"Two," I said. "One at the forge, and one at the stable." Saying the words made me even colder inside.

"Two for me also," she said, "but neither was Kirthan."

For what do you fight? I had asked Dern. I had never asked Tice.

At dusk, we gathered at the base of the waterfall. We wore dark clothes and had blackened our faces and hands with charcoal. Soft leather boots gave our feet protection but allowed us to use toes and arches to grip. I would climb first, then Salle, and Freya at the rear. The last report from the women keeping guard around the forge had told us what we expected: the men inside had drilled holes through the walls, on all four sides, to keep watch. Other than that, nothing had changed. Six horsewomen ranged around the forge, and as many archers and swordswomen.

I checked my parcel of fatwood one last time before climbing onto the first boulder. The air temperature had dropped, and the water, initially warm against my skin, felt cold. I moved upward. I could hear Salle behind me, but the sound of the water obscured most of our noise.

At the rockface, I stopped to catch my breath. The weight on my back affected my balance. I found the rope and began to climb the sheer face. My feet slipped on the wet rock. I hung by one arm from the rope, fighting back panic. My searching hand found a protrusion in the rock and grabbed it. I hung on, trying to remember what the rockface looked like as water splashed into my eyes. The knob of rock under my hand felt roughly triangular. In my mind, I saw another piece of rock jutting out, above it and a bit to the right. I reached up to the next knot in the rope and hauled myself up. My foot found the triangular hold. I pushed upward.

I finally hauled myself onto the ledge and lay panting. The sweat of fear and exertion cooled against my skin. My injured arm ached. I counted to ten before tugging on the rope, the signal for Salle to begin climbing. My eyes had fully adjusted to the dark. In the starlight, I could just make out the movement of water. I climbed onto the next boulder.

As I neared the top, I found a dry spot to wait. Salle arrived a few minutes later, then Freya. I felt their parcels of wood—dry. I touched both on the hand and met their eyes. Both nodded. I crawled forward, keeping to the thorn bushes, trying to move and breathe silently.

Over the sound of the water, I could hear the horses moving. The guards rode at a slow walk around the forge, keeping out of range of a surprise attack. Their noise would help muffle ours. We reached the meadow. The forge lay about ten strides away.

I had the right side, as we faced the building, Salle the left. Freya had the back. In open ground, now, we went at our own speeds, waiting until a horsewoman appeared to catch the attention of any watchers. I crawled a body length, stopped, waited, crawled again. It took ten minutes to cover the distance.

Huddled against the side of the building, I unstrapped the parcel of fatwood and unwrapped it. The greased leather fell open silently. I found the flint and tinder, pushing them into the pocket of my leggings. I counted out five sticks of fatwood by feel, and built a pyramid, carefully, quietly, against the boards of the wall.

I did this five times. I could hear movement and voices inside the forge. Whenever the footsteps or voices seemed too near, I lay still. I had no idea how long I was taking. I built the last pyramid, then took the flint and tinder from my pocket.

I moved into a crouching position. I struck a spark, lit the tinder, then held the frayed end of a fatwood stick into the small flame. It crackled, and shrivelled, and caught.

On my feet now, I thrust the burning fatwood stick into each pile of kindling, forcing myself to wait until I saw the flames licking upward in the pyramid. At any second someone inside would notice the flickering light through the spy-holes. As I lit the last one, a shout came from inside. I ran for the waterfall hearing the crackle of the fires behind me.

In the shelter of the bushes, I turned to look back. Through heavy smoke, I saw growing flame. Salle dropped beside me. "Where's Freya?" I hissed.

"Don't know," she gasped, coughing. She had breathed too much smoke. At the forge, the rear door swung open, and men ran out, swords drawn. I heard an arrow fly, but no one fell. The horsewomen closed in. I saw a shape crawling towards us, awkwardly: Freya. I crawled forward, grabbing her shoulders, ignoring her gasp of pain, and pulled her to the bushes. The smell of burned flesh assaulted us. "I waited too long," she murmured. "My arm...." I pulled her to the stream's edge and pushed her arm into the water. She moaned.

"Leave it there," I said.

The crack of timber snapping shot through the night. I looked up to see the forge collapse. It fell slowly, the sod roof breaking through the burned rafters, the flaming walls spreading out. Sparks spiralled upwards. Like fireflies.

Grainne rode over to us. "There were only four. The others may have tried to shelter in the metal store, but we won't know until tomorrow."

My job—our job—was not done, then. "Freya needs help. Her arm is burned." Grainne nodded and rode away. I sat with Salle and Freya, keeping Freya's arm in the water. The heat from the fire had died. Freya began to shiver.

My sister arrived with a torch and two others bearing a stretcher. We moved

Freya gently onto the stretcher, covering her with a blanket. "You did well, Lena, keeping her arm in the water," Kira said. She moved the torch closer. "Are you all right? Whose blood is that?"

"Not mine," I said.

"You're shivering. Go and get warm. There is soup at mother's. You too, Salle," she said authoritatively. We did not argue.

We walked down the hill. The cut on my arm from the Lestian soldier pained me, but it would wait till morning. At my mother's, I drank hot soup and found some dry clothes to change into. I gave Salle some of Kira's clothes. Tice came to the door.

"Kira told me you were here," she said.

"We're not finished," I said, trying to muster some energy.

"I know. Grainne told me. Tonight?"

"Later," I said. I needed rest. "After midnight. Tell the cohort to meet me here in four hours." After she left, I sank into a chair, holding my soup mug in both hands. I wanted to sleep, but when I closed my eyes I saw the eyes of the boy I had killed. So young, and so thin, and so scared. Had he thought to gain glory? Would his mother ever know what had befallen him, on what shore the waves had claimed his ashes? I hugged the steaming mug, staring into the night.

At midnight, a wispy seafog gathered. Most of the women would sweep the village from the harbour upward, but Tice and I would be on lookout. We had the best eyes at night.

"I want us in the trees," I said. "Looking over the village and the fields. Look for movement, listen. If they have hidden in the fields, they might choose now to move."

"Can you climb with that arm?"

I shrugged. It throbbed, but I could ignore it. "I climbed the waterfall. I can climb a tree."

She looked at me levelly for a moment then grinned. "Let's go."

Our best vantage points lay about twenty strides apart, close to where the willows bridged the stream. Tice looked toward the village and the harbour while I peered outward, to the fields. Stars glittered in the cold air. Wisps of fog gathered in the lower areas. I waited, flexed my muscles to keep from stiffening, and watched.

I could hear the occasional murmur of conversation from the guards at the meeting hall. The moon, half-full and high, gave a faint light. I heard a fox bark, high in the hills, and saw a barn owl hunting along a hedge.

An hour passed, and another. My arm ached. I moved it, trying to keep it supple. The barn owl rose from its perch on the hedge to fly straight across the field. I could see nothing in its talons. A rustling noise came from the far side of the hedge. I stood, stiffly, and moved along the branches, trying to see beyond the bushes.

I swung clumsily into the next tree, hearing Tice moving towards me across the bridging branch. A small field barn stood at this end of the field, partly shrouded by hanging fog. Tice crouched beside me.

I stiffened. A figure moved toward us, hugging the wall for concealment. The clothes and the long, braided hair told of Leste, yet I hesitated. Something about the way he—or she?—moved, and the planes of the face, that sent a stab of recognition as sharp as a knife-thrust through my gut. Maya? It couldn't be... And then I realized. I touched Tice's arm. She followed my gaze and immediately drew her knife.

He stepped away from the barn into the moonlight. I heard Tice's indrawn breath, and the barely audible name she spat: "Kirthan." She raised her arm to throw. I grabbed frantically at her arm, catching it on the downward arc. The knife veered high into the barn over his head. He froze, looking up. I dropped from the branches, hands open and empty.

"*Garth?*" I said.

Tice dropped beside me.

"Garth?" she said, disbelievingly.

"Garth, son of Tali, brother to Maya?"

"How did you know?" I could see his confusion and fatigue. He seemed, at that moment, very young.

"Your sister is my partner. You move like her, look like her, too. For a moment, I thought you were her."

He stared at me in the faint light.

"I am Lena, Gwen's daughter. Garth, we played together."

"I remember."

"Do you remember me?" Tice said fiercely. "I knew you as Kirthan."

He shook his head. "I have been Kirthan for so long now. Where did we meet?"

"At Jedd's farm. In the barn, one afternoon," she said bluntly. He said nothing for several heartbeats.

"In Karst. I remember," he said. He gestured helplessly. Tice strode forward to pull the knife from the boards of the barn. She did not sheath it.

"Have you a weapon?" I asked. He drew a small knife from his boot, handing it to me. His hand shook. I waited.

"That's all. I had a sword, but I left it back there," he pointed up the hill, "in the caves." I must have looked puzzled. "When we came ashore at dawn, I left the others—it was easy, in all the confusion—and climbed to the caves. I remembered where they were. I've been there ever since. The women hiding in the large one didn't see me." He met my eyes. I remembered the movement I had seen from the branches of the willows yesterday morning.

"Put your hands behind your back," I said. He did so, and I tied them, my fingers trembling. Tice stood silently, her knife still in her hand. "I am taking you to the meeting hall," I said. "You can tell your story there, to the council, and your mother."

"Why not kill him?" Tice asked, coldly. "He has proved thrice a traitor, to the Empire, to Leste, to us. Why should he live?"

"He surrendered," I said, keeping my voice level. "And if there is retribution to be made, for deserting the Empire's armies, that is not for us to demand." I looked at Tice, her face in the moonlight pale, and hard with anger. "Cohort-second, continue with the patrol. There is still a man to be found. I will take Garth to the council. You may speak to them later, and privately, if you wish."

For a moment, I thought she would refuse, but she nodded. "Cohort-leader," she said formally, turning back into the willows, her knife still in her hand. I looked at Garth.

"Come," I said, unsheathing my own knife. "You have a story to tell." In the moonlight, I could see tears in his eyes. He swallowed hard, and at my gesture, began to walk along the path, toward the footbridge. I walked a few steps behind, watching him. We crossed the bridge, following the path uphill, toward the council hall. He stumbled more than once. At the hall, a fire burned, and lanterns lit the porch. A figure rose to meet us.

"Tali, I bring you a prisoner."

CHAPTER ELEVEN

"MOTHER."

"Garth?" Tali stopped, raising her lantern higher. In its flickering light, her face reflected disbelief followed by a joy that was quickly quenched. Her lips trembled. "You look like Mar. Now I understand why Dann said we bred traitors."

Garth shook his head, a barely perceptible movement. He stood a little straighter, goaded by her words. "Are you a council leader, Mother?"

Tali laughed, a short, sharp sound. "Does it matter?"

"Yes," he answered. "I may speak of my role only to the council leaders." He had gained some control over himself. His voice sounded clearer, more assured.

"By whose orders?" Tali asked, her lips thin.

"My orders come from the Empire. I report to Dern, Captain of *Skua*."

"Dern," I scoffed, incredulous. "His orders?"

Garth turned slightly to look at me. "I must speak to the council."

Suddenly I remembered the night—so long ago, it seemed—when I had demanded to know why Dern had really come to Tirvan. He had referred obliquely to new information the Empire had received about the invasion. This must be what he meant. "He tells the truth," I said.

"Gwen is here," Tali said. "Gille and Sara are sleeping. I will send someone for them." She turned to her son. Her face momentarily softened. "If what you say is true, it would be unwise to take you into the hall where you will be seen by the other prisoners. Lena, will you stay with him on the porch for a moment?" She disappeared back into the lit hall. I gestured to Garth, and we climbed the few steps onto the wide porch.

"You may sit, if you wish," I said. He sank down onto a bench, leaning back against one of the pillars that supported the roof of the porch. He closed his eyes. Even in the lantern light, I could see lines of fatigue deeply etched on his face. Such weariness came from a longer struggle than just a day and a night without food or sleep.

Tali reappeared with Gwen, carrying a cup. She held it to Garth's lips, and he drank deeply. "Thank you," he said. Her fingers lingered on his cheek.

My mother knelt beside him. "Are you hurt?"

He blinked at her. "No."

She took his wrist, felt his pulse, then laid the back of her hand on his forehead. Tali watched intensely.

"No fever," my mother finally proclaimed. "He needs sleep, water, and food."

"You are my aunt, I think," he said quietly.

"I am," my mother said. "Gwen. Try to sleep."

We waited in silence as Garth closed his eyes, dozing. Tali sat beside him, not quite touching him. I sheathed my knife, watching him, seeing again the resemblance to his sister. I wanted him, very much, to be telling the truth.

Sara and Gille arrived about twenty minutes later. Garth opened his eyes at their approach, and stood, clumsily, his bound hands hindering him.

"Garth," Tali said, fighting to keep her voice even. "Once of the Empire's seventh regiment. My son. He says he reports to Dern and can speak only to you three." She turned to go back into the hall, but Gille stopped her.

"Stay," she said. "You too, Lena."

"Gille," Tali said. "I can't."

"Come over here," Gille said, walking Tali further down the porch. Snatches of their words reached me.

"I cannot let myself believe him," Tali said. Whatever Gille replied I did not hear, but Tali shook her head.

"...not after Maya," I heard.

"You will witness," Gille said clearly. "I request it, as council leader."

I thought Tali would refuse, but she just nodded, letting Gille lead her back to where we waited. I looked away. I did not want Tali to know I had overheard.

Gille addressed Garth. "I am Gille, and this is Sara. We are the council leaders, along with Gwen. Whatever you have to say to us, Tali, as your mother, should hear, and I think Lena should, too."

He nodded, slowly.

"I was to speak to the council, but also to anyone else you chose to be present." He paused, searching for words. "What my mother said is true. I report to Dern."

"You are a spy?" Gille spoke calmly without a hint of surprise in her voice.

"I am. One of maybe a half-dozen on Leste. How I came to serve the Empire in this way is not a pretty story, but I am to tell you the whole of it." He straightened, looking from Gille to the others. "I was taken from here unwilling, and unwilling I was schooled as a soldier. I had—I have—no talent for fighting. The regiment saw this and offered me training as a medic. But even that was not to my liking. At fourteen, I ran away."

Tali gasped.

"The seventh were on the move along the south coast. There was a trading ship from Leste preparing to sail from one of the retirement farms. I found my way aboard at night. They were happy to take me. Leste does not love the Empire." He cleared his throat. "May I have some more water?"

Sara held the cup to his lips. He drank, then thanked her and went on. "For over three years, I worked on that ship and on the jetties of Leste. I grew to like the sea, and I learned the language. Then, nearly four years ago, while we were trading in a harbour along the south coast, *Skua* arrived. I thought I was safe, dressed as a Lestian, my hair long, and speaking their language. Somehow, Dern recognized me. He had me captured and taken to him. The penalty for desertion is death. He offered me an alternative." He spoke flatly, without emotion. I hugged myself, listening, thinking of what Dern had told me all those weeks before, of the price paid by those boys who could not bring themselves to serve.

"For these last few years, I have spied on Leste for the Empire. We trade frequently with the retirement farms, which made it easy enough to leave messages, and I was privy to much of the planning of the invasion. Kolmas trusts me. Also, I am betrothed to his niece." That startled me. Betrothed? He went on. "Dann was more suspicious and did not want me to be aboard ship, but Kolmas insisted. With my medic's training, I could care for the wounded."

"What did you tell the Lestians about Tirvan?" Tali asked, her voice just barely audible.

"Nothing." Garth shook his head. "They do not know this is my birth village. I claimed to have been born inland, so they were not interested. Kolmas had traded here, before I was part of his crew. The invasion plans were based on his recollections."

"What were your instructions for the invasion?" Gille asked quietly.

"To help the village if I could. I was supposed to stay with the catboat; I was going to burn it, but at the last minute Dann ordered me to go with him. He wanted me where he could watch me, I think. I pretended clumsiness on the path and fell twice. Dann lost patience with me and sent me to Kolmas. I slipped over the wall into the field and worked my way up to the caves. I thought if the battle went against you, I might be able to be of use."

"What were you promised, if the Empire was victorious?" My mother spoke.

"A second chance to serve the Empire, aboard *Skua*," Garth said, quietly.

"And you wanted this, or were you more afraid of death?" Tali asked.

Garth met his mother's eyes. "When Dern first found me, and offered me the choice of spying or court-martial, I agreed to spy because I knew that the alternative was death. But when Leste began to plot against the Empire, I realized where my allegiance truly lay."

"And your betrothed?" I said.

He flushed. "I had to behave like any Lestian man of twenty to remain unsuspected. I regret the betrothal. She is a gentle girl, who does not deserve such deception. I have done many things I am not proud of in these past few years. I will make redress where I can, if I can."

Gille spoke. "The council will confer. Tali, please join us. We will not be long, Lena." As they walked into the night, I could hear the murmur of their voices, but not the words.

"Kirthan," I said, testing the name. He smiled, just a brief movement of his lips.

"That is how 'Garth' is rendered in Lestian. Tice is your friend?"

"And my cohort-second," I said. "I don't know if you can make sufficient redress, there. That is between her and you, and the council."

I leaned back against the wall of the council hall. My reaction to him confused me. He confused me. He is so much like Maya, and yet not. A gentle breeze moved the air. The moon sank closer to the sea. Inside, I could hear movement, and the occasional moan from an injured prisoner.

"Where is Maya?" Garth asked suddenly.

I straightened. "Gone. She chose exile, rather than fight."

"But you stayed?"

"You are not the only one looking for a second chance, Garth," I said angrily. "When this is over, I will find her."

"I missed her so much, those first years. I hoped to see her again."

When the council returned, Gille spoke. "We think it best," Gille said without preamble, "that you are kept in custody, Garth, for two reasons. While we are inclined to believe your story, until we have confirmation from Dern, we cannot be entirely convinced. And secondly, were you to be given your freedom, your role would become immediately apparent to the other prisoners. We would not endanger your life. We will chain your hands and feet, loosely enough to allow you some movement, and confine you to a cottage under guard."

"It is fair."

"No it's not," I said, indignant. "Mother, Gille, he's telling the truth. I know he is."

"Is he?" Gille said sternly. "He admits to a web of lies, Lena, going back many years." She softened. "I said we were inclined to believe him, but you must see we have to be sure."

I looked from her to Garth. "It is fair," he repeated.

The spurt of anger Gille's words had engendered subsided. If Garth thought it fair, why should I argue? I nodded. "Where?" I asked.

"The forge cottage," Gille said. "It's far enough from the hall and easy to guard."

Tali chained his feet, loosely enough to allow him a shuffling walk, her deft fingers finding ways to touch her son briefly. I unbound his wrists and let him eat the bread and cheese and apples Sara brought. Then Tali loosely shackled his arms again, and we escorted him to the forge cottage, matching our pace to his slow shuffle. He stumbled once, and I put out a hand to steady him. My fingers tingled where I had touched him.

At the cottage, he lay down on the bed, chains clinking, and closed his eyes. Tali covered him with the blanket.

"We'll send someone to keep watch," Gille said. "Tali, Lena, watch him till then."

Do they not trust me alone with him? Then I saw Tali's face, watching Garth, trying for impassivity and failing. "He is so like Maya," I said. She nodded. Did she see the resemblance to Maya, or to Mar, their father and her dead love? Or just her son. In the normal course of events, she would never have seen him again after he was sent, drugged and unknowing, with the men. I left her with him and went out into the night.

When a swordswoman came to take the first watch, I briefed her on the limits of his freedom. Tali joined us outside. The first hint of dawn lightened the eastern sky as we walked down the hill. At the meeting hall, I poured a cup of tea from the ever-present kettle, going back outside to where I could see the training ground from the porch. I sat on the bench, sipping the hot, sweet tea. My arm throbbed, and I could not get warm. I looked at my hands. I had killed two men in the last twenty-four hours, cut both their throats, one in a fair fight, one in pity. I had trained and practiced, yet the last day felt like a dream. Months of training seemed to have more substance than one day of battle.

I should not have refused Dern, I thought. I had wanted love, not realizing that the comfort, and perhaps the pleasure, would have been enough. I wish I had said yes. When had I last touched someone, except to correct a hold, or to console? Or to kill.

I sat, struggling to sort out my feelings, as Salle approached from the northern edge of the village. I greeted her and sent her in for tea. One by one, the women of my cohort arrived. When most were present, we moved out to the training ground. The eastern stars had faded quickly. Somewhere a cock crowed. Ten of us stood on the field. Freya, wounded and resting, made eleven.

"Has anyone seen Tice?" I asked. No one had. Somewhere out there, the last man waited, hidden. "Sleep," I ordered. "Half of you until noon, half until tonight."

I sent the cohort to their beds, with much grumbling from Camy and Aline, and waited for Tice. As the sky changed from dawn grey to blue, a knot of apprehension tightened in my gut. I waited another ten minutes, then reported to Gille, to begin a different search.

I walked down under the willows, wondering if Tice had fallen asleep in the branches. Finally, I spotted her leaning against a trunk, not sixty feet from where I had sent her back on patrol. "Tice," I called. "Wake up!"

She did not move. "Tice," I shouted again. A wave of fear washed through me—fear and cold certainty. I grabbed a branch to swing myself up into the tree, climbing quickly. I put out my hand to touch her, feeling the chill of her dead flesh.

"Tice!" I tried to turn her towards me. My hands found the knife, embedded in her back. "Oh, Tice," I moaned. I leaned forward, resting my head on her shoulder. My hand found hers and held it.

I had sent Tice back on patrol when I knew her anger might distract her. Clearly and coldly, I analysed what I had done. I had sent her back when I should have sent her home, and I had done so to prevent a confrontation between her and Garth that I did not want to have to handle. I had failed as a leader. The thought turned my heart to lead. I let go of her hand, placing it so it did not dangle helplessly, and sat up. I pulled the knife from her back. The blade gleamed with blood. A drop fell on my hand. I threw the knife into the earth beneath the tree, wiping my hands on my tunic. I could not move her by myself. I would wake Salle. My cohort alone would handle this.

Salle and I lowered Tice's body carefully down from the willow, placing it on the stretcher. Then we carried her through the village to her cottage. My mother waited. I had gone to tell her, and fetch the stretcher, while Salle dressed. We laid Tice on her bed, and then I sent Salle away. I removed her clothes, and my mother and I washed the body and dressed it again. We worked in silence except for brief words of instruction or direction.

When we finished, we sat at the kitchen table. The cat was nowhere to be seen. "Mother," I said. "Tice told me of her son."

"We will send word to Karst. Do not worry yourself. You are exhausted and need sleep."

"There is more, though. Did Tice speak of the father to the council?"

"Only that he was a Lestian trader," she replied. "We did not need to know more, as he was not of the Empire." She sighed. "Tice was very private, Lena, as you must know."

"Yes, but she told me the father's name. She said he was a young Lestian, called Kirthan. But the boat was Kolmas's, Mother, and Kirthan is the Lestian form of Garth."

My mother looked at me, startled. "Are you sure?"

I nodded, tiredly. "Yes. She told me of it weeks ago, a few days before *Skua* sailed. But when she and I captured Garth, Mother, she called him Kirthan, and he acknowledged her."

"He will have to be told of the child," my mother said, slowly, "but not yet."

"Will you tell Sara and Gille?"

"Yes," she said. "But not Tali, not yet. Nor must you, Lena."

"I won't," I said. There were footsteps outside. Casse came in the door.

"I will sit with her, Lena," she said quietly. "You need to rest."

"Thank you, Casse," my mother said, before I could protest. She touched my shoulder. "Come, Lena. You must sleep."

I let my mother lead me away as if I were a child again. My body, heavy and cold and slow, seemed to take a long time to respond to my thoughts. Outside in the cool morning breeze, I stopped on the path. "I can't sleep," I said, almost petulantly. "We have a hunt to finish."

"You must sleep," my mother said. "You are wounded and exhausted. I am ordering you, Lena, as a council leader. Name a cohort-second." I stared at her, shocked, before the simple practicality of her words sank in.

"I would have chosen Freya, but it will have to be Salle, now."

"Then tell her," my mother said. "Brief her on tactics, if you can think clearly enough. Then I'll treat that arm and give you just enough poppy to let you sleep for a few hours. You can lead the search this evening if it's still needed."

I agreed, reluctantly, and with my mother beside me went to wake Salle for the second time. We found her sitting on the porch of the cottage she shared with her sister, Kelle.

"I need you to be cohort-second, Salle," I said, after she had greeted us. "And

I will need you to lead the search this afternoon."

"What would you have me do?" she asked, calmly.

"Concentrate on the edges of the village, the outbuildings and field barns." I struggled to think past the fog in my brain. "He's probably been watching. He'll have seen us searching in the village." She nodded, understanding. "Work in pairs. I want no one on her own." Too late, a voice in my mind said.

"Grainne and the horsewomen are patrolling the higher fields," Salle said. "The women preparing graves are guarded by archers. And we'll be searching the village. Our man will feel harried. Perhaps he'll make a wrong move."

"Perhaps." Fatigue closed in on my muscles and my mind. I let my mother lead me away. She took me home, to the room where I slept as a girl, and gave me a small cup of wine, warmed and dosed with poppy and other herbs. I did as she told me, though I felt like a husk, hollow and dry. She undressed me, bathed my arm, and bandaged it. Somewhere during that treatment, I slept.

When I woke, the sun had begun its western descent. In the half-light of the room, a fragment of dream still made disturbing images in my mind: Maya coming home, changed almost beyond recognition. Then I remembered. *Tice.* The hollow inside me widened into an abyss. I sat up quickly. The room swam. I waited until it stopped then stood, stripped off my clothes, and washed.

Dressed again, I went out to the kitchen. A kettle simmered on the stove, and a mug with dried leaves and honey sat ready on the table. I poured in the water, stirred. My arm felt stiff, but less painful. I flexed it tentatively. I sipped the tea. Anash. I reached for the honeypot to spoon in more, to counteract the bitterness.

Outside, the day was cool, with a slight haze and a strong on-shore breeze. I walked up to the meeting hall. Around the inner periphery of the octagonal hall, Lise and Casyn had drilled eyebolts deep into the structural timbers. The prisoners stood or sat, shackled to the eyebolts. The severely injured lay on pallets in the centre of the hall. Six women stood guard, escorting pairs of prisoners, chained at hands and feet, out to use the privy and get some exercise. Casyn had estimated that *Skua* would not return for five or six weeks. We could not keep healthy men constantly chained to the wall for that long a time. These Lestians were no soldiers. Dann and his men would have struggled against the chains, but they had died at the forge. These others, shocked by their defeat and seeing their captain cooperate with Gille, followed his lead.

Gille was studying a list as I came in. "Food stores," she said briefly. "We have twenty-odd extra mouths to feed." Her face softened. "Lena, I am so sorry. Tice found a friend in you, I think, as well as a cohort-leader."

"Thank you," I said, my voice trembling.

She looked at me sharply. "Are you all right?'

"I dreamt Maya came home, but I almost couldn't recognize her. From the poppy, I suppose."

"Probably," Gille agreed. "And not surprising, given how much Garth looks like her."

Garth.

"Lena?' she asked, concern on her face.

"I had forgotten about him." Confusion flooded through me. Yesterday, he had been all I could think of. "How could that happen?"

"You were shocked and exhausted, and we gave you poppy. He became confused with Maya in your sleeping mind. Nothing more, or less, than that, Lena."

"Is he still at the forge cottage?" I could see him in my mind, in the moonlight, with Tice's knife vibrating in the wall of the barn above him. I remembered her anger, and my response.

"We need to call the cohort-leaders together to explain about Garth," she said. "He looks enough like Maya, and like his father, for those who remember, that tongues are already wagging."

"What will you tell them?"

She shrugged. "The truth, as much as we know. We are inclined to believe his story. Casyn told us there were spies, but we are waiting for his story to be confirmed by Dern."

My thoughts had started to clear. "How is Tali?"

"Confused," Gille said. "Angry at him for deserting, proud of him for taking the second chance, if he is telling the truth, that is, and happy that he is alive. She's with him now."

"What guard will you want tomorrow, for the burials?"

If my question surprised her, she did not show it. "If you do not find the last man before then, we will need archers and horsewomen, in a circle around the graves, facing out. And two from your cohort, to guard the dead and their bearers, on their way to the burial ground."

I calculated. "That will mean only two from our cohort can bear Tice's body." Four women usually bore a body to burial. In the absence of family, the cohort would do this instead.

"I realize that," Gille said, "but it will have to be. Half-a-dozen women will have to remain behind, on guard. I have asked for volunteers, and one to guard Garth, as well. Although I think Tali will do that."

I left the hall to walk to Tice's cottage. Casse sat beside the still form. She said my name in greeting, but nothing more. Tice looked peaceful. I touched her cold face.

"I am sorry," I whispered. I said goodbye to Casse, walking up the hill. The forge was now only a pile of ashes and burned timbers, the anvil and stove sitting blackened in their midst. The guard walked back and forth near the cottage, sword in hand. Through its open door I could see Tali and Garth sitting at the table. Two-day old stubble darkened his jaw, blurring his resemblance to Maya. I stopped at the door.

"May I come in?"

"Surely," Tali said. I entered, leaning against the wall. Garth smiled at me. I looked away, and then back.

"Tice is dead," I said bluntly. "She was stabbed in the back, in the willows."

He closed his eyes. "I am sorry."

"There is only one man left at large. Do you have any idea who it is?"

He thought a moment. "How many were with Dann?"

"Four."

"It may be Cael," he said. "He was one of Dann's men, but he always kept apart from the others, somehow. Dann and the other three had served together for some time, but Cael was a stranger to them and did not always seem to take his orders from Dann."

I nodded. "Thank you."

Tali stood. "I have stayed long enough. Lena, I will walk with you."

We left Garth at the table. Outside, the guard came over to speak to me, words of consolation. I responded, somehow.

We walked some distance from the cottage before Tali spoke again. "His first questions were about Maya."

"Do you believe his story?"

She considered. "Yes," she said finally. "Perhaps it is just a mother's blindness, but I do." She did not ask me what I thought.

CHAPTER TWELVE

WE DID NOT FIND OUR MAN THAT AFTERNOON, or that night. Late in the afternoon, we lit the pyre at the water's edge. Gille escorted Kolmas, shackled like all the other men, to the site, so that he could speak a few words over his dead kinsman and bear witness to the flames. He surveyed the pyre, and the bodies, nodding solemnly.

"This is good," he said. "We burn our dead, or, if death finds a man at sea, we give him to the waters. They will go to our gods this way. I thank you."

He said a few words in his own language, raising his shackled hands up to the sky, as far as he could, then bowing to the ocean. Gille strode forward to push the lighted torch into the wood of the pyre. Drenched in oil, it caught quickly. The wood crackled. Smoke rose, almost straight up. For a while, it smelled only of wood. Then a smell of roasting meat overpowered the clean smell of the woodsmoke, and I could hear the hiss of fat. Around me, women turned away with hands over their mouths. I swallowed the rush of cold saliva but did not move.

The stars shone in the western sky before the pyre had burned to the strand. The incoming tide would wash the beach clean. Tomorrow, we buried our dead.

I slept for a few hours between dawn and mid-morning. When I woke, the first of the heavy autumn fogs hung, grey and cold, over the village. I washed in cold water, shivering, and dressed in clean clothes before walking up to Tice's cottage. Salle met me there, along with Casse and Dari, who had volunteered to be the other two bearers.

"I spoke to Gille and Sara about postponing the burials because of the fog," Casse told us. "They debated it and decided we must go ahead. The fog could last for days, and we need to bring the mothers and children down from the caves. They cannot stay there indefinitely."

"They're guarded," I said, "and Cael does not know the village. The fog will provide protection for us."

"Let us hope so," Casse answered.

We wrapped Tice's body in a woven sheet of deep blues and reds, the colours of her pots, and placed it on the stretcher. Then, each taking one corner, and, guarded by Aline and Camy, we carried her up to the burial ground. We walked carefully and slowly, gauging where we walked by the familiar curves of the path and the shapes of trees and boulders that loomed out of the fog. Focusing on my steps took my mind away from our burden.

As we neared the burial ground, I heard the voices of other women.

"Lena?" I heard my sister ask.

"Here," I answered, stopping. Kira stepped out of the fog.

"Let me guide you," she said, glancing down at the stretcher. "The graves are to your left. Come up higher, this way." We followed her, laying the stretcher where she indicated. The other dead lay in place.

"You're the last," Kira said. "We are all here, now."

"Thank you, Kira." I heard my mother's voice but could not see her. Droplets of water condensed on my hair and ran into my eyes. I put a hand up to brush them away. My mother appeared in front of me. "Lena, will you do the rites for Tice?"

"I will." She handed me a small, stoppered flask containing water from the sacred spring. I would place a few drops on Tice's forehead, eyes, and lips, and then place the flask between her hands before we buried her. I slipped the flask into the pocket of my tunic, wondering as I did what the rites of Karst were, and whether it mattered.

Voices and the sound of hooves and jingling harness floated down from above us as the women from the caves, and their guard, descended the path. A baby cried. Suddenly, a woman shouted, and a child screamed. I heard Grainne snapping commands amidst more screams. I ran, past the dug graves and up the hill path, pulling my knife from its boot sheath.

I found the women not more than fifty paces above the burial ground. They had formed a ring around the children and Minna, and they too had drawn knives. Dian sat her horse just above them on the path.

"What happened?" I asked, panting.

"The Lestian snatched one of the children," Dian said grimly. "Grainne and Rasa have gone in pursuit."

"Which one?"

"Pel," Mella said from the circle. She held her child with one arm, her knife in the other hand. "He was supposed to be in front of Ranni—we were keeping the children between the adults—but someone slipped on a wet rock, jostling him, and he ran out of the circle. Cael grabbed him almost at once."

"How did Cael know we were here?" Kelle asked. Other women from the burial ground had reached the group now.

"He must have been following us," Dian said. "In this fog, we wouldn't have seen him."

Rasa rode up. She shook her head. "Nothing," she said. "I think he's gone into the caves, with Pel as hostage."

"Get the rest of them to the burial ground," Dian said. She turned to me. "Where is Pel's mother?"

"On guard duty at the hall," Gille said. "Take them down to the burial ground. We will bury our dead," she said grimly. "There is little we can do in this fog. He won't harm the boy if he wishes to bargain."

We brought the women and children down to the graves. Lara ran to Dessa, burying her face against Dessa's breast. Dessa rocked her, tears streaming down into Lara's hair. Around them, mothers found their children, comforting the little ones who sobbed with fright and cold. It was some time before we could begin the rituals.

Dessa stepped forward first, holding Lara's hand. She knelt beside Siane's body, uncovering her face. Lara sobbed once, then controlled herself. Dessa handed her the flask, removing the stopper for her. Guiding Lara's hands with her own, together they let a drop or two of sacred water fall onto Siane's forehead. Lara touched it. "Be at peace, mother," she said, her voice barely audible, but not breaking. Dessa, too, touched Siane's forehead. "Be at peace, my love," she said. Then she dropped water onto her own fingers to touch Siane's closed eyes and lips. Then they drew back the covering blanket to tuck the flask into Siane's hands, before covering her again and stepping away.

Other hands lowered the stretcher into the grave. We repeated the ritual three more times. Tice was the last. Carefully, I rolled back the blanket to touch the water to her forehead. "Be at peace, Tice," I said, "my friend, my cohort-second." I touched her eyes and lips with my wetted fingers and placed the flask in her hands.

The council and the cohort-leaders gathered at my mother's house in the early afternoon. The sun, a pale disc, barely showed through the fog. We gathered around the fire in my mother's sitting room. Tali sat with a shawl over her shoulders, staring at the flames.

Gille had ridden with Grainne and Dian into the hills, hoping to find the cave where Cael held Pel. My mother made tea. Subdued by burials and loss, we said little as we sipped the hot, sweet liquid. Finally, Sara spoke.

"Some of you know what I have to tell you already," she began. "Two nights ago, Lena and Tice took a prisoner. This man is not Lestian, though he sailed with them as part of their force." She glanced at Tali before she continued. "This man is Tali's son, Garth."

"What?"

"Are we sure it's Garth?"

"A traitor?"

I felt a wave of anger at this comment. Sara held up her hand, and the group quieted. My mother sat beside Tali, putting an arm around her. "Hear me out," Sara said. "He is Garth, and he claims to be a spy for the Emperor, under Dern's command. This is consistent with information that Casyn told Gille and that Dern told Lena."

"Yes," I confirmed.

"We are inclined to believe him," Sara went on, "but until we hear from Dern or Casyn, we hold him guarded at the forge cottage."

A harness jingled outside announcing Gille's return. She strode in, water droplets condensed on her wool cloak. "Cael is in the large cave," she announced. "Pel is unharmed, but Cael will let him go only if we release our prisoners and give them boats to sail to Leste. He gives us a day before he kills

Pel." My mother took her cloak and hung it to dry.

"Could Kolmas reason with him?" someone asked. Gille shook her head.

"We could try," she admitted, "but he is not one of Kolmas's men. Kolmas says he barely accepted Dann's leadership. I don't think it is worth the time it would take."

The cave, defensible from inside, had no other entrance. Cael had Pel for hostage and shield. For all my cohort's skill at stealth and the knife, we faced an opponent at least our equal, and more likely our master. Sara spoke. "Garth is our only chance."

"Explain," Gille said.

"We send Garth to the cave. Cael will think only that he has also eluded capture and will not be on his guard. Garth can kill Cael, or wound him, and let Pel escape."

"Or we will find ourselves up against two holding Pel hostage, not one."

"I think Garth is telling the truth," I said, "but Cael may have seen him captured. We would have to make it look as if he had escaped. I agree with Sara. Garth is our best chance."

We debated for another twenty minutes, but in the end, even the most reluctant agreed. Gille stood. "Who will go with me? Tali? Lena?"

Tali looked up. "No," she said lifelessly. "I can't. Lena, you go."

I found a cloak, and Gille and I walked up the hill to the forge cottage through the fog. Garth sat in the kitchen, playing cards with Salle. "Leave us, please," Gille said to Salle. When she was gone, Gille began. "Cael holds your brother, Pel, captive. He took him this morning at the burials."

"What does he want?" Garth asked.

"He is giving us a day to release the prisoners and give them the means to sail away, or he will kill him," I answered. "We need your help."

"How?"

"If we release you," I said, "and make it look like you escaped, will you go to the cave and set Pel free?"

"Kill Cael, you mean?" He said softly.

"If that is what it takes."

He hesitated for a few heartbeats, looking from me to Gille, and then back to me. He raised his chin.

"I will."

We cut the leg chains, leaving the shackles around each ankle and a small piece of chain trailing. We unlocked the shackles on his arms, tying the hasps with blackened string. He would say that he had overpowered his guard on the way to the privy and fled into the fog.

We could not follow him. The fog shifted as we waited with our questions. Would Cael believe Garth's story? How long would it take Garth to find the cave in the fog? Would be able to overpower Cael? Would he even try?

When it grew dark, we fed the animals and the prisoners. Tali sat in my mother's kitchen, watching her make bread. I stayed for a while, then went out into the night. I could not be still. The breeze had risen, and the fog thinned. I walked up to Tice's cottage, lit a fire in the kitchen stove, and opened the window. I waited.

With a soft chirrup, the tortoiseshell cat jumped onto the windowsill. I put the fish I had brought into her bowl. She jumped down to feed. When she finished, I stroked her gently, my hands smoothing her fur, accustoming her to my touch. I picked her up, feeling her muscled warmth. She struggled a bit. I held her tightly with one arm and bent down to pick up her bowl with the other. "Shhh," I said.

I carried the cat, with some difficulty, down to the house I shared with Tali. I put her in my bedroom, with her bowl, and closed the door. Tomorrow I would bring a rug or two from the cottage. Perhaps the familiar smells, and food, would convince her to stay with me. I realized I did not know what Tice had called her.

At midnight, I went to do guard duty at the hall. My sister tended the wounded, two of whom had died earlier in the day. She looked up as I came in.

"No news," I said. "Will these men live?"

"I think so," she said, brushing her hair back from her eyes. "One or two have a mild fever, but there is no other sign of infection, and they're responding to willow bark tea." The wounded men lay on pallets, bound by chains at their wrists or ankles. Most slept. The other prisoners slept around the outside of the room, huddled in whatever position of comfort their chains allowed. They had a blanket each, and a thin sack of wool for a pillow. Fires burned in the fireplaces. They would have little to complain of, I thought, when we turned them over to the Empire.

The night passed. When I took one man outside to the privy, the fog was mostly gone and the air was frosty. Inside, I locked his chains again, making a tour of the room before joining the other guards playing a game of chance at a table.

We had played three games when Dari came to the door. "They are back," she said. "Pel is safe and unharmed. Go to them, Lena. I'll take your place, here."

I ran through the night to my mother's house. In the sitting room, Tali held Pel. He crackled with excitement, self-importantly the centre of attention. As I came through the door, he squirmed from his mother's arms to run to me.

"Lena," he said, hugging my legs, his words spilling over, "the enemy captured me and took me to the cave. This man rescued me! He killed the other man. I saw the blood on his knife." Pel looked up at me. "He says he's my brother." I looked over Pel's head to where Garth stood. He smiled, and this time his smile reached his eyes. His eyes, not Maya's. A faint warmth, a barely glowing ember, flickered in the void inside me. I picked up Pel, holding him close, and buried my face in his hair. When I looked up again, Garth was still watching me.

"He is your brother," Tali said. "His name is Garth."

"Who do you serve with, Garth?" Pel asked, always the first question of the boys to the men, spring and fall. Garth hesitated.

"He serves with Dern," Gille said, from behind us. "Welcome him home, Pel."

††††††

Two days later, I stood at the top of the village, waiting for Garth. Below me, women went about their business, save for those on guard in the meeting hall. We had prevailed. Much of what we had feared and made ready for had not happened: no barns had been burnt, no animals slaughtered, no women raped. But we had lost four women to death and one to exile, and we had killed nearly twenty men. Could we go back to tending fields and catching fish, to Festival and raising children, and slowly forget?

Brilliant sunshine washed the village. The last of the heather shone purple on the ridge where Sella and the smaller girls herded the sheep. Garth climbed the path to join me. I had asked him to walk with me, sending Pel to tell his story of capture to Freya. Pel had, not surprisingly, attached himself to Garth. His new brother was a prize to brag about to his friends. Garth took patiently to being followed by a gaggle of small boys, but I had spoken firmly to Pel, and we walked through the fields alone. I had one more duty, apart from the guard rotation, to fulfil.

Tali had cut his hair, which diminished his resemblance to Maya, but I could still see her in the tilt of his cheekbones, and in his eyes. The palpable tension that had marked him during his first few days with us had faded. We walked along the edge of the fields, eating handfuls of berries from the brambles that grew there, climbing higher, away from Sella and the sheep. As the rocks grew steeper, I held out a steadying hand to him. His skin was warm and dry. A buzzard hunted over the ridge, its screams loud in the clear air. At a group of rocks, warm in the sun, I stopped. "Shall we sit?" I asked.

We sat, looking out over the village and the sea beyond. He stretched, and his arm brushed mine. I closed my eyes.

"Garth, we need to talk about Tice."

He pulled away slightly. "I had hoped to make redress, if I could."

"You can," I said, gently.

"How? She died hating me. She would have killed me, that night, had you let her." Overhead, a lark hovered, singing.

"She hated you, Garth," I began, and stopped. "No, she hated Kirthan because he had been the tool with which she shaped a future different than the one she had thought she wanted. But she was a grown woman, Garth, and free to choose. She hated you because she thought you would never have to accept the consequences of an afternoon's pleasure." I picked a dried grass stem from beside the rock, weaving it between my fingers. "That afternoon meant exile for her, and one other. She bore you a son."

I heard his sharp intake of breath. I played with the grass for a moment more before looking up. He stared blindly out to sea, tears on his cheeks. I knelt beside him, holding him while we both wept, for the betrayals, and the lost, and at the cruelty and joy of hope.

Finally, he sat up, brushing the back of his hand over his eyes. "Where is he?"

"His name is Valle. He is being raised in the slave quarters of Jedd's retirement farm. Tice said there was no other choice for a son with no father to claim him."

"I had left the message for Dern high in the rafters of the barn," Garth said, his eyes distant, remembering. "When I found her there, climbing the rafters to amuse herself while she waited to see Jedd's accountsman about some wine business, I was afraid she would find the message. So, I set about distracting her. It went further than either of us meant it to, I suppose. I gave no thought to a child."

"And Valle?"

"I will claim him, as soon as I am able. But who will raise him?"

"Tice's mother, or sister, or aunt—a woman of Karst, anyhow. You will need to speak with the council there." I hesitated. "After *Skua* comes and the prisoners are dealt with, I will leave Tirvan to find Maya. We could ride together for a while."

"I'd like to have some time with you, Lena. But I don't know what Dern will say."

"Nor do I," I said, "but he is a compassionate man." We walked again, in silence, each lost in our own thoughts. A light breeze rippled the grasses. I could hear the distant calling of sheep in the high pasture. I slipped my hand into his. He stopped for a moment, smiling down at me. We followed a path that led into a small grove of trees. In the shade of the branches, I stopped. "Garth," I said softly. He turned toward me. I put my hand up to his face, to the shape of Maya's face under his skin. "I love your sister, and nothing can change that. But she isn't here, and you and I are, and we are both in need of comfort. We could be that for each other, for a while." He smiled, slowly.

"Are you sure?" he whispered. I nodded. He brought his lips to my hand, and I heard his breath catch. I stepped closer. We stood like that, drawing warmth and strength and life from each other, until I felt desire rise and moved my mouth to find his. He tasted of blackberries, of earth and water and sun distilled into sweetness, the taste of harvest and celebration, and of the end of all the summers of childhood.

PART II

If the past is not to bind us, where can duty lie?

George Eliot

CHAPTER THIRTEEN

I SLID THE LAST FOLDED SHIRT INSIDE THE SADDLEBAG, buckling it closed, my fingers stiff in the morning cold. I checked the bedroll, tied behind the saddle on my sturdy Han mare. Beside me, Garth and Casyn did the same. The horses snorted and stamped, their warm breath steaming in the frosty air.

A crowd had gathered to see us leave. I caught my mother's eye. She smiled back at me. I had said my private good-byes, to her and to my sister, and Tali, earlier. I waved to Freya, and to Pel and Sarr, watching our departure in sulky silence.

I swung up into the saddle. My horse moved restlessly, eager to get warm on this cold morning. Garth mounted, steadying Tasque with hands and voice. Dern and Casyn exchanged some last words and embraced before Casyn turned to mount Siannon. Then he raised his hand, in salute and farewell, and we started up the path.

We rode slowly, letting the horses pick their way up the narrow, stony track. Hoarfrost whitened the ground as we climbed higher. A grouse, already half-moulted into its white winter plumage, rose from the heather beside the track. At the top of the ridge, we stopped. Below us lay the village, the smoke from the hearths hanging over the houses. Ahead of us, still out of sight, ran the paved road. The thought of it brought a tightness to my throat. I looked down at the village. It already looked so small beneath us. I swallowed.

"Come, Lena," Garth said after a minute. "You won't forget." I turned my horse to ride east, further into the hills.

Ten days before, in the early afternoon, I had gone in search of my mother. I found her, alone, hanging herbs from the beams of the kitchen.

"Lena," she greeted me from the top step of a short ladder. "Can you give me a hand? Kira has taken a salve to Ranni for the baby, and this is easier with two."

"Of course," I said. The bundles of fresh herbs lay on the table, already tied. I began to hand them up to her. "I wanted to talk to you."

"What about?" my mother asked, her eyes on the job.

"The men should be back soon, right?"

"I believe so."

"Once they've come, and we no longer need to guard the prisoners, I'm going to look for Maya."

She said nothing immediately, but her hands stopped tying the herbs. Then she looked down. "I thought you might," she said. "Leave those for now," she added, indicating the herbs. She climbed down the ladder to put her arms around me. I leaned into her. She smelled of lavender, as she always had. She held me tight for several heartbeats, then gently stepped back. She put out a hand to stroke my hair. "When I bore you, and Kira afterwards, I remember being thankful you were both girls, so that I wouldn't have to say goodbye," she said. My throat tightened. She smiled. "You will need money and warm clothes, and maps. And what about camping supplies, and food? Have you made a list?"

I laughed, relieved that she wouldn't try to dissuade me. "Not yet. Let's get these herbs hung, and I'll tell you my plans as we work. You hand them up to me. I'm taller than you, anyhow," I said. I climbed up a couple of steps of the ladder, taking the bunch she handed me, tying it to one of the many small hooks that lined the beam. "I will ride," I said. "Dian and Rasa will sell me one of their horses. They have a little mare I like. I can buy her if Dessa will lease *Dovekie* from me for a year." I glanced down to take another bunch of herbs.

"She might," my mother said. "But even if you find Maya, she cannot come back for three years, remember."

"I know." I had my own thoughts on that, but they weren't ones I wished to share yet, not with the council, or even with my mother. "I'll give myself a year to find her. If I don't, I'll come home. If she wants, Freya can fish with me. Her apprenticeship will be done by then." I had lain awake last night, listening to Garth's soft breathing beside me, thinking this out.

"And if you do find her? What then?"

"I don't know," I said. "I can't make those plans now. I can only plan the looking." I tied the next bunch, knotting the string with a sharp tug. I reached down for another bunch.

"That's all of them," my mother said. "There is something else you could do, Lena, on the road."

I climbed down the ladder. "What's that?"

"Ride to Karst," she said gently, "to tell them of Tice's death. Exile or no, she has family there, and they should know. I had thought to send a letter, next Festival, or even to ride out to the first inn to send word from there. But it is news that would be better given by someone who knew her and knew how she died."

I did not want to do this, but I knew my mother spoke the truth. I had a responsibility. "But what if Maya went north, towards the Wall?"

She considered. "You'll only know that by asking at the inns, so ride south first. If at the first inn, they have no news of Maya, leave a letter there, to be taken to Karst. The first inn is no more than a day's ride, or so I am told. But I hope she went south, Lena. It will be winter soon."

An hour later, I walked down to Dessa's workshop. The doors stood open to the afternoon sun, revealing Freya and Dessa planing planks for a new hull. Two of the village boats had burned with the catboat; it would take much of the winter to replace them. The smell of freshly shaven wood made the air pleasantly spicy. The women looked up at my footsteps.

"Hello, Lena," Dessa said quietly. She spoke and moved with less confidence now, and I thought her hair had greyed. But she worked, and directed her apprentices, and came to council. Lara, Siane's daughter, watched from a corner of the workshop.

"Did you want me?" Freya asked, straightening.

I hesitated. "Yes, but if you're busy—"

"I can spare her," Dessa said.

"I came to see if you would like to go sailing with me. Not to fish, just to go out on the water." I wanted to talk to her away from the village and other ears. Beyond that, a general restlessness made me want to take *Dovekie* out.

"I'd like that. Let me get some warmer clothes, and I'll meet you at the wharf."

We sailed south, something I rarely did, keeping the coastline in sight. For a while, we said little. Seabirds followed us, and clouds scudded along the horizon.

"How is your arm?"

"Healing well," Freya said. "It's not bothering me much." She rolled up her sleeve to show me. I saw new skin, pink, shiny, and slightly puckered at the edges. "It's still a bit tender, but I can work. I have to rub salve into it several times a day to keep the new skin from tearing."

"Good."

"Kira says you kept it from being much worse by putting my arm in the stream." Freya said. "I don't believe I've thanked you."

I shrugged. "It seemed the right thing to do. I'm glad it helped."

"Dessa thinks I'll be able to fish without problems in the spring."

"How is she?"

Freya sighed. "She's quiet, as you saw, and subdued. She doesn't talk about Siane much, except to Lara. And she works all the time."

"And Lara?"

"I worry about her," Freya admitted. "She cries often, and she doesn't like to be out of Dessa's sight. I wonder if she's afraid Dessa will disappear, too, or if she thinks she needs to take care of her."

The breeze blew Freya's hair back off her face. She looked older, I thought, no longer a girl. "Probably a bit of both," I suggested, steering with my knee against the tiller, feeling the currents of wind and water against the boat.

"What will happen to us, Lena?"

"What do you mean?"

"Tirvan. All the villages. Can we go back to the same rules, the same way of living?"

I adjusted the tiller to slow a bit. "Do you want to? I guess I haven't thought about it too much. I've been thinking about finding Maya."

"But that's part of it. The old rules say three years must pass before she can return. Do you think that's right?"

I had considered this. If the Emperor could change the rules for deserters, why could not the village council change the rules for exiles? If—when—I found Maya, I planned to bring her back to Tirvan to make this argument at council.

"No," I admitted.

"What does your mother say?"

"We haven't talked about it. But I'm leaving to find Maya, as soon as I can."

"You really are going, then?"

"Yes. Do you think Dessa would lease *Dovekie* from me for a year?"

"As I said, all she does is work," Freya answered. "She got those hulls started before anyone else had even begun to think about it. I think she'll do it."

"Good," I said. "I'll talk to her in the morning."

Freya started to answer, but an unexpected gust of wind caught the sail, and her attention went to the lines. I looked up to see if her arm constrained her, if she needed my help, but that thought vanished. Far out on the ocean, beyond the calmer waters of the coastal coves, I saw the triple sails of a large boat. *Skua.*

We turned *Dovekie* around, running her back to the harbour on the strong off-shore breeze. *Skua* could not be seen yet around the southern headland. We docked and tied *Dovekie* quickly. Freya ran to find the council leaders. I went to find Garth.

He had saddled the smallest of our hill ponies for Pel and Sarr. They rode on leading reins in a circle around him on the common, learning to balance with only knees and thighs. The riding lessons had begun a week ago. Garth needed something to do, and the boys shadowed him constantly. Dian had suggested it. Both boys, in the normal course of events, should have gone with their fathers, or their father's proxy, after autumn Festival this year, but Festival would not happen now.

He saw me coming and said something to the boys. He gathered in the leading reins to bring the ponies to him. I reached the common and stood waiting while he unclipped the long reins from the head collars and slipped on the bridles.

"Ride up to and around the hill fields," he said to the boys, "then return the ponies to the barn. Rub them down well. Check their hooves and clean the tack. I will inspect both ponies and tack later, and I expect to find both spotless. Understood?"

"Yes, sir," they chorused, and rode away.

"*Skua* is coming." I said. "She'll be here in a couple of hours at the most."

His dark eyes widened slightly. He took a deep breath. "So, I will learn my fate."

"It can't be bad," I argued, as I had more than once before. "Gille will speak for you, and Tali. All of us will. Pel would have died without you. You have done what Dern asked of you."

"I hope you are right."

I wanted to put my arms around him, but I couldn't, not here in the sight of the village. He slept at his mother's house, as did I. Only Tali and my mother truly knew that the second bed in Pel's room went mostly unused. What others assumed, seeing the time we spent together, I did not know, nor did I care.

"You will tell them about Valle?"

He sighed. "I will, when the time is right," he said, glancing up at the hills. "I need to see that Pel and Sarr have got the ponies back safely, and return this harness. Will you walk up to the barn with me?"

I glanced at the sun. "I can't. I'm on guard duty soon, and my blades and leathers are at the house. Perhaps at supper?"

"Perhaps," he said. "We'll see what the tide brings." We separated; I walked across the common to Tali's house, where I put on my leather boots and jerkin and strapped on my sword. The secca I slipped into its boot sheath. In the days since their capture, the prisoners had given us no trouble. They remained chained inside the meeting hall, loosely enough to allow them to stretch out on their pallets and sit in some comfort to eat. We guarded them around the clock, eight women, one always a Cohort-Leader, six hours in the watch, escorting them to and from the privies, bringing food and water. Mostly, we fought off boredom. *Skua*'s arrival meant the end of this duty. The prisoners would become the soldiers' responsibility.

Walking up the hill to the meeting hall, I stopped to look westward out over the sea. I could just see *Skua* now, her sails catching the afternoon light. I wondered who else had seen her. I met Tali on the path, bringing two men back from the privies.

"Ah, Lena, good," she said. "I wanted to talk to you, and you're late."

"Am I? I'm sorry, Tali. There is news."

She raised her eyebrows. We shackled the men on the porch, then walked a distance away. "Look," I said, indicating where with a tilt of my head.

Tali looked. "*Skua*! Does Garth know?"

"That's why I'm late. I went to find him. Freya and I saw her when we were out sailing. Freya went to tell the council leaders."

A shout came from the porch, followed by a babble of Lestian voices. "You had best tell Kolmas," Tali advised. "Send for help if the prisoners are too restive. I'll see if Grainne or Dian can send another couple of horsewomen over."

I found Kolmas inside, standing at the full length of his chains. "What is happening?" he demanded.

I held up a hand. "A minute." I said. To the other guards in the room, I said "*Skua*'s back. She should make the cove in an hour or so. I've told Tali. We'll have help if we need it."

"Will Casyn be on her?" Aline asked from across the room.

"I don't know." I turned to the catboat's captain. "Tell your men to be quiet." When the hall no longer rang with voices, I spoke.

"*Skua* will make our cove within the hour. She and her men were here for many weeks in the summer, helping us prepare to defend Tirvan. Her captain is called Dern. We have been waiting for them to return, to hand you and your men over. You will be their prisoners, now."

Kolmas licked his lips. "I have heard of this boat and captain," he said. "But I heard the general Casyn's name, too."

"He may be on board. He sailed away from here on *Skua* and planned to return. Tell your men."

He pitched his voice to be heard throughout the hall and onto the porch. The hall once again filled with voices, their tones questioning and sharp. Kolmas answered firmly. Slowly, the men quieted, dropping into conversation with their neighbours.

"What do you know of Casyn?"

"He is great general, they say," Kolmas replied cautiously, "who won many battles."

I nodded. "He is a fair man. We will tell him that when you saw the battle was lost, you surrendered, and that you have helped as much as you can. I do not think you need to worry if you accept the Empire's victory."

"If the Empire can feed us, many will accept," he replied, so quietly I had to strain to hear. "Some men said, ask the Emperor to lead us, not fight, but our king said no, fight. So we fought. But to say our king is wrong is treason, so I do not say that. What I think, I keep here." He touched his chest.

"Say that to Casyn."

Skua sailed into the cove to drop anchor an hour later. So many prisoners requested the privy once she had anchored that we set up a rotation, taking them out in pairs to see the ship. When the small boat launched, even from our height, I thought I could recognize Casyn and Dern.

The hours passed. We brought all the men inside to feed them. We gave them tea, adding the spices they liked. Their little shows of bravado had given way to a subdued acceptance, and mostly they sat, blankets around their shoulders against the chill of evening, sipping their tea. Kolmas watched them. I had grown to respect him.

I heard the footsteps on the path outside and straightened. The west door opened, and Casyn came in. Dern followed him, and behind him, Gille. Dern's eyes searched the room. He smiled when they found me. I grinned back, all restraint gone in the relief of seeing them safe. Casyn saw me, too, just a hint of smile touching his eyes.

"Lena," he said. "You lead the guard, tonight."

"I do," I said, hoping I could keep my face suitably schooled.

"I have spoken with the other Cohort-Leaders already," he said. "Well done.

I know there has been sorrow for you, and for the village, but across the Empire the women's villages prevailed, and the Empire stands. Be proud, Cohort-Leader."

"Thank you," I said, unexpected tears pricking at my eyes, all levity gone from me. Casyn's eyes moved to Kolmas.

"Do you lead these men?" Casyn asked.

"I am Kolmas. I was captain," he answered. "These men were mine, yes. Some were my crew before. Some came to my boat only to fight. Some were sent to me, soldiers, but they are dead. I did not lead them. But these, yes." He spoke evenly, with neither pride nor humility. Casyn, nodded in his grave manner.

"I am Casyn, General of the Empire. Leste has fallen. Your king is our prisoner. Your women and children are unhurt. Your men have two choices. Swear fealty to the Emperor and the laws of the Empire, and we will take them home to freedom. Refuse, and they become slaves. Death awaits a rebellious slave."

"Freedom?" Kolmas said. "To farm and trade, as we have always lived, or to be soldiers of the Empire?"

"You must swear to the laws of the Empire," Casyn replied. "The Empire requires all men to be soldiers."

"And our women?" Kolmas asked.

"Will learn to farm and fish, and work metal and wood, as all women of the Empire do," Casyn said patiently.

"Only this, or slavery?"

"Why should there be choice?" Casyn asked, reason in his voice. "Leste was the aggressor. You invaded. We fought back, and not only kept our own lands but conquered yours. Enslaving you all would have been fair. But instead we offer you freedom for fealty."

"Freedom? This is not freedom, but I will swear, Casyn General, and I will advise my men to do the same. I do not see choice. Our woman and children are hungry. Do I bend my knee to you?"

"No," Casyn said. "Speak to your men, first. Tomorrow, we will hear your oaths." Kolmas nodded, sinking onto his haunches, his eyes shadowed. Casyn turned to me.

"Cohort-Leader," he said, "you and your guard are relieved. *Skua*'s men will stand watch tonight." He stepped aside to let the soldiers who had waited outside enter. As they filed in, Danel flashed me a quick grin.

"Anwyl leads this watch," Dern said. "Lena, will you explain your routines?"

As succinctly as possible, I told Anwyl, who greeted me with a quick grin, how we managed the guard. Five minutes later, I stepped out onto the porch of the hall where Casyn and Dern had waited.

Casyn stepped forward to grip my shoulder, a military gesture. "I am glad to see you safe," he said, his smile broader now.

"And I you," I said. Dern swept me up in a hard, brief hug, which I returned fiercely.

"I heard how Tice died," he murmured. "I am sorry, Lena."

I looked from one to the other. "Have you seen Garth?"

"We have," Casyn said, "but only briefly. We have much to talk about. You need not worry for him."

"Will he be chained again?" I asked.

"No," Casyn said. "He will face some hard questions, but no more."

"Tali," Dern said, "was most persuasive." He grinned, his teeth flashing white in the night. Tension drained from my shoulders and neck. I looked down toward the harbour. On the common, bonfires blazed, and I could hear music and laughter. Sudden joy bubbled up in me. It was over.

"Shall we join the celebrations?" I suggested, grinning. "I think I need some wine."

I pulled myself out of bed the next morning well after the sun had risen. Garth had slept in Pel's room last night. He had been quiet at the bonfires, leaving early but bidding me to stay.

Downstairs, I drank two mugs of water then set the kettle to boil. I stretched, considering food. I heard footsteps on the porch, and Tali came in, bringing cold air and the tang of woodsmoke with her.

"Good morning," she said. She had a mug in her hand. "Are you making more tea?"

"Yes, do you want some?"

"I could use another cup." She put her mug on the table.

"Have you had breakfast?"

"No," she said. "I don't want much. What about you?"

"I thought maybe some bread and jam."

"That would be good." She took the bread from the bin and sliced it. The kettle sang. I made the tea, setting the table with butter and blackberry jam. Tali brought the plates and knives, and we pulled up chairs.

I spread butter and a spoonful of blackberry jam on the bread and took a bite. The sweet-and-sour of the jam burst against my tongue. I had helped pick the blackberries only a few weeks before. "Lena," Tali said, when she had eaten her slice of bread and jam, "there is something I want to say to you before you leave."

"Yes?" I sipped my tea.

"Do you remember how upset Maya was when I had Pel?"

"She thought you should have been loyal to her father, even though he was dead. We had a big fight about it. I told her she was being stupid." I remembered the shouting and the tears, the extreme passions of twelve-year-olds. We hadn't spoken for days. In the hugs and kisses of reconciliation, we had taken our first tentative steps towards becoming lovers.

"We had similar arguments," Tali said. "I would be careful, Lena, of ever letting her know about your relationship with Garth."

"But we talked about liaisons," I protested. "We both accepted it. It won't change things between Maya and me."

"If this were truly a Festival liaison, I would believe that. But what is between you and Garth seems like more."

"No," I said, shaking my head.

She held up a hand. "Let me finish. Only you can know what's between you and my son. But can't you see that Maya would have difficulty accepting it for many reasons? For you to take another lover might be hard enough, but for that lover to be Garth, her beloved and lost brother? She will feel that you have both betrayed her."

I sat silent. The truth of Tali's words hurt. "Tali," I said finally, "it is only because he is Maya's brother that I could be with him. I said no to Dern. But I won't tell her. And he too will keep the secret."

"I think that is wise."

I sighed. "Perhaps I should have said yes to Dern and not turned to Garth. But I couldn't keep being strong alone, Tali, in those days after the killings, and he reminded me so much of Maya."

"I am not blaming you. We all need comfort and love, and memories are rarely enough. I waited twelve years to have Pel, but his father was neither the first nor the last man I held in my arms during Festival, regardless of my love for Mar. Perhaps Maya will have learned this, too, on the road."

"Maybe," I said. The thought had occurred to me in the night hours when sleep would not come. "I hope so. I'd be happier if I knew she was not alone."

Tali stood. "Come here," she said. I went into her arms, and she held me tightly for some moments. "Go safely, and be strong. And come back. We need you here."

"I will," I said, fighting tears. "I will."

When she released me, I saw tears glinting in her eyes as well. She smiled. "And now I had best get to work."

"I need to see Dessa," I said. "If she won't lease *Dovekie*, I'm not sure how I'll pay for this journey."

"Oh, I imagine she will," Tali said. She drained her mug and put it down, turning to leave the room. "I'll see you tonight."

"Tali?"

"Yes?" she said from the door.

"Thanks."

She nodded continuing on her way. I rinsed plates and mugs, put the remaining food away, then went down the hill to speak to Dessa.

"Aye, I'll take her," Dessa said. "But you'll need to clean her up. I don't have the hands to do that with building two new boats." We agreed on a price. I borrowed Freya again and we paddled *Dovekie* around to a small shingle beach where we could haul her out of the water. Using roller logs, we dragged the little boat well up onto the beach, gently laying her to one side. Barnacles encrusted her bottom. I would need to scrape them off and check the boards and caulking for damage.

"Thanks, Freya."

"Any time," she said. "I hope Dessa lets me sail her." We walked together back to the village before I left her to return to the workshop. Climbing up the hill to the field where the Han horses grazed, I saw Dian and Rasa working in the open door of the barn, Grainne with them.

"Lena!" Dian greeted me. "Have you come to bargain?"

"I have. Good morning, Rasa, Grainne."

"Good morning," they answered. Packs and harness lay scattered on the floor of the barn, and two of the horses stood tethered. The mare I wanted grazed in the field.

"It's Clio you want, am I right?" Dian said. I nodded. She went out into the field to catch the little mare, clipping a rope to her head collar. She walked her over. I put out my hand for her to smell me, then rubbed her neck. I liked the look of her, her compact body and calm eye.

"She's seven," Dian said, "well-schooled and gentle, for all she's trained to war. Let's get her saddled, so you can try her out." Rasa brought over a saddlecloth and saddle, quickly tacking up the mare. I swung up into the saddle, riding her out into the fields. She obeyed my hands and legs without protest.

After a few minutes, I turned her head to bring her back to the barn. "She's an easy ride," I said, dismounting.

"And built for travel," Rasa said, patting the mare.

"How much do you want for her?" I asked. Dian looked at Rasa.

"You'll need the tack, too, right?" Rasa asked.

"Yes."

Rasa named a price. "The Empire would take her for more," she said, "but they have more money. If you ever want, bring her back to Han, and we'll take her back."

"Or Tirvan could keep her as a broodmare here," Grainne said, "to improve the stock."

Rasa laughed. "We've given you ideas," she said. She slipped an arm around Grainne for a quick hug. Grainne leaned into her.

"Lena," she said, her voice diffident. "You should know. I'm going with Rasa and Dian to Han. I want to learn more about breeding horses and training them. You won't be the only one leaving Tirvan."

Surprise made me speechless for a moment. "Does the council know?"

"I told Gille yesterday."

"Well," I said, "I wish you luck and safe journey, Grainne. Will you send word, somehow, if you learn anything of Maya?"

"Of course," she said. "I wish you luck on your journey, too. I hope you find her."

I walked back to *Dovekie* without seeing the path. The changes have started already. How strange to think of Grainne leaving. Before this summer, she would have kept on working her hill ponies and talking to the men, spring and fall, about their mounts. If Spring Festival and her ponies' seasons coincided, she might even breed one or two to a small stallion, if the chance arose. But she never would have talked of leaving, or even thought it possible.

My steps brought me to *Dovekie*. I surveyed my boat. Not too bad, I thought, assessing the barnacles. I found a comfortable bit of driftwood to use as a stool and took up the scraper. Gulls screamed overhead, and waves lapped the shore rhythmically. I bent to the task.

An hour later, I heard the crunch of footsteps on the shingle. I looked up to see Dern approaching. He wore a leather jacket with the fleece turned inward. I sat up, and he smiled down at me.

"Don't let me keep you from your work."

"If I had a second scraper, you could help," I answered.

"I've scraped my share of boat's bottoms," he said, grinning. Then his voice changed, losing the levity. "How are you? Truly?"

"I'm...all right. I'm leaving Tirvan to find Maya."

He nodded. "Your mother told me. She also told me how Tice died. I'm sorry, Lena." He sat down on a piece of driftwood

"It was my fault. I shouldn't have sent her back on patrol when she was so angry."

He sighed. "I too have made bad decisions, as I told you once, decisions that cost friends their lives. So has Casyn. You bear some of the responsibility, Lena, but not all of it. Tice let her anger distract her. Or perhaps the man who killed her was simply better with a knife. You will never know. All you can do is accept the choice you made, grieve for Tice, and go on."

"I'm trying."

"It takes time. Going to Karst will help. I'm glad you will have company on the road," he said. I looked up, startled.

"You gave Garth leave?" Hope leapt inside me.

"I did. He told us of his son. I have given him six weeks, plenty of time to ride to Karst. He is to meet us in Casilla after that."

I stood. "Thank you, Dern."

"He earned it. He's been on duty, in a dangerous situation, for three years. Much of our most valuable information came from him. He earned his pardon and his leave." He half smiled. "You care for him."

I nodded. "We both love Maya. It's a bond, and Tice is, too, in a way." I thought of the dreams I awoke from, dreams where the boy whose throat I had cut became Tice. Garth brought me back from those dreams, most nights. I straightened, looking down at him. "Dern...."

He shook his head. "There is no more you need to say." He stood to take me briefly in a soldier's embrace. "Take care, Lena." I watched him walk away along the shingle, the crunch of his boots on the pebbles fading as he neared the rocks on the headland. I felt tears in my eyes, for the small sorrow of what I could not be for Dern, and for the joy of what he had given Garth.

CHAPTER FOURTEEN

TWENTY MINUTES LATER, I SAW GARTH RUNNING toward me along the beach. I put the scraper down, standing to meet him. He flung his arms around me and swung me, radiant with relief. "Dern told me," I said, wrapped in his arms. "I'm so pleased, Garth."

He kissed my hair. "Did he tell you I will be Watch-Commander on *Skua* when I join her at Casilla?"

I pulled back so I could look at him. "No," I said, "He didn't. I don't know what that means, Garth."

"I'll command a watch, six men. It's a junior position, but not too junior for my age."

"An officer's rank, then?"

"Yes," he said. "It's so hard to believe, Lena. I never thought I would have a second chance." He looked suddenly younger. The wind caught his hair, and he laughed. "I never thought I would be so happy to be a soldier, either," he said. "But I've learned where my allegiance lies. I will serve the Empire honourably."

"You will." I took his hand. "I bought the mare this morning. We need to practice riding."

"Dern offered me Tasque for the journey. Casyn is going to check his shoes. You should ask him to check your mare's, too." He spoke rapidly, the words bubbling out of him. Like Pel.

"I will. She's called Clio." I looked back at *Dovekie*. "If I don't finish these repairs, we won't be able leave when we planned. I need few more hours here, at least."

He grinned. "I will see to the horses. See you tonight." He kissed me again, a long kiss. I felt my legs soften.

"Go," I said, but called after him as he started off the beach. "Garth!"

"What?"

"Have you told your mother?"

"She's next!" he called back, breaking into a run.

That night, Casyn came to Tali's house. We sat in the kitchen near the fire, Tali mending Pel's jacket. She hated sewing and scowled over the work. Garth and Pel played *xache*. Garth had chosen to teach him the game of war, in part to mollify Pel's disappointment over having to wait until spring for his father to come for him. I sat watching the two brothers moving the game pieces. The tortoiseshell cat, dozing on my lap, purred as I rubbed her ears. She had adopted Tali, not me, but I had the only free lap. I felt as lazy as the cat.

Tali welcomed Casyn, glad of an excuse to stop her mending. He accepted wine, pulling a chair up to the table. We talked casually of the village's food supply, the health of the prisoners, strategies in *xache*. When Garth and Pel finished their game, Tali sent Pel to bed over his protests.

"I'll take him up," Garth offered, swinging Pel up out of the chair to carry him up the stairs. Casyn watched them go.

"He is good with the boy," he said. "When he has served some time on *Skua*, he would make a cadet-master."

"You were Dern's cadet-master, were you not?" I asked. The fire and the wine had made me sleepy. Had Casyn not been there, I would have followed Pel to bed.

"I was," he said, with his slow smile. "He was nine. He had a good mind, even then. His class was my last before I moved on to other roles." He took a sip of his wine. "I must ride south, now, Lena. The Emperor's winter camp lies in that direction, and I must report to him within the month. If you would be willing, I would ride with you and Garth until our paths diverge."

"I would be honoured," I said, sitting up in my chair. The cat, disturbed, jumped down to wash her face in front of the fire. "And glad of your company and your guidance on the road. But I can't speak for Garth."

Garth came back down the stairs. "Speak for me on what?" Casyn explained. "Of course you are welcome, sir," Garth said, "but we'll be slower than you. Neither of us are accustomed to long hours in the saddle."

"No matter," Casyn said. "I can make up time after our ways part, and I should not push Siannon too hard for the first while anyhow. How long do you need, Lena, to finish your work on your boat and prepare?"

I thought. "Five days? Is that too long?"

"Not at all," Casyn said. "Five days it is."

Later that night, I woke wondering whether Gille had asked Casyn to accompany us. The thought disturbed me in a way I could not quite define. Garth, always a light sleeper, stirred beside me. "What is it, Lena?" he asked. I told him my thought. "If so, what of it? We're both glad to have Casyn with us, just as much for his company and as for his knowledge of the road. I doubt Gille thinks either of us need protection. Go back to sleep," he said gently. He rolled over. I fitted myself along the warmth of his back and drifted into a dreamless sleep.

†††††

The track widened, allowing Garth and me to ride abreast, behind Casyn. Looking back, I could no longer see even the smoke from Tirvan's chimneys. Stop that, I told myself. Look around you. This is new. The plateau we rode on was rocky, heathland and bog, without trees. A raven croaked from a boulder.

We came to the road. I had expected a cobbled track, but the builders had made it wide enough for two wagons to pass. Paved with squared stone, it spoke of permanence and age. Casyn signalled a stop. We rode up beside him.

"North," he said, pointing, "the road goes to Serra and Delle, and beyond it to Berge where it turns east again to run below the Emperor's Wall on the northern border. South, it meets the sea near Karst, and then again turns east to Casilla. The closest inns are an easy day's ride in either direction."

A map nestled in my saddlebag, drawn by Casyn, showing the villages and inns on the road. If no one at the first southward inn had news of Maya, I would accompany Garth to Karst, riding northward again as spring approached. The northern road, Casyn had counselled, would be treacherous for a lone traveller in a matter of weeks.

"Is there an eastern road?" I asked. When Casyn had brought me the map, I had focused on the inns, knowing that I was most likely to find Maya—or at least hear word of her—at one of them.

"No," he said, "or, at least, not a true road. A beaten track runs at the edge of the plain from the eastern end of the Wall to where the mountains meet the sea. There is a fort there, and the paved road runs out from Casilla to the fort, but the route north from there is used only by patrols, or messengers with urgent business. It is a lonely ride and dangerous. I have done it once or twice. Wolves and bears roam the mountains." He looked up at the sky. "It is going to snow. Shall we ride?"

We turned south, riding side by side on the hard surface as Casyn talked, telling us stories of other journeys on this road, in other seasons. The snow began, large flakes that melted on the ground. No wind blew, and I heard little sound beyond the horses' hooves on the cobbles and our voices.

After two hours, we stopped where a spring bubbled up into a pool. Someone had dug it out, modifying the flow so that the water rose into a clay-lined basin to run down into a broader pond. "Let the horses drink from the lower pool," Casyn directed. "We can take water from the upper." The water was cold, tasting of iron. I stretched, flexing the stiffness out of my upper thighs and stamping my numb feet.

When the horses finished drinking, we returned to the road. The land had changed from the flatness of the plateau to a series of gentle hills. The road rose and fell as we steadily lost altitude. Trees grew in small clumps. The snow stopped.

At the bottom of one hill, the road bridged a fast-flowing river. Beside the river, on the northern bank, a path wound into the hills to the west of us. "Where does that go?" Garth asked.

"There is a valley, about three hours ride from here, where the hunting is reliable," Casyn replied. "A hunt party comes most autumns to take venison, and sometimes boar." I felt as I had the night Tice told me about the south, ashamed of my ignorance about the world beyond Tirvan. The men knew a wider world, but women rarely left their home villages except to take up work in another. Tonight's inn lay only a day's ride from Tirvan, but I could think of no one who had ridden out to it. Our safe harbour will become a prison, I had said to Maya, long months before. Perhaps it already had.

We stopped again at noon near a small stream in open woodland that bordered the road. Casyn removed the horses' tack, leaving on rope head collars that allowed them to graze unimpeded. The clouds had thinned a bit under a weak sun. I gathered twigs and, in a blackened ring of stones, built a small fire to boil water for tea. Garth shared out dried meat and cheese and apples.

We ate without hurry. The heat from the tea in the tin mug felt good against my hands. "Where is the Emperor's winter camp?" Garth asked.

"At the southern edge of the grasslands," Casyn answered, "there is an area of rolling hills and small lakes before the land changes again to the fertile fields of the south. His camp is there. It's reasonably warm, and there is good hunting and fishing."

"What's he like?" I asked. The Emperor's name was Callan. He had been elected to the role some eight or nine years back by the senior officers of the Empire. Beyond that, I knew nothing of the man.

Casyn considered. "He's a bit taller than me, with dark hair, although it is mostly grey, now. He has great tactical knowledge, and sound and considered judgment, but he does not let himself be bound by tradition. He approved the recruiting of spies and asking the women's villages to defend Tirvan was his idea."

"You seem to know him well," Garth said.

Casyn smiled. "I suppose I do. He's my brother."

I laughed. "I said to Dern, once, that I did not think you were quite the average soldier. I'm glad to have been proven right."

Casyn leaned forward to pour himself more tea from the pot in the coals of the fire. "Being the Emperor's brother does not confer much status, except that I am also one of his advisors. And I have known him since I was seven and he was eight, which may give me a bit more knowledge of how he thinks, and why. We were in the same regiment until our early twenties."

We finished the tea. Garth brought water from the stream to cool the ashes of the fire. We re-saddled the horses, mounted, and returned to the road.

We kept the horses to an easy pace, but after another hour of riding, my legs and back ached. I shifted in the saddle, trying to find a more comfortable position. The mare slowed, tossing her head, not understanding my unintentional signals. I tightened my thighs, ignoring the pain, and took a tighter hold of the reins. The day grew dark, the clouds bringing an early dusk. My thighs and shoulders burned with soreness. Just when I thought I could stand it no longer, we came to the inn. It sat to the right of the road, a long, plain, two-storey building, with an archway at the midpoint leading into an interior courtyard. I had expected a smaller building, built of wood as Tirvan's houses were, with maybe a paddock and a stable, but the inn was built of stone and slate. It looked as if it had stood here a long, long time, growing over the years to house many men and horses. The sense of age disturbed me, somehow.

We rode through the archway into a cobbled yard. A woman came out from one of the buildings that enclosed the courtyard. "General," she said, "we haven't seen you since the spring."

"Mari," Casyn said. "Is all well here?"

"Aye," she said. Casyn dismounted easily. We followed his lead, Garth steadying me when my numb feet threatened not to take my weight. Mari stepped forward to take the reins.

"These are my companions: Lena of Tirvan, and Garth, Watch-Commander of the Empire's ship *Skua*." Casyn said, giving Garth the courtesy of the rank he would soon hold. "We've ridden from Tirvan today, at an easy pace, so the horses need only the usual ration of grain and hay. We'll be staying only one night, weather allowing."

"Aye," Mari said again, and with a nod to us, led the horses into the stable. We walked across the cobbles toward the inn. My leg muscles quivered with exhaustion. Casyn opened a door. We stepped into a hallway that led into the main room of the inn. I blinked in the sudden dimness. A bit of light came from a fire burning in a massive fireplace at one end of the room, and a bit more from small windows near the low ceiling, its crossbeams darkened by years of smoke. Under my feet, huge flagstones lined the floor. Tables of equally darkened wood, with benches on either side, took up half the room, and some chairs stood near the fireplace. The room was empty.

"Livia," Casyn called. A door opened in the far wall, and a young woman came through. She was about my height, with close-cropped hair and broad shoulders.

"General," she said in a tone of surprise. "I didn't hear anyone ride in." Her eyes flicked to Garth and me. "You'll want some supper."

"And beds for the night," Casyn agreed. "But right now, drinks for us all." He introduced us as he had before. I stood swaying slightly with exhaustion.

"Welcome," she said, disappearing back through the door. We took off our fleece coats and our gloves. Casyn motioned us to the chairs near the fire.

Livia returned with a tray bearing three pewter mugs. I took a deep draught: cider, cellar-cool. On a low table, Livia placed a plate with some cold sausage wrapped in pastry. "Supper will be a couple of hours," she said. "This will help tide you over."

Garth took a piece, handing it to me. "Eat."

"Thank you," Casyn said to Livia. "All is well here?"

"It's been quiet," Livia said, leaning against the back of a chair. "A group of women from Han rode through a week ago, but they only stopped long enough to water their horses and to give us the news of victory. A number of men left this morning, so you just missed them. Bren of the tenth was here two days back, coming down from Delle. He left a message for you. I'll get it." She left the room. I could hear her talking to someone. I took another mouthful of cider. After a minute or two, she came back, to give Casyn a folded and sealed note.

Casyn broke open the seal to read the note, nodding to himself. He slipped it into the pocket of his tunic. "Before we leave, I'll give you a message for Turlo," he said to Livia. "He was at Berge, so you should see him in the next few days."

"Bren left a message for him, too," Livia said. She turned to me. "There is a hot pool," she said, "if you would like to ease your muscles after the ride. Find me when you are ready." I considered, my mind working at half speed. The thought of a hot soak was appealing, if I could find the energy to walk anywhere. My feet tingled with cold inside my boots, even by the fire. Casyn had told me a day or two before that the inns maintained the same strict rules that the villages did for all but the two weeks of Festival. I would bathe and sleep separately from the men. I wondered if perhaps the rules had changed here, too, this autumn.

I ate another sausage roll and finished my drink. Sighing, I pushed myself up. "I'm going to the baths," I said. I walked across the stone floor, feeling the stiffness in my legs. The door opened into a kitchen where Livia sliced carrots with a small boy playing near her feet. She turned as I came in.

"Ready for the pool?" She bent to pick up the boy. "My son," she said, smiling. I followed her out into a low brick hallway with arched ceilings. A short way down this passage, she opened a door, releasing a waft of sulphur. The oval pool was four paces across. It bubbled up from its underground source into a brick-lined basin, spilling out at the far end of the room into a shallow, tiled channel before disappearing under the wall. Wooden benches lined two walls, and robes of undyed wool hung on pegs beside towels.

"This is the last inn to have a hot pool on the way south," Livia told me. I remembered the Han riders' appreciation of Tirvan's baths.

"I always took them for granted," I said, and "I'm glad of this one." I sat on a bench to pull of my riding boots.

"Is this your first time on the road?" Livia asked.

I looked up. "Yes. I seek my partner, Maya, who chose exile rather than fight. Did she come this way?"

Livia considered. "Dark haired, travelling on foot?"

"Yes. Long hair, halfway down her back?" I struggled to speak calmly.

"I remember her. But she wasn't alone. She was with a woman from Berge: Alis, I think her name was." The child in her arms fussed, and she stroked his hair.

"Do you know where she was headed?" I asked, suddenly not tired.

"South," Livia said. "The southern inns are busier. They would likely have found work once they were past the Grasslands road ten day's ride from here— three weeks on foot. You will find her," she said, unconcerned.

"Gan!" the boy said, struggling.

"Yes, all right," Livia said, putting him down. "Find your Gran. She is in the linen-room." He ran off down the corridor. "He does not like to be still. May I stay and talk to you while you soak?"

"Yes," I said. She sat on the bench. I finished undressing and stepped into the pool. Under the surface of the water, a step, or platform, ran around the circumference of the pool. When I sat, the water came to just below my chin. I cupped some water into my hands, washing my face, running my wet hands through my hair. "What is life like at the inns?"

Livia laughed. "I can only speak for this one. I was born here. Eight of us live here, and three children. We farm a bit and make cheese and cider. We keep horses for the post riders and hold and pass on messages. Spring and fall, in a usual year, it's busy. In between, there are always messengers, officers like the General about the Empire's business, and hunt parties. And a few women, moving from one village to another."

"What's a post rider?" I stretched my legs as the heat penetrated my muscles.

"A messenger on urgent duty. They ride from one post, or inn, to another, changing horses at each so that the animal is fresh. The Empire pays us to stable a few horses for them and keep them exercised and shod."

"Are all the inns a day's ride apart?"

"A day's easy ride. Two days walking. The post riders stop at three inns in one day, eighteen hours in the saddle, six hours to eat and sleep. They can ride from the Wall to the Eastern fort in about ten days if they must."

"I can barely ride at a gentle pace for a day," I said ruefully.

Livia laughed. "What did you do, in Tirvan?"

"I fished. Maya and I have a boat, called *Dovekie*."

"You fought?" I heard no judgment in her question.

"Yes," I said. "I killed two men with a knife. If I wake in the night, shouting, it's because I am dreaming of it." Not quite the truth, but it would do.

"I'm sorry," Livia said, flushing. "I shouldn't have asked."

"It happened. I'm trying to learn to live with it. What were you to do in the invasion?"

"Nothing directly. If you hadn't been victorious, if the first people on the road again had been men from Leste, I was to ride north to the Wall. There are ways across the hills. I too learned how to kill with a knife, to protect myself. But I didn't have to do it." The water draining away gurgled in the silence of the room

Livia broke the silence. "The young officer—Garth?" I nodded. "He looks like your Maya, if I remember her rightly."

"He's her brother."

She stood. "I should get back to the kitchen. Mari will have taken your saddlebags to your room. I'll show you where it is when you want. You may use a robe and leave it in the room." She hesitated. "Your room adjoins the men's, and no one else will be on that floor to see who sleeps where. If there were other travellers, I wouldn't tell you this. I would rather not be woken by your bad dreams, if there is a cure." She smiled. "I can make you anash tea in the morning if you wish."

I looked away, embarrassed. "How did you know?"

She shrugged. "He's too solicitous, and you watch each other. Mari, who misses nothing, saw it first. With only us, it means nothing, but were there other men here, there would be consequences. I imagine," she went on, gently, "that the General has let him know, while they are alone."

"Casyn did caution us," I said. "I'm sorry."

"There's nothing to be sorry for. Stay in the pool as long as you like. Supper will be ready in an hour."

I soaked for another ten minutes, then dried off and put on one of the robes, enjoying its warmth and softness. I left the wet towel hanging near the door, picked up my clothes, and walked barefoot down to the kitchen. Livia stirred a stew while an older woman kneaded bread at the centre table. The kitchen smelled wonderfully of lamb, rosemary, and yeast.

"This is Lena, from Tirvan," Livia said. "My mother, Keavy." Keavy smiled a welcome and pummelled the dough. I followed Livia up a narrow stair to the next floor. "These are the back stairs. You don't want to go back out into the common room. It's cold." She showed me to a small room overlooking the courtyard. It held a wide bed, a washstand, and a woven rug on the floorboards. My saddlebags sat neatly on the floor beside the washstand. I could see a chamber pot tucked under the bed. "When you're dressed," Livia said, "turn left out of the room. You'll come to the main stairs. Call when you come down, or just put your head through the door, and someone will get you a drink." She left. I dressed in lighter, woven trousers and shirt, rather than the felted wool of my riding clothes. Those I hung from pegs on the back of the door. I found my comb and ran it through my hair.

A knock at the door surprised me. I opened it, expecting Livia, but instead Garth stood in front of me. He smiled. "I'm just going to the hot pool, but I wanted to talk to you first." He closed the door. "I've been paying you too much attention, Casyn tells me."

I flushed. "Livia said as much to me at the pool."

"I thought I was being careful. If I've embarrassed you, forgive me."

"I'd rather be embarrassed, here, than for you to have problems with other officers, later."

"In Leste, men are gentle with women in public, putting their needs first. I had forgotten how different it was, outside of Festival, in the Empire." He stroked my hair. "I suppose I need to learn again."

I leaned into his hand briefly. "Livia also gave us leave to sleep where we choose tonight as long as Casyn is not offended."

"Do you want me with you?" Garth asked, smiling.

"Yes," I said. "This first night, in a strange place, who knows what my dreams will be?"

He bent forward to kiss me lightly. "I'll speak with Casyn." He turned to go.

"Garth," I said. "Maya was here. She went south with a woman from Berge."

He turned again, his face alight, and stepped forward to hug me. "Good." He released me, smiling. "We'll find her, Lena. I promise."

We ate lamb stew and fresh bread for supper in the common room, with more cider. Afterwards, Keavy brought us a bowl of apples. I ate one, then took a second and walked, with Casyn and Garth, out to the stables to see the horses.

They stood in loose boxes, with a good bed of straw. I fed Clio her apple. Someone had curried her, and she had a rack of hay and a bucket of water in her stall. Four horses, other than ours, all in good condition, shared the stable. "Are these the horses kept for the post riders?" I asked Casyn.

"For the Empire," he said, "yes. If Siannon were to become lame, I could leave him and take one of these four. Mari would keep Siannon until I could claim him or send someone for him."

"And if it were Clio who was lame?"

He shook his head. "You could, perhaps, make a private arrangement with Livia. They have a few hill ponies of their own. These horses are the Empire's, and Keavy and Livia are paid well to house them and keep them in condition for the Empire's soldiers."

"But you pay for Siannon's feed and stall?" I asked, trying to sort this out.

"No, nor for my own room and board. The same is true for Garth, now he is attached to *Skua*. If I wanted, say, boar and mushrooms seethed in wine for dinner, then yes, I would pay for that, as it isn't the usual fare. If I am content to eat what Keavy puts in front of me, and drink the wine she offers, I pay nothing."

"But I do," I said. "How much?" He told me, and I thought about the coins I carried. I could travel for a long time.

I yawned, tired from the long ride and the good meal. "Bedtime," I said.

Casyn fed Siannon the last piece of apple. "Keavy distils a brandy from their apples that is worthy of a glass," he said to Garth. "Will you join me?"

We walked back across the cobbled courtyard to the inn. Stars gleamed above us. I said goodnight to the men and walked up the stairs. I stopped at the top, disoriented. Left or right? I pictured Livia leading me up here earlier, and turned left.

In my room, I studied the window. I wanted to open it to the night breeze, but I couldn't see how it worked. I pulled at it. Nothing happened. Frustrated, I pushed against the frame, and it moved slightly. I took a step back to examine the window again. Thin cords ran upward from the lower frame. I pushed up, and the lower window rose smoothly.

I undressed, leaving my clothes on the floor, slipping under the covers. The mattress, stuffed with straw, made small rustling sounds as I moved. My hips and lower back ached, even after the baths. The sheets and pillowcase smelled of lavender. I fell asleep to the chirp of crickets and the murmur of voices from the room below.

I woke to Garth moaning in the throes of a nightmare, tossing his head on the pillow. I began rubbing his shoulder. "Garth," I whispered, "wake up." His restless movements calmed a bit. "Wake up," I repeated. He rolled towards me, opening his eyes. "You were dreaming." When he moved closer. I could smell the sharp sweat of fear on him. "The same dream again?"

"I don't remember all the images, but I was trapped somewhere again, tied up, I think, and I couldn't escape. I was so frightened and confused. I wish these dreams would stop."

I massaged his back. "They will," I murmured. Gradually, his breathing slowed and his muscles relaxed. His hands began to move gently on my skin. I slid my hands along his back to his hips and raised my mouth to his, offering and taking what I could against the memories and the night.

CHAPTER FIFTEEN

I WOKE AT DAWN. OUTSIDE, A COCK CROWED. Smells of fresh bread and frying sausages rose from the kitchen. Garth had gone. I got out of bed to wash at the basin before dressing again in my riding clothes. I packed my other clothes into the saddlebag.

Downstairs, Casyn stood, writing a note at the common room table. I put my saddlebags by the hall that led to the courtyard and went into the kitchen. Livia cooked sausages at the stove.

"Sleep well?" she asked.

"Thanks, yes."

She handed me a mug of anash tea. "There's honey on the table." She gestured with her head, her hands busy turning the sausages.

Casyn finished his writing and sealed the note with wax. I spooned honey into the tea, stirring it.

Garth came in from the courtyard. "It'll be sunny today," he said, "but not warmer."

Livia brought in bread and sausages and a bowl of scrambled eggs. After we ate our breakfast, I paid her.

"I hope you find your Maya," she said, smiling. "Good luck on the road."

In the courtyard, Mari had the horses ready. I slung my saddlebags behind the saddle and mounted. Livia brought her son out to wave goodbye to us. We clattered out through the archway, and onto the road.

For the next three days, we rode south through an unchanging landscape. The riding itself became easier as we and our horses became conditioned to the saddle and the long hours. On flat stretches, we could trot or sometimes canter. At about noon each day, we stopped to build a fire and eat. I brewed my anash then, drinking it bitter, without honey.

In the late afternoon each day, we came to an inn. They all seemed much the same. None had baths. I ate with the men, but slept alone, usually on a different floor. Each innkeeper remembered Maya, and Alis of Berge, but none could tell me where they had gone. "South," they all said.

On the third day, we woke to heavy skies and a cold wind from the west. "Rain," Casyn said. An hour later, it started. The cold, stinging rain blew into our faces and across the open road. We pulled our hats down, tugged our collars up, riding into it. Clio dropped her head, and I let the reins lie loose on her neck. Water dripped off her mane, running down my coat to soak my legs.

In the early afternoon, we stopped in the shelter of some evergreens. The rain had not subsided, but the trees cut the wind. Casyn pulled a cloth bag of oats from his leather saddlebag. "Put the horses' head collars on," he said to me, "and then share this among them."

"We'll never get a fire lit," I said, unbuckling Tasque's bridle, my fingers clumsy with cold.

"Probably not," Casyn said. He sounded unconcerned. "Are you cold, either of you?"

I tossed Garth the end of the tether rope. He tied it around a branch. I poured a third of the oats onto the wet ground. Tasque bent his head, lipped the grain, and began to eat. "I'm fine out of the wind," I said. My felted wool trousers were soaked, but the leather coat and hat and my riding boots had kept me mostly dry. We finished feeding the horses.

Casyn gave me cheese and dried apple. "No point in trying to eat bread in the rain," he said.

We ate standing, half under the branches. Garth took a small flask from his pocket. "I bought some brandy from Keavy the first night. I think we could all use a mouthful." The brandy, resinous on my tongue, warmed my stomach and made my fingers tingle.

The rain fell all afternoon though the wind dropped. The horses plodded along the road, their hooves making small splashes with each step. Water ran along the stone channels at the edge of the road and stood in puddles in every dip of land. A buzzard sat miserably on a dead tree, its feathers striped by rain. By mid-afternoon, I began to shiver, and my teeth started to chatter.

"Dismount and walk," Casyn directed me, "until you are warm again."

I gave Clio the command to stop and swung off the saddle, my legs not wanting to obey me. Garth and Casyn dismounted as well. We began to walk. This is what Maya did, I reminded myself, feeling the stone through the soles of my riding boots. Rain dripped off my hat. Casyn set a brisk pace. Warmth soon spread, first under my coat, and then to my thighs, and finally to my feet and hands.

After about half an hour we remounted. At dusk, we came to the inn. We had walked for short stretches twice more, and Garth had given us another sip of brandy about an hour earlier, but now cold pervaded my body. Clio's dun coat looked almost black with water. We rode into the courtyard and dismounted, I leaned against the mare.

Casyn glanced over at me. "Go in. I want to look at Siannon's feet. I thought he was favouring his off hind this last while. Garth, find us a stable hand." The stable was connected to the inn by a roofed porch that ran the length of both buildings, widening at the stable to create a sheltered area for saddling and unsaddling. When we led the horses under the roof, their heads rose at the smell of grain. Tasque blew out a long breath, shaking himself like a dog.

Garth and I walked toward the inn door. "I can't remember ever being this cold," I said, wrapping my arms around me. I could not control the shivering.

"Get your coat and boots off and find the fire," Garth said. "Do you want more brandy?" I shook my head. Under the overhanging eaves we took off our hats and coats, my fingers clumsy on the buttons. Just inside the door were pegs and a brick floor with a drain. One leather coat hung there, dry. We hung our dripping coats beside it, leaving room for Casyn's, and went into the common room.

A man, middle-aged and bearded, wearing the dun-coloured travelling clothes of the Empire, sat by the fire studying a map. He looked up as we came in. Garth saluted. "Watch-Commander Garth, of *Skua*, sir."

The officer stood to return the salute. "Bren. Major of the Tenth. Come in by the fire. It's a wicked day for travel."

"Lena, of Tirvan," I said. I thought I saw a flicker of reaction, quickly controlled. We walked closer to the fire and its warmth.

As we came closer, Bren studied Garth's face. His hand found his belt knife. A muscle flicked in Garth's jaw as he endured the man's scrutiny. "I know that face," Bren finally said. "Son of Mar, of the Seventh?"

"I serve with Dern, on *Skua*, now."

"You deserted," Bren said coldly. "How can you claim you serve anywhere?" Garth said nothing. His papers, I knew, wrapped in oiled cloth, lay deep inside his saddlebags. "Answer me, man."

"We travel with Casyn. He is outside with the horses." I said, my voice wavering. "He will tell you." My voice sounded too high, too uncertain.

"Casyn?"

"Peace, Bren," Casyn said calmly from the door. He walked across the room to clap Bren companionably on the arm. "Garth has served the Empire honourably and well these past three years, providing us with information from Leste. He carries a letter of leave from his captain, and a pardon signed by me on the Emperor's behalf. Much of our most valuable information came from this man." Garth flushed at Casyn's words, but I could see him relax, almost imperceptibly

"So, he's one of yours, General," Bren said. He turned to Garth, hands out, palms up, in front of him. "My apologies, Watch-Commander. I should have realized, when you said you served with Dern. Casyn and Dern between them recruited the spies." He extended his right hand to grasp Garth's upper forearm. "Well done, soldier."

Garth nodded, grasping Bren's arm to return the formal greeting. "Thank you, sir," he managed.

The innkeeper came in with a tray of mugs. "Broth with wine," she said." She looked at me with a critical eye. I had sunk down onto a bench. "You're shivering," she said. "Sit by the fire and drink this. When you're done, I'll show you to your room, so you can change. Bring me back your wet clothes, and I'll dry them by the kitchen fire." The pottery mug was warm in my hands, and the broth smelled wonderful. I took a sip, then a larger swallow, feeling the heat coursing into my body. I drank it down as the fire warmed my legs.

The men spoke of war. I felt superfluous, and wet. When I finished my broth, I took the mug to the kitchen. The innkeeper stood at the sink, washing a pot. She looked up.

"Ready? I'm Aasta, by the way." She wiped her hands on her apron. "Follow me." She took me down a hall and up a flight of stairs to the women's bedrooms. The room, floored in wide planks, had a chair and table as well as the bed and washstand. A mug stood on the table, and a canister of tea. "I'll send Sari with some hot water, and she can bring back your wet things. Do you want the fire lit? This room's above the kitchen, so it's always warm."

I shook my head. "No, thank you. I'm warming up. The broth was wonderful." Aasta smiled, and with a nod of her head, left, closing the door behind her. I sat down to pull off my boots. I had just stripped off my damp socks when I heard a knock at the door. A girl of about twelve came in, carrying a pitcher of hot water.

"Hello," she said, a little shyly. "I'm Sari." She had long brown hair, braided back off her face. She put the water jug on the washstand.

"I'm Lena, from Tirvan." I took off my trousers, reaching for the towel that hung on the wall.

"Tirvan!" Sari said. "Do you know Maya?"

I stopped drying my legs. "She's my partner. I'm trying to find her. Do you know where she went?"

The girl shook her head. "No, not really. South. She was here for two days in the spring. If you find her, will you give her a message for me?"

"Surely," I said, curious.

"I'll write it out this evening, then," she said, smiling. She bent to pick up my wet trousers. "Your tunic?"

"It's dry. Is there nothing more you can tell me? Was she well? Was she alone?"

"She was well," Sari said, "save for a twisted ankle. That's why they stayed two days. She was with a woman named Alis, from Berge. There were two other women here, and they all left together."

With a wave, she left the room. I used some of the hot water she had brought to brew my tea, leaving it to steep while I washed, thinking of Maya. Four women together would be safer. I drank the tea, grimacing against the bitterness, and dressed in dry clothes.

"Lena," Casyn said, looking up. "Bren has a story I would like you to hear." The room was warm. Casyn poured me a cup of wine from the jug in front of him. Bren seemed to be gathering his thoughts. I waited.

"The Empire's ship that came to Berge for provisioning had been in the south in midsummer," Bren said finally, glancing at me and then away, "at a retirement farm. One of the junior officers rode out to the nearest inn, to pick up messages. His horse cast a shoe on the journey and had to be reshod. It was a bad-tempered beast, so the woman who was doing the job asked him to hold its head. There were two stable-girls talking in the barn, apparently unaware that he could hear them.

"They were talking about a plan being made by some of the women who had chosen exile over fighting. They spoke of organizing themselves into a group, with chosen leaders. When the fighting was done, those leaders would go to the Emperor to ask him for a place where they could build a new village—a village true to the tenets of Partition and open only to those who chose exile. The girls also discussed who the leaders were likely to be." He paused.

"Maya was one of them?" I asked. He nodded. "That's—unexpected."

"Which part?" Bren asked.

"She wanted the rules of Partition to keep governing us, even though most of us voted the other way. In her mind, when we voted to fight, we betrayed tradition. But to lead a petition to the Emperor..." I shook my head. "Maya was never a leader."

"Perhaps," Casyn said gently, "exile has changed her."

Garth spoke. "When I was seven, Maya was my shadow, my playmate in everything. I did not want to leave Tirvan or her. I promised her that I would run away from the soldiers and come back for her. We would go beyond the Wall, or into the mountains, and live there secretly. It was a child's plan, but neither of us ever forgot it. When I did run," he went on, embarrassment shading his voice, "in the back of my mind I always thought I would go to Tirvan for Maya, someday, to take her away."

I turned to Casyn. "Can she petition the Emperor?" I could not remember ever hearing of a woman doing so.

"Yes," Casyn said thoughtfully, "but it is irregular. A woman's village, or an inn, or a trade guild, may petition, but not an individual. The women's councils, not the Emperor, deal with women's individual grievances. If Maya's band of exiles form a guild, and duly register that guild, then, yes, they can petition."

"A guild?" Garth said.

"Guilds," I explained, "are our governing bodies."

He frowned. "I thought that was the council?"

"Well, yes and no. The council is elected to make sure the rules of the guild are followed. At Partition, the group of women who founded Tirvan decided what village's rules would be and how we would live. They formed the guild that is Tirvan."

"So village rules are different from one place to another?" Garth asked.

"Some of them," I said. "But some were set once by larger guilds that operated over many villages. There used to be a fishing guild, and in theory I—and Maya—belong to it."

"What did it do?"

I thought back, trying to remember what Dessa had taught me all those years ago.

"It set the term of our apprenticeships, so they would be the same in all villages. Dessa told us that at one time, a small part of what we earned would have gone to the fishing guild. If we had needed money to buy *Dovekie*, or had a disagreement over fishing grounds that could not be settled by the village council, we would have sent word to Casilla, and representatives would have come to settle the issue. But that stopped a long time ago."

"Are guilds described in the Partition agreement?" Garth asked.

"Yes," Casyn said.

"Could a new village guild be formed?"

"Would the Emperor grant such a request?" I asked Casyn.

"To answer you both," Casyn said, "there is nothing to stop a group of women from requesting permission to start a new guild and a new village. As far as whether Callan would grant such a request," he went on, "I don't know." He leaned back in his chair. "Callan does not see himself as bound by tradition, which could lead him to reject a claim made on the basis of the rules of Partition. On the other hand, he might see it as fair recompense. The problem for this new guild would be twofold: where to find land for such a village and what the Empire's responsibility towards it would be."

We fell silent. I sipped my wine, trying to imagine a village open only to those who had chosen exile. Would chance have given them the right mix of skills? What would Maya, whose trade was the boats and the nets, do in a land-locked village? What would I do?

Nothing. I had not chosen exile. Maya was planning a future that did not, could not, include me.

The men resumed talking, but their words swirled and eddied around me, unheard. Aasta brought dinner: rabbit stew and dark bread. My stomach growled, reminding me that I needed food. I took the bowl Aasta offered me and a slice of bread from the basket.

The men talked of inconsequential things at dinner, Bren and Casyn telling stories of their younger days on the Wall. They had all of Garth's attention, and I found myself drawn in by the tales. Bren rarely looked my way, speaking only to Garth and Casyn. The rain fell steadily, and even through the thick walls of the inn, we could hear water running in the gutters and splashing on the cobblestones.

Sari came to clear the plates, bringing us dried fruit and biscuits, and, at Casyn's request, another jug of wine. "We'll stay here tomorrow," he said. "One day of riding in the rain is enough, and the horses could use the rest. Siannon has a bruised frog. He'll benefit from a day on straw."

I accepted another cup of wine. Without it, I reasoned, I doubted I would sleep tonight. My initial shock had passed; now anger crept in to replace it. Perhaps I should just go to Karst with Garth, and then—what? Go home? Ride to the Wall up the eastern track, braving mountain storms and bears? I looked up. Casyn and Bren spoke quietly together, but Garth was watching me. I took a mouthful of wine, avoiding his questioning eyes.

CHAPTER SIXTEEN

I WOKE LATE THE NEXT MORNING, WITH A DULL HEADACHE and heaviness in my muscles. I lay in the bed until the need for the chamber pot forced me up. Downstairs, Aasta gave me tea. After the third cup, heavily sweetened, I began to feel better. I ate a piece of dry toast. In the common room, Bren and Garth played xache. Outside, the rain continued.

I wandered around the room. Like the other inns, this one had low ceilings and a flagged floor. The walls were whitewashed between the timbers. Small windows under the eaves on either side looked out on the courtyard and the road. I had no idea how to pass the time. At home, we spent wet days in the repair of nets and traps or other chores. A long wet spell in winter usually meant a few days of games and stories. I played *xache* fairly well, I thought, but I had no one to play with. In any case, I suspected Bren and Garth had the only set the inn owned.

After some thought, I went out through the kitchen and along the corridor that connected the inn with the outbuildings. In the stable, I asked the ostler, Dorys, where to find Clio's tack. Dorys showed me the harness room where I found the saddle soap and the necessary brushes and rags. I sat down on an upturned bucket in an empty stall to set to work.

The saddle had started to gleam under my ministrations when I heard Casyn calling my name. "In here!" I called back.

He came to the stall.

"How is Siannon?"

"Better," he said. "He'll be fine for tomorrow, if the rain stops. May I talk with you while you work?"

"If you like," I said. He left in search of another bucket. I sat down to re-soap the cloth. I had started on the bridle when Casyn returned. He sat, hands resting on his knees, watching me in silence for a little while.

"I sat by the fire for a long time last night, thinking about Maya and what she and the other exiles want. I thought about what we asked of all of you, and how that has changed what the Empire is. Two hundred and thirty-three years have passed since the last assembly of men and women in the Empire. I think it is time for another."

I stopped rubbing soap into leather to look up, frowning "Another assembly?" I said. "With all of us? Where?"

"Probably the winter camp site," Casyn said in an amused tone. "And no, not quite all of us. The entire population of the Empire was not at the Partition assembly. Men and women were chosen to represent the views of larger groups." He leaned forward, intent on his vision. "Maya has a point. Both men and women have consciously chosen to change the precepts of the Partition agreement. Surely, we must forge a new contract, and what better time than now? For the first time in ten generations, men and women have lived together, worked together, and trained together. Dern, Bren, and I, and for that matter Callan, all think differently of women than our fathers did. Lena, can you say that you see us, men and the Empire itself, in the same way as you did in the spring?"

I shook my head. "No," I said slowly. "I have been thinking about this, a bit, while we have been riding. It seems to me that we—women, I mean—are schooled not to think beyond our village, its needs and customs. There's so much I do not know about the Empire, or even about the next village. Some of it is my own fault. I should have listened more at lessons, but some of it I was never taught."

"I am not much of a scholar," Casyn said, "but I have read what histories there are. The women's villages have become more inward-looking in the past few generations. There used to be, according to the records, more travel between villages, and the guilds met once a year. A trader's guild moved from village to village, bringing goods and news and ideas, and there were travelling musicians."

"What happened?"

"You know what happened. This lesson you did learn, Lena."

The tunnels, I thought. Late springs, early winters, little food, not even enough to provision the men. Only a few children born, because the village could not afford more. "The heavy snows. Of course." He nodded.

"I always thought it was just the north. But the histories say otherwise. That was when the Wall was built to keep the northern people penned in. They were starving and beginning to raid southward."

"How long did the cold last?"

"Maybe thirty years," he said. "Long enough to change how the villages functioned, to make self-sufficiency their first concern. When the weather warmed again, the village councils needed every woman to farm and fish. Travel would have been discouraged as well as, consciously or not, much teaching about the world beyond the village." He stood. "Please keep this to yourself, for now, Lena. We will talk again before our ways part." He smiled down at me as he left, his grave, slow smile. His hair was greyer than it was in the spring. Did Gille miss him? They had partnered only briefly, a month or two, but much longer than the Festival liaisons. *We live apart and die apart*, Casyn had said in the spring, in a voice shaded with regret. I wondered, for the first time, if we had to.

When the bell rang for the noon meal, I had not finished cleaning the tack. After Casyn left I had sat, bridle in hand, trying to make sense of what I had heard in the past day. How could we give Maya and the other exiled women what they wanted, and at the same time shape a new contract between the villages and the military, and maybe even between women and men? Maya's group wanted the old ways. Casyn was thinking of something new.

The rain had stopped. The clouds moved east, and the day brightened. I walked across the wet courtyard. Sari came out of another building. The laundry, I thought, from the smells that came from the opened door, falling into step beside me.

"I have the message for Maya. May I give it to you at the meal?"

"Wait till the end, so as not to have it food-stained." A thought struck me. "Sari, does this have anything to do with Maya's plans for a new village?"

"You know about it! I wasn't sure. Yes, of course it is. The note is just to say that I would like to join them when I am adult and can choose."

"And this would be allowed?"

"Yes, of course," she said impatiently. "I couldn't choose exile because I'm too young. But I would have. I did not want to fight, and I'm glad I did not have to. Fighting is for men."

"I fought."

"Then why are you looking for Maya?" she demanded. "You won't be welcome. I better go," she said in a different tone. "Aasta will need me." She veered off towards the kitchen. I watched her run, trying not to resent the doubts her comment had surfaced. Would Maya even want to see me? I had fought. And killed.

We ate barley soup with goat cheese and bread at the long table. "We can ride tomorrow," Bren announced cheerfully. He had beaten Garth twice at *xache*.

"Will you play with me, this afternoon?" I asked Casyn. I had things I wanted to ask him. He looked surprised but agreed.

When Sari came to clear the table, she brought me the sealed note. I slipped it into the pocket of my trousers and went to the kitchen. "May I have a mug of hot water?" I asked Aasta. "I have a headache and would take some willow bark. I have some in my pack." She poured water from the kettle, giving me the mug without comment. I went down the hall to my room to make my anash. The bitterness, without honey, no longer bothered me. I wondered if I still needed to drink it, and if the irregularity of the hour each day I did drink it would have consequences. I would know in a few days. Beyond that, I refused to think. I took the note from my pocket and put it inside my pack.

I won the toss. We sat alone in the common room. Bren and Garth had gone to see their horses. I made my opening move. Casyn countered. We worked through a standard opening. Casyn knew his game and would beat me, I realized, but no matter.

"Casyn," I said quietly, "At the Partition assembly, what happened to those who did not vote for Partition?"

He slid a piece along the squares. "Some accepted the choice and lived out their lives under the new order."

"And others?"

"Exile from the Empire," he said. "Slavery, for some."

"Where did they go?" Exile from the Empire meant leaving the bounds of the Empire forever. I moved a piece; a bad choice. Casyn took it. "North, or over the mountains. They were given six weeks to get beyond the borders. After that, they would be captured and killed, or enslaved."

"And the men castrated, as Garth would have been?" I asked. I could not help myself.

Casyn put down the taken rider. "Garth was being trained as a medic," he said calmly. "Medics serve in the field and are part of the army. He would not have been castrated. How do you know of this, Lena?" I reddened.

"Dern told you," he surmised.

"We were talking one night about killing, about sending others to kill or be killed," I said. "It was very late, and we had drunk more wine than was wise."

"It is a barbaric practice," Casyn said, with an edge to his voice. I looked up, surprised. "The forces of the Empire accept change very slowly, and with much resistance. The threat of castration overcomes most boys' fears about fighting. That is the argument and the justification. But if one studies the records, for the generations we have kept them, the number of boys who cannot bring themselves to serve in the field has not changed. There are always a few. The refusal to fight has not been bred out of them, which is the real thinking behind the practice."

I moved a *xache* piece almost randomly, not thinking about the game. "Are you speaking for yourself, or as the Emperor's advisor?"

"Both," he said after a moment. "Callan feels as I do, but that cannot be said to anyone, Lena, not even Garth, or Dern, were you to meet up with him again. Our father, who was a brave man and a good soldier, fathered a third son, Colm. It was clear from the earliest days that he would never make a soldier. He is a scholar and a historian. He taught Callan and me what we know of the Empire's history, but he paid a high price." I could hear the bitterness in his voice.

He looked at the board. "We aren't really playing, are we?" he asked. I shook my head. He leaned back in his chair. "Perhaps this invasion by Leste was a blessing," he said. "Perhaps now we have a reason to talk of change."

"Did you talk of this, with Gille?"

"A bit," he said. "It was her idea for me to ride with you, so that we could talk. If you were to choose maybe half-a-dozen women to represent Tirvan at an assembly, Lena, who would you choose? Beyond yourself, and the council, of course."

I considered. "Tali," I said after a moment, "and Dessa. Maybe Kyan. And Casse, for her long experience." I thought a while more. "I would have chosen Siane, too. Her views were shared by only a few others in the village, but they should be heard."

Casyn nodded. "You will be a fine council leader one day, Lena."

"But never a general," I said lightly. He looked at me appraisingly.

"Would you be, if you could?"

I thought of the blood spilling over my hands, and of Tice's body in the willow. I shook my head. "No."

"I would have said the same at eighteen," he said. I wanted to ask him to explain, but he continued on. "When you stop at the inns, after we part, you might plant the thought of an assembly, just a hint, a suggestion made over wine and talk, nothing more. My brother needs to be seen to be serving the wishes of his people, not calling for a new order from the chair of the Emperor." He reached out to move a piece one square forward.

We played out the game, Casyn winning in five moves. I could not find a way to ask him to explain what he had meant about not wanting to be a general. It seemed too private a thing for me to probe. When we had finished playing, I went back to the stable to finish cleaning my tack, and to think. I thought I understood, a little, how Maya had felt in the spring, her world shifting toward an unrecognizable future. The familiar task provided comfort, and I gave myself up to it.

In the late afternoon, the rattle of hooves on the cobblestones broke the stillness. A lone rider came through the archway and dismounted, handing his reins to Dorys. She led the horse, a bay gelding, wet with sweat, into the stable. I went to help her. "Who is it?" I asked, unbuckling the bridle.

"Major Turlo," she said. "He's ridden hard today." She called to her apprentice. "Walk this horse till he cools, then curry him down well. I'll make up a bran mash for him. Keep him away from that water trough," she warned. The girl grinned at her, taking the horse by his bridle.

Turlo, I remembered, had been the soldier sent to Berge. I put my tack away and washed the smell of saddle soap off my hands. Then I crossed the yard.

The day had brightened considerably through the afternoon, and the common room seemed dark. The men stood near the fireplace. As my eyes adjusted to the dimness, I saw that the newcomer had the reddest hair and beard I had ever seen. I stopped, uncertain. Red hair belonged north of the wall. I remembered what Casse had said about the raids, and the rapes. I stepped forward.

"Lena," Casyn said, "this is Major Turlo. Lena was a Cohort-Leader and instrumental in winning the battle at Tirvan."

Turlo shook my hand. Younger than Bren and Casyn, he had bright blue eyes. "Good for you, lass," he said. "I wouldn't have wanted to be on the wrong side of the women of Berge. They fought well—only lost four, and the whole thing was over in a few hours."

"We lost four, too, but it took nearly three days to finish it. And without Garth, I am not sure what we would have done."

Turlo looked from me to Garth. "There's a story here. Let's have some wine and hear it." He strode over to the kitchen door. "Aasta," he called, "some wine, if you will, and five cups. And something to tide us over till supper. I've been riding since before dawn, and you don't want me keeling over on your hearth." I laughed. I liked this man. He seemed genuinely interested in what had happened at Tirvan, unlike Bren.

We arranged ourselves in chairs near the fireplace. "The invaders came at dawn," I started, "although we'd seen the sails the day before and were ready. All our cohorts lay in wait, hidden, and when the Lestians landed we let them move up into the village before we began the defence." Aasta came out with a tray bearing wine and small savouries. She put the tray down on the table, but she did not leave again, seating herself on a stool to the left of the hearth. I continued. Turlo listened without comment until I described recognizing Garth. He whistled, low and long.

"Luck was with you, Garth," he said, reaching for the wine flask. "Go on," he said to me. I took a sip of my wine before continuing on. I did not look at the men, but stared into the flames, trying to remember the order and the details of those hours and days. I told of the search for the Lestians, of Tice's death, of the raid at the burying.

"When Pel was taken, we decided we had no choice but to ask Garth to rescue him. Only he could get close to Cael, so we cut his chains to make it look as if he had escaped. He brought Pel home safely. And that is all the story I have to tell." Without thinking, I finished with the words Xani or Gille used when they told the stories of our history.

Aasta stirred. "A fine story," she said. "Brave women, brave men, and brave deeds. You're a rare storyteller. I'd hear that again, given a chance. Now I'd best look at the stew." She pushed herself up, to disappear into the kitchen.

Turlo looked at me thoughtfully. "It is a good story, and you did tell it well. Someone should write it down, though. Casyn, tell it to Colm when you get to the winter camp. He'll do it properly."

Casyn stretched. "I will. But Lena, you should find ink and paper to record it, too. Whatever I tell Colm will be my version of your story, and not the same. To be accurate, history needs many voices. Or so my brother would tell me."

Could history ever be accurate? I wondered, raising my wine to my lips. All the talking had dried my throat. Who decided which stories were told?

In the morning, Turlo announced he would ride with us. Dorys had come in at first light to tell him his bay needed to rest. "Two, three days, at least," she had said.

"Well, he'll get more than that," Turlo said, unperturbed. "I'll leave him here for you to doctor, Dorys, and take another. He's not mine, as it happens. My poor old fellow was a casualty at Berge, took an arrow in the throat. The bay's a post horse from the northern inn, so it's fair exchange."

The thought of his company pleased me, but Bren also rode with us, and that made me uncomfortable. He remained distant and humourless, and I could not forget his challenge to Garth that first night. We said our farewells to the inn-folk and mounted in the cobbled courtyard. Clio whickered at the post horse, a sturdy chestnut. "Is yon a Han pony?" Dorys asked, pointing her chin towards Clio. I nodded. "So is this one," she said. "Seems they know each other." The two horses blew gently at each other. We rode out of the courtyard and back onto the road.

A fair day had dawned, and the clear sky was dotted with a few small clouds. The officers rode abreast, with Garth and me following. Turlo wore a quiver and carried a short bow, a hunting bow, for small game or birds. Odd, I thought, for an officer.

As the sun rose higher, the air warmed. We stopped at a stream to let the horses drink, stripping off outer tunics and cloaks. I stretched. "Why do you carry a bird bow?" I asked Turlo.

"To hunt," he said simply. "I've a taste for wild meat, and if I can get a brace of hare, or grouse, well, that's a fine meal."

"Turlo," Bren said, surprising me, "is barely civilised. Were he not riding with us, he would probably forgo the inns entirely, except to check for messages and buy wine, to spend his nights camped under a tree, roasting rabbit over a fire and singing barbaric northern ballads to the moon."

Turlo grinned. "Aye, I would," he agreed. "And glad you've both been, a time or two, of my prowess with bow and arrow. Shall I tell the young folk?"

For the next hour he told us detailed, and, I suspected, highly exaggerated, stories of hunt parties that would have failed and Wall garrisons that would have starved, without his hunting skills. He must have spent much of his service on the Wall. His stories made me laugh, and I welcomed the distraction.

We halted at noon at a rocky hillside scattered with pines and the scrubby oak of the highlands, to eat cold meat and apples before stretching out in the shade. The horses grazed the sparse grass between the trees. A jay called, then another, a harsh sound. Turlo raised himself on one elbow, raising a hand for silence. The jay called again. Turlo pointed, slowly. On the rocks above us, a wildcat sat, gazing down at us with its deep golden, unblinking eyes. The tip of its tail moved slightly. "A young one," Turlo whispered, "this spring's kitten. Smelt our meat, most likely." He sat up suddenly, and the cat vanished. "Don't want it thinking man and food go together."

"I've never seen one before."

"Nor I," murmured Bren.

"I have," Garth said, "before my father came for me. I was climbing in the hills above Tirvan, and I came across a litter. Their eyes were barely opened. The female must have brought them out for some sun. She snarled at me, and the kittens fled, but, oh, I wanted one. I planned to go back to capture one, but then it was Festival and the end of Tirvan for me."

"Just as well," Turlo said. "They're not to be tamed, and the female would have gone for your face. But I know how you felt. I had the same plans until my mother caught me dragging a fishing net into the hills and gave me a scolding I've never forgotten. 'Wild things are meant to be wild,' she said. 'You can't change their nature. If you want a pet, there's plenty of barn kittens.' She said a wild thing taken as a babe is never truly tame but can never be truly wild again either. It will only be a shadow of what it should be. I never tried to tame anything again."

"It would do a lot of men good to learn that lesson," Casyn said. He looked at the sun. "We should ride."

In the afternoon, the men's talk turned to war. I lagged behind. The land had changed again. Elm and ash stood among the oak, their leaves fading from green to yellow and brown. My hands rested on Clio's withers, the reins loose between them. Clio followed the horses ahead of her, needing no guidance from me. I thought about what Turlo had said, about not trying to tame something wild. The Empire had forced Garth to go against his nature. Turlo too might have been meant to roam the bogs and hills of the borderlands, unconstrained by the uniform of the Empire. Yet he seemed content, even happy. How could that be?

We rode south, bypassing inns except to water the horses and have a meal for ourselves, making camp instead. Turlo proved as adept with his hunting bow as he had claimed, so we ate well those nights, roasting rabbit or partridge over the fire. On the road, I often rode slightly apart while the men talked of war, strategies and mistakes. Strategy had interested me only when it concerned Tirvan and its defence.

I thought often of Maya. I envisioned her rapturous at our reunion, begging my forgiveness. I saw her on the other side of the Empire, writing letters that reached me twice a year, and always six months late. I saw myself working at the closest inn or fishing port, riding up occasionally to meet her outside the village. I thought of many ways we could wait out the three years of her exile from Tirvan. Very occasionally, I let myself think about what life might be like, without her, forever.

Whenever that thought intruded, I purposely began to think of Casyn's proposal for a new assembly. I thought again about whom I would choose to represent Tirvan, weighing the strengths of Tirvan's women in my mind. Casse would speak her mind, calling on long experience, but could she make such a journey? Would Dessa consider coming now, if it meant leaving Lara? The assembly would have to be in the summer, so the village delegations could camp on the way because the inns could not cope with large numbers. In this way, the miles passed.

About mid-morning of the next day, Casyn dropped back to ride with me. He reined Siannon in until we rode at a slow walk. The others pulled ahead.

"What is it?'

"Bren makes you uncomfortable."

"Yes," I said. "I don't think he likes me being here."

"Bren is never easy among women," Casyn said. "His life is soldiery, as is true of all of us, but for him it is everything. He simply does not know how to talk to you."

"I don't fit."

"Exactly," Casyn said. "Bren is more rigid in his thinking than your Maya,

Lena, but he is a good soldier and a fine strategist. His campaigns are planned meticulously, down to the last horseshoe nail needed. He has taught us all how important details can be."

"And I am not one of those details."

"Not one he has ever had to consider before," Casyn said with a chuckle. "He helped plan the invasion of Leste and then went north to manage the Wall garrisons. Their numbers were down, and he was the best man to organize the defence there. He opposed the involvement of the women's villages because he could not understand how it might work."

"Does he now?"

"I think he is beginning to," Casyn said. "But there is something more."

I eyed him curiously.

"His discomfort with women extends to Festival," Casyn said. "He cannot make himself understood or attractive to women. Twenty years ago, I convinced him to go to Tirvan for Festival. He met a woman he wanted to know better, but it didn't work out. Her attention was given already to another man."

"Because I am from Tirvan, he is even more uncomfortable."

"Yes."

"Do you know who she was?"

"No," Casyn answered. "He never told me."

I looked forward to where Garth rode between Turlo and Bren. "I wish you'd told me this days ago."

"I should have," Casyn said. "I thought you both might relax just by riding together."

"We've barely spoken, and I've been riding behind."

"That's why I told you," he said.

I nodded. "I'll try to join in."

At our mid-day break, Turlo offered to teach Garth to use the hunting bow. The day had turned glorious, the sky a clear blue with a light breeze. Garth accepted with alacrity.

"I'll come to watch," Bren said, standing. Garth nodded a welcome. He clearly liked Bren. After my talk with Casyn, I could see his distant manner in a new light. I no longer felt rejected by him, but I remained ambivalent.

"And you, Lena?" Turlo offered. I shook my head. My monthly bleeding had begun, and a general lassitude had settled over me. I stretched out in the warmth, drowsing as the hunters went off over a ridge. After a while, I stirred to see Casyn sitting on a nearby rock, a mug of tea in his hands. I rolled over, sitting up.

"I thought you had gone hunting," I said.

"Four is too many."

"May I ask something? About Turlo?"

"Bren this morning, Turlo now?" he teased.

"It seems to me that Turlo is much like Garth. He is happier hunting, or wandering the wilds, than anything else, yet he holds a commission and serves the Empire." I stopped, not sure how to continue.

"You are wondering why Turlo became an officer while Garth chose to desert," he said gently. "There is no easy answer to that. Turlo, for all his love of the wild, came willingly. His father was on Wall duty, a scout, and his tales of that life probably had the boy enthralled. Also, the Wall is a place where Turlo's skills and interests are needed and encouraged. By the time he came to the cadet camps, he was already a talented borders scout. But Turlo is also a born leader. He understands men much as he understands animals, instinctively, and we fostered that in him. Garth is a different man, and his opportunities were different. If Mar had been in a borders regiment, then, yes, perhaps he would have reconciled to the army, but perhaps not. I doubt that Garth will ever be truly happy leading men, but I think he will teach boys with care and discipline and with a greater sensitivity than he received." He sighed. "I am not sure I have answered your question, Lena, but it is difficult to talk about what might have been when we are speaking of men. I prefer analysing tactics."

"I've noticed," I said drily. "Although you're not quite as bad as Bren." He laughed. "I still wish things had been different for Garth."

"And for yourself, and for Maya," he said gently. "As I do. But we cannot shape the circumstances to fit our lives, only our lives to fit the circumstances. What defines us, as men and women, is how we respond to those circumstances. Courage comes in many forms, Lena, and I think perhaps Garth, in trying to reconcile his nature to the expectations of the Empire—and ultimately his own expectations of himself—is more courageous than Turlo."

A gentle breeze rattled the dry leaves. I could hear the horses cropping grass. Casyn sipped his tea. I lay back again in the sun. "When do our roads part?" I asked.

"Two days from now. About midmorning on the second day, we'll come to a track that runs south-easterly, while this road swings to the west. We'll say our farewells there. The easterly track will bring us to the winter camp more quickly than the southern. Your errand takes you south, and neither should be delayed."

I nodded. I would miss him, but part of me wanted to be alone with Garth again, to talk to him of Maya and the future, and to camp under the trees and moon. I heard voices; looking up, I saw the men climbing over the ridge, rabbits swinging from their hands. Garth was grinning. A light breeze blew, his hair back across his forehead as he held up his brace. "Dinner tonight," he said. He looked relaxed, his eyes lit up with pride in this new skill.

"If we can buy some root vegetables, pot herbs, and perhaps a loaf of bread at the next inn," I said, "I'll stew those rabbits tonight, as a change from roasting them." This brought appreciative noises from Turlo, but then, anything to do with food usually did. We doused and scattered the fire, re-bridled the horses and tightened the girths before mounting, turning south again into the red-gold afternoon.

Two days later, in mid-morning, we rode up from the bowl of a grassy valley between two ridges of land. We urged the horses up to the crest. As Clio came abreast of the larger horses, I reined her to a stop to look out. I gasped.

Beyond this final ridge, the land fell away quickly in a series of declining hills. A sea of grass extended far beyond sight toward the horizon. From this height, we could see the roll of the land and the sweep and ripple of the pale, sere grasses. The sky soared above us, and the boundary between land and air looked like a hazy blur on the distant edge of vision. As I gazed at the space and enormity of the grasslands, an unrealized tension eased. I felt an inner expansion, the loosening of constraint. I could live down there, I thought, suddenly, fiercely, wanting it. I could lose myself in that land, below that sky, in all that emptiness.

"I had no idea," I said. "Rasa and Dian tried to describe it, but I didn't understand the immensity. It looks as if the grasslands go on forever."

"Not forever," Bren said. "Eventually, the land begins to change again, sloping down to the fertile fields of the south."

We sat our horses, looking down at the rippling grasses. A long-winged hawk hunted over the plain. I began to sort out features—clumps of trees in valleys, the occasional glint of a stream. The road itself stood out clearly, winding over hills and into valleys until it disappeared into the haze on the horizon. Another track branched off from it toward the east.

"The eastern road," Casyn said, following my gaze. "Let's ride."

A series of switchbacks led us gently down into the grasslands. We wound back and forth at a walk, reins loose, letting the horses choose the pace. The sun rose higher in the sky. Turlo and Garth talked about the game to be found on the grasslands and the best places and times to hunt. The sea of grass grew closer until we rode into it, the wave and ripple of the grasses in the breeze creating a constant susurration like waves on a beach. Small birds trilled among the grasses, darting rapidly from one clump to another or flashing high into the sky. When the sun had nearly reached its zenith, we came to the place where the roads diverged.

Just to the north and east of the fork, a small stream running out of the hills had been channelled into drinking basins. A rough ring of small boulders and logs marked the common resting point. We dismounted, removed bridles, let the horses drink from the lower pool, then hobbled them for grazing. Turlo built a fire. We made tea and ate cheese and bread.

Casyn stood, brushing the crumbs from his legs. After looking to me for permission, he pulled the map from my saddlebag to spread it on a flat piece of ground, weighing the corners with small stones. He beckoned us over. "We are here," he said, pointing. He traced the line of the southerly road. "There's an inn here, at the river. You could reach it by nightfall. Or there is a good camp some miles before that, in a stand of trees by a stream, just here." He pulled a blackened twig from the fire, making a mark on the map. "In another seven or eight days of easy riding, you'll reach Karst. Try not to push the horses. They—and you—will need to drink more often through the grasslands. The air is dry here. Groom them well at night." He stood, refolding the map before handing it to me. "It's time."

We smothered the fire and prepared the horses. I filled water skins. We had divided the food and camp gear that morning. When I handed the skins to the men, Turlo grinned at me.

"You'll do fine, lassie," he said. His mood buoyed me, and I grinned back.

"The evenings will be quieter," I said. "Don't drive the others mad with your stories."

Turlo laughed. "They've heard them all, and told them all, so many times, they can't tell my lies from theirs." He held out a hand, suddenly serious. "Go safely, Lena," I clasped it in the soldier's grip. He turned to Garth while I shook hands with Bren. I held out my hand to Casyn. He took it, holding it between both of his.

"Go safely. I will see you again."

"Go safely, Casyn." I had too much to say, and to ask, and time had run out. I turned away, willing my eyes dry, and mounted. Garth saluted Turlo and Bren, then Casyn, before mounting Tasque. I turned Clio's head to the south, raising a hand in farewell.

Clio's ears pricked and her stride lengthened as we rode south. I reined her in, waiting for Garth to come abreast of me on the road. "Clio wants to run."

"She must have memories of running free in the grasslands," Garth replied. "Still, why not?" We gave the horses their heads, pounding along the road. I bent low over my mare's neck, urging her on, feeling my own spirit rise with hers. I laughed with the sheer joy of life and sunshine and freedom.

We rode through the afternoon, watering the horses frequently. The sky soared above us, the blue unbroken save for a few small clouds in the west. We scared up grouse and hare, and once, cresting a small rise, we saw a herd of deer far in the distance. Garth sat his horse easily, relaxed and confident. He turned to say something and caught my eyes on him. He smiled.

"Camp tonight or the inn?"

I smiled back. "Camp."

We reached the campsite an hour before sunset. A stream ran beside a stand of trees under a rocky outcropping, providing a windbreak. We unsaddled and groomed the horses thoroughly, washing the dust from their eyes and nostrils. The western sky glowed red and orange and pink by the time we finished. I ran a hand through my hair. "I need a wash," I said. The shallow stream did not allow for swimming, but I stripped to wade in. Cold water came up to my knees. I dug my toes into the sandy bottom. Kneeling, I used my hands to cup water up and over my head, washing the dust from my hair and body. I felt Garth behind me. He poured water from his hands along my back. I gasped at the cold.

As his hands left my back, the gasp became a moan. I turned to him. We kissed with increasing need until Garth broke away, taking my hand.

"I built a fire and spread the blankets. Let's get warm." He led me to the fire, and we made love with urgency and passion under the cobalt sky.

Later we ate more cheese and dried fruits and bread. The horses rested at the edge of the trees, standing head to tail and slouching on three legs. Stars fogged the sky. I lay back, looking for the constellations I knew. I found the hunter with his dogs, and the bears, and from there the north star. I could follow it home to Tirvan, I thought, if Tirvan is still home.

I propped myself up on one elbow. "Did Casyn say anything more to you about what will happen now?"

"I know my orders. Casyn is going to rejoin the Emperor in a little while, and there will a meeting of the senior officers. Why?" He reached forward to add a log to the fire. "Did he say something to you?"

"In a way. Garth, what if there were another, honourable, thing for you to do, other than the army? What if you could build roads or buildings, or trade, not as part of the army but as a free man, sanctioned by the Empire. Would you do it?"

He considered. "Not now," he answered finally. "I think I see a place for me, a way I can serve that I can live with, perhaps even be proud of. But if another way had been possible, and had been offered, yes, I'd have taken it. What are you thinking of?"

I hesitated. If Casyn had not told him of my task, to incite the women of the Empire to demand a new assembly, should I? "If Maya and her group can become a new guild, petition for a new village, with different rules from the rest of Tirvan, then why can't there be an equivalent guild of men, bound by different rules but still legitimate under the Empire? At twelve, you choose— land or sea. Why isn't there a choice to leave honourably and openly, to serve the Empire in a different way? You ran, Garth. You risked your life rather than submit to that choice. Others submit to worse."

He looked away. "I didn't know you knew about that," he said eventually. "But that is the law. The Empire won't change it because they need to breed men who will fight."

I shook my head impatiently. "This Emperor has already changed the rules. You are proof of that. We aren't horses, bred for the cart or the saddle, for strength or speed. We are human and capable of thought and choice and change. The rules of Partition, determining the fate of deserters, or at least some deserters, have been overturned. Surely this is the time to change other rules, too?" I took a breath. "What choices do you want for your son?"

The firelight shadowed his eyes. "More than I had," he said quietly. "I never planned to father sons for the Empire's army. I was to marry a trader's daughter, on Leste, and father sons for the boats and the trade."

"Maya swore she would give no sons to the regiments, either. But Valle is alive, and he's nearly three. Today you ride to claim him. In four years, you will ride to Karst again to take him to his place as a cadet."

He made an impatient gesture with his hand. "That's the way of our world." He stood, looking down at me. "Would you bear my child, knowing, if it were a son, that his future was pre-ordained?"

I had thought about this, riding the southward road. I shook my head. "Not if there are no choices for the child beyond what is circumscribed." In the flicker of the firelight, he smiled bitterly. He touched my hair.

"I need to think. I'll be by the stream." I watched him walk into the darkness, toward the sound of the running water. An owl called. In the clear, cold sky above me, the hunter followed his course, fixed, unchanging, with his dogs at heel.

CHAPTER SEVENTEEN

CLOUDS HAD BLOWN IN OVERNIGHT. They were not yet threatening rain, but by evening I guessed we would be glad of an inn's roof above us. Garth looked tired. I wondered when he had returned to the fire to sleep. We ate without referring to last night's conversation. I doused the fire and rolled up the bedding while Garth tacked up the horses. When our eyes met, he did not look away, but he did not smile.

We rode at a walk, letting the horses warm their muscles. The grasslands stretched ahead of us, undulating in broad swells of land bisected occasionally by small streams. Grouse foraged at the side of the road, sometimes taking to wing at our approach but more often scuttling into the longer grasses, which moved constantly, a soft background rustle.

"I thought about what you said, last night," Garth said, after we had ridden for half an hour. "Maybe I should leave Valle where he is. Perhaps the life of slave is better. He would be safe and fed, and if he's capable, he could rise high. Why should I give him to the Empire?"

"Leave him in slavery?" I said, shocked. "That gives him no choice at all."

"He has none now! Neither of us do. I go to Karst and say, 'This is my son. I acknowledge him. In four years, I will come back to take him away to learn to be a soldier.' Why isn't that slavery, too?"

I recalled Kolmas's words in response to Casyn's offer: *This is only another sort of slavery.*

"It would disrupt nothing to leave him alone. No one has prepared him for me. His life will just go on as it is now."

"He will be named fatherless, unwanted. You can't do that to him, Garth. Like it or not, he is your responsibility. Or are you running away again?"

Garth's face blanched, and I wished the words unsaid. He reined his horse in. I swung Clio around to look at him.

"Go away," he said, his jaw clenched. A chasm opened inside me.

"Garth—"

"Go!"

I closed my eyes for a moment then turned Clio south. I dared not look back, but after a few minutes, I could hear Tasque's hooves on the road behind us. How could I have said that? Garth had no inkling that the Emperor might change the laws. I had to tell him. He had risked his life for the Empire, in secrecy and silence, these last years. Gradually, I slowed Clio. When I could hear Tasque close behind me, I stopped.

"Garth," I said quietly. "I was wrong to say what I did. I have something to tell you. Will you listen?"

He looked grim, but he nodded.

"I have a task on this road, beyond seeking Maya. Casyn charged me with speaking privately to the girls and women of the inns to plant the thought of a new assembly, one at which a new set of laws, for all the Empire's men and women, would be written."

His eyes narrowed. "The Emperor wants this?" he demanded. "Casyn told you this?"

"Not exactly," I admitted. Clio shifted under me, feeling my tension and wanting to move. "But he did say the Emperor wants a new assembly, to make a new agreement between women and men. I have been instructed to plant the idea at each inn we pass, so that it arises from the villages and the inns, and not from Callan." A corn bunting called, clear and sharp, from atop a swaying stem. Tasque snorted.

Garth stared at the horizon. "He must have his own agenda. Did Casyn say what it is?"

I hesitated. "He alluded to it," I said finally. "But he made me swear I would tell no one." I met his eyes. The anger had vanished, but wariness lingered. "I will tell you, if you want." I felt my heart beat.

"No," he said after a moment's pause. "Keep your word, Lena. I have trusted this Emperor, or his proxies, for some years now. I'll trust you, too."

"I don't know the Emperor, but I trust Casyn."

"As do I," Garth said. He half-smiled. "They say that the Emperor can hold a battlefield in his mind, each dip of land, each outcrop, each copse, and see how the battle will go, before it is fought. He chooses his strategy and deployment based on this picture in his mind, a picture that changes with season and weather, or time of day, and yet he always knows what will happen."

"I would like to meet him, some day."

"Perhaps you will," Garth said, glancing at the sun. "We should ride. Karst is still some days ahead."

We rode on. Garth's reaction, his instant suspicion of the Emperor's motives, surprised me. His years of keeping secrets, of twisting the truth, had influenced how he saw the world. Something about our conversation niggled at me, a vague disquiet.

The sun rose higher, a pale disc behind the clouds bright and warm enough to burn the mist away from stream valleys and bring the first of the hawks up into the sky, hunting effortlessly over the plain. The clop of our horses' hooves accompanied the ripple of the wind and the faint, high scream of the hawk. At mid-morning, I heard the clink of metal and the murmur of women's voices from the inn.

Unlike the others we had passed, this inn was a wooden structure, long and low, with outbuildings roofed with turf. Stone formed the foundation, but above that, broad wooden planks, overlapping, comprised the unpainted and weathered walls. Behind the inn and its outbuildings, the post horses and some smaller horses, like my Clio, grazed, sharing the grass with a herd of goats.

One of the inn's horses caught our scent and whinnied a greeting or a challenge, wheeling to crowd against the fence closest to the road. Tasque returned the call. A woman stepped from an outbuilding, raising a hand in greeting. We rode into the yard. Chickens pecked in the dust. "Welcome," she said.

We dismounted. "Lena of Tirvan,' I said. Her eyes narrowed, but she said nothing.

"Garth, Watch-Commander of *Skua*."

The woman was in early middle age and stocky, with short hair and fine wrinkles around her eyes. She nodded. "I'm Zilde, the inn-keeper. There's feed and water in the stables for your horses, or a spare paddock if you want to turn them out. I'm afraid there's no one to take them for you. My girls have gone, leaving only myself, my mother, and my aunt, and they are too old to handle horses. Are you staying?"

I shook my head. "No. But the horses could use grain, if you have it, and if you have bread to spare, I'll buy some."

"There's bread," she said, "fresh-baked, and grain in the bin. Come in when you're ready." With a lift of her chin, she indicated the door into the common room of the inn. We led the horses over the yard and into the dim, cool stable where we stripped off their harnesses and found grain and water. As we worked, I considered Zilde's reaction when I mentioned Tirvan.

"I wonder if her girls chose exile." I said, half to myself.

"We can't exactly ask," Garth answered. "Will you do what Casyn asked of you?"

"I'm not sure," I said.

When we had seen to the horses, we crossed the yard to the common room door. We took seats at a table, and Zilde brought a jug of steaming liquid and mugs on a tray. She put the tray down on the table, pouring a dark, malty drink into the mugs. An older woman carried in a plate of bread rolls with hands twisted and swollen with the joint-ill. No wonder we had to see to our horses ourselves, I thought. A second woman came out with butter and a fruit preserve. "My mother, and my aunt," Zilde said. We introduced ourselves. Again, I saw a fleeting reaction to the mention of Tirvan.

We ate. The bread was still slightly warm, melting the butter and softening the tangy fruit preserve. Quince, I thought. The drink had a grain base, and Zilde, pouring herself a mug too, added a chunk of butter to it. "Where are you headed?" she asked.

"Karst," I said. "Garth goes to see his son before rejoining his regiment, and I have news to bear to the village." Zilde visibly relaxed at my answer.

"I thought, as you are from Tirvan, you might be going to join that Maya," she said. "She a friend of yours?"

"Yes," I said neutrally. "But I haven't heard much of her since she left, just some stories at other inns about a group of exiles."

Zilde snorted. "Stories is right. Stories about petitioning the Emperor for a new village for those what didn't fight. Or who wouldn't have if they'd been old enough to choose. My own daughters have gone off to find her, to join this group. They slipped off one night with their ponies, and me with no one to send after them. As if a bunch of stripling girls can build a new village, supposing the Emperor was foolish enough to grant the petition."

"Do you think he might?" Garth asked.

"How should I know?" Zilde retorted. "What do I know of the Emperor? You'd know more than me." She eyed him. "Well?"

Garth shook his head. "I've been on frontier duty for many years."

Zilde sipped her drink. "An Emperor who would ask women to fight could do anything," she stated finally. The two older women nodded in agreement.

"Maybe Maya's right to ask for change. Maybe we all should. The old rules have been broken. Maybe it's time to make new ones." I tried to keep my voice level, almost disinterested, a tired traveller just passing the time in an inn. Zilde shook her head.

"I always heard those long winters bred strange talk in the north," she said. She looked at me appraisingly. Suddenly her face softened slightly. "Did you fight?" I nodded. "Kill anyone?" I nodded again. She held my gaze. "Then I shouldn't be judging." She stood up. "I'll get that bread for you."

One of the older women bent to pick up the tray. "I liked the old rules," she said.

They left us to finish the meal. Garth looked at me quizzically. I shrugged. I had done what Casyn had asked.

We let the horses rest for another half hour while we drank second mugs of the grain drink. Garth wandered around the common room. I sat, watching him. His hair had grown out a bit, and he needed a shave. I no longer saw Maya as easily in his features. Finally, he swallowed the last of his drink. "Ready?" In answer, I put my own mug down, and we went back out into the day.

As we saddled the horses in the yard, Zilde came out, blinking in the light. "Will you take a message for me to the inns and villages? Tell them I've a place for an apprentice or two."

"Of course," I said, paying her for my meal.

She nodded her thanks. "Good luck on the road." She lifted a hand in farewell as we swung into the saddles and turned the horses. We scattered chickens and dust as we trotted through the gates and onto the road. The horses, rested and grain fed, wanted to run, but I held Clio back.

"Garth," I said, as soon as we had ridden out of earshot of the inn, "do you think Maya encouraged her girls to leave?"

He reined Tasque in to walk beside me. "No," he said, after some consideration. "She wouldn't. The girls were too young."

We rode on in silence, but the thought nagged at me. Garth had told me what he thought I needed to hear. He didn't know Maya. But did I?

The road ran straight south. From the tops of the undulating rises in the land, we could see it gleaming in the winter sun. The days grew steadily shorter until we had a brief eight hours of light in which to ride each day. We stopped at the inns to buy bread or cheese or just to pass on Zilde's request. This made it easier to bring the talk around to Maya and her dreams, and from there to the suggestion of change for us all, since someone always asked what had happened to Zilde's daughters. On the road, and sometimes in the middle of the night, my thoughts returned to the question I had asked Garth. Had Maya encouraged the girls to leave?

Late on the afternoon of the sixth day, the clouds that had been building all day released a cold, slicing rain with ice in it. From the last small rise in the land, we saw the smoke of an inn, two miles or so distant. We reined the horses off the icy stones of the road into the grass, riding into the teeth of the wind. By the time we reached the inn, ice coated the horses' manes and our hats, and our bodies shook with cold.

In the yard, I slid off Clio, leading her, on numb feet, through the wide door into the barn, not waiting for the innkeeper or the ostler. Garth followed behind me. I stripped off my sodden gloves and stuffed them into the pockets of my coat, and with stiff fingers worked at the girth. The leather had tightened with the damp, and my fingers stung. I felt helpless, frustrated, and suddenly tired of the road and strange inns and strange people. I missed Casyn. I felt the hot sting of tears behind my eyes. I took a deep breath, leaning my head against Clio's warm neck, ignoring the wet, rubbing my hands together.

"I'll take her," a voice said behind me, "and the gelding. You two get into the inn." I turned to face a woman of about my age. "Go," she said. "I'll take good care of them,"

I handed her the reins. "Thanks," I tried to say, but it came out as a croak. "She's Clio," I managed. The woman nodded.

"Tasque," I heard Garth say behind me. I saw surprise cross her face, and she looked at the grey more closely in the dim light.

"So he is," she said softly. She looked at Garth. "And why you have Captain Dern's horse is a story for the hearthside, when you're warm and have food and drink inside you. Go. I want to hear this story sooner rather than later!"

We stepped out of the doorway into a covered walk. The stable block attached at right angles to another block, which in turn ran at a right angle into the inn itself, creating a three-sided structure surrounding the yard. The covered walk ran along the fronts of all three buildings, the angled roof attached directly to the structure and supported by beams every eight feet or so. I walked gratefully along the dry cobbles, sheltered from the wind.

Inside, apprentices showed us to rooms, bringing hot water and hot drinks. I collapsed on the bed, not caring that I made the quilt wet. I held the mug of tea in my hands letting the warmth seep through. I want to go home, I thought. I want the baths, and the sea, and to be alone.

Some time later, washed and warmed and in dry clothes, I came down to the common room where a fire burned in the hearth. Rain slashed at the windows.

Two women playing a game—not xache—at the fireside looked up as I came towards the fire. "A nasty day," one said. "I'm Karlii, and this is Sherron. We're from Ballin." Karlii looked about my age, dark and not tall. Sherron bore her a strong resemblance: a sister, or cousin.

"Lena from Tirvan, heading for Karst." I included my destination to try to head off the now-usual reaction to the mention of my village. I didn't want to talk about Maya. Sherron's face lit up.

"I have a sister in Karst. She went to learn to be a wine-maker. Will you pass my greetings on to Hilar of Ballin, and tell her that I am well, and Karlii, and that we ride to Han?"

"I will," I said, "if you will take my greetings to Han, to Grainne of Tirvan, who travelled there after the fighting, and to Rasa and Dian. Tell them I am well, and that Clio is as good a horse as they promised. What takes you there?"

"Sad news. The women who rode to assist us were both killed in the fighting."

I nodded, feeling a pang of grief for Rasa and Dian. "I ride for the same reason," I said. "Our potter was from Karst. She was killed under my command." No one spoke.

Finally, Sherron shook her head. "There must be many of us on the roads, riding to bring sorrow."

"Or reassurance," Karlii said. "We've met one or two women who were going home to see how their families fared, and to show that they were unharmed. We carry messages of safety, too, to send north. We should resurrect the old messenger's guild," she said, smiling, but not, I thought, entirely in jest.

"You like the road?"

"I like not herding cows," Karlii said, making a face.

Sherron laughed. "And I like not making cheese, at least for a while," she said. "That's what we do in Ballin: herd cows, breed cows, milk cows, and make cheese and butter to send to Casilla. I'm a cheese-maker, and generally I like doing so. Karlii chose to be with the animals. The dairy was too confining for her." She smiled at Karlii.

"I thought about apprenticing to the herds and hunt," I said, "but for us it's mostly sheep, and days up on the hills watching for foxes and eagles after the lambs. I liked that part, but I hate sheep, so I apprenticed to the boats instead and learned to fish."

"Boats!" Karlii said. "On the sea?"

I nodded.

"I've never seen the sea," she said longingly.

"I had never seen the grasslands, nor the grape fields, nor Casilla. But I will."

Sherron pushed the draughts board to one side, pointing to the wooden settle. "Shall we sit?" She took a pewter mug from the mantle behind her, pouring me a drink from the jug on the table. I sipped: ale, rich and smooth.

"Thank you." I sat on the bench with one leg tucked under me.

"I have been to Casilla," Sherron said, "to sell cheeses. It's a day's travel from Ballin in the cart. I'm not a good trader, so I only went the once. It was an adventure for a young apprentice, I tell you, travelling the roads, staying at an inn, going to the market. I'd never seen so many people, women and men, in one place."

"Women and men?" I asked. "Was it Festival?"

Sherron shook her head. "No. Casilla is divided into two parts: the women's town and the Empire's quays and barracks and training grounds. The market is in the women's town, but the quartermasters and cooks from the barracks come to buy provisions and supplies. They purchased most of our hard cheeses."

"In Tirvan, we saw men only at Festival, but I remember, Tice—our potter from Karst—saying that they traded regularly with the retirement farms."

"You had men living with you in your village all this past summer, didn't you?"

"Yes. And I travelled south with men. But once the messages have been carried, we will return home. The men are even now returning to their regiments and companies. I have wondered whether life would return to normal."

"I don't want it to," Karlii said passionately. "No one asks each generation if they want to live by the rules of Partition. We must abide by the rules or leave. But even in leaving, we're only trading one village for another, and the rules stay the same. What if I want only to live with one man and bear his children and keep both sons and daughters by my side to raise?" In the firelight, I could see the glint of tears in her eyes. From behind the kitchen door, I heard Garth's voice, and then a woman's sudden laugh.

"My partner chose exile," I said, suddenly irritated, "because she did not want change. To her, the rules were sacred, and in choosing to fight, our village betrayed her. How can we make a world where both you and she are satisfied?"

"I doubt we can," Sherron said. Karlii said nothing. I looked from one to the other.

"But we must try." I took a deep swallow of the ale. "Perhaps," I said quietly, "it's time for a new assembly." Karlii's eyes glinted again in the firelight, but now it was with challenge and interest. "Take that thought north with you," I said, "to Han, and the inns along the way. Speak it quietly and only to women. If enough of us want it, the Emperor must listen."

"Do you really think it's possible?" Karlii asked, hope flickering in her eyes.

"I do," I said, realizing I meant it. "But be subtle, Karlii. Not all women agree." She nodded thoughtfully. "I believe that."

The next morning dawned sunny, and the ice and snow melted before we had finished breakfast. Sherrin gave me a letter for her sister. I tucked it into

MARIAN L THORPE   183

my saddlebag then we walked out to the stable together. I introduced them to
Garth, who had brought Tasque out onto the cobble to saddle. I tacked up Clio
while Sherrin and Karlii did the same with their ponies. The four of us rode out
of the courtyard together before taking our leave.

Sherrin turned her pony's head north. "Good luck," she said. "Don't forget
that letter."

"I won't. Be careful on the road."

Garth raised a hand in salute, and we turned south.

"Good company?" Garth asked. He had not joined us in the common room.

"They ride to Han, with the same sort of news as I carry to Karst—two dead."

"A difficult duty," he acknowledged. We rode slowly, letting the horses'
muscles warm.

"They will speak of a new assembly on their ride north."

"I left you alone last night, in part, because your conversation looked fruitful.
My presence would have ended any discussion along those lines."

"What were the other reasons?"

"I thought it would look wrong. I need to behave with propriety, now. There
are many officers on the road."

He spoke the truth, yet it rankled. The world had changed. Why couldn't we
all change with it?

"I suppose," I said, urging Clio forward into a trot.

A few hours later, we came to the end of the grasslands. Soon after leaving
the inn, we had seen the land change: outcrops of rocks and patches of marsh
became more common, and the grasses grew thinner and shorter. The large
rolls of land broke into small hills with shrubby growth in their folds. Broad-
leaved plants appeared beside the road. We saw our first trees—oaks, but
different from the ones at home. Their pointed leaves hung brown and
desiccated. Intermixed with the oaks, we saw other trees, leafless. Under the
trees, among the dried leaves, sparse grasses grew.

We came to a track leading east. It had rained recently, and hoof prints
pocked the mud of the unpaved road: shod horses, and large. I remembered
what Casyn had said on our first day out from Tirvan, of the Emperor's camp
at the transition between grasslands and grape fields.

"A hunting party, perhaps," Garth speculated. "Or riders bearing provisions
from Karst or Casilla. Those horses were heavily laden and walking. I wouldn't
be surprised to meet the like in the miles between here and Karst, and I think
the inn tonight will be busy." He caught my look. We had stayed away from inns
when the weather was good. "We are done with camping, Lena. The inn we will
reach tonight is the last on the road south. After that, farms and villages provide
for travellers. Tomorrow, we ride to Karst."

I nodded silently. Our time together, as more than companions on the road,
had run out. Tomorrow, we would pick up the threads of our separate lives: he
to claim Valle, I to pass my sad tidings to Tice's family and council. From there,

Garth would ride to Casilla and *Skua*, and I would go—where? I had spoken privately to the innkeeper the previous night. Maya had not stopped there. Nor had Karlii and Sherron seen her at Ballin. If no one at Karst knew of her, I would ride on with Garth to Casilla, but we would be no more than companions on the road. I thought of Karlii and her fierce love for her soldier. Sherron had told me later that he had been one of the men sent to Ballin to train the women. He had left under orders immediately after the battle, but reluctantly. His attachment to Karlii was as strong as hers to him.

I held out my hand to him. He took it.

"I'll miss you," I said. We had become lovers out of grief and loneliness, for comfort, but for me, at least, it had become more. Tali had been right. "I love you, Garth."

"And I you," he said, smiling. "I will never forget our time together." He tightened his grip on my hand, briefly, before releasing it. He leaned forward in his saddle to kiss me. I returned the kiss.

"You have no doubts about Maya?"

"Of course I have doubts," I said, impatiently. "She's planned a whole future in this village of hers, one that I can't be part of. I don't know what she's thinking, but I have to find her."

"And if she says, 'Go away'?"

"Then at least I will know." I did not voice the thought that slid unbidden into my mind: then I can go home.

An hour later, we met a hunting party riding north. The packhorses carried deer carcasses, gutted and bled. We reined to a halt. As Garth rode forward to speak with the leader, I waited, letting Clio relax. Garth pulled his papers from his saddlebags, offering them to the other man, who shook his head. He gestured to me, and I rode forward. The older man's tunic bore the insignia of a captain.

"Captain," I said. "I am Lena, from Tirvan."

"Martin," he said, offering his hand, "from the twelfth. That's a good Han pony you're riding—a good choice for a long ride. I know who you are. I was in Casilla a week past, and Captain Dern asked me to look out for you on the road. You've taken good care of his horse, Watch-Commander."

"Did Dern have news for us?" I asked.

"No, just asked me to look out for you. He told me you both acquitted yourselves very well in the fighting. Did you meet anyone else on the road?"

"We rode with General Casyn," Garth answered, "and met the Majors Bren and Turlo. They joined us, but left us at the grasslands road."

"They hadn't arrived when I left for Casilla two weeks back," Martin said. "I'll be glad to see Turlo. He always brightens up a camp." He glanced up at the sun. "We must ride. I'll let General Casyn know I've seen you. Good luck to you both."

"Sir," Garth said, formally, saluting.

We allowed the laden pack animals and the rest of the hunting party to pass.

Garth watched them for a minute.

"I wonder what Dern told him."

"About you?"

"Yes." He urged Tasque back to the road, and I fell in beside him.

"Well," I said, trying to be practical, "he must have said something of what you did. Otherwise, where have you been for the last five years?"

"Turlo told me to look men in the eye, answer civilly, and never lose my temper. There have been rumours about him all his life. His red hair tells of his northern blood, and he probably has been sent to spy north of the wall because of it, which makes his loyalties suspect to some."

"Turlo is well-loved," I said. "You heard what Martin said just then."

"Yes, but Turlo is known. I'm an unknown young officer with a questionable past."

"As Turlo was once, too," I argued. "It will be all right, Garth. You have the trust of Casyn, and by extension the Emperor. That must count for something."

"I suppose," he said, falling silent. He looked troubled. I too felt uneasy, disturbed by our earlier conversation and the thoughts it had engendered. I craved solitude, not the crowds and conversations tonight's inn promised.

The inn was indeed bustling. Our horses shared a box stall, and the apprentice showed me to a room in which two people had already stowed their coats and saddlebags. The beds, a washstand, and some hooks on the wall comprised all the furnishings, save the rush matting on the floor. The apprentice brought hot water so I could wash. I was drying my hands when the door opened and two women came in. We smiled hello. After retrieving something from a saddlebag, they left again. I ran a comb through my hair. It needed cutting. I put the comb away to go down to the common room.

Only women occupied the tables and benches. The men had a separate room. Here in the south, where villages and farms crowded closer together, and with regular traffic on the road between Casilla and the Emperor's camp, custom kept men and women apart. Voices and bodies filled the room. I went to the serving bar to order ale and food. When it came, I paid, then made my way to an empty place at the far end of a table. My roommates sat at the opposite end. They each raised a hand in greeting but made no effort to include me in the conversation. I ate my stew, listening.

I heard talk of crops and herds, of a good year for wine, of births and deaths. Women bet on a dice game at a table behind me, and someone played a stringed instrument of some kind in the far corner, quietly and without accompaniment. I thought of the map Casyn had drawn for me, trying to picture this inn. As far as I could remember, it sat at the hub of several roads, leading out to a semi-circle of villages—Ballin, Karst, two or three others. When I finished my food, I turned slightly to watch the dice game behind me. It seemed friendly, with much laughter and joking. One of the women looked up. "D'you want to join us?"

I shook my head. "I've never played. May I just watch?"

"Sure," she answered. "But where are you from, that you've never thrown the dice?"

"Tirvan."

"Well, isn't that something. I go my whole life without meeting anyone from Tirvan, and then I meet two women in a month. It's a long trip south. What brings you here?"

"I have business in Karst. This other woman from Tirvan, was her name Maya?" My voice sounded odd to my ears.

"That sounds right. What's your business in Karst, if you don't mind me asking? That's where I live. I'm Daria," she added, extending her hand to me. She was middle aged, dark-skinned like Tice, with greying, cropped hair. As we shook, I tried to order my thoughts.

"I must take my message to the head of the council."

"That's Anya," she said. She gave me a long look. "It'll be bad news, then." She closed her eyes, briefly. "I hadn't heard of any of us going so far north. I won't press you, child. I'll know soon enough."

"Please, when did you see Maya? And where?"

Daria stood, handing the dice to another player. "Keep my spot warm," she said, sliding onto the bench across from me. "A couple of weeks back, in Torrey. It's a village to the west where the river broadens out into marshland." I remembered that Danel, Freya's love, had come from Torrey. "They weave baskets there, and we buy them to hold the grapes at harvest. I'd ridden over to place an order for next year."

"Do you think she's still there?"

She shook her head. "I know she's not. We travelled a bit together the next day, but it's hard to ride to the pace of a group walking, so I left them after a while. She was going to see the Emperor. She said she wants her own village, she and her friends. Did you know?"

"Yes," I said. *Going to see the Emperor.* I realized Daria had asked me a question. "Sorry. What did you say?"

"D'you agree with her? About the village?"

"I don't know."

"Can't see what harm it would do, myself," Daria said. She stood up. "You ride to Karst tomorrow?" I nodded. "I've another day's business here, but I'll be there the following day. It's about four hours in the saddle if you're easy on the horse. Look for the bell tower and the hall. That's where most will be around mid-day, sharing a meal. Now," she called to her fellow dicer, "hand them over." She returned to her game.

I sat, feeling tears prick my eyes. Gradually, my thoughts cleared. Tomorrow I would ride to Karst to deliver my news. I would stay one night, then ride north again. If the weather held, and I pushed Clio, I could be there in two days, three nights. I had to tell Garth.

"Daria," I said, urgency in my voice. She looked up. "I need to speak to one of the men. I don't know what is done here."

She gestured toward the serving bar with her head. "Tell Fryth who you need to speak to, and she'll get him. There's a room between the two common rooms where you can talk,"

"Thanks," I said. I crossed the room and caught Fryth's eye. "I need to speak with Watch-Commander Garth. Could you fetch him?"

"Aye, that I will. Wait in there." She pointed to a space opening from the servery. The door that adjoined the men's common room was closed. A bench stood against one wall, but I could not sit. I paced the small space until Garth entered.

"Maya has gone to the Emperor's camp," I said without preamble. "Two weeks ago. "

"Then she'll still be there." A mix of emotions crossed his face. "And I won't see her," he said quietly. I looked at him, shocked. I had not thought of this.

"Oh, Garth."

He shook his head. "But you will, and you'll know what to say to her, of me." He hesitated. "Do you want me to take word of Tice to Karst, so you can leave for the camp tomorrow?"

"No," I said, reluctantly. "Tice's death is my responsibility, and the news is mine to bear. But I won't linger in Karst, though I will be with you, if you want, when you claim Valle. I would like to meet him." I saw him relax, infinitesimally.

"I'd hoped you would be there," he said. In the half-light, I could not read his eyes. I wanted to put my arms around him. A burst of laughter came from the soldier's side. "I better go," he said.

I went back to my table, picking up my half-full mug of ale. I remembered a bench, outside, and found my way there in the cold night. No clouds obscured the sky. The stars glittered. I sat on the bench, drawing my knees up for warmth. I found the bear and then the north star. I could follow them home. So could any who had apprenticed to the boats. I had heard fireside tales about the different stars in distant lands. If you travelled far enough, how did you find your way home?

I shivered as the night's chill seeped into me. I went back inside to mount the stairs to my room. Stowing my saddlebags under my bed, I stripped down to my shirt and pulled back the covers. The blankets, woven of good wool, warmed me, and I gave myself to their comfort and to the oblivion of sleep.

CHAPTER EIGHTEEN

I SLEPT DEEPLY, NOT STIRRING EVEN WHEN MY ROOMMATES came to bed. I woke when the first hint of light showed in the eastern sky. The morning star shone above the horizon. I dressed quietly and picked up my saddlebags.

Downstairs, Fryth was already at work at the servery. "The Watch-Commander is up, too," she said. "There's bread and cheese for you here and a mug of tea. Drink that, at least. It'll be cold on the road this early."

I thanked her, giving her the coins for the night's lodging and my breakfast. I sipped the hot, sweet tea carefully, feeling its warmth spreading inside me. I folded the bread around the cheese and took a bite, then stuffed it in my tunic pocket. I could eat on the road. I drank down the remaining tea, ignoring the heat.

"Good luck to you," Fryth said, turning back to her cooking fire.

I picked up the saddlebags, going out to the stables where the horses, saddled and waiting, snorted in the cold air. I pulled on my riding coat and gloves, then swung the saddlebags up and secured them. Garth emerged from the stable.

"Ready?" Awakening sparrows chirped in the eaves of the stable.

"Ready," I answered, though my mind shied from what the day would bring. We mounted and clattered out of the stable yard. The wide, paved road ran south from the inn to where two narrower roads branched off.

We took the westerly road at an easy pace until the sun rose high enough to melt the frost off the paving stones. I nibbled at my bread and cheese. Here and there, I could see the work of woodcutters. The road began to slope downward, snaking into a series of switchbacks. We turned a corner and stopped.

Below us, the forest gave way to fields, each planted with precise, parallel rows of trellised vines. Dirt tracks ran between the fields, houses, and outbuildings scattered among them. Smoke rose from the houses, and in the far distance, I spotted a larger building with a tower: the central meeting hall. Beyond that were more fields, and then a shimmer at the horizon: the sea. The sea. I looked away, back to the neatly ordered land, and the memory came to me of the grace and precision of Tice dancing.

We urged the horses to a canter as we passed the rows of grapes. A few were neatly pruned and tied, but the majority grew thick, hanging loosely over the trellises. Winter work, I remembered Tice telling me. We came to a house with a workshop beside it. The air smelled of freshly cut wood from a row of newly-manufactured barrels lined up outside the building.

A woman came out, her clothes powdered with sawdust. "Strangers!" she said. "I thought you might be Daria, although I couldn't think who the second horse would be. What can I do for you?"

I introduced us. "We have business in Karst. What is the way to the meeting hall? I must speak with your council leader—Anya."

She nodded. "Keep on this road until it forks then go right. At a canter, you'll be there before noon. Anya will be there." She looked at us both. "I'll expect to hear the meeting bell this afternoon. Would you like water before you ride on?"

We let the horses drink and accepted water ourselves without dismounting. The cooper handed us mugs with the same economy of movement that Tice had had. I drank the cold water and handed the mug back. We reined the horses back to the road.

The sun was high when we reached the hall—a low building, built of silvered wood on a stone foundation, with a bell tower rising high from the centre. A porch ran around the front and sides, covered with twining grapevines. Trees I did not recognize, gnarled and bent, grew to one side.

We dismounted. The horses sidestepped nervously, reacting to our tension. I stroked Clio's neck, damping down my jitters to calm my horse. A girl of nine or ten came running from inside the hall, stopping when she saw us.

"Is Anya within?" I asked her. She nodded. "Can you hold our horses while we go to speak with her?" She nodded again and came forward, holding out her hand for the horses to sniff. She stroked their muzzles. When I believed them to be calm, I handed her the reins. "This is Clio, and this is Tasque. They will stand for you, or you can walk them up and down, if you like." She took the reins, leading the horses towards the back of the hall. We went inside.

I had been expecting dark, but the hall swam with light from a series of windows high in the walls above the porch roof. Long tables ran across the room, and fireplaces took up most of the walls. Several women readied food at the far end. They looked up as we walked across the hall. One woman, grey-haired and tall, walked forward.

"I am Anya, Council Leader. Are you looking for me?"

"Yes," I said, meeting her brown eyes. "I am Lena, from Tirvan in the north. This is Garth, of *Skua*, who fought with us there. May we speak with you?"

"Privately?" I nodded. I saw her face tighten. "There is an office through here," she said, indicating a door to our right. "Please come."

Inside was a long table, covered with papers, two chairs, and a bench. Anya closed the door behind us. "Please sit," she said. She took the chair behind the table. Garth sat on the bench, leaning forward, tension in every line of his body. I sat on the edge of the other chair, my heart pounding. Anya looked at me. "This is not good news you bring."

"No," I said. I thought of my mother, instructing Kira on how to deliver bad news. *Be direct,* she had said. *Be honest.* "Our village potter died in the fighting. She was from Karst, and her name was Tice." Anya closed her eyes and was silent for a long moment.

"How did she die?"

"I was her Cohort-Leader," I said. "She was my cohort-second. After the main battle, some invaders were unaccounted for. I sent her to patrol alone, and she was stabbed." I swallowed hard. "I made a mistake, and it cost Tice her life. She was my friend." I waited. Anya's expression did not change.

"I am glad she found a village to take her in and a friend," she said. "Were you friend enough to know her story?"

I nodded. Garth looked extraordinarily calm.

"I am part of that story," he said. "I am Valle's father, and I come to formally acknowledge him."

Anya looked startled. "Tice told us the father was Lestian trader."

"She knew me as Kirthan. I was a spy for the Empire. I have a letter from my captain in my saddlebags to confirm this if you wish to see it. That afternoon, I thought Tice was going to uncover a message I had left, a message of significant import to the safety of the Empire. I offered her wine, instead, and myself. I didn't think of the possibility of a child."

Anya bowed her head for a moment and sighed. Then she looked up. "I will see that letter. I don't doubt you, but others will, so it's best that I have read it. I ask that you speak of this to no one until I have met with the rest of the council. You too, Lena," she added. "I'll tell Tice's mother and sisters myself this afternoon. The others will have guessed there is bad news, but Tice is not the only woman from this village to have sought a different life in the last years. I will call meeting tonight, so all may know. I'll ask you to speak then, if you will."

Garth cleared his throat then spoke in a firm voice. "I swore to make redress for my wrongs, where I could. Tice died before I knew of Valle. She tried to kill me."

"Was she trying to kill you or an invader?"

"Tice recognized him and called him by his Lestian name. I stopped her because I also recognized him." Anya raised an eyebrow. Like Tice. "His sister is my partner, and they look enough alike to be twins."

Anya returned her gaze to Garth. "Valle has your eyes. What redress would you make, soldier?"

"Whatever I can," he said, "beyond simply claiming the child. What would you have me do, council leader?" I heard the thread of anger in his voice, remembering that first night, so many weeks ago, when he had responded to his mother's insinuation of treason with the same controlled fire. Maya has the same steel within her.

Anya nodded, once. "Go now," she said, "and see to your horses. There is a paddock on the far side of the hall. Come back into the hall through the stables, and you'll find yourself in the kitchens. I'll find you a place to eat and wait. I think it's best if you do not mix with the village yet."

We did as she asked, walking silently back through the bright hall with the eyes of the women upon us. The horses, already unsaddled, cropped grass in the paddock, their tack hanging neatly on the fence. The child had disappeared.

"You seemed very calm," I said.

"As did you. But we still have Tice's family to face and the meeting tonight." He looked around. "It's so ordered. Tamed. It reminds me of Leste. No land is wasted."

He had never spoken of Leste before. I did not know how to respond, but he did not seem to expect a reply. He took his saddle and bridle off the fence. "Let's find the stables." I picked up my tack to follow him.

We found our way to a tack room, and then through the dark stable, down a hall to the kitchen where Anya waited for us. She took us to another room, with a table and chairs, bringing us food: wine, fish stew, bread, soft cheese, and small, wizened fruit I did not recognize. Then she left us. I took a mouthful of the stew. It was rich with chunks of a white-fleshed fish and shellfish and onion.

I could taste a spice I couldn't name. I ate hungrily, wiping the bowl clean with crusty bread to get the last drops. I put the bowl to one side and reached for the fruit. I bit into one, tentatively: sweet, and chewy. "What is this?"

"A fig. There were trees outside."

"It's sweet," I said. I spread some cheese on the bread. Sherron had said the hard cheeses went to the army, mostly. Garth stood to look out the small window. He had eaten his stew but nothing else. I could see the tension in his shoulders. "Have some wine."

He shook his head without turning. I poured some for myself. It was a pale golden colour, the colour of the winter grasslands. Above us, a bell tolled, three deep rings, then a pause, then three more.

Garth moved away from the window. "I feel helpless. All those weeks of riding and now to sit here in this little room, waiting."

"There's nothing else we can do," I said, looking around. I spotted a box sitting on a shelf and reached for it. "I'm wrong. We can play *xache*." Garth shrugged.

"Why not? It will pass the time." Garth poured himself some wine, and we tossed. He won, and we began the ritualised game, designed, Casyn had told me, to teach men to think of war in terms of tactics and consequences, and of acceptable loss.

I had conceded one game and was winning the second when Anya returned. "Tice's mother and sisters are here. Before you see them, it is only fair I tell you a few things." She sighed. "Tamar, Tice's mother, is a woman of strong views and considerable pride. She was Council Leader for many years before the illness in her joints made it too difficult for her. When she learned Tice was pregnant, she became very angry. She forbade communication between Tice and her two sisters, and she would not see the child, nor Tice, even to say goodbye."

"How could she be so cruel?" I said, shocked.

"As I said, she is a woman of considerable pride. She saw Tice's pregnancy as a source of shame." Anya spoke with studied neutrality.

"Then who will raise Valle?" Garth said suddenly. "Is that not a sister's role, or a grandmother's?"

"Usually," Anya admitted. "Would you take him, Lena?"

"Me?" I tried to think. "How could I? I am going back on the road to find my partner. I can't take a small child with me."

"But once you find her?" Anya asked.

"I don't know." I took a breath, willing myself to calm. "If I am needed, I will come back for him as soon as I can and take him home with me to Tirvan."

"I am sure," Anya said, "that we can make arrangements for him here for a while if we need to. You might also take him to Casilla. Tevra, who was Tice's partner, might have him."

"Are we to pass him around, like a wineskin?" Garth said angrily. "This is ridiculous. Better he stays where he is than shove him from one place to another, never knowing where he belongs. I will not acknowledge him unless I know he will be taken care of."

"I will take him," I said firmly, "and keep him with me until he is seven if there is no one in Tice's family who will." I would think later about how I could do this, and what it might mean, for Maya and me.

We followed Anya out into the hall. At the fireplace at the far end, two women stood beside an older, seated woman with a cane across her knees. I judged Tice's sisters to be both older and younger than Tice. The older looked nearly thirty and the younger more or less my age. Tice had never spoken of them.

Tamar had a face that spoke of pain. Deep lines ran from her nose to the edges of her mouth. She regarded us levelly but made no gesture of greeting. Her daughters nodded slightly. The younger of the two had reddened eyes.

"Tamar, Joce, Ianthe" Anya began, "this is Lena, of Tirvan, who was Cohort-Leader and friend to Tice. And this is Garth, Watch-Commander of *Skua*." She turned to us. "Tamar is Tice's mother, Joce and Ianthe her sisters. Shall we sit?" It was not a request. We sat.

"Tell me how my daughter died," Tamar said, her voice cold.

"With respect," I said, hesitating, "I think you need to hear Garth first. Ours are not separate stories, and it begins here, with the begetting of Valle."

Tamar made a small pinched movement of her mouth. Her eyes flicked to Anya, and then to her daughters. Ianthe—the younger sister—made a small gesture with her hands.

Garth told them the bare facts, unadorned with reason or excuse. The women listened without interrupting until he told them of the meeting at Jedd's farm, and his need to keep Tice from the intelligence hidden in the rafters of the barn.

"Watch-Commander," Tamar said, "I knew my daughter's anger and wilfulness all too well. She made a choice, too, with the knowledge that a child could well be conceived. I cannot condone your actions, but I understand why you acted as you did. Why Tice did, I will never know." Her voice remained expressionless. Garth did not respond.

I wished I did not have to tell this cold woman anything. I glanced at the sisters. Ianthe fought tears, so I looked at her as I spoke. "I didn't know why Tice had come to Tirvan, except that we needed a potter. I didn't know her well until this past summer. She kept herself apart. When I was chosen Cohort-Leader, I chose her as my cohort-second, so that she could teach us to move the way she did. She handled a knife as if she had held one all her life." Ianthe smiled, slightly.

"We became friends. She told me of Valle, and how he was fathered. She told me she had acted out of jealousy and anger towards her lover who had had a child the year before." At that, Ianthe sobbed audibly, and Joce put her hand on her arm. Tamar did not move. I steeled myself for the next part.

"After the fighting, all but a few of the invaders were captured or had surrendered. Tice and I were patrolling for the few who still roamed the village when we saw Garth. She named him as Kirthan, and threw her knife to kill him. I had also recognized him, so I deflected the knife. He looks very much like his sister, my partner, Maya, who had left Tirvan in the spring. We took him captive," I stopped, swallowed. "And then I made a terrible mistake. Rather than argue with her about whether to kill Garth, I sent her back on patrol. She was angry and upset, and I should not have done so. She was stabbed in the back, distracted, no doubt, by her anger. I take responsibility. I am so very sorry."

Only the muffled sobbing of Ianthe broke the silence. Garth shifted beside me. Finally, Tamar spoke. "You have done your duty," she said. "For that, I thank you." She started to stand, Joce immediately supporting her.

"Wait!" Garth said. "My son, Valle. What of him?"

"He is nothing to me. Come, Joce, Ianthe. I wish to rest." She began to move away, Joce at her elbow. Ianthe turned to follow, and then stopped.

She stepped away from her sister and mother. "I will raise him," she said. "I will raise Valle if you acknowledge him, Watch-Commander." I felt a wave of relief, followed by an odd pang of disappointment.

"Not in my house, Ianthe," Tamar said. "I forbid it." Then she turned, to walk slowly away. Her footsteps, and those of Joce, and the slow tap of Tamar's cane echoed in the hall.

We stood silently until the doors had closed behind them. Anya spoke first. "Are you sure, Ianthe?"

"Yes." Her voice wavered, but she swallowed, straightening her shoulders. "I am. I won't let my mother's pride sacrifice a child's future." She smiled. "He is a lovely child, Watch-Commander. I see him occasionally, when I have a reason to be at Jedd's farm. He doesn't know I am his aunt, of course."

"You are welcome at my cottage, Ianthe, you and Valle." She made a face. "Tamar won't approve, but I am Council Leader. It's my decision."

"How can I help?" Garth asked.

"Come to us at Festival, if you can, to be with him," Anya said. "Anything else would set him apart even more. There will be whispers and gossip, but we'll do our best to counter that. And we'll talk to him of you, so that he can brag of his brave father, as all the small boys do."

Garth smiled. "For all I did not want to be a soldier, I remember telling the others what a great fighter my father was." He sobered. "What will you tell him of his mother?"

"That she was my sister, and I loved her, and that she died in the fighting," Ianthe said. "And I'll show him her pots."

"Tell him she danced," I said. "To music, and with a sword, and both were beautiful."

"I believe that," Ianthe said.

"I had best send a message to the farm," Anya said, briskly. "We'll need Valle here, tomorrow morning, for the claiming ceremony. Ianthe, will you go?"

"Yes, of course," she said eagerly.

"Wait just a moment, and I'll write it. Lena, I was going to have you lodge with me tonight, but now I think Ianthe will need the bed. Old Ione keeps beds for men who come on business and for messengers. I'd already arranged for Garth to stay with her, and she will find a bed for you, too. Let me get this note written, and I'll take you there." She disappeared into the office.

"Ianthe," I said, before Garth could speak. "You don't have to do this and estrange yourself from your family. I will raise Valle, either here, or back in my home village."

"No," she said firmly. "Thank you, Lena, but no. He is my sister's child. I loved her, and I owe this to her. I'm used to my mother's ways, and Joce isn't as distant as she seems. She'll find ways to see me and Valle." She smiled. "You'll always be welcome if you wish to visit, to tell Valle of his mother's time in the north."

"I'd like that."

Anya reappeared with a sealed note in her hand, which she gave to Ianthe before turning to us. "Follow me."

Old described Ione well. I judged her to be eighty, at least. Our rooms—on different floors—were sparsely furnished, but the sheets smelled of lavender and sunshine, and the scrubbed floors shone. We fetched our own water from the well for washing, at Anya's quiet suggestion.

I shook out my cleanest clothes and washed in the cool water. The soap smelled of lavender too. I realized I would have no opportunity to talk to Garth before dinner, and that thought did not altogether displease me. I needed time to think about how I had felt when Ianthe said she would raise Valle. I understood why I was relieved, but why was I also disappointed?

I let the thought sit in my mind, not trying to find an answer. I dried myself with a towel that was old but neatly mended, and dressed. I brushed my hair and hung up my riding clothes. I would need them again tomorrow. If I had stayed for Valle, I thought, then I would not be leaving tomorrow. I might never have seen Maya again. Maybe that would have been best.

"Why?" I said out loud. I sat on the bed for a while, waiting, but no answer came. I lay down, drifting into sleep and jumbled snatches of dreams until the meeting bell rang across the fields.

Nearly a hundred women crowded the meeting hall, sitting in rows of benches arranged along the long axis of the room, facing east. Anya and two other women—both also olive-skinned, with grey in their hair—stood under the windows, conferring. Tamar sat in a high armchair to one side, a concession to her illness, I guessed, with Joce beside her. I did not see Ianthe.

When Anya saw us enter, she motioned us to a bench against the wall. "Sit here," she said as we approached. "Mikelle, Roxine, this is Lena of Tirvan, and Garth, Watch-Commander of *Skua*. Mikelle and Roxine are council leaders." Each woman took our hands in both of theirs, smiling a greeting. Their hands felt dry and cool; mine were damp with sweat and nervousness.

We sat with a hundred pairs of eyes on us. I tried not to look at the floor. Garth scanned the room then turned his attention to the council leaders. I did the same.

"Women of Karst," Anya called. Voices stilled.

"Women of Karst," Anya said again, her voice quieter. "Our guests have brought news." She turned to us. "Please stand, so all may see you." We complied. I looked out over the rows of women, but the brightness of the western windows made it hard to see faces. "Lena, of Tirvan village, and Garth, Watch-Commander of *Skua*, have ridden south with news of one of our women." Anya said levelly. "It is sad news they bring, although not entirely. You may sit," she said to us.

"Tice, daughter of Tamar and sister to Joce and Ianthe, was killed during the invasion of Tirvan," Anya said. A wave of voices spread across the room. One woman slipped off the bench to go to Joce and Tamar, kneeling to take Tamar's hands. Tamar shook her head. The woman rose to speak to Joce, reaching out to her. Joce stepped away from the embrace.

Anya continued. "She was stabbed, on night patrol. I am told she died quickly."

"Has word been sent to my sister, in Casilla?" The woman who had gone to Tamar and Joce asked.

"Not yet, Tevian," Anya answered. "The Watch-Commander rides there to join his ship in a few days. I had hoped he would take the letter, although I had not yet asked him. Unless you wish to go to Tevra yourself?"

"I wish I could," Tevian said, "but as you know my babe still needs the breast, and she's too sickly to withstand the ride to Casilla." She turned to Garth. "Will you take the letter, Watch-Commander?"

"Of course," Garth said. He sounded older, as if in the last days he had grown into his new roles: officer of the Empire, father.

"The Watch-Commander," Anya said to the room, "supported the defence of Tirvan. The ship on which he serves has sailed from there with the Lestian prisoners, but he sought his captain's permission to ride south with Lena. He, too, brings a message. While disguised as a man of Leste, and on the Emperor's service, he fathered Tice's child, Valle." Faces reflected surprise, disbelief, shock. Voices rose.

"What?'

"No!"

Anya raised a hand for silence. The room obeyed. Like Gille, she commanded respect. "The webs the goddess weaves brought them together again at Tirvan, long enough for this to be confirmed. He has come to acknowledge his son."

Chatter broke out again. Eventually Anya raised a hand again, asking for quiet.

"Who will raise him?" Tevian asked.

"I will," Ianthe said. She had been standing at one end of the hall, beside the fireplace, hidden in the shadows. "I have told the Watch-Commander—Garth— and my mother and sister. I will take Valle. The claiming ceremony will be tomorrow morning. We will live with Anya." As she spoke, she walked into the light of the room. I could see her trembling even from my distance. Brave, I thought. So brave.

"Bring him to me when you need to," Tevian said. "He's nearly of an age with my Kinley. They can play together." She strode over to Ianthe to hug her, murmuring something too quietly for anyone but Ianthe to hear.

"Women of Karst!" Anya called, pulling attention away from Ianthe and Tevian. "You have heard the news. Meeting is over. There is tea, of course, but please respect that Lena and Garth have ridden a very long way and are tired. For those who wish to witness, the claiming ceremony will be two hours after dawn."

We all rose. Mikelle and Roxine walked over to us, smiling.

"Thank you," Roxine said, "sounds quite inadequate, for what you have both done."

"What have we done?" Garth asked quietly. "Valle will have a different life, yes, and a father, but what of Ianthe? She's lost both her mother and her sister."

"I think," Mikelle said, "that perhaps Valle has provided the reason for Ianthe to leave her mother's house." She spoke slowly, choosing her words with care. "Do not worry for her, Watch-Commander, not on that front, at least. She and your son will be safe with Anya, and most of the village, even Joce, in her way, will support them, as we do with all our children."

"All your legitimate children," Garth said. Mikelle inclined her head, accepting the statement.

"Yes," she said. "But that isn't our choice. Had the child been a girl, Tice could have kept her. What does a village do with a fatherless boy who has no place in the Empire's armies?"

"I do not know," Garth said heavily. "Forgive me, Mikelle. I didn't mean to give offense."

"I took none," she said. She laughed. "Council leaders are thicker-skinned than that, Watch-Commander. Now, would you both like tea?"

A few minutes later, I had a mug of tea in my hand and a group of women about my age around me. I expected questions about Tice, but these women had other interests.

"Would you tell us of Tirvan?" one of them asked shyly.

"With pleasure," I said, relieved. I could handle this. "Not that there's a lot to tell. We are a northern village, but I suppose you know that. There is Berge, close to the Wall, and then Skeld, and Delle, and Tirvan. All are coastal villages, so we fish. I had a boat," I said, "with my partner. Many women fish, but others tend the herds—sheep, and some cows—weave, or work in wood or metal. We're isolated, so we must be masters of all trades."

"How big is your village?"

"About forty houses," I said. "And the barns and stables and workshops, and the docks and fish sheds. The village fans out from the harbour up into the hills." I thought of the sea I had glimpsed today, and a sharp pang of homesickness assailed me. "It's very beautiful in the spring when the meadows are in flower, and in the autumn, when the heather blooms."

"Who came to you, to ask you to fight?" a slightly older woman asked.

"Casyn," I said. "He is a general, but he was born in Tirvan. I think that was the way of things."

"Yes," the older woman said. "The man who came to us, Rolan, was born here. He is Anya's brother. I wondered if that had been the case everywhere."

"We were lucky," the older woman went on. "We lost no one. The defence was easier than you might think. We're bordered on the south, where the land meets the sea, by sheer cliffs of chalk, nearly impossible to climb. We concentrated our defences at the harbours, with riders moving between. Other cohorts guarded the roads to Casilla and to the Four-Ways Inn. We attacked from above, with arrows and spears, and burned their boats. They surrendered quickly." The older woman spoke with calm precision, and, I thought, deep passion.

"Were you a Cohort-Leader?" I asked.

"Yes," she said. "As you were, from what I have heard."

There is talk, I thought. Of course there is. "Yes. Our tactics were very similar, but we lost four women."

"Would you do it again?"

"Oh, Halle," someone said impatiently, "Do you have to bring this up now? I want to hear about the north. I want to hear about snow."

"If you mean, would I defend my village again, and in a leader's role," I said slowly, "then, yes. But I have no love for fighting and less for killing."

"But now we know we can, if we must," she said quietly, "and we can wield weapons and think tactically. Can we forget this, to go quietly back to what our lives were before?"

"Most of us will," I said. The younger women listened, their eyes flicking between us.

"But not all," she said. "I'm Halle," the older woman said. "May we speak in the morning, before you leave? Anya will tell you where to find me."

"If you like." She unsettled me. In truth, I did not want to speak with her again, but could think of no way to refuse her. I crossed over to where Garth sat with Tevian and Ianthe.

Together, we walked out into the starry night. A warm wind blew from the south. I could smell the hint of salt from the ocean. Bats flew and chattered overhead, hunting insects.

"The *siraca*," Tevian said. "The wind from the south. It's never winter here, or not for long. Tomorrow will be glorious."

CHAPTER NINETEEN

THE DAY WAS GLORIOUS, INDEED. Two hours past dawn, I walked outside without my coat, marvelling at the warmth of the breeze against my skin. At home, the peaks above the village would have been white for weeks now, the ponds frozen. Snow might even be forcing us to spread ashes on the pathways and resort to brooms to keep porches and doorsteps clean. Fires would burn day and night in the houses. Here, it smelled like spring, with the winter solstice still more than a week away.

I had awoken early after a night of deep and exhausted sleep. I crept out to the pump, hoping I would not disturb Ione, to wash my hair under the cold stream. By the time I took a bucket back to my room, bathed, and dressed, the sun had risen.

I stood at my window, letting my hair dry, watching the sun light the rows of vines, dyeing them pink, creating long shadows. I heard Ione rise and go out to the kitchen; I heard Garth come downstairs and then go back up. A while later he came down again. A bird called, a squeaky mix of notes. I watched a hare lope along the edge of the field. The breeze carried the faint smell of the sea.

I found my comb, tidied my now-dry hair, and went out to the kitchen. Ione drank tea at the table.

"Th' wa'ch commander's gone," she said. She had no upper teeth in front, so she slurred some words. "A' th' hall."

"I'm going there as well, but I'll come back later to change and pack. Should I pay you now or later?"

She shook her head. "No char'e. Tice was my gran'-niece. No charge, for ei'er of you."

I nodded, my heart in my throat. "I'll give the coins to Ianthe, then, for Valle." I offered. She smiled, showing her gapped teeth.

"Tha's good."

At the hall, Garth stood speaking to Ianthe and Anya. A dozen or so women sat on the benches, Tevian among them. Mikelle and Roxine came in just after me.

"Lena, good morning," Anya said. "Will you stand as witness this morning?"

"Yes." A claiming ceremony needed three witnesses. I wondered who the other two were.

"Do you know the words?"

"I think so. I've attended claiming ceremonies before, but never stood as witness. In Tirvan, after the mother states the father's name, the witnesses state their names and that they have witnessed. Is it different here?"

"No," Anya said. "Ianthe will speak in Tice's stead, and I'll leave your witnessing to last, so you can hear the others speak. Is that all right?"

"Yes," I said. "We always do the father's witness last in Tirvan."

Outside, hooves clopped on the path. Anya went to the door to open it. A tall man, not heavy, but soft-looking, came in carrying a small boy. I heard a soft gasp from Ianthe. The child did not cry, but he had one thumb firmly clamped in his mouth. The man handed the boy to Anya before bending to kiss the child's forehead.

"You are his father?" he addressed Garth with an undercurrent of challenge.

"I am," Garth said mildly.

"I am Alister," the man said, "under-steward at the farm owned by the General Jedd."

"You have helped to raise my son till now?"

"We all have. He's a good boy, and clever." He glanced over at Valle, but the child had burrowed his head into Anya's shoulder. She rocked him, murmuring.

"Then I owe you my deepest thanks," Garth said. "I am Garth, Watch-Commander of *Skua*, and if there is ever anything I can do for you, I will, if it is in my power." He extended a hand to Alister, who took it, looking mildly surprised. They shook. Alister took one last look at Valle, inclined his head to us, and left.

Anya came forward, carrying the boy. Valle raised his head, looking at us doubtfully, still sucking his thumb. His skin glowed olive, and his hair curled tightly around his scalp like his mother's, but Anya had spoken truly: his eyes were Garth's.

"That was well done," Anya said to Garth. "Valle, this is your father. Can you say hello?"

He shook his head, turning his face back to Anya's shoulder. He said something.

"Valle?" Anya said. "Tell me again?"

He looked up at her. "No father," he said. He looked ready to cry.

"Is that what they told you? They were wrong, Valle, but only because they didn't know. This man is your father. His name is Garth. He's been away a long time, but now he's come to see you. Say hello."

Valle looked at Garth. "Tholdier?"

"Yes," Garth said, smiling. "I'm a soldier. Would you like to ride on my shoulders?"

"Yeth," Valle said, holding out his arms. Garth took him, swinging him up on his shoulders. I remembered him picking Pel up the same way. Valle laughed, putting his hands in Garth's hair. Garth looked up at his son and grinned, his face suddenly alight.

You are not, I told myself sternly, going to be jealous of a child.

"Are we ready?" Anya asked.

"Yes," he said.

We arranged ourselves in a half-circle, facing Anya.

"We are here this morning," Anya began, "to witness the claiming of this child, Valle, by his father, Garth of *Skua*, soldier of the Empire." She smiled. "While it is usual for the child to be present, and often for the father to hold him, it is not usually on his shoulders. But no matter. We will continue." She handed Garth a piece of paper. "Garth of *Skua*, please read the words written here, and, if you agree, speak them to us all." Garth unfolded the paper awkwardly, balancing Valle with one hand and skimmed it. Then he nodded.

"I, Garth of *Skua*, son of Mar of the Seventh and Tali of Tirvan," he said clearly, "acknowledge this child, Valle, to be mine, borne by Tice of Karst. He will be raised by his aunt, Ianthe of Karst, until he is seven, and then I or my proxies will send for him, to serve the Empire."

Ianthe stepped forward, smiling up at Valle. "I, Ianthe of Karst, in proxy for my deceased sister Tice, daughter to Tamar of Karst and to Theron of *Petrel*, recognize that Garth of *Skua* is father to this child and has acknowledged him. I will raise him to know his father, and his duty to the Empire, and prepare him to serve it." Her voice caught slightly at Tice's name, but her words rang clearly in the hall.

"I, Tevian of Karst, witness this."

"I, Roxine of Karst, Council Leader, witness this."

"I, Lena of Tirvan, witness this."

Valle sat on his father's shoulders, his hands in his hair, looking up at the rafters. I wondered what they had done with him in the slave quarters. He seemed resilient and cheerful. Very likely, they had made a pet of him. What would he make of a world of women for the next four years?

Garth swung him down, keeping a hold of one hand. Ianthe took the other. He looked up at her.

"Hello, Valle. I'm Ianthe. Let's go eat. Are you hungry?"

We walked to breakfast at Valle's pace. I walked beside Tevian, trying not to feel left out.

We ate sausages and eggs, and warm biscuits, and figs in honey, as the sun shone through the windows of Anya's house. Ianthe fed Valle biscuit pieces drenched in honey and gave him a spoon for his scrambled eggs. I watched, smiling. I spoke with the others, feeling myself growing hollower inside, a space the meal could not fill. Finally, I pushed my plate away and stood up.

I had no reason to linger. Garth would stay for a few days. Twice a year, for a week, many sons saw their fathers. Fathers and daughters were almost never united, unless like Maya they had a brother in the same village. Between visits, the boys heard stories of their fathers, of soldiering and the Empire, to prepare them. Garth would come back, if he could, for the next four years, spring and fall. And Ianthe would be here, with his son.

Garth turned my way. "You're not leaving yet?"

"Not quite. I need to change and pack. I'll say goodbye before I go."

I walked the short distance between Anya's house and Ione's. In my room, I changed into my riding clothes, found my coat, and packed my saddlebag. In doing so, I found Sherron's letter to her sister. I had forgotten it. I looked around the house and yard for Ione but could not find her. I would ask Anya to say goodbye for me.

I carried the saddlebag and my coat to the hall, draping them over the paddock fence. Clio trotted over. I rubbed her neck and led her into the stable to tack her up. I worked methodically, focusing only on I what I had to do, and not what came next.

The girth tightened, I swung my saddlebag up and secured it, then strapped my coat behind the saddle. I picked up each of Clio's feet to check for stones. When I could find no more reason to delay, I opened the paddock gate to lead Clio out. Tasque whickered at her.

"I'm sorry, Tasque," I said to Dern's horse with tears pricking my eyes. I will not cry over a horse, I thought. Clio walked obediently behind me as I led her over to Anya's house. I tied her reins to the porch and went back in, the letter in my hand. Everyone still sat around the table, but Valle now lay stretched across Ianthe's lap, sleeping. Garth stood up.

"Anya," I said, "I nearly forgot this. Would you give it to Hilar, who came from Ballin? It's from her sister."

"Of course," Anya said. "Must you go?"

"I must. I, too, have someone to find." She put out her arms, and I hugged her. I said my goodbyes to the other women, taking one last look at Valle. Then I turned to Garth.

"I'll come out with you," he said. We walked out into the sunshine. Clio whickered at him. He held out his arms, and I stepped into them. He wore only a light shirt, and I could feel his muscles and his warmth. He smelled of lavender soap, and his own, so-familiar scent.

We stood like that for several heartbeats before I pulled back. "He's beautiful, Garth."

He smiled. "His eyes are like Maya's. Did you notice?"

"Like yours, too. Take care of yourself." I hoped he could hear beyond the words.

"And you," he said. "Tell Maya I've never forgotten her,"

"I will."

"I'll see you again," he said, putting out a hand to caress my face. "Perhaps not for a few years, but I will. That's a promise, Lena."

I smiled. "If you don't, I'll come to find you. Farewell, Garth."

"Farewell." He watched as I mounted Clio and turned her head north. We each raised a hand in goodbye.

I pushed my little horse harder than I ever had. We galloped until we reached the end of the grape fields, which forced me to focus on the road, my balance, and nothing else. The cooper called out to me as we galloped past, but

I only raised a hand.

At the climb back up into the forest, we slowed. Even then, feeling my urgency, Clio broke into a trot wherever she could. At one switchback, I paused to give her a breather, looking for the first time back down through the trees to the fields below. Beyond the vines, I could see the glint of the sea. Suddenly, I remembered I had told Halle I would speak with her this morning. There was nothing I could do about it now.

When the land flattened again, I kicked Clio back to a canter. We ate up the miles steadily, and gradually I calmed. I forced myself to think of Maya. Jays called at us as we rode through the trees. In the distance, I could see the glimmer of a stream. I slowed Clio. She needed to be cool before she could drink.

When we reached the stream, I allowed Clio a few mouthfuls before I tethered her away from the water. The altitude made it cooler here. I unstrapped my coat from behind the saddle, shrugging it on. I ran my hands up and down Clio's legs, but found no heat or swelling. Clio pricked her ears and whickered. I looked down the road to see a horse and rider approaching.

"Ho, Lena," Daria called, dismounting. "I did not expect to see you on the road again so soon. Where's your companion?" She led her horse to the stream to let him drink.

"He stayed in Karst," I said. "He'll ride to Casilla from there in a few days." I told her briefly what had passed. She said nothing, only raising an eyebrow when I told her Garth was Valle's father.

"I am sorry," she said, when I finished. "Both for Tice—I liked her—and for Tamar. She has driven another daughter away with her pride. But the child will do well with Ianthe. I always thought she'd find a reason to break free some day. What about you? You'll have a cold and dangerous ride to Tirvan, this time of year."

"I ride to the Emperor's camp, to find Maya."

"Why?"

"I left Tirvan to find her."

She regarded me steadily. "Did you?" she said finally. "But you've known about her new village idea for a while. There will be no place there for you, you know."

I looked away. Daria pulled her horse's head up, away from the grass he cropped. "Don't mind me," she said. "I speak my mind. I'd best be on my way."

"Will you take a message for me? I was supposed to speak with Halle this morning before I left, and I forgot. Would you tell her that I'm sorry, and it wasn't intentional?"

"Halle the fisherwoman?" She mounted her horse. "There are two Halles at Karst."

"I don't know. Maybe a bit younger than you? She asked about the fighting at Tirvan."

"That's her." Daria snorted. "What did she want? To talk about how to change our lives, now we know how to fight? She's like your Maya, wants something new, only completely opposite. Halle wants to live among men and be a soldier. She spent too much time with Rolan." She looked down at me. "I'll give her your message. Good luck to you." She raised a hand in farewell and clattered onto the road.

I watched her go, wishing obscurely that she had stayed longer. I had craved solitude, but now that I had it, I wished I didn't. I took Clio over to the stream. As she drank deeply, I thought about what Daria had said. Maya had made her choice. She wanted a life without me.

As clearly as if she stood beside me, I heard Tali's voice, speaking to my mother all those months ago when Maya had chosen exile: *She said that she would go to look for Garth.*

Garth had unknowingly given Maya the idea—and the courage—to choose exile, but she had not found him. I had. I felt suddenly lighter. I laughed, startling Clio, who snorted and sidestepped. I made soothing sounds at her, and she bent her head back to the stream. I would go to the winter camp and ask to see her. I would tell her about Garth, and Valle, and I would say goodbye. And then? Then I would go home.

Riding under the bare limbs of trees, Clio broke into her rolling trot. I let her pick the pace, no longer feeling the urgency of this morning, glad again to be alone. I wondered if I would have a chance to speak with Casyn at the winter camp. I wanted to tell him I had done as he had asked.

From what Daria had said, Halle wanted something even more radical. Had she formed her ideas on her own, or had they been suggested to her? I could not be the only one charged with spreading the idea of change, I realized. Casyn had no way of knowing how far south I would reach in my search for Maya, or what villages I would visit.

The sun had not quite begun its downward arc. I would reach the Four-Ways inn in another hour, I thought, if we maintained our steady pace. I could buy food there and grain for Clio, enough for the ride to the Emperor's Camp, where I would stay a day or two, let Clio rest, make my reports. The thought of seeing Maya no longer made me anxious now that I knew I did not come to plead with her.

I felt Clio's shoulder drop and shifted my weight to compensate for the stumble. She slid a bit on the stones of the road, then stopped. I dismounted. She held her near forefoot off the ground.

I ran my hands down her leg, but it seemed sound. Her hoof appeared undamaged, but the shoe hung loosely, and I could see where a nail had worked free. I had checked for stones with half my mind trying not to think of Garth. I could easily have not seen one missing nail.

Cursing, I pulled at the shoe, but I could not remove it. I led Clio a few paces down the road. She showed no sign of injury. I couldn't ride her, but we could walk. I loosened her girth, swapped the bridle for the head collar, and led her on.

We limped into the courtyard of the inn about two hours later, the loose shoe making an odd rhythm to Clio's steps. I took her into the stable yard where a very young apprentice came out to meet us.

"Your horse has a loose shoe."

"I know. Where is your stable-master? I'd like her reshod as quickly as possible."

"Bad luck," the girl said. "She's gone to Casilla to trade for nails and such. She won't be back for a day or two." She bent to pick up Clio's hoof, examining the shoe.

"Is there no one else?" I asked. My boots pinched, and my stomach growled. I had hoped for an hour's rest and refreshment, while Clio's shoes were seen to.

"The other apprentice went with her. She could do it, but I can't. I'm not big enough. Sorry."

I sighed. "Can you stable her, then, and give her some grain and water? She's cool enough. We've been walking for two hours." The girl nodded leading Clio away. I turned toward the inn.

I found Fryth at the servery, and the inn busy. She greeted me by name. I asked for food and ale, and for a word with her when the custom slowed. She nodded. I took the meat pie and mug of ale over to a table. I had eaten little at breakfast, and hunger had gnawed at me for the last hour. I wolfed the pie. About half an hour later, Fryth came over.

"You weren't long at Karst," she said, sitting opposite me. "How can I help you?"

"How far to the Emperor's camp, from here?"

"On horse? About ten hours. You'll not get there today. Better to stay here and start early tomorrow."

I explained about Clio.

"Ah, I see," she said. "I expect Alda back the day after tomorrow, but it will likely be late. I've beds and stalls enough for you to stay here, though. If you're short of money, I can always use another pair of hands."

"It's not that. I just don't want to delay. My obligations at the Emperor's camp will only take a day or two, and then I can ride north. There's an inn in the grasslands, the first after the highlands, where I can work this winter and be that much closer to home when spring comes." I had thought this out, walking Clio along the road. Zilde would give me a bed and work, I hoped.

"I see," Fryth said. "Then you won't want to dally. The grasslands are no place to be in winter. We've had post riders in here who've lost fingers and toes to frostbite riding through them."

"Do you have a horse you would trade me for Clio? She's a good horse, bred in Han." I did not want to give up my little mare, but I saw no other choice.

Fryth considered. "I'd rather not. There's another solution, maybe. I learned my trade at a smaller inn a bit north of here, and I can turn my hand to most things. I can't shoe your mare, but I think I can take her shoes off. At least the loose one," she amended. "Then I'll lend you a horse. You can lead your mare behind you and get her reshod at the Emperor's Camp. Someone will be riding this way, and they can bring my horse back then. Will that serve?"

"Very much." I wanted to hug her.

She stood up. "Let's give it a try."

Pulling off the loose shoe turned out to be simple. With something to give me leverage, I could have done it myself, on the road. Removing the three others took more skill. The apprentice walked Clio around the stable yard a few times while Fryth and I watched.

"She'll do, I think," Fryth said. "You've not far to go on stone, as the track out to the camp isn't paved." I remembered the hoof prints in the mud. She turned to the apprentice. "Which of our horses will Lena's tack fit best?"

The girl considered. "Plover. He's freshly shod. He was going to be ridden to Casilla, but then Alda decided to take Sparrow instead because he can carry more weight. He's in the paddock. I'll get him ready." She handed Clio over to me, running out of the stable yard.

"Chatterbox, that one," Fryth said, watching her fondly. "She's my granddaughter. I wanted her to learn to cook, like her mother, but it was horses from when she could walk. Do you need food for the road?"

"Yes. And a bit of grain, if you have it."

"Grain's in the bin," she said. "Take what you need, then we'll settle up for that and the food."

Piebald Plover stood half a hand shorter than Clio, with feathering around his hocks. Endurance, not speed, was what this one would give me, but if I had to lead Clio, then it didn't matter. The apprentice had put my saddle on him, but a different bridle. "He likes this bit better," she explained.

I thanked her, giving her an extra coin. I swung up onto Plover's back, and she handed me Clio's lead rope. I wanted to tie it to the saddle, but she would not let me. "You need to be able to let go of her if something happens. What if a bear attacks you?" I thought it unlikely, but I saw her point. Plover stood calmly. "He won't kick your mare," Inge assured me. She patted his neck. "Be good," she said to the pony. "He likes to be scratched between his ears."

"I'll take care of him," I promised, signalling him to walk. He moved away obediently, Clio following. She had come to Tirvan on a lead rein, I remembered.

We rode north through the afternoon. I discovered Plover had a gentle mouth and an uncomfortable trot. Mostly we walked, though, for Clio, and because I felt suddenly battered with exhaustion. I rode in an almost trance-like state, feeling as if I had left pieces of me behind, in Tirvan, in Karst, on the road, and only a shell straddled the pony beneath me.

I reached the wide track to the camp at dusk. The sun had set about half an hour before, and the western sky still glowed a deep pink. The evening star hung over the horizon. I guessed I still had a bit of time to ride until it was too dark to see, and the track looked dry and level. I turned Plover's head to ride eastward among the trees.

Half an hour later, I had to stop. I could see almost nothing now, and I still had camp to make. I heard water to the left of the track. I dismounted, tying the horses to the nearest tree, then walked in the direction of the sound until I found the stream. A level patch near the stream would do for the tent. I led the horses to the stream; while they drank, I unsaddled Plover and found the bag of grain, pouring half of it out on the ground in two piles. I led Clio to hers and tethered her, then returned to Plover. I took his bridle off, and put on his head-collar, knotted the rope around a branch and left him to eat.

By starlight, I gathered fallen wood and chose a place for a fire. Once it was burning steadily, I found my bread and cheese and ate. Then I sat by the fire, wondering what to do. I still felt this odd sense of being split into many pieces. Despite my exhaustion, I did not think I would sleep. I made tea, sipping it slowly.

Pitching the tent seemed like too much effort. I spread the saddle blanket on the ground, curling up on it with my blanket wrapped around me. The darkness pressed down on me. I had never slept outside alone before. I could hear the stream and the horses' breathing, and from far off the call of an owl. The wind rustled the dry leaves of the oaks. I drifted into sleep.

I awoke a few hours later, needing to empty my bladder. When I opened my eyes, I could see each tree clearly. The moon had risen, full and bright. I unrolled myself from the blanket, moving a short distance away from my bedding to relieve myself. I could see the horses standing head to tail. Plover raised his head. I thought my movement had awoken him, but he swung his head left and snorted. Clio too looked left. What was out there? I had no weapon. I stayed crouched with my heart beating in my chest, watching the horses. They continued to stare into the night, ears pricked. Whatever they sensed interested them, I decided, but either they did not think it dangerous, or its scent came from some distance away.

I straightened, considering. The sense of dislocation had left me somewhat while I slept, and I could think a bit more clearly. The sound could simply be another horse, or even a person on foot, but that seemed unlikely. Suddenly, a long, wavering wail broke the night. I gasped, and then laughed in relief. A rabbit had just lost its life to a hunting owl or a fox.

I considered building up the fire and trying to go back to sleep, but I doubted I could. You are being scared by the words of a twelve-year old, I told myself. If there were bears, or wolves, Casyn—or more likely Turlo—would have told you.

"Enough," I said out loud. I doused the embers of the fire, rolled up my blanket, and prepared the horses. I led them back out to the track before mounting Plover. He swung his head towards the west and home, but when I asked him to walk east he did so without balking.

After a while, Plover's easy pace let me doze in the saddle. The moon rose high in the sky and began her descent. The night grew colder, and the wind picked up slightly. My fingers on the reins, even inside my gloves, grew stiff. I was thinking about dismounting and walking when the next gust of wind brought the scent of wood smoke. Plover pricked his ears, picking up his pace. Through the trees, I could see the faint glow of banked night-time fires. Clio whinnied.

I heard a male voice, and an answering whinny from the darkness ahead of me. The fires brightened, as if newly fed with dry fuel.

"Name yourself," a voice commanded. In the sudden brightness of the replenished fire, I could see nothing. A good defensive move.

"Lena of Tirvan. I seek the Emperor's camp."

I heard footsteps, and then a young soldier holding a torch approached me. Plover shied at the proximity of the torch, and I gentled him.

"We were told to expect you," he said. "Have you ridden all night?"

I shook my head. "I slept a while. What time is it?"

"About four hours to dawn. Come. I cannot leave guard duty, but there is a place you can rest, and food and water for you and your horses."

"Can I not ride on?"

"No," he said. "Such are our orders for anyone not of this company. And there would be no point at this time of night. Better to sleep."

Disappointment washed over me, but knew I could not argue. I dismounted, stiff with cold, and followed the young soldier. He showed me a tent.

"There is a camp bed in there on which you may rest. The latrine," he said, and I heard a shading of embarrassment in his voice, "is just over there." He seemed very young. He pointed north. "I'll picket your horses and feed and water them. I am relieved an hour before dawn and will wake you then."

"Thank you. And your name?"

"Darel. Of the third."

"The piebald is Plover, and the dun Clio." I went inside the tent to the promised camp bed and a small brazier, not lit. I pulled off my boots and stretched out. The bed cradled my aching body. In a few hours, I would see Maya. I closed my eyes and slept.

Chapter Twenty

When Darel wakened me, the sun had not yet risen. I found my boots in the dark, pulling them on. Darel had Plover tacked up and Clio on her leading rein. His own mount, a bay with the look of a Han-bred horse, stood ready to go. He did not introduce me to the soldier now on guard duty. I raised a hand to the man from across the camp, and he acknowledged me with a nod.

"It's about a quarter of an hour to the Emperor's camp," Darel volunteered once we had started out. "The woman's camp is another bit beyond that. I am to take you to General Casyn, though. Those were the orders."

"How long has the General been here?" I asked to make conversation. "I rode south with him to the grasslands road where we parted eight or nine days ago."

"He arrived three days ago, he and Major Turlo." Something in his voice as he said Turlo's name caught my attention. I looked at him more closely. In the dawn light, I could see his fox-red hair.

"And the women," I asked. "How long have they been here?"

"About two weeks. The Emperor gave them tents and food. They're camped in a small valley east of our camp. We're not allowed to go there."

"How many women are there?" Ahead I could see the shape of tents and fires, and figures moving. Voices carried in the still air. I heard a laugh, boisterous and familiar: Turlo.

"Perhaps three dozen," Darel said.

We rode into the camp: a village of tents, set up in orderly lines. Men moved outside the tents, getting ready for the day. I saw them looking up at me. Darel sat his horse with a straight back and a serious look on his face, riding directly for a group of larger tents on a slope some yards ahead. I looked around, curious, to see a figure striding towards me. I reined Plover in, grinning.

"Lena!" Turlo shouted. I dismounted. He lifted me off my feet in a hug. I wondered, breathless, what the watching soldiers made of this. Turlo put me down and stepped back. "Cohort-Leader, welcome to the winter camp," he said. "Let me take you to Casyn." He looked up at Darel. "Well done, cadet," he said, smiling. Darel flushed. "Take care of the Cohort-Leader's horses, please." He turned to me. "What happened to your Han mare?" I explained. "Cadet!" he called to Darel, who had begun to lead horses away. Darel turned in the saddle.

"Sir?"

"Get the mare reshod, please. Come," he said to me, striding ahead. I followed him into one of the large tents. "Casyn, look who I've found!"

"I think the whole camp heard," Casyn said, rising. He too stepped forward to embrace me, in the formal soldier's manner. "Welcome, Lena. I am very glad to see you." He smiled at me, and I smiled back. "Have you breakfasted?"

"No."

"Turlo?"

"I'll not say no to food."

"Why does that not surprise me," Casyn said drily. I laughed, feeling ridiculously glad to see them both. Casyn called to someone for food and drink, bidding me sit while we waited. "No debriefing until you've eaten, Cohort-Leader." I sat on the stool he indicated, looking around. Unlike the small sleeping tents we had used on the road, this tent was tall enough to stand in, and not just in the centre. A screen blocked part of the space, but the rest of the room held a desk and chair, several stools, and a couple of chests. A lit brazier provided warmth. This was not luxury, but certainly comfort, more than I had envisioned.

In short order, tea, bacon, and bread fried in the bacon fat arrived. The soldier who brought it unfolded a small table, placing it in front of me, and another for Turlo. I ate hungrily, Turlo leisurely. Casyn drank tea.

When I had finished and held a mug of tea, Casyn spoke. "You know Maya is here?"

"Yes. I had news at the Four-Ways Inn."

"But you went to Karst first."

"Garth offered to take the news of Tice's death, to let me come straight here, but it was my duty. And I wanted to be there for Garth, to witness his claiming of Valle. I'm glad I did." I told them, as concisely as I could, of what had transpired at Karst.

Turlo muttered "Stupid woman!" when I told them what Tamar had done, but Casyn simply listened.

"Karst breeds proud women," he said when I had finished. "And men. But it sounds as if the boy will be safe and properly raised."

"Yes," I said.

"And what of your task for me?" Casyn asked. Startled, I glanced at Turlo. Then I relaxed. Of course, he knew.

"I did as you asked. The suggestions that we could ask for a new assembly proved of great interest to some, laughable to others, and I think one or two women thought me mad. One woman I spoke to wanted even more, to be a soldier, living and fighting beside the men."

Casyn raised an eyebrow. "An idea fraught with difficulties. But your sense, overall, is that there is support for change?"

I wanted to answer him accurately. I sorted through all the impressions I had gathered. "There are certainly those who just want life to go back to what it was, but most women seem to realize that it can't, or won't, and many don't want it to."

"And then there is Maya and her compatriots," he said. "How do we resolve these divergent wishes?" I sensed this question was rhetorical and did not reply. I swallowed the last of my tea.

"May I go to her now? If you have more questions for me, I will be glad to answer them later."

Casyn looked up. "She will not see you," he said gently. "She has told me so." I started to speak, but he held up a hand. "I won't stop you from trying. Indeed, I have no authority to do so, but I wanted you to know that she will have you turned away. You should also know that her first question to me was to ask about your safety."

"I am not surprised that she has said she won't see me. I heard enough on the road to expect that." Even so, I had held on to a vestige of hope. "Did you tell her about Garth?"

"No," Casyn said. "I felt that was yours to tell, and perhaps a reason for her to see you after all."

"Thank you for that. It was, in the end, why I came."

Casyn studied me. I needed to say these words to someone, to make them real before I said them to Maya.

"I realize there can be no future for us," I said steadily, "but her last words to Tali were that she was going to look for Garth. She's missed him all these years. I have to tell her he is safe."

Casyn nodded gravely.

"I have a note to give her from a girl at one of the inns," I said. "I'll write my own note, saying I have news of Garth, and deliver them both. Do you have pen and paper I could use?"

"Of course." Casyn showed me his writing box, and I sat beside the brazier in the tent to write a short note.

Maya, I am at the Emperor's Camp. I would like to see you, if only for this: I have news of Garth. He is safe and well, and I have a message from him. I read it over. It sounded cold to me, but what more could I say? I signed my name, folded the paper, and sealed it.

"I'll take her," Turlo said, unfolding himself from his stool. We walked out of the camp between rows of tents, along a path that ran up to the top a small rise. Below, in a small valley beside a stream, stood a dozen or so tents. I could see several women working around the tents, but not Maya. Turlo put his hand on my shoulder. The gesture almost made me cry. I wanted to lean into him, to be comforted.

"Come back to the General's tent when you're ready." I nodded my thanks, and walked down towards the tents, my body tense with apprehension.

I saw someone notice me at the encampment. Hands pointed, and women conferred. Two began to walk towards me. They met me on the path, still a good distance from the camp.

"Hello," the older of the two said. She had short hair and kind eyes. "I am Lena of Tirvan."

She held out her hand. I took it. "I'm Alis, originally from Berge," she said, "and this is Kirthe, from Torrey. Will you talk with us a minute?"

I decided to take the lead. "I don't expect Maya to see me." I saw the flicker of surprise in Alis's eyes. "I've heard enough of your plans, on the road, to understand why." I hoped my voice sounded calm. "But I have two notes for

her. One is from a girl at one of the inns on the grasslands. One is from me." I
handed them to Alis. I saw her glance at Kirthe. "Please tell Maya that the note
from me concerns her brother."

"I'll tell her," Alis said. "I'll give her these when she wakes. She and some of
the others were planning late into the night."

"Thank you." I hesitated. "She is well?"

Alis smiled, fine lines fanning out around her eyes. "She is well."

Walking back up the hill, I remembered Garth saying how helpless he felt,
waiting at Karst for Tamar to react to our news. But I didn't feel helpless. I felt
like I did late in the summer, ready to face what was coming, but still
apprehensive. Part of the way up, I turned to watch Alis and Kirthe. I hoped to
see which tent they would enter, but they joined a group of women washing
clothes at the edge of the camp. I realized they could see me watching.

I thought about crouching at the top of the hill, to watch the camp for a
glimpse of Maya, but the idea seemed childish. I walked back between the rows
of smaller tents. Men looked at me curiously, but no one spoke to me. The air
smelled of wood smoke and horse dung and rang with the clang of metal and
shouted commands.

Casyn sat writing outside his tent, the brazier beside him. He looked up as I
approached.

"I've left the messages with one of the women," I said. "They saw me coming
and walked up to meet me on the path."

"Be patient. I think she will see you."

"For news of Garth."

"That will be what she tells the others," he agreed. "Now, I have been
thinking of what to do with you. You need a place to stay, and you are neither
of this camp nor the women's. I think it would be best for you to camp just
slightly apart from us. I'll have a tent issued to you, and a camp bed and brazier,
and my aide will show you where to raise it. Following Turlo's lead, wise man
that he is, you will be called by your rank of Cohort-Leader in public. As you
should call us by rank, outside of private conversation. The men will follow our
lead."

He stood, and almost immediately a middle-aged soldier appeared. I
recognized him as the man who had brought breakfast. "This is Sergeant Birel,
my aide. Sergeant, this is Cohort-Leader Lena, from Tirvan. She needs a tent
and the usual fittings."

"Yes, sir. If you would come with me, Cohort-Leader?"

I followed Birel through the camp. We stopped at a large tent, with wagons
covered in canvas behind it. He went inside, to come back out with a folded
tent. I took it, surprised at its weight. Blankets came next. "I'll show you your
campsite and then we'll come back for the rest of the things."

We walked beyond the periphery of the tents to a small grove of trees. I
looked around. The trees gave me some privacy as well as protection from
wind and rain. After we put up the tent, I followed Birel back to the stores for

the brazier and charcoal, and then for the camp bed. He showed me how to put the bed together. Wooden pegs held the frame, and a rope strung through holes in the frame supported the sleeper. More trips gained me water jugs and other necessities. My little camp came together quickly.

"I'll detail some soldiers to dig you a latrine pit and put up wattling around it."

"I can do that."

He shook his head slightly. "Best not. No officer would, in camp. The General would like you to join him for the midday meal after you refresh yourself."

I looked down at myself. I had ridden hard and long yesterday, and slept rough, and it showed. I had not even considered this when I had gone to the women's encampment. Briefly, I wondered what Alis and Kirthe had thought, but then dismissed the thought. What of it? "I'll be there. Thank you for all of this," I added, gesturing to the camp.

"Not at all," he said briskly. "Shall I give you some time before I send the team over?"

I could stand in my tent, but only near the centre. I moved the washstand, filled the bowl, and stripped. I realized I should have lit the brazier when I felt the water. I washed and dressed quickly. As I combed my hair, I wondered if the camp's barber would cut it for me.

As I stepped out of my tent, a team of two soldiers approached, one with a spade over his shoulder, the other carrying wattle panels.

"Cohort-Leader," the one with the spade addressed me. "Sergeant Birel sent us to dig your necessary. Do you want to say where?"

"I'll leave that to your judgment." Did you thank soldiery for such work? Then I remembered Casyn's unfailing politeness to his subordinates. "Thank you."

I walked back up the short path into the main camp. I hoped I could remember how to find Casyn's tent. A few men nodded to me, and a young officer, passing, greeted me by rank.

"Lieutenant," I said, glad that I could recognize his insignia. "Can you direct me to the General Casyn's tent?" He pointed. "Thank you."

Birel was waiting for me there. "Please come with me," he said, without further explanation. We ascended a slope to where a large tent stood, somewhat apart. Birel pulled open the flap.

"Cohort-Leader Lena, sir," he said, gesturing me to go in. I stepped under the flap into the interior. Three men rose to greet me: Casyn, and two others I did not recognize, both roughly Casyn's age. One wore unrelieved black, and the other, the brown uniform of the Empire. I glanced uncertainly at Casyn. He turned slightly toward the man in uniform.

"Callan, may I introduce Cohort-Leader Lena, of Tirvan. Lena, this is Callan, our elected Emperor."

I had absolutely no idea what I was supposed to do. Callan smiled.

"Welcome, Cohort-Leader." I had expected him to look like Casyn, and around the eyes I could see a resemblance. But he stood half a head taller than Casyn and carried less weight on his lean frame.

"Thank you, sir," I said, just audibly, through very dry lips.

"And this is my advisor, Colm," he said, indicating the other man. The third brother, I remembered, the historian and castrate. He looked quite a bit like the Emperor, but less defined, with watchful eyes. He returned my greeting with only a hint of a smile.

"Shall we sit?" Casyn said. I waited for Callan to sit first. Casyn, I thought, you could have warned me. Young officers are trained in protocol. I am not.

"Casyn has told me what happened at Tirvan, both at his arrival and during the fighting," Callan said. "I will not ask you to elaborate on that unless there is something you particularly want to tell me." He paused.

"No, sir," I said. "Except that without Garth, now Watch-Commander of *Skua*, more lives would have been lost, a child's among them."

"His acts are known to me," he said, nodding. "Tell me, if you will, what you heard on the road from other women at the inns."

I repeated what I had told Casyn. Colm took notes, and Callan listened intently. When I spoke of Halle, and her desire to be a soldier, he smiled.

"She would envy you, then," he said lightly.

When I finished speaking, he glanced at his brothers before turning back to me.

"What do you know of the Partition agreement?"

"What all women know," I said. "Two hundred years past, an assembly was called to resolve the differences between what the men of the Empire and the women of the Empire wanted. They talked and argued for nearly two weeks, and in the end, voted for what we have today: the women's villages and the Empire's army, and all the rules and the customs that have grown up around those."

"Do you know how many women and men voted for Partition?"

"No," I said, surprised. "I don't." I had never thought to ask.

"It was a majority of both men and women, but not quite six in ten were in favour. Nearly half the Empire's people did not want Partition, but preferred a free choice in how to live."

"And they had to abide by Partition or choose to be exiled." He looked surprised. "I asked Casyn: I wasn't taught it."

The Emperor shook his head. "None of us were. Until Colm found the records in a storeroom at the eastern fort, it had been completely forgotten. Very likely, the actual result of the vote was never widely known. But I have known now for nearly a decade, and over those years, I have found myself wanting to know if we—all of us, the Empire—still want to live this way."

He chooses his strategy and deployment based on a picture in his mind, a picture that changes with season and weather, or time of day, and yet he always knows what will happen, Garth had said. It had niggled at me, then.

"May I ask you something, sir? If this is presumptuous, please forgive me. I am not schooled in the correct protocols."

He grinned. "In this private conference, you may speak freely."

"Someone told me, once," I said, choosing my words carefully, "that in planning a battle, or a campaign, you always seem to know what will happen. When you planned the campaign against Leste, did you see in asking the women's villages to fight, that when it was done, we would have little choice but ask for a new assembly, either to affirm Partition or create something new?" I took a breath, suddenly, deeply angry. "Were we pieces in your game, Emperor?"

He took it calmly, with a brief glance at Casyn. "Yes," he said simply, "and no. The need to have the women's villages defend the Empire against Leste was real. The reasons Casyn gave to you at Tirvan were the truth. But did I see the outcome you spoke of? Yes. But I did not, and I swear this on my honour as the Emperor, I did not manipulate the threat to us from Leste. The Lestian invasion was not of my making."

"And if it hadn't happened? How would you have brought about a new assembly?" I could feel Casyn watching me. I wondered if Colm was still recording our conversation.

"I do not know," he said. "Perhaps I would have just asked if it was wanted."

"I think we would have said no."

"Probably," Callan agreed, "but the seed would have been planted. If the question was asked again, two or three years later, the answer might have been different."

I heard a cough at the door. Colm got up to open the flap, revealing Birel and another man bearing trays of food and wine. They came in, to arrange the food on low tables, add coals to the brazier, and silently leave. Colm poured wine for us all. My anger had gone, vanquished by the Emperor's calm reason.

Bread and cheese, apples, walnuts were handed around. Callan, it seemed, ate much as his men did, although I doubted they drank wine of this quality. I felt uncomfortable.

"Sir," I said suddenly, "please forgive me. I overstepped."

He took a drink of his wine. "Not at all," he replied, easily. "Those who advise emperors should be able to challenge them as well. It would concern me if you did not want to know the mind of the man whose ideas you were spreading. Casyn told me to expect no less."

We ate. Our conversation, it seemed, was over. Afterward, Casyn stood. "I will walk with you, Lena." We emerged into the midday sunshine.

"You could have warned me."

"I could have," he agreed mildly, "but then you would have thought about what you wanted to say. I preferred the conversation to be unrehearsed. You did well."

"I challenge the Emperor, and you call that doing well?"

He stopped. "Yes, Lena, I do," he said. "You are not under his command, for all that we will treat you as a soldier while you are here. You owe him courtesy, which you have given, and honesty, which is what he heard from you. If there is to be a new assembly, women must be prepared to speak their minds and not defer to the title."

I could see Casyn's logic, but it still made me a bit uncomfortable.

"Casyn...General," I amended, as we were in public. "What am I to do, here? You've said you will treat me as a soldier, but where and how should I spend my days? I can't always eat with you. Should I spend my time alone?"

"There is no reason you cannot mix with the younger officers when they are off-duty. Darel, for one, would be glad of your company. Your ponies will need exercise, of course, and I thought you might like to spend some time with Colm, when his duties allow. You might find it interesting to learn more of the Empire's past."

"I would," I said slowly, "but has he the time?"

"He will find a few hours, I think."

After we parted, I walked back to my tent to change into my riding clothes. I found the horse-lines, and Plover, but no Clio. I asked the soldier on duty.

"Gone to be reshod, Cohort-Leader. A nice little Han mare, if I may say so."

"She is," I agreed. "I'd like to curry the piebald. Is there a brush I could use?" He brought me one, seeming unsurprised by the request. I thought of Casyn with Siannon, and Dern with Tasque. Officers, it appeared, frequently took care of their own horses. I gave Plover a good currying while he stamped and snorted with pleasure, rippling his skin under his coat. I remembered what Inge had said, and rubbed him between his ears, breathing in the warm smell of horse. The grooming soothed us both.

The day was sunny and cool, with a light breeze. Back at my tent, I built a fire pit, and from the firewood someone had stacked by my tent, I made a fire, heating water to wash my clothes. The sun had dropped well down in the western sky, and I had just hung the last shirt over the line I had strung between two trees when I heard footsteps.

"Cohort-Leader," Colm greeted me. "Are you busy?"

"I'm just finished." I hesitated. "I don't know how to address you."

"The men call me Advisor, but in private my name will be fine. My brother tells me you would like to learn some of the Empire's history."

"I would," I said, marvelling once again at Casyn's generosity. With everything he must have to do, he still found time to talk to Colm about me? "I'm beginning to realize how little I know. Casyn has told me a few things, and of course I was taught a little as a child, but much seems to have been missed."

"Where would you like to begin?"

"Let me build up this fire, first" I said. "I have wine, if you like?" He assented, and after I had put a few more logs on the fire, I ducked inside my tent to find the bottle and two cups I had received earlier from the stores tent. He pulled two rounds of wood close to the fire to make rough seating. I poured the wine, handing him a cup.

"Thank you," he said, sipping. If he noticed the rougher quality compared to what he drank with Callan, he made no sign.

"What was life like, before the Partition agreement?"

"That is a difficult question," he said. "There is nothing written to tell us exactly how people lived. But I've made a study of old records, from before Partition—tax rolls and tally sheets, the court records. Such things tell a story, if you know how to hear it. It would seem that men and women, for the most part, lived their lives together in the villages that now belong to women. They owned land, separately or together, and learned and practiced trades. The army was then a trade like any other: a choice for men, not an obligation."

"Only for men?"

"I think so. I find women's names mentioned rarely in the army's records, and even then, it's not clear what their role is. I think perhaps some of the cooks and launderers may have been women, and even perhaps the horse-masters. But I don't think they fought."

I watched Colm as he spoke. In the sunlight, I could see more resemblance to Callan, but his features lacked Callan's definition and strength. He reminded me of Siane, after her leg was smashed, and she could no longer farm; softer, a blurred copy of her previous self.

"What happened to bring about Partition? I was taught only that it came about because the men wanted to invade north, and the women didn't." I had accepted that, all my life, but no longer.

"There's some truth in that. The Emperor of the day, Lucian, offered free land in the north to any man who joined him in the conquest of those lands. Many chose to join him. The Empire at that time had grown crowded, as unlikely as that seems now, and arable land was in short supply. But then Lucian had to tax the villages more to feed his larger army, and the villages, depleted of much of their workforce, had difficulty providing the food. The headwomen of all the villages—for women have always run the village councils—objected. They banded together and approached Lucian to demand an assembly. From that assembly came Partition and our lives as we know them today."

"But we didn't take the north," I said, frowning.

"Many who would not live under the rules of Partition fled north, so when Lucian marched beyond what is now the Wall, he found an organized resistance and a larger fighting force than he had expected. Some of them had been trained in his army and knew his tactics. His invasion failed, and the border was set. We patrol it to this day."

"When word of the planned invasion by Leste came, did you remind the Emperor of Lucian's failed invasion?"

He smiled. "You are quick. I did not need to. Callan forgets nothing."

We talked for some time. Colm told me of Lucian's successor, Mathon, who had built the road, and expanded the eastern fort. He described the small forts that predated the Wall and then the building of the Wall, when the increasing cold led to more border raids. "Some accounts indicate that before the Wall was finished, women and children slipped through the border patrols and begged for refuge at Berge where they were taken in. The red hair of their Northern fathers remains not uncommon in Berge to this day, as you have seen in Turlo." He glanced at the setting sun. "I must go. Casyn and my twin will be looking for me."

"Your twin?"

"Callan and I are twins. He is the older, by six minutes, something he never let me forget when we were children."

It explained so much—not only Colm's apparent acceptance in the camp (although who could argue with the Emperor about whom he chose to be his advisors?) but also Casyn's conviction that parentage alone did not make a soldier. I wondered if Garth knew.

"If you like," Colm said, "I'll introduce you to some of the junior officers. It would be good for you to have some companions in camp."

We walked together to a large tent set among smaller sleeping tents. "This is the common area for the junior officers when they are off duty," he explained. The door flaps were tied back, and inside I could see three men playing dice.

"Advisor," one man said, standing.

"Lieutenant," Colm said. "May I introduce Cohort-Leader Lena, from Tirvan. She will be in camp with us for some days and needs to learn our routines. Cohort-Leader, this is Finn, Lieutenant of the Fourth." With that, he was gone. Finn looked to be in his early twenties, stocky and pleasant-faced.

"If you would rather I did not join you, Lieutenant, I'll go back to my tent."

"Not at all. We would be glad of your company. Our own gets a bit stale after a while." He introduced me to the others. They seemed genuinely pleased to have me there. I accepted a cup of ale and found a chair.

"Tirvan," Finn said. "That's quite far north. How fared you, in the fighting?"

"I'll tell you, if you like, but would you answer something for me, first?"

"Certainly, if I can."

"How is it decided who comes to the Emperor's camp? You're from the Fourth, Lieutenant. The young soldier on guard duty the night I arrived was from the Third. And you, "I gestured to the others, "are all from different regiments."

"We're seconded to the Emperor's Regiment for a year," Finn explained. "It's part of every officer's training. Cadets like Darel are sent if they are considered to have potential as officers. I was here as a cadet. I think most of us were. If a senior officer comes to serve with the Emperor, he may also bring some men along."

"How big is the camp?"

"There are one hundred and sixty men, and ten officers, not including the Emperor. And various officers who come and go, like Major Turlo, and General Casyn, although he will stay, now, I think." He paused. "You know the General,

I believe?"

"He came to Tirvan in the spring to ask us to learn to fight, and then stayed, to help train us, and be our blacksmith for a time. I had no idea he was a general for the longest time."

"Almost all the men who went to the villages were senior officers, but they did not want that known. I imagine the council leaders knew, in each village, but otherwise it was felt that the villages would rely too much on their expertise and not develop their own. Tell me of your defence plan, and how the fighting unfolded."

I explained, painting them a picture of how Tirvan sat on its hillsides, and the harbour and coves, and how we had planned to use the tunnels and hiding places in the village. I told them of the waterfall, of learning to climb up it, and of burning the forge. I told them of the caves in the hill fields, and how they had almost been our undoing.

"When Pel was taken, we weren't sure what to do." I paused. "But one man we had captured during the fighting was not truly of Leste. He was a spy for the Empire."

"A spy!" one of the other officers, Gulian, exclaimed. "I heard rumours of this. How did you know he was telling you the truth when he claimed to be such?"

"I recognized him. We were children together in Tirvan. He agreed to try to rescue the child, and did so, killing the invader in the process. And that was the end of it."

"Casualties?" Gulian asked.

"Four dead," I said. "And some wounded. One was seriously burned when we set fire to the forge."

"It sounds a fine campaign."

"Did you go to Leste?" I asked. Dern had told me a bit about that part of the fighting. As in the villages, it had been quick and fairly bloodless, except for some of the King's Guard.

Finn shook his head. "Not I. I was here as part of the Emperor's Guard. But Gulian and Galdor went."

They spoke of the island. They described the long and low terrain, terraced with grapes and other fruits and spices, and they spoke of the fear of the women and children in the towns and villages. Only old men and boys remained in Leste to defend the island. When it became clear that the Empire's soldiers had orders not to kill, but to subdue—"Hard, that was, learning to wound rather than kill," Galdor said—most surrendered quickly. Only the King's Guard fought with conviction, and they were outnumbered five to one.

"Of course, we have garrisons there now," Gulian said. "I hope to serve on Leste after my time here. I'd like to be warm again," he added, with a mock shiver.

"But it is warm," I protested.

"Perhaps to a northerner," he grumbled. "I was born in Casilla."

A steward came in with food, spreading it out on the long table. If my presence surprised him, he did not show it. He lit more lamps, placed them on the table, and set four places. We ate roast fowl, and potatoes, and nutty, spiced parsnips with a good wine. Afterwards the steward brought tea, and tiny squares of honey-soaked pastries stuffed with walnuts. I had rarely eaten so well.

"Is the food always this good?" I asked, refusing another pastry.

"Here at the camp, yes," Finn said. He took the pastry I had turned down. "But not on campaign."

"Or up at the Wall," Galdor added.

After dinner, they offered to teach me to dice. Forbidden real gambling, they played for points, "and glory," Finn said. Four dice were tossed from a cup, and the one who came closest to twenty-one, but not over, won. The game involved no skill, just pure chance, and we played as if the future of the Empire hung on the outcome.

Galdor won. Hugely pleased, he laughed a deep, rumbling laugh. Finn stood. He seemed to be the leader, whether by length of commission or by natural leadership, I didn't know. "We're on duty an hour before dawn, so it's time to retire. If you're up that early, Cohort-Leader, please join us for breakfast. Otherwise, we would be pleased to have you join us again, tomorrow afternoon."

"I've enjoyed this evening," I said truthfully. They had demanded nothing of me, the conversation remaining on military matters, food and drink and the dice game. When had I last simply had fun? I said goodnight, walking through the dark camp to my tent.

I stretched out on my camp bed, not yet ready to sleep. Someone had lit the brazier in my absence, and the tent was comfortably warm. I chuckled, remembering Gulian's complaints of the cold.

I thought about what he had said of garrisons on Leste. Was Leste now subject to the Partition agreement? How could I not have asked Casyn this, or Dern? If not, could the Empire have two provinces, with different ways of life? Surely that would breed discontent. I would have to remember to ask.

Chapter Twenty-One

I AWOKE TO THE TRUMPET ANNOUNCING WATCH CHANGE, an hour before dawn. The sides of my tent flapped, and I heard water dripping. I swore, remembering my washing.

I put my head out of the tent. The air had turned colder, and a fine, light rain fell. I pulled on my heavy pants and found my jacket. After visiting the latrine, I made my way to the junior officers' commons. None of the officers were present, but a steward appeared almost immediately.

"Would you like breakfast, Cohort-Leader?" he asked. Not by a flicker of an eye or expression did he indicate that he found my presence unusual or inappropriate.

"Please. And may I have tea?"

"Right away."

He brought me tea, a mint-based infusion, and shortly afterwards eggs and toasted bread, butter and honey, and a dish of apples and figs. By the time I finished eating, several other young officers had come in, but none I knew. To a man they greeted me politely, and by rank, but they ate together at the other side of the tent.

I walked back to my tent. The rain had stopped, and the wind whipped the clouds along. With luck, it would clear, so my washing would dry. I needed to move. I had slept well, and sitting about had never appealed to me.

At the horse-line, I found my tack neatly stowed in a brush shelter nearby. I saddled Clio, who idly browsed on a biscuit of hay, and mounted. We headed for the hills above the camp. I had noticed other riders there yesterday, not in formation but out for exercise. A clear trail, pocked with hoof prints, showed the way. On the hilltops, the wind blew fiercely, making me glad of my fleece coat. I set Clio to a gentle canter. She needed little urging, after two days not under saddle. We followed the trail that ran below the ridge-line away from the camp.

The camp sat in a natural bowl, shallow-sided and sheltered. If it were in danger of attack, the hillsides would have to be patrolled at all times. I wondered if that had happened during the invasion.

Below me, the hillside flattened into fields cleared of brush. Training grounds, I decided: places for drill and practice. Hearing voices ahead, I followed the trail around a pinnacle, and saw, in the field below, men practicing archery with bows nearly as tall as themselves. In the wind, many arrows went wide of the butts. I assumed shooting in the wind was the purpose of the exercise. I watched for a while, my hands itching to hold a bow again.

I turned Clio to head back. The wind made my eyes tear. Back at the horse-line, I unsaddled and brushed Clio before returning her to her place on the picket. The exercise had settled me. If my clothes had dried—if they haven't blown halfway to Casilla, I thought—I would do some mending. I would need to light the brazier, though, and warm the tent, or my fingers would be too cold to hold a needle.

A cadet met me on the path. "Advisor Colm asks if you would meet him at the Emperor's compound, Cohort-Leader. Do you know the way?"

"I do. Thank you, cadet." I turned up the slope, wondering what Colm might want.

The Advisor waited for me outside the tent. "Good morning, Lena. You have a visitor." He gestured to the tent.

"Maya?" My gut churned.

"Yes," he confirmed calmly, "and a companion." He opened the flap, and I stepped inside.

Maya's hair was short, as short as mine. She looked even more like Garth. "Your hair..." I said, through dry lips. She looked thin and tired.

She put a hand up to it, shrugging. "It was more practical for travelling." Alis stood behind her, near the corner of the tent. She caught my eye, smiling slightly.

"Lena, why are you here?" Her voice held the steel she shared with her mother and her brother.

I took a breath to steady myself. "To bring you news of Garth." My throat felt tight.

"Truly?" she said, with a thread of hope in her voice. "That wasn't just a ruse, to make me see you?"

"Maya!" Alis whispered. Maya ignored her, her eyes on me, challenging.

"Have I ever lied to you, Maya?"

Her face softened. "Forgive me. I couldn't let myself believe it."

"We should sit," I said. "I have a lot to tell you." We found chairs, and I sat facing the two women. Maya and Alis sat close together. Alis took Maya's hand for a moment, giving it a squeeze. Once, that would have elicited anger from me, or at least jealousy. Now, I felt nothing but a numb acceptance.

I took a deep breath. She would not like all of what she would hear, but I would speak the truth. "I was leader of one of the cohorts at Tirvan," I began. I could see her recoil slightly. That hurt, even now. Alis took Maya's hand again. "Tice, the potter, was my cohort-second. We captured Garth on the night of the invasion. He had been serving aboard the Lestian catboat as a spy to the Empire." I heard her gasp, but went on. "He had long hair, braided in the Lestian style, and I recognized him because he looked so much like you."

"He serves, then," she said. I could hear the undercurrent of disappointment in her voice.

"He does," I said. "His current rank is Watch-Commander, aboard the ship *Skua*. But this wasn't always the case. Before he became a spy, he deserted."

"The punishment for desertion is death!" Her voice rose with panic. "How is he alive and serving?"

"He found passage away from the Empire on a Lestian trader, and lived and worked on Leste for some time. Eventually he was captured by the Empire and offered an alternative to the usual punishment: to serve the Empire by gathering information on the Lestian plan. To be a spy. He agreed and did so for three years. We may owe our success this autumn to Garth, Maya. You should be proud of him." I hoped she would not hear the struggle for control in my voice. I heard myself defending—no, praising—Garth to his sister. It told me where my allegiance lay.

I looked into Maya's hazel eyes, so much like Garth's. They glittered with unshed tears.

"Did he speak of me?" She sounded so very young.

Part of me wanted to say no, to hurt her, to dash her hopes. But I had loved her. In some way, I still did. I loved them both, and I could not be cruel. Garth had trusted me.

"He said to tell you he had never forgotten you." Her face blazed with happiness. "One night, he told me that in the back of his mind, when he ran, he always hoped to come back to Tirvan for you, forgetting you would be an adult, with a life of your own."

"I wish he had."

Suddenly, I grew angry. "You can't have it both ways. If you want tradition, Garth should be dead, executed for desertion. The only reason he isn't is that the Emperor Callan recognizes that tradition has its place, but people must move forward."

"Maya and I, all of us, had the right to say no and choose exile," Alis said, her voice edged with anger.

"At Partition, those who would not live by the agreement were exiled beyond the boundaries of the Empire. Would you accept that, if an assembly so ruled?"

"Yes," Maya said, raising her chin. "If a full assembly so rules. But as you said, this Emperor sees that tradition is not all, and the villages have made their feelings towards the Partition agreement clear. Why shouldn't we be allowed to stay within the Empire?"

My anger fled, replaced by a wave of tenderness. "I hope you are," I said gently.

"Truly?" She sounded surprised.

"Oh, Maya, our lives may have separated, but I want you to be safe."

She did not meet my eyes, but simply nodded. After a moment, she looked up. "And I you, Lena. What will you do?"

"I don't know," I admitted. "Go home, I think, but not until spring. Perhaps go to Casilla, so that I can say I have spent a season in the city. Or work the winter at an inn."

She stood. "Thank you for the news of Garth. I won't see you again unless the Emperor commands it."

"Wait," I said hurriedly. "I have more to tell you, about Garth."

"More!" She sat down again.

"We rode south together. In fact, I left him only three days ago, in Karst. We've been together since the invasion."

"Why?" She frowned.

"We both had business in Karst. Dern, his captain on *Skua*, gave him permission to ride down and meet the ship at Casilla, at midwinter. It made sense for us to ride together. Casyn rode part of the way with us, too."

"You went to tell them about Tice?"

"That was my mission. And Garth went to acknowledge a son he did not know until now he had fathered. I bore witness for him. He's there now, getting to know the child."

"Oh," Maya said. She seemed confused, as if she could not assimilate this. Perhaps she can't, I thought. Garth is an ideal to her, not quite real. Alis studied Maya, looking just a bit worried. I took a breath to steady myself and gave her the last gift I had to give.

"Garth will likely be at Karst, spring and fall, for the next few years, duty allowing. His son is three. You have four years."

Hope bloomed in her face. "Oh," she breathed. "Yes. Yes. Thank you, Lena."

I stood. "There's one more thing."

"What?"

"We never said good-bye."

She looked at me for a moment, then stood. I stepped forward and put my arms around her, lightly. She felt as unsubstantial as a bird. "Farewell, Maya," I whispered, and let her go.

I had known, at some level, what would happen at this meeting since the night at Aasta's inn. I had wept for Maya, the night she left, and many times since. I did not weep now. I walked out of the tent into the wind and clear air, feeling whole for the first time in many weeks.

Back at my camp, I took my lighter clothes off the line and went into the tent. I lit the brazier, and did my mending, then folded and packed away shirts and underclothes, readying myself to leave. The sense of calm, of something completed and concluded, remained with me. I realized I needed a drink. I sat on the bed and was reaching for the jug of water when I noticed a book beside it with a note tucked inside. I opened the note.

"This is my own history of the Empire," the note read. "I thought you might like to read it." It was signed "Colm."

I picked up the book and turned to the first page. In neat, upright script, I read. "In the third year of the reign of the Emperor Lucian..."

I read, or thought about what I was reading, until mid-afternoon. Like learning knife-play, it was an exercise in attention. If I kept my attention on what I read, I did not have to think of my future. When the slant and colour of light told me that evening fast approached, I put the book down to walk to the commons.

Galdor and Finn welcomed me. With a mug of ale in hand, I threw dice, laughing, and nibbled on pickles and bread. The evening had become night when suddenly both Galdor and Finn shot to attention.

"General," Finn said. "Please come in."

"At ease," Casyn said. "I won't disturb you, but I would like to speak with the Cohort-Leader. Can you spare her from your game?"

I excused myself and followed Casyn out into the night. He did not speak until we had walked a few yards away from the commons.

"You have seen Maya," he said gently.

"She wanted news of Garth, and I gave it. I won't see her again."

"That is her choice?" Casyn said.

"It's not mine," I said sharply.

"Forgive me," Casyn said. "Are you all right?"

I swallowed and nodded. "I am. I was prepared for this."

"Have you thought what you will do now?" he asked.

"A bit," I said. "I could go back to one of the inns, Zilde's, near the end of the grasslands. She needs help. I could winter there and ride home in the spring. I haven't really made a decision."

"The Emperor asks that you stay until Midwinter's Day. He would like your counsel, and your presence, for some proclamations he will make that day."

"My counsel?"

"Think about the number of women you would want to attend an assembly from each village, and about how they should be chosen. We spoke of this on the road, if you remember." I nodded. The request reminded me of what I had meant to ask.

"Is Leste bound now by the Partition agreement? And if so, will they have a voice in this assembly? Or are there different rules for Leste?"

He smiled. "If you are not council leader at Tirvan by the time you are thirty, I am no judge of young officers," he said. "That exact question has taken up much of my brothers' time, and mine, in the last days. We have a plan, but," he said, "it is for no one's ears, until Midwinter's Day. By then, the governor of Leste will have arrived with his advisors to hear the future of his province."

Leste's former king now governed in name only. All the decisions came from his advisors, senior officers of the Empire. Galdor and Finn had explained it all to me over dice. "When will he come?"

"Soon. The wind yesterday would have made for good sailing from Leste. If they land tonight, as I think they will, they will arrive the day after tomorrow."

"I'll stay." I wanted to see this once-king of Leste. I wanted even more to know what Callan would say, to Maya and the others, in response to their petition. Even with the delay, I should be able to reach Zilde's inn before the worst of the winter set in. Staying would give me a bit more time to think, too.

"I'll tell the Emperor. Will you go back to the dice?"

I considered. I felt oddly light-hearted. "Yes, I was winning."

The odd euphoria lasted through the night, only seeping away when I returned to my camp for the night. Lying on the bed, in the light of the brazier, I tried, unsuccessfully, not to think of Maya. I could see that she and Alis had become more than just travelling companions. As I had with Garth, she would have looked for warmth and comfort in a changed and frightening world. I could not find fault, there. I wished she had not cut her hair. I wanted Garth. I began to cry, then—not the racking sobs of new bereavement, but the slow, trickling tears of old grief. I curled up, hugged the thin pillow, and let the tears come.

Several days passed. Garth, I calculated, would have left Karst to meet *Skua* at Casilla. I wondered if Tali had done this, tracking in her mind what she could imagine or guess of Mar's movements. The Governor of Leste did not arrive. I rode most mornings, spent the afternoons reading, or talking to Colm when his duties allowed. I met some of the other junior officers, and, with permission, went with them one morning to practice archery at the butts. To my pleasure, I outshot half of them.

Turlo came to my camp one afternoon. I was sitting outside my tent, reading in the hazy sunshine and cool air. I had a small fire burning to counter the chill.

"Hello, Cohort-Leader," Turlo called, from several strides away. I looked up, smiling, happy as always to see him. "What are you reading?" he asked, sitting beside me.

I showed him. "Colm's history," he said, surprised. "You're honoured. He doesn't usually let that out of his sight. How are you, Lena?"

"I'm fine. Really," I added, to his quizzical look. I spoke the truth. I felt peaceful, accepting.

We talked of inconsequential things for some minutes. After I laughed at something he said, he looked at me thoughtfully.

"Who's your father, Lena?" he asked then laughed at my startled reaction. "I have a reason to ask. Beyond the usual, I mean. I am far too old to ask you for that reason, more's the pity."

I flushed. "Galen, of the Third." A thought struck me. "Your regiment."

He grinned. "I thought so. You laugh exactly like him. I know Galen well. He's on borders duty. Do you want to send him greetings? I'll see him when I ride north again."

"I wouldn't know what to say. I've never met him."

"Pity," Turlo said. "He's a good man. May I tell him of you?"

"If you like," I grinned. "But try to tell the truth, Turlo."

He laughed, deeply. "I only lie about hunting."

Turlo had left, and I had returned to reading when Colm arrived. I had begged pen and ink, and paper from him yesterday, wanting to write down thoughts, or questions that occurred to me while reading. I greeted Colm.

"I haven't written much," I said.

"That isn't why I have come. The Emperor would like to see you."

"Now?"

"If it's convenient," he said, smiling. I had grown to like him very much in the last days. Grave and thoughtful, like Casyn, he tempered his considerable knowledge with an undercurrent of humour and endless patience with my questions.

After carefully placing my book on the table inside, I accompanied him to the council tent. Callan had a document in his hand, reading, but he put it down as we entered.

"Cohort-Leader," he said. "Thank you for coming,"

"How may I assist you, Emperor?"

He gestured me to sit. He looked tired. Colm found his writing materials.

"If we were to hold a new assembly, perhaps next summer, how many women from each village should attend?"

"Three," I replied. "From most villages, these would likely be the council leaders. But I also think that there should be a way for those women whose views might not be that of their leaders to have their voices heard."

"Go on," he said.

"In my village, there was one woman, Siane, whose views were not those of the majority. She found the taking of life, any life, abhorrent, to the extent that she ate no meat or fish. She died in the fighting, but if she hadn't, I think her opinion should have been heard. Perhaps letters could be written, to be presented at the assembly?"

Callan nodded. "That could be done. Why did not this Siane join the other women who chose exile?"

"She voted against fighting, but she came to realize that she would fight and kill to protect her daughter. She refused refuge with the children during the fighting."

"Bravery comes in so many faces," Callan said. I heard an echo of something someone else had said to me, once. "What else, Lena?"

"What about the inn-keepers?"

"We had thought of that. There is an inn-keepers' guild though, like most guilds, it is inactive. It could be revived and three women chosen from within it to represent them."

"Will there be time?" I asked.

"It will be difficult," he admitted. "I had originally thought to hold the assembly at mid-summer, but I think it will have to be a few weeks later to give the inns and villages time to prepare."

"May I suggest one more thing?"

"Of course."

"When you send word of the assembly, if you can find a way to do so, send a copy of Colm's history to each village. In Tirvan, we have forgotten—if we ever knew—much of what is written there. To make informed decisions, everyone should have the chance to learn what you and your advisors know."

He raised his eyebrows. "An interesting idea," he said. He turned to his brother. "Could we do so?"

Colm considered. "Not the full history," he said finally. "But if it was summarised, leaving out some of the details, then, yes, I think we could. There is a copy at the cadet school. I could send a messenger, asking them to condense the last chapters while I begin on the early ones."

"Write the order, and I will sign it."

"Do you need your book?" I asked Colm.

"No," he said, "I have another copy."

"Thank you, Cohort-Leader," the Emperor said. I took my leave. Outside, in the thin sunshine, the flag of the Empire—a white horse before a wall outlined in grey and black, against a green background—snapped in the breeze. From my reading, I now knew the flag had once had only the horse as insignia. I wondered when the Wall had been added. I walked back to my tent. I wanted to be at this new assembly. I had helped to shape it, and I wanted to see the outcome.

CHAPTER TWENTY-TWO

ELON, THE DEPOSED KING OF LESTE, ARRIVED THE NEXT DAY. I stood among the officers as he and the soldiers guarding him entered the camp under grey, afternoon skies. Elon had a thick cloak wrapped tightly around him against the biting wind. A hood covered his head, and he wore fur gloves. I could hear him coughing. Finn snorted. "He doesn't look much of a king."

"Have you even seen a king before?" I asked.

"No," he admitted. "But I expected a soldier, like the emperor. Not a sick old man."

I shook my head. "Leste barely had an army. Why would he be a soldier?"

Finn shrugged. "I just expected it, that's all."

They rode to the council tent. We watched as the effort of dismounting brought on a bout of coughing that nearly bent him double. One of his escorts took him by the upper arm, helping him into the tent.

I walked with Finn back towards the junior officer's common.

"Who are the officers guarding him?" I asked Finn.

"Majors Blaine and Nevin," he replied. "I don't know them, really. I spoke to Nevin once when I was delivering weapons to his section of the Wall. They both held Wall posts until a year or so back when the Emperor brought them south. Blaine commanded the troops that took the palace on Leste."

"And they've been there ever since?"

"Yes. There's a lot of work to be done there, and Elon had to be well-guarded. My guess is they'll go back with him to be the Empire's force behind the king's nominal governorship." He grinned. "That should suit them after years and years on the cold Wall. Although maybe not," he added, "they were born up there, somewhere. They have the same mother, but different fathers, I think. Nevin's son now holds the garrison that his father used to. Maybe they like the cold. Like you," he said, giving me a gentle poke.

I twisted away from his teasing fingers, smiling. It felt good to be treated casually. I liked Finn. The somewhat staid and formal character he had presented when we first met hid a well-developed sense of humour and a keen understanding of men. I guessed that senior officers were always the topic of much gossip and speculation among cadets and junior officers. I wondered what they said about Callan and his brothers, Colm especially.

"Quite a job they'll have," he said, "bringing the Empire's ways to Leste."

"Will they have to abide by the Partition agreement?"

Finn nodded. "There can only be one set of rules. Anything else would breed discontent, both here and there."

"But men who have never fought and women who have never learned the trades—surely it can't happen all at once."

"Probably not," Finn agreed. "But we can't leave the men to start plotting rebellion. They'll have to be brought into the army somehow."

"What happens to the trading ships?"

"They live by the agreement," Finn said firmly." A burst of laughter from a row of tents caught his attention. "I'd best get those men working. See you tonight?"

I nodded, continuing to the commons. I wanted some tea, and I had nothing particular to do this morning. When the steward brought my tea, I settled down at one of the tables. Finn did not even consider that the women of Leste could start a rebellion. Nor had I, I reminded myself, until this year.

Midwinter's Eve dawned cloudy and cold, the coldest day of the winter so far. Light snow fell. Today, the leaders from the women's camp made their formal petition to the Emperor, and Callan had asked me to be present.

"Maya won't like that," I said to Colm, when he came to tell me.

"But the Emperor will. Callan has the right to choose his advisors, and his audience," Colm reminded me. "You won't be asked to speak, but your presence is requested."

The meeting began an hour after mid-day. I had slept badly, lying awake in the small hours, wondering if Garth had reached *Skua*. I spent a restless morning, grooming Plover and Clio, attending to small chores. At mid-day, I washed and combed my hair, before walking down to the junior commons. Finn's orders required his presence at the petition hearing as part of his education, and we had agreed to meet beforehand.

"This could be long," he said. "Better have something to eat." I helped myself to bread and cheese, and an apple.

"What's the protocol?"

"Follow the lead of the senior officers. Stand if they stand, and sit when they do. We'll be seated by rank with junior officers at the back, so just do what I do."

"That's assuming I'll be sitting with you," I said.

"Where else do you think you'd be?" He grinned. "As long as you're here, Cohort-Leader, you're one of us, even if we don't make you drill troops and ride guard."

"I'd be happy to ride guard. I wish you'd suggested that earlier. It would have given me something to do."

"You still could. I can speak to the officer in charge."

I shook my head. "No point, now. I'm leaving after the Midwinter ceremonies."

"Going home? That's too bad. I'll miss you." He pushed his chair back. "We'd best go. Doesn't do to be late."

At the council tent, the women had not yet arrived. The Emperor's chair of state stood centred against the long wall, flanked by chairs for Colm and Casyn. Three rows of seats extended out from and behind them. As Finn had predicted, we sat at the back behind the senior officers, facing a half-circle of chairs.

I heard voices outside then several men entered. I recognized Elon and two of his guards. "Why is he here?" I whispered to Finn.

"To witness the Emperor's judgment," Finn whispered back.

They sat in one of the front rows. From behind, I could see the governor's greying hair, curly and close-cropped. He wore a shimmering blue-green robe. When he turned to speak to his guard, I saw a thin, lined face. He coughed, but not as badly as he had on his arrival.

Other officers came in, Turlo among them, to take the other chairs, until only the Emperor's chair and the two flanking it remained empty. It no longer felt appropriate to whisper to Finn, so I sat quietly, watching.

Six women entered, Maya, Alis, and Kirthe; the others I did not know. They had dressed in their cleanest clothes, but they looked worn, and their boots were covered with scuffs and patches. The women sat in the half circle of chairs facing us. I hoped they could not see me. We waited.

Finally, the tent flap opened one more time, and Callan entered, followed by his brothers. Callan wore dark grey, with a robe of the same colour, trimmed with white fur. His head was bare. We all stood. The women glanced at each other, unsure, and followed our example.

Callan sat in the chair of state, resting his hands on the carved arms. Casyn and Colm took the chairs flanking him, and the rest of us sat. When the room quieted, Callan spoke.

"We are here today to hear a petition for the founding of a new village." At the side of the tent, I noticed someone writing, keeping the record. "Who speaks to this petition?"

Three women stood.

"Name yourselves," Callan said.

"Alis, formerly of Berge." She sounded calm.

"Maya, formerly of Tirvan." Her voice did not waver, but she spoke quietly.

"Kirthe, formerly of Torrey." All three met the Emperor's gaze.

"Have you the guild document?" Callan asked.

"We have." Alis came forward, and Colm rose to accept it. He unrolled it, read it through, then handed it to Callan, who did the same.

Callan nodded. "These are in order." He looked up at the women. "Who will speak?"

Alis stood. "I will begin." She took a moment. "In the spring of this year, messengers were sent from the Empire to ask the women's villages to break with the Partition agreement and learn to fight, to defend the Empire. I, the other five women here, and the thirty waiting at the camp, said no, choosing exile.

"Those who are here today chose to go south, hoping to find a village to take us in, one that had voted against the Empire's request. We found no such village, but as more women joined us, we began to talk of forming a new village that would be true to the tenets of Partition.

"As we travelled, our numbers continued to grow. We went to Casilla, thinking we might find a corner of the city where like-minded women had gathered, but we could not find one." She paused as Elon broke into a bout of coughing. Then she continued. "We travelled east to the edges of the Empire, and then north again, on the track that runs along the mountains. Eventually, we found a valley where we thought we could camp and be safe. We spent the rest of the summer there, hunting for game and fishing. We survived." She stopped. "I will let Kirthe speak, now."

From my seat at the back, I could not see the reactions of the officers. I glanced at Finn, trying to read the expression on his face. He looked thoughtful.

Kirthe, short and square, looked to be in her late twenties. She spoke clearly: "In the autumn, after we had been in the valley perhaps eight weeks, an Empire's Messenger stopped to tell us the invasion had been thwarted, and the Empire was safe. He was riding north to the Wall, but took the time to deliver this message to us. We thank the Empire for this courtesy." Callan inclined his head, and Hedda continued. "We decided then that the time had come to petition for the right to form a new village. We debated sending only the three of us, but in the end, we wanted our numbers seen, so we are all here."

The Emperor held up a hand. "You are exiled only from your home villages. Why do you not seek work and a home in another village now that the fighting is done? To build a new village—plough unbroken land, clear forest—is an enormous task."

"For two reasons. First, we have been together now since late spring," Hedda said, "bonded by our shared beliefs. And we are mostly young, strong, and skilled in many trades. We would prefer to stay together."

"Why did you not all arrive together?" Callan asked.

Maya stood. "I will answer that," she said. I watched her closely but could see no sign of apprehension. "One of our number, Willa, from Ballin, died of a fever in the late summer. Three of us went to Ballin first to bear news of her death. Two others were late arriving because they had gone north to take two girls home. The girls were too young to choose to join us, and we would not let them stay." Zilde's daughters, I guessed.

"Why did you not send them home immediately?"

"They came to us late in the summer. With the invasion imminent, we felt they would be safer with us."

"Your plan is to keep this village true to the Partition agreement," Callan said. "But what if a new assembly changes the law of the land, and the Partition agreement is obsolete? Will you abide by the law, or choose to be exiled beyond our borders?"

"That will depend," Maya said, "on what the law is. If we cannot live by it, I suppose at least some of us will look for another land where we can live in peace."

"Exiled," the Emperor said again. My heart clenched at the word.

"Perhaps," Maya said evenly. I could see the resolve in her face and hear the iron in her voice. Like Garth, I thought.

Callan nodded. "I would hear the second reason you wish to build a new village."

Maya glanced at Alis, and then over at me. Alis started to stand, but Maya shook her head, once.

"No one village could take us all, and wherever we were, our beliefs would once again place us in the minority. We would always be waiting for the next time an Emperor's Messenger arrived, always waiting for the next time we would have to choose exile. We are not prepared to do that. If our petition is refused, many, if not most of us will choose to leave the Empire, sir." Now I could see the signs of strain in her tight jaw, and the tiniest tremble of her muscles.

"If your petition is granted, and the Partition agreement stands," Callan said, his voice breaking into my thoughts, "your village will follow it. You would provide food and other goods to the Empire's armies and bear children by her soldiers?"

"As a village, we would," Maya said. "Whether or not a woman chooses to bear a child would remain her decision, as it is now."

An evasive answer, but not one Callan could dispute. I wondered how much of this he knew already from his previous meetings with these women. He bent to Colm, asking him a question. He listened, nodding. Then the Emperor straightened.

"One last question," he said. "If I choose to grant this petition, I also must decide what land to grant with it. Did you raise buildings at the eastern valley?"

"A few," Maya replied, "but none of any permanence. Brush and log shelters, for the most part."

"I will consider your petition, and tomorrow I will give my ruling. Please return here at mid-morning." He stood. We followed suit. He saluted his officers, inclined his head to Elon, and walked out of the tent, his brothers just behind. Elon followed them, flanked by his two guards. The women left last.

Outside, a weak sun had broken through the clouds. I asked Finn to excuse me, following the path the women had taken away from the council tent. On the far side of the camp, I called to Alis. All six women stopped and turned.

"May I speak with you?" She looked at Maya, who shrugged. They conferred in low voices, then the other women continued on while Alis waited.

I took a leather purse from my pocket as I approached. I held it out to her. "Maya and I held a boat in joint ownership in Tirvan. I leased the boat out for a year when I left. By law, I can't give her half the lease money, but nothing prevents me from giving it to you."

She looked at the purse, and then at me. "I'd be foolish to say no. We'll need money, whatever happens." She took the purse, began to leave, then turned back. "Thank you."

The petition hearing had not taken very long, after all. I wondered what to do now. Tonight, there would be some merriment at the junior commons, Midwinter's Eve being a traditional time of fun and feasting. I thought about the games and song and food I would miss tonight in the meeting hall at Tirvan. Even the littlest babies came, and toddlers fell asleep on benches or the floor as the night progressed. Traditionally we stayed awake long into the night, sleeping late the next day.

Finally, I went back to my tent to nap. I slept fitfully and lightly, disturbed by dreams. When I awoke, it was dark. I washed my face and brushed my hair, then walked through the rows of tents. Already the camp seemed noisier than usual with voices raised in song and laughter. Inside, the junior commons smelled wonderfully of food. Gulian, seeing me come in, poured a cup of something and handed it to me. It steamed, smelling of spices. I sipped carefully, tasting cider.

We ate roast pig and goose with winter vegetables, followed by nuts and dried fruits. Spirits ran high. "I'd rather be me than the Emperor, tonight," Finn shouted in my ear at one point. "He has to entertain the governor of Leste. It'll be all protocol and politeness, there."

After we had eaten, the stewards and some of the officers moved the tables back, leaving a clear space in the centre of the tent. Instruments—an elbow pipe among them—squeaked and moaned in discord while their players tuned them, and then a lively, irresistible jig began.

I let myself be pulled onto the dance floor. The dance had steps, and I worked them out after a minute or two—a pattern of back and forth, meetings and partings. No one minded my missteps, and when that dance ended and another began, I kept dancing.

Later, hot and sweaty and thirsty, I stood beside Finn when the pipes changed their tone to something low and mournful. The tent fell silent. One man stood alone on the floor. When the drummer began a low, slow beat, he began to dance, slowly and formally, his hands raised, his fingers gesturing. I did not understand what I saw, but my throat tightened.

"What is it?" I whispered to Finn.

"The *Breccaith*," he whispered back. "It is always danced this night, and at Midsummer, to remember those who will never feast with us again."

I watched the dance, and the faces of the men I could see in the firelight. Some shed unabashed tears. The stewards moved silently among us with trays bearing filled cups. Finn handed me one, indicating with his fingers not to drink. The music slowed, and the drumbeats ended. On a last wail of the pipes, the dancer sank to the ground.

In the silence that followed, Finn raised his cup. "To our fallen brothers."

"To our brothers," the tent echoed.

"And sisters," I said quietly, drinking the toast. The dancer stood to join his friends, and the music began again, now softer, less insistent. The men danced in pairs or small groups. Finn touched my shoulder.

"Will you dance with me?"

We moved onto the dance floor. He took my hands, showing me the steps.

"You dance well."

"I was taught by a woman from Karst," I said, remembering the lessons on the playing field at Tirvan, all those long months ago.

"The one who was killed?"

"You remembered."

"We're trained to," he said simply. "Every man, every officer. And not just to send the messages back to the women's villages or to brothers or sons in other regiments, but so their lives and deaths are not without meaning. It is what an officer must do. We live our lives to honour those who died."

I wanted to point out that I wasn't an officer, but I stopped myself. I had been one when Tice died, and Finn thought of me as such.

The dance ended and another began. Finn guided me through the first steps again, his hands warm around mine. We had just repeated the steps again when another man, one I did not know, came up behind Finn.

"Don't keep her all to yourself. My turn, now."

"Josan, you're drunk," Finn said shortly.

"No matter. She's the only woman here. You don't get her all night."

"I am not dancing with you," I said. "I don't know you, and I don't want to. I'm dancing with Finn."

"More'n dancing, too, I'll bet." Josan said. He lunged forward, grabbing at my breasts. I took a step back. Finn took Josan by the arm.

"Leave us be." Others had stopped dancing now to watch.

"I outrank you," Josan growled, pulling free of Finn's grip. He lunged at me again. Without thinking, I pivoted, ducked, and came up under his outstretched arm to punch him hard in the stomach. He doubled over. I shoved him hard. He fell and lay groaning.

A round of applause made me look up. "Well done!" Galdor called. I stood panting a minute. Josan moaned again, pushing himself up. Suddenly he vomited, to the disgust of the men nearest.

"Come," Finn said, pulling me away, back to the tables. He found me wine, and I sat on the bench.

"I think," Finn said, looking at me with respect, "Josan is lucky you did not have a knife."

I took a mouthful of the wine. "He is lucky. I didn't even stop to think."

Finn nodded. "He isn't a bad officer except when he's been drinking, and then, well, you saw what he's like. Are you all right?"

I nodded. "I am. But, Finn, do others think that you and I—?"

He shrugged. "I doubt it." He hesitated. "I'm not a man for women, Lena, and most here know that. Even Josan knows that when he's sober enough to think."

"Oh," I said. "I didn't realize—"

"Why would you?" The music had started again, but this time without the elbow pipes, just the drum and stringed instruments. Someone began to sing.

"Shall we join the singing? It's good fun."

"Yes," I said, "let's."

The commons still rang with song—somewhat off-key—when I excused myself and left. The watch had changed an hour ago. The newly off-duty junior officers had appeared at the commons, wanting food and drink, determined to make up for the four hours they had missed. We had all eaten again and joined them in more toasts. I was beyond satiated, and more than somewhat drunk. At my tent, I stripped off my outer clothes, falling onto my camp bed, my head spinning. I heard a voice coming from the camp, young and true, raised in solo song:

> *The swallows gather, summer passes,*
> *The grapes hang dark and sweet;*
> *Heavy are the vines*
> *Heavy is my heart*
> *Endless is the road beneath my feet.*

Was Tice's song mine now, too?

I slept through the watch-change bugle in the morning, waking only when the sun rose high enough to brighten my tent. I had a raging headache and felt more than slightly sick. I wondered how long the revels had gone on.

I drank some water and prepared myself for the day. At the council tent, people had already gathered. Last night, before the merriment had completely taken over, Finn had told me to get here early.

"By custom," he said, "any off-duty soldier can come to hear the Emperor's proclamations, and they will. It's something to talk about, to tell their sons and their lovers, so expect crowds."

The entire front of the council tent had been opened to allow a standing crowd to hear, if not see, the proceedings. I wondered if I would have to stand, too, but Birel saw me, showing me to a chair inside. Today, only the chair of state and the two advisor's chairs stood at the far end of the space. Rows of chairs for the audience faced them, with two tables for secretaries at the far edges. Some of the junior officers from the second watch joined me. One of them yawned. His pale hair looked uncombed.

"What time did you get to bed?" I asked.

"Maybe an hour before dawn. We broke up when the first watch left to prepare for duty. You left earlier, didn't you?" I nodded. "I should have, too." He groaned. "Maybe I can sleep a bit after this." He brightened. "I heard you really laid into Josan last night," he said, grinning. "Good for you. He's a pain when he's drunk."

The space filled quickly, but the front row remained empty, reserved for the petitioners and for the governor of Leste. Maya came in with Alis and Hedda.

The other women would listen from outside today. I guessed, turning in my seat to try to see—then wishing I hadn't moved—that most of their camp had come to hear the Emperor's decision.

The governor wore the same sea-coloured robe over his tunic and leggings. When he coughed, he reached inside his robe for a handkerchief. He did not sound well. The same two senior officers walked slightly behind him: Blaine and Nevis, I remembered.

Canvas rustled behind the chair of state, and Callan entered through a door I hadn't seen before, followed by his brothers. We all stood. He too wore the same robes as yesterday, with the addition of a pendant of silver. Casyn wore his uniform, and Colm had dressed in his usual black. He held papers in his hand. They took their seats. We sat, and the tent and the crowd outside settled into silence.

Callan relaxed into his chair. I thought he might stand to speak, but he did not. I wondered if the crowd outside could hear.

"We gather this Midwinter's Day, the eleventh year of my election to Emperor, to hear my ruling on a petition as well as other decisions of mine that affect the Empire. These rulings are being recorded, and copies will be sent to all regiments and villages. I will speak first to the petition, then on several other issues that pertain to the Empire as a whole, and, finally," he inclined his head, slightly, to the governor, "on the future of our newest province, the island of Leste."

"To the petition, then." The three women stood. As he looked at them, I thought I saw the barest hint of a smile around his eyes. My head pounded. "In the matter of the petition for a new village, I grant the petition." I heard a gasp from the women and cheering from outside. Thank you, Callan, I thought, watching Maya's face. She did not smile, but I saw the look of strain replaced by one of quiet acceptance. She had reached for Alis's hand, before Callan spoke, and she held it still. I saw Alis squeeze her fingers.

When the crowed had quieted again, Callan continued. "I grant the petitioners the land in the eastern valley where they camped this past summer." He shifted his gaze to address the women direction. "You are charged with following the Partition agreement, or any other agreement that becomes the law of the Empire. If you refuse, you will be cast out. You will be exempt from providing food and other goods to the Empire for a period of five years while you establish your village, but are expected to honour the twice-yearly Festivals beginning in the autumn of this year. I offer you the choice of returning to your village lands now or remaining where you are camped until the spring. If you choose the latter, I will also make available to you the forge and carpentry of this camp, when my men do not need them, to begin to prepare for the construction of a new village. You need not decide this now," he continued. "Is there any reply you would like to make?"

"Thank you, Emperor," Alis said. "May we divide our women, send some back to the valley to clear trees and hunt while others remain here?"

"You may," he said. "You are now the women of your village, whatever you choose to name it, and your decisions on how you order your village business are your own."

"We are grateful for your ruling," Alis said simply. She smiled, looking from side to side at her companions. They sat.

Callan looked over to Colm.

"I now turn to the other matters. It has long been my intent to build a permanent road from the eastern fort to the Wall, at the foot of the eastern mountains. Construction will begin in the spring and will take many years." A new road, and Maya's village would stand right beside it. I wondered who had suggested to them that they look for a place to camp on the eastern track.

Alis frowned. The three women conferred with whispered words and gestures, until Colm cleared his throat.

"In the beginning," Callan continued, "the work will be done by those men of Leste who would not submit to my authority and are now slaves." At the mention of Leste, I glanced at the former king. Elon's eyes narrowed. "But in the future, it will not be so. Already, we teach boys to design and build those structures needed by the Empire—roads, bridges, canals, but they learn this trade as soldiers. Now, this trade will be one of the choices cadets can make at twelve years of age. It will be considered an equal choice to the others, in service to the Empire, and will carry with it all the rights of those in Empire's service. Like the choice of becoming a medic, it will be without the requirement to learn the arts of warfare beyond self-defence."

Now Valle has a choice, I thought. Watching the men, I saw surprise, even astonishment, in the quick glances to each other. Several eyes went straight to Colm. Did they think him the architect of this? Outside, I heard murmuring. I wondered what the senior officers thought.

The Emperor waited, watching us. When he had our attention again, he spoke once more.

"There is one more proclamation," he said, "addressing the Partition agreement. When I asked, in the spring, that the women's villages be active in the defence of Tirvan against the threat from Leste, I was also asking them to break with the agreement made at the Partition assembly. They did so. Therefore, it is my belief, and, I understand, the belief of many women in the villages and at the inns, that a new assembly is required, either to reaffirm the Partition agreement or to create a new agreement. The assembly will take place three weeks after Midsummer. Three women will be chosen from each village, three will represent the inns, and we will have an equal number of men. This will," he said, with a nod to Alis, "include the newly-formed village. The new assembly will be held here."

This proclamation drew more glances, but less surprise, among the men. The women again conferred in whispers. The officer beside me leaned over. "By the god," he whispered, "there'll be lots of talk in the commons and the tents tonight. These are enormous changes, Lena, more than any Emperor has decreed in decades, centuries, maybe. And not popular with all, I think." His brow furrowed as he spoke.

Colm rose to speak to the secretaries. I saw them find new paper and check their nibs. When Colm returned to his seat, Callan spoke again. "Now I will speak to the future of Leste. This fair island is now a province of the Empire. The former king, Elon," he inclined his head to him, "governs there, assisted by a council chosen by me. But if Leste is a province of the Empire, then its laws must reflect those of the Empire. To this end, all Lestian men and boys between the ages of twelve and fifty-five will enter military service in the spring. Next year, we will take boys at eleven, and the following year, ten, until boys leave their home villages at seven to be prepared for service. Men beyond the age of service will be charged in teaching women the skills and trades that will be required of them. Of changes in taxation, and the laws of marriage and inheritance, I will speak privately with the governor and his council." He looked to Elon. "Do you wish to speak?" Elon stood, the effort making him cough.

Suddenly, I heard commotion and shouting, the jangle of harness. Callan raised a hand for silence. The tent flaps parted, and a soldier came in, dressed for riding, and splattered with mud. In his hand, he held a folded piece of paper.

"Emperor," he said, without hesitation, his eyes on Callan. "The Wall has been breached, and the north is attacked. Here is the report." Officers stood at the words, blocking my view. I slid along the seats, ignoring the nausea the motion caused to move to the side of the tent, where I could see. The messenger strode forward, handing the paper to Callan.

Callan broke the seal, scanned the paper quickly, then handed it to Casyn. "Our thanks, soldier," he said. "Senior officers, Advisor, attend me. This audience is over."

Casyn looked down at the paper. He said something, one word, I thought. A name? I saw Callan hesitate, a moment of indecision. He glanced at his brothers before all three turned.

The conquered king of Leste stood, coughing, slightly bowed, a handkerchief at his mouth, with Nevin and Blaine at his side.

"Nevin," Callan said, his voice oddly gentle, shaded, I thought, with grief. "Your son, so recently commander in your stead, opened the gates to the northerners. Why?" I looked from the Emperor to his officers, trying to understand.

Elon straightened. His hand dropped from his mouth, returning the handkerchief to a pocket of his robe.

"No!" Casyn roared. He grabbed Callan by the shoulders, pushing, turning him away. The Emperor twisted desperately, hampered by his heavy robes. A knife flashed, turning end to end across the small space. Soldiers moved quickly, pulling out weapons. A body leapt, blocking Callan from the blade. I heard a gasp, a truncated scream. Chairs fell around me, and men shouted. Frozen, I stared at the man dying in his brother's arms. The blood soaked, unseen, into the black fabric of his tunic.

Callan's face contorted as he looked down at his brother. "Colm," he said, the sorrow and love in his voice palpable, "Oh, Colm. I saw the meaning too late. I am so sorry, my twin, my little brother." Gently he lowered his brother's body to the floor and stood to embrace Casyn. They stood with bowed heads for a moment. I looked away. Nausea threatened to overwhelm me.

The Emperor turned to the room. A second dead man lay on the floor: Elon, his throat cut. Callan looked down at him coldly.

"I would like to leave him on the hills for the carrion birds," he said, anger in every syllable. "But his body must go home to Leste. Otherwise, they will say he is not dead, and he will become a hero waiting to free them from bondage." He glanced at the two men who had guarded Elon, standing defiantly beside the dead king. Blood gleamed on the blade in Blaine's hand. Callan turned to his soldiers. "Take them," he said. Nevin shifted, as if to run, but he had no chance.

"As for those who plotted with the king of Leste," he said, pitching his voice to clear steel, "death is their reward. Major," he said, looking to Turlo. "See to it at once. Then join us for a council of war." His eyes dropped to Colm's body.

"My brother will be buried here, with the full honours given to those who die in service to the Empire," he said, his voice gentle now, but still commanding. "Two hours from now, on the hill. Then we ride north." Callan and Casyn lifted Colm's body together to carry him out of the council tent.

I pushed forward through the jumble of chairs and people, ignoring my headache. Officers hurried from the tent, shouting orders. The three women huddled together. A spray of blood stained Alis's tunic. She had been closest to Elon when Blaine had cut his throat. Maya and Hedda seemed shocked. "Come outside." I shepherded them through the confusion of the crowd outside. Maya clung to Alis and would not look at me.

I found the rest of the women standing together, confused. One woman, seeing the blood, turned Alis toward her, searching for injury.

"Are you a healer?" I asked.

"A midwife," she said. "Is Alis hurt?"

"No, just shocked. The blood isn't hers. Take them back to the camp and give them hot tea with lots of sugar. They just saw two men killed."

"Dear goddess," the midwife whispered. "We don't belong here." She began to shepherd the others away.

I called after her. She turned. "There is war coming again. From the north, across the Wall. This camp, these men, will be riding north in a few hours. Look to your safety."

She looked frightened. "Where should we go?"

I shook my head. "I don't know." I saw other women turn to look at me. "I don't know where you might be safe. I don't know what these invaders, and those of the Empire who helped them, want. You must make your own choices." I knew my words sounded cruel, but I had nothing else to give them, not right now. "If I learn more, I'll try to bring word," I added, to soften the message.

Later, I walked down to where the junior officer's tents had stood. Finn and Galdor were overseeing the collapse of the camp. They greeted me, but their orders occupied them, and they made no attempt at conversation. I stood for moment, undecided, before speaking.

"How did the Emperor know, Finn? About Nevin and Blaine?"

"The paper the rider brought," he said slowly, "must have said exactly where the Wall was breached. Nevin's son commands a section of the Wall. And Blaine..." He stopped.

"Was Nevin's brother."

He nodded.

"Why?" I said softly. "And why did Blaine kill Elon?"

Finn shook his head. Galdor shrugged. "The second question is easier," he said. "Elon was their co-conspirator. With Elon dead, there would be no one to bear witness against them. As to why, I don't know," he admitted. "But this is older than the Emperor's proclamations today, older than the battle with Leste this year. I've heard it said Blaine wanted to be Emperor, but realized he stood no chance against Callan in the vote."

"They'll have to increase the garrisons on Leste, now," Finn said. "There will be uprising because of this. Gulian may have his wish for warm weather granted."

I watched them directing their men, and the rapid, disciplined way in which the camp came down. These men knew their work.

"I didn't know him well," I said, after a while, "but I liked Colm."

"We all did," Finn said.

"Not all," Galdor said quietly.

Finn frowned. "What do you mean?"

"I've overheard talk, once or twice. Some of the men thought it unnatural that the Emperor had a castrate as his advisor, brother or no."

"But he taught most of the officers," Finn said dismissively. "And every one of them at camp will be at the burying."

"True," Galdor said. "And many of the men as well."

"I wonder who the Emperor will appoint to govern Leste," Galdor said.

"Casyn," I said, without really thinking.

"The General?" Finn considered. "You might be right. But that would deprive the Emperor of both his advisors, so perhaps not. Bren, maybe." He turned to me.

"Will you be leaving us now, Lena?"

"Yes," I said, "but I'll stay for the burying. I pray you prevail, again, in the battles."

Finn shook his head. "A winter war," he said, "and against our own men. There is no easy victory, this time."

"This is Lucian's war all over again," Galdor said. My heart contracted. The comparison fit. Could we win this war? I needed to go home, I thought, right away. Would I be in time to defend Tirvan? And what would happen to Maya? I shuddered. I felt helpless, tiny. I wanted, more than anything, for someone older and wiser to tell me what to do.

We stood at the burying ground on the windy hillside. The day had turned grey, but no snow or rain fell. I shivered in my fleece coat. As Finn had predicted, many of the officers and not a few of the men had come to witness the brief ceremony. I looked around.

"Where is Turlo?" I whispered to Finn, standing beside me.

"Gone north to scout out the invaders."

I nodded. Who else, for that task?

A piper played a sad descent of notes. We turned to watch four officers, one of them Casyn, bearing Colm's body to the grave. The bearers walked slowly under a double line of crossed swords. They laid the covered pallet by the dug grave, turning the sheet back to reveal Colm's face. As a man, they turned east and bowed. Callan stepped forward. Bareheaded, he raised his voice against the wind. "Colm had no rank, no position in the Empire's service, beyond being my advisor," he said. "But he died a hero. He gave his life for me, and therefore for the Empire. We honour that today." He knelt to place a hand on Colm's brow. "The god of soldiers receive you, my brother, or I will know the reason why when I stand before him myself." He, too, turned to the east, but did not bow, although he inclined his head. The bearers stepped forward again, carefully lowering Colm's body into the grave. The piper played the same sad notes. Callan bent to take a handful of earth. "Farewell," he said, throwing the earth into the grave. Casyn followed suit. Then they turned and walked down the hill. They had a war to plan.

I packed my saddlebags, leaving out only my heavy riding clothes. Outside my tent, I could hear the creak of leather and the clang of metal as the troops rode out. In my hand, I held the history Colm had given me. I walked out of the tent to go in search of Birel. I found him supervising the loading of boxes at the council tent.

"Wait here, please," he said, after I explained what I wanted. He ducked inside the council tent, emerging a minute later. "Go in."

The tent, stripped of Callan's things, seemed even larger. More boxes waited for the supply wagons. Casyn stood, a map in his hand. He looked up. I could see the lines of fatigue and grief around his eyes.

"Casyn. I am so very sorry."

"I will miss him all the days of my life," he said simply. "It should have been me, protecting Callan. But for once, Colm was faster than I."

I handed him the book. "Colm lent it to me." He opened it, reading a few words. Then he closed it and handed it back.

"Keep it. Colm meant you to. He told me he wished all his pupils had your mind."

"He taught me so much." My voice caught, and I looked away.

"And me," Casyn said. He straightened. "What will you do?" I heard an odd hesitation in the question. I looked up at him. His brother had died violently this afternoon, and yet he went on, defending his Empire, putting his grief behind him. How we respond to circumstance is what defines us, he had told me once. I owed him so much. I realized I loved him, as I supposed I might have loved a father. I took a deep breath. There were too many choices, or only one.

"What would you have me do, General?" I said. I glimpsed a brief smile in his eyes.

"Look at this map with me, Cohort-Leader," he said. He spread it out on the big table still standing against one wall. "We are here," he said, pointing, "and here is where the hills of the north give way to the central grasslands. You remember?" I nodded, remembering how my heart had lightened at the sight of the sea of grass below me, so many days and weeks before. "We need to engage the rebels well north of this escarpment. If we are on the grasslands and they are in the hills, they will have the advantage of ambush and retreat into the valleys and rocks, and we will be open to them, to be picked off like deer at the autumn cull. We may already be too late, but we must try, and that means a fast ride north. At the same time, we must send more men to Leste. Insurrection there is a certainty." He smiled, grimly. "We are again where we were when I first came to Tirvan, but this time we have an enemy both within and without and not the strength of men to meet both. The planned response to an invasion from the north, a breaching of the Wall, was made years ago, but that plan was known to Blaine and Nevin, and has doubtless been passed on to Nevin's son, who opened the gates to the northerners. We must use another plan, but there is no certainty of success."

"You need every man."

"And every woman. But this is harder than asking you to fight against Leste. Now we fight, in part, against our own people. I cannot compel anyone, and I would not try. But every woman who would choose to come, whether to battle or to serve as messengers and medics, grooms and cooks, everyone is needed, if we are to hold our Empire."

And if we didn't, Tice and Siane and Colm had all died for nothing. *Live your life to honour those who died*, Finn had said. I thought of Halle, in the council hall at Karst. She would come. How many others?

"There is no one to protect Maya and her women," I said slowly.

He shook his head. "We cannot spare anyone. I sent a cadet to tell them, to advise them to try for Casilla. The city will be safer, I think."

"Thank you," I said. That would have to do, for now.

"I am sending cadets east to Casilla and the eastern fort with messages, but we would not send even those, if there was another way. Will you ride west, Lena? Ride to the Four-Ways Inn, and back to Karst, as Emperor's Messenger?"

"Where do women go, who would join you?"

He pointed down at the map. "Here," he said. "Where the hunting trail meets the river. Tell them to bring provisions, extra horses, heavy clothes, tents if they can."

I nodded. "I need an hour to break camp and to pack."

He looked at me steadily for a minute. "Make it half that. I will have Birel bring you the letter naming you as Emperor's Messenger. He can help you pack. Ride your mare. The pony will keep up if led behind unburdened. You can leave him at the Four-Ways Inn and ride even faster. Go now, Lena."

I swallowed and nodded, turning to leave. Tears burned hot behind my eyes. I had just ducked through the tent flaps when Casyn called to me.

"Cohort-Leader," he said. "Will you come north?"

I turned to face him: a dark figure against the canvas of the tent. I could see the motion of his hands as he rolled the map.

"I don't know," I said. "If.... if I can, General."

The wind moved the tent flaps behind me. I saw him nod.

"Go," he said. "And thank you."

In my camp, I packed Colm's book, and with it the paper and writing instruments he had given me, into my saddlebag. I had begun to write an account of these last months, beginning with the day Casyn had arrived. I had thought I would have time to work on it at the inn or in the grape fields.

Birel arrived, bringing the letter with the Emperor's seal. I stowed it in my saddlebag as well. We collapsed the tent, rolling and tying it.

A soldier led Clio up, with Plover on a leading rein. She carried my tack, and my travelling gear. Clio whickered at me. I rubbed her nose. Birel threw my bags over the back of the saddle. I mounted and took the reins, glancing east, towards the women's camp. Already the sky grew dark. The winter sun was low on the horizon.

"Go with the god, Cohort-Leader," the sergeant said. The soldier's benediction. He saluted me. I returned the salute. Then I turned Clio's head west, toward the setting sun, and rode.

THE CHARACTERS OF EMPIRE'S DAUGHTER

Aasta – an innkeeper
Alda – an ostler
Aline – a member of Lena's cohort
Alis – an exile from Berge
Alister – a servant on Jedd's farm
Anwyl – a crewmember of Skua
Anya – a Council – leader of Karst
Ava – an apprentice
Binne – a fisherwoman of Tirvan
Birel – Casyn's soldier – servant
Blaine – an officer of the Empire
Bren – a Major of the Empire
Cael – a solder of Leste
Callan – the Emperor
Camy – a member of Lena's cohort
Casse – a retired Council – leader of Tirvan
Casyn – a General, brother to Callan
Cate – a weaver of Tirvan
Colm – Callan's twin and advisor
Danel – a crewmember of Skua
Dann – a soldier
Darel – a cadet, Turlo's son
Dari – Kyan's partner, a cohort – leader
Daria – a trader from Karst
Dern – the Captain of Skua
Dessa – a boatbuilder at Tirvan
Dian – a horse warrior of Han
Dorys – an ostler
Elon – the King of Leste
Ferhar – a crewmember of Skua
Finn – a Lieutenant of the Empire
Freya – a girl of Tirvan, Dessa's apprentice
Fryth – an innkeeper
Galdor – a Lieutenant of the Empire
Galen – Lena's father, a border scout
Garth – Maya's brother
Gille – a herdswoman, Council – leader of Tirvan
Grainne – a horsebreeder of Tirvan
Guilian – a Lieutenant of the Empire
Gwen – Lena's mother, Council – leader & midwife
Halle – a woman of Karst
Hilar – a winemaker of Karst

Ianthe – a woman of Karst. Tice's sister
Ilene – a cooper of Karst
Ione –   a woman of Karst, Tice's great – aunt
Jedd – a retired General of the Empire
Joce – a woman of Karst, Tice's sister
Josan – a Lieutenant of the Empire
Karlii – a cheesemaker of Ballin
Keavy – an innkeeper
Kinley – a child of Karst, Tevian's son
Kira – a girl of Tirvan, Lena's sister, apprentice midwife
Kirthe – an exile
Kolmas – a ship captain of Leste
Kyan – a woodworker of Tirvan
Lara – Siane's daughter
Largen – a crewmember of Skua
Lena – a fisherwoman of Tirvan
Livia – an innkeeper
Mar – a soldier of the Empire, Maya & Garth's father
Mari – an innkeeper
Martin – a Captain of the Empire
Maya – a fisherwoman of Tirvan, Lena's partner
Mella – a woman of Tirvan
Mikelle – a Council – leader of Karst
Minna – a retired potter of Tirvan
Nessa – a woman of Tirvan
Nevin – an officer of the Empire
Pel – a boy of Tirvan, Maya's brother
Rai – a girl of Tirvan, Lena's cohort
Ranni – a woman of Tirvan
Rasa – a horse warrior of Han
Roxine – a Council – leader of Karst
Salle – a woman of Tirvan, Lena's cohort
Sara – a Council – leader of Tirvan, Lena's aunt
Sari – an apprentice
Sarr – a boy of Tirvan
Satordi – a crewmember of Skua
Sherron – a cheesemaker of Ballin
Siane – a recordkeeper of Tirvan, Dessa's partner
Tali – a woman of Tirvan, Maya's mother, Lena's aunt
Tamar – a woman of Karst, Tice's mother
Tevian – a woman of Karst, Tevra's sister
Tevra –   woman of Karst, Tice's ex – partner
Tice – a woman of Tirvan, potter, Lena's cohort – second
Tiernay – a crewmember Skua

Turlo – a General of the Empire
Valle – Tice's son
Xani – woman of Tirvan, Casyn's mother, deceased
Zilda – an innkeeper

EMPIRE'S
HOSTAGE

for
Drs. Tomer Feigenberg, John Radwan, and Sarah Rauth,
&
the entire team of surgery, nursing, and radiology staff
at the Carlo Fidani Cancer Centre,
without whose expertise
I would not have been alive to write this book.
'Thank you' seems completely inadequate.

†††††

The swallows gather, summer passes,
The grapes hang dark and sweet;
Heavy are the vines,
Heavy is my heart,
Endless is the road beneath my feet.

The sun is setting, the moon is rising,
The night is long and sweet;
I am gone at dawn.
I am gone at day,
Endless is the road beneath my feet.

The cold is deeper, the winters longer,
Summer is short but sweet;
I will remember,
I'll not forget you,
Endless is the road beneath my feet.

-Tice's song

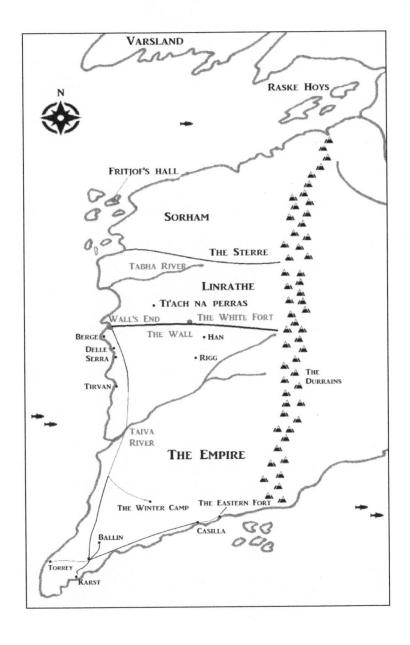

There are roads which must not be followed.

Sun Tzu

CHAPTER ONE

THE RAIN SLASHED DOWN UNCEASINGLY, half ice, stinging exposed skin and making it nearly impossible to see anything in the grey light. When the sun, hidden now behind the thick layer of clouds, set—not long now, I estimated— the stones of the Wall and the native rock would lose what warmth they held, and begin to ice over. Night watch would be treacherous, tonight. I counted it a small blessing that my watch had begun after the midday meal.

I wiped a gloved hand over my eyes yet again and scanned north and eastward, not focusing on anything, but looking for motion, or for something that didn't belong, as Turlo had taught me; something that moved against the wind, or a shadow that hadn't been there yesterday. I listened, too, to the sounds beyond the noises of the fort and the babble of the stream behind me: the hoarse cry of a raven, the soft chatter of sparrows settling into their roost. No alarm calls. I walked the few steps across the watchtower to begin my scan again, to the northwest.

Footsteps sounded on the wooden stairs. I did not turn. Only when my relief stood beside me, looking out, could I look away.

"I think the minging gods have forgotten it's the first day of spring," Halle said. "Anything I should know?"

"There's a raven in the usual tree," I answered, still looking outward, "but it's just making conversational croaks occasionally. I saw a fox about an hour ago, when I could still see, and its mind was on finding mice in the rocks. No owls today, but maybe they're not hunting in this rain. There could be forty northmen out there, and as long as they moved with the wind and stayed low, I wouldn't know. But I don't think so. I'm guessing there is one, or maybe two, watching us, no more."

"Wrapped up in their cloaks, under some rocks or furze," Halle said. "I'd rather be here."

"So would they," I reminded her.

She laughed, but without mirth. "Go and get warm," she said. "The hunting party brought back a deer, so there's venison stew to be had." I glanced over at her. Her eyes were on the land beyond the Wall, watching.

"Good luck." I took the stairs down from the watchtower as quickly as I felt safe; the movement warmed me, slightly. At the bottom, I stepped over the gutter, running with rainwater, and onto the cobbled walkway that ran along the inner side of the Wall. The Wall itself broke the wind, and the rain fell with less force. Still, I pulled the hood of my cloak over my head as I walked to the camp.

All the discipline of the Empire could not build a finished fort in a time of war, and while the tents and a few stone and timber huts stood in orderly rows, most of the roads and pathways between were earthen—or mud, right now. Since the skirmishes had died down, some weeks earlier, work had begun on paving the main thoroughfares through the camp. A narrow, cobbled track ran from the Wall to the centre of the encampment, just wide enough for two people to pass. I noticed it extended a few feet further into the camp than it had when I had left for watch duty. I stepped off its comparatively clean cobbles onto the slick surface of the hard-packed earthen path. It had been built to drain, and two ditches ran on either side of it, but I could feel mud sticking to my boots.

At the kitchen tent, I scraped the mud off my boots on the iron blade mounted outside, and shook the worst of the rain off my cloak. Ducking inside, I met a blast of welcome heat. I stripped off my gloves and cloak, and the thick tunic I wore beneath the cloak, piling them on a bench. A gust of cold air told me someone else had come in. I turned to see Darel already loosening the clasps of his cloak. He'd been on watch duty at the tower east of the camp.

"Quiet?" I asked. He nodded, concentrating on pulling his tunic over his head.

"Very." His red hair, streaked with rain, stood up in clumps. He sniffed the air. "I hear rumours of venison stew," he said. Caro, on servery duty, spoke up.

"More like thick soup," she said, "but, yes, it's venison. With some root vegetables and barley in with it. Sit down, and I'll bring it over." We did as directed, and soon enough two bowls of food stood in front of us, with a loaf of dark, hard bread. Darel cut the loaf in half with his belt knife, passing one piece to me. I ripped off a chunk, and dipped it in the soup, eating hungrily.

Caro brought over two mugs of thin beer, and for a space of some minutes we did nothing but eat. Others had come in as we ate, and the smell of damp wool began to overpower the scent of venison stew in the tent. No one said much; another day of rain and cold and mud dampened spirits as much as it did hide and stone. I'm sick of rain, I thought, listening to its ceaseless drum on the tent. If the sun would come out, I'd feel better.

Caro put more fuel in the brazier and then slipped onto the bench beside me. We had ridden north together, from Casilla, half a year earlier, when Dian had come south to requisition food and horses and other supplies for the army. I hadn't really known her. She had worked at one of the small food stalls near Casilla's harbours, and sometimes on my way to or from my work on the boats I had bought something from her.

"How's the soup?" she asked.

"Fine," I said. It was; thick enough to be satisfying, and reasonably spiced.

"It was only a yearling," she said. "Not enough meat to go around, really, so we had to make soup."

Food, I knew, was becoming a problem. At the end of the winter, with almost all the army ranged along the length of the Wall, game within a day or two's hunting was scarce. Sending men—or more likely women—south to the villages for provisions meant fewer of us to defend the Wall if another raid occurred. The truce, called ten days ago, could end at any moment; the Emperor and his advisors spent their days at the White Fort, east of our camp, negotiating with the leaders of the northmen. Fifteen months of war: eight to drive the invaders back beyond the wall; another seven, now, keeping them there, until the ravages of winter, little food, and the deaths of so many, on both sides, had led to the request, and agreement, to parley.

"Who brought it in?" I asked idly.

"Dian," Caro replied. "They got two, both yearlings, but one went to the White Fort. Have you had enough to eat?"

I shrugged. "Enough," I said. Food was for energy, nothing more, and what I'd eaten would suffice. "Is there any tea?" Darel looked up.

"I could eat more," he said, "if there is any?" Darel was so young, and growing, and thin as a starveling cat. All the cadets looked the same.

"There's a bit," Caro said judiciously. "Give me your bowl, and I'll bring it back, and your tea, Lena." She slid off the bench to return to the servery. Darel stretched. "Dice?" he suggested. "After we're done eating?"

I shook my head. "Not tonight," I said. "My tunic needs repairing. One of the shoulder seams is splitting." Caro came back, and Darel fell on his bowl as if he hadn't eaten the first helping. I curved my hands around the mug of tea. It smelled of fruit: rosehip, I thought.

I sat, sipping the tea. It warmed me, as much as anything did, these days. Darel finished his soup, wiping every trace of liquid from the bowl with the last piece of bread, and pushed his bench back. He took his beer and joined a pair of cadets at another table, pulling out his dice. They would sit here, playing, all the rest of the evening, if Caro let them. The servery tent was warmer than the barracks, and there was always the chance of some scraps of food.

I finished the tea, idly watching the dice game. "Minging dice," one of the cadets growled.

"Language!" Caro warned. She allowed no obscenities in the kitchen tent: another slip and she'd make the cadets leave, and they knew it. I'd got used to the casual swearing among the troops; 'minging', a lewd term for urination, was one of the most frequently heard. I even said it myself, now. I stood to take the mug back to Caro, along with Darel's forgotten bowl. Suddenly, the clatter of hooves on the cobbles rang out in the night. "Who?" Caro breathed. The cadets dropped the dice, standing. The tent flap parted, and Turlo—General Turlo, now, and advisor to the Emperor—strode in. Darel straightened even more: the presence of his father always made him conscious of his decorum.

Turlo blinked briefly in the light of the tent. "General?" Caro said. "Would you like food, or drink?"

He smiled at her. "We ate well enough at the Fort," he said, "but thank you. No, I came in search of two soldiers, and I've found them. Guard Lena, Cadet Darel, please go to your barracks, pack your possessions and come back here as quickly as you can. You two—he nodded to the other dice players—go to the horse lines, please, and bring back two mounts. And then retire to your barracks," he added. "Go!" he said, not unkindly; the cadets scurried to do his bidding.

Darel had not moved, but looked over at me. "General?" I said. "What is happening?"

"I will tell you," he said, "when you return with your packs. Bring anything you cannot live without, and your warmest clothes and boots, if you are not already wearing them. Quickly, mind!" It was mildly said, but still an order. I glanced at Darel; he had already turned to put on his outdoor clothes.

We dressed hurriedly and went out into the night. The cadet barracks lay in the opposite direction to mine—the Guards being the women who had come to support the army of the Empire—but Darel hesitated. "Lena," he whispered, "what do you think is going on?"

"No idea," I said. "But we have orders to follow, and very little time to do it in. Be quick, Darel!"

I half-ran to the Guards' barracks, trying not to slip on the slick path. I was in luck; the three women I shared my room with were somewhere else. Halle, at least, was on duty; I wasn't sure about the other two. No questions to slow me down. I pulled my pack from under my cot, looking inside: spare underclothes and socks, another pair of breeches and a shirt lay folded. The pack doubled as storage in this small space. I picked up my indoor slippers, putting them in the pack. From the small wooden chest beside the cot I took a few other things: my comb, my sewing kit, the soft absorbent cloths I used every month during my bleeding, the small supply of anash from which I brewed a tea to lessen the cramps that came with the bleeding, my pen and ink. Then I picked up the last two items that lay inside: two books. One was the history of the Empire, given to me by Colm, the Emperor's advisor and castrate twin; one was my own journal. I stuffed them down inside the pack, buckling it closed.

Outside the servery tent two horses—my Clio, I noticed, was not one of them—stood saddled and bridled beside Turlo's horse. Inside the General sat alone, a mug of beer on the table. Caro had gone. Turlo looked up at me without smiling, nodding for me to sit. Darel came in a minute or two later.

"Now," Turlo said, "I will be brief. The talks have been fruitful: there is a truce that both the Emperor and the Northmen's leader, Donnalch, can agree to. *Teannasach* of the North, he styles himself; so be it. I remember when he was a stripling leading raiding parties for sheep, but no doubt he remembers when I was a stripling too, scouting up their glens. If you do this long enough, old adversaries are almost friends." He grinned. Nothing, ever, seemed to keep Turlo's spirits down. "But the treaty, my lad, and lassie," he added, "requires hostages. Donnalch's son, and another, to us, and two children of our leaders, to them."

Darel found his voice first. "We are to be hostages? Sir?" he remembered to add.

"But I am not a child of our leaders," I protested, not understanding.

"Aye," Turlo said. I wasn't sure which one of us he answered. He looked at Darel. "You are my son," he said, "and therefore must stand as hostage. And you, Lena," he said, switching his gaze to me, "Casyn asked for you to stand as his surrogate daughter. His own daughters are in Han, with their own children, and the Emperor has fathered no sons, or daughters, for that matter, in all his years."

Casyn had asked for me. The words echoed in my head. I had met my own father only once; he served at one of the easternmost postings on the Wall. In the almost two years I had known and worked with and served the General Casyn, I had come to regard him, and to love him, I had acknowledged, as I might have my own father, had I known him. I had had no conception that he might have thought of me in a similar light. Something pushed through the dullness of my spirit. This time, I thought, you will not fail him. This time, you will go.

"What does it mean, to be a hostage?" I asked. I saw something flicker in Turlo's eyes. He grinned again.

"Exchanging the children of high rank as hostages is an old and honoured tradition," he answered, "although not one we have respected, in some generations, and in truth needed to be reminded of. We'll treat Donnalch's son, and the other boy they are sending—his brother's son—with every courtesy. They will lodge in the White Fort for now, and then be sent south to the Eastern Fort when the weather improves, to learn with our senior cadets. Darel, you will basically live the life that Donnalch's son would have, whatever the education, in arms and tactics and books, they deem appropriate. That is the gist of it: we exchange our heirs, in surety for each side's good behaviour. You will not be mistreated, but, understand, neither will you be truly free."

"And me?" I asked. "I cannot see the northerners teaching me arms. And I am not a child."

"You are right, of course," he said, his voice graver. "I must be honest and say I do not really know. We have not concerned ourselves, over the years, in gathering much intelligence on how the women of the north folk live their lives, except to know they live with their men, and perhaps divide the responsibilities of daily life much as we did here once in the Empire, before Partition. But," he said, his voice brightening, "you will bring us back much valuable information, as a result."

"Am I to spy, then?" I tried to keep the exasperation out of my voice.

"Of course," he said simply. "Both of you. Do you not think that the northern boys will be doing the same?"

I realized the truth of what he said. "Why must we go so quickly?"

"I will tell you as we ride," he said, standing as he spoke. "Mount up, now."

Once we had ridden past the tents of the camp Turlo spoke again, his voice raised slightly against the wind and rain. "You asked about the need for haste," he said. "Donnalch would brook no delay. The exchange had to be done tonight, before he would sign the papers of truce. Callan had little choice but to agree, since Donnalch's son and nephew were already at their camp, close to the Fort on the northern side."

"I wonder," I said thoughtfully, "how long those two boys have known they would be part of the truce?"

"And what their instructions have been?" Turlo said. "As always, you are quick, Lena. If Colm had been here," he said, a trace of grief in his voice, "he would have seen the probability that an exchange of hostages would be part of any agreement, I believe, and we could have prepared the two of you too. But we did not see it, until earlier today, and there was no way to let you know."

"Is the truce fair?" Darel asked.

"It is," Turlo answered. "I cannot tell you much tonight; the proclamation will be tomorrow at mid-day, at the White Fort. You'll be there, front and centre, by the bye, as proof to all the good will between our two sides, so hold your heads up and be proud ambassadors for the Empire, when all the eyes are on you."

"I hope they let us have baths, then," I said.

Turlo laughed. "No doubt they will."

We rode through the gates of the White Fort, stopping outside a large stone building. Soldiers—cadets, really—stepped forward to take our horses. We dismounted, shouldering our packs. The horses were led away. I glanced at Darel: he looked as nervous as I felt.

"General," I said. "How long are we to be hostages?"

He looked from me to his son. "Half a year," he replied. That long? I thought. But Turlo still spoke. "Half a year, from now till harvest, to give the northerners a chance to plant and harvest: food runs short on both sides of the Wall. Time for us to hold Festival, and let the villages know our needs for food and supplies. And in that time Callan and Donnalch—and advisors on both sides—will hammer out the terms of a final peace, or not."

"But this is an order, and my duty," Darel said, his voice steady. "I understand, General."

"Good lad," he said. "And you, Guardswoman?"

A mix of emotions roiled through me: a thread of pride, fear, reluctance. When I had ridden north to the Wall the previous autumn, I had sworn fealty and service to Callan, the Emperor, for the duration of the conflict with the northmen. He had not released me from this, and therefore I too had an order and a duty to follow. I had thought I might die as a Guard, so why was I of two minds about this? But when was the last time I had really wanted to do anything?

"General," I said, "will it be known, that I shall be a hostage to the northmen?"

Turlo's eyes softened. "You are thinking of your mother, and your sister?"

I nodded. "Yes," I said.

He understood. "My belief is you will be allowed letters," he said, "at least to your family and other women. I will find a way to send word, to Tirvan. Will my word suffice?"

"Of course," I said, grateful for his comprehension and compassion.

"Is there anything else?" I hesitated. "Tell me," he insisted.

"Well, if I could, if it's allowed—could I have my mare? Clio?" At least she would be something familiar. My stomach roiled. Why had Casyn asked this of me?

He laughed. "Is that all? Of course you can; you'll need a horse, no doubt. I'll have someone bring her over in the morning, and her tack. Darel, is there a particular horse you would like?"

Darel grinned, his teeth bright in the moonlight. I saw the resemblance to Turlo in that grin. "I rather like the skewbald with the white eye," he said, "but so does Rikter. Still, I don't suppose he'll have much chance of revenge, if I'm away with the northmen."

Turlo reached out to cuff his son lightly on the shoulder. If he had heard the fear behind the bravado, he didn't acknowledge it. "Good man," he said. "The skewbald it will be. Now, they are waiting for us, and we can delay no longer." He pulled open the great wooden door, beckoning us inside.

We walked into a hall. Torches in black iron sconces gusted high in the rush of air from the open door, and then subsided to flickers against the grey stone. Turlo led the way to another pair of doors, his boots loud to my ears on the stone flagged floor. Apprehension knotted my stomach. He knocked, but, not awaiting an answer, pulled the doors open and strode inside.

I stopped, Darel beside me, just inside the door. Like the hall, stone blocks formed the walls, but the ceiling curved above us, twice the height of the hall, huge beams supporting it. Fireplaces burned at both ends of the room, and torches, this time in gleaming bronze sconces, lined the walls. But the floor! It was flagged, around the periphery, but otherwise an intricate picture, in tiny fragments of stone and ceramic and glass, made up the rest of the surface. The colours gleamed in the firelight. Faces and sea creatures and designs—and under my booted feet I could feel warmth. Into my dazzled mind the words carved on the stone gates of Casilla came unbidden: 'Casil e imitaran ne'. 'There is only one Casilla' was the common understanding of the words, which were in no language of the Empire, but a very old woman I had met in the marketplace had told me a different translation: 'Casil this is not'. I had puzzled over those words, but something about this room resonated with them. It did not look as if it belonged to the Empire I knew, but to something older, perhaps greater.

I forced myself to look up at the men seated at a long table. I saw the familiar face of Casyn, and beside him his brother, the Emperor Callan. Beyond Casyn, the empty chair that should have been Colm's: it was Turlo's, now. On the other side of Callan sat a man, tall but slight, with greying dark hair and no beard, dressed in a woven, woollen tunic and breeches, a cloak, also of wool, over one shoulder. The cloak was pinned to his shoulder with an intricate, enamelled pin, and around his neck he wore a twisted gold ring. Like the floor, the brooch and the gold of the torc glittered in the firelight. Two more men sat beside him, one clearly a close relation; the other, younger and light-haired, and stockier. And beside them, two young men, bracketing, I thought, Darel in age. My heart beat hard against my chest. I willed my breathing to slow.

Callan stood. "Thank you for your speed, General," he said. "Guardswoman Lena, Cadet Darel of the third, welcome to the Council of the White Fort, where after long days we have agreed to a truce between the Empire and the Northmen. Has the General Turlo explained your roles?"

Callan had named me, the elder, first. "He has, Emperor," I replied, hoping my voice was steady. He nodded.

"Yes, Emperor," Darel answered. He had served at the Emperor's winter camp, in the time before the invasion, and was less in awe of his Emperor as a result than some of his fellow cadets might have been. Darel shared many traits with his father, I was beginning to realize, and Turlo rarely stood on ceremony.

The slight man spoke, his voice surprisingly musical, and conversational. "This is your son, Turlo, then? Not that I need to ask: I can see it in his face. Who is his mother?"

"Arey, her name is, from Berge," Turlo replied. "And before you ask, Donnalch, her hair is brown and Berge's records say her forbears, for as many generations as they have records, are from south of the Wall." Donnalch grinned.

"Aye, but who would tell of a child got by a northman who had slipped over the Wall?" he said. Then his voice became serious. "And the woman, Casyn? You ask for her to stand surrogate for your own daughters?" My breath caught in my throat. I swallowed.

"I do," Casyn said, in his grave voice. "If Lena will have it so. My daughters are both mothers with small children; even so one might have agreed, but they are several days' ride away in Han village. And had I the right I would be proud to name Lena my daughter." He smiled at me, with those words.

"Hmm," Donnalch mused. "Lena," he said, in his lilting voice, "You are from Tirvan, am I right?" 'Teeerrvaan', he pronounced it, not our shorter, flatter 'Turvan'. I nodded. "How old are you?"

I cleared my throat. "Nineteen," I replied. I could not remember the title Turlo had mentioned. "Sir," I added, in case he thought me lacking in courtesy.

"And you have skill with weapons, I am told," he said.

"Some," I said. Hold your head up, Turlo had said. "I have learned the sword, and the use of a secca, in these past two years. The hunting bow I learned as a girl. I am reckoned a good shot with a deer bow," I added.

He studied me for some time, without speaking. I kept my eyes on him.

"But I cannot put you with the boys," he said, half to himself. He paused. "Will you read? And write?"

"Of course I can," I said, too startled to be more polite.

"No, lassie, that's not what I asked," he said, spreading his hands. "I asked if you will. Do you like to do such, I should perhaps have said."

"Yes," I said slowly, with a quick glance at Casyn. "I have learned to like both; I have been reading the stories of our Empire, and I keep a journal, a private record of the happenings of my life."

"Then," he said, with a quick confirming look to his advisors, "I know what to do with you. You were a bit of a puzzle, lassie, but now I have it: I will send you to a *Ti'ach*; a house of learning, as we do with one of our own sons or daughters who are drawn to the written word. Will that suit you?"

He was asking me where I would like to go? I glanced again at Casyn, and this time saw him make the briefest of nods. "Yes, sir," I said. "It would suit me."

"My title is *Teannasach*," he said easily. "But 'sir' will do fine, until your tongue is more comfortable with our language. Now, these two youngsters"— he indicated the two boys—"are my son, Ruar, and his cousin Kebhan. They go as hostage to your Empire, to be cadets. You two come as hostage to the North, to Linrathe. We of the North hold to more of the old ways, and not all the agreement between us can be of the Empire's shaping. So, this exchange of hostages is a symbol, but it is also a surety, for us both, that the agreement we have made here will hold from planting to harvest. If it does not, then the lives of our heirs—of Kebhan and Ruar, or of Darel and Lena—may be forfeit. Is this understood?"

I swallowed. I looked at Darel; he had paled, but his face was resolute. Then I glanced over at the two northern boys. They looked solemn, but not shocked. They had known in advance, I thought. "Yes, sir," I answered.

"It is growing late, *Teannasach*, and there is much to do if our truce is to be announced tomorrow." The Emperor spoke; his voice sounded weary, but not strained. I regarded him: even in the forgiving light of the torches, he looked tired. His face held more lines, and his hair more grey, than when I had first met him over a year earlier. Time had brought betrayal and loss, and the relentless battle to push the northmen back and reclaim the Wall for the Empire. But he had done it, against enormous odds.

"Aye," Donnalch agreed. "Shall we have a few minutes with our children, to say our farewells, and then we can commit this agreement to paper, and sign our names to give us a season of peace?" He pushed back his chair to stand. Immediately his two companions and the boys followed suit. "We will leave this room to you, Emperor," he said. "As it's your fort," he added. I watched the five of them leave the room by a door in the far wall. It closed with a click of its latch.

"Darel, Lena," Casyn said. "Please, come, and sit. Leave your packs." We did as we were told, taking the chairs just vacated by the northmen. My legs felt suddenly weak. Casyn poured two glasses of wine, passing them to us. "There is food, if you would like," he said. I shook my head, as did Darel, which surprised me. He must be as nervous as I am. Casyn poured more wine, for himself and Turlo and the Emperor. He glanced at Callan, who nodded.

"You will be wondering why we agreed to this, and with such haste," he said. "We have been talking, now, for nearly twenty days. At first, we were trying to create the terms for a lasting peace, but there is too much we do not agree on. What we could agree on was the need for a hiatus, for the reasons stated, so we began talking about the terms for a temporary truce. We had reached an agreement late this afternoon, and then Donnalch made the demand for hostages."

"I could not let the truce fail on such a request," the Emperor said. "The

Teannasach, I think, needed to put his mark on this agreement, and as he proposed his own son and his brother's son as their hostages, saying that his people would see this as binding, in their tradition, I believe he offers this in good faith."

I had a dozen questions, but none could be asked, here and now. I wished I had some time with Casyn, alone; I needed advice. I gathered my thoughts.

"May I ask a question, sir?" I said.

"Of course," Callan said.

"What am I—we—to pay attention to, wherever we are sent?"

"Ah," Callan said. "I could answer that better for Darel than for you, Lena. For you, Cadet," he said, turning to Darel, "there are two things: the state of their supplies, whether it is food or weapons or men, and, perhaps more importantly, what the men are saying. They will forget, eventually, to hold their tongues in front of you, and the boys your age will repeat what they hear from their fathers and uncles. Commit it to memory: do not write it down in plain words, at your life's peril. Now, go with the General Turlo—your father," he amended, in a rare acknowledgement of the relationship, "who will tell you what you can write, if you are allowed letters."

Turlo beckoned Darel over to a corner of the room. The Emperor turned his eyes to me. I had seen those eyes gentle in compassion, pierced with anguish, cold in anger and judgment. Now I just saw fatigue, and perhaps a mastered regret.

"Donnalch said he would send you to a house of learning," he said. "What we know of these is limited. There is no code to brief you on, no knowledge to pass on, or even much advice I can give you. Listen to what is said, about Donnalch's leadership, about the war, about what they wish to change. Exchange views on Partition, on your life as a woman of the Empire, our histories. Colm would have known more," he added, "and I believe he would have envied you this opportunity."

"I will do my best, sir, to remember that." I felt the prick of tears behind my eyes. Colm, who had just begun to show me complexity of our own history, and the cost and consequences of our choices. I could not fail him, either.

The Emperor regarded me in silence for some moments. I waited. "Listen to your instincts, Guardswoman," he said finally. "You will do well, I believe."

"Yes, sir." I hoped he was right. I heard footsteps crossing the room: Turlo and Darel. They joined us. The two men stepped aside to confer in hushed voices. I looked at Darel. He tried a grin.

"Another adventure," he said, in a passable imitation of his father.

Fatigue and apprehension began to dull my mind again. The northmen joined us, and after some further conversation among the leaders, Birel— Casyn's soldier-servant—led us through a warren of dark lanes to our beds for the night. Darel's bed was in a shared room, but I had a small, dark chamber to myself. The room felt clammy, but when I pulled back the blankets to climb into the narrow cot, I realized someone—likely Birel—had put a heated stone wrapped in cloth in the bed.

I pulled the blankets over my shoulders and wrapped my feet around the stone, then doused the single candle standing on the small table beside the cot. The mattress below me rustled, a thin pallet of straw on a rope web, suspended from a wooden frame. If I were lucky there would be no vermin sharing the straw. Where would I sleep tomorrow night? I shivered, more with anxiety than cold, burrowing deeper into the blankets. I would not think about tomorrow. Instead, I began to count in my mind all the beds I had slept in, this past year, since I left the one I had shared with Maya, and then Garth, in Tirvan.

The first had been the bed at Keavy's inn, a day's ride from Tirvan, with Garth beside me in the night. Then more inns, and camps, for several weeks, and then? The shared room at the Four-Ways Inn, I remembered, and then the bed with old Ione at Karst. My camp bed at the Emperor's Winter Camp. Back to the Four-Ways Inn, riding as Emperor's Messenger now, a brief sleep in Freya's own bed. Then Karst again, and then Casilla: one night in a hostel near the gates, and then months in the Street of Weavers, sharing a house with Tevra and Ianthe, and Garth's son Valle, and Maya, after she joined us. The memories of these rooms and houses and beds blurred and shifted. Sleep claimed me.

I awoke to a knock on the door. The room held no light, and I had no sense of the time. "Yes?" I called.

"Time to get ready, Guardswoman," I heard Birel say. "I've brought wash water. Shall I leave it outside the door?"

"Wait," I said, pushing back the blankets to sit up. I fumbled on the table, and by feel lit the candle. Then I walked the three paces to the door, opening it. I stood aside, holding the candle high, to allow Birel to bring in the water.

He had also brought soap and a towel. "I'll return shortly," he said, "to guide you back to the great hall."

This part of the White Fort had only communal latrines for the men, and so I used the chamberpot before washing. I combed water through my hair and dressed in my clean clothes. Then I repacked my pack, and waited for Birel.

He returned promptly. I shouldered my pack, following him through the damp morning. Around one corner he stopped to knock on another door. Darel opened it, and stepped out. He too had dressed in clean clothes, and smoothed down his red hair.

"Good morning," I greeted him. "Sleep well?"

"Of course," he said. He had learned the soldier's knack of sleeping anywhere and anytime, whether in a shared barracks or curled up under the Wall during a brief halt. "And you?" he asked.

"Yes, fine." I had slept, solidly, fatigue trumping apprehension, and my sleep had been dreamless, as far as I remembered.

We followed Birel to the great hall. This morning the light came from the high windows, and the floor, while still magnificent, did not shimmer and glitter; the images lay still. Sleeping, I thought, and then dismissed the fancy. The men of the Empire and the North sat at the long table, but the focus at this moment was breakfast, not diplomacy.

Turlo greeted us by name. "Come and sit," he said, "and eat. There's fresh bread, and some dried fruit. Eggs and cold venison, too." Places were found for us, and food brought, and I made as good a breakfast as I had had for some months. Birel, unasked, brought me tea, smelling of mint.

I saw Birel take Casyn's plate and pour something steaming into his cup. Turlo nibbled dried fruit. The Emperor's place had been cleared; he studied papers before him, a pen in his hand. At the other end of the table the servers repeated the work, clearing plates, pouring drinks. The Emperor looked up.

"Now," he said, "we had better talk of today." I saw, from the corner of my eye, Birel gesture to the servers. They left the room, Birel alone staying, standing against the wall.

"Keep eating," Callan said, as Darel moved to push aside his plate, "but listen." The Emperor looked down the table at the northmen; they stopped their conversation to focus on Callan. Donnalch rose.

"I'll sit with you," he said easily, and walked along the table. Casyn, with a glance at his brother, shifted over. Birel brought another chair, and Donnalch took the place beside the Emperor. The gesture, with all its implications, made me uncomfortable. I could not think of this man as the Emperor's equal.

"We are lucky with the day," Donnalch remarked, as he sat. "The sun is shining, and by all the signs there will be no rain before the afternoon. It's best if we can do this outdoors, where as many men can see and hear as possible."

Callan acknowledged this statement with a nod of his head. "If we speak from the watchtower west of this fort," he said, "the land is nearly flat for a good space on both sides. Will that serve, do you think, *Teannasach?*"

"Aye," Donnalch said. "Your messengers are ready to ride?"

"They are," Callan said. "And yours?"

"Mine also," Donnalch agreed. "The copies of the treaty are ready too, the ones entrusted to my scribes, and yours also, I believe?"

"Done," Callan said, "and the exchange has been made: the copies are here." He indicated the papers in front of him. "I have read and signed them; there are no errors that affect the meaning of the truce; your scribes are to be commended." He spoke quietly and politely, but I thought his voice lacked spirit. He did not quite sound defeated; resigned might be a better word. I wondered what the treaty said.

"And yours," Donnalch said. "I read through the copies from your scribes earlier, and wrote my name on them all; I wake early. So now, Emperor," he challenged, "how will we determine the speaking order? Who has precedence?" He smiled as he said this, but something in his face told me this was a serious question. Donnalch's men, I noticed, had become very still.

"*Teannasach,*" Callan said calmly, "as you yourself said last night, it is my fort. And my wall, and my watchtower. Your incursions into the Empire were repelled, and you and your men retreated to your historic lands. I think our positions are clear, and therefore the precedence. Would you not agree?" He kept his eyes on Donnalch as he spoke. The hall was very quiet. I had the sense that this conversation had happened before

Donnalch held Callan's eyes for several heartbeats. Then he inclined his head, a half-smile on his lips. "As you say," he said, his voice courteous. "I will give precedence to the long years of history, and the remnants of the greater Empire that this room reminds us of." I frowned. What did he mean? I glanced at Casyn. He looked grim. I repeated Donnalch's words in my mind, and heard this time the subtleties: precedence not to the Emperor, or even to his superior military position, but to history. I watched the men, holding my breath, feeling the precarious balance in the room.

Callan stood, his hand lightly resting on his sword, his eyes still on Donnalch. I heard chairs scrape as around both men their supporters stood too. Belatedly I realized I too had better stand, although I had only my secca on my waist. I could hear Darel's breathing beside me, not quite even, and the thumping of my heart. Very slowly, Donnalch came to his feet.

"The remnants of a greater Empire we may be," Callan said, "and myself a pale echo of those Emperors who came before, but the soldiers of the Empire do not forget. If it is that history you would acknowledge, then will you face east with me, and bow to that memory, and to what may still lie beyond the mountains and the seas?"

"I will," Donnalch said, "and my men with me. We do not forget either." The men moved out to the centre of the hall, facing the windows where the morning light was brightest. Callan and Donnalch stood beside each other, their swords in front of them. I followed Darel to stand behind the men. I had absolutely no idea of what they spoke, or what this meant.

Callan's voice rang out. "To the Empire unconquered," he proclaimed, bowing deeply. I followed suit, a memory surfacing of Colm's burial: Callan and the soldiers facing east and bowing. What did they bow to? What greater Empire? Where?

The brief ceremony seemed to be over, but the men remained standing. Donnalch turned to Callan. "Perhaps, Emperor," he said, "we should make this acknowledgement again, when we announce our truce. It would help, I think, to remind both sides that we come from a common history, although we have taken different paths. Perhaps, one day, we can find a road that we can all walk on, without enmity, and the truce we sign today may be the first step on that road." He spoke simply, with no trace of the challenge or posturing I had heard earlier.

Callan nodded. "Perhaps."

A line from Colm's history of the Empire came back to me: 'When there had been silence from the east for many years...'. I had thought, when I read it, that it had referred to a previous threat that had gone quiet, and had not asked Colm about it, although I had meant to. I wracked my brain. What did I know about the east? The mountains, the Durrains, which formed the eastern boundary of the Empire, and were said to be uncrossable. The Eastern Fort, where I had never been. Something more: the Eastern Fever. I heard the words in my mother's voice, but I couldn't place the context; something, perhaps, overheard as she instructed Kira. And what had the Emperor just said? What still may *remain beyond the mountains and the seas?* What was he talking about? I shook my head in frustration.

The movement caught Turlo's eye. He turned to look at me, frowning slightly. I coloured: did he think I disagreed with Callan, or Donnalch? I made a small gesture of placation; he nodded slightly, returning his attention to the leaders. Callan and Donnalch still faced each other, silent. Finally, Donnalch inclined his head slightly, a faint smile crossing his lips, and turned again to sit.

The men spoke quietly now, looking at papers. I watched for some minutes, but when I saw Kebhan and Ruar begin whispering to each other, I turned to Darel.

"Darel," I murmured, "this bowing to the east, what's it all about?"

"Don't you know?" he whispered back, surprise evident even in the hushed tone.

"No," I said. "Would I be asking, if I did?"

He remained quiet for a moment. "I suppose," he whispered finally, "it doesn't matter, to the women's villages. I can't tell you everything here, so this must do for now: once, many hundreds of years ago, maybe longer, we were part of a larger Empire, whose Supreme Emperor ruled from a city far to the east. What happened to that city, and those Emperors, we do not know. But what we know, the men, I mean, of command and strategy, and of fighting, we learned from them, and Callan and our Emperors before him take their titles in subservience to the Eastern Emperor, whether he lives or not, and remembers us if he does live."

I stared at him. "But what happened?"

He shrugged. "I told you, we don't know. Just that all messages, emissaries, trade, they all stopped. A very long time ago. We learn about it as cadets, and then we forget about it again, except in ceremonies, and at burials."

"But why does Donnalch know about it, and honour the memory? The north is not part of the Empire."

Darel shook his head. "I don't know. Maybe they have learned it from us in the long years there have been soldiers on the Wall?"

"Maybe," I murmured. My mind went back to a conversation I had had with Colm, months before. We had spoken of the building of the Wall, and how the northern armies had included men who had chosen to move north, rather than live under the rules of Partition. Perhaps, I thought, they brought the knowledge of the Eastern Empire, and the traditions around it, with them, and they have been maintained there to this day, as they have been here.

And what did it matter? This Eastern Empire had been gone for centuries. Rituals called upon many things: some invoked gods I did not believe in, and a long-disappeared Empire wasn't that different. I would take the knowledge north with me: perhaps it would help in finding common ground with those who would be charged with my keeping. It might be useful to know this, in a house of learning. I felt glad, suddenly, that I was not the village girl I had been before the day, nearly two years ago, when Casyn had ridden into Tirvan. I had known nothing then of our history, beyond a few bare facts, and nothing at all of the world beyond the borders of Tirvan. Since then I had learned to defend the Empire, ridden its length, lived in Casilla, served the Emperor. I had learned lessons of the heart, too, I thought, about love and loyalty, duty and obligation, and how difficult it was to separate them. I would take all that north, and learn what I could, for my Emperor, and for myself.

CHAPTER TWO

A WEAK SUN BRIGHTENED THE DAY, but gave little warmth. The stones of the road and the Wall gleamed damply, drying in the stiff northwest breeze. I rode beside Darel in the middle of the entourage. His attention was mostly given to controlling the wall-eyed skewbald that had waited for him, tacked and restless, when we left the White Fort. I had been glad to see my Clio, although I needed both my voice and hands to keep her calm.

Darel's horse shied, skittering sideways over the flagstones. Clio danced away from the larger horse. I heard Darel swear, hands and heels efficiently bringing the skewbald back into line. I felt the northerners' eyes on us; they sat their rougher hill ponies easily, and would know that our mounts' skittishness came in part from our own apprehension. Although, I noted, Kebhan and Ruar's ponies trotted calmly.

Ahead of us the commanders and their advisors had noticed nothing. As we approached the watchtower where the proclamation of truce would be made, the crowd of soldiers deepened. We slowed to a walk, and then pulled up. Dismounting, I handed Clio's reins to Birel, who had appeared beside me; he took the skewbald from Darel as well, motioning us forward.

I followed Darel to the base of the watchtower, and up the wooden steps. I could hear more footsteps behind us, echoing on the thick planks. As I turned the corner onto the top of the tower, the cold wind snatched at me, carrying the scents of smoke and pitch: the beacon-fires had been lit, to call the people in. My eyes watered. I looked northward. A horde of men and some women stood on the moorland below the tower, looking up. Southward, an equal number watched, although almost all were men.

Watchtowers held, usually, one to three men: eight of us crowded the space. The Emperor, and beside him Casyn; Donnalch and his brother—whose name, I realized, I did not know—and the four of us who stood as hostage. From the end of the platform I saw a red head on the top of the Wall below: Turlo, with more men beside him. I guessed the Wall ramparts on both sides of the tower supported men, watching, guarding. The crowds on both sides shifted; voices rose and fell.

Casyn had told us, before we left the White Fort, what we were to do: step forward when our names were announced. Beyond that, nothing. Given the wind and the crowds, all proclamations were to be made twice, once facing north, once south, repeated by both the Emperor and Donnalch.

From the wall rampart below us came the wild moan of the elbow pipe, a sound that belonged to these windswept moors and valleys. The crowds on both sides of the wall gradually fell silent, except for the shifting of bodies. Together, Callan and Donnalch stepped forward, to the north, first. My gut tightened. I looked at the backs of the two men, Callan a head taller than Donnalch, and heavier. Neither man wore armour. Callan's grey cloak, trimmed with white fur, hung to his knees; around his neck was the silver pendant denoting his rank. Donnalch's robe encompassed the greys and fawns and purples of the moor, as effective a camouflage as the feathers of a grouse hen. The gold torc caught the light. His dark hair lifted in the breeze.

"People of the north," he said, his voice pitched to carry. He followed it by something in a language I did not know, the words sliding together, sounding somehow as wild and sorrowful as the pipes. "People of the north," he said again. "I stand here today—no, we stand here today, to announce a truce, between myself and Callan, the Emperor of the lands south of the Wall, and between our peoples. Listen now, as together we tell you, in our common language, of the terms of this truce." He turned slightly to face Callan. "Emperor," he said, gesturing.

"My thanks, *Teannasach*," Callan said. "These, then are the terms. For six months, we will lay down our arms; your people will return to your villages and your fields, to your byres and pastures, and mine will do the same, before starvation finds us on both sides of the Wall. I give my word here, and the *Teannasach* will give his, that no raid nor battle will be undertaken by either side during this time of truce, nor any action that leads to the death by violence of a man or woman of our opposing side." He stepped back slightly. The mass of people remained, for the most part, quiet. Waiting, I thought, to hear more. Donnalch raised his voice again.

"In those six months, I and Lorcann, and the Emperor Callan and his brother the General Casyn, will meet, and talk, with the intent and the hope to find a way to a permanent peace between us; a peace, mind you, not a treaty that makes one side a vassal state to the other. Only if we are equals, in the tradition of the fallen Empire of the East that both our lands revere, can there be true peace. In surety of this truce, and our hopes for a lasting peace, I send my son Ruar, and my nephew Kebhan, to live with the cadets of the Southern Empire." At a nod from the man I now knew was Lorcann, the two boys stepped forward. Now the crowd did react: no one shouted, or cried out, but a slow murmuring began. Donnalch raised an arm, and slowly, it subsided. The boys stepped back beside Darel and me.

Callan spoke again. "I have no children," he said, calmly, "to my sorrow. The Empire sends Darel, son to the General Turlo, and Lena, who stands as surrogate daughter to the General Casyn, to live and work and learn with you, and as hostages to the Empire's intentions. Here they are." I took a deep breath, and with a brief glance at Darel, stepped to the edge of the watchtower. Hundreds of eyes looked up at us.

"Thank you," I heard Casyn murmur, and we stepped back. I let my breath out. Donnalch spoke again.

"Look," he said, holding up a rolled paper, "here is the truce. Watch, now, as the Emperor and I sign it in your sight." He unrolled the paper, spreading it on the rampart of the watchtower. The wind caught at it. Casyn and Lorcann held in down, and first Donnalch and then Callan signed the document. It would have to be signed twice, I thought, for both sides to see. The paper was rolled again, and held up in Donnalch's hand.

"This truce begins now," he cried, "and the penalty for any man or woman who breaks it is death: not only yours, mind, for you may be willing to make that choice, but remember that you could be choosing death for my son and nephew too, and that is not your choice to make. As your *Teannasach*, chosen by you to be your leader, I command you: uphold this truce, and leave here today with nothing more in your hearts and minds than your families and the sowing of your crops. We have made history here today, with you as witness; remember that and rejoice." He said something else, in the same tongue, with its undercurrent of music and mourning, and handed the scroll to Callan.

We all turned, then, to face the soldiers and guards of the Empire. Callan and Donnalch repeated the same words, Callan announcing the truce, and then Donnalch giving the terms. Only in the minor changes needed for the speaking order and the audience did the speech differ from what had been said to the northerners.

"I send Darel, son to General Turlo, and Lena of Tirvan, who stands as surrogate daughter to my brother the General Casyn, to live and work in the north, as hostages to the Empire's intentions," I heard Callan say. Again, I took a deep breath, and stepped forward. The eyes before had been those of strangers, assessing, curious. Now the eyes of those I served with, my companions and friends, looked up. I saw Halle in the crowd, met her eyes. She smiled, gave a quick nod. I swallowed. I did not look for anyone else.

I heard Casyn's quiet cue to step back. The same formal signing of the document occurred, with Lorcann and Casyn holding the paper against the wind. Callan said the final words, reminding our people that my life, and Darel's, were forfeit to truce-breaking. I heard the words, but I could not make them real. I wondered where Callan and Donnalch would meet; here, on the Wall, I supposed. Who would guard the Wall now? Soldiers from both sides, surely?

A clatter of boots roused me. The Emperor and the *Teannasach* descended the steps from the watchtower, followed by their supporters. Darel stepped forward just at the same moment as one of the northern boys—Ruar, I thought. They both stopped.

"It is your Wall," Ruar said softly, and with a slight bow. "You go ahead."

Darel hesitated. He looked at the steps, and then back at Kebhan. "The way is wide enough for us both," he said. "Shall we walk together?"

Ruar smiled slightly. "A diplomatic solution," he replied. He wore woollen clothes like his father's, woven in shades to blend with the moorland, and deerskin boots, and this close to him I could see Donnalch in the shape of his chin and his eyes. He turned to his cousin. "You will walk with the lady Lena, Kebhan," he said.

"I am not called lady, Kebhan," I said, "nor are other women you might meet in the service of the Emperor."

He glanced at Ruar. "That is good to know," he said. "How should I address you, then?"

"By my rank, which is Guard," I said, "or just by my name. You may also meet women who serve the Empire's army but are not part of it. Such a woman you would call by her role: Cook, or Smith, if you did not know her name."

"I see," he said in his soft voice. "In our lands, La...Lena, a woman of rank, and you must have such, if you stand as surrogate to the General Casyn's daughters, is addressed as my lady, or Lady. You should expect this."

I frowned. "Rank in the Empire does not come from our fathers," I said, "so if I had any rank, it would be from my mother, who is a council leader in our village. But we do not use such terms: rank and titles belong to the Empire's armies, not the women's villages."

"We both have much to learn," Ruar said. "We must all try not to take offense at usages and customs not our own." I frowned again: *was he chastising me?* But he turned away. "Come, Darel; Cadet Darel, yes?" he said. "We should follow our *Teannasach* and your Emperor down these steps. Are you ready?"

Darel grinned. "Ready, Cadet Ruar." They descended shoulder to shoulder, heads high. I looked down at Ruar. Eleven, maybe twelve, I thought. In the Empire, he would be choosing his path to service, whether on the boats, or as a cavalry cadet, or training to be a medic, just as I at twelve had chosen my apprenticeship. I wondered what the customs were, in the north.

"Come, then, Guard Lena," Kebhan said. A quick learner.

"Cadet," I replied, and we turned and walked together down the stairs.

†††††

Clouds scudded across the hills. We rode with the east wind in our faces, the thin spring sunlight holding little warmth. The track we followed was muddy; we kept the horses to a walk, and even so could not avoid being splattered.

Near mid-morning our leader, Ardan, held up a hand to stop. Turning in his saddle, he called to me. "Lena, ride up beside me." I did as he asked. We had stopped at the crest of what had felt like a gentle rise, but below us lay a long, deep valley, and in that valley stood a complex of buildings, built of grey stone. An L-shaped hall made one side of the complex, standing three storeys high and roofed in lichened, mossy slate; from each of its wings ran lower structures, and two or three free-standing smaller buildings surrounded the central courtyard. Trees sheltered it, and the rocky valley side. It looked, to my eyes, very old.

"The *Ti'ach*," Ardan said, gesturing. "Also called *Ti'ach na Perras*, for Perras, who heads this house, and to distinguish it from the others. Here you will live, for the duration of the agreement, and be treated as any other woman who had come here to learn."

Looking down, I swallowed my apprehension, studying the buildings to make sense of what I saw. Smoke rose from several chimneys. Someone came out of one of the smaller buildings, a basket in her arms, and began to peg out washing on a line. Others worked in what I thought was probably a garden plot, preparing the ground. It looked peaceful, nestled in its valley, undisturbed.

We rode down a switch-back path and over a stone bridge. The stream below ran rapidly, in full spring spate. In the paved courtyard, we dismounted. I held Clio's reins, looking around me. On seeing us riding down the path, the woman hanging washing had left her basket to go into the large house, calling something as she went, so by the time we reached the courtyard several people had emerged from inside. I saw two young women—one no more than a girl—and a man a few years their senior, flanking a grey-haired man leaning on a stick, and an upright older woman beside him.

It was the older woman who spoke. "Ardan," she said. "Welcome back. We were not expecting you. Are the talks completed then? Is there peace?"

"My lady," Ardan said. "There is a truce: six months to replenish our food supplies, on both sides of the Wall. Our *Teannasach* and the southern Emperor have proclaimed it, and during this truce, they will negotiate a longer peace, it is hoped. For surety, hostages have been exchanged. One has been sent here. I bring her to you: this woman, Lena, who stands hostage for the General Casyn."

As Ardan spoke I stepped forward, Clio obediently following. In the silence, I could hear her mouthing her bit. The older woman smiled.

"Welcome to *Ti'ach na Perras*, Lena," she said. "I am Dagney, and this," she gestured to the man beside her, "is Perras, *Comiádh* to this house. Ardan, will someone take Lena's horse, please?" I felt Clio's reins taken from my hand, heard her turn away. "Come," Dagney said, beckoning. She and Perras turned to walk back into the house. One of the younger women waited. "Come," she repeated. "I am Jordis. Are you tired, from your ride?"

I bristled at the implication of weakness. "No, my lady," I answered. "I am used to riding; I am a Guard in the Emperor's troops, and have ridden the length of the Empire twice. A few hours in the saddle is nothing."

"Oh, dear," she said, flushing. "I have offended you. But, a Guard? I did not know women served in the troops. Please forgive me...will you tell me more?" I realized she was flustered, and younger than I had thought. I stopped bristling.

"It is I who should apologize," I said. "You only asked what anyone would of a traveller. I am happy to tell you more, but," I looked over at the doorway, "should we not go inside, as the Lady Dagney indicated?"

"Oh. Yes," she said. I followed her up the shallow steps into the house. The door opened into a wide hall, lit only by small windows. The air smelled of stone and a smoke that was not woodsmoke, but something sharper. As my eyes adjusted I could see a long table and chairs standing on the flagged floor. At one end of the room a huge fireplace dominated; cabinets lined the opposite wall. Perras and Dagney, and the other man and girl waited, standing, at the table. The room was cold.

"Jordis," Dagney said gently. "Please go and fetch tea. Lena, will you sit?" Chairs were drawn. I took the one that Dagney indicated, draping my cloak over the back. Everyone sat, the young man last, after helping Dagney with her chair.

"Let me introduce you," Dagney said. "This is Niav," she indicated the girl, "and," nodding to the man, "this is Sorley. They are students here, as, I assume, you are to be?"

"I suppose I am," I said, "my lady. Your *Teannasach*," I stumbled a bit over the unfamiliar title, "said I should come here." I tried to remember his words. "He said he would send me here, because I like to read, and write, and this is where sons and daughters of your land come, if that is what they are drawn to."

"The *Teannasach* was a student here himself," Dagney said, "for a while. He still visits, when he can. Now, Lena, tell us a bit about yourself. Where are you from?"

"Tirvan," I said. "It's a fishing village, on the coast, south of Berge and Delle." I saw Perras nod. "I had a boat there, with my partner. We were separated, in the preparations for the invasion by Leste, and later I went south, to find her, and for other reasons. The search took me to our Emperor's winter camp, and I was there when..." I hesitated. What did I say to these people? It had been their men we had fought against.

"When the *Teannasach* took his men through the Wall," Perras said, his voice precise and measured.

"Yes," I agreed. "When that news reached us." I warmed to Perras, coming subtly to my aid as he had.

"And you came north, to the fighting?" Dagney asked. "I also did not realize women fought at the Wall."

I shook my head. "Not at once. I was given a task to do, to ride to the southern villages, to ask for women to ride north. I came north, to the Wall, later." That would do, I thought. They did not need to know all my history.

"The General Casyn is your father?" Perras asked. "You are hostage in his name, did I hear?"

"I am," I said, "but he is not my father." I saw Jordis return, carrying a laden tray. "He asked me to stand instead of his daughters, who are mothers with small children, and some distance from the Wall. It was Casyn who trained us, at Tirvan, and we rode south together, for part of the way. Now he is—" I stopped. "Was, I suppose," I amended, "my commanding officer."

Perras nodded. Jordis put the tray on the table and for a minute or two the distribution of tea and small oatcakes, spread with a soft, pungent cheese, occupied us. I sipped the smoky, unsweetened tea.

"What languages do you speak?" the young man—Sorley, I thought—asked.

"Only that of the Empire," I said. He raised an eyebrow, but said nothing.

"What books have you read?" Jordis asked.

"Schoolbooks," I shrugged. "My mother has books of healing—she's a midwife—but I haven't read those. There were not many books in Tirvan, except those, and some on husbandry."

"But why, then, were you sent here?" Sorley asked. "Forgive me if I sound rude, but you have less learning than one of our children in their tenth year."

I put my cup down and took a breath. "I came late to an interest in books," I said, trying to remain calm. "In the weeks I spent at our Emperor's winter camp, I was given a history of our Empire by the Emperor's brother and advisor, Colm. Reading that, I began to want to know more. So, I may know very little, but I am eager to learn."

"Colm's history?" Perras said, his voice a shade less measured. "You have read Colm's history?"

"I have," I said, "and discussed it with him, just a little."

Perras shook his head. "He and I exchanged a few letters. His loss was more than unfortunate," he said. "What do you remember? Could you write it down?"

"I could," I said. "But I have a copy, if you would like to read it."

Perras put his cup down. No one spoke.

"You have a copy of Colm's history?" Perras said. I could hear the disbelief.

"Yes. Colm gave it to me to read, and after he was killed, the General Casyn told me to keep it. He said the Advisor had meant for me to have it. It's in my saddlebag."

"I would be..." Perras hesitated, "most grateful if you would let me read it. Would you consider allowing it to be copied?"

What would Colm think? I wondered. He and this man had corresponded. "Yes," I said, "I would, as long as it is done here. And I can keep an eye on it," I added.

"I will do the copying myself," Perras said. "As I read it; it will help me in considering and remembering what is written, and allow me to annotate as I go. Is that acceptable, Lena?"

"Of course."

"Would you like more to eat or drink?" Dagney asked. "If not, then I will have Jordis show you to your sleeping chamber, and you may wash and change after your ride. And then," she smiled, "perhaps you could bring the book down to Perras. He will be in his workroom, waiting as patiently as he can." I heard the gentle teasing, and the affection behind it. I glanced at Perras. He acknowledged me—or Dagney's comments?—with a nod. I smiled.

"I will be as quick as I can," I said, standing to turn to Jordis.

"This way," she said, pointing. I picked up my cloak, following her out of the room and up a flight of wooden stairs. The sound of my riding boots echoed against the stone walls; Jordis, I saw, was wearing deerskin slippers. We reached a landing. At the third door, she stopped.

I stepped through the door. My saddlebags sat on a low chest against one stone wall. A narrow bed, covered by a woven woollen blanket, faced a small fireplace, with a sheepskin on the flagged floor. A table and chair filled the space under the one window, and a wardrobe and washstand lined the other wall. Simple, but more than adequate, and much better than my shared quarters at the Wall.

"I am next door," Jordis said. "Is there anything you need, Lena?"

I shook my head. "Just a few minutes to change, and perhaps to wash my face and hands. Is there water in the jug?" I stepped over to the washstand. The jug was full, and a towel hung on the bar. "I see there is. Then, no," I said, and then realized there was. "Wait," I said. "Yes, there is. Jordis, I assume there are no servants here? We empty our own slops, and the chamberpot?"

"Yes, of course," she said. "Except for the *Comiádh*, because of his infirmity. I

275 MARIAN L THORPE

will wait for you in my room. When you are ready, knock on my door, and I will show you the back stairs, and the well and laundry." She hesitated. "Are you used to servants, Lena?"

"No!" I said. "I am far more used to doing for myself, and happy to do so, once I know the house. But should I not take the book to Perras first? And is that what I call him?" There was a familiarity to this, learning the protocols and ways of a new place. I had grown used to it, over the past year.

"*Comiádh* is better," Jordis answered, "at least at first. The older students, those who have been here for some time, often call the *Comiádh* by his name, but I am not comfortable yet doing so. I think I am waiting for him to invite me to." She coloured a little.

"Com-i-ath," I tried. "Is that right?"

"Almost," Jordis said. "The emphasis is on the last part, though—Com-i-ATH. Do you hear the difference?"

"*Comiádh*," I stressed the last syllable of the title.

"Good," she said. "And yes, take him the book first. We can do the other later. Should I wait for you, or can you find your way back?"

"If you don't mind waiting," I said, "while I think I can find my way back to the hall, I do not know where the *Comiádh* will be. Will you show me? I'll be quick in changing; soldiers learn to be."

"I'll wait. I'm that side," she indicated with a movement of her head. She closed the door quietly behind her.

I took a deep breath, valuing the brief solitude. I walked to the window. It had a view over the yard. The wind had picked up a bit, and the laundry billowed in the weak sunshine. I looked out, beyond the valley, to the hills where the play of cloud and sun dappled the grey-green of their slopes. A lone bird—a buzzard, I thought—rode the air.

I stepped away from the window to pull off my riding clothes. Quickly washing in the cold water, I dressed again in my clean tunic and trousers. Hair freshly combed, I pulled my indoor slippers onto my feet, and picked up Colm's history.

Jordis had left her door open. I knocked lightly; she turned from where she sat at her table. I saw she had been reading. "That *was* quick," she said. She looked down at what I held. "Is that the history?"

I held it out to her. "Do you want to see it?"

Her eyes widened. "Not before the *Comiádh*," she said, with a quick shake of her head. She stood. "Come."

I followed her down the stairs and through the hall. She led me to a door I hadn't seen, obscured between the cabinets by shadow, and knocked lightly.

"Come," I heard Perras say. Jordis opened the door, ushering me in before her.

Perras sat in an armchair beside a fireplace, where a fire glowed, warming the room and giving off a rich, unfamiliar smell, not unpleasant. On both sides of the fireplace, shelves held many books, and some objects. Writing tools and paper, and an open book lay on a large table.

"Lena," Perras said. He stood carefully, steadying himself with the arms of the chair. "You were very quick."

I held out Colm's history. "I thought it important to you." And I have been trained to not keep those who outrank me waiting, I thought, but did not say. Perras took the book from me. He turned slightly to the firelight, and opened it. I knew by heart the words that began the first page: 'In the third year of the reign of the Emperor Lucian...'.

We stood in silence as Perras read, turning pages carefully. After a few minutes, he sighed, closing the book. "I must not be greedy," he said, "but I have waited a long time to read this work."

"You never met Colm?" I asked.

"No," Perras answered. "We exchanged a few letters, as I think I said, a few years ago, about what our records and our memories say about the building of the Wall, but we never met. I had hoped we would. We would have had much to discuss." He glanced down again at the book in his hands. "So much," he echoed. Then he raised his head to smile at me. "Please sit; it is easier for me." he said, his voice firmer. He nodded toward a second chair, facing his, on the opposite side of the fireplace.

I did as I was bid. Perras settled himself back into his armchair, looking up at Jordis. "You may go," he said gently. "My thanks for bringing Lena to me."

"My pleasure, *Comiádh*," she answered, and slipped from the room, pulling the door firmly closed.

I waited for Perras to speak. The warmth and flicker of the fire threatened to make me sleepy. I suppressed a yawn. The *Comiádh* appeared deep in thought.

"I think," he said, "that I would like you to sit with me each day, for a few hours, as I copy this history. That way I can ask questions of you, and discuss what you remember, as I read it." He smiled. "And you can keep an eye on your book, as you requested. Does that seem reasonable, Lena? I can see the book is precious to you."

"Yes, mostly because Colm gave it to me, and because both the book and he taught me things I had never known about our history." I stopped. Perras regarded me intently. I felt a need to explain. "In our village school, we learned just the simple facts: that the Partition Assembly was held, and some of the reasons why, and why we now live the way we do. That was all I wanted to know, at ten or twelve. But now—" I stopped.

"But now the facts are not so simple, and you are questioning whether they are facts at all." Perras finished for me.

"Yes," I said. "*Comiádh*, as we go through this book together, would you tell me what you know, from beyond the northern Wall? I would like to hear your side, too."

I saw a flicker of surprise in his eyes. "It will not make things simpler," he warned. Then he smiled again. "Beyond the northern Wall," he repeated. "Perhaps that is the first thing we must question." I frowned, puzzled. "Turn around, Lena," he said, "and look at the map."

I turned my head. On the wall behind me hung a large map. I looked at it, not recognizing anything. I stood to examine it more closely. A blue expanse to the right of the map was water, I realized, and there was blue, as well, at the top edge and at the bottom. I saw the pointed symbols for mountains running down the centre of the map, veering left. Islands of brown dotted the blue near the bottom of the map. I frowned.

"Where is this?" I asked. Perras stood, slowly, making his way over to stand beside me. He laid one hand on my shoulder, pointing with his cane.

"Here," he said, "is what you call the northern Wall. And here we are," he pointed to a spot below the line he had called the Wall, "and here is your home village, Tirvan." He indicated a place on the right-hand side, where the land met the sea.

"But," I started to say, and then I saw. "It's upside down," I said, in wonder.

"From what you are used to, yes." Perras agreed.

He had taken his hand from my shoulder, and so I took a step forward. I scanned the map. I found the roads I had ridden, and Karst, and followed the road with my eyes back to the Wall. Then I let my eyes travel down toward the bottom of the map. I could not read the names, but I could see the line of another wall, and named villages, and then a gap of ocean where the islands lay, and then just the edge of another land.

"There is another Wall!" I said. "And what lands are these, here?" I pointed to the bottom of the map.

"The land to the far north, at the bottom, is Varsland, and the islands belong to it." Perras said. "The other Wall—it is not a stone wall, or not mostly, but an earthern dyke for the greatest part—is The Sterre. The land below it is called Sorham—the South Home of the men of Varsland, for to those people it is south; and between The Sterre and the Southern Wall is this land, Linrathe."

I stared, trying to take it all in. Questions swirled in my mind. I didn't know what to ask first. My eyes returned to Tirvan, trying to fix a point in this new image of my world. I heard Perras make his slow way back to his chair and settle himself. I traced again the road to Karst, and found Casilla, and let my eyes come back to the Wall. I followed the Durrains from the sea to where they bent eastward, and studied the islands and the northern lands, then brought my eyes up again to where The Sterre was marked, dividing the land from the Lantanan Sea on the west to the mountains.

"Does the map show the same distances everywhere?" I asked without turning. "Would it take as long to ride from The Sterre to the northern sea as it does to ride from the Wall to Casilla?" The distances looked the same to me, on the map.

"Were there roads of equal quality, and the land equally flat or hilly," Perras said, "then, yes. The map is accurate, or as accurate as our mathematics allows it to be."

"Then," I said, "Sorham is as big as The Empire, and this land—Linrathe?— only half the size of either. Am I right?"

"You are," he answered. "Come and sit down, Lena, and tell me what you are thinking. Turn your chair, if you like, so you can see the map."

I did as he asked; I was being rude, standing with my back to him. I moved the chair so I could see the map with a turn of my head.

"What are you thinking?" Perras repeated.

"Too many things," I said. "That the world is not what I thought I knew; and how can I not have been taught this, at home or by Colm? That your land is walled between two larger lands, so why then do you raid south and not north? Who are the Varslanders, and why have they not sailed south to the Empire?" I shook my head, like a horse trying to dislodge an irritating fly. "Too many things,"

"Good," Perras said gently. I looked up. "Now I know what we should teach you in your time here. You will find more questions, as we work together, but we have a starting place. But that is enough, for today. Can you find your way back to your room?"

I wanted to object, but I knew Perras was right; I had learned more than enough for today. "I can," I said. I stood up. "Thank you, *Comiádh.*" I hoped I had got the pronunciation right.

"Thank you, Lena," he said. I crossed the room, pulling open the door. I glanced back before I closed it; Perras had Colm's history open on his lap, his face rapt.

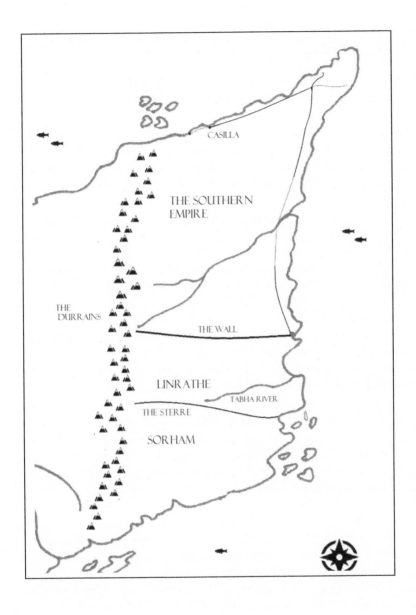

CHAPTER THREE

THE HALL WAS EMPTY. I walked across to the outside door to pull it open. The sun had begun to wester, but I estimated several hours of daylight remained. I wanted to check on Clio.

Outside the clouds were still moving quickly across the sky. It had rained briefly at some point; damp patches showed on the flagstones. I looked around, wondering where the stables were.

I had better find someone to ask, I thought, setting out for the nearest range of outbuildings. I poked my head into an open door: the laundry. No one was here, but I could hear voices close by. I walked along to the next door, and opened it. As my eyes adjusted to the dim interior light, I realized I had found the bathhouse.

Ardan lay in a large metal tub, his legs hanging over the end. Gregor, another of our party, occupied the tub beside him. A jug of something—I guessed beer—sat on a table between them, and two large mugs. I averted my eyes. "My apologies," I said. "I was looking for someone to tell me where the stables are."

"Walk down to the end of these buildings, and you'll see a path that goes off to the north," Ardan said. "Follow it, and you'll find the stables. But your mare is in the field behind the stables; I gave her a rub-down, and an hour or so in the stall, and then turned her out." He sounded unperturbed by my presence.

"Thank you," I said. "I like to see her, in a new place."

"Aye, you're well trained," he said. "Close the door as you go, to keep the warm in, if you would." I recognized the dismissal, and did as he asked.

The path took me to the stables, as Ardan had said it would. Just below the crest of a slight rise, Clio stood among a group of horses, one hip cocked, resting. When I called her, she ambled over to the fence and blew happily as I scratched her poll and withers. Tatters of hair hung from her heavy winter coat. After a few minutes, I gave her a gentle slap and she wandered away from the fence, back toward the other horses. I went in search of her tack.

I found it hanging in a space that doubled as tack and feed-room, neatly stowed, and cleaned, albeit the quick cleaning of a working day. I wondered if Ardan or Gregor had cleaned it. I needed to thank them. I would give the tack a thorough cleaning—and Clio a thorough grooming—as soon as I could.

I heard a sound from the end of the stables, the familiar scrape of pitchfork on stone. I walked down the range; at the end stall, I found Sorley clearing out soiled bedding.

"Hello," I said. "Sorley, isn't it?" He looked up, straightened.

"Lena," he said. "Can I help you?"

I shook my head. "I came to see my horse," I said. "Although, would you know where Jordis is? She was going to show me around."

He glanced up at the sun. "She'll be with the Lady Dagney, in lessons," he answered, "for another hour, I would think."

"Oh," I said. "What should I do, then? Do I have time to curry Clio?"

"You should," he said. "Did you see the tack room?" I nodded. "You'll find what you need there, but why don't you bring her down this end—you can tether her there," he said, pointing to a ring in the wall between two stalls, "and talk to me at the same time. If you would like," he added.

"All right." I went to fetch Clio and the currycomb. By the time I brought her back, Sorley had finished cleaning the stall, and was propping a barrow up against the end of the stable.

He looked at Clio. "She's a nice little mare."

"She is," I agreed. "Her name is Clio, and she was bred at Han, in the north of my country." I began the task of easing out the undercoat. As I worked, sparrows flew out from under the eaves of the stable and began to pick up bits of hair for nest-building. After a few minutes, I glanced at Sorley. He sat on an upended bucket, watching.

"Tell me how things work here. What are the days like, and who decides what we do?" I thought he might give me a more balanced view than Jordis; he was older, exuding calm and competency.

"The *Comiádh* and the Lady Dagney decide what we do, if you mean with whom we study. What we study depends on our own interests, for a large part, although there are some common subjects, such as how to write well, and how to take care of books and scrolls. Did the *Comiádh* say who your tutor would be?"

"I am to work with him."

He looked mildly surprised. "Then it is history, and politics, that interest you?"

I considered. "I suppose. History, anyway. What does the Lady Dagney teach, then?"

"Languages, and music, and the *danta*."

"What are *danta*?"

"Long poems set to music," he explained, "that tell stories about past kings, or battles, or other things; our history, in a way, but with a lot of other things— magic, and giants, and winged horses—mixed in. Sometimes they are fairly horrible, like the song about Ingjol, who killed his enemies by burning down the hall they slept in, and sometimes they are more like stories for children."

I moved to Clio's other flank. "And are there other teachers?"

I saw the negative movement of his head. "No. Although sometimes a student who has been here for some years, like me, will work with newcomers, if we are asked."

"I see," I said. "How long have you been here, Sorley?"

"Five years. It will be time for me to leave, soon."

"To do what?" I wondered if my question was an intrusion.

"I will go back home," he said. "Help my father, instruct my brothers and in the school a bit, learn be the *Harr*...I do not know how to say that, in your language. Leader? Of the family, and the village?"

"I don't know, either," I said. "In our village, we had headwomen, but they were elected by the council, and the title was council leader. But I think I understand."

Clio flinched as I tugged on a mat of hair, and I realized I had not been paying attention to the task. I soothed her with voice and hands, giving my attention to detangling the knot.

"How do you learn, then? You do not have places like the *Ti'acha?*"

"No," I said. "In my village, in Tirvan, girls go to school from the time we are seven, until we are twelve. We learn to read and write, and do sums, and some history. We learn the rules that were set down at Partition, both for the Empire's men and women, and for the villages. In our last year, we choose an apprenticeship, and after that we learn as we work, practical skills."

"And if a girl truly wanted to learn more, from books, I mean? Is it against the rules?"

"I don't know," I said slowly. "It has never happened, as far as I know. Although my mother—she is the midwife and healer, as I said—sometimes said she wished she knew more, or had more books." Would she have gone beyond the village to learn, if the chance had been there?

"If we can find peace, beyond this truce, I mean," Sorley said, "then she could go to the *Ti'ach na Iorlath*, where healing is taught, for a season, if she would be allowed to."

"But she is more than twice my age," I said.

He shrugged. "Age does not matter," he said. "The *Teannasach* himself comes here when he can, to discuss and debate matters with Perras, and the Lady Dagney, and to read more books, which leads to more discussion and debate." I heard the bucket scrape as he stood. "The lesson will be nearly done. Do you want to turn your mare loose again, or stable her?"

"Turn her loose. She has spent too long picketed, or in stalls." I untied the lead rein to walk Clio back down the stable block to the paddock, stopping briefly at the tack room to put away the currycomb. She looked a lot better, I thought, as I watched her trot away across the field. I turned to Sorley.

"She will need shoeing before too long. Who does that, here?"

"There's a smithy a few miles north of here," he answered. "But will she need shoes? You won't be going anywhere; couldn't you just take her shoes off for now?"

Anger spurted through me. Who was Sorley, to tell me what I could or couldn't do? I bit back a sharp retort. He was right, of course. Although...

"Do you not ride to hunt? I am skilled, both with the hunting bow and with a knife. I would like to help with that, if I could."

He looked down at me, raising one eyebrow lazily. "Women don't hunt here," he said, "except for hawking. Can you fly a kestrel, or a sparrowhawk?"

"No," I said coldly. "But I can take down a deer with one arrow, and I have killed both game and men with my knife." I looked up at him. "Your women may not hunt, Sorley, but I am from the Empire, and the Empire's women hunt."

He flicked his eyes away from mine. "The decision will be Perras's," he said. "My understanding of a hostage is that you live by our rules, while you are with us. But I may be wrong."

Casyn had told me much the same. "You are probably right," I admitted. "I am not accustomed, yet, to this role of hostage."

"Nor do we really know how to treat you." We walked a few steps back toward the house in silence. "Have you really killed a man?" he asked, suddenly.

"Yes," I said. "Two, actually. But I would rather that was not common knowledge. I don't like talking about it." I no longer had nightmares, but the memories were not good ones.

We rounded the corner of the outbuildings that held the bathhouse and laundry, and there was Jordis. "Lena! I was looking for you."

"I was at the stable, seeing to my horse."

"I can show you around now," she continued. "Sorley, the Lady Dagney is waiting for you."

"Then I better go. I will see you later, Lena." He walked off in the direction of the hall.

"Where do we start?" I asked.

I spent the best part of an hour with Jordis, first touring the rest of the outbuildings—fuel-store, toolshed, cidery—there was an orchard somewhere—and the chicken coop, where the hens that provided eggs for the *Ti'ach* were housed at night, against weasels and foxes. Then we went inside, and I was shown the kitchen, and the stillroom, and Lady Dagney's teaching rooms and the adjoining music room, where Niav was practicing a stringed instrument. We did not go to the third floor—the male pupil's rooms, Jordis explained, and off-limits to the girls and women of the *Ti'ach*. That part, at least, reminded me of the inns of the Empire, where men's rooms were also separate, and often—as here—with a separate staircase for access.

Finally, the tour was done. We had returned to the kitchen; at about this hour every day the household gathered for tea, Jordis explained. Two trays were waiting in the kitchen: one with a large pot of tea and mugs, one with a plate of buttered bread and another of oatcakes. We each took a tray, carrying them through to the hall. Jordis went back to the kitchen to return with a third tray, this one with small plates. She distributed them around the table: I counted nine.

"Nine?" I said to Jordis. "I haven't met everyone, then?"

"Oh," she said. "It's only Cillian, from the *Ti'ach*. He is a pupil of the *Comiádh*, like you, but he is older. I don't know who the other two plates are for—perhaps some of your escort?"

My question was answered as the household began to gather. Ardan and Gregor came in from outside; Sorley, Niav and Lady Dagney from her rooms. At a look from Dagney, Sorley walked over to Perras's door, knocking before opening it. "Tea, *Comiádh*," I heard him say.

We took our seats. Dagney looked around. "Where is Cillian?" she asked.

"He rode over to the smithy," Sorley said, "several hours ago."

"We won't wait," Dagney decided. She poured mugs of tea and we passed them around the table, followed by the plates of bread and oatcakes. Following the lead of others, I took one piece of each. My stomach had been rumbling for a little while. I wondered if I had missed the mid-day meal, or if morning and afternoon tea replaced that meal here.

"What have you done this afternoon, Lena?" Dagney asked me. I gathered my thoughts.

"After I met with the *Comiádh*, my lady," I answered, "I went to see my horse; I like to do so in a new place. She needed grooming, so I did that, and talked with Sorley, who was also at the stables. And then Jordis found me, and showed me around, until just a few minutes ago."

"And what do you think of our *Ti'ach*?" she asked. I wondered what the question really meant. I doubted she wanted a polite, meaningless answer.

"It seems very peaceful," I said, "and organized so that there is time for both learning and work in and out of the house. The way the building is designed reminds me of some of the inns which I have stayed in, on the road, except for the stables being more distant than would be usual. Beyond that," I shrugged slightly, "it is only my first afternoon, but those are my impressions."

"I am glad you find it peaceful," Dagney said, smiling. "We do strive for that. It will be a change for you, will it not?"

"It will, my lady."

"Lena is to study with me," Perras said to the room. He looked around. "But it appears you all knew that—except, perhaps, you, Niav?" She nodded. "It will be good for me to have a second pupil, and one who brings a different knowledge than most. But, Lena, you should also spend a few hours a week with the Lady Dagney—I am thinking of languages—you speak only one, and it would be useful if you had at least a basic understanding of our language, and that of Varsland."

"If you wish." A thought struck me. "Am I making you all speak my tongue, because I do not understand yours?"

Dagney smiled. "Not entirely. When a student leaves here, it is our hope that he or she will be comfortable in speaking three languages: our own; that of the Marai, the people of Varsland, and yours. So, in conversation at mealtimes, and in lessons, we may speak any of the three. We will speak your language for a week or two, both for your benefit, and for Niav's, as she has had no chance to converse with a native speaker." I glanced at Niav, who coloured slightly.

"Also," Perras added, "many of our books are written in your language, or a version of it, so it is important that students learn to read it, as well."

I wondered how many of our soldiers could speak or read these other two languages, or at least the language of Linrathe. Turlo, perhaps, and borders scouts, and those with long service on the Wall? It could not be wise to deal with an enemy who could communicate in your language, without learning theirs, too.

"I will be off in the morning, with your leave," Ardan suddenly announced. I looked his way, but he was addressing Perras. "Gregor will stay, as the

Teannasach directed. I see no reason to leave two men."

"Nor do I," answered Perras. I frowned. Why was Gregor staying? But then I realized: he was my guard, to ensure I did not leave. I opened my mouth to protest, and then closed it. As the *Teannasach* directed, Ardan had said. Ardan could not change the order, even if he had wanted to. Darel would be guarded too, and, I reflected, so would Kebhan and Ruar, on our side of the Wall.

The room was darkening, and I heard rain against the window. Niav brought candles from the sideboard and lit them. I glanced toward the window. "*Comiádh*, sir?" I said. "May I go to stable my horse? I would prefer her not to be out all night in the rain, as there is a stable for her."

"We'll go," Ardan said, before Perras could answer me. "No point in us all getting wet."

"Thank you, Ardan, Gregor," Perras said, but even as the men stood the hall door opened. A tall man stepped in, his dark hair dripping rain onto a heavy sheepskin jacket.

"Cillian," Dagney said. "You are late. Is all well?"

"Yes, my lady," Cillian replied, his voice soft. He walked into the low candlelight, and for a moment I thought he was someone I had seen before— but where? "Just that the rain has come from the north, and so I rode back from the smithy at a walk as the path was slippy, and then I took the time to stable the horses that were in the paddock, and ensure they had a bite of hay. But a hot mug of tea would be welcome."

Niav had gone to the kitchen at Dagney's words. Ardan and Gregor hesitated, and then sat again. "That was kind of you," Perras said. "You have saved these two soldiers a wet trip." The two men murmured words of thanks, but Cillian shrugged them off. "No matter," he said, shedding his wet coat and hanging it on the back of an empty chair. No, I decided, I did not know him.

Niav returned with hot water to fill the teapot. She brought Cillian a mug, and the last of the bread and oatcakes. He smiled at her. The room was silent.

After a mouthful of tea, he looked up. "I am being rude," he said. "We have visitors."

"Ardan and Gregor you will remember," Perras said, "as soldiers of the *Teannasach's* guard." Cillian nodded. "And this is Lena, Guardswoman of the Empire, one of the two hostages exchanged in surety for the truce. The *Teannasach* has sent her here, and she will be studying with me, so you have interests in common."

I saw the flash of surprise in his eyes, followed by a cold, evaluative look. "Another student of history, and a woman of the Southern Empire at that," he said. "You will be busy, *Comiádh*." He spoke no word to me.

"Now, Lena," Dagney said. "The hours between our afternoon tea together and supper are not scheduled; this is time for all of us to use as we please: in study or practice, conversation, or solitude. There is a rota for the duties of the house each day, but you will not start on those until tomorrow. You are not bound to the house; you may, in this time, exercise your horse or see to her other needs, if you wish, but the *Teannasach* has asked Gregor to accompany you if you ride out by yourself or with others of the *Ti'ach*. We are glad you are with us, but scholars and teachers of the *Ti'ach* cannot be responsible for your safety; that is Gregor's job. I hope this will not distress you?"

"No, my lady," I answered, glad I had realized Gregor's role earlier. I might have been less calm, otherwise. I had had little to do with Gregor on the ride here, but he had always been polite. I judged him to be about thirty, a lean man of middling height with a relaxed air to him. I wondered how he would find life at the *Ti'ach*, guarding one woman in a school. Ardan—or the *Teannasach*— must have had reasons to choose him, I thought.

Niav and Jordis rose to gather the plates and mugs. Sorley stretched, speaking to Dagney. "My lady, will I disturb you if I practice the *ladhar* for an hour? I can take the instrument to my room, if it will."

"It will not," she said. "And the practice room will be warmer."

I stood too, uncertain of how to take my leave. "Thank you," I said finally, "my lady, *Comiádh*, for such a welcome to the *Ti'ach na Perras*. I am looking forward to my time here."

Dagney looked surprised. "Your presence here graces us," she said. "We will learn together, for you have things to teach us, too."

"I am eager to start tomorrow," Perras said.

I smiled. "Thank you," I said again. I smiled, too, at Cillian, making the overture.

Then I walked up the stairs to my room, pulled off my boots, and collapsed on the bed.

I drifted into a light, dreamless sleep for a while, but the room was cool and I had not pulled the blanket over me. I woke to cold hands and feet. No fire had been laid in the hearth. I remembered Dagney's words to Sorley about the practice room being warmer, and guessed that fires in our rooms were reserved for the coldest months alone. Fires had been a luxury in the barracks, too. I was used to the cold. I lit the candle on the table.

I pulled my journal out of my pack; pen and ink stood in a stand on the table, beside the candle. But I was not ready yet to write down my feelings and impressions. I turned my pack out onto the bed, putting my few possessions away in the wardrobe and chest. Then I sat at the table, opening my journal.

But still I did not write. I stared out into the darkening world, past the candle's reflection, letting the thoughts and impressions of the last week swirl through my mind. Casyn's request that I stand as hostage in his daughter's stead; the room at the White Fort, with its floor of pictures; the rituals that invoked an Eastern Empire; the map on Perras's wall. A world turned upside down.

CHAPTER FOUR

IN THE END, I WROTE ONLY A FACTUAL ACCOUNT of the past few days. I could not marshal my thoughts to do more. I had not had a chance to write since Turlo had come to the servery looking for Darel and me, and so even the facts took a long time. My hand ached as I reached the end.

I glanced over what I had written, and picked up the pen again. *Why have I never heard of the Varslanders, when they are closer than Leste?* I wrote. *Why do they not trade with us? What peace treaty exists between them and the Northmen—the people of Linrathe?* All questions I could ask Perras.

There was one more thing. *Ask Perras about the Eastern Empire.* Not yet: for some reason, I felt it was not something I could broach with him, until I knew him better. But the ritual at the White Fort haunted and frustrated me. I felt like a child again, kept from grown-up mysteries.

From downstairs, a deep ringing 'boom' sounded. I guessed it was the signal for supper. I lifted the candlestick and in its flickering light made my way down to the hall.

Supper was mutton stew and barley bread, and more oatcakes served with cooked apples. A thin beer accompanied the food. Perras and Dagney led the conversation, directing questions at the other students about recent lessons, and what conclusions they had drawn from what they had learned. I guessed this was the usual pattern at the evening meal.

But at the end, as we were finishing the oatcakes and apples, Perras cleared his throat. "Tonight, we will not have our usual entertainments after supper, for there is something you all should hear: the words of the treaty our *Teannasach* and the Southern Emperor have signed. So, let us have the table cleared, and, I think, wine poured for everyone, and then I will read the treaty to you."

"Do we ask the kitchen-folk to join us?" Jordis asked, already gathering plates.

Perras shook his head. "No. I will gather the *torpari* tomorrow, and they will hear it then."

Cillian went to one of the cupboards and brought back goblets that caught the firelight, making several trips with the fragile objects. As he placed them on the table, I realized they were glass, something I had never seen except for some tiny, square, medicine bottles my mother had. From the same cupboard, he brought a flagon made of glazed pottery, and poured a small amount of dark wine into each glass. He did not distribute them.

Ardan moved a candle from the centre of the table closer to Perras, and handed him a tied scroll. The older man loosened the ties, and unrolled it, reading the words to himself. I saw him nod, slightly, and then he looked at me.

"Lena," he said, "you among us, save for Ardan and Gregor, will have heard these words before. When I have read them, I would appreciate it if you would tell us how they were received, by the gathered soldiers of the Empire. I will ask Ardan to do the same, for our men."

"I will do my best," I murmured, glad of the forewarning.

"'Herein are the terms of the truce between Linrathe and the Southern Empire, agreed this first day of spring at the White Fort, between Donnalch, *Teannasach* of Linrathe, and Callan, Emperor of the South,'" Perras read. I listened, hearing the words again, letting them wash over me as I watched the faces around the table: Dagney intent, focused; Sorley frowning occasionally; Jordis nodding. Only Cillian showed no reaction, his face set, although a muscle jumped in his jaw at the mention of the Eastern Empire.

"'The penalty for the breaking of this truce by any man or woman, from Linrathe or the Southern Empire, is death for the transgressors, who also risk the lives of the hostage of their land. Remember this, and maintain the peace.'" Perras paused. "It is signed by both the *Teannasach* and the Emperor," he finished. No one spoke.

"The wine, now, I think," Perras said. Cillian and Sorley rose and distributed the glasses, Cillian serving the end of the table away from me. I watched how Perras cradled his, cupping the bowl in his hand gently. I copied him, the glass feeling cool and smooth against my hand. I held it lightly, afraid of its fragility.

"To a temporary peace," Perras said, "and may a lasting one arise."

"To peace," Dagney said, and took a sip of her wine. The rest of us followed her lead. The wine, rich and smooth, warmed my throat. I put the glass down carefully.

"Now, Lena," Perras said, his voice conversational. "What can you tell us of the reaction, from the Empire's men? And women," he amended.

"I had only a few minutes to see," I said slowly, "and you must remember that soldiers are trained not to show reaction to orders, and the truce, read out by our Emperor, is an order. So, I may be guessing here, a bit, but what I think I saw was relief. We have been at war for over a year; many have died, and food is scarce. I think nearly everyone wanted and welcomed a truce."

"And did you?" Perras asked.

"Yes," I said. "For the same reasons." And because I had begun to think the war unwinnable. I did not say that aloud. I suspected many on the Wall felt the same.

"Ardan?" Perras said. "What did you see and hear?"

"Much the same," he answered. "I also saw pride, when the *Teannasach* spoke of a treaty of equals. They—we—have great faith in him, and look to this as a beginning of change for Linrathe, in our dealings with both the Southern Empire and with Varsland."

"Lena," Perras asked, "what will happen now, for your soldiers? Where will they go? The treaty speaks of returning to fields and villages, but that is not your way, is it?"

I shook my head. "No," I said, "not for the men."

Niav leaned forward. "Is it true," she asked, her voice hushed, "that women do not live with men in your land, by law? And that they do all the work of men?"

"It is," I answered. I saw her eyes widen in the firelight.

"But why?' she asked.

I glanced at Perras. "Go ahead," he said. "The others know what our history teaches; it will be instructive for us all to hear what you were taught about Partition."

"I would have told a different story, not too long ago," I said. "But briefly, then: many long years ago, men and women of our Empire did live together, much as I imagine your people do here. But military service was mandatory, and the Emperor of the time, Lucian, wished to expand his Empire, except that he needed the approval of the people to do this: those were the laws, at the time. Village councils were in the hands of women, as so many men were away so much of the year, and those councils overall did not want the Empire to be expanded at the cost of more lives. So, the Emperor called for an assembly, and, after long discussion and debate, a proposal was made that divided the laws that govern men and women: women would live in the villages, farm and fish and provide food, much as they already did, and be governed by their councils. Men would fight: the army would govern them. It is called the Partition Assembly, as it divided not just our laws, but our lives."

I glanced at Niav, watching me, wide-eyed. I took a breath. "What I did not know, until this past year, is how many objected. For many people of the Empire, men and women, Partition was not the answer. But by our laws, those people either had to submit to this new decree of the Empire, or choose exile. Many chose exile, and most, I believe, crossed into these lands. Some of us in this room may share common ancestors; your *Teannasach* and our Emperor may be distant cousins, for all I know. But to live separate lives has been our lot for twenty generations or more, and it seems normal to us now." Or it had, until the invasion from Leste. "Does that answer you question?" I asked Niav.

"Yes," she said. "So, you can do everything? Build a wall? Shoe a horse?"

I laughed. "Well, not me personally. But in my village, in Tirvan, there were women who did those things, and who built boats and houses, and ploughed and harvested the fields. I fished, with my partner, from our boat."

"And you can fight," Sorley said. "After all, you are a soldier now."

"Yes," I answered. "I can fight, and I have. I can handle a sword, and a bow, but my specialised training is with the secca, the knife, in close combat."

"Sorley," Perras said quietly, "we are diverging from our purpose here tonight, with these questions. You will recall I asked Lena what would happen now, for the soldiers of the Southern Empire."

"My intent was to remind us that there are now women among the Empire's soldiers," Sorley said, "and that perhaps what happens for male and female soldiers might be different."

"As it will be," I agreed, not waiting for Perras to speak. "Women will return to their home villages, to the work they left. The men will return to their duties, whether that is teaching cadets, or patrolling the Wall or the Durrains, or building roads, training horses, or making swords, I suppose."

"But they will continue to be soldiers, training and planning, for the next six months, while our men will not, for the most part," Cillian said. "Which could be giving the Empire an advantage."

"Do not underestimate the *Teannasach*," Ardan said sharply. "Do you think he would not have thought of that?"

"The Southern Empire has had professional soldiers for many generations," Perras pointed out. "And yet we have fought to an impasse. Will one summer change that?"

"Is not the point," Jordis said, "that there should be no more fighting? The *Teannasach* and the Southern Emperor will spend this summer talking, looking for a permanent peace. And another winter war? Remember what Halmar wrote:

war in winter sends sorrow soaring;
hunger hurts, cold kills:
ravens rejoice, wolves wait;
men moan, women wail:
death in darkness, glory gone...

"And if the intent is to find peace, then perhaps the *Teannasach* did not see harm in the soldiers of the Southern Empire returning to their usual duties?" she finished. Her insight surprised me—unfairly so, I admitted to myself, as I barely knew her.

"Do you think the *Teannasach* can negotiate a permanent peace, under the conditions he has laid down? An agreement of equals?" Perras asked. It was Sorley who answered.

"If he does," he said, "then surely it would challenge the terms of our peace with Varsland, with the Marai?" he said. No one responded.

"Forgive me," I said, "but I do not understand. What are the terms of the peace with Varsland?"

Dagney answered. "Linrathe pays tribute, or tax, if you like, to Varsland," she said. "In return, the Marai—the ship-warriors of Varsland—do not raid into Sorham, and leave landholders such as Sorley's father, and my brothers, in peace. It was not always so."

"Is that why there is another Wall? The Sterre?" I asked, remembering the map.

"It is not why it was built," Dagney answered, "but now, yes, it defines the border between Sorham and Linrathe. The Marai do not cross it, although they may enter Sorham for peaceful purposes, seeking trade or marriage. People of Sorham travel north, too, to Varsland or the islands, for the same reasons. My own mother was born on Naermest, one of the islands of Raske, or the Raske Hoys, as they are named there. Many—if not most—of the folk of Sorham carry the blood of the Marai."

"So," I said slowly, working through it, "Linrathe has a peace treaty with

Varsland, but by the terms of this treaty Linrathe is," I hesitated, looking for the right word, "subservient to Varsland. The Marai are paid to leave Sorham in peace. But is it Linrathe, or Sorham, who pays the tribute? Who does Sorham belong to, if not itself?"

"Long years ago," Perras said, "Sorham was conquered by Varsland, if conquered is the right word. The Marai moved south from Varsland, settling on some unclaimed lands, raiding into claimed lands, taking wives and fathering children. But folk also moved north from Linrathe, especially when our numbers swelled at the time of Partition in the Southern Empire. Conflict ensued, and after some years the current agreement was reached: the Marai withdrew with the promise of peace, leaving Sorham to Linrathe, for a price."

"I believe our *Teannasach* thinks," Cillian interrupted, "that if he can negotiate a treaty of equals with the Southern Emperor, then it will be time to challenge the terms of our treaty with the Marai. Their king is old; there will be a new one soon, so what better time?"

"Aye," Ardan spoke softly. "That is how I see it, too."

"If our two countries find peace," Cillian said, "then is not the very reason for the Southern Empire's army gone? What happens to an army when there is no enemy to fight?"

No one replied. I took another mouthful of wine. Candles and shadows flickered in a small movement of air, from beneath the door or a loose window. Cillian was wrong, I thought. Enemies could still arise, as Leste had.

Perras broke the silence. "I think that is enough discussion for this evening," he said. "Perhaps one song, before we retire? Lena, is there a song of the Empire you could sing for us?"

I had not expected this. "I have not much of a voice," I said, stalling.

"No matter," Dagney said. "Sorley, would you fetch a *ladhar*? Sorley will follow you on the instrument," she explained, as he went toward the practice room, "or accompany you, if the tune is one we know."

"I hope you can recognize it, if it is," I said. I wondered what to sing, reviewing in my mind the songs sung at Tirvan. Only one stood out.

Sorley returned, and moved a chair back from the table. He ran his fingers over the strings of the *ladhar*, and adjusted one tuning peg. Then he nodded. I stood.

"This is not a song of my village," I said. "I learned it from our potter, Tice, who was from Karst, at the southernmost reaches of the Empire." I took a breath, and began.

The swallows gather, summer passes,
The grapes hang dark and sweet;
Heavy are the vines,
Heavy is my heart,
Endless is the road beneath my feet.

I heard the notes of the *ladhar*, as mournful as the song. I glanced at Sorley;

he nodded. I continued, the instrument now in time with my voice.

The sun is setting, the moon is rising,
The night is long and sweet;
I am gone at dawn.
I am gone at day,
Endless is the road beneath my feet.

The cold is deeper, the winters longer,
Summer is short but sweet;
I will remember,
I'll not forget you,
Endless is the road beneath my feet.

Sorley plucked a few more notes from the *ladhar*, letting them fade away into the night. Silence held, for a minute.

"Thank you," Dagney said. "The tune is known to us, but not those words. Would you write them down for us, Lena? And anything you know about the song?"

"Of course," I said. "Tice said she had learned it from a retired general of the Empire. And I heard it sung at the Emperor's winter camp, but that is all I know. I think it is a southern song, though, because of the line about the grapes."

"You may be right," Dagney said. "You will find paper and ink, and a pen, in the box on the table in your room. If you should run short, just ask for more. And now, I think, it is time for us to retire. Lena, you will hear the breakfast bell in the morning; before that, your time is your own, as is the time now until you choose to sleep." She stood, as did Perras. "Good night to you all," she said.

"Good night," Perras echoed. "Don't stay up too late, children." A smile flickered on Cillian's face as he stood to fetch Perras a candle, a smile that brought again the feeling that I knew him from somewhere. He saw my eyees on him, and the smile vanished. Perras, organizing himself with candle and stick, looked from Cillian to me. "Cillian," he murmured. "Would you light me to my room? I find myself unsteady tonight." He handed the candle back to the younger man, and together they walked slowly to Perras's study door.

Ardan had also risen. "Bed for me too," he announced, "I've an early start. Sleep well, all." Gregor, with a nod to us, accompanied his commanding officer.

No one spoke for a moment, until Sorley broke the silence. "Cillian holds a grudge against the Empire," he said quietly. "It's not personal, Lena."

"I'm glad to know I wasn't imagining it," I said tartly. "Am I allowed to know what that grudge is?"

The students looked at each other. "I suppose so," Sorley answered. "We all know. His mother—she was very young—died after giving birth to him. His father was a soldier of the Empire, but whoever he was, he never returned to see how his lover had fared. Cillian has not forgiven him, and, by extension, the Empire."

"I see," I said.

"Perhaps," Jordis said, "if he had known you were coming, he might have had time to prepare himself."

"I think the *Comiádh* is speaking to him now, about this," Sorley said quietly. He stretched. "I am going to practice the *ladhar*," he said. "Niav, do you want to join me?"

The younger girl shook her head. "I would rather talk to Lena," she replied, and then shot a doubtful look my way. "If that is all right?"

Did I want to talk? Inwardly I sighed. But I had had my time alone, and my journal, and I did not think I had anything more to write tonight. "Of course."

Sorley grinned. "Niav loves stories," he said. "She'll turn them into songs, though, Lena; be warned." He left us, raising a hand in farewell as he did.

"What would you like to know?" I said to the two young women sitting with me.

"Everything," Niav burst out. "What your village is like, and how you learned to fight, and about your travels. And how it feels, to be told you must live in these villages, and not marry."

"That is too much for one night," I said slowly. Is that how she sees us?

"Tell us about your travels," Jordis suggested. "Tell us about Casilla—you have been there?"

"How do you know about Casilla?" The question surprised me, but I welcomed the change of topic.

"It's on the map," Niav said, as if it were obvious. "We learn the geography of your country too, as well as ours, and Varsland." She sounded put out, as if I had under-estimated her. Then again, I thought, I had.

Casilla. How to begin? "When the wall was breached—" I stopped. "When it was opened to your soldiers," I amended, "I was at the Emperor's winter camp, for the Midwinter celebrations and proclamations. As the army prepared to ride north, I was asked to ride as messenger, to the southern villages, to ask women who were willing to ride north too. That task took me some time, and when I was done I stayed for a while at Karst, the grape-growing village of the south."

"Why did you not ride north?" Niav demanded.

"Hush, Niav," Jordis said. "Lena will tell us what she wishes. Do not pry."

"It's all right," I said. "I did not know, yet, if I wanted to fight again. Defending my village was one thing; it was personal, and those threatened were my family and my friends. I was not yet sure I could raise weapons in a larger cause."

I remembered my conversations—arguments, really—with Halle, who had seen no choice but to ride north. Nor had she wanted one: she wished to be a soldier, and could not understand my reluctance. I had not liked her then, and could not tell her how my actions as a cohort-leader, which had led to the death of my friend and cohort-second Tice, had made me doubt myself. I did not want to tell this to Niav and Jordis, tonight.

"So," I said, resuming my tale, "I stayed in Karst for some weeks. My cousin Garth had a son there, and I stayed with the woman raising him—his aunt—

and another friend. The child's grandmother, however, made life difficult for the child and his aunt, and when she decided to go to Casilla, I chose to go with her." I paused.

"Casilla is walled," I continued, "with enormous gates to let in the trader's carts. The gates and the watchtowers are of stone, and they gleam white in the sunshine, and the flag of the Empire flies at each tower, snapping in the wind from the sea. Inside the gates there is a wide road, running down to the harbours: it divides the city in two, into the women's section, and the men's. At one point, there is a wide square where the market is held." I stopped, unsure if I was being clear, trying to marshal my thoughts.

"Harbours?" Jordis said. "More than one?"

"Yes. The fishing harbour, on the women's side, and the quays and anchorage for the ships of the Empire, on the men's side, and between them the traders' quays." Saying this, I remembered the scream of gulls, and the shouts of men and women working on and around the boats, and the salt, pungent smell of the sea and of fish.

"This divided life." Jordis said, "It's hard to imagine. Everything must be duplicated, then? Cookhouses and bakeries, shops and inns?"

I nodded. "Yes. There are two cities, really, and the separation is maintained, except at the market, and during Festival. I had wondered, too, how it might work, but the rules of Partition are held."

"How strange," Jordis murmured. Niav said nothing, but instead sang a stanza, softly:

O we forbid ye, maidens all,
with flowers in your hair,
To go or come by Kertonhall,
for young Fintaill is there.

The tune was haunting. "That's lovely," I said. "Is that from a *danta*?"

"Yes," Niav answered. "It's from a long song, that tells how a maiden won her true love back from the fair folk, angering their queen in doing so. The Lady Dagney says it is very old, and that we share the story with the Marai. I will learn it in their language, soon. But how did you know about the *danta*? "

"Sorley told me," I explained.

"Tell us more about Casilla," Jordis said, a shade impatiently, I thought.

"On the main gates," I said, "there is an inscription, in no language I know. It says *'Casil e imitaran ne'*."

"'Casil this is not'," said a voice behind us. We all turned to see Cillian standing there. He repeated the words I had spoken, but his inflections made them sound very different. "Or," he continued, "'Casil is not equalled here', if you prefer a more elegant translation."

"So, the old woman was right," I said, half under my breath.

"What old woman?" Niav demanded.

"In Casilla," I said slowly, "those words are generally taken to mean 'There is only one Casilla', but an old woman I met there told me they meant exactly what Cillian just said: 'Casil this is not'."

"And they do," Cillian said. He pulled out a chair and sat. "Do you not learn Casilan?" he asked.

"No," Jordis said sharply. "There were no languages taught in Lena's village. We talked about that over tea, before you arrived."

"And it would seem that is true throughout the country, if the inhabitants of Casilla believe the gate inscription to mean 'There is only one Casilla'," Cillian commented. "Casilla, Lena, is a diminutive, meaning 'Little Casil'. Perhaps once it was meant to rival Casil, but the gate inscription indicates that someone realized it did not."

"And where is Casil?" I asked. But as I spoke I realized the answer. "In the Eastern Empire?"

Cillian raised an eyebrow.

"So, you have learned some things," he said. He was, I thought, striving to be polite. I wondered what Perras had said to him. I shook my head.

"Not really," I admitted. "I heard of it only in the last weeks; it was something Donnalch—your *Teannasach*," I added, stumbling again over the unfamiliar word, "and our Emperor spoke of at the White Fort. They gave an oath to 'the Empire Unconquered'. Darel—the other hostage, a cadet—told me it meant the Eastern Empire."

"Is that all he told you?"

"Cillian, is this not what the *Comiádh* will instruct Lena in?" Jordis said quietly.

He looked at her. A small muscle in his jaw twitched. He nodded.

"Jordis is right," he said. "You should discuss this with Perras, not with me."

"No!" I said, too forcefully. "Please, can't we talk about it now? It has been puzzling me."

Cillian sighed. "Tell us what you know, then."

I thought back to what Darel had said. "There was an Empire in the East," I began slowly, "and a Supreme Emperor, to whom the Emperor here owed allegiance. He—the Supreme Emperor—ruled from a city in the East—that would be Casil?" Cillian nodded. "And then one day all trade and communication—all contact—stopped. But the Emperor and the troops still pay homage to the memory." I shook my head. "That's all I remember."

"It's a fair summary," Cillian said. "But Perras will tell you more, and be glad of your interest." He stretched, and ran a hand through his hair.

"Was Linrathe part of that Empire?" I asked, remembering what had puzzled me at the time.

Cillian shook his head. "Not that I was taught," he said. "Ask Perras, Lena; he has the stories. I am no lover of Empires, lost or current." The chill had returned to his voice. He stood. The chair scraped on the flagged floor. "Sleep well, *daltai*. I will see you at breakfast." He stalked away, not to the stairs, but to the door. A breeze, a taste of night air, and he was gone.

CHAPTER FIVE

I SLEPT WELL. I HAD GONE TO BED SHORTLY after Cillian left, pleading fatigue, and had fallen asleep almost immediately. I woke to the chatter of sparrows outside my window, and faint sounds from the house.

Downstairs, I helped Jordis and Sorley bring food from the kitchen to the hall: bowls of thick oat porridge, jugs of milk, dried fruit. Niav took a tray to Perras's rooms, Dagney explaining quietly to me that he was stiff and sore in the mornings, and preferred to eat alone. There was little conversation over the meal, at least until the food was finished and most of us were drinking a second cup of tea.

"Now, *daltai*," Dagney said, using the same plural of 'student' that Cillian had the night before, "most of you know your duties or lessons for the morning. Lena, Perras wishes you to go to him, but he will not be ready for you for another hour, and unlike the others you do not have work to be getting on with. So, Sorley, will you take Niav for her lesson in the first hour, and then I can work with Lena?"

"Of course, my lady." The others excused themselves, heading off to work, practice, or lessons. Cillian had said nothing during the meal, and did not look my way as he left. I waited for Dagney to speak.

"Shall we go to my rooms?" she asked, rising. I followed her from the hall and through the music practice room, into the teaching room. Like Perras's room, this appeared to be her study as well as her teaching space. Many bookcases stood against the walls, but here the shelves held instruments as well as books. Larger instruments hung from pegs. She gestured me to a chair facing her desk.

"We had spoken of you learning at least the basics of our language, and perhaps that of Varsland. Does this seem sensible to you, Lena?

"It does," I agreed, "at least, it does for your language. I am not sure about Varsland's, not at the same time, unless they are very similar?"

"They share some words," she said, smiling, "but, I see your point. You have not learned another language, even a few words, at all?"

I thought back to the weeks guarding the Lestian captives. Had I picked up any words? Not really, I admitted to myself.

"No, my lady." I explained about the Lestians. "I don't think I even thought to try to learn their words. I just let their captain translate."

"So," she said, "it is unlikely you have a predisposition to learning languages. But no matter; it will be more work for you, but far from impossible. You are older than most who learn another language, and that will slow you down. You are in for a challenge." She smiled. "Let us begin, then. We will start, as you did so long ago, with the letters and the alphabet—we do not use different letters than you do, do not worry—but we do pronounce them differently, and use them in different combinations and with different accents, and those are the first things you should learn." From a drawer of her desk she brought out a written sheet and handed it to me.

For perhaps forty-five minutes I learned the alphabet again. I expected to just say the sounds, but Dagney had me think about how my mouth's muscles and my tongue worked to make the sounds, and what happened when I used them differently. "Good," she said finally. "You can practice with Niav: she can correct your pronunciation, and you hers in your language. But there are three words I would like you to learn before we end. Can you guess what they are?"

I thought about what I would want to be able to say. Food? Water? But I could point to those, or make signs.

"Please and thank you?" I hazarded.

"Very good!" Dagney said. "Yes, those two, and one more—'sorry'. Those three allow you to be polite, and good manners smooth many an awkward discourse."

"They do, my lady," I answered, thinking of Casyn, always thoughtful, always polite.

"So," she directed, "repeat these after me, and then try to use them as often as is reasonable. 'Please' is *'allech'i'*."

"*Allech'i,*" I repeated.

"Further back in your throat," Dagney prompted. I tried again, generating a more liquid sound and a nod from Dagney.

'Thank you'—*meas*, and 'sorry'—*forla*—took up another quarter of an hour. Finally, Dagney sat back.

"Enough for today. You have been a good student. Go to the kitchen now, and ask for tea with honey; your throat needs it. Perras will be expecting you, but have your tea, and do whatever else you need to, before going to him."

"Thank you, my lady," I said. She smiled in response, but I could see her mind was already elsewhere, her eyes slipping down to a musical score on her desk. I closed the door quietly behind me and went, as directed, to the kitchen. It was empty but for one woman, who sat at the long table peeling root vegetables.

"Hello," I said. I didn't remember seeing her earlier. "I'm Lena. The Lady Dagney sent me here for tea with honey, for my throat."

"Yes, my lady," she replied, her accent thick. She stood and went to the stove, moving a kettle forward and opening the door to give the coals inside a poke. She reached for a mug, and from a canister added something dried. The kettle sang; she poured hot water into the mug, and a spoonful of honey, before handing it to me.

"*Meas,*" I hoped my accent was passable. She smiled. "*Allech'i,* may I know your name?" I added.

"Isa," she answered. "I am Isa, my lady."

"*Meas,* Isa," I said. "But in my land, I am not addressed as 'my lady'. Just by my name, Lena."

"But you are in our land now, my lady, and I must. It is the custom."

I nodded. "Yes, of course. *Forla.* I should have realized." I should have, too, I thought, hoping I hadn't embarrassed Isa. But when I glanced at her, she had returned to scraping parsnips, unbothered. I took a tentative sip of the tea: rosehip, the traditional winter tea for colds and sore throats. The heat and sweetness felt good on my slightly scratchy throat. I stood awkwardly, not knowing if I should stay or go. Isa looked up.

"Sit, if you would like, my lady," she said. I pulled out a chair and sat, cradling the mug. Isa smiled at me. "Are you here to learn music, like my niece?"

"Your niece?" I asked, puzzled.

"Niav," she answered. "She is my sister's youngest. She came for a visit last year, and the Lady Dagney heard her telling stories and singing to the little ones, and offered her a place here at the *Ti'ach*. We were all pleased, but I lost my helper with the babies." She laughed. "But there are always girls for that! So, are you here to learn the songs and stories?"

"No," I said. "I will learn history while I am here, with the *Comiádh*. But he and the Lady Dagney thought I should learn your language as well, so I will be working with her as well." I took another swallow of the tea, thinking back to what Kebhan had said when he too had called me 'lady'—'a woman of rank.' Did being a pupil at a *Ti'ach*, a *dalta*, confer rank? Or was it my status as hostage, guarded by a man of the *Teannasach's* troops? I thought of asking Isa, but somehow it did not seem appropriate.

"Like Cillian, then," Isa said. I noted the lack of any honorific.

"A better balance," I said lightly. "Two students for the *Comiádh*, three for Lady Dagney." A thought struck me. "Are there usually so few students, Isa?"

"Nae," she answered, shaking her head. "There should be half-a-dozen more, but the war took them; the boys away to fight, were they old enough, or to home to do the work of those who went. The girls also went for home, to be another pair of hands on the farms, or in the workshops. So, we are not what we should be, here at *Ti'ach na Perras*," she finished, her voice sorrowful. "Only the lady Jordis, and Niav and Cillian, and the lord Sorley—and I hear he is soon for home too, and now you, my lady."

Well, I thought, I had my answers, to both questions. I finished my tea and put the mug on the table. "*Meas*, Isa," I said. "I should go to the *Comiádh* now; he is expecting me."

"*Allech'i*, wait a moment, my lady." She got up. "I will make tea for you to take to him. Would you like a bitty more, as well?"

I declined, and in a minute or two left the kitchen carrying a steaming mug for Perras. I knocked at his door.

"Come," he called. I opened the door and went in.

"I have brought you tea, *Comiádh*," I said.

"Ah, Lena, welcome," he said, from his seat at the table. "And thank you for bringing my tea. You have had some?" I nodded, and he took the mug from me and placed it on the desk before him. A banked fire warmed and scented the room.

"I have been transcribing the history," he told me. "Now you are here, I suggest we do this: I will read to you what I have transcribed, and you will follow along in the history, and tell me if I have made an error. And please, ask questions as we go. Do you think we can do that?" He handed me the volume of Colm's history, gesturing to another chair at the table.

"Of course, *Comiádh*," I answered. I sat across from him, and opened the book. He took a long swallow of his tea, and straightened the papers on the table.

"To begin," he said, and began to read.

"'In the third year of the reign of the Emperor Lucian, when there had been silence from the East for many years, consideration was given to the expansion of the Empire's lands, as the villages and towns grew crowded. The Emperor's eyes turned to the northern lands, bleak and mountainous as they were, and he offered free land there to any man who would join him in the conquest.'"

Perras read the words, but it was Colm's voice I heard. Tears pricked my eyes. I did not need to check the text in front of me; I knew these opening words off by heart. I realized Perras was waiting.

I nodded. "That is correct," I said.

"Any questions?" he asked. I shook my head.

"Not now." I wanted to ask about the East, but it seemed too soon.

Perras nodded and continued to read. This time I did drop my eyes to the book I held.

"'Many joined Lucian, for the offer of land was tempting. But they did not find the conquest of the northern lands easy, for the inhabitants knew well the hills and valleys, forests and caves, and used them to their advantage to repel Lucian's army.'"

"Go on," I said. Perras cleared his throat. His voice, I thought, was strong for a man of his age.

"'After several years of skirmishes and small battles, a spring came that was cold and wet throughout the land, and crops and cattle suffered.'"

"Stop." He looked up. "The text says, 'both cold and wet,' I explained, and you read 'cold and wet'." He nodded.

"Thank you." He made the correction before continuing to read.

"'But there were many men to feed in the troops, and Lucian, his thoughts fixed on the northern lands, decreed a higher tax of food from the villages and farms. The headwomen of the villages said 'No' to this tax, almost as one voice, arguing thus: You have taken our strongest men; the rain and cold are unceasing; how are we to feed you? They demanded an Assembly, and the Emperor, bound by the laws of the Empire, had to grant it.'"

"Now I do have a question."

"Yes?" he encouraged.

"What Colm wrote here, that the tax of food from the villages came before the Partition vote—this isn't what I learned, at Tirvan. There, I learned that the army fed itself for some years, before taxing the villages."

"You did not ask Colm about this?" Perras asked.

"No," I answered. "We talked of other things that day. I had meant to," I finished.

"Someone wrote once that those are the saddest words that can be said," Perras said gently. "I too had meant to talk more to Colm." He sighed. "We must shoulder that regret, and go on. I think the answer to your question may be two-fold, Lena. Firstly, in your village—was this history written?"

"No," I said, "not that I know of. It was told to us; we learned all our history that way."

"Tales spoken, even when those who tell them believe them to be true, can often stray from what actually happened. But they often retain much of the truth, and it is possible that there were two sets of taxes; the one before Partition vote, and one, later, that increased the tithe even further, and that over the years the two have become confused, conflated into one event. We may never know," he finished. I could hear what I thought was a trace of frustration in his voice.

"Is there nothing in your books that speaks of this?" I asked.

"No," he said. "Those who wrote our histories were not terribly interested in what was happening in the southern Empire. Although the Partition vote and its results—the laws dividing your lives into women's villages and compulsory army life for boys and men—did warrant mention. It was rather drastic," he added.

"I suppose. It was just normal, for us, until these past two years."

"But it was not normal, at the beginning," he reminded me. "Shall we go on?"

"'For ten days and nights women and men met and debated,'" he read. "'The men supported the Emperor in his quest for more lands, arguing it was needed. The women argued there was land enough; careful husbandry would make it sufficient. Finally, Lucian suggested a parting of the ways: men would fight; women would fish and farm. A vote was taken and by a small margin passed.'"

"Not quite six in ten," I said. Perras looked up, his eyebrows questioning. "That is what the Emperor told me," I explained.

"How did he know this?"

I thought back, to that first meeting, and the unexpected turn the conversation had taken. "He said Colm had found the records. In a storeroom, somewhere."

Perras leaned back in his chair. "I think," he said, "I will include that, as a footnote. I did not know how close the vote was, and it is worth recording." He wrote for a minute.

Should I tell him, I wondered, that Callan had planned a new Assembly, to consider and vote again on the Partition agreement? Nevin or Blaine would have sent word of this north, had they both not died that Midwinter's Day, executed as traitors. And there was my answer. I was not a traitor; I could say nothing. I regretted even making the comment about the vote. But the Emperor had told me to exchange views on Partition and our histories—did that mean I should talk about it? No, I told myself firmly. It's not our history; it's our future. And he told me to trust my instinct, and my instinct tells me to say nothing.

Perras finished his writing and looked up again. I hoped my confusion did not show in my face; to hide it, I glanced down at the book in my hands. "This next paragraph," I said, forestalling any comment from Perras, "I have always wondered about what it says." This was not strictly true: it had been Niav's comment last night, about marriage, that had caused me to wonder.

"Let us check my transcription," he said, "and then please ask what you wish; if I can answer your questions, I will."

"'But the decree from the Emperor after the Partition vote was not to the liking of many men and women, not even some men senior in the army and long trusted by Lucian, even though that disagreement meant their death by the laws of the Empire'," he read. "'All men would serve in the Emperor's armies, whether they wished to or not; all women would fish and farm, or run the inns and workshops. Marriages were ended and families sundered. Twice a year only, war allowing, could the men visit their homes. Many fled the lands governed by Lucian, going east over the Durrains, or taking boats south; some even fled north, to the wild lands and people there.'"

"It is correct?" he asked. I nodded. "And what did you want to ask?"

"Several things," I said, prevaricating. Suddenly I did not feel I could ask what I had originally wished to, about marriage; not yet. "The people who fled east," I said instead, "across the Durrains. Where would they have gone? What lies beyond the mountains?" I turned, to look at the map that hung on the wall behind me. It showed the Durrains, but the land beyond them was blank.

"Ah," Perras said. "It is not on that map, Lena. But if you go to that third shelf," he pointed at the bookshelf to the right of the fireplace, "and get down the blue box, I will show you." I stood to do his bidding. I pulled the blue box from the shelf and placed it on the table. The Comiádh opened it, taking out a rolled paper, tied with faded ribbon. He loosened the bow and spread the paper—the map—out, weighing the edges with the box on one side and his inkwell on the other.

"Come and stand beside me," he said. I did as he asked, peering down at the map. It was old; the paper browned and spotted, the colours faded.

"Here are the Durrains," Perras said, indicating a line of marks on the map. It was oriented in the way I was used to, the mountains running down the map to the sea at the bottom. But to their right, where the map Casyn had drawn for me long months before had ended, more land was shown; land and rivers and towns, occupying most of the sheet. In large letters, extending over most of the lower portion of the map, was the word cadenti.

"What does that mean?" I asked, pointing at the word.

"Conquered," Perras said.

"Conquered?" I said. "By whom? When? What language is that?"

"By the Eastern Empire," he said, "half a thousand years ago, at least. And the language is Casilan, the language of the East, the archaic version of your tongue, to answer your questions in order."

I stared at the map. "I did not realize. I thought we were part of that Empire, yes, but conquered by them? Who were they?"

"The Casilani ruled much of the known world," Perras said. "They were, from all we know, a people of order, literate and learned, who sought to expand beyond their borders, perhaps at first to feed their growing population. From this city, here," he pointed to the far-right edge of the map, where 'Casil' was inscribed in faded gold lettering, "they marched and sailed armies east, and conquered almost all the lands you see here. They brought learning and order with them. They established subordinate Emperors in their colonies—your Emperor Callan is heir to that position—to oversee the army and the food shipments and the taxes. And then, quite suddenly, they disappeared."

This was much as Darel, and then Cillian, had told me. I looked at the map again, noticing this time that the lands to the north of where the Durrains bent eastward were shaded in grey, not the faded green of most of the map. I moved my eyes to the left, where the land I recognized as my own lay: it too was shaded green, but to its north, the map again was grey.

I pointed to that grey. "Is this Linrathe?"

"What is Linrathe now, yes," Perras answered.

"Does the grey mean it was not conquered?"

"It does," he said.

"Why not?" I demanded. "How did these lands hold out, if my own did not?"

"For much the same reasons, I believe, that your Emperor Lucian's armies could not: 'they did not find the conquest of the northern lands easy, for the inhabitants knew the hills and valleys, forests and caves well, and used them to their advantage'. It is a wild land, Lena, and very difficult, and more so as you go north. But they did try; the Sterre, the other wall you noticed yesterday on the wall map: they built it, but could not hold it for more than a dozen years, if that. Their armies retreated south, and left these lands in peace, more or less."

As Lucian had, and now as Callan needed to. Was it just the land that made Linrathe so unconquerable?

"At the White Fort," I said slowly, "the morning of the proclamation of truce—I was there. The Emperor, Callan, and the *Teannasach* debated who should speak first, at the proclamation. Callan claimed precedence, and Donnalch granted it, but I didn't understand his reasons." I struggled to remember. "He said that we came from a common history, and that he and his men did not forget the greater Empire either. What did he mean, if Linrathe was not conquered?"

"Sit, Lena," Perras said, "and I will attempt to explain." I did as he asked. When I was seated, he went on.

"Linrathe—or what would become Linrathe—was not conquered, no," the *Comiádh* answered. "But in the dozen years the Empire of the East's armies occupied this land, the leaders here saw much to admire in the Empire's ways, although they had no wish to be ruled by Casil. They sought—both during and after the occupation, for the Eastern Empire continued its presence in your lands for another two hundred years—to learn from the East, from their writings, from observation and likely from the interchange of ideas, and adopted what seemed good and appropriate for our people. These schools, for example, are part of that tradition. So, yes, the *Teannasach* spoke truly, when he spoke of a common history, although we have moved on from that common history in very different ways."

"I see," I said slowly, my thoughts whirling. My confusion must have shown on my face, for Perras put down his pen.

"I think," Perras said, "that is enough for today. You have much to think about, and the mind does not learn if it is force-fed. There is still over an hour until the mid-day meal. It is your time, of course, but perhaps you might go riding? I used to ride after lessons, especially difficult ones. It helps settle one's thoughts."

My mind cleared at the thought of riding, of action and movement. Clio would be sufficiently rested. I stood.

"*Meas, Comiádh,*" I said. "It is a good idea."

"*Meas,* Lena, for helping me with the transcription," he replied. "Come to see me at the same time tomorrow, and we will continue."

I closed the door quietly behind me. The hall was empty. Upstairs, I changed into my outdoor clothes and boots. From my bedroom window, the sky gleamed grey; not threatening rain, I thought, just a grey day.

After a quick visit to the latrine I began to walk toward the stables and paddock. A moment later, I heard footsteps behind me, and turned to see Gregor following me. Of course, I thought. I won't be alone; he has to go with me.

"The *Comiádh* told me to go for a ride," I said, "as a break from my lessons. Since you must come with me, do you know this area well enough to lead me somewhere to gallop? I am in the mood for a run."

"I can do that, my lady," he answered. I didn't bother to correct him. We walked in silence to the stables. The horses grazed in the paddock, but as always Clio came to me when I called her. I scratched her head, wishing I'd brought her a piece of bread, and led her out of the field and to the tack room.

Gregor followed with his solid bay, and tacked the gelding up with the economical, practiced moves of a cavalry soldier. He mounted, not waiting, I was glad to see, to offer me a leg up. I swung onto Clio's back and followed Gregor away from the stable.

The path ran down along the edge of the stream, its surface pocked by the hooves of sheep. The stream itself gurgled and splashed along a bed of dark rock, running fast with the early spring rains and the melting snows of winter. A small brown bird with a brilliant white throat hunted in the moving water, walking into the stream and diving below the surface.

"What bird is that?" I called to Gregor. He reined up and looked where I was pointing.

"A *snámh'a,*" he said. "I don't know its name in your language." He shrugged. "It swims? That's what its name means."

"Swimmer?" I hazarded. "Swimming bird?"

He nodded. "Something like that."

"*Meas,* Gregor," I said, and was rewarded by a moment of surprise on his face. Mentally I chastised myself for forgetting to use 'please' before my question. Next time, I told myself.

Ahead I could see a stone bridge spanning the stream; beyond it, the track led into a wide valley, with the stream at its right edge. We clopped over the bridge; at its far side, Gregor glanced back at me. "We can gallop here," he said. "Do you want to set the pace?"

"No," I said after a moment's consideration. "You know the land better. We'll follow." He nodded, and urged his bay into trot, and then quickly into a gallop. Clio tossed her head, and galloped after them.

When was the last time I had galloped for pure pleasure? Somewhere in the grasslands, riding south with Garth, I thought. It felt like a lifetime ago. I leaned a bit further forward, and gave myself up to the sensation of speed and power.

It took us about ten minutes to reach the far end of the valley, and sweat lathered along both horses' reins when we pulled up. The valley had narrowed toward the end, the land rising more steeply on the left side. Gregor pointed up the hill. "If we go up there," he suggested, "there's a good long view. It might interest you."

"Let's," I said, and Gregor turned his horse's head to the hill. We followed a track that zigzagged back and forth across the slope to reach the top, an easy climb. The hilltop was flat. Sheep grazed, scattered across the plateau, and a strong wind blew from the west.

I gazed northward. I could see a line of hills a long distance away; snow lay on their peaks; the highest were shrouded in cloud. I thought I saw a glint of water before them. Gregor spoke.

"I was born in those hills. That's home, or was. My *Athàir*—my da— has sheep, like most there, and my *Mathàir* and the women weave the wool."

"Some women in my village were weavers, too," I said. "They made blankets, and sails, and material for clothes. Is that what the women in your family made?"

"Not sails," he said. "But the other, yes."

"Do you miss them?" I asked impulsively. He did not answer immediately. "*Forla*, Gregor," I said. "I should not have presumed to ask that."

"It's fine, my lady," he said, and the tone of his voice told me he was not just being polite. "I was just collecting my thoughts. Do I miss them? Yes, I suppose I do; although there is no real place there for me. My brother helps my da with the sheep, and there is not a living there for all of us. So, a soldier I became, when the *Teannasach* asked for men."

I looked up at him, sitting easily on his horse beside me. He was looking north, the wind blowing strands of his dark hair across his face. Why was he a soldier, and not Cillian? They were the same age, more or less. 'I am no lover of Empires,' Cillian had said. Surely someone who felt like that would have joined a fight against my Empire? But was that what the invasion was about? I realized I didn't know. I had never questioned, never asked.

"*Allech'i*, Gregor," I said. "What does the *Teannasach* want with the Empire's lands? Why did he breach the Wall?"

He looked down at me. "Don't you know?" he said, the surprise evident in his voice.

"No," I said, "I don't. I thought it was to support a faction of our soldiers who wanted to overthrow the Emperor, but it can't just be that. There must be something more for the *Teannasach*, and your people. Is it for land?"

"No," he replied. "Not for land, or for any prizes. We invaded to give you back what your Emperors have taken from you. You live in tyranny, my lady, whether you realize it or not: men and women are meant to live together, to marry and raise families, to work together. And you cannot. There are many here in Linrathe whose ancestors, mine included, escaped your lands to freedom here, and for many generations they have been asking our leaders to free the southern lands. This *Teannasach* has listened, and acted. So, it is all for you, my lady Lena, and not for us at all."

CHAPTER SIX

I STARED UP AT GREGOR, SPEECHLESS. All for us? But why did they think we wanted this? I thought of Nevin and Blaine: was this what they had wanted? Was this why Nevin's son had opened the gates to Linrathe's soldiers? Did the Emperor know? How could he not, after all the long talks with Donnalch? Too many questions. I had wanted to gallop, to clear my head, but now it pounded with confusion and doubts.

Gregor had turned his horse around, facing back the way we came, to scan the horizon, his soldier's training making these actions automatic. I opened my mouth to ask to return to the *Ti'ach*, to talk to Perras, or Dagney. I had just started to speak when he held up a hand to stop me.

"Look," he said, pointing south. "Horses and riders, moving fast." I looked outward, to where he pointed; two horses on the hilltop above the *Ti'ach*. "That's the *Teannasach*: I recognize his horse. And Ardan with him, I've no doubt. We must go back, my lady; I might be needed."

The horses picked their way back down the hill. As soon as we reached level ground, the walk became a gallop, back across the valley and over the bridge, slowing only as we reached the narrow, muddy, uneven path beside the stream. At the stable, we both had our horses unsaddled and turned out in minutes. The day was cool and we had walked the last distance, so they would come to no harm. I strode with Gregor up the path to the house; we reached the courtyard just as Donnalch and Ardan clattered in.

Gregor said something I did not understand, although I thought I caught the word '*Teannasach*'. The two men dismounted; Gregor took the reins of Donnalch's horse, and again said something, this time to Ardan, who laughed.

"No hurry at all, except that we were hungry," he answered, glancing at me, "and wanted to get here in time for the noon meal. If there is one. Have you eaten today since breakfast, Lena?"

"No," I said. "And there is a noon meal planned."

"Good," Donnalch said, "for a piece of bread at dawn has not much staying power." He grinned, turning toward the hall door. As he reached the first step, the door opened. For a moment, against the dark of the room behind, I could not see who stood there.

"Welcome, *Teannasach*," Cillian said. "Food is nearly ready, please come in." A very formal greeting, I thought. I glanced back at Gregor, wondering if I should help with the horses. He shook his head and began to lead the two horses away. I followed Donnalch and Ardan into the hall.

As when I had arrived—only two days before, I realized—everyone came out to greet the guests. Donnalch had a word for everyone, even Niav, who blushed and giggled when he spoke to her. Dagney sent her out to the kitchen, and I went with her.

"Two more mouths," Isa said from the stove. "Well, there's plenty bread.

Niav, cut a bitty more, will you not?" Niav did as she was asked, slicing a loaf with practiced skill. She piled it into a wooden bowl.

"What can I do?" I asked.

"Take the bread out to the hall," Niav answered. "One bowl at each end of the table."

Out in the hall the elders and Donnalch had gathered at one end of the room. Neither Ardan nor Cillian were to be seen. I placed the bread as Niav had directed. Jordis and Sorley were setting the table, bringing spoons and mats from the sideboard where the glass drinking vessels were kept.

We moved back and forth from the kitchen, bringing a round of cheese and bowls of soup. My stomach rumbled. Jordis went to stand beside Dagney. "My lady?" I heard her say. "The food is ready."

She nodded, and spoke quietly to Perras and Donnalch. They broke off talking to come to the table, Donnalch pulling out Perras's chair and making him comfortable before seating himself beside Perras. He looked around. "Where is Ardan?"

"I sent him and Cillian for ale," Perras said. "I thought you would like a draught. Ah, here they are," he added, as the outside door opened. But it was Gregor who entered.

"Did you see Ardan, and Cillian?" Perras asked.

"No, *Comiádh*, I did not," Gregor answered, coming further into the room. "Shall I go to look for them?"

"No, sit," Donnalch said. "Ardan had something to say to Cillian; they will come when ready."

"Then let us begin," Dagney said. "Cold soup is not to anyone's liking. Sorley, will you take those two bowls back to Isa, and ask her to keep them warm on the stove?"

The soup, creamy on my tongue, tasted of the parsnips Isa had been peeling earlier, and of a pungent spice I could not name. As I ate, I watched the people around the table, curious as to how they treated their leader. Donnalch, I saw, ate with hunger, seemed happy with the simple food, and spoke to everyone in the same open, unassuming manner. Niav, who appeared awestruck at sitting at a table with her *Teannasach*, watched him closely, and without being asked, slipped into the kitchen at one point to return with more bread. As she put it on the table beside Donnalch, the outside door opened again. I looked up. Ardan and Cillian came in, carrying two earthenware jugs. Cillian looked pale, I thought, and distracted.

"There you are," Perras said. "Mugs are on the sideboard; who would like ale, in honour of the *Teannasach*'s visit?"

Mugs and ale were distributed, but I took only a small amount. The soup for the two men was brought from the kitchen, and we continued eating. I tried the ale. It tasted much like any other ale, I thought; I preferred wine, but had learned to drink what was offered in the last two years. I glanced over at Cillian. He seemed to be eating little, but had drained his ale and was pouring more.

"*Teannasach*, forgive me if I overstep—" Perras began.

"You cannot," Donnalch said. "But I can guess what you want to ask: why am I here, and not negotiating with the Southern Emperor, am I right?"

"You are." Perras nodded, a slight smile on his lips.

"It came to my mind that I needed to visit the *Ti'acha*, and the *torps*, to see what our people thought of the truce, and to hear what they wanted from a permanent peace, if we can reach that goal. Callan of the South accepted this; in truth, I believe he wanted much the same, time to consult his advisors and the villages. So here I am. Shall we go hawking this afternoon?"

"Do you not want to discuss the treaty?"

"I would like to speak with you, Perras, but I am also ready for some fun. We can talk in the dark of evening, and into the night."

Perras raised an eyebrow. "As you wish, *Teannasach*," he said. "The fawkner has kept the birds ready; your falcon was flown last a few days ago, I believe. Will you take the young people, if they wish?"

"Oh, yes, please," Niav breathed. Donnalch laughed. I wondered if she wanted just to be near him, and if he knew that.

"How could I say no?" he teased. "Yes, of course. Who would like to go?"

"I will," Sorley said. He, I thought, was at ease with the *Teannasach*, but I supposed he had met and spoken with him before. Cillian shook his head, but said nothing. A direct question from the *Teannasach*, and he didn't bother to speak? But Donnalch showed no sign of offense.

"And you, Lena?" he asked. I hesitated. I really wanted to stay, to ask Perras about what Gregor had said. I was troubled, too, by what the *Teannasach* had said about Callan: time to consult his advisors and the villages. Would he announce a new assembly, like he had planned...and I not there to be part of it? But I cannot refuse Donnalch, I thought; I am not Cillian, long part of the *Ti'ach* and known to the *Teannasach*.

"Yes," I said. "If I may. But I don't know anything about hawking."

"You don't need to. Just come and watch."

We all went, except Cillian, who had remained silent and withdrawn throughout the meal. Ardan and Gregor accompanied us—Ardan to guard the *Teannasach*, and Gregor to guard me, I thought—and the fawkner, a sturdy, sandy-haired man in his forties called Tómas. I followed the others to a long, low building on the west side of the courtyard; Jordis had pointed it out to me yesterday, calling it the mews. Where the hawks are kept, she'd said.

Ardan led Donnalch's horse out, and Sorley followed with his own and a sturdy pony, saddled but also laden with saddlebags and rope. He handed the pony's reins to Gregor. The *Teannasach* and Sorley mounted, then swung their right legs up over the pommels of their saddles, to allow Tómas to fix a wooden support—a straight piece of wood crowned with in a curved piece set at right angles to the base—to the saddle on the right side. I frowned. What was that for? I watched Donnalch gather his reins in his left and, and lay his right arm in the curve of the wood. Tómas came out from the mews with a falcon, hooded, and with leather straps dangling from its legs, handing it up to ride on the

Teannasach's gloved fist. It moved from Tómas's wrist to Donnalch's easily, sitting calmly and quietly.

"Even the weight of a falcon can prove tiring, over an afternoon, with the arm always held up," Gregor said in my ear. "The *tuki* takes the strain and gives the bird a smoother ride. A calm bird will hunt better."

I glanced over at him and smiled my thanks. I didn't know if I should speak; he had not whispered, but his voice had been pitched low. "What are the leather straps?" I murmured.

"They're called jesses," he replied, keeping his voice quiet, but not whispering. "They stop the bird from flying from the hand until its handler wants to release it."

Sorley's bird—smaller, I noted, than Donnalch's, although I thought it the same kind—was handed up. He spoke to it soothingly. It had not, I noticed, transferred quite as well as Donnalch's, shifting its weight back and forth on Sorley's wrist. Sorley stroked its back with one finger, and the bird settled.

"We will wait for you by the stream," the *Teannasach* said. Tómas emerged from the mews with a third, much smaller bird, and swung up into the saddle of the pony. He had no *tuki*, but moved the bird to ride on the saddle's pommel in front of him. They rode off at a walk.

Gregor motioned us forward, and we walked down the path to the stables to saddle our mounts. I wondered how Clio would react to the falcons. Are the Han horses trained to falconry? I wondered. Do officers of the Empire fly hawks?

As if he had heard my thoughts, Gregor came over to me as I tacked up Clio. "Has she experience of falcons?" he asked.

"I don't know," I admitted.

"Then stay at the back, away from the *Teannasach* and the Lord Sorley," he said. "A frightened horse could scare the birds, and we don't want to lose one." It made sense. I nodded my agreement, and swung up into the saddle.

We rode down the track Gregor and I had followed earlier in the day, and across the same field. Where the land rose, Donnalch turned his horse up the hill, and again we climbed to the flat, windy plateau from where we had seen the *Teannasach's* arrival this morning. There we halted. I guided Clio away from Donnalch and Sorley, to the back of the group, and caught Gregor's eye. He rode over to me.

"Should I dismount, and hold her?" I asked him in a whisper.

He considered. "Not a bad idea," he said. He glanced over at Donnalch, who was conferring with Tómas and Sorley. "Do it," he said.

I swung down from the saddle to stand at Clio's head, stroking her neck. She blew at me, then dropped her head to nose at the thin grass. I held her reins, watching the men.

Donnalch removed the hood from his falcon and raised his arm. The bird launched itself in one powerful push and flew, not high but directly away from us, across the ground. Clio raised her head and sidestepped, rolling her eye slightly. Automatically I calmed her, my eyes never leaving the falcon. The initial rapid wingbeats gave way to a flat-winged soar, the leather jesses trailing. Suddenly the bird twisted and flew upward, rapidly gaining height, and then folded its wings and arrowed down. I held my breath. Surely it would crash into the ground? At the last moment, I saw its wings and legs extend. Fur exploded into the air.

"A hare," Donnalch said. Tómas nodded, and went to the bird. I saw him offer it a piece of meat, then slip a hood back over its head. He raised it to his arm, picked up the hare with the other hand, and returned to the group, handing the bird back to Donnalch.

Gregor too had dismounted and now led his horse over to me. "A good start," he said.

"I thought it would hit the ground. It came down so fast," I answered. Niav and Jordis were talking in normal voices to Donnalch and Sorley, so I didn't bother to whisper.

"You've not seen a *fuádain* hunt before?"

"No," I said. "There are seabirds that dive like that, straight down, but they are going into water. Does it ever miss and crash?"

"She," he said. "That's a female bird; you can tell by its size and colouring. The smaller falcon the lord Sorley flies is the tercel, the male. And yes, they do miss sometimes, especially when they're learning to hunt. Sometimes one is badly injured and dies. But not often."

Sorley unhooded his bird and I watched again as it flew, rose, dived, taking another hare. Clio did not react this time to the flying bird. A weak sun had broken through the clouds, and the wind had lessened. The *fuádain* took two more hares.

"Shall we move?" Donnalch asked. "I've a mind to try for *cailzie*, and for that we need to be closer to the forest. The cock birds will be thinking of the hens, now, and perhaps out from the trees."

"Aye," Tómas answered. "And perhaps the lassies can fly the *merliún* there, for *colúir*."

I remounted, and we rode east toward a band of dark forest. The land rose as we approached, and at one end of the trees a scarp of clay and rock rose like a wall. Crumbled soil and boulders lay at its foot. I could hear the coo of pigeons from the trees.

We stopped some distance from the trees. Donnalch unhooded his bird and it flew, quartering the ground between the forest and us. The pigeons fell silent. The bird circled, went higher, and then plunged at something I could not see against the dark of the trees.

I lost it for a moment, and then she flew up again, close to the evergreens. A pigeon broke from the shelter of the branches and the falcon was on it, pursuing it towards the wall of rock and clay. She rose, stooped, and falcon and pigeon together hit the side of the escarpment, tumbling down to a tiny ledge.

I heard Donnalch swear quietly. Tómas walked rapidly towards the scarp, swinging something that looked like feathers, wings, fastened to the end of a leather strap. He whistled at the falcon, swinging the lure. She looked up;

clearly unhurt, she had begun to pluck the pigeon. Tómas whistled again and held up his arm. She rose on her legs and raised her wings, pushed off—and spun helplessly, twisting on a snagged jess.

Donnalch swore louder. Tómas dropped the lure and ran to the base of the scarp, looking up. "Caught on a root," he said. "Up to the top, and lower me down on the rope."

"That scarp's not safe," Donnalch said. "And the rains will have made it softer."

"Aye," Tómas said. "But you and the other men, and the horses if need be, can take my weight. You nae wish to lose the bird, *Teannasach*?"

"I'm thinking we'd have to be well back from the edge," Donnalch replied. "Do we have enough rope?"

The falcon gave a wild flutter, trying to free herself. Niav and Jordis turned away from the sight of the struggling bird. As the men debated I studied the scarp, my eyes searching the surface. "There's another way," I said. Donnalch turned to me.

"What do you mean, lassie?" he asked.

"I can climb up to her," I said. I pointed. "There's enough of a slope, and hand and foot holds, to reach where she is." Donnalch studied the cliff face.

"Aye," he said after a minute. "I see what you mean. But, Lena, it's a soft clay, and the face will crumble if it's climbed. Better to see if we have enough rope, and send back for more if it's needed. Tómas has rescued birds from worse places than this, over the years."

A shower of clay and pebbles fell. The falcon battered the cliff face with her wings. Tómas made a worried sound.

"She's not hanging calm," he said. "She's bound to break a leg, if she keeps that up." At his words, the falcon beat her wings again, and this time a feather fell with the clay. Donnalch frowned.

"You said you could climb up to her?" he demanded.

"Yes," I answered. "I am trained, and experienced, in rock climbing. There are cliffs at Tirvan, and we had to climb them, in the dark, when Leste invaded."

"If we rope you, can you climb down?" I heard Tómas make a sound of protest. "Lena is lighter than you by a third, at least," Donnalch said. "With the cliff so soft, it will be safer. If you are certain, Lena?"

"I am," I said, "except that I have never handled a hawk."

"Sorley, give me your bird," Donnalch ordered. Sorley passed his hooded tercel over. Tómas, who had gone to his pony, dug in the saddlebags to hand up a pair of heavy leather gloves. "Put those on," Donnalch said. I complied.

"You'll need to hood her," he explained. He slid the leather hood off Sorley's bird and then back on. "Like this. Get your arm where her feet can grasp it; she'll hold on, and right herself as soon as she can. Then hood her. She's upset, so she'll likely go for your hands, or try to, so keep the gloves on. She'll go quiet once the hood is on, and we can pull you up."

He had me unhood and hood Sorley's bird several times. I was clumsy, and tentative, but after a few tries he deemed it good enough. He looked up at the cliff face, where his falcon was still fighting her jesses. I realized the men had already ridden to the top of the cliff, and the girls had withdrawn to somewhere I could not see. Perhaps they had ridden back for more rope, just in case.

I wondered, as I rode to the top of the cliff, if I truly could do this, and why I had offered. The rocks of Tirvan's waterfall had been stabilised and ropes added in the weeks before the Lestian invasion, in preparation for climbing; as well, I had climbed it so many times I knew each rock and crevice. This crumbling cliff face was something very different, and so was the situation. I had climbed the waterfall to defend my village. I was risking my life here for a bird. Maybe there won't be enough rope, I thought.

But there was enough rope, Donnalch judged, to lower me. Tómas tied the rope around my waist and shoulders, knotting it in front. Then he knotted the other end around his waist. "You're sure?" he said, quietly, so only I could hear. I nodded. I knew my actions were foolhardy. I knew I was trying to prove something to these men. He held my eyes for a long moment. I wondered if he could see my doubts. Then he too nodded. I walked to the cliff, turned my back to the drop, and when I felt the rope tighten, stepped off.

The rope taut under my hands, I scrabbled for footing on the cliff-face. The unstable clay shifted and crumbled. I had no grip. I pushed off, swung. Pebbles and clods of earth dropped from above, where the rope bit into the cliff edge. I looked up, and then down at the struggling bird, and swallowed my terror. "There's no footing at all," I called. "You'll have to take all my weight."

Foot by foot the men lowered me. More soil and rock fell from above. I swung, pushed, dropped slowly. The bird grew closer.

Suddenly a large chunk of soil fell, barely missing me and trailed by a shower of pebbles. I heard someone shout from above. "Hold on, Lena," Donnalch called. "We need to get something under this rope." I hung, waiting. Looking down, I could see the small ledge and the broken root that the falcon hung from. She had gone quiet. I spoke to her, soothing noises, hoping she was not injured.

"Lena!" Donnalch called.

"Yes?" I shouted. The bird fluttered.

"We must pull you up a bit; we're putting a saddle under the rope, to stop it cutting the cliff edge. If you can brace yourself at all, when we tell you, it will help."

"I'll try," I called. The rope tightened even more, and I was pulled up. I tried to keep my feet against the cliff-face.

"Now!" Donnalch called. I braced my feet against the wall, seeing a large rock protruding at eye height. I leaned in and grabbed for it, catching it under my gloved fingers. It didn't move. I hung on, waiting, breathing hard.

"Good!" Donnalch called. "Down again now." I let go of the rock, and let myself be lowered. No more soil fell from above me. I slid down the cliff face, and my foot found the ledge.

"Stop!" I shouted. I manoeuvred over and got both feet on the ledge. It held. Slowly, slowly, I moved to turn my body on the ledge, shifting my feet and my weight in tiny movements. When I stood with back and hands flat against the cliff, I called up. "Give me just a little slack."

The rope loosened. I slid down to a crouch, my hand reaching out to the root. I extended one leg, and then the other, until I sat on the ledge. I pushed the dead pigeon off the edge to give myself more space. The falcon dangled beside my right leg. Murmuring to her, I grasped the root with my left hand, leaning until her talons could reach my leather-clad right arm.

She grasped my arm immediately, the strength of her claws and feet evident through the leather. She scrabbled around, righting herself on my arm. I straightened as much as I could. The men had the rope just slightly slack. I needed now to let go of the root, and hood the falcon.

I leaned as far back as possible and took my hand off the root, reaching slowly for the hood in my shirt pocket. I couldn't straighten entirely; the jesses were not long enough to allow it. I found the hood, turned it in my fingers, brought my hand to the falcon's head, watching her cold yellow-ringed eyes. She moved on my arm. I held my breath.

But she did not flinch from me. I slipped the hood over her head. She stopped moving. I held my arm up and leaned forward again, finding my balance, my left hand exploring the leather jesses tangled on the root. A slit in the leather had snagged on a small, upright rootlet. I slid the jess up and over.

I sat on the ledge, breathing heavily, thinking. I could not stand again from this position; the men would have to pull me up from where I was. I would need to get my left hand behind me, to avoid scraping against the cliff face, and then turn in the air. Or should I? What would be safer for the falcon?

"Is she free?" Tómas voice, from below me. I looked down. He stood at the base of the cliff. He must have run down once I was on the ledge, I thought.

"Yes," I called. The falcon did not move.

"Unhood her," he called. "I'll whistle her down to me."

It would be better to be pulled up the cliff-face without the bird, I realized. I reached over and plucked the hood from the falcon's head. She looked around, her curved and pointed beak too close to my face for my liking.

A sharp, cutting whistle came from below. The *fuádain* swivelled her head, and at a repeated whistle raised herself to launch into the air, gliding down to where Tómas stood, swinging the lure. I watched as she dropped gracefully onto his out-stretched arm.

I took a breath. Sounds from above told me the *Teannasach* and the others had seen the falcon return to Tómas. A pebble fell; I looked up. A face looked down. Sorley. He must be stretched out on the cliff top, I thought.

"Magnificent, Lena!" he called. "Are you ready to be raised up?"

"Yes," I answered. "I can't stand, though; you'll have to pull me from here."

His face withdrew. In a moment, I felt the rope tauten, and I grasped the knot with one hand. I extended my other arm and, once I felt my body leave the ledge, pushed off from the cliff, trying to position myself so I could use my legs to keep from scraping along the scarp. I swung, turning from side to side for a minute, but being pulled upward at the same time. The weight of my body took me hard into the cliff-face. I cried out in surprise and pain as my extended wrist took the brunt of the impact. The upward motion stopped. "Are you all right?" Donnalch called.

I tried to flex my wrist. Sharp pain ran up my arm. "I've hurt my arm," I called. "I hit the cliff-face too hard. Let me see if I can get my feet against the wall, before you pull again."

I swung my body, cursing myself. Whatever I had set out to prove, I was now injured. Nothing but a fragile woman. Cradling my throbbing arm to my body, I manoeuvred around until my feet were firmly against the face of the cliff. "Now," I shouted.

Slowly but steadily they pulled me up. My feet slipped twice, jarring my arm and bringing tears to my eyes, and more pebbles and soil from above. But then I was at the cliff-edge. Hands reached down for me, held me under my armpits, dragged me over the edge. My wrist throbbed. I lay on the grass, panting, tears streaming down my face, too drained to worry about looking weak.

"Come, Lena," Donnalch said gently. "We need to get away from the edge." He extended a hand down, and I let him help me to my knees, and then my feet. The other men stood some distance off. I walked beside him, the rope dragging, to where they stood, brushing away the tears with my gloved right hand. The women, I saw now, sat on their horses in a little group behind the men.

Sorley stepped forward to undo the knots of the rope harness, freeing me. I winced as he pulled the loop down over my left arm. Pain radiated up from the wrist to the shoulder. Donnalch saw my grimace. He took my left arm in his hands and pulled off the heavy glove. Then he probed. I bit my lip.

"Turn it," he ordered. I moved the wrist, gasping involuntarily. He felt along the bones.

"Not broken," he said, "but a bad sprain. It will need rest and binding. Bravely done, Lena. *Meas*, for rescuing my falcon, although those words are inadequate."

"Aye," Gregor said. "I doubt any of our girls could have done what you did today."

Something broke in me. "And you think we need freeing?" I cried. "That we live in tyranny, and have no choices about how we live our lives?" I felt the tears on my cheeks, and heard the rage in my voice, but fear and pain and anger overwhelmed reason. "I can climb a cliff and rescue your falcon; I can advise Emperors and speak in council meetings; I can sail a boat and kill men with a knife. Your women can do none of these. And you think the women of the Empire need freeing because we cannot marry? How dare you, *Teannasach*, Donnalch of the North? How dare you presume to know what we want?"

CHAPTER SEVEN

I CHOKED BACK A SOB, willing myself not to break down completely. I stared at Donnalch. He regarded me thoughtfully. Then he turned to look at the rest of the men. I saw Gregor flush.

"*Forla, Teannasach,*" I heard.

"*Deir'anaí,*" Donnalch answered, his voice firm. Gregor nodded. Donnalch turned back to me. I wiped my face with the back of my hand, and swallowed.

"Well, *Teannasach?*" I said.

"Did you speak to the Emperor Callan in this way?" he asked, his voice amused. I blinked in surprise.

"Yes," I replied. I almost smiled. "Once," I amended. "Only once, in anger, *Teannasach.*"

"And what did he say?"

"He said, 'Those who advise emperors should be able to challenge them as well'," I answered. I had my anger under control now, although I could feel the aftermath of emotion in the slight trembling of my body. I hoped it was not visible to Donnalch.

"Aye," he said thoughtfully. "That sounds like Callan. Well, lassie, I did not think of you advising me—although I am no Emperor—but perhaps I should have. Now, Ardan, give Lena a sip or two of the *fuisce* you carry, and then we had best go back; Lena needs tea and honey, and the falcon needs her mews."

Ardan appeared beside me with a leather flask. I took a sip of the spirits; smoky and rich on my tongue, the *fuisce* warmed me at once. After a second sip, I felt stronger, the trembling subsiding. I handed the flask back to Ardan. Gregor led Clio forward, and I mounted, holding my left forearm against my body. It was awkward.

"Gregor," I said quietly as I put my foot in the stirrup. "Are you in trouble now, because you told me why Linrathe was invading?"

"Aye," he replied. "And I should be."

I grasped the pommel of the saddle with my right hand, and hauled myself up, half prone across the saddle. Clio moved slightly, flicking her ears. Gregor soothed her.

"What will happen?"

He made a small movement of his head. "Whatever the *Teannasach* decides."

I swung my leg over and sat up in the saddle. My wrist throbbed. I looked down at him. "*Forla,*" I said quietly. "I truly did not mean for this to happen."

We rode back to the hall at a walk, Gregor staying close beside me. Donnalch spoke quietly to Ardan, and the others rode in silence. By the time we reached the courtyard I was trembling again.

Donnalch swung off his horse and bounded up the steps, shouting orders.

Gregor helped me dismount. "Go in," he said. "I'll see to your horse."

Dagney came out from the hall. "Lena," she ordered, "go straight to the *Comiádh*'s chambers; they are the warmest in the house. Isa will bring tea, and I have liniments for your wrist. *Allech'i*, Jordis, go with her."

Perras's door stood ajar. The fire blazed in the hearth, and I sank into the chair offered me. Jordis found a blanket to tuck around my legs. The tea arrived, Isa clucking her concern. I took the cup gratefully. I sipped. Hot and sweet, with just a thread of a bitter aftertaste: Isa—or someone—had added willow-bark for the pain. My mother would have done the same. I held the cup, drinking the tea slowly.

Dagney arrived with a basket, and sat in front of me. I held out my arm, and gently she pushed back my sleeve and touched my wrist. I winced, shook my head at her murmured apology. "It is a sprain, as the *Teannasach* thought," she said. She dug in the basket, bringing out a pot of liniment. She spread it over the wrist, rubbing it in with circular motions. It smelled astringent. "Heather and witch-hazel," she explained, "and an herb called *mot'ulva*, that we get from the Marai. It will help." Then she bound the wrist tightly with a linen bandage, and finally fashioned a sling for my arm from more linen. "You'll need to keep it bound and in the sling for a week," she announced. "We will salve it three times a day."

She poured me another cup of tea. "What were you thinking, Lena?" she asked gently as she passed me the tea.

"That the falcon needed rescuing, and I was the best person to do so," I said bluntly. As much as I liked Dagney, or thought I did, I was in no mood for lectures on what was right—or wrong—for me to do. Dagney must have heard as much in my voice, for she gave me an assessing look, saying nothing for a moment.

"It was brave," she said, after a pause. "I am sorry for your injury, though."

I shrugged. "I've had as bad, or worse, from fishing, over the years." I was being rude, as truculent as a child. "Thank you, my lady, for your ministrations," I said, trying to make my voice less brusque. "*Meas*," I added, remembering. "My mother would be interested in this salve; the herb you mentioned—*mot'ulva*?—is not one we know, as far as I can remember, or at least, not by that name."

"It is also called *arnek*," Dagney said, "but the herb grows only in the northlands and the highlands, so perhaps she would not have access to it. I can send some home with you, when it is time for you to go. But I did not know you were interested in herbs and healing, Lena."

"I'm not, not really, but I have helped my mother in the herb harvest and still-room as a little girl, and some of it I remember."

"A bit of healing lore is always useful," she said. She stood, gathering linen and scissors back into her basket. The pot of salve she left on the table. "*Allech'i*, Jordis, will you dress Lena's arm again this evening, and three times tomorrow?" she asked. "You saw what I did? Then I will look at it again, in two days."

"Yes, my lady," Jordis said. "I can do that."

A knock at the door, and then it opened a crack. "Can I come in?" Donnalch's voice.

"Yes, *Teannasach*," Dagney answered. "We are done; Lena is resting."

He came into the room, bringing the scent of the outdoors with him. "The *fuádain* does well enough," he said. "A few days of rest, and she will be fine, although right now she favours the leg she hung from. Tomas will tend to her. As the Lady Dagney has done for you, Lena, I see. You also are well enough?"

"*Meas, Teannasach,* I am," I replied. "As you said, it is a sprain and I will heal much as your falcon will."

"Salve and willow-bark, and binding and rest is what Lena needs," Dagney said. I though I heard a warning in her voice. Donnalch was looking at me, though, and I shook my head slightly. A smile twitched at the edge of his mouth.

"I'm thinking she's a bit tougher than you give her credit for," he said. "I'll not be long, Lady, but I want a few minutes with our hostage." Gently said, but it was the *Teannasach* that spoke, reminding both Dagney and myself of my status.

"As you will," Dagney said formally. "Come, Jordis."

"Warm in here." Donnalch pulled his outer tunic off. As he spoke, I realized I too was hot, and pushed the blanket away from my legs, letting it drop to the ground.

"I would offer you tea," I said, "but it has willow-bark in it, and there is not a second mug."

"No matter." He sat in the other chair.

"I am glad the falcon is not seriously hurt," I said. "Does she have a name?"

"Grasi, I call her."

"And it is fine for Grasi to hunt, and kill, even though she is female?"

"It is her nature; she was born to hunt and kill," he said evenly. "But she was also born to mate, and raise her chicks with her tercel. As she will, in another season. I would not deny her that right; it would be cruelty, to go against her nature so completely."

"And if her tercel is gone, will she raise those chicks alone?"

"Aye, of course," he said. "Although only because she must. And almost certainly less successfully."

"Because they are solitary birds," I said, "and no other female will help her raise that brood. But think of foxes, *Teannasach*, where the young from a previous year help feed the new litter, so even if the dog fox is gone the young are raised successfully. What is the nature of one animal is not that of another. And we are neither falcons nor foxes, bound to the roles nature gives us, but thinking, reasoning humans. Why should we not choose how we live?"

Donnalch shook his head. "I see I did right in sending you here," he said. "You argue as if you had been taught by Perras for many years. Where did you learn this, Lena?"

"From the women of Tirvan. Do you think we do not argue, in council and out of it?" And from Casyn and Colm, I thought, but I was not about to admit that, not at this moment. "And you are changing the subject, *Teannasach*," I added.

"Aye, I am," he said easily. "Because you are hurt and tired, whether you choose to admit to such or not. I am truly interested in your thoughts, but I would like them to be considered and calm, and I doubt you can stay so, right now." I started to protest, but he stopped me with a raised hand. "I have two things to say, or, more exactly, one to say and one to ask. Will you listen?"

"Of course, *Teannasach*," I replied, remembering my place here.

"Sometimes," he began, "a leader must find ways of making a task understandable to minds less versed in history, and what Gregor told you was how I explained my incursion against your Empire to the shepherds and fishermen of Linrathe. Gregor told you there are those amongst them who have been agitating for such a sortie for generations?"

"He did," I confirmed. "Is it not true, then?"

"Not entirely," Donnalch said. "But it brought men to the cause, and bound them to me as a leader who listened to their dreams. I channelled that desire to support my own plans."

"Which were what?" I asked, bluntly.

"Ah, lassie, I'm not about to tell you that, not now." He smiled. "Would you expect me to? I'm only telling you this much so that you don't kill yourself in my care, trying to prove the women of the Empire are a match for our men," he went on. "It was a brave thing you did today, and it will have done the girls here—and the men, too—no harm to have seen you do it. But now, my question. Could you ride, do you think, in two days? Or even one? Long days in the saddle, I mean, not a ride for pleasure or exercise. Answer honestly, please, Lena."

I flexed the wrist again. It hurt, but not as much as it had before it had been salved and bound. "Yes," I said, "if the riding is not at speed, I could manage it, I think." I wanted to ask why, but did not.

Donnalch pushed his dark hair off his forehead with one hand, his manner suddenly more serious. "I would like to talk more with you, but I am constrained by time: I have given myself a bare fortnight to make this journey. But I want to hear your thoughts before that, and so I can see no choice than to have you accompany me, and we can talk on the road." He stood. "I'll find the Lady Dagney, and make the arrangements. We'll be a small party, and all men, unless you want another woman along?"

I shook my head. I was used to travelling with men, alone, and had no concerns about their conduct towards me. On the ride north from the Wall to the *Ti'ach na Perras*, the men had treated me with respect. "If someone can bind my arm for me, for a few days," I said, "and see to my pony's tack." Donnalch had not, I noticed, asked me if I wanted to go. I was his hostage, I thought, so I suppose he doesn't need to. I was his to command. Did I want to go? I wasn't sure.

"Gregor can do that," he answered. "Rest, now, Lena. We will leave the morning after next."

†††††

Dagney spoke forcefully: either another woman went, or I did not. "It is not your honour I am concerned about, Lena," she explained. "Many who learn of your presence will already have their own thoughts about that, unfortunately," she added, with a small grimace, "but the *Teannasach* cannot be seen to ride alone with a woman." She paused. "I will come," she said. "It has been some years since I went north." She smiled at my expression.

"Don't look so shocked, Lena," she said. "I am capable of the ride, and I will be regarded as a chaperone without peer."

I felt myself blush. "My pardon, Lady," I said. "I wasn't thinking you were too old; I just didn't realize you would leave the *Ti'ach*."

"But how else would I find my *danta*?" she asked. "The songs are not written down, or not all the versions of them, anyhow. Almost each village or *torp* has a slightly different version, of the words, or tune, or both. I visit, and talk, and sing with the people, and write down what I hear. I have recently turned my thoughts to a set of ballads about two sisters, and so I will do my research while we travel. Two pots on one fire."

Privately I wondered what Donnalch would think of this: would it distract from his own purpose? I said nothing, though; it was not my decision. We sat in Dagney's teaching rooms after another lesson in language. I had added a few words—predictably food—*be'atha*, and water—*vann*—and learned to ask for both. My arm ached. I had slept poorly, not finding a comfortable position, and the lesson had gone slowly.

Dagney had gone herself to the kitchen to ask for tea, and Isa had brought it through some minutes before. I held my mug in my good hand and sipped.

"Should I go to the *Comiádh* now?" I asked.

"Soon," she said. "Let us talk a bit, first, about what it is you will say to Donnalch, as we ride north."

"How can I decide that, until I know what he asks me?"

"You know it will be about how women of the Empire live, about your right—or lack of it—to marry, to raise children with their father present, to be part of a family."

"Or," I argued, "about the constraints put on the women of Linrathe, to marry, to have and raise children only with a man, and to believe that is the only family."

"Well," Dagney replied, her face impassive, "even your villages haven't found a way for a woman to have a child without a man, have they?"

I stared at her for a moment, and then began helplessly to laugh. Somehow, I put my tea down without spilling it, wiping the tears of laughter from my eyes. Dagney laughed with me. It took us both a minute to gain control. But even as I laughed, a thought had come to me.

"Tell me," I said when I could speak again. "Is it shameful, here, for a woman to bear a child when she has no man to claim the child? To be the father?"

"It is," she answered, sober again now. "There is shame both in bearing a child without an acknowledged father at all, and in bearing a child to a man outside of a formal partnership, even if he acknowledges the child as his."

"And are these formal partnerships—marriages—permanent?"

"Not always," she said slowly. "A marriage can be dissolved, if both man and woman agree. It is rare, though."

I gathered my thoughts. "So perhaps we are not so different. Our children also need to be conceived in a partnership; children born outside of an acknowledged partnership are shameful for us too. The difference is the length of our partnerships with men; they may last only the week of Festival, or, as in my aunt's case, for many years, until her man—Mar—died. Even though they only saw each other twice a year, they were partnered only with each other. And the men, or their designates, are responsible for their sons, by law."

Dagney considered. "It is an argument," she said finally. "But it does not get to the heart of the question: you have no choice in this. You cannot live with your man, even if you wanted to."

"And can you choose to live without a man?" I said. "Are there not restrictions on our choices on both sides?"

"We can choose to live without a man," Dagney said. "I am proof of that. What we cannot choose to do, honourably, is to have a child in that situation."

"And that is why Cillian is so angry," I said, remembering what Sorley had told me.

"It is," Dagney agreed. "And speaking of Cillian, Lena, I think you should know: he will be accompanying us. The plan was made before the *Teannasach* chose to include you as well."

"That will be awkward. He doesn't like me."

"It's not personal, Lena."

I nodded. "That's what Sorley told me, too. I'm sorry for Cillian. I have some experience of what it means for a child to be unacknowledged in our lands; it is not easy. I expect it is not here, either."

"It isn't," Dagney agreed. "Many come—or are sent—to the *Ti'acha*, because it is thought, rightly, that here we care about scholarship, and not lineage. What should matter now in our country is where Cillian trained; he has even now the right to call himself Cillian na Perras, telling all that he is a scholar, trained in this house."

"Should matter?"

Dagney sighed. "Cillian himself makes it difficult. He will not let his anger go, and accept his life as a scholar. He has a very good mind. Perras tells me he is highly skilled in analysing strategy, and the tactics of battles and their outcomes over time, which is why, I expect, the *Teannasach* has commanded him to ride with him as he visits the villages. But he has been disagreeable ever since Ardan told him he was to go. He dislikes acknowledging any authority, seeing himself as separate, somehow, from our laws and our life, an observer and commentator, and a cynical one at that." She shook her head, frustrated. "I am not expressing myself very well." she said. "I have known him over thirty years, almost since he was born, and I love him, but I worry for him. He is not happy."

There was nothing I could say to that. Dagney also said nothing for a minute, her eyes unfocused, thinking. Then she smiled, brisk and contained again. "Go to Perras now," she said, "if you are finished your tea. Leave the mug there; Isa will come for it, soon."

I rose, a bit awkwardly, my balance uncertain with my arm slung against my body. "Thank you, Lady."

I left the warmth of her teaching rooms and crossed the colder hall out to the even colder latrines, fumbling there with my clothes, one-handedly. Then I reversed my steps back into the hall to knock at Perras's door. "Come," he called, and I opened the door to step inside. The room was warmer than Dagney's had been. Perras sat close to the fire, transcribing Colm's book.

"Lena," he greeted me, putting his pen down. "I understand you are to ride north with the *Teannasach.*"

"I am. He has requested it, and I can't say no." I hesitated. "I would rather stay here," I said, wondering if I was being imprudent, "to learn from you. There is so much I wanted to ask."

"And I was looking forward to our talks, too. But what the *Teannasach* wants he will have, and so it must be. You will not be gone that long. This is only an interruption in our learning." He glanced down at the page in front of him. "But I must ask this, Lena: will you leave me Colm's history, while you are gone?"

I took a deep breath. I had been expecting this question. "I cannot," I said softly. "I am truly sorry, *Comiádh*, but I cannot. He trusted me with it, and it is all I have of him."

He smiled, sadly, I thought. "I thought that would be your answer. In anticipation, I have been transcribing as much as I could, last night and this morning. At least I have now had a chance to read it. You leave the morning after next?"

"Yes."

"Then I think I can get it done, with Cillian's help in the transcription when my hand grows tired. But it will not leave us time to talk, which I regret."

I bowed my head. "As do I, *Comiádh*."

"But it is only for a short while," he answered, "and the Lady Dagney knows our history well. As do Cillian and the *Teannasach*. You will have time to talk, on the ride."

"I suppose so," I said. Privately I wondered if either man would entertain my questions: Donnalch had his own reasons for taking me along, and I thought Cillian would avoid me as best he could. I doubted my questions about the history of the northlands and the Eastern Empire would be a priority for either man. But Dagney would indulge me, I thought.

"My hand needs a rest from writing," Perras said, "so we may talk, for a little while, now. I will leave my questions until you return. So, this is your chance, Lena: what can I tell you, that you would like to know?"

Of all my questions, there was one that puzzled me the most. "What happened to the Eastern Empire?" I asked. "I know all communication stopped, but why? Do you know? How could they just disappear?"

"Ah," Perras said. "The answer to that—or more accurately the answer to why you do not know—lies in fear and superstition. The actual answer is quite simple, but it is hidden, because to speak of it might bring it back."

I looked at him, not comprehending.

"Disease, Lena," he said. "The Eastern Empire fell because of disease."

"Disease?" I repeated. And again, I heard my mother's voice: *the Eastern Fever...* "The Eastern Fever?" I asked. "It killed them? All of them?"

"How do you know that name?" Perras asked sharply.

"My mother," I answered, confused by his tone. "She is a healer. I heard her talk of it once."

"Openly?" he probed, his tone less severe.

I struggled to remember. "She was talking about anash." The memory played at the edges of my mind...the council meeting, when we had debated the use of the contraceptive tea for young girls, against rape by the Lestians should our defenses fail. "Yes, openly," I said. "In meeting. She was giving her opinion about anash's safety for young girls, and she said it had been used against the Eastern Fever, and therefore was likely safe."

"That was all?" Perras queried. "And did anyone ask about the Eastern Fever?"

"No one," I answered. "It wasn't part of the discussion, and nobody seemed interested."

"Is that all you know?"

"Yes," I said. "It didn't seem to matter. If I thought about it at all, I suppose I thought it was an ague, or a summer fever, that's all."

"I wonder," Perras said thoughtfully. "Have the women's villages forgotten, both the fever and the prohibition against speaking its name? So, you do not know what else your mother might know of it?"

I shook my head. "No."

"How I would like to talk to her, or another healer," he murmured. He sighed. "Dagney will tell you the rest, child, as you ride. I will speak to her. I had best return to the copying, if I am to get it done."

Chapter Eight

Fog obscured the world, a fine icy fog that spangled our cloaks with tiny droplets and hid the land on either side of the track. We rode at a walk, letting our horses pick their footing, following Gregor. His horse, he had said, knew this track, and he trusted it to find a safe path.

Occasionally a shaft of sunlight cut through the mist, illuminating moorland or mountainside for a moment, showing us a terrain of grey rock, silver-green heath, pewter water. Except for the quiet clop of hooves and the occasional jangle of a bit, silence reigned. Not even a curlew's mournful cry broke the stillness. I sat Clio passively, my gloved hand holding the reins loose and low on her neck, as I had for the past two hours, being carried.

Ahead of us, Gregor called a halt, his voice muffled by the fog. "Ride up," I heard Donnalch say. He had been riding behind Gregor, followed by Cillian. Behind Cillian was Dagney, and then me, and behind us, taking the tail position, Ardan. "There's space here for us all." I gathered my reins to heel Clio forward, edging in among the other gathered horses and riders. We stood on a platform of rock, bare but for the orange and green of lichens, pocked with depressions and fissures. Beyond and below us ran a wide stream, rushing downhill.

Clio shook herself, a shiver running through her skin from head to tail. "This is the Tabha," Gregor said. "It's too fast and too wide to cross here, so we're going to follow the track downhill awhile, until we can ford it safely."

"But a mouthful of food and drink first," the *Teannasach* said. "Dismount, to rest your horse a minute, and warm you." We did as we were told, my movements awkward due to my injured arm. Clio stood stolidly, used to this now. I took a package of food from my saddlebag, my one hand stiff and clumsy on the leather straps, and unhooked the water skin. I wedged the package of bread and cheese into my sling, and, carrying the water skin in my good hand, found my way over to Dagney. I carried the food for us both, her saddlebags taken up with her *ladhar* and writing tools.

She was checking the wrappings on her instrument, ensuring the oiled cloth beneath its woollen bag was keeping it dry. Apparently satisfied, she turned to me, reaching for the food. "You are not in too much pain?" she asked quietly, unwrapping the package. I shook my head, scattering water droplets from my hood.

"Just a dull ache," I said truthfully. She held food out to me. I put the water skin on the ground and took the bread, layered with a piece of cheese. I took a bite. The bread was dry and stale, but the cheese, earthy and pungent, made from sheep's milk, compensated.

"This damp does it no good," she said, the concern in her voice reminding me of my mother. The memory pained. I pushed it away. Dagney glanced around. "I wish you had seen this in sunlight," she said, as she chewed. "The

Tabha tumbles down off Beinn Seánfhear, sparkling and splashing over the rocks, and when the *liun*—the heather—is in flower, in the late summer, it is glorious. Even now, in sunshine, it has a bleak beauty."

"Is there a song about it?" I asked, swallowing the last bite of food. I reached for the water skin to wash it down.

"Yes," she answered, "it is mentioned in several, but there is one specifically about the battle fought here, long ago, and the river's role in ending it."

"Tell me," I said impulsively. The lack of opportunity to talk frustrated me: when the track wasn't too narrow to ride together, the wind or rain had made conversation impossible. Last night I had been too exhausted to talk, falling asleep as soon as I had swallowed some food and Dagney had seen to my arm.

"Not now," Dagney answered. "But once we ford, the land is drier, and if we can ride side by side I will tell you then, or sing it, if I can. A story always lifts hearts, even if my *ladhar* is too damp to play."

"Always?" I heard Donnalch's voice ask. "Even when the chorus speaks of *an abhaínne geälis dhuarcha ag fóla?*"

"Yes," Dagney answered evenly. "For the Marai sing the same line: *Tien lissande flodden, mattai af bluth.* Both sides found the cost here too high, as you well know, *Teannasach*, and so we have peace. Is that not enough to lift our hearts?"

"Is it?" he said. "I wonder." He raised his voice. "Time to ride. Mount up!"

"What does the chorus mean?" I asked Dagney as we mounted. She hesitated. "'A shining river dulled by blood'," she replied, and then she was behind me on the path. Inwardly I shivered at the description. Peace bought with blood. I leaned back in the saddle to balance my weight as Clio began to descend the narrow path.

The fog began to lift as we came down from the heights. As the visibility improved, I saw that the Tabha flowed rapidly across its rocky bed, swollen still with the meltwaters off the high peaks. I wondered how we were to cross it. But when the land flattened, so did the river, widening into a slower and shallower channel. Waterfowl took to wing as we approached, calling, circling back to land in the river behind us. The faint jingle of a bell drifted across the moorland; somewhere, a flock of sheep grazed. Gregor called a halt: we had reached the ford.

Shallower the river might be, but I judged it still over Clio's knees, and perhaps deeper in the middle. My little mare was obedient, and plucky, but she did not like water, and I had only one hand and arm with which to control her. "Gregor," I called.

He turned in his saddle. "Lena?"

"Clio will need to be led over," I said. "She is not good with deep water."

"Will she carry you, or should you come up behind one of us?" A reasonable question. I considered. I wasn't sure what Clio would do, but neither could I see how I could mount up behind another rider with my injured arm. "She'll carry me," I said finally, hoping it were true.

Gregor turned his horse to ride up to me. Dismounting, he took a rope from his pack and looped it through the bit rings on Clio's bridle, knotting it with deft moves. "She knows my horse best," he said, although nobody had spoken. Then he swung himself back up into the saddle, signalling to his bay to move forward, down the shallow bank and into the water.

Clio snorted as the water lapped at her hooves, but she moved forward obediently. Gregor kept his gelding to a slow walk, letting it pick its own route across the stony bottom of the ford. The water reached higher on Clio's legs. She faltered, swinging her head against the tautening lead rope. I urged her forward with my feet, encouraging and, I hoped, calming her with my voice at the same time. Another step forward, and another. I could feel water, cold against my boots. Clio flattened her ears. I brought my hand down to the pommel of my saddle.

My mare stopped, water lapping at her belly, her muscles tensed. Gregor felt the lead rope go tight and halted his horse, turning slightly to see what was happening. As he turned, the lead rope slackened a tiny bit, and at that Clio sidestepped and sprung forward, heading for the far bank, wanting to be out of the water.

Gregor dropped the lead rope. I tightened my legs against Clio's belly and held on as she scrabbled across the stones, hooves sliding, water splashing, beyond my control. A front leg slipped. She stumbled, throwing me forward against her neck, my bad arm pushed against my body, shooting pain up to my shoulder. Somehow, she kept her footing, scrambling upward onto the far bank. She stopped, shaking herself like a dog, her sides heaving. I sat, hand still tight on the pommel, gasping with pain and relief. Gregor appeared beside me, reaching for Clio's bridle.

"Are you all right?" he asked. He led Clio—totally obedient now—further away from the bank.

I nodded, took a deep breath. "Yes," I managed. "Banged my arm, that's all."

"We'll need to strap it tighter," I heard Dagney say. "And you are wet, and will chill, and that will not be good for you or your arm." She brought her mare to beside me, reaching out to touch my wet breeches as she spoke.

"If she cannot get a horse across a ford without Gregor's help," I heard Cillian mutter, "how can she claim not to need men?"

I bit my lip. If I reply, I thought, I might cry, and I will not cry in front of Cillian. But even as I looked mutely at Dagney, Donnalch spoke, his voice cold in rebuke.

"Hold your tongue, Cillian," he said, not raising his voice at all, but the anger and command still evident in his sharp, measured tone. "Her mare's fear of water is not a reflection on Lena's abilities, especially riding with one arm."

I reined Clio sideways and looked at Cillian. He was staring at Donnalch. "I think you make a heroine of this girl, *Teannasach*," he replied, his voice as cold and angry as his leader's. Suddenly, in the timbre of his voice, and the planes of his face in anger, I saw—and heard—the resemblance that had been plaguing me. I had a knack of seeing the overlay of one face on another, the way the women from Han could identify the bloodlines of their horses from their looks and the way they moved, a skill that had saved my cousin Garth's life during the Lestian invasion. But now I nearly spoke my shock aloud. He looked—and sounded—like Callan, cold and fierce in the aftermath of betrayal.

"I am of half a mind to send you home," the *Teannasach* said. "Mistake me not, Cillian; you are past insolence now, for all our tradition of free speech to our leaders. I brought you along to hear what our people have to say, and to give me your thoughts, but if you cannot keep from voicing your prejudices then you will be of no use to me at all. Less than no use; you will be dangerous, planting ideas in the minds of the people. So. You will not ride at the back with Ardan any longer, but beside me and Lena as we talk. And you will keep quiet, unless I ask you a direct question. But be prepared to speak with me in the evenings, in reasoned discourse. If you cannot do that, I will send you back to the *Ti'ach*."

I saw Cillian take a deep breath. Then he nodded. "As you wish, *Teannasach*," he said, his voice flat.

Donnalch moved his head to look at me. "We will ride a bit ahead," he said. "The Lady Dagney will bind your arm again and help you to change into dry trews—you have such?" I nodded; the word was unfamiliar, but the meaning clear. "Be as quick as you can," he said to Dagney.

My mind spun. How could Donnalch, who knew both the Emperor and Cillian, not see the likeness? What did it mean? I thought of Turlo, seeing my father in me when I laughed. How could he not have seen this? He was too keen an observer, and he ignored nothing. Dagney had dismounted; I realized she was waiting for me to do the same. I slid off Clio.

Dagney helped me out of my boots and my wet breeches, and into the spare pair I had packed. Then she unbound, salved, and rebound my injured arm, tying it closer and more firmly to my body. I gritted my teeth and stayed still.

"Ready?" she said, packing away the salve.

"No," I said. "I need to check Clio's legs and feet." I bent to the task, running my good hand along her legs. Should I say something about Cillian, about what I had seen? No, I decided. That was for Donnalch, if it were for anyone. I straightened. "She seems fine," I said.

Dagney helped me mount, steadying me as I swung up onto Clio. The men had ridden ahead at a slow jog, keeping the horses moving against the chill of the river fording. We did the same. I was glad of Clio's smooth trot, and Dagney's tighter binding of my arm.

We caught up to the men after a few minutes. Donnalch slowed the group to a walk. "Ride by me, Lena," he said. I moved up beside him. The plateau we rode on was gravel and scrubby heath, the ground firm. The fog had lifted, revealing a cloudless blue sky. We rode a while without speaking. I had the impression Donnalch was gathering his thoughts. Cillian rode on his other side, silent, looking forward. I kept glancing at him, looking again for the likeness to Callan. If he noticed, he ignored me.

I decided to break the silence. I'd had enough of not talking. "Tell me more about the battle at the river," I said, "if you would, *Teannasach*."

"It was the last battle between Linrathe and the Marai," he said, "fought in the autumn, after a summer of war. The Marai had been raiding since the spring, all along the coast and up the rivers. The *Teannasach* at the time, Neilan, had divided his men, sending some to the coast and some to defend the lands and people along the rivers. But most Linrathe's men were at the coast." His voice took on a rhythm, a thread of formality. I recognized the cadence of a tale told to instruct.

"Word came that the Marai were up the Tabha," Donnalch continued. "The summer had been wet, wetter than normal, and so the boats of the Marai could be rowed up the river much further than usual, nearly to this spot. They found naught but sheep; the shepherd lads or lasses had fled at the sight of the boats. But one of those lads at least was fleet of foot, and so word reached his *torp* quickly, and from there a man and horse rode out across the hills, to find Neilan's army at the coast."

Gregor and Ardan had moved closer, Gregor's leg nearly brushing mine as he rode beside me. They would know this tale well, but I guessed they had not heard their *Teannasach* tell it; this would be a memory to tell their grandchildren, some day.

"That army marched and ran and climbed, across the mountains and the bogs, and came to the Tabha in two days, under cover of night. They hid in those hills." The *Teannasach* pointed, up to the hills to our left. "As the sun rose they saw the Marai on this plain below them. The weather had cleared, and the sun shone, and not knowing their enemy were in the hills, the Marai were at ease, eating and drinking, sleeping, playing games, in the sun on both sides of the Tabha.

"Neilan said to his men: a quarter of you stay here, in the hills; come only if the battle goes not our way. Then he signalled to the rest, and down they ran out of the hills, swords out, shouting, to take the Marai by surprise. For some time, it looked as if Neilan would take the day: they drove the Marai back across the Tabha, killing many, for they had been without their helms and shields, most able to put hands only to their axes and swords as the men of Linrathe raced down upon them."

Donnalch paused, clearing his throat. We had slowed to an amble. He glanced at us, and went on.

"But Halvar, the leader of the Marai, rallied his men and took them up the beginning of the hills, so that Neilan's men must come at them uphill. True and valiant as the men of Linrathe were, they had run for two days through deep bog and steep mountains to reach the battle, and exhaustion began to take them. The hidden men, seeing this, made their charge, and they were fresh and rested, and again the day looked to be Linrathe's.

"The Marai boats were moored some miles downstream, where the river became to steep to row up. Halvar had left men with the boats, and by some means the news of the battle had reached them." A wry smile crossed Donnalch's face; his eyes were distant. He can see this battle in his mind, I realized, here on the land where it took place.

"So again, just when the battle had turned to Linrathe, Marai reinforcements arrived, and these with armour and shields. In the end, the battle was not ours, but neither was it theirs. The men fought on and on, into the afternoon. Halvar died, an arrow piercing his throat, and his place was taken by his son-in-law Orri.

"But as the men fought the skies dimmed, the weather itself matching the darkness of that fight. Huge clouds rose over Beinn Seánfhear, and lightening flashed. The rain in the mountains must have been ferocious, for the river rose in spate, and water rushed down the hillside, breaking the Tabha's banks and flooding the plain. Men from both sides fell; many drowned. Marai clung to Linrathan; men who had been fighting to the death only a moment before helped each other to higher land. It is said that it was Neilan himself who led Orri to safety, at least," he added, with a glance to Dagney, "by our bards." He shrugged. "It may have been so. For Orri agreed to a peace, standing on a hillock with Neilan by his side, and by the time the waters had receded both sides had agreed on the Sterre as the boundary between Linrathe and Sorham, and Orri and Neilan took what remained of their armies away."

He was done. No one spoke. I looked around me, at the plain and the mountains, and thought about what had happened here, the blood and bones lying beneath the soil.

"It was long, and bloody, but necessary," Donnalch said suddenly, in his normal voice. "They wanted our lands, to farm and to settle. To enslave us and displace us, neither of which we could allow."

"To impose their way of life," I said.

"Aye," Donnalch agreed. "But the flaw in your argument, Lena—for I can see where you are taking this—is that no one in Linrathe asked the Marai to come. No more than your Empire asked Leste to invade. But the gates of the Wall were opened to us, do not forget."

"By a treasonous few," I replied. "They had no right to do so, no authority."

"They would have said they had a moral authority," Donnalch said. "For while it might not have reached your village, Lena, closer to the Wall, where there is more congress between our peoples, authorised or not," he smiled slightly as he spoke those words, "there is more wish to see an end to the division of our lands."

"And so, you invaded, to free the Empire's women? Without knowing if that is what most of us wanted?"

"That was only one reason, as I have told you," he said calmly. "But, Lena, do you know what most of you want? Or do you think there is only one way to live?"

"What of your women?" I snapped back. "They lack the choice to live as I do, as the women of the Empire do. Surely, they should have that choice too? You sent only boys as hostages: were you afraid of what a girl, a woman, might learn?"

"That," Dagney said from just behind me, "is a very good question, *Teannasach*."

"Aye, it is," Donnalch said finally. He fell silent. My own thoughts roiled. Change: it was what the Emperor had wanted as well, what I had been charged with speaking of, to women, as I rode south after the successful repulsion of Leste. I did know what most women wanted, at least those of the villages and inns I had visited. But could I tell this to Donnalch? Could I trust him, this man who had led his men into our lands, and had suborned some of our soldiers to his way of thinking?

In my mind, I heard a junior officer speaking, after the assassination attempt on Callan: *Blaine wanted to be Emperor.* Blaine's nephew had opened the gates to Donnalch. Had Donnalch and Blaine made some sort of agreement, only to have Blaine fail in his attempt to become Emperor? Was opening the gates the contingency plan?

I couldn't ask. But surely Callan had, in the long days of talk that had led to this truce of which I stood as surety. Callan, who wanted more choices for his people, men and women. Free choices, I reminded myself, choices made by us, at Assembly, framed by our laws, not imposed by conquest, by the wishes of a few. But if Blaine had become Emperor, what would have happened? He would have acted within our laws too, surely?

And if so, how many might not have died?

The thought horrified me. I could not bring myself to believe it. Blaine, who had colluded with not only Donnalch, but with the king of Leste; Blaine, who had orchestrated—or at least made possible—the assassination attempt on Callan. I had no reason to believe he would have acted within the law.

My question—or Dagney's comment—had silenced Donnalch for the present. I dropped back slightly, trying to piece together understanding from surmise and rumour, partial explanations and memory, and failing utterly. "Only one reason," Donnalch had said. What were the others?

I felt like screaming, like kicking Clio hard and galloping away. I didn't understand these people, and I wasn't getting the chance to learn. I went where I was told, and tried to make sense of the bits and pieces of information I got, but I couldn't. The pieces didn't make a whole. 'Listen to what is said, about Donnalch's leadership, about the war, about what they wish to change. Exchange views on Partition, on your life as a woman of the Empire, our histories.' my Emperor had instructed me. These were orders, I reminded myself. Calm down, listen, and eventually a story, a pattern, will emerge.

Behind me, I heard the strings of Dagney's *ladhar* being plucked. I turned in my saddle. She was tuning the instrument, her horse led by Ardan to free her hands. Satisfied with the tuning, she began to sing.

The purple heath, the yellow broom,
Made glad the eye as out we rode,
To meet and fight at river's edge,
To hold our lands against the foe.

A river gleaming on the hill.

From down the ben the river splashed,
The Tabha bright in morning sun.
The Marai north and Linrathe south,
To fight until the day was done.

A river gleaming on the hill.

Ardan's voice, rough but true, joined Dagney's on the chorus.

A sword was raised, the arrows flew
Across the burn as thick as rain.
Below the hill, where field is flat,
The air was rent with cries of pain.

A shining river dulled by blood.

The battle raged, the sun rose high,
Knee-deep in water men fought on.
The Marai boats moored down the stream,
Linrathe's best men up on the ben.

A shining river dulled by blood.

By now all the men—even Cillian—were singing the refrain. I stayed silent, listening.

When bodies thick served as a bridge
And neither side could take the day,
The hidden men came forth to fight
Among the fallen where they lay.

A river red and thick with blood.

As evening fell and still they fought,
Both sides with numbers grievous few,
A shout came from the river's flow:
"Enough!" the cry, a voice none knew.

A river red and thick with blood.

Swords fell from hands; men stood as stone
As from the river words poured forth:
"I say enough. Go from this place,
And live in peace, both south and north."

An angry river flowing red.

"For red my waters flow today,
And silver only should they be.
Bury your dead here on my banks,
Forget not what you heard from me."

An angry river flowing red.

"For peace I want and peace I'll have
Or watch my waters rise and flow
To drown this land and all within,
Both north and south, both high and low."

A peace enforced by river's god.

Both sides obeyed, the cairns were raised
Against the raven, kite and crow.
The Tabha's peace has long remained,
No man would dare not keep it so.

A peace enforced by river's god.

A river gleaming on the hill.
A shining river dulled by blood.
An angry river flowing red.
A peace enforced by river's god.

No man would dare not keep it so.

The notes of the *ladhar* died away. The call of a curlew drifted over the moor, over our small and silent band, over the burial mounds I could now see on either side of the path, mournful, ancient, eternal.

Chapter Nine

"Of course," Cillian said, after we had ridden in silence for some minutes, "the river did not speak. The minds and voices of men spoke, seeing the futility of the battle and the loss, but better it be remembered that they obeyed a spirit of the waters than admit to conceding the day."

"Maybe," Gregor said. "But you were not there, Cillian, and I myself have heard voices in the wind and water more than once. I would not be too quick to doubt."

"Whether the voice was that of a river god, or that of the conscience of men," Dagney added, "the battle ended when the river rose, and we have kept the Tabha's peace." Her voice trailed off. She was looking ahead, her brow furrowed. I glanced at the men; they too stared ahead. Donnalch raised a hand. We halted. Across the plateau, I could see a pair of horsemen, galloping towards us.

"They are Marai," long-sighted Gregor said, "wearing the colours of King Herlief."

The men exchanged glances. "He is dead, then?" Donnalch murmured. No one replied.

The horsemen galloped closer. We waited. When they were still some distance away, Gregor spoke again. "Their cloaks are bordered with black points. These are the Earl Fritjof's men, *Teannasach*, not the King's, and one of them is not Marai, but Linrathan."

"Fritjof sailed west two years ago," Ardan said, "looking for their promised land of grapes and honey. I had not heard he had returned."

"King Herlief forced him to go," Donnalch said quietly, "after he nearly killed his brother in a fight. Over what, I cannot recall."

I saw the men push their own cloaks back, making it easier to reach for their weapons. What was happening? I transferred Clio's reins to my left hand, holding them as best I could. I would need the right for my secca.

The approaching men slowed their horses to a trot. Hands on reins, they showed no sign of reaching for weapons. Both men were of medium height, with close-cropped light hair. Over a tunic and breeches of brown they wore cloaks of blue and green, pinned with large circular brooches and edged, as Gregor had said, with a black border patterned into points.

The *Teannasach* walked his horse forward a few steps. "Niáll," he called, "what brings you into Linrathe, wearing the livery of Earl Fritjof?"

"*Teannasach*," one replied. He reined his horse in, inclining his head to Donnalch. "We came as messengers, not expecting to find you riding out in the land. We bring news: King Herlief is dead. Fritjof is king now. He asks that you make haste: he wishes your presence at the burial rites and his crowning, but neither can be delayed." His eyes flicked to Dagney and me. The second rider reached for something. My muscles tensed, but he brought a rolled paper from the top his saddlebag, holding it out.

"The King himself wrote this," Niáll said. Donnalch rode forward to take it. Circling back, he returned to his place between Gregor and Ardan before unrolling it. He read quickly, then bent his head to say something to Ardan, who nodded.

"I am honoured that your King has asked me to be present at these ceremonies," Donnalch said, his voice formal. "But there is one of my party who is injured and cannot ride at speed; nor would I ask such of the Lady Dagney. We will need to make arrangements for them, before I ride north with you. Twenty minutes, and I will be ready."

Fritjof's two men glanced at each other. The one who had spoken nodded. "As you wish, *Teannasach*," he said. "We will wait for you at those trees ahead. There is a stream there, to water our horses." They reined their horses round and rode off at a trot.

When they were out of earshot, Ardan spoke. "Do you trust them, *Teannasach?*" he asked.

"Herleif's death was expected," Donnalch replied, "and the seal is Fritjof's. I would not recognize his hand, even if he did write the words himself. I believe the men are from Fritjof; I had heard that Niáll had taken Fritjof's coin. Whether I trust them—or Fritjof—is another question; not really, is the answer. The Earl was ever a plotter, subtle and fluid in his allegiances, but his eye was always on the throne. He has it now, over his brother, it appears. I wonder if Ásmund, too, is dead," he added quietly, as if to himself.

"Why should it matter if you are there for the rituals?" Ardan growled. Clearly, he was unhappy with this turn of events.

"It gives legitimacy," Cillian said. "If Fritjof is crowned in the presence of another country's leader, this will be seen to be wider acknowledgement of his right to rule."

"Aye," Donnalch said, nodding. "And therefore, his right to treat with me. I am guessing that not all Marai wanted Fritjof as their king. His brother would have had supporters. Personally, I, too, would have preferred Ásmund, but that," he warned, "cannot be said to anyone, mind."

"Now," he said briskly. "Gregor, you will stay with the Lady Dagney and Lena. Will you return to the *Ti'ach*, Lady?"

"Not immediately, unless Lena wishes to," Dagney replied. "Having started, I would like to continue with my plans to collect *danta*. There are three *torps* I had hoped to stop at. If Lena and Gregor are willing, we could visit each for a day, and then return to the *Ti'ach*. The riding will not be strenuous, Lena; they are only an hour or two apart, and they will be generous to us, as travellers and a *scáeli*. And you will see a bit more of our land, and our people."

I considered. Why not? It would give me time alone with Dagney, and surely now we would be able to talk, if not while riding then when we stopped. "Yes," I said, "I would like that."

Donnalch nodded. "Good," he said briefly. "But when you return to the

Ti'ach, ask Perras to spread the word of Fritjof's accession. It should be known, at least among the *Ti'acha*."

"Of course," Dagney said. Should the Emperor know? I wondered. Would he care? Did he even know who ruled the Marai, or even of the Marai? There was no mention of them, in Colm's history of the Empire.

"Cillian," Donnalch said. "You will come with me. You will keep your eyes open, and listen and remember. Watch who speaks to whom, who is unhappy, who is angry. But give no opinion, even if asked, and above all put no words to paper. If something troubles you, find me. You understand?"

"I do, *Teannasach*," Cillian said. He looked, I noted, happier than I had seen him look before. Or if not happy, then interested. Intrigued. That was the right word, I thought. Intrigued.

Donnalch took Gregor aside, speaking to him quietly. Dagney and I waited. "Where do we go now?" I asked.

"Just a bit further north," she answered, "on the same path that the *Teannasach* will ride, for a little way. We take a track that branches off to the left, back up a bit into the hill. There is a *torp* there, the one these sheep belong to, and they will feed us and give us a place to sleep tonight, and we will sing and tell stories. But I was hoping that Cillian might stay with us, to write down the words of songs we will hear tonight. Otherwise, I must do it from memory." She smiled a bit ruefully. "And that was easier when I was twenty. But I will manage."

This was nothing I could help with: I barely recognized half-a-dozen words. "What's a *torp*?" I asked, remembering Donnalch had used the word earlier.

"A farm and its collection of cottages. Not a village, but not a lone house, either," she answered. "The farmer—the *Eirën*—holds the land; the cottagers, or *torpari*, work for him, but have a bit of land for themselves. Much like the *Ti'acha*, in fact," she added.

Gregor rode back to us, his face grim. I wondered what Donnalch had said to him. Dagney, with the ease of authority and long acquaintance, simply asked. "What's wrong, Gregor?"

He shook his head. "Marai, riding bold as hoodie crows into Linrathe, with a Linrathan to guide them. I don't like it, Lady. The Sterre's been unguarded, or under-guarded, for too long."

"And is not the *Teannasach* sending you for more men to do so, now Fritjof has claimed the throne?" Dagney spoke in an undertone, not looking toward the small party of men.

"Aye, Lady, but I must see you safely back to the *Ti'ach* first, and you have places you wish to visit. So, it will be a ten-day before our men reach the Sterre, and that's too long."

Dagney made a gesture of impatience. "I have ridden these hills for thirty years. What do I need an escort for now?" Gregor looked uncomfortable.

"It's not you, Lady," I said. "It's me, the hostage. Gregor is charged with keeping me safe, and with ensuring I don't escape. When we are back at the *Ti'ach*, I am guessing Sorley will be asked to take on that role, so that Gregor can ride to the Wall. Am I right, Gregor?"

He looked even more uncomfortable, but nodded his head. "You are," he murmured.

"And if I give my word? Would that be enough?" Our eyes met. He assessed my words, his gaze level.

"It would be for me," he said finally. "But it's not my decision."

"*Teannasach!*" Dagney called. "A word, before you ride?"

Donnalch said something to the two Marai, reining his horse away from them. He trotted over to us. "Lady?" he asked.

Dagney kept her voice pitched low. "Let Gregor ride south," she said. "Lena will pledge her word to not try to escape. Surely that is enough?" He hesitated. "Fritjof's men riding freely in Linrathe, and one of them knowing every inch of this land?" Dagney echoed Gregor's words. "You need more men at the Sterre. Which is more important, Donnalch?"

The jangle of a bit caught my attention. I looked over to see the Marai riding towards us. Donnalch saw them too. "You are right," he whispered. "Gregor, as soon as you can, ride south. Ignore what I say, now," he finished. Raising his voice only slightly, he said, "and do not tire the women, Gregor. Keep the pace slow and the distances short. I will see you at the *Ti'ach* in a ten-day." He held a hand up to the messengers, who had stopped only a pace or two away from us, Ardan behind them. "Find some new songs, Lady," he said. He raised his voice. "And now I must ride to bid farewell to one king, and honour another." He swung his horse around, signalling it with heels and hands. It leapt forward, galloping across the heath, Fritjof's men, taken by surprise, lagging behind. We watched them for a minute, until Dagney spoke.

"Come," she said. "We should follow them; one might just look back. You will know where you can leave us, Gregor."

"Aye," he said. "There's more than one path from Bartolstorp to the Tabha. Greet my mother for me, will you, Lady, and my father and brother? I would have liked to have seen them, but this need is greater."

Half an hour later, in a fold of the hill, Gregor raised a hand in farewell and turned off the track we followed, onto what looked to me like a sheep trail along the side of the valley. "Ride safely," Dagney called to him, reining her mare to a stop. I followed suit. She looked at me. "Another half-hour to Bartolstorp," she said. "How are you feeling?"

"I'm fine," I said. She nodded, and we began to walk along the track again. After a minute, Dagney began to speak.

"Gregor's family have held this *torp* for many generations," she said, "long before the borders were set, and his *torpari* have been mostly the same families for all those years, as well. I will be asking them about a *danta* called '*Sostrae lys yn dhur*'; that is 'the dark and pale sisters', in your tongue. It tells, in its simplest meaning, of the drowning of the pale sister, the younger, by the older one, for the older one wants the younger's lover. The dark sister takes the younger one to the sea, where she drowns her, then tells her lover that the girl has run away with another. The body floats down a river, where it is found by a miller, who recognizes her and tells her lover, who in the meantime has wed the dark sister in despair. The grieving lover strings his *ladhar* with the pale sister's hair, but he will never again play the instrument for his dark wife, reserving it for when he is alone, to hear his true love sing to him."

"How horrible," I said. "Sisters, drowning each other over a man?"

Dagney laughed. "You forget," she said gently, "that here a man confers status and protection to his wife, and a dark mind might see that as a reason to commit murder. But I do not believe that is what the song is about at all, except on its surface."

"What, then?"

"I think it is about one people's conquering of another, probably in a sea battle, and how the conquered people keep their beliefs and ideas alive in secret, by song and story and custom, hidden from their overlords."

I considered. It made sense, in an obscure way.

"What peoples? What battle?" I asked, genuinely curious now.

Dagney shook her head. "That is what I am trying to find out. If I can transcribe different versions of the song, from here in the south to the versions sung in the Rathe Hoys, I can look at the details, and perhaps work it out. It is very old, and I already know it varies greatly in the tellings: sometimes the girls are the daughters of a king, sometimes of a farmer. While both a king or a farmer represent the land, I think the versions with a king may be older, closer to the truth."

We rode on. I thought about what Dagney had said. Songs, for me, were just verses sung around a fire, stories set to music, but I had never thought about what they might mean. Was the song I had learned from Tice anything more than a soldier's lament for leaving his lover? What was it Colm had said? Something about tax rolls and court records telling a story, if you knew how to hear it. If history lived in those dry documents, did it also live in songs?

A shout from ahead of us brought me out of my reverie. I saw a shepherd hurrying towards us, his dog at his heels. "*Scáeli* Dagney," he said, and then much more, but I could understand none of it, the words soft and sibilant, running together like music. Dagney replied to him, gesturing. I heard my name. The shepherd looked up at me. I smiled a greeting. He nodded, and then, turning back to Dagney pointed down the track.

"*Meas*," Dagney said. She turned in her saddle to me. "Torunn—that's Gregor's mother—is at the house. Bartol and his older son, who is also named Bartol but is called Toli to distinguish him, are out on the hill with the men, mending walls. The shepherd will send his son to tell them we are here. Bartol has some words of your language, and Toli more, if I remember rightly, but I doubt Torunn has any; this will be awkward for you, Lena, but it cannot be helped. I will do my best to help you understand what is being said."

We rode into the *torp* a few minutes later. It was not dissimilar to the *Ti'ach*, as Dagney had said, with a largish farmhouse and a courtyard of outbuildings, but here there was no doubt that the concerns of sheep and cattle over-ruled all. It was not dirty, precisely, but the air echoed to the constant bleating from a pen of ewes and lambs, and the remains of a depleted stack of hay slumped to one side of the yard. Pigeons flew up from the muddy flagstones as we rode in, circling to land on the house roof. A sheepdog yipped from where it lay beside the sheepcote, but did not approach us.

A woman appeared at the open front door to the house, shading her eyes against the sun. "*Scáeli* Dagney," she said, and then a torrent of words I could not understand. Dagney dismounted, indicating to me to do the same. I did, fatigue suddenly washing through me.

A boy appeared to take our horses, leading them off somewhere. "Lena," Dagney said to me, "this is *Konë* Torunn, wife to Bartol, who heads this *torp*." I smiled at the tall woman, her dark hair braided and pinned over her head; her frame lean and wiry. Her sleeves were rolled up, and an apron covered the dark dress she wore: she had been working. Dagney said something to Torunn: I caught Gregor's name. Torunn smiled, her blue eyes crinkling, and said something, a question, I thought, from the inflection. Dagney laughed, and nodded. "She asks if he is well," she said to me.

Gesturing, Torunn led us into the house. Like the *Ti'ach*, it had a big central room, but unlike the *Ti'ach*, this was both kitchen and hall. A long table ran widthwise across the room; behind it were the hearth, where a pot hung over the flames, and the table itself was crowded with rising bread, a sack of grain, a platter of soup bones. A young woman was chopping root vegetables at one end of the table. From her build, and her face and eyes, I took her to be a close relation of Torunn—a daughter?—but she seemed too young. At Dagney's direction I sat, my arm throbbing. It had been improving, but this morning's accident had worsened it. I flexed my fingers, feeling pain shoot up the arm.

"Lena, this is Huld, Torunn's grand-daughter. Gregor's niece," Dagney added. Huld smiled at me. "Welcome," she said in strongly accented tones.

"*Meas*," I remembered to say, surprised that she spoke my language. My surprise must have shown, for she smiled again.

"I learn to speak your words," she said haltingly, "My *Athàir*...my father...he teach. My many-times mother's mother come from your land."

Gregor had alluded to that, I remembered.

"You learn our words?" Huld asked.

I spread my hands, shaking my head. "Only one or two," I said. "*Forla*," I added.

"We practice," she said. Torunn said something to her, and she ducked her head and went back to the vegetables, glancing at me occasionally. I wrapped my hands around the mug of tea Torunn had placed in front of me, welcoming the warmth, almost too tired to sip it.

Dagney and Torunn spoke at length. I let the sounds slip by, not trying to recognize anything, slowly drinking my tea. Through the open door, I heard the sheepdog whine, and footsteps, and a moment later two men entered the room. Gregor's father, Bartol, I thought, and his brother Toli.

Bartol strode forward to hug Dagney, an enveloping hug of real welcome. She was well-known here, I realized, as Toli also embraced her, if not as enthusiastically as his father. The room filled with talk and laughter. I finished my tea. Its warmth had revived me briefly, but now I felt tiredness overwhelming me again. It had been days since I slept well, the pain and awkwardness of my arm waking me every time I moved in my sleep. I shifted my stool, trying to find a more comfortable way to sit, the scrape of the wooden legs along the flagged floor sounding loudly and discordantly. Heads turned my way.

"Lena," Dagney said, "forgive me. Your arm needs tending, and you need to rest." A word to Torunn had us being ushered up a flight of stone stairs to the sleeping chambers, where Torunn opened a door to a small room. One narrow bed, and a chest, was all the furniture it held.

I sat on the bed as Dagney unbound my arm and examined it. She tutted. "Give me a moment," she said, and left the room. A minute or two later she returned, carrying my saddlebags, followed by Huld carrying a bowl of water.

Dagney eased my tunic over my head and gently pulled it free of my arms, and then did the same with the linen undertunic I wore. I shivered slightly in the cool of the room, but the water Dagney bathed my arm in was warm, and the salve made my skin tingle. I felt Huld's eyes on me, but I did not look up. Dagney's ministrations were gentle, but I could feel tears threatening.

My arm salved and rebound, Dagney helped me dress again and sent Huld away with the bowl of cooling water. As soon as Huld closed the door behind her, I could not keep the tears away. Dagney, murmuring words of comfort, put an arm around me, and let me cry.

"I'm sorry," I said after a few minutes, snuffling. She handed me the cloth with which she had bathed my arm, and I found a dryer corner to wipe my eyes and blow my nose. "It's just—"

"All new. You are not here by choice, and you cannot understand what is being said. And in addition, you are in pain and tired. All very good reasons to cry," Dagney said. I forced a smile. "Now," she went on, "I think you should rest. Sleep, if you can. I will explain to Torunn, and we will not expect you at dinner, but someone will bring you soup and bread later. All right?"

I nodded. It was exactly what I needed. I lay down on the bed and let Dagney remove my boots and pull a blanket over me. She stroked my hair briefly before she left me. I did not sleep immediately, but lay, feeling the throbbing in my arm subsiding, thinking. I felt so alone. I had spent much time by myself before, riding between villages and inns, during watch-duty on the Wall, but at the end of the day there had almost always been someone to talk to, if I wished, or just to listen to others' conversations. Even if I had purposely remained on the periphery, I had still been part of what was happening. I had not realized what a barrier not understanding what was being said would be.

On top of this, I was frustrated. There was so much I wanted to know, both for myself and to take back to the Empire, and every time an opportunity presented itself to learn more it was thwarted. I was failing in my task. I shifted on the bed, rolling over on one side. I will just have to get Dagney to talk to me, I thought, as I drifted into sleep.

The sound of a *ladhar* drifting up from below woke me some time later. No light came in through the small window. The sun had set. I sat up. My bladder twinged. Reaching under the bed with my good hand, I felt around for the chamber pot; finding it, I crouched beside the bed to relieve myself.

A soft knock at the door came just as I adjusted my breeches. I pushed the chamber pot under the bed. "Yes?" I called. The door opened. Huld came in carrying a tray. She pushed the door closed again with her hip, putting the tray on the chest.

"Food," she said, gesturing.

"*Meas*, Huld," I replied. The soup smelled good: lamb and barley, I thought, and the bread looked fresh-baked. There was nowhere except the bed on which to sit, so I sat on the edge. Huld put the tray on my knees, and I picked up the spoon. One spoonful reminded me how hungry I was. I ate with appetite, trying to not gulp my food. Huld perched on the side of the chest, watching me.

When I was done, she took the tray from me. "Come for music?" she asked. I hesitated. I felt grubby, travel-stained, not fit for company.

"*Allech'i*, Huld, *vann?*" I asked. "To wash," I added in my own language, pointing to the washbowl on the end of the chest.

"Ahh, *ja*," she replied, jumping up. Taking the tray, she went back downstairs, to return five minutes later with a jug of steaming water, a towel, and a chunk of soap.

"I help?" she asked, as I struggled with my tunic.

"*Ja*," I replied gratefully. I could handle my breeches, but pulling a tunic over my head one-handed was a challenge. She lifted the outer tunic, and then the under, over my head carefully. "*Meas*," I said, and bent to my washing.

After a few minutes, she took the soap from me. I looked at her questioningly. She smiled, and began to wash my back. Her hands on me were firm, and after the first surprise I let myself enjoy the feeling. I had last had a bath at the *Ti'ach*, some days ago now. While I had grown accustomed to brief washes and long gaps between baths on the Wall, I preferred to be clean.

When Huld had dried my back, I reached for the drawstring on my breeches. Huld took a step back. "I go," she said. "I come back, help you dress, *ja?*"

At Tirvan, like all the women's villages of the Empire, and on the Wall, there were no nudity taboos among women. I had bathed and swam and washed among girls and women of all ages since I was a toddler. Huld's modesty startled me, especially as she had had no problem with either seeing or touching my naked upper body. "You can stay," I said. "I don't mind."

She blushed. "*Ja?*" I nodded, stepping out of my breeches and under-breeches. I washed, feeling Huld's eyes on me. I glanced over at her as I dried myself. Music floated up from the hall. Her lips were slightly parted, her eyes wide. I felt an answering tug, deep and low, and looked away. Did she even know what it was she was feeling?

I dressed again, in cleaner clothes, and followed Huld downstairs to the hall. The meal was clearly over; Dagney and Tori sat on tall stools in front of the table, *ladhars* on their laps; around the periphery of the room men and women sat or stood; children sprawled on the floor. The fire in the huge fireplace glowed, giving off the same smell I remembered from Perras's room. Wall-sconces lit the rest of the hall. We found a space, and a stool for me, on the outer wall. I saw eyes turn my way: I guessed my presence and my role as a hostage to the peace had spread among the folk of this *torp*. Or perhaps, I reflected, it was simply that I wore breeches. Most folk, I saw, had on what looked like their best clothes. To honour Dagney, I realized.

Tori said something to Dagney, and they began a song, the melody jaunty, quickly repeated. The smallest children began to dance to it, jumping up and down, twirling, slightly older ones attempting a few more complex steps. My foot began to tap. Hands started to clap, and then one or two couples stood to dance, hands and feet in rapid motion.

After a few bars Dagney began to sing, the words, like the music, simple and repetitious. Voices from the room began to sing the chorus. The music gained in speed; hands clapped faster, feet moved rhythmically and rapidly. Voices sung louder. The music reached a climax of beats, and ended.

I realized I was grinning. It did not matter here that I couldn't understand the words. Music was its own language, not needing translation. After another song, not dissimilar to the last, Dagney changed the tuning on her *ladhar*, and began a slower melody.

"Women's dance," Huld said in my ear. "You try?" I hesitated. "Is slow," she added.

Why not? I liked to dance, even if I did not do it well. I followed Huld out onto the floor, joining maybe a dozen other women. We lined up in two rows, facing each other. The women began a slow clap, matching the beat of the music, advancing to meet each other. I followed suit, clapping my good hand against my thigh. When we met, we held our hands high to clap against our partner's, then linked arms to circle around each other. A few steps backward, still clapping, and we repeated the moves. I was awkward at first, with only one free hand and arm, but as the *ladhar*'s melody became a little faster, we met its challenge, our feet and hands moving more quickly. On the third time our hands met, we held them up to allow the furthest right couple to move under our linked hands.

When it was our turn to duck under the canopy of hands, Huld kept my right hand firmly in her left, her skin warm against mine. Our hips brushed as we ran to the end of the line. As we took our places she caught my eye: her face was flushed, her eyes dark, and she smiled in delight. I smiled back, unable not to, feeling the beat of the music reverberating through me.

The dance was done. Huld kept my hand in hers, leading me outside into the cool night. Stars whitewashed the sky, the night cloudless. Huld led me behind an outbuilding. In the shelter of its walls she turned and kissed me, hard and urgent. I felt desire shoot through me. How long since I had taken comfort in lovemaking? Weeks, now, maybe months, brief interludes with other Guards, affirmations of life amongst the deaths. Huld's hands had begun to move. I pulled away. "No?" she said. I could hear the puzzlement in her voice.

"How old are you?" I whispered.

In the starlight, I saw her smile. "Eighteen years," she said. "A woman. I choose this, yes?" She paused. "And you not first," she added.

Her kisses had told me that. "Is this accepted?" I whispered.

"No," she said. "But no one sees; they all dance, or if out in night like us, what they do is secret too." She drew a finger down from my lips, along my neck, and lower. I shuddered.

"Then, yes," I said, sliding my hands down her back, drawing her to me, my lips finding hers. This time she pulled away.

"Come," she said. I let her lead me again, through a door and up, by feel, a wooden ladder, into the loft of a byre. Below us cattle slept, warming the shed. I felt hay beneath my feet, and sank to my knees, pulling Huld down beside me. Faint music drifted in from the hall. We fell into the hay, lips joined, hands exploring, touch and scent and sensation our only guides in the utter blackness of the night.

CHAPTER TEN

IN THE MORNING, Huld was not among those gathered in the hall to bid us farewell. Late in the night we had slipped back, separately, to our own rooms, when voices outside told us the *torpari* were returning to their cottages. Finding hay still in my hair this morning, I hoped we had been unseen.

After the lovemaking Huld had curved herself against me, one finger stroking my cheek. "Tell me of her," she murmured.

"Who?" I asked, already drifting into sleep.

"The woman who hurt you. You make love for the body, for pleasure, yes? Not for heart. You hold back what inside you."

I rolled away from her, staring into the darkness. Huld put out a hand to touch me. "I not upset," she said. "Just say what think. I wrong?"

"No," I said slowly. "You are not."

"Tell me," she urged. "Talk is good."

Was it? "Her name is Maya," I said. "When Tirvan—my village—voted to fight against the invasion from Leste, she chose exile from Tirvan rather than fight. I stayed to fight, but when it was over, I went to find her."

"And she not want you?"

"No," I answered, "She didn't, because she had found like-minded women and they were going to start a new village, one open only to those who had been exiled from their home villages. There would have been no place for me."

"Is sad," Huld said.

"I understood that, though," I said into the night. "It was the second time, later, that I could not understand."

"You join up again, then?"

"Not quite," I said, hesitating, looking for a simple way to explain. "After Linrathe invaded, I stayed in the south. I had a male lover for a while, and he had a son in a village that grew grapes and made wine, and so I went there, to help raise his son."

"So, you not fight again?"

"Not at first, no. The woman who was raising Valle—the boy—decided to go to Casilla, our one city, to live with a friend, who had a child of about the same age. I went with her. We weren't lovers, but I didn't have anywhere else to go. I found work on the fishing boats—Casilla is on the coast—and helped support us. And then Maya came looking for Valle, too, because his father was her brother. She moved in, and after a while, she asked me to leave. She told me I had no reason to be there, and she wanted me to go."

"So, your man, he your Maya's brother?"

"Yes," I said.

"She know?"

"No," I said. "I never told her."

"Then why send you away?"

"I don't know," I said. "I don't know." I felt the mix of anger and humiliation I always did, when I thought of that time. Huld lay silent for some minutes.

"Was only pleasure with this man, too?" she asked.

It was easy to speak the truth in the dark. "No," I said. "It started as comfort, but by the end, when he had to leave for his ship, I loved him."

"Then we try for comfort, again," she whispered, running her hand down my arm. I turned back to her, to the taste of her lips and the heat of her skin against mine.

At breakfast, Dagney had not asked where I had disappeared to the night before. Dressed for riding, she ate hungrily, speaking only of the *danta* versions Toli had transcribed for her, and where we would ride to tonight: another *torp*, the *Eirën* named Sinarr. Sinarrstorp, she said, was a good day's ride to the east, across the hills, but Bartol had sent a boy on a pony at dawn, to tell them we were coming.

I also ate with hunger. My arm pained me less, and I could move my fingers and wrist more easily. Free of intense pain, and buoyed by last night's lovemaking, I had an appetite. We ate porridge and bacon, and barley bread with honey, all tasting wonderful to me. What sky I could see through the narrow windows was blue. I looked forward to the day's ride with only Dagney. Perhaps I would get some of my questions answered.

I smiled and said *meas* to Bartol and Torunn and Toli, and to anyone who spoke to me. I did not look for Huld. She had told me early this morning when she had come to help me dress that she would not be here. "I go red," she had said, as she salved and bound my arm, "and others see, maybe remember we gone from dance. It not shame, *leannan*; but for me and you only. You understand?" I had assured her I did. I felt much the same. At the Wall and throughout the Empire, all pairings were accepted and unremarkable, unless the age difference was too great, but I did not understand the structures and mores of Linrathe. I too, I thought, would 'go red', if anyone were to guess what Huld and I had been doing in the hayloft. Or even in my room this morning, although we had had time for little more than a few kisses.

The thought must have made me smile, because Dagney suddenly spoke. "You are looking much better this morning, Lena. I was glad to see you dancing last night; it has done you good. You slept well?"

"Very well," I said truthfully. "And my arm hurts much less this morning. Look," I added, wiggling my fingers.

"Pleasure helps the body heal," Dagney said. I felt my face grow hot. She continued, either not noticing or choosing to ignore my flush. "Now, are you finished? We have a long way to go today, and should get started."

We rode through the early morning sunshine along a reasonable track, the route, Dagney told me, that traders took with their pack animals between the *torps*. The boy who had ridden to Sinarrstorp at dawn on a sure-footed hill pony would have taken a different route through the hills, faster, but also easy to lose, or be lost on.

"If Sinarrstorp is so close," I asked, "won't their *danta* be the same as Bartolstorp?"

"Not necessarily," she answered, turning her head to talk to me; the track, while good, was not quite wide enough for us to ride abreast. "It will depend, in part, on where the families came from, originally; if most share an ancestral village with Bartolstorp, then, yes, the *danta* will be much the same. But if not, and I do not know if they did or didn't, then the *danta* may be very different."

Where they came from originally? "Haven't these people been here, well, forever?" I asked, genuinely curious. "Where would these ancestral villages be?"

"In the north," she said. "When we spoke of this, when you first came to the *Ti'ach*, perhaps we made it too simple. The Sterre is the boundary between Sorham and Linrathe, and Linrathe pays tribute to Varsland for Sorham, but by the time of the battle of the Tabha, many with northern blood had settled in these lands as well. They chose to stay, when the Marai withdrew for the last time, and it is those people who farm the torplands hereabout."

"And everyone lives peacefully?" I asked.

Dagney laughed. "Yes," she answered. "It was all so long ago. Bartol and Toli and Sinarr, and their *torpari*, if you asked them, would tell you they are Linrathan, not Marai, or even Sorhaman, although they likely have distant family there. There is trade between us, and people do move back and forth, but their allegiance is to the *Teannasach*, not to King Herlief, or rather, Fritjof, now."

I thought of Gregor's reaction to the Marai soldiers; certainly, he had not been pleased to see them in Linrathe. And why should Dagney not know how her own people thought? But even those who appeared most loyal could have secret sympathies, or else Linrathe would not have found the Wall open to them two years past. I kept my thoughts to myself.

"Well," Dagney said after a minute. "We have a long ride, the weather is good, and so we have the time and opportunity to talk. What would you like to know, Lena?"

I had so many questions. Part of me wanted Dagney to explain how relationships—between men and women, or otherwise—worked here in Linrathe, enlarging on the conversation we had started. On the other hand, I might find myself flushing again, and Huld had asked for privacy. Our brief liaison could not be known; I had no idea what the punishment—for her or me—might be. My thoughts went back to my last conversation with Perras.

"The Eastern Fever," I said. "Perras told me the Eastern Empire fell because of it, but we did not have time for him to fully explain. He said you could, on the ride."

She said nothing for a moment, and then, unexpectedly, began to sing.

A ring around, a ring around

A ring of blossom hiding thorn,
We dance and dance but only one
Will stand alone now all forlorn.

"Do you know that song, Lena?" she asked.

"Yes, of course," I said, puzzled. "It's the ring-game song; I played it as a child. But what has that to do with the Eastern Fever?"

"That is what it is about," she said. "Like the *danta*, it is more than a child's game-song. It is a memory of how the red rash of the fever killed almost everyone. When you chose the one who would stay standing at the word 'now', you were playing at being the lone survivor of ten or a dozen or even more in a village or farmstead."

"That's horrible," I said, grimacing. "But I never liked the game. I hated to be the one left standing, fingers pointed at me, and the others going on without me."

"On to death, and to whatever lies beyond," she said. "but that is how it was supposed to make you feel, bereft and terrified, as the lone survivor at a *torp* might."

"Where did this fever come from?" I asked, "And why did it go away?"

"I can answer the first to some extent," Dagney said. The path had widened slightly, and I could ride beside her now. "It began in Casil, the capital of the Eastern Empire, and then its outposts and colonies. It was probably spread by those who were sent as messengers, or perhaps by people fleeing Casil. In either case, it killed almost everyone, including, we must assume, the Emperor and his heirs. But how it got to Casil is not known to us, although some writings suggest it came with traders from countries even further east. And why it disappeared? That I do not know, although perhaps it has something to do with the cold. For while there were deaths, in Linrathe and in the Empire—and more in the Empire than in Linrathe—north and east of the Durrains only a comparative few died."

I thought about something she had said. "Deaths in the Empire, and Linrathe, but not further north?"

She shook her head. "No. Or if there were, they were negligible. That is why the Marai rebuilt the Sterre, to keep us out, to keep the fever from their lands. It is also why they have never travelled south to your lands, because, as I said, the fever was worse there than it was here in Linrathe. Did Perras tell you of their prophecy? They were to explore to the west, to find there a land of grapevines and honey and mild weather. They believe they were spared from the fever to fulfill that prophecy, but only if they never go east or south?" I nodded. "So," she went on, "even though they are great sea and river-farers, they have not ventured south or east, but only west, for all these years."

"So, no one knows," I said, after a minute or two of contemplation, "what might be left now, over the mountains?"

"None who have travelled that way have returned to tell us," she said. That meant, I realized, that people had travelled east, beyond the Durrains. I wondered if any of the Empire's men had done so; I knew of soldiers who had scouted into the mountain range, but beyond it? I opened my mouth to ask Dagney more about these travellers, when I saw, riding rapidly towards us on the path, two mounted men, wearing the colours of Fritjof. I also saw their drawn swords.

I reined Clio to a halt. Beside me, Dagney did the same with her mare. Metal clinked behind me. I turned in the saddle to see two more riders approaching. The same livery, the same drawn weapons. This was an ambush.

How had they known where we were? Thoughts of Gregor's loyalty, and then of Bartolstorp, flitted through my mind. But no: more likely they had simply followed us, waiting until we were in a good spot to be taken easily. No betrayals. I met Dagney's eyes. She shook her head, made a small gesture of resignation with her hands, both almost imperceptible. My secca was on my waist. I pulled my tunic over it.

The men surrounded us, blocking the path from all directions. One spoke to Dagney, in a tongue more guttural than that of Linrathe; the language of the Marai, I assumed. She replied. I caught nothing in the flow of words, but another man spoke again, this time addressing me.

"You will come with us, my ladies. King Fritjof wishes to extend his hospitality to include you both, and we are to escort you at all haste to his crowning." Polite as the words were, I knew we had no choice. Had the boy sent to ride to Sinarrstorp made it, I wondered, or had he been intercepted? If he had reached his destination, then we would be missed this evening. If not...

"We will come," Dagney said, as politely as if the invitation had been real, although I could see a tiny flutter in her cheek. "I am honoured to be invited, as I am sure Lena is too." She looked toward me. I could see the warning in her eyes.

"I am honoured," I said, hoping my voice was steady.

"That is good," the leader said. I thought I recognized him: he had presented Fritjof's letter to Donnalch, yesterday morning. Niáll, I remembered, the Linrathan. Who escorted Donnalch now? Two of the men rode forward, grasping the bridles of our mares and attaching a lead rein to each. All pretense of an invitation accepted vanished. Clio tossed her head, protesting. I soothed her with voice and hands, inwardly matching her protest.

We rode north at pace, stopping occasionally to relieve ourselves, and for food and water for us and the horses. The men were courteous but firm. The sun sank behind the hills, forcing us to ride more slowly, and eventually to stop, in the shelter of boulders beside a small stream. My arm ached steadily, and I could see the fatigue on Dagney's face.

We were allowed to go a distance off to empty our bladders. At the campsite, one man guarded us as the others built a fire and saw to the horses. Niáll walked off beyond the campfire. He returned a few minutes later.

"There are many stars, and no sign of rain," he said. "No tents are needed tonight."

"We have no blankets," Dagney protested. Whatever was in the pot over the flames was beginning to simmer, the scent of broth rising.

"We have blankets for you," he said. "You will be warm enough, beside the fire, if you sleep side-by-side." I knew, from my days and nights on the road and on patrol, that he was right. I wondered where we were, in relation to Sinarrstorp, and whether the *Eirën* would send out men to search for us. Frustration rose. I could not even ask Dagney, because Niáll spoke the language I would have to use. I realized, suddenly, that that was why Dagney had requested we speak my language, to let me know that anything I said would be understood by our captors.

Later we were given bowls of broth, thick with barley and beans, and chunks of a dark bread. Fair trail food, and tasty enough; the hard-cooked eggs and cold mutton of lunch had been hours ago, and the porridge of breakfast even longer. We ate, and then went briefly out into the night again, returning to blankets spread by the fire, with rolled sheepskins for pillows. Dagney helped me pull off my riding boots, and I hers, and we settled onto the ground, wrapping the blankets around us, Dagney closest to the fire at my insistence. Under the cover of the blanket, I moved my secca to where I could easily reach it. We had not been searched for weapons. I guessed they would not think to: we were women. From beyond the firelight an owl called, a long, wavering cry. Fatigue seeped into my bones and my mind. I slept.

For the next three days, we rode north and west at a steady but not gruelling pace. The weather, thankfully, held, although it grew colder as we moved north. Ice edged small ponds in the mornings. The men were generous with the night-time fires, and with food; it was clear we were not to suffer privation.

Behind a boulder on the second morning, crouched to urinate, I whispered to Dagney. "What do they want from us?"

"You, I think," she whispered back. "I cannot think what value I might have to them, so it must be you."

But why? I turned that question around and around in my head as we rode, reaching only one answer: King Fritjof wanted me for what I knew of the Empire. He had no faith in prophecy, and no fear of fever: he planned to invade. I grew more sure as I thought it out. But if that was why he wanted me, why did he want Donnalch? To ask him to join in this attack? And if he said no—then what? Donnalch's life would be forfeit, I thought, and the Marai would sweep down through Linrathe, its army scattered by our truce, and into the Empire.

I murmured this to Dagney, again as we emptied our bladders, the only time we had to exchange thoughts out of hearing of the men. Her face paled, but she whispered calmly, "I had the same thought. I think you are right; it fits with what I have heard of Fritjof. But the Marai will not send all their men through Linrathe to the Wall. Some, yes, but it will be boats, along the coast and up the rivers, that make up their greatest force."

I straightened, hands automatically tying my breeches, tucking the secca into its hidden position along my groin. My mind focused on what Dagney had just said.

"Come, Lady Dagney, Lena!" Niáll shouted, closer than I had thought him. But not close enough to hear, I reassured myself. Whatever orders the men had been given, they must have included giving us no chance to complain of any indignity to our bodies or our privacy. They were scrupulous in leaving us alone. But I said no more.

We had repelled an invasion just two years ago. Could we do it again? But that time we had had six months' warning, six months of preparation and planning. If there were any chance, then word had to get to the Wall. Gregor would bring the story of Marai riding freely south of the Sterre to the Linrathan commanders at the Wall, but would they tell the Empire's Wall commanders? And even if they did, what would those men make of it, knowing nothing of these people, of their command of boats and the sea?

At the camp that night, after we had eaten, Niáll stood over us by the fire. "Play for us, if you would, Lady?" he asked Dagney. I saw the quick look of surprise on her face, followed by acquiescence.

"If you like," she said. "I will need a minute to tune my *ladhar*, though." She fetched the instrument, plucking the strings and adjusting the tension on the pegs until she was satisfied. Then, quietly, she began to play.

After a few minutes of the *ladhar* only, she started to sing, in a language I thought must be that of the Marai. Sometimes the men joined in, sometimes they simply listened. After an hour or so, she began a song I thought I recognized, the preliminary notes she played bringing back the words of the chorus to me: 'A shining river dulled by blood'. Niáll stiffened.

"Not that one," he said sharply. "That's enough music. We should sleep now."

†††††

I could smell the sea long before I could see it. We rode to the top of a ridge, and there before us was the ebb and swell of waves, and the scream of gulls. An archipelago of islands dotted the sea, separated from the mainland by a tidal channel. On the largest of these islands a long, low building dominated.

The tide was going out, revealing with each ebb a causeway linking the mainland with the largest island. An hour, I estimated, before we could ride across safely. My thought was echoed by Niáll. "We wait," he said, "but not long. Dismount."

Four days earlier we had crossed the Sterre. The building on the island reminded me of that boundary wall: not stone, like the southern Wall, but primarily timber and sod, reinforced with stone buttresses. The hall, from what I could see, echoed this construction. It looked new, the wood not yet weathered grey, standing on the highest land on the island. Below it, straggling down to the tideline, were other buildings, workshops and houses, I guessed, all sharing the yellow gleam of new wood.

I swung down off Clio. I could use both arms now, and wore no bandage nor sling. Loosening her girth, I looked over to Niáll.

"I'll have to walk my mare across," I said. "She doesn't like water."

He nodded in acknowledgement. A shout came from over the water. We had been seen. Words were exchanged, with much gesturing. I saw a man running up to the hall. Delivering the news of our arrival, no doubt.

I watched the tide receding, and the red bills of the big black-and-white sea-pies probing for food along the exposed rocks, just as they did at Tirvan. Smaller brown plovers ran on the shingle, picking up things too small to see. Homesickness flowed into me, an almost physical pain. I turned to look along the headland to hide the welling tears. Just south of where we stood, a small jetty nosed out into the sea. Moored to it, listing into the shingle with the retreating tide, were two small rowboats. Somewhere over on the island would be another jetty, and more boats, for crossing when the tide was high. I heard my name, and looked back at the group. Dagney and Niáll were talking.

Dagney left his side and came over to me. "Walk a bit along the shingle with me," she said. "There are things you need to know, before we cross, and Niáll feels I should tell you now, and beyond the hearing of the other men."

I frowned. I handed Clio's reins to one of the escort and followed Dagney. What could the men not hear? At the jetty, she stopped. "Here will do," she said.

"What is it you need to tell me?"

"Wherever it is Fritjof has been for the last two years, he has brought back customs new to the Marai, ones that concern us. He houses his women in a separate hall now, and rarely, and only at his command, are they allowed into the men's presence, to dine, or in my case, to entertain. Your clothes will be taken: women are forbidden breeches, so if you can find a way to hide your secca, do it, although I think our belongings will be searched. And if it is your time to bleed, Lena, you may not come into the presence of the men at all, but stay in the women's hall."

What did it matter if I bled or not? But Dagney was not done. "If Fritjof were to take an interest in you," she hesitated, "he is giving women no choice, if he decides he wants them."

"But I am not a Marai woman!"

"True. That may work in your favour. And the *Teannasach* is pledged to your safety, for whatever that is worth here. But you needed to know."

I saw her point. I wondered if our captors' scrupulous respect of our privacy and our bodies on the ride here meant that I was already seen as belonging to soon-to-be-king Fritjof. The thought made me shudder. I swallowed. "Is there anything else?"

"Yes." Her voice dropped to a whisper. "We are still in Sorham. Fritjof is choosing to be crowned in lands ceded to Linrathe in exchange for tribute long years past. He is making a statement that all can understand. And perhaps equally as frightening, no one from Sorham has told the *Teannasach* that he has built a hall here." So perhaps my earlier fears of treachery were not far off, I thought. Dagney continued, her voice at a natural pitch again. "Follow my lead in all things; I doubt they will separate us, as they will need me to translate for you. Now come, Niáll is signalling. It's time to cross."

I led Clio across without incident, the occasional wave lapping over the cobbled causeway. Probably I could have ridden, but I wasn't willing to take the chance. Niáll rode ahead of us, the other men following Dagney and myself. On the island shore I remounted, riding at a walk to the open area at one end of the hall.

A tall man waited for us, flanked by two guards. He towered over them both by at least a head, his pale hair tied back from his bearded face. We dismounted. Niáll said something; the tall man made a gesture of acknowledgement. His eyes travelled to Dagney.

"*Scáeli* Dagney, *Härskaran*," Niáll said. Dagney bent her knee, her eyes down. So this was Fritjof. He had cold eyes.

"*En mathúyr?*" Fritjof said. "*Mer heithra, scáeli.*[1]" He said something else, and Dagney stood. Fritjof's gaze turned to me. I saw his eyes narrow. He glanced at Niáll.

"Lena," he explained, "*Gistel te Teannasach, fo handa marren, Härskaran.*[2]"

I inclined my head, but did nothing more. Fritjof frowned. He snapped an order, jerking his head to the left.

"*Härskaran,*" Niáll replied. "Come with me," he said. "I will take you to the women's hall. There you can wash, and proper clothes will be found for you. Take your saddlebags, but leave your horses."

---

[1] "A musician? I am honoured, bard."

[2] "Hostage to the *Teannasach*, from the south, King."

CHAPTER ELEVEN

THE WOMEN'S HALL STOOD DOWN THE HILLSIDE, in a flat area sheltered by cliffs on two sides. At a doorway Niáll halted. He knocked and called out, but did not open the door. A moment later it swung open, and a girl of perhaps twelve looked out at us. She gasped when she saw Dagney and I, and ran back in, calling.

A woman, perhaps in her thirties, came to the door, dressed in a rich embroidered tunic and skirt. She looked at us both, and then at Niáll, questioningly. I caught our names in the exchange, and I thought the word *Härskaran*. Dagney added something, and the woman beckoned us into the hall.

"Just follow my lead," Dagney said to me. "They will make us welcome here, and I have told them you do not speak the language, so they will not expect you to understand them. I will translate."

We were shown to seats on a bench covered with furs, and wooden cups filled with a hot tea brought to us. The women crowded around while Dagney and the headwoman, as I thought of her, spoke. I sipped the tea, looking around.

One long room made up the central portion of the hall, its roof supported by tall pillars and arches of wood, not dissimilar in structure to the meeting hall in Tirvan, although that had eight sides, whereas this was a rectangular building. Beyond the pillars, where the roof dropped lower to meet the walls, the space had been partitioned, and divided from the hall by curtains, mostly of woven wool, although I saw one or two that were fur. Private spaces. Underfoot, the floor was of wide boards, covered with woven rugs. Hearths burned along the central space, warming and lighting the hall.

"Lena," Dagney said, putting an end to my observations, "this is Rothny, wife to Fritjof and the highest-ranking woman of the Marai. I have explained who you are, and why you are with us. Be respectful, be friendly, but do not trust too much." A smile never left her face as she spoke. "Greet Rothny, if you will; the words are *'Mer heithra, Fräskaran Rothny'*."[3]

I turned to face Rothny. Inclining my head as I had for Fritjof, I repeated the words as best I could. Rothny smiled. "*Glaéder min halla.*"[4]

Dagney stood. "Come now," she said to me. "The women have prepared baths for us, and fresh clothes, and I for one will welcome both." I followed her again. Behind one of the woven curtains two baths, looking like oval half-barrels, waited, steaming slightly. I put my saddlebag down, waiting to see what Dagney did. The women who had led us to the baths left the space, pulling

---

[3] "I am honoured, Queen Rothny."

[4] "Welcome to my hall."

the curtain closed, and in the dim light we undressed and climbed into the baths.

The water's heat penetrated my limbs, easing aches I had grown accustomed to on the ride. I heard Dagney sigh with relief. We soaked for some time without speaking. I found soap on a small shelf near my head and washed, submersing myself completely to rinse off, and to wash my hair. Two women slipped in, each with a bucket of steaming water to add to the baths, disappeared again, and returned with clothes and towels. I lay in the water until it began to cool, then stepped out, reaching for the towel that had been left on a small stool, folded on top of the clothes.

"What happens now?" I said to Dagney, who was also drying herself.

"We go to the hall to eat the mid-day meal with the men; the *Härskaran*—Fritjof—has asked for us. The *Fräskaran* will accompany us," she answered, the last muffled as she pulled a tunic over her head. I picked up the clothes left for me from the stool. A woollen tunic, and a skirt of the same fabric. I dressed. The skirt, falling nearly to my ankles, felt confining, for all it was loose enough.

I looked around for my saddlebag, which held my light shoes. I could not see it, nor the clothes I had so recently taken off. "Where are our things?" I asked.

"Probably at our sleeping quarters," Dagney said. "Did you hide your secca?"

"It's in the boot sheath," I answered. "But that won't fool a determined searcher for long."

"I don't think the *Fräskaran's* women will be looking for a weapon," Dagney said. "Unless Niáll has let it be known you may be armed, and there is no reason he would know that; he has been serving Fritjof since before Leste attempted its invasion of your country. So, hope that Rothny's serving women don't decide to clean your riding boots." She ran a bone comb through her hair, wincing at a tangle.

The curtain slid back, and one of the serving women beckoned to us. We followed her along the central space to another curtain. The woman pulled it back, showing us two beds with a table between them. The contents of our saddlebags had been neatly arranged on shelves over the beds. My boots and my slippers stood at the end of the left-hand bed, Dagney's at the right.

"*Takkë*," Dagney said. She sat on her bed, combing her hair dry. The serving woman spoke, gesturing at the comb; Dagney shook her head. "*Takkë*," she said again, this time with clear dismissal in her voice. I had no trouble understanding that exchange, I thought.

"I should have insisted you learn the language of the Marai," she said. "At least you'd have a few words. *Takkë* is thank you; *vaëre*, please. Have you looked at your boots?" Her tone remained conversational.

I bent to check the hidden sheath. My secca remained in place. "Should I leave it there?"

She shook her head. "No. Somewhere safer, if you can think of a place."

I looked around the room, and then at the items on the shelves. A small bundle caught my eye, beside my journal and Colm's history. "Dagney," I asked, "what is the custom here, for blood cloths? Would I wash them myself?"

She followed my eyes. "A good thought," she said. "Yes, custom here too says each woman washes her own, unless she is very ill; even the *Fräskaran* would not usually ask that of her serving women. No one will touch them. I am a bit surprised they were even unpacked, but I suppose they had orders to completely empty the saddlebags, and they are in a case."

"Good." I untied the soft leather case, then wrapped my secca in the stained cloths it held. Once the package was returned to the shelves I slipped my feet into my indoor slippers. The skirt caught at them, irritating me. I couldn't remember the last time I had worn skirts. At the ceremony binding me to my apprenticeship? I wondered. It seemed unlikely.

I heard soft footsteps approaching. A question, in Rothny's clear voice. "*Ja*," Dagney said, tying back her hair. A hand moved the curtain aside. "Time to eat," Dagney said to me, standing. The *Fräskaran* waited for us, in the same embroidered tunic as earlier, but now with bracelets on both arms and several rings on her fingers. Braids encircled her head like a crown. She gestured. "*Vaëre*." As we moved toward the centre of the hall, she held up a hand. "*Din ladhar, scáeli*," she said, "*vaëre*." Regardless of the 'please', I didn't think this was a request. Dagney nodded, and retrieved her instrument.

Fritjof's hall rang with voices as we entered. As my eyes adjusted to the gloom, I saw a long table set crossways to the length of the room, raised on a wooden platform about two-thirds of the distance down the hall. Fritjof sat in a tall chair, facing the lower tables and benches, an empty chair to his right. Donnalch sat to his left. His face lit when he saw us, but as I met his eyes across the space I saw warning in them, after the relief.

I could not see Cillian, nor Ardan. We walked toward the high table; nearly at the platform, Rothny stopped, pointing at two empty spots on the bench. "*Takkë, Fräskaran*," Dagney said. I echoed the '*takkë*' and slid into the spot furthest from the high table, allowing Dagney the end spot; she would have to stand to play at some point. Rothny walked on, mounting the platform to take the chair beside her husband.

The hall had fallen silent as we—or rather the *Fräskaran*—approached the high table. Fritjof stood as his wife joined him, remaining standing after she had taken her chair. He waited a moment, then began to speak. His words sounded to me precise, brooking no argument or dissension. I felt my skin prickle. Dagney turned to me.

"He says," she murmured, "that now all witnesses he required are present— he means us, or at least you, by that—then his coronation can proceed, tomorrow. And then he bade us to eat, and enjoy ourselves."

Servers began to bring platters of meat and bread to the tables. "Who are the other men at the high table?" I whispered to Dagney.

"Two are *Härren* of Sorham, landholders and leaders; the others I do not know. Marai, I presume. Fritjof's brother, Åsmund, is not among them. I wonder what that means."

The man across from us looked up, catching Åsmund's name. He frowned.

Dagney, seeing his reaction, said a few words to him. He nodded, and made a gesture of dismissal with his hand.

"I told him I was only explaining Fritjof's lineage to you," Dagney murmured. "There is tension here, about the brother."

The server reached between us to place a platter on the table. When I looked up, he handed me a short knife, set into a wooden handle, a tool for cutting meat. I realized there were no other implements on the table, save for an intricately carved wooden spoon at each place. "*Takkë*," I said, glancing at Dagney.

"Every Marai carries his or her own table knife," she explained. "These are ours to keep, and to bring to each meal. They are used by women to cut spun wool, and small hides, to skin rabbits and gut fish, and whenever a small blade is needed. There is a pocket in your sleeve—see?—to carry it. Use it, and not the pockets in the skirt; otherwise you will cut yourself. Now, Fritjof's table has been served, so we may eat."

She reached over to spear a piece of meat from the platter, transferring it to her own plate and reaching for bread. A dish of stewed berries sat beside the platter. Dagney spooned it liberally over the mutton. I followed suit. The berry sauce was tangy, almost astringent, but it balanced the strong, salty flavour of the sheep's flesh.

Ale splashed into the earthenware beaker above my plate. At the parallel table, I saw the servers moving along the rows of men, pouring the drink. One caught my eye: Cillian. I schooled my face to impassivity, barely moving my head. He poured wine for Niáll, who barked something at him. Cillian nodded. Putting down his jug, he went away, returning in a minute with a bowl. I saw Niáll spoon sauce over his meat.

Cillian moved along the table, not looking at me. I concentrated on my food. After the mutton and bread a sweeter bread, rich with dried fruit, was brought. For the lower tables, at least, that was the end of the meal.

I looked around the room, catching several people staring at me. Well, I thought, I am a stranger, and hair is short, not like these women's. I sipped the last of my ale, moving my gaze to the head table. Donnalch looked our way occasionally, but when his eyes caught mine they did not linger; he watched the room constantly, I noted. The others paid us no attention at all.

A server bent to speak to Dagney. She nodded, standing, picking up her *ladhar*. "I must play," she said to me. A stool had been placed for her on the platform; she sat on it, tuning her instrument. The servers brought more ale. Benches scraped as men pushed back from the tables, making themselves comfortable.

Niáll took Dagney's place beside me. "I am here to translate, should it be needed," he explained. I nodded. Dagney began to sing, a melody I had heard played before. After a moment, I leaned towards Niáll. "What song is this?" I asked.

"In your tongue," he said, "something like 'Sisters Dark and Light'."

"*Meas*," I answered, thinking about what Dagney had said about this song.

Was she taking a chance playing it, sending a message? Or was it just a familiar song to please the crowd?

Dagney played three songs. Niáll told me the names of each, but said nothing else. Occasionally, from the corner of my eye, I glimpsed Cillian clearing tables and pouring ale, but he stayed away from our table. I did not look at him. During the last song, Niáll shifted in his seat as if he were uncomfortable, distracting me. Glancing at him, I saw beads of sweat on his face. Suddenly he got up, walking rapidly out of the hall. Too much ale, I decided.

When Dagney finished her last song, to much stamping and cheering, Fritjof stood. Whatever he said resulted in more stamping and cheering. He turned on the dais and bowed to Rothny, extending a hand to help her rise. I watched as she smiled at the other men at the high table before descending. Were we to go with her? I looked at Dagney; 'stay there', she gestured. I waited. After a moment, she beckoned to me. I slid along the bench, inwardly cursing my skirts, and stood. A tug on my sleeve made me turn. The man who had been sitting on my far side held my eating knife out to me. "*Takkë*," I said, smiling at him. I found the sleeve-sheath, and slid it in.

I climbed onto the platform. Donnalch stood. "Lena," he said, "I am glad to see you well; your arm is better?" His voice was formal.

"*Teannasach*," I replied. "It is much better, thank you."

"I am glad to hear it," he said. "King Fritjof wishes to speak to you, to learn more about the Empire. I will translate, and my clerk will transcribe, so that there is a record."

His clerk? That had to be Cillian. Fritjof, I guessed, would have little regard for those whose work was to read and write, except to use them as needed. "Of course."

We followed Fritjof towards the back of the hall, partitioned off with walls of wood to make a private room. Inside, a fire took the chill off the room, and several chairs faced the hearth. Sheepskins lay in front of each chair. Unshuttered windows set in the end wall let light into the room, far more comfortable than anything I had yet seen in the women's hall.

Cillian, summoned from his serving duties, caught up with us just as we entered the room. The door shut behind us. Fritjof gestured us to the chairs, choosing one closest to the fire for himself. Donnalch sat opposite to him; Dagney and I in-between. Cillian did not sit, but prepared to write at a tall desk near the windows.

Fritjof asked a question. Dagney shook her head, as did Cillian. Dagney turned to me. "Lena, where is Niáll? He came to translate for you, when I was singing."

"He left in a hurry," I said. "I thought perhaps he felt sick, too much ale? He did not look well." She translated this for Fritjof, who scowled. He had wanted him here, I thought, to verify that what I said was correctly translated.

Fritjof began to speak. Donnalch explained rather than translated his first sentences, welcoming me to his lands and his coronation, the first person of the Empire to have witnessed this. I saw a small muscle twitch beside Donnalch's eye when he spoke the words 'his lands'. Then the questioning began.

"How large is the Empire?"

"About the size of Sorham," I answered, "if my understanding of that is correct." Fritjof nodded when this was relayed to him. Had he known that, and was only testing me?

"How many boats does the Emperor command? How big are they?"

"I do not know the answer to the first question," I said. Donnalch relayed this. Fritjof frowned. "As to how large—maybe fifteen paces long?" I said, purposely underestimating, looking at Donnalch as I did. He moved his head slightly, a tiny negative gesture. "No, wait," I said, as if I had reconsidered, "maybe longer, maybe twenty, twenty-five paces. Thirty men, and their officers." I had been warned; I was to speak the truth. Or, I thought, at least I should be truthful, if Donnalch will know if I'm not.

The questioning continued. I was asked about rivers, about harbours, about towns and roads. I pleaded ignorance when I could, and carefully minimised what I said about Casilla. I was not asked about the Wall; Fritjof had other sources for that information. Nor, I noted, was I asked about the women's villages, other than to confirm that was how we lived.

I had no doubt that Fritjof planned an invasion. I was also certain he had reclaimed Sorham for Varsland, and that Donnalch was a guest in name only.

Finally, Fritjof leaned back in his chair with a grunt. He looked over at Cillian, who still wrote. When Cillian put down his pen, Fritjof said something, clearly a command. Cillian walked over to a sideboard to pour wine for us all.

I took the cup. I was thirsty from all the talking. As Cillian handed it to me, he murmured something: 'tonight', I thought. "*Meas*," I replied, hoping he would know I had heard him.

Dagney and Donnalch began to talk, in the language of the Marai. Fritjof did not react, but sipped his wine, listening, his eyes sometimes straying to me. Suddenly, Dagney switched languages. "And I bring you greetings, *Teannasach*, from Einar and Bartol, and also from Ingold; he asked to be remembered."

"*Marái'sta!*" Fritjof barked. Dagney turned to him and bowed, speaking words in a contrite tone. He stared at her, then turned again to Cillian, who repeated the words in Fritjof's language, or so I guessed: I could only pick out the names. Was she telling him where we had been, or planned to go? Why had she spoken so that I could understand?

After another minute of scrutiny Fritjof dismissed us. I put down my wine cup, standing. In one swift movement, Fritjof stood beside me. He took my chin in his hand, firmly, as I instinctively pulled away. He tilted my head upward, studying my face. After the first glance, I kept my eyes downcast. I felt his eyes travel up and down my body, his hand moving from my face to my arm. I willed myself not to flinch. "Hm," he grunted. He let me go.

Trying not to tremble, I followed Dagney out of the room and the hall. The sun shone. I blinked, adjusting my eyes. "Are you all right?" she asked.

I took a deep breath. "Yes," I said. "I think so." *Was I?* I had never been looked at like that in my life, assessed as if I were a pig at market. "The last time," I said to Dagney, "a man attempted to make me pay attention to him against my will, I punched him until he was sick."

She raised her eyebrows. "Good for you. But punching Fritjof might not be diplomatic."

I stared at her for a moment. Her mouth quirked. I started to laugh. I covered my mouth with my hands, knowing the laughter was a release of tension, not wanting to draw attention to myself. I focused on what I had sensed in the room.

"Dagney, is the *Teannasach* a prisoner?"

She looked around. We were alone. "I think so. Cillian, if he can keep calm, and not go off hot-headed, should be safe. Fritjof thinks he is just a clerk. As for Arden—" She shook her head. "I am afraid of what Fritjof is planning for Donnalch."

I thought about what she had said to the *Teannasach*. "Who is Ingold?" I asked. "Was it his *torp* we were to visit, after Sinarrstorp?"

She smiled. "No, although it is not an uncommon name, and there is an Ingoldstorp, much further east. Ingold—or Ingjald, to give it its proper pronunciation—is a character in a *danta*, a king who invites other kings to a feast in his new hall, and then, as they sleep that night, burns it down, killing them all."

I had heard this before somewhere. "A warning, then."

"A warning," she agreed, beginning to walk towards the women's hall. "Donnalch would know which *torps* I could reasonably visit, and Ingoldstorp is not one of them. And he knows the *danta* well."

We returned to the women's hall, to spend the afternoon outdoors, on benches along the western face of the building, overlooking the sea. The Marai women spun wool, their drop spindles in constant motion. They had offered me a spindle, but I did not know how to spin, a fact which led to much chatter. Dagney played her *ladhar*, singing occasionally, but mostly allowing the notes of the melodies to weave among the women's talk. A few women rocked cradles with one foot, and small children played around the benches. Seabirds circled and cried, wheeling and gliding in constant motion.

I wondered where Clio was, and if I would be allowed to see her. I wondered if Ardan were safe, if any of us were. I played clapping games with the children, and gave in to encouragement to use a spindle, resulting in uneven, lumpy yarn and much laughter; even the little girls could spin better than I. The waves swelled and retreated. I watched the flow and eddies, how the rocks were exposed and covered, where the weed grew thickest, thinking about how to fish these waters, how to navigate them, my years of training guiding my thoughts. It was something to do.

CHAPTER TWELVE

BEFORE WE WENT BACK TO THE HALL for dinner that night, one of the women brought me two silver bracelets, and a pendant of a clear, honey-coloured stone. She touched my hair, making a 'tsk' sound, but there was nothing to be done with it. Dagney refused bracelets, explaining, I thought, from her gestures, that she could not play the *ladhar* with them on, but accepted an enamelled comb for her hair, and a brooch.

"I will not sit with you tonight," she told me as we waited for the rest of the women, "I am directed to play during the meal." For this occasion, several of the other women would be joining us in the hall. They had been busy dressing hair and comparing jewellery for the last hour. I remembered what Dagney had said: that here a woman's status came, usually, from her husband. Whose wives were these, to be invited tonight? Or did they all 'belong' to Fritjof?

"Dagney," I said, quietly, "are these women accepting of this new way of life? Surely they find it restrictive, if they used to live and work with their men?"

"I do not know," she replied. "I have not heard any complaints: the *Fräskaran* seems to accept it, and the others take their cue from her. But I wonder where his brother's wife is, and her women: I fear for them."

"You think they are dead?"

"Or perhaps held captive elsewhere. In either case, it appears to be enough to keep these women silent, even if they dislike the changes in their freedom."

Her answer left me unsatisfied. I tried to imagine Huld in this setting. Could she submit to this isolation, this reduction in her freedom, her life? Perhaps, I thought, when the alternative is death. But I thought too that she would find a way to resist.

The hall glowed with lantern light; I recognized the odour of burning whale oil. Candles gave further light to the head table. I followed the other women to a table near the side of the hall, but not too far from the head table. As we sat, Cillian slipped into the seat beside me.

"I am here as your translator," he said. "There will be speeches tonight."

"Niáll is still unwell?"

"He should be," he said, his voice conversational. "I put enough holly berries in his sauce to make him sick for several days. The other men who shared that bowl are also ill, but not as severely. He took most of the holly, as I intended. It shouldn't kill him, but he won't be going far from the latrines for a day or so."

I smothered a laugh. "That was well done," I said. I noticed a glance or two towards us.

"We shouldn't talk," Cillian said. "When I translate, I will add a sentence, or two, to the end of each translation. If you must respond, make it sound like a question; both languages use an upward inflection for questions, so those around us will think you are asking only for explanation. Now, I am going to make some signs of worship, as if we had been praying. Repeat them after me."

He touched his forehead, lips, and breast. I did the same. I wondered whose god this honoured.

A few minutes later we all rose, as Fritjof and Rothny entered to make their way to the high table. Both, tonight, wore robes of fur, Fritjof's trimmed with the pelts of winter weasels, pure white except for the black-tipped tails; Rothny's with the feathers of the snow owl, white with black barring. Behind them came a boy of fourteen or fifteen—Fritjof's son?—and then the same men, the Sorham *Härren*, who had sat with them at the mid-day meal, and finally by Donnalch. Two guards followed the procession. When all were seated, they took their places, each at one end of the dais.

Fritjof stood again, gesturing to us to stay seated. He spoke briefly, sounding cheerful and relaxed.

Cillian translated. "Enjoy the meal. Drink heartily. *Did you note how he is treating our leader?*"

I smiled and nodded. Fritjof had given the Sorham *Härren*, mere landholders, precedence over the *Teannasach* of Linrathe. It was a subtle but clear insult, and, I thought, a message: he is sure of Sorham, or at least where these men hold sway.

The meal was impressive, especially for early spring. The high table ate fish, followed by platters of small birds—the shore plovers, I guessed—and then a haunch of venison. The lower tables fared nearly as well. We too ate fish, and then deep pies made from the lesser meats and organs of the deer, rich with gravy. Where the head table had wine, we had ale, and we were given only dried fruits to nibble on after the pies, but it was by far the best meal I had eaten in a very long time.

When the platters had been cleared and the cups refilled, Fritjof stood again. Benches scraped as we stood for the *Härskaran*. Fritjof raised his glass and shouted a toast. The room shouted back.

"To the Marai kingdom restored," Cillian said. "*He is claiming this land.*"

I watched the two *Härren*. Their pleasure in toasting Fritjof looked real to me. What will Sorley think? I wondered, remembering him telling me that he would be coming home soon, to this province, to learn to be the head of his holding. Was either of these two men his father? I slid my eyes to Donnalch. He held his cup high, his face impassive.

At a word and gesture from Fritjof, we sat. Fritjof began to speak.

"Tomorrow, I will be crowned," Cillian translated. "*He has killed his brother, and many of those loyal to his brother. A new day dawns, one that will see the Marai returned to their rightful place as lords of sea and land, not just in the north, but south as well. Our leader is a prisoner, a guest in name only, and his guard is dead.*" The room had begun to murmur at Fritjof's mention of the south.

He held up a hand for silence. Cillian followed his words in a quiet undertone. "Yes, the south. We know the stories are no more than old wives' tales and meaningless prophecies. We sailed west for many years, many generations, and found nothing, until only I had the courage to sail east. Rich lands lie close at hand. *I am going to plead illness tomorrow morning, and escape while all eyes are on the crowning."*

"I will come with you?" I said, remembering to make my statement sound like a question. "Did he say he sailed east?"

"Linrathe we have, or at least we have their leader, and without him they will turn from the fight easily," Cillian translated, his eyes on Fritjof. *"He did, although I do not know what he means by that. And I will be better alone."*

"Not necessarily."

He frowned. "He is speaking of you," he whispered. "Listen. And for the lands south of Linrathe, south of the Wall, lands we know only from stories, I will hold as hostage the woman Lena, sent to Linrathe from the southern Empire to ensure the peace between them. More than hostage; on his birthday, when he becomes adult, I will give her to my son Leik as his wife."

What? Heads turned to look at me. I looked up at Fritjof, hatred and fear welling. I glanced once at Donnalch, whose eyes told me nothing. Had he agreed to this? I looked at Leik. He gazed back, interest on his face. Then, slowly, I turned my gaze back to Fritjof, and bowed my head. Let him think I accepted it. "When is the boy's birthday?" I whispered to Cillian.

"In a few days," he said. Fritjof was speaking again. Cillian translated, the explosion of cheers and shouting in the room almost obscuring the last sentences. "Tomorrow I am crowned. Three days after that, Leik reaches his manhood. We will celebrate that, and give him time to enjoy his bride, and then we will take to our boats and sail south, Marai once again, masters of the sea, conquerors. Now, bards, music! *I will take a rowboat when all eyes are on the crowning, and cross to the mainland. I will try to steal a horse somewhere."* The music began, a fast, bright tune.

"Steal a fishing boat from a harbour. You can sail faster than riding," I said.

"I can't sail a boat."

"Then you need me; I can. I will find a way to stay back. And I will not be that boy's wife." Cillian said nothing. I glanced at him, to see him staring at Donnalch, indecision on his face.

"If you are at the jetty soon after the crowning begins, then, yes," he said finally. "But I will not wait."

"I will be there." But how?

After that, the night was music and drinking. The women talked, ignoring me. Men drank and gamed. A server bent to speak to Cillian. "I am summoned," he said to me. "I must go." I watched him leave the hall. Who had asked for him? Why? A thread of fear tightened around my thoughts.

One of the musicians—a man—stood, calling something. The room quietened. The three musicians, Dagney among them, I knew, although I could not see her—were seated at the far side of the high table. This man had stepped up onto the dais to make himself heard. Once the room was close to silent, he began to sing.

The tune rollicked, and the audience sang along. At the end of every verse, they thumped the tables and drank. A drinking song. We had those, too. I could not sing the words, but I joined in the drinking, although I swallowed very little. I wanted to look as if I were trying to fit in. But sips of ale and table-thumping did not keep the fear at bay. To distract myself, I thought about what Fritjof had said. He had sailed east, and returned to tell his tale. No fever had ravaged his men, and he had found a people whose customs he liked enough to copy. What did this mean?

At the end of the song, men left the room singly and in pairs, a few from each table. One of the women tapped me on the shoulder. I looked around. She stood beside me. She cocked her head, and mimed squatting slightly, then pointed at me. "*Ja*," I answered. I followed her out into the night.

Our bladders relieved, I lingered, looking up at the stars and the sliver of the moon, the cool breeze off the sea welcome. No hint of poor weather on its way, although I knew as well as any coastal dweller how quickly that could change. There might be fog in the morning, I thought; the breeze was slight, and dying.

My companion tugged on my arm. I followed her again, back into the light and heat and noise of the hall. When we got back to our table, Leik sat on the bench, talking to the other women. He stood at our arrival, politely gesturing for me to sit. I did my best to smile at him, and took my place. He sat beside me, offering me a cup of wine.

He looked more like Rothny than Fritjof, except for his eyes. Those were Fritjof's, and they looked at me the same way, assessing, the undercurrent of desire evident in the heaviness of his eyelids and the set of his lips. Manhood might be official in three days, I thought, but he had experience of women. He took my hand, running a finger over my wrist and along the vein. I pulled my hand back, unthinking. He frowned, and grabbed it, holding it tightly. I forced a smile, and dropped my eyes, playing the shy maiden, anger coursing along every nerve of my body.

Leik laughed, and stood. He put his fingers under my chin, forcing my head up. I kept my eyes down. He ran a finger along my neck, to where the tunic began. He said something, holding up three fingers. Three days, he was telling me. I nodded. "*Ja*," I whispered.

He walked away. The other women chattered at me. I drank the wine, willing the trembling to stop. I wanted to talk to Dagney. I wanted to not be here at all. I had agreed to be hostage to the Empire's truce, but this had gone beyond what I thought was expected of me. I must escape.

The men were getting louder, the laughter more raucous. At the tables where dice were thrown, tempers flared. I could feel sweat between my breasts and on the nape of my neck. On the far side of the hall, a man stood suddenly, shouting, clearing the table in front of him with one sweep of his arm. The women beside me said something, my earlier companion grasping my arm. When I looked at her, she swept her head towards the doors. Time to leave.

No one blocked our departure, or bothered us on the path back to the women's hall. No one took any notice of us at all, I thought, although men were coming and going from the feast. The breeze had dropped, the still air cool on my skin. Wisps of mist or low cloud floated over the stars. I could hear the lap of waves on the shore, and the faint bump of a boat against a jetty. Just as we reached the hall, I took a last look out across the water, along the mainland. A light flickered, very faintly, somewhere south along the coast. A house? On the coast like that, they were likely to be fisher-folk.

Inside the women's hall the fire was banked and glowing. Women who had not attended the feast sat around it, drinking tea. When we came in, they jumped up, clearly asking questions. Someone pointed me towards the fire, handing me a mug. I sat, glad of the tea, but as I sipped it, fatigue dragged through me. The women chattered. I noticed eyes turning my way. Finishing the drink, I stood, pointing towards my sleeping chamber and miming sleep. Heads nodded; one word—probably good night, or the equivalent—was repeated. "*Takkë,*" I said, "*takkë.*"

They are talking about me and my 'betrothal' to Leik, I thought as I undressed in the small space, lit by one candle. If women here take their status from their husbands, then I will be more important than any of them but Rothny. They won't like that.

And perhaps no one would be upset if I couldn't attend the coronation. But how to get out of it? My eyes roamed around my sleeping area. A glimmer of an idea came to me. I would sleep on it, I thought, and see if it still seemed a good idea in the morning.

Dagney came in, very late, barely disturbing me. Just before dawn, the seabirds already calling, I opened my eyes, wide awake. I lay, listening, hearing the first stirrings of other people. There were fires to tend, food to prepare, and much else to do, on this momentous day.

When the voices in the hall grew louder and more numerous, I got up. I went out to the latrines, came back in, accepted a mug of tea. Dagney yawned her way into the room, cupping both hands around her mug as if in need of the warmth. Her face sagged with tiredness.

"Did you hear what the king said last night?" I asked, as soon as I could. "About sailing east?"

"I did," she said. "If he speaks the truth, it changes so much."

"Do you doubt him?"

She shook her head. "Not really. But who are the people he found? Will they follow him here, to be yet another threat, either from disease or by arms? What does it mean, for us, for the Marai, for your Empire? There is no one I can ask," she finished, and then brightened slightly, "unless I couch it in terms of *danta*, of songs—maybe that would work, if they thought my interest was only that of the *scáeli*, wanting to write a song in honour of the voyage. Perhaps I will mention it to Fritjof later."

"Do you play again today?" I asked.

"Yes," she said. "Lena, I must tell you this: I spoke to our leader briefly last night; we had only a minute. He wants you to know he did not betray your presence in our lands to Fritjof purposely; he and Ardan were overheard, when they thought themselves alone and free to speak. A mistake, and one he regrets deeply."

"Had he any words of advice?"

She shook her head. "None. Or perhaps no time to speak them; Fritjof called him away."

"And Ardan is dead," I said. She looked startled. "Cillian told me."

She closed her eyes. "Dear gods," she said.

"And you are caught in this too," I pointed out. She made a gesture of negation.

"I may have been anyhow," she said. "Fritjof knows me as a bard, a *scáeli*, and might well have demanded my presence here." I thought she was making excuses, but I let it go; I couldn't carry that guilt right now. I needed to be focused.

"What will you do?" she murmured.

"Better you don't know," I answered. She held my gaze a moment, then nodded slightly and turned away to pour more tea.

"By tradition," she said, "there is no food served until after the crowning. And do not drink too much: the ceremony is long, and no one can leave. I am glad it is spring, and the sun not too hot."

"Where is the crowning?" I asked, keeping my voice casual.

"On the highest point of the island. Fritjof will face north, towards the lands of the Marai; the witnesses—which will be everyone on the island—also face north. During the ceremony, we see only his back. The priest who crowns him is the only one to see his face until the crown is on his head. Only then will he turn to greet his people."

"Thank you." Information I needed; the chance of me being seen slipping away towards the mainland, to the east, were negligible, if I kept to the cliffside. I took my mug to the table, then stopped, frowning slightly. I rubbed my lower belly. The girl serving the tea held up the mug, asking a question. I shook my head. "*Na, takkë.*"

We dressed and donned ornaments, more than for last night's feast. I, Dagney explained, was to walk just behind Rothny, as befitted my status as Leik's betrothed. She and I, and her serving girls, would come last, after everyone else had gone to the ritual grounds.

I slipped the eating-knife into its pocket in my sleeve. We would go from the ritual to yet another meal, a simple one of smoked fish and bread, so that the kitchen-folk could be at the crowning. The feast tonight would make up for it, Dagney assured me. Then it was time for her to go, to play as the people gathered. She touched my arm, gently, and left.

I sat, waiting. Women began to leave in groups. When only a few remained, I slipped out to the latrines. Very carefully, I drew the long skirt of my gown up, and with my woman's knife I made a small and shallow cut, high on my thigh, wincing at the pain. I hoped I had judged the cut right: deep enough to bleed, but not too quickly. I wiped the knife, returning it to its pocket.

When I returned to the hall Rothny stood alone, except for her two servants. She gestured to me; we needed to go. I nodded, and followed her out of the hall.

We walked up the path, past the feasting hall, climbing towards the broad summit of the island. When we about half-way, I stopped, clutching my belly, moaning. Rothny frowned. I looked up at her, trying to look regretful. I pulled up my skirt just enough for her to see the blood trickling down my leg.

She said something, sharp and angry, shaking her head. She turned to the youngest servant, giving orders; the girl looked stunned, bursting into tears. Rothny gave her a push, looking at me, pointing back to the women's hall. The message was clear. The girl was to accompany me back to the women's hall, missing the coronation. She was small, and young, no match for my skills. And by sheerest luck, no other woman was at her bleeding time, or if she was, she was watching the crowning from some hidden place on the island. The hall was empty. I could make my escape.

The girl grabbed my arm, pulling me along the path back to the women's hall. I let it happen, allowing her to think she was in charge. At the hall, she shoved me towards my sleeping chamber. I took one stumbling step forward, then pivoted, keeping my body crouched, and lunged upwards at her, punching her in the stomach. She gasped, doubling over, but she had no air in her lungs with which to scream. I had her on the ground, my hand over her mouth, before she could take a breath.

She stared up at me with frightened eyes. I pulled a strip of cloth from the pocket of my skirt, a strip cut from my lighter riding tunic early this morning, and gagged her. Then I rolled her over, and with more cloth strips I tied her hands and feet. I dragged her into the sleeping chamber, put her on the bed, and tied her to it. She would come to no harm.

I felt her eyes on me as I stripped off the skirt and pulled on my riding breeches and boots. I reached up to the shelf for my few things: the wrapped blood cloths, my comb, my books. The books were gone. When had I seen them last? There was no time to think about it. I pushed things into my saddlebags, slung them over my shoulder, and started for the door.

CHAPTER THIRTEEN

I SCRAMBLED DOWNHILL, keeping behind boulders and in dips of the ground whenever I could. The breeze was in my face; it would carry any sound I made towards the crowd watching the crowning, but they would be, I hoped, too engrossed in the ceremony to care.

Cillian waited at the jetty. He had untied the small rowboat, his small pack already stowed under the seat. Wordlessly I slipped onto the boat, pushing my saddlebags against Cillian's pack, steadying the boat against the dock with one hand. Cillian climbed in, the boat rocking as he took his seat. I pushed off, and began to row.

The oarlocks squealed. Cursing—Cillian had had time to remedy this, had he known to—I stopped rowing to dig in my bag. I found my blood cloths, pulled the oars up, and wrapped and tied cloths around the shafts. Cillian offered no help. I shoved the empty case back into the bag and picked up the oars again. The tide was rising. We reached the other jetty in a matter of minutes. Cillian clambered out to tie the boat. I unwrapped the cloths from the oars and stuffed them in my bag, not bothering with the case. I pulled Cillian's pack out from beneath the seat, handed it to him, and stepped up to the jetty. Without speaking, we climbed the angled path to the top of the cliff. At the top, Cillian broke into a run. I kept pace, the leather saddlebags bouncing on my shoulder, following him east and south until my side stabbed me with every breath. Only when we reached a small stand of pines did he stop.

"We need to find a *torp*," he panted. "We need horses."

I shook my head. Hadn't he listened? "Too risky. Too slow. We steal a boat. We can sail faster than riding. A lot faster."

He stared at me, a muscle working in his jaw. "Where should we go?" he said finally.

I had thought about this. "Berge. Or, not Berge, but the fort just north of it, at the Wall. There will be ships there, almost certainly, and it will be easy to get word to the White Fort, if that is where our leaders are."

"Gregor should have reached the White Fort by now," Cillian argued. "Miach will be leading men north already."

"But not fast enough, and Fritjof will be sailing south, not marching. We need the Empire's ships to be waiting, and the Emperor must command that. He will believe me, Cillian, but we need to get to him as quickly as we can. And we are not doing that if we stand here arguing!"

I saw the flicker in his eyes as he acknowledged the truth of what I said. We began to run again, angling west, back toward the coast.

In mid-afternoon Cillian spotted a small cluster of buildings in a cove ahead of us. My eyes found ropes and floats, a pile of traps, the paraphernalia of fishing. I glanced to the sea; the tide was out, which meant the boat would be too. We would have to wait. Cillian scowled when I told him this, but said nothing. We found a group of boulders, warmed by the sun, and sat against them. Cillian dug in his pack, handing me a piece of bread. "There isn't much," he said, "but we should eat a little."

I chewed it, calculating. The tide would turn soon. I expected the boat back in late afternoon, although it could be later, if the fishing had been good; there were still five or six hours of light. If we waited until a couple of hours after dark, we stood little chance of detection, and the tide would be nearly high again. But we would need to hide until then. I looked around.

"What are you looking for?" Cillian asked. I explained. He frowned again. "Why don't we just keep going? This can't be the only fisherman's hut on this shore. And if they've sent men after us, they'll find us in that time."

He had a point. I glanced again at the buildings. The shed at the shore stood open, back and front, no boat inside. No boat pulled up on the beach. Cillian spoke the truth: we needed to keep going. I finished the bread. "You're right," I said. "Let's go."

We circled wide of the cottage, but even so a dog yipped from the buildings, shouted down by a woman's voice. I hadn't expected a dog at a tiny fishing settlement; in Tirvan, all the dogs were for the sheep and for hunting. They had no place around the boats. Perhaps this one was a pet. We would need to be careful.

We passed by another fishing settlement, and another: they seemed to be evenly spaced along the shore, sharing the waters. If they were, I estimated, we should reach the next just about at dusk. We continued, alternately walking and running, keeping close to trees and rocks wherever we could. The land underfoot was a sandy heath, sometimes soft enough to make movement difficult, sometimes firm. We saw no one. What sheep we saw were gathered along the tideline, eating seaweed, no shepherd or sheepdog guarding them.

The light began to fade. Ahead of us, the land rose, the curve of the beach below us giving way to cliffs where seabirds circled and screamed, landing on narrow ledges in the rock. I cursed. There would be no fishing huts here; we would need to clear this headland. My stomach growled. "Cillian," I said, "we need to stop."

"It's getting dark," he objected.

"I know. But we need a bit more food, and water. Then we cross this headland, and hope there are fisher-folk in the next cove."

He handed me another small piece of bread, and the water-skin. We would need to find fresh water again, I thought: it was at least a three-day sail to Berge, and that would be with favourable winds. Food we could do without, if we must, and we could always trail a baited line, but water we would need. I took a scant mouthful to wash down the bread, and then another, and handed it back to Cillian. "Drink sparingly," I warned.

We started off again. There was no track to follow; whatever dealings these fisher-folk had with each other, it was by boat, not by land. There had been tracks leading inland from each settlement, probably to the *torps* that each served, but nothing between them. The land rose. We climbed, the coarse heath scratching against our boots. A huge bird, white-tailed and pale-headed, soared up from the cliffs and over our heads. I ducked, reflexively, then stared up at it. It was enormous, larger even than the golden eagles that hunted the hills above Tirvan. "What is it?" I asked.

"Sea-eagle," Cillian said. "Keep going."

We reached the crest of the headland. Beyond us I could see the curve of another cove, and another cluster of huts. I closed my eyes in relief. Every inch of me ached, fatigue was sapping every muscle, but I could make it to that settlement.

Half an hour later we crouched in the heather and bracken, watching and listening. The boat—a small fishing boat, single-sailed—lay anchored just off-shore, its sail lashed to the mast, rocking gently on the swells. In the larger hut, the flicker of firelight and the smell of frying fish told of the family preparing for the evening meal.

"Pull your breeches' legs out of your boots and then down over them," I murmured to Cillian. "It helps keep the water out of your boots," I explained, at his puzzled look. I pulled my secca out of its boot sheath, tucking it into my belt, and adjusted my breeches. "Now," I continued, "we wade out to the boat. It won't be deep: the moon is nearly dark, so the tide is low, but be prepared to get wet. When we get there, throw your pack in, then lean over it and grab something as close to the far side of the thwart as you can—the far edge of the seat," I clarified, seeing his frown, "and then step in. I'll keep her steady. Stay close to the far side to let me climb in. Then haul up the anchor, but stay near the centre of the boat. I'll start rowing. We won't put the sail up until we're out a bit." He exhaled, loudly. "A problem?" I asked.

"At least we could both ride," he said.

We crept along the shore. The waves were gentle, not making enough noise to muffle our steps. I rolled my weight on my feet as Tice had taught me, all those months ago, but Cillian had no skill in walking quietly. The cot was almost dark now, just the soft light of a banked fire glimmering through the shutters; they'd be up early to sail as soon as the tide allowed in the morning. With luck, the inhabitants had eaten their supper and were soundly asleep.

We were approaching the water when Cillian stepped on a something— driftwood, I guessed—that snapped loudly. We froze. A dog barked, sharply, from the cot. I took a step back and sideways, avoiding the wood, cursing. A voice called a challenge. "Go," I hissed at Cillian. "Get on, and get that anchor up." We both began to run, heedless now of sound. A shape emerged from the cottage, silhouetted against the faint glow, and then another, the dog growling nearly at our heels. We would make the boat before them, I estimated, trying to angle my direction to reach the boat as quickly as possible. Waves slapped against my legs. The dog barked from the waterline. Cillian was at the boat, reaching over, climbing on—and my left ankle caught the anchor rope. I fell, heavily, the water over my body and my head, flooding my mouth and nose. My bags slipped from my shoulder. I blew out, pushing up with my arms, trying to stand, when arms caught me from behind.

I struggled, but the man's arms were strong from fishing and he held me tightly. I heard the splash of another person's strides behind him. He was shouting something, angrily, pulling me around to face him. One clutching hand fell on my left breast. He stopped. His hand groped. He called something to the other man, and then shoved me around, ripping at my tunic.

His hand was rough against my skin, and he stank. There in the waves, he caught a nipple between thumb and finger, squeezing. He raked his fingernails, ragged and sharp, across my breast; I gasped. He laughed. His other arm was tight around my waist, but one of my arms was free. He brought his head down to my neck, half-biting, half-sucking, the one hand kneading my breast, the other dropping lower to my buttocks, pushing me against him. He was hard, even in the cold water. I willed myself to become limp. I let my free arm drop slowly, to take the secca from my belt. Raising it, I stabbed him in his exposed neck, once, twice, rage powering the thrusts. He gurgled, moving his hand from my breast to his neck, and then he fell into the sea.

I looked up. The other man was no man at all, but a boy of perhaps twelve years. He stood in the sea, staring at the body. His father, probably. Behind him, the dog whined. I pushed the secca back into my belt, turned, and pulled myself onto the boat. "Go," I said to Cillian. "Go!" I screamed, as he hesitated, looking at me. He turned, pulling the anchor up as I pushed oars into their locks. As soon as the anchor-stone was out of the water I was rowing, all my fear and anger channelled into the action, taking us away from that place.

When we were out deep enough, I pointed the boat into the wind and stopped rowing. Cillian had hunkered down in the stern. I shipped the oars and stood. "Need to get this sail up," I panted. "Stay there. You'll only be in my way." I glanced back shoreward. In the last vestiges of light, I thought I could make out the shape of the boy, crouched over his father's body at the sea's edge. No one else.

I unfurled the sail, a simple square, clipped the lines in place, and hoisted the yard. There was no moon. The breeze was mild, but enough for us to sail. But I did not know this coast. If the man had done any night fishing, there might be a lantern. I could see a shape under the thwarts that could be a chest. I pushed it out. It held a lantern and candles, a loop of rope tied to the top of the lantern. I ducked under the sail and hooked the lantern in place at the bow; it hung above the water, giving me a chance of seeing rocks, or the change in wave pattern that told of submerged rocks. But even as I hung the lantern, I debated my choices. Night sailing was risky, and I had never done it alone. Cillian would be of no help, more likely a hindrance. We had a long way to go, and haste was needed, but if we lost the boat—and ourselves—to rocks, then word would never reach Berge. The boat was still headed into the wind, and we were drifting slowly backwards. I needed to decide, but my mind was fogged with exhaustion.

"Cillian," I said, "do you know this coastline at all? Can you tell me about rocks, small islands, anything?"

"There are a lot of islands," he said, "big and small. Further south there are fewer, except in one place; the coast is flatter there, with long beaches of sand, but not here."

"I don't know what to do," I admitted. "We need to get away from this cove, at the very least, but there could be another settlement in the next. We should get out into the deeper water and anchor, so we can start sailing at first light, before other boats come out, but we risk hitting rocks in the dark."

"Wouldn't it be safer to row?"

"It would be," I said. "But I don't think I can." The spurt of energy engendered by the attack had gone, leaving me drained. And my arm was aching, a deep, nauseating ache, adding to my fatigue and confusion.

"Show me how," he said. I hesitated.

"It's not that simple," I started.

"Show me," he insisted. I nodded, then realized he couldn't see my acquiescence.

"All right," I said. "Come up to the thwart. Keep your body low as you move."

The boat rocked as he made his way to the rough seat. When he was seated, I moved behind him and helped him place the oars in the locks. "Hold the oars here," I said, indicating the grips, "with your hands on top, right, good," I added, as he grasped the oars in a serviceable manner. "Don't let the oars go too deep," I said, as he moved them down toward the water. "Right now, just hold them, while I drop the sail."

When I had the sail down and furled, I came back to the thwart. "Now, lift the oars out of the water and bring them forward." Cillian did as I said. "Keep the angle shallow as you drop them and pull back evenly and steadily." The boat moved forward. "Not too far back," I instructed, as I tried to see his movements in the dark. "Now lift them, bring them up and forward, back in, good." We slid through the water, not smoothly, but it would do.

"Can you keep that up?" I asked.

"For a while," he said.

"Don't grip too hard, or pull too hard, you'll tire yourself too quickly," I said. "Just row steadily. We don't want speed, anyhow. I'm going back up to the bow, to watch for rocks."

The oars splashed too much, but there was no one to hear. Cillian kept the boat to a straight line while I peered forward into the pool of light the lantern created. The sea to all sides was black, no other lights on the water, no lights on land, only the stars to differentiate sea from sky. We moved forward. Suddenly I saw, or felt, rocks looming up ahead. "To larboard!" I shouted.

"What? How? Tell me!"

"Dig in hard with your left oar!" I shouted, cursing Cillian's ignorance and my own stupidity. "Get the right out of the water, now. Keep rowing with the left, hard." I felt around for something to push off the rocks with, finding nothing. The little boat swung left. I scrambled to the stern, just as the boat bounced off the rocks. Ignoring its roll, I reached out and pushed, hard. We moved away from the rock. I slid forward to balance the boat, hoping the side of this rock was straight and clean, with no sharp angles below the waterline waiting to hole us.

We were swinging too far larboard, spinning round towards the rocks again. Cillian had not steadied the course; the starboard oar was still out of the water. I pushed in beside him, picking up the oar. "On my count," I panted. "One, two, three—" Our oars splashed into the water nearly in unison. We surged forward, almost straight. I said a silent prayer to any god listening and kept rowing, away from the rock.

Nothing holed us. After a minute or two I told Cillian to stop rowing. We drifted, rocking gently, while I studied the sky. In the effort to get away from the rocks, I had lost track of our direction. I found the twin stars, high above the hunter: south. The bow of the boat was pointing west, towards the land.

"Drop the anchor," I said. "We need sleep. We will sail at first light." Cillian said nothing, but he pulled up his oar and laid it along the boards before lowering the anchor-stone overboard. I steadied the boat against the pull of the anchor until the stone hit bottom. Cold seeped into me. I was wet and exhausted, and all my spare clothes had been in my saddlebag.

I slid off the seat and onto the boards. "Come here," I said to Cillian. "We need to share body heat."

"I'm all right," he said.

"No, you're not," I answered. "You're wet, and now you've stopped rowing, you're going to get cold. Did you bring any dry clothes, anything we can put over us?"

"My riding cloak," he said. "It's in my bag." He fumbled at the ties of his bag, cursing at his clumsiness, but after a minute he freed the knot to pull out the woollen cloak.

"You have it," he said. "I don't need it."

"Cillian," I said, exhaustion blunting my voice. "Don't be stupid. Get down here. I need your heat, even if you don't think you need mine. If I die of exposure, what are you going to do?"

That silenced him. He crawled down beside me; we spread the cloak. It didn't quite cover us, but Cillian was still a hand's-breadth away from me.

"Closer," I said, feeling the first shivers beginning. He edged closer, still not touching me. I sighed. "Roll over." He did as I asked, dislodging the cloak. I wrapped it around us again, and then put my arm over him, pulling my body against his until there was no space along our lengths. He tensed, but as the cloak and our proximity began to warm us, he began to relax. I slowly stopped shivering. I tucked my head in against his neck, and fell asleep.

CHAPTER FOURTEEN

I WOKE, STIFF AND SORE, to a faint paleness in the eastern sky. I had roused several times in the night to pull the cloak back over us, and once to make my way to the gunwales to relieve myself, falling back into a shallow and fitful sleep again each time. But now I was fully awake, and it was time to sail.

"Cillian," I said, "wake up." He grunted, and stretched, rolling onto his back.

"Lena," he muttered.

"Time to get moving," I said, sitting up. I looked around. The stars were clearly visible, and already seabirds were skimming the waves, hunting. No fog, but a stronger breeze, blowing from the north-west. Exactly what we needed.

Cillian got up, uncertainly moving toward the stern. I glanced at him; he was undoing his breeches. "Pay attention to the wind direction," I told him. I turned my back on him—there were basic courtesies on a small boat—and opened the lid of the chest again, looking for water. An earthenware pot, stoppered with a woollen rag, looked promising. I picked it up. It sloshed, but it sounded and felt half-empty. I removed the rag, sniffed, and sipped. The water tasted of the pot. I allowed myself two small swallows, before passing the pot to Cillian, who had come forward again, tying his breeches.

"A couple of mouthfuls, no more," I warned. "We will have to find more water somewhere."

With the water re-stoppered and stowed, I used an oar to swing the boat into the wind again. "Hold it there," I said to Cillian, and raised the sail. He pulled up the anchor-stone, and we began to move south slowly, the light wind just sufficient to propel the heavy boat. But until it was fully light, this was enough.

As the day brightened, I could see we were among a line of islands, creating a wide channel between the open sea and the mainland. Other boats would be on their way out soon. We needed to stay as far out from the mainland as was safe, and even that course was predicated on none of the islands being inhabited. And somewhere, we needed to go to shore for water. I would worry about that later. The wind was freshening, promising a long reach. I adjusted the sail for the increased wind. "Sit there," I directed Cillian, pointing to the opposite gunwale. He complied, although a glance over showed me his face was set and his knuckles white.

The little boat ran with the wind for some time, needing little adjustment of sail or tiller. But looking ahead, I could see the line of offshore islands was ending; we would lose our shelter from stronger winds. Dark patches in the water beyond the last island told of stronger waves. "Cillian," I said, as I shortened the sail, "be prepared for some rougher water, and move as quickly as you can if I tell you to." I reminded myself to use terms he would understand.

The wind hit the sail with more force than I had expected, the boat heeling sharply. I reefed the sail, shouting at Cillian to move to the other side of the boat as I did. I felt the boat settle. A few more adjustments to sail and lines, and we were sailing at a fair clip, the little boat taking the waves remarkably well. I rested one hand lightly on the tiller, and glanced over at Cillian. He held on to the boat with both hands, his shoulders tense, his eyes moving from the land to the waters behind us, and back again.

All the rest of that first day we sailed with a favourable wind. I showed Cillian how to steer, and how to make small adjustments to the sail, having him take over when I needed to relieve myself, or to move to stop my muscles cramping. I had seen line and hooks in the chest, so when we switched places again, I set up a line, baiting the hook with dry bread, and gave it to Cillian, explaining as best I could the difference between how a nibbling fish and a hooked fish would feel. He lost the first fish, but hooked the second with a firm tug. I filleted it with my secca, and we ate the firm, wet flesh, me hungrily, Cillian doubtfully. He kept it down, though, even with the swells, although I saw him swallow hard a time or two.

Hunger had been satisfied, and the boat ran fair with the wind, needing little attention. "Cillian," I said, "what of these lands to the east, where Fritjof claims he sailed? Could he be telling the truth? Did he talk about his travels to the *Teannasach*?"

"Not when I was there," Cillian said, 'but, yes, he could have travelled east, I think. I have been trying to recall the maps. There are rivers that reach down into the eastern lands, and the Marai boats are shallow. It is possible he could have rowed down those rivers."

"He would go against the prophecy, and convince others to go with him?"

Cillian laughed, wryly. "In a moment. The *Teannasach* and Fritjof's older brother, Åsmund, were friends; King Herlief sent Åsmund to Linrathe as a boy for a time, to the *Ti'ach na Perras*, and he and Donnalch would hunt and hawk together, as well as have lessons. It was why Donnalch thought he could renegotiate the terms of our treaty with the Marai, once Herlief was dead. But from what I have heard, Fritjof was wild even then, wanting what Åsmund had—not the schooling, for that was never Fritjof's interest—but his hawk, his horse, even when the animal was too large and strong for him. He could never wait, or be counselled by wise words. The King sent him away, finally, after he tried to force himself on the girl being considered for Åsmund's bride, and then nearly killed his brother in a fight when he intervened."

I shuddered. "And his men?"

"If you had been at the *Ti'ach* longer," Cillian said, "you might have heard some of the *danta* that concern themselves with the exploits of the Marai, of their raids and battles and the glory those brought. There were—are, no doubt—those among the Marai who thought they had grown soft and land-bound under Herlief, weak. Fritjof would have had little trouble in convincing that faction to support him."

"And now they all must support him, or die," I said.

We saw the occasional other fishing boat, but they were well in from our position, fishing the more sheltered waters. In mid-afternoon, a headland reached out towards us; as we passed it, I saw the half-moon curve of a long cove, and the sparkle of a stream running down the cliffside. I could see no buildings, and no boats. "We're going in," I said, through lips chapped now from the salt air, the wind, and thirst. I gybed the sail. "Prepare to row," I ordered Cillian, bringing the sail down as we reached the beach. He rowed us in fairly smoothly; when I could see the bottom close, I jumped off, to haul her up to the beach. As I did, I felt a sharp pain in my upper chest.

"Be quick," I said to Cillian. "Drink your fill, fill the water-pot, and we'll get off this beach before someone sees us." While he knelt at the stream, I untied the top of my tunic and felt my chest where my attacker had scratched me last night. The skin was tender, and felt puffy. I cursed. I had, in my haste and fear, forgotten a basic principle: I had not soaked the ragged cuts in sea water. Over the years, I had escaped infection from hooks and spines, rock scrapes and knife-slips, by immersing the injury in the ocean for several minutes. There was only one thing to do.

"Cillian," I called. He looked up from filling the water jug. "Come here, will you, when you're finished that?" I walked to the sea edge, bending to wash my secca thoroughly, holding it in the waves. Cillian approached me. "Put the water-pot in the boat," I directed. "Then I need you to do something for me."

When he stood before me, I said, "Look." I pulled open my tunic, pushing aside the torn pieces to expose my breast. He looked away. "I'm injured," I said bluntly. "The man last night scratched me, and the scratches are infected. Tell me what you see." He brought his eyes to my breast.

"There is pus, here," he said, reaching a finger out and then pulling it back.

"I thought so," I answered. "Take my secca, and cut the scratches deeper." I saw the look of horror on his face. "I can't do it myself," I said, "and it has to be done, or the infection will spread. The secca is clean. I will hold my breast taut, but you must make the cuts. And if you must touch my breast to do so, then do it. Can you do this?"

He looked at me for a long moment. "I can," he said. I flattened my breast down with my hands, feeling the tug and stab of the infection as I did. He brought the knife tip down. I closed my eyes, biting my lip against the sharp, exquisite pain of the blade. He made three cuts. I did not cry out.

"Thank you," I said, when he was done. Blood dripped down my breast, staining the tunic. He handed me back the secca. "I will soak it now, in the sea." I told him. "Then I will get a drink, and we will go back out."

I waded out into the water, crouching down so the sea would cover my chest. I steadied myself with one hand, and with the other massaged the cuts, pushing pus and blood out, letting the sea-water in. It stung, worse than the initial cuts. Involuntary tears sprung to my eyes.

When I felt I had soaked long enough, I stood and walked back out of the water. At the stream, I knelt and drank deeply, resisting the desire to rinse the cuts in fresh water. I retied my tunic as best I could, and we pushed off, rowing back out to deep water.

The sun and wind dried my clothes, and as I sat by the tiller I wrapped Cillian's cloak around me until I was warm again. Cillian caught more fish for supper. As the sun set in the west, I saw him gazing out at the mainland. The breeze was dropping with the sun; we sailed slowly now.

"I know where we are," he said. "That is Linrathe, now. You were right, Lena. Even on horseback we would not have got this far, so fast."

"If that is Linrathe," I said, "we could make land, find a cove or even a settlement."

"Not tonight," he answered. "These waters are called the Maw: along these cliffs there are submerged rocks, sharp and frequent as teeth, for many miles; a barrier to landing. Some say that is why the Sterre is built where it is, to extend the sea barrier on the land. But tomorrow, yes, further south, we can get water and food, and send word overland, perhaps."

"I see," I said, feeling the disappointment. "We should anchor soon. If this is the Maw, then we cannot afford to be caught amongst the rocks in the dark."

We dropped the anchor stone, and ate the fish Cillian had caught. The little boat rocked gently on the waves. The evening star appeared on the horizon, and streams of gulls headed back towards land, over our heads. The approaching night felt peaceful, but my thoughts were not. All afternoon I had considered what Cillian had told me about Fritjof, and the threat to both Linrathe and the Empire. Our two countries must work together, if were we to defeat the Marai. Cillian knew this better than anyone else, but he hated the Empire. He needed to hear what I had to tell him.

"Cillian," I said, "I have something to say, and I think it will make you angry. Will you hear me out?"

In the fading light, I could not read the expression on his face. "I suppose," he said flatly.

"My first night at the *Ti'ach*," I said, "I asked Sorley why you seemed to resent me." That wasn't quite true, but I wanted to deflect any reaction away from Sorley. "He told me about your mother." I paused.

"He shouldn't have," Cillian said. "It was not his story to tell."

"Nonetheless," I said. "It is done. I have a question, and it might be important. Do you know nothing of your father?"

He did not reply at first. Overhead, gulls continued their arrowed flight back to land, silhouettes now against the darkening sky. "Nothing," he said finally, "except that he was a soldier of the southern Empire. My mother was sixteen. She lived just north of the Wall, on a small steading. Whoever he was, he took advantage of a young girl, and then deserted her."

I had one more question. "How old are you, Cillian?"

"Thirty-three. Why?"

A fish jumped, splashing back into the water off the bow. I did the calculation: thirty-four years ago, Callan would have been seventeen. "I think,"

I said slowly, "that the Emperor, Callan—he might be your father. You have a strong look of him."

I saw his head turn towards me. "You know the Emperor well enough to say this?" It was not the response I had expected.

"I think I do," I answered. "I have spent some hours in his company. I have seen him when he is pleased, and when he is angry, and it is when you are angry you look most like him. But even that first night—I thought I knew you, but it is your likeness to Callan I was seeing."

"More proof of the malevolence of Empires, then," he said.

"That isn't fair!" I said. "Callan would have been a soldier then, a cadet, actually, nothing more. He may have been posted away from the Wall, without ever knowing your mother was with child."

"But he never came back," he said into the night. I had no answer for that.

"Cillian," I said after a moment, "this goes beyond you. The *Teannasach* and the Emperor together paid homage to the Eastern Empire, to what it once was. Many of my people crossed into your land at Partition; we share blood and history, and you more recently than most, perhaps. We must remember that, and work together, if we are to defeat Fritjof." I waited. There was no answer, only the steady slap of the waves, and the beating of wings overhead, in the dark sky.

He tucked up against me more willingly that night, under the heavy cloak, although he kept his back to me, afraid, I surmised, of his body's involuntary response to mine. He held no attraction for me, and I doubted I truly did for him, but we are not always captains of our bodies' reactions. I woke heavy-headed and aching, to a grey morning; a light fog hung over the sea, beneath a clouded sky. "We will have to sail with the land in sight," I told Cillian as we prepared the boat. "If we lose the land, we can lose all sense of direction, and the wind is no help; it can change in a moment." The wind, in fact, still blew from the north-east, but it was gustier, possibly presaging a storm. I would be busier with the sails today.

As I reached up to adjust the sail, pain shot through my breast. The area had been throbbing when I awoke, but I had ignored it, telling myself it was just the throb of any cut. But the pain said otherwise. When I had the sail set and the lines fixed, I touched my breast, feeling beneath the fabric of my tunic the inflammation of infection. I shivered. If draining and soaking the scratches yesterday hadn't cleared the infection, doing it again would not likely help. The salve which might have had been in my saddlebag. I pushed the fabric aside, looking down. Red streaks extended from the cuts, too far to be just the usual redness of healing. I closed my eyes. "Cillian," I said. Something in my voice alerted him.

"What's wrong?" he asked.

"My scratches are infected," I said, as calmly as I could. "Badly. The seawater did not help; I did it too late. I must show you how to sail, alone, because you may need to do so. We'll head for land as soon as it's safe, and I should be able to sail until then, but you need to know how. So, come, sit beside me."

He came forward. As the sun rose behind the clouds, and the fog slowly dissipated, I taught him the basic theory of sailing. I showed him how to judge the wind by the thin tell-tale strip tied to the mast; I explained how to trim and let out sail, how to tack, how to gybe, and when, how to furl and tie the sail before taking to the oars. Then I sat back and let him do it, watching, suggesting, correcting, feeling the throb in my breast deepen as the first signs of fever invaded my body.

Sweat beaded my brow and I was wrapped in the cloak against deep shivers by mid-day. "We must be past the Maw by now," I said. "We should find a harbour." The wind was strengthening, the gusts coming more frequently, and I was afraid for the boat under Cillian's hand if we had to run in front of a gale. One misjudgment and we would capsize, and that would be the end.

I turned my head to look at the sky behind us, and caught my breath. On the horizon, further out than us and still a good distance behind was a boat, a ship, much larger than us, square-rigged and moving fast.

"Cillian," I croaked. He looked at me; I raised an arm to point, ignoring the pain that shot through my breast as I did.

"That's a Marai ship," he said.

"After us," I said.

"Can they see us?" he asked.

"Doubt it," I said. Talking took effort. "Maybe in the sun, but everything is too grey today."

"What do we do?" His mind was off the sails. A gust hit, swelling the sail, pushing the boat forward and sideways, rocking it violently.

"Trim the sails," I gasped. "Quickly!"

He leapt to the lines. As he did, another gust hit, this time on the opposite side of the sail. The wind swirled. The boat swung, sails flapping. A wave broke over the bow, soaking us. I pushed myself up, shedding the cloak, reaching for the lines, ignoring pain, ignoring weakness. Cillian stumbled, falling against the gunwale, grabbing desperately for something to hang on to. He scrabbled against the boards, found his feet, reached for the sail. I crawled forward, and together we furled and tied the sail, leaving the little boat drifting on the growing swells.

I fell against the gunwale. "You'll have to row in," I said. My head spun. I crept to the centre of the boat, where a dead weight would best lessen pitch. "Give me the cloak," I muttered. I felt the weight of the cloth cover me; I heard the creaking of the oars in their locks, and then I knew nothing at all.

CHAPTER FIFTEEN

OR ALMOST NOTHING. I have confused memories of being moved, of voices and pain, and then truly nothing until I woke—when? where?—in a bed, under warm blankets, in a dim and quiet room. I blinked, even the muted light causing my eyes to hurt. My mouth felt parched, tasting foul. I moved my head, looking for water.

"Lena?" My mother's voice. What was she doing in Linrathe? I'm dreaming, I thought, but then she was bending over me, her hand on my cheek.

"Lena," she said again. "Can you hear me?"

I focused on her face. She looked worried. "Yes," I whispered. "Thirsty."

She smiled. "Let me help you up," she said. She put one hand behind my shoulders and pushed me up, propping me on pillows. I tried to help her, but I was as weak as a newborn mouse, and sitting up brought a spasm of coughing, deep and painful. When the coughing stopped, I was exhausted. The room spun. My mother held a cup to my lips. "Slowly," she warned. I took a sip, and another, the water cool on my raw throat.

"What happened?" I croaked. She shook her head.

"Later," she said. "A sip or two more, and then you should sleep again." I took another tiny bit of water. Then I closed my eyes to let sleep take me again.

When I woke the second time, I felt stronger, and the room stayed in one place. My mother was at my bedside in an instant—she must be watching me constantly, I thought—this time with a bowl of warm water, with which she washed me, as if I were a baby, before dressing me again in a clean, warmed nightgown, rubbing my back when the change in position brought on the coughing again. She still wouldn't let me ask questions, but this time, even in my weakness, I felt myself getting annoyed.

I let her brush my hair and feed me some broth, but when I felt myself slipping back towards sleep, I pushed the spoon away and said as firmly as I could, "Where am I?"

"Berge," my mother said.

"How?"

"Cillian brought you," she answered.

I tried to shake my head, but the movement hurt. "No," I said. "He can't sail."

"He didn't," she said, smiling. "He rowed the boat you took into a cove, and by blind luck it had a fishing settlement. Cillian convinced the fisherman to bring you both to Berge. How, I am not sure."

"Why are you here?"

The smile disappeared. "Oh, Lena," she said. "Casyn sent for me. He thought you were dying, and in truth so did I, when I arrived. You had an infection raging in your blood, from the scratches on your chest, and another in your lungs. You have been very ill, Lena, so ill it took all my knowledge to keep you alive." Tears shone in her eyes.

"But you did it," I whispered.

"Only because you are so strong," she answered. Something she had said came back into focus.

"Casyn is here?"

"Not right now," she replied. "He'll be back soon. That's enough talking, Lena. Rest again. The Empire is safe, and Linrathe, and that is all you need to know."

My mother was right. It was all I needed to know then. For the next few days I slept, waking to eat a bit, be washed, and after the first day, be taken to the latrine and made to walk a few steps. This took all my strength, of body and of mind. Anything else seemed unimportant, and very far away. But I coughed less every day; soon I could sit up on my own, and eat porridge and soft-cooked eggs by myself, and as my body grew in strength, my mind moved away from self-absorption. I was allowed no visitors, and this made me wonder.

"Mother, why can't I see Cillian?" I demanded one morning. "Or is he hurt, or sick, too?"

"No," she said. "Cillian is well. But right now, Lena, your body is still weak, and you could catch any illness very quickly. Until I am sure you are strong enough, you cannot risk visitors." Her voice was firm, the healer, not the mother, speaking, but she *was* my mother, and watching her hands automatically retying her hair, and the small lines between her eyes, I knew there was something she was not telling me.

"How is Kira?" I realized I had not asked about my sister yet. Was that what she was keeping from me?

Her face cleared. "Kira is well, very well," she said. "I have left Tirvan in competent hands, that I know. She will have four deliveries to cope with this spring, and Casse is failing, I'm afraid, but I think she will live through this summer, and perhaps see one more autumn hunt."

"Kira is seventeen now," I said slowly. "A woman."

"She is," my mother said. I could hear the pride in her voice, for the daughter that had been her apprentice and was now her equal.

"She will stay in Tirvan?" I asked. She would have the choice, now, to leave for another village, to be their healer and midwife, if she so wished.

My mother laughed. "What do you think?" she asked.

I smiled, thinking of my sister. "She'll stay," I agreed. "What else has happened in Tirvan? I've been gone so long now. Tell me what everyone is doing."

For the next hour, my mother recounted the doings of my home village in the nearly two years I had been gone. My small cousin Pel was gone, now, of course; the men had come for him last autumn, a year late, but the need to concentrate the Empire's forces on the Wall had kept the soldiers from Festival and from claiming their sons. Even last autumn, my mother told me, only a few men had come, and all the boys, the village had been told, were to be taken to the Eastern Fort, as far away from the fighting as possible.

"Your aunt was glad, in a way, to see him go. He was growing headstrong, and we have no experience with raising boys over seven. He needed the discipline of cadet school," my mother said. "And he—well, not just Pel, but all the boys of age—were wild to be gone. They threatened to take the ponies and find the army themselves, when no men came in the spring," she added.

"Pel would have done it, too," I said, contemplating. "Especially after Garth taught them to ride. How did you stop them?"

She laughed. "It was Casse. She rounded them up and told them, in no uncertain terms, that the ponies belonged to Tirvan, they were needed for the hunt, and if they took them, they would be guilty of theft. And thieves, she pointed out, were punished severely in the army; not only would they have disappointed their fathers, they would have robbed themselves of any chance of advancement. I am not sure if it was those reasons, or when she told them bluntly that their only work in the army would be digging latrines and cleaning them, too, that convinced them, but convince them she did."

I laughed. "Good for Casse," I said. "And Dessa? How is she?" Dessa had been my apprentice-master on the boats. Her partner, Siane, had been killed in the failed invasion by Leste, leaving Dessa to raise Siane's daughter.

"She is better," my mother said. "And Lara," she added, brightening, "is apprenticed to me, or to me and Kira, I suppose, as of last autumn."

I raised an eyebrow. "I can see Lara as a healer," I said, "but I did not think she would leave Dessa. Before I left, she was like her shadow."

My mother nodded. "She was. But in the spring after the invasion, when Dessa began fishing again, Lara was sick with worry every time she took the boat out. It was Kira who began to spend time with her, taking her to pick herbs, talking to her, reassuring her. So, when she turned twelve, and asked the council to let her apprentice with us, well, we could not say no. And Dessa approved. Lara is slight, as you know. The boats would not have been a wise choice."

"I'm glad," I said. I was suddenly homesick, the stab of longing a physical pain. I wanted to see Tirvan again, the unpainted clapboard houses on the hill, the jetty and the boats, my upstairs bedroom in my aunt Tali's house. I wanted my boat back, my *Dovekie*, built for a crew of two. I wanted to soak in the baths and watch the golden eagles hunting over the high fields where the sheep grazed. But I could, I realized. I could go home now, when I was well enough, surely?

The next morning my mother came in with something in her hands. I was standing, restless and unsettled, looking out the window at the glimpse of the sea beyond the roofs and streets of Berge. I turned as my mother came in.

"I have something for you," she said. I looked at what she held out.

"Colm's history!" I gasped. "How? It was taken, at Fritjof's hall." I recognized the other book, too: my journal. I took them from her, turning them over in my hands.

"Cillian had them," she said. "They had been given to him to begin translating. He knew they were precious to you—and to Perras, he said—so he took them. I thought it was time you had them back."

I stared at the books. Even if they had not been taken from me, they would have been lost with my saddlebag, the night we stole the boat. Cillian had saved them. My hands trembled. Tears stung my eyes, and then I was sobbing, deep, racking sobs that brought back my cough. My mother put her arm around me, and guided me to the bed, sitting with me, holding me, as I cried, and coughed, and cried some more.

"Clio," I said, or rather wailed, when I could speak at all again. "I left her there. I had to, but I miss her—and what will they do with her?" I said between sobs. "They will have ridden her to war, and she could have been killed."

"Shhh," my mother soothed. "You had no choice, Lena. You did the best you could, and you did well."

Anger took the place of grief, suddenly and violently. I pulled away from my mother. "You are right," I shouted. "I had no choice. I was a hostage. I was meant to be at a house of learning, not forced into marriage with a prince of a people I didn't know existed. I said I would go, I would be the hostage, because I didn't...I couldn't disappoint Casyn again. I owed him that. He said I was like a daughter to him—how could I say no? But I went to learn..." I stopped. Even through my flaring anger I knew what I was saying was wrong. I had not known what being a hostage entailed when I agreed. And how could Casyn have known what he was sending me to? I shook my head, my anger turning against myself. My mother was murmuring something.

"Don't listen to me, Mother," I said wearily. "I know it's not Casyn's fault, or the Emperor's. It's just how things turned out. They couldn't have known."

"You are allowed to be angry," she said. "None of this—none of the last two years—is what you thought your life would be: there have been forces beyond your control, as well as the consequences of your own choices." I swallowed, nodding. She went on. "And when we doubt our own choices," she said gently, "it can be easier to let others make the next decisions for us, or do what we think they would want us to do. It's why there are three council leaders in the women's villages, Lena, so our decisions are never made alone, and two of us must agree."

"But how do you know your choices are right?" Even to my own ears, I sounded about ten. But my mother just put her arm around my shoulders, and pulled me to her.

"We often don't," she answered. "Lena, do you want to tell me what happened with Maya?

I shook my head, tears leaking from my eyes. My mother rocked me gently. "Your letter reached me, although it took a very long time," she said. "You sounded so hopeful, when you wrote: Maya had come to Casilla, and you had found work on the fishing boats, and there was Valle to raise. I thought you were still there, you know, until Casyn's first message came to tell me you had been sent north, as a hostage to the peace. Why did you leave Casilla, Lena?"

"She sent me away," I whispered.

"Maya sent you away?" I heard the surprise in my mother's voice.

The tears rolled down my cheeks. I did not try to check them. "She wanted Valle to herself, because he was Garth's. She could accept Ianthe; she was Valle's aunt, too. But I didn't have a claim, she told me, so I didn't need to stay. She and Ianthe could raise him, without me."

"Did she know about you and Garth?"

"I don't know," I admitted. "I never told her, but maybe she guessed, from all the time we spent together on the road. Or maybe Garth told Ianthe, and she told Maya. I don't know," I repeated.

"Oh, Lena," my mother said. "Why didn't you just come home?"

I sat up, wiping my eyes. "I was going to," I admitted. "And then Dian came, looking for supplies and recruits, and she told me how hard the fight was on the Wall. And Casyn had asked me to come north, and I hadn't. I thought about how I had had a choice, but Garth and Daryl and Finn and all the other young men didn't—and I could be useful. So I went."

"To where you were wanted, and where you didn't have to make choices," my mother said gently.

I pulled away from her slightly. "Yes," I admitted slowly. "But it was more than that, Mother. Casyn had trusted me to be a leader at Tirvan, and a messenger on the road, and had made me privy to some of the inner thoughts of the Emperor. The Emperor himself had trusted me. Even when I was working in Casilla, helping to raise Valle, the thought was at the back of my mind that I had betrayed their trust. So, I went to the Wall."

"Did you never think that we needed you in Tirvan?" The question was asked gently, without accusation.

"No," I said. "Tirvan was fine without me." She sighed.

"You are so like your father," she said, surprising me.

"My father?" I said.

"Yes," she answered. "The Festival you were conceived, he told me right from the start he wouldn't be back to Tirvan. If I birthed a boy-child, he'd come back to claim him at the appropriate time, but otherwise, no. He liked seeing new places, he said. In reply to my letter telling him of your birth, he sent a doll—do you remember it?" I nodded. "And I never heard from Galen again."

"I met him," I said.

"Did you?" She sounded surprised. "So he's still alive."

"Well, he was around midwinter," I clarified. "He'd ridden in from the eastern end of the Wall, where it meets the Durrains, for supplies and probably with information. Turlo introduced us. He seemed likeable. We talked for a few minutes; he asked about you," I remembered. "I have a sister, he told me, in Rigg, and two brothers at the cadet school at the Eastern Fort. Then he wished me luck, and rode away." I shrugged. "But why do you say I'm like him?"

"Oh, Lena," she said, a trace of amusement threading her voice, "adventure. Do you remember asking me why you couldn't ride away with the men, when you turned seven?"

"Did I?" I said. "I don't remember that." But her words brought back, not a memory, but a feeling, an inchoate longing, mixed with a vague sense of failure.

"And then later you always wanted new coves to fish, new directions to sail. And you certainly didn't get that from me! I've never been out of Tirvan in my life, until now."

"But I wanted to come home," I protested. "I was going to, until the Wall was breached, and Casyn needed me to ride south to ask for help. And I'm coming home with you now, when I'm well enough."

"If the Emperor will let you," she said gently.

I frowned. "What do you mean?"

"You are still sworn to his service, you know, and bound by the terms of the truce between him and Linrathe. For which you stood hostage, Lena. Just because we gave—are giving—aid to Linrathe against a common enemy does not mean the truce is superseded. The Emperor may choose to send you back to the house of learning you first were at, and is within his rights to do so."

"I don't think he would, though." I answered. "Callan is a just man."

"He is also an Emperor at war," my mother said. She sighed. "Try not to worry about it, Lena. Do you want to read now? Or write in your journal? I'll leave you in peace, if so."

"Maybe I'll try to write a bit," I said. "A lot has happened. I'm not sure I can remember it all."

"It may come back, as you write. I often found that, when I wrote notes about childbirths." She stood. "Tomorrow, if the day is dry, I will take you outside. You need to begin to walk, to build up your strength."

I smiled at the thought. "Then I hope the day is dry," I said. "I'm feeling like a newly-sheared sheep. I just want to get out of this pen and back to my fields."

She laughed. "Good. One more day, and you can be out in the air again."

When my mother had left, I opened my journal. I had written nothing since my arm had been injured the first time, saving Donnalch's hawk. So much to remember. I would make a list, I decided, to begin with, and then fill in the details. I picked up the pen, dipped it in the inkpot, and began.

Chapter Sixteen

THREE MORE DAYS PASSED. True to her word, my mother took me out, first into a walled courtyard that caught the sun, and then for longer walks, into Berge itself. We stopped a lot, sitting on whatever was at hand: sometime the steps of a house, sometimes a low wall. But by the third day, I could walk to the harbour overlook, although my mother would not allow me to attempt the long descent down to the sea itself.

Berge itself felt both familiar and unfamiliar. The village was perhaps twice the size of Tirvan, and unlike my home village, which straggled down a reasonably gentle slope to the harbour, Berge had two sections: the houses and workshops on the top of the cliff, and those at the harbour. A track angled down steeply between the two halves of the village, with a few buildings along it. More stone had been used in building here, especially at the harbour level, perhaps for strength against the wind and tide. The Wall could be seen easily from Berge, its line along the northern horizon following the contours of the land, extending from the fort at the land's end, down the cliff, to end at the military harbour. From my vantage point at the top of the cliff, I could see several ships at anchor. One of them, I thought, might be *Skua*.

The on-shore breeze brought with it the smell of fish, and I could hear voices from the harbour and the occasional jangle of rigging. Seabirds soared along the cliffs, their grace in the air changing to clumsiness when they landed at their ledge nests. Out to sea, I watched the gannets fishing, their black-tipped wings folded as they dove vertically into the water, almost always coming up with a fish in their beaks. Some fisherwomen hated them, thinking they competed for fish, but I loved watching their precision and skill.

But as much as I wanted to watch the birds and the sea, my eyes kept returning north, to the ships and the fort and the Wall. I thought of the conversation my mother and I had had, sitting on a stone wall in the morning sunshine the day before.

"Why hasn't Cillian come to see me?" I had asked again.

"Lena, think," she had answered. "This is a women's village of the Empire. Cillian is a man of the north. How could he come?"

"Oh," I had said, feeling stupid. "Of course. I wasn't thinking." But the exchange had reminded me of something else. "Why was I brought to Berge, and not treated by the Empire's medics, anyhow?" I had asked. "At the White Fort, Guards weren't sent to the nearest woman's village if they were injured or ill."

"Who nursed them? Not the actual treatment, but who dealt with their personal needs, if they were unable to take care of themselves?"

"Women," I had admitted. "So here, with Berge so close..."

"Exactly," she had said. "The medic had drained your cuts, and poulticed them, exactly as Marta or I would have done, but you needed constant care, and the women of Berge could do that better than the army could. Remember, you had brought word of imminent invasion, and all hands were needed to respond to that." She had sighed, then. "I know you are restless, Lena, and you have questions that I cannot answer. But you must be patient."

I was not good at patience. I felt almost as much a hostage here in Berge as I had at the *Ti'ach*: I had little choice in what I could do, and my future depended on what Callan—or more likely Casyn or Turlo—determined. I needed something to do, and I knew I lacked the strength to make the walk down the cliff to the harbour and back, even if I could have been useful once I was there. I was writing my journal, slowly, but I could not do that all day. I looked north, one last time, and stood to begin my slow walk back to Marta's house.

This was the first day my mother had allowed me out alone. I was grateful for that: I needed space and solitude, and while I was surrounded by houses and other people out about their business, their brief greetings did not intrude on my thoughts, and the long views sufficed to make me feel less cooped up. As I walked back through the upper village, I resolved to ask for some light work, something that would occupy my hands for a few hours a day, at least.

The mid-day meal was ready when I arrived, bread and smoked fish, and some spring greens, served at a table on the broad porch of Marta's house. I had my appetite back, and I ate hungrily. When the meal was over, I stood to carry dishes to the kitchen.

"Lena, you don't need to do that," Marta, Berge's midwife and healer, said. "Kyreth can do it." Kyreth was her apprentice, a girl of fourteen, who had brought me drinks and food when I was still bedridden, and listened while my mother and Marta had discussed my progress.

"No," I said firmly. "I need something to do. Let me clean up, so Kyreth can do other work. I have caused you enough extra work, these past weeks. Let me start to make up for it."

"All right," Marta said, with a glance at my mother. "But let Kyreth bring the water from the well. You should not be carrying the bucket yet."

I conceded this point. While I moved from porch to kitchen with the plates, Kyreth fetched water to fill the kettle simmering over the banked fire. Then, with a brief "Thank you, Lena," she disappeared, leaving me alone in the kitchen.

When the kettle steamed again, I swung it away from the fire, carefully lifting it off its hook. It was the smaller kettle, the one used to heat water for tea, but even so the weight of it tugged at the scars on my chest. I rested it on the kitchen table before I took the last steps over to the counter where the basin awaited, put it down again, and counted to twenty before I lifted it again to tip the water into the basin.

Washing dishes had never been such hard work. Four plates, knives and forks, and a few serving bowls, and by the time they were washed, dried, the wash-water poured away and the kettle returned to the fire, I needed to sit. I had done little that used my upper body in the last weeks. My chest ached. I explored the area with my fingers: no bleeding, just the tenderness of healing tissue after use.

I rested, looking out the kitchen window to where Kyreth worked in the herb garden. I wondered what else I could do. Washing hung on a clothesline, moving slightly in the gentle breeze. I would fetch that in, when the warmth of the day began to fade, I decided. I got up and went outside, to tell Kyreth.

And so it went, for a week, ten days: I did household chores, more each day, and began to run errands for Marta, delivering salves and teas, finding my way around Berge. The scars hurt less, and I grew stronger. When it was sunny and dry, I would linger at the top of the cliff, watching the sea, breathing in the familiar smells. I thought about returning to Tirvan. The thought made me oddly uncomfortable, and I tried to analyse what it was. Surely I wanted to go home? It was all I had thought about, many times, on the Wall, and as a hostage. But when I turned my mind to my village, to my little boat *Dovekie,* to the work out on the sea and at the jetty, I felt the inertia of reluctance underneath the pull of the familiar.

On a clear afternoon, I sat on the wall above the harbour watching a small boat, in design and size almost identical to *Dovekie*, sailing in to the jetty, crewed by two women, working together with the competence of long practice. Observing them, I realized the source of my vacillation about going home. Who would I fish with? Or live with? As I analysed this thought, I saw it was deeper than that. My life in Tirvan had been, since earliest childhood, shared with Maya. We had been friends, then lovers, then partners in life and work. In the weeks between her exile and when I had left Tirvan to search for her, invasion, and aftermath had distracted me. While I had missed her, deeply and intensely, there had been too much else to think about and do. I had not considered what my life there would look like without her, forever. Now, confronting that truth, I wondered if it was truly the life I wanted. There would be a thousand reminders of her at Tirvan. But if I did not go home, then where? What would I do? Stay a Guard on the Wall? Go to Han, and learn to breed and train horses? Go back to Casilla and the fishing fleet there?

"Lena!"

I turned to see Kyreth running towards me. "What is it?" I called, standing.

"There is a soldier, come to see you," she said breathlessly. "An older man, with a beard."

Casyn. I followed her through the village, walking quickly, resisting the impulse to run. He was standing outside Marta's house, by its low wall, looking down the track towards us.

"Lena," he said, and opened his arms. I went into them, hugging him tighter than the soldier's embrace called for, resting against his strength. It was he who pulled back, just slightly, and I took the cue and stepped away, looking up into his lined face.

"I hoped I would see you," I said. He smiled.

"You look well," he said. "Very well. Your mother is skilled in healing. When Cillian brought you to the harbour, we thought you were dying."

"I know," I said. "I think I was. Casyn, thank you for sending for her." The words were inadequate, but he understood.

"It was Marta's idea. She said if anyone on this side of the Wall could save you it would be Gwen of Tirvan, and the fact she was your mother was even better. One of the fisherwomen here went, by boat, to save us sending a fighting man. Or woman," he added.

How did Marta know of my mother? But there was a more pressing question. "What happened, Casyn? You turned Fritjof back, I know, but how? Where?"

He smiled again. "Shall we sit?" he said, indicating the steps leading down to the road. Kyreth had disappeared. We sat side by side. The stones were warm from the afternoon sun, now beginning to wester over the sea. Casyn said nothing for a minute, collecting his thoughts.

"When Cillian—or rather Piet, the fisherman, with Cillian and you on board—reached the military harbour, we had three ships at anchor: *Skua*, *Osprey* and *Petrel*, with crews totalling just under a hundred men. Cillian told us there was one Marai ship in pursuit, possibly, if they had not turned back, believing you dead; he guessed that ship was lightly crewed, perhaps no more than ten men."

"Wait," I said. "Why would they have believed us dead?"

"Ah, of course," he answered, "you wouldn't know. Cillian persuaded Piet to bring you here in his own boat. The one you took was towed out behind until the waters were deep, and then overturned, in the hope the pursuing ship would find it and think you drowned. As far as we know, it worked."

"That was good thinking," I admitted.

"It was," Casyn agreed.

"Fritjof had said he would sail south three days after his crowning," I said. "We must have been three days getting here, and the winds were with us. So you must have met him off the coast of Linrathe."

Casyn shook his head. "Do you not remember? The weather was changing, the night you fell ill. The winds switched to the south. Cillian and Piet rowed here as much as they sailed. It gave us the advantage. We met them further north, and we took them almost entirely by surprise. They turned inland, rowing up a river to escape our larger ships, and were caught by Linrathe's men: Lorcann, Donnalch's brother, had been riding north at all speed, once he had gathered his troops. By pure chance, we came together nearly at the same place."

"Is Fritjof dead?"

"No. He escaped north, back into Varsland. Lorcann tells me there are a hundred islands and inlets where he could have hidden. We chose not to pursue him."

Lorcann tells me. A chill arose inside me. "Casyn," I said. "What has happened to Donnalch?"

I saw the flash of pain on his face. "He is dead," he said gently. "Fritjof killed him."

I put up a hand to my mouth. The *Teannasach*, dead. "Dagney said he would,"

I said after a moment.

Casyn raised an eyebrow. "Did she?"

"She tried to warn him, with a song she sung." Casyn's face showed doubt. I frowned. "Did you think it was because of *me*? Because I escaped?"

He spread his hands. "You and Cillian. It may have been part of the reason."

"Dagney tried to warn him." I repeated, my voice rising. "Did Fritjof kill Dagney too?"

"No. She is safe. Lorcann said that Fritjof would not kill a...a singer—although he used another word, or he would bring down the wrath of all their gods on his people."

"A *scáeli*," I said. "More than a singer. They keep the history of their people, in the songs and stories." Emotions battled in me; relief for Dagney, sorrow for Donnalch. And Ardan, I remembered, who Fritjof had had killed earlier. Who else, either on the island or in the battle?

"Lena," Casyn's voice was solemn. "There is more, and this will be even harder to hear. Should I call your mother, to be with you?"

I stared at him. Was Callan dead? Or Garth? *Skua* had been among the ships in battle. I searched Casyn's face: it was grave, and I could see sorrow in his eyes, but not, I thought, what I would see if his brother had been killed, or if he had to tell me that Garth was dead. I shook my head. "Tell me," I said.

He sighed. "Fritjof taunted the men of Linrathe with Donnalch's death. He had beheaded him, and carried his head with him on his ship." I swallowed, hard. "He told them Donnalch was dead because he, Fritjof, had claimed you as hostage and bride for his son, and you had broken that treaty." I must have made a sound, because he put out a hand to touch my shoulder. "He was trying to turn them, Lena, by telling them that you were untrustworthy, and by extension all the Empire as well. He failed: for the greatest part, the men of Linrathe stood with their leader and with us, and we prevailed against the Marai." He fell silent. Cold emanated out from my core.

I forced the words through my lips. "For the greatest part?"

"There were some who believed him." He took a breath. "Lena, do you remember the terms of the truce signed on the Wall? That your life was forfeit, were the truce to be broken?"

I nodded. "But the truce was not broken, not by us."

He hesitated. "You killed a man," he said finally.

"A man who tried to rape me! And that was not in Linrathe!"

"But it was in Sorham, which is Linrathe's. But even without that, Lena, even if that killing could be explained and excused—which it is, in my mind—Fritjof claimed he killed the *Teannasach* as a direct response to your escape. Yours and Cillian's." He looked away.

"And?" I whispered. "What is it you aren't telling me, Casyn?"

"Two men left the fight after hearing Fritjof's words," Casyn said, his voice almost a monotone. "They rode east, and south, to where Darel was."

"No. Not Darel. No..." I started to weep. "How could I have foreseen this?" I said between sobs. "I was trying to save Donnalch, Casyn...oh, Darel..."

"By the terms of the truce Linrathe had the right," Casyn said bleakly. "Although the right did not reside in those two men, and Lorcann has had them killed."

"That will be little comfort to Turlo," I sobbed. Casyn took my hand. We sat on the cooling steps as the sun dipped further into the sea and the light dimmed. Slowly, a cold truth crept into my battered and grieving mind. I took a deep breath, and another, and wiped my eyes and face with my free hand. "General." My voice rasped with weeping, and a bout of coughing kept me from speaking for some minutes. Casyn took his hand away, straightening. I stood. He too brought himself to his feet. I looked up at him, controlling the coughs. "By the terms of the truce," I said, "my life is forfeit too."

His grey eyes never left mine. In them I saw regret, and deep pain, and the clear honesty I had always seen. "Yes, Guardswoman," he answered.

I forced myself not to look away. "Better that I had died, then," I said. "Does my mother know?"

He shook his head, a tiny motion. "No."

No one has told her, I thought, but she is a council-leader, and she will know what the truce said. She can work it out. "Will you send her away, before...before it is done?"

"There will be a trial," he said. "For you, and for Cillian, although he will be tried by his own people, of course. Do you not want her here, for that? I cannot force her to go, Lena. She is a guest of Marta, and of Berge."

He was right, of course. It was only my life he could order. "The trial is a formality," I said. A shadow of indecision passed over his face.

"Much rests on it," he answered. "Lorcann—he will be *Teannasach* soon, and is now save for the ceremony—thinks more in black and white than his brother did. He will, we are nearly sure, sign a permanent truce with the Empire, for we are not the enemy snapping at Linrathe's heels, but rather an ally, now. And we too need Linrathe, as a buffer between us and the Marai. But before that, we— Callan—must prove he is a man of his word."

I was a piece in the game, I thought, not for the first time, a piece of little worth, to be sacrificed to the greater plan. I remembered accusing Callan of treating the women's villages that way, all those months ago at his winter camp, after the Lestian invasion. He had not denied it then, not entirely. I should have remembered that, when I agreed to be a hostage.

I took a deep breath against the welling anger and fear. "Thank you, General. Will I be told when the trial is?"

"Of course, Guardswoman. Expect it to be another week; I was here in part to judge if you were strong enough to be tried. My judgement is you need a little more time."

"I am not strong enough to be executed?" I shot back.

He sighed. "Not that. But do you not want time with your mother, time to write letters?"

"No!" I snapped. "I do not want my mother to know. Better she thinks I died another way, a relapse perhaps. Can you grant me that, General?"

He spread his hands. "I could—but if she is still here, in Berge?"

"She won't be," I said. "I will find a way to send her home. Cannot I be tried at the White Fort?"

"Perhaps," he answered. "I will suggest it." His face softened. "Lena..."

"No, General," I said, as coldly as I could. "We must be Guardswoman and General, now." He held me in that grave, assessing gaze, for a heartbeat, and another. Then he nodded.

"Farewell, Guardswoman," he said. "I will make my recommendations. Please let me know your mother's plans."

"I will, General," I answered. "Farewell."

I watched him walk away to the north. Suddenly my legs gave out. I sat, hard, on the steps, cold now in the dusk, and took several deep and unsteady breaths. Darel, I thought, tears starting again. Brave, funny, irreverent Darel. I hope it was a quick death. He was only fourteen, and so like his father. So like his father...the thought reverberated in my fogged mind. I must tell Casyn about Cillian, about his likeness to Callan. In the horror of what he had told me, I had not thought of it. Perhaps it could save his life.

"Lena?" My mother spoke from the porch. "Come in. It's getting cold."

I stood, wiping my eyes, wondering how to face her. But she had seen my hand go to my face, and came towards me. "What's wrong? What did Casyn say to you?"

"Just...deaths," I said. "He came to tell me of deaths. The *Teannasach* of Linrathe, and Turlo's son, Darel. The other hostage."

"Oh, Lena," She put her arms around me, holding me. I took a deep breath, and started to cough again. I pulled away to cover my mouth, unable to stop the deep racking spasms. "Into the house," she ordered, "and into bed. Now, Lena."

She helped me up to the porch and up the stairs to my room. I undressed. She pulled a thick nightdress over my head and pulled back the covers for me. I climbed in, letting her tuck the blankets around me as if I were a child, piling pillows behind me so I was half-upright. "Tea, soup, and sleep," she said. "Tea first, and a salve for your chest. I will be back in a few minutes."

But it was Kyreth who brought me the tea, tasting of honey and herbs, warm and soothing for my raw throat. The coughing subsided. The salve my mother brought smelt of the same herbs, and it too warmed me where it was rubbed into the skin of my chest. I submitted to all these ministrations calmly, glad at some level of the distraction. But after I had drunk my soup, and another cup of tea, had had a heated stone tucked into the bedcovers at my feet, and the curtains closed against the night, I was left alone with the stark truths Casyn had told me. I was responsible for two deaths, of people I had known and liked. For that, I too would have to die.

CHAPTER SEVENTEEN

I SHOULD NOT HAVE SLEPT, but there must have been poppy in that last cup of tea, for I did, for some hours. It was past midnight when I woke. I got up to use the chamberpot, afterwards pushing the curtains aside to look out into the night. Stars gleamed from between clouds, but there was no moon.

I would be sentenced to death, in a week or so. Cold words, to match the cold inside me. Oddly detached, I thought about what that would mean. How was it done? A knife to the throat? Hanging? I shivered. I would prefer the knife, I thought. Something quick. I remembered the gurgling, coughing death of the boy whose throat I had cut, when Leste had invaded, and that of the fisherman in the water. Maybe not. Although it would be only fair, somehow.

Only fair. What was fair about this? The cold in me coalesced into the ice of anger. I had risked my life to bring word of the Marai plans to the Emperor, and this was how I was rewarded? Should I have just allowed them to invade, while I myself became an unwilling bride?

The anger grew. I wanted to smash something, or scream, or both, but some vestige of civility, here in Marta's house where I was a guest, kept me from doing so. I paced the room, the word 'unfair' pulsing in my mind.

Finally, I sat on the bed, drained and numb. I looked up at the window again, and as I did so my eyes fell on my books: my journal and Colm's history.

I went to the shelf, took the history, lit a candle. In its flickering light, I leafed through the opening pages. I thought I knew these words by heart. I read, once again, the description of Lucian's reign. In the third paragraph, a line caught my attention:

But the decree from the Emperor after the Partition vote was not to the liking of many men and women, not even some men senior in the army and long trusted by Lucian, even though that disagreement meant their death by the laws of the Empire.

I read quickly.

The northern people, beset by the same conditions unsuited to crop or cattle, began a series of skirmishes south, raiding for whatever food could be taken. As the days shortened the Emperor gathered his troops and rode north to meet the enemy, but three things were against him: the cold and snow of an early winter; the lack of adequate rations for his men, and the presence, in the enemy's bands, of men of the Empire, who had trained and fought with Lucian and knew his tactics. Among these men may have been the generals who had disagreed with Lucian, for he had commuted their sentences of death to banishment, outcast beyond the Empire's borders, as was his right as Emperor.

I stopped reading. Was there a chance for me, here? I thought back to Callan, pronouncing summary justice on Blaine and Nevin, after their betrayal, the cold steel in his voice. He had shown his rogue commanders no pity, no generosity. Would he deal with me in the same way?

Part of me could not believe it. Blaine and Nevin had been complicit in a plan to kill the Emperor, an act of treason. I had broken a truce and a promise to bring word of a planned attack. Surely these would not have the same punishment? But I had violated an oath given in the Emperor's name. Was that not also treason?

I slept a bit more, fitful dozing rather than deep sleep, but when the sun rose I was awake, a few decisions made. I would use Colm's history to plan my defense, and I would tell my mother as little as possible. I would try to get her to leave, even if it meant telling her lies. The anger remained, coiled and cold inside me, and beyond that, deeper and even colder, the terror of what was to come, but I would ignore them both, for now. I dressed and went downstairs. The day was damp, a fine misty rain falling. I took a shawl from a peg in the kitchen to cover my head and shoulders as I went out to the privy to empty the chamberpot, shivering slightly in the cool air.

Back inside I met my mother on the stairs. "Lena," she said. "Why aren't you in bed?"

"Because I am awake, and feeling fine," I said. "I'm not even coughing." Which was true, apart from a few shallow coughs when I first got out of bed. "And I'm hungry. All I had for supper was the broth."

She regarded me, her hands moving to re-pin the knot of her hair. "All right," she said. "But stay indoors, near the fire, and rest this afternoon. And tell me if you start to cough again."

"I will," I promised.

I washed and dressed and went back downstairs, to find Marta in the kitchen. "There's tea," she said, indicating the pot keeping warm on the stove. I poured myself a cup, sliced some bread, and sat at the table to eat.

"Marta," I said, "did you know of my mother, before she came here to tend me?"

"Of course," she said. "Gwen of Tirvan is an honoured name among midwives and healers, did you not know? We have exchanged letters over the years, sharing what we know of the uses of healing herbs, and other ways of treating illness and injury. Her knowledge of the uses of anash, for example, goes far beyond what many others know, myself included. We have had some long talks while she has been here."

I shook my head. "I had no idea," I said. "She is just my mother, and our healer and midwife."

Marta laughed. "It is always so," she said. "What made you ask?"

"Something the General said, when he came to see me yesterday," I answered. "Shall I do these dishes, Marta, and then chop vegetables for soup?'

I spent the morning doing kitchen chores. These tasks seemed unreal, but they were something for my hands to do, and my mind. If I did not focus hard on the steps, I forgot things, forgot even what I was doing, sometimes. When the bread was rising and the mid-day soup simmering, I poured myself tea and sat at the kitchen table. I leafed through Colm's history, looking for other instances of Emperors choosing to banish a wrong-doer, rather than execute them. If I were given a chance to speak in my defense, I needed to know this history.

I found a brief reference to the exile of a murderer in Mathon's reign, clemency granted because the Emperor thought the killing, retribution for a physical attack, a form of self-defence. Had I not killed the fisherman for the same reasons? I read the passage again, committing it to memory.

In the late morning, the skies cleared a bit, the fine rain giving way to a weak and watery sunshine. I took the book back to my room and went outside to gather greens and radishes for the meal. When I came back in, my mother was in the kitchen, setting the table.

"What else did Casyn say yesterday?" she asked. "Something has upset you. Will you be allowed to go home?"

I hesitated. I had planned what to say, when she asked this. "No," I said, and saw her face fall. "Not yet. There will be a hearing, for me and Cillian, a formality, Casyn says, and then I will either be sent back to the *Ti'ach*, if the peace still requires hostages, or allowed to leave the Emperor's service." Half a lie.

"I see," she said. "You must be disappointed, Lena. You wanted to come back to Tirvan."

"I did. Or I thought I did, when I was first recovering. But I'm not sure, now." "Why not?"

What would she believe? "I'd like to see everyone," I said. "But I don't know how to live there without Maya. Everything we did, apprenticing, fishing from *Dovekie*, we did together. I don't know if I can go back to that life." And I never will, I thought, glad of the cold that numbed me, keeping tears from my eyes.

"Had you not left Tirvan, you might have found a way," she said thoughtfully. "And you may yet, but I think I understand." She held out her arms, and I let her hug me, and did my best to hug her back.

"Mother," I said, when we had stepped apart, "should you not be going home, yourself? I am well, or nearly so, and I think you are worrying about Tirvan, regardless of how competent you know Kira to be."

She laughed. "You are right. But I was more worried about you. And I still am."

"But I am fine," I insisted, hoping she could not see the lie in my eyes. "And the fishing boats will be growing busier as the weather warms; if anyone is going to make time to sail you home, it needs to be soon. I will be going back to the Wall, to the White Fort, for the hearing and the decision." If she thought the hearing would not be here, at the coastal fort, she would have no reason to stay.

"Perhaps you are right," she admitted. "You are past danger. I will stay, though, if the fisherwomen will bear with me, until you leave for the Wall. And you will send word?"

"Of course," I promised.

"Oh, my dear," she said. "I hope you find what you want, wherever you go."
I tried to smile. "So do I," I said.

How, I wondered, could I get a note to Casyn, once my mother's plans were
made? I could ask my mother how she had sent word of my health, if I told her
I wanted to send greetings to Cillian. But I did not need to: after the mid-day
meal, Casyn's soldier-servant, Birel, arrived, leading a compact chestnut
gelding behind his own horse.

"Guardswoman," he greeted me, swinging down off his bay. "The General has
sent you this horse and its tack, as compensation for the loss of your mare. He's
newly shod, and a good steady horse. I've ridden him myself, at times."

"Hello, Sergeant," I said. "This is unexpected." Did this mean I would be
riding to the White Fort? I stepped off the porch to go to the horse's head. I let
him smell me, rubbing his neck. He snuffled my hand, blew out, and stood
quietly. "What's his name?" I asked. He was slightly taller than my Clio, with
heavier legs.

"Suran. He'll serve you well, I've no doubt. I was also to tell you: his food and
stabling will be paid by the General, while you are in Berge. And now I should
be getting back."

"Wait," I said, adding quickly "if you would. I'd like to send a note to the
General. I won't be five minutes."

"Of course," he replied. He stood at ease, holding the two horses. I ran inside
and up the stairs to my room. Writing as quickly as I could, I thanked Casyn for
the horse and then made my request: could he, somehow, call me back to the
fort some days before the trial? My mother would leave Berge then, I wrote. I
signed the note, folded it, sealing it with wax from my candle.

Back outside I handed it to Birel. He slipped it into his tunic pocket. "I'll see
he gets it, Guardswoman," he said. Then he held out his hand to me. Surprised,
I took it. "You're a brave soldier, Lena," he said roughly. "There'll be many
who'll speak for you, if necessary. Don't lose heart."

So he knew—but of course he did. Men like him, who served the senior
officers, were privy to many secrets. The unexpected kindness touched me.
"Thank you, Birel," I said. He nodded, mounting his bay to ride back to the fort.
I watched him leave, then turned to the horse whose reins I held. "Well," I said,
"what to do with you?" I looped the reins around the gatepost, and went in
search of Marta.

She was mixing a salve in the still-room, instructing Kyreth. "Keep stirring,"
she said to her apprentice. "What can I do for you, Lena?"

I explained about the horse. "Where can I stable him? The army will pay; I
am still a soldier."

She nodded. "They sent money for your care and food here, too. Our own
ponies are pastured at the top of the village, and there is a barn for poor
weather, but it won't be an army stable."

"It will be fine," I said. "Army horses are adaptable; they are often picketed outside, in all weathers. Who do I see about it?"

"Risa. She's probably up with the sheep, in the fields. If not, her apprentices will know where she is."

"Thank you," I replied. I went back out, looking east; there were sheep grazing on the uplands. I untied Suran, adjusted the stirrups, and using the steps as a mounting block, swung up into the saddle. He stood steady as I mounted, and obeyed the reins without hesitation.

I tested his paces as we rode towards the pasture, finding he had a comfortable trot and a rolling, easy canter. My own muscles ached even from this brief test, so I brought him back to a walk as I approached the lower fields where a group of ponies grazed. The breeze was off-shore, and their heads went up as we came closer, the wind carrying the smell of a strange horse to them. They trotted up to the wall. Three of them were heavily in foal. I brought Suran closer, letting them smell each other; if he was to share a field with them, the sooner they got to know each other, the better.

No one seemed to be around. I surveyed the higher fields, and there I could see two figures and a dog, working the sheep. I followed a track up between the walls.

"Are you Risa?" I called, as I approached them.

"I am," she called back. "Give me a minute; we're nearly done with this group." I watched, recognizing the task she was at: dagging, clipping dried dung off the flanks of the sheep. Now the weather was warming, the dung attracted flies, which would lay their eggs in the dung; when the larvae hatched, they would burrow into the sheep's flesh. I remembered why I hated sheep.

I dismounted, letting Suran drop his head to graze. Risa finished her work and, after a word to her apprentice, came over to me. "Lena, isn't it?" she asked.

"Yes," I said. "I've just been assigned a horse, to get me back into riding shape before I return to duty. I'll need a place to pasture him and store his tack, for a week or so. The army will pay. Can I turn him loose with the ponies?"

"He'll need some hay, too, if you are going to be riding him daily," she said. "But it's there in the barn. There's a tack room. Will you be taking care of him?"

"Yes."

"Good; we're busy right now, as you can see. There's a small paddock just by the barn; put him there for a day or so. It adjoins the geldings' field. I don't want him in with the mares; they're too close to foaling. Does that suit?"

She reminded me of Daria, from Karst: plain-spoken, practical, and good-hearted. "Yes, of course," I said. "Can I ride around here for a bit, before I turn him out?"

She shrugged. "It won't bother the sheep."

"Thanks," I said, and with a wave to the apprentice, I kept riding. The track curved up to the higher pastures. Near the top, I stopped. North of us, I could see the line of the Wall, following the landscape. I was high enough to see a couple of the watch-towers, spaced along its length. The coastal fort spread out southward from its line, itself walled and towered, and below both, ships stood at anchor in the harbour. One of them could be *Skua*. I hoped not. I did not want Garth, or Dern, to witness my trial. But maybe it would be at the White Fort. Why else would Casyn have sent me a horse?

I had tried to be a good soldier. From the first day Casyn had ridden into Tirvan, I had done what he asked. Except once, I reminded myself. 'Will you come north?' he had asked, in the hours after word of the Wall's breaching had arrived. And I had not, not for long months. But when I did, I thought, I served the Emperor well, on the Wall and then as hostage. The anger in me twisted. Why had I done what Casyn had asked, and Callan, so blindly, so trustingly? Tears rose in my eyes. From the wind, I told myself. What a fool I had been, seeing only the adventure, and not the cost.

I rode back down to the barn and paddock. I unsaddled and curried Suran, turning him out into the paddock with a biscuit of hay. The geldings in the next field trotted over to examine him; nothing untoward happened, so I went back into the dim barn to put away his tack. My back and legs ached from the riding, and my thigh muscles trembled. I was glad the walk back to Marta's house was downhill.

"The army has sent me a horse," I told my mother at supper that evening, "so that I can re-accustom my body to riding. I would think I will be called back to the Wall in about a week, and then on to the White Fort."

"I hope they do not ask you to ride all day," she said, frowning.

I shrugged. "They know I have been very ill. I am to tell them when I can ride for half a day," I lied, "so that is what they expect." I concentrated on the fish on my plate. I had no interest in food, but I knew my body needed fuel.

"Don't push yourself," she warned. "I spoke with the fisherwomen today. Elga, who fetched me from Tirvan, is willing to take me back in a few days. While she was waiting for me to pack my things when she came to find me, she spoke with Dessa, and there are some ideas about boat design she'd like to discuss with her. So, she is happy to take me back, but as you guessed she wants to do it soon. I will tell her tomorrow to choose a day."

"If the seas allow," I said, the fisherwoman's caution coming automatically to my lips.

The weather held, only small showers of rain blowing through, not enough to keep the boats off the water. I rode Suran daily, rain or no, testing his trot and his canter, strengthening my muscles and building my endurance. I wanted no weakness to prevent me from riding to the White Fort. I ached from the effort, and part of me wished Berge had baths like Tirvan's, to soak my tired body in at the end of the day, but no hot springs bubbled out of the ground here. There was a bath house, but using it meant building fires to heat water, and I couldn't be bothered to go to that effort.

I found no more mention of banishment in Colm's history. I thought of the books on Perras's shelves, at the *Ti'ach*, and wondered what the punishment for treason would be in Linrathe. I knew what it was in Varsland, under Fritjof.

Was there an argument there, that we were better than the Marai? I turned that around in my mind, examining it from every side. I could not decide. Who could I ask? The only possibility was Cillian, were I allowed to talk to him. Where was he?

I needed to get to the Wall, I thought, frustrated. I was well, and the advice I needed now could come neither from my mother, nor the women of Berge. That afternoon, I turned Suran's head north. A tower stood where the fort's wall turned back toward the Wall. A lone soldier looked north, his eyes moving from the sea to the lands beyond the fort, and back again. He did not look south: what threat could be expected, from Berge?

"Soldier!" I called. He turned rapidly.

"What do you want?" he called down.

"I am Guardswoman Lena, lately of the White Fort garrison. I have been recuperating from injuries at Berge. I need to send a message to the General Casyn that I am well and can return to my duties. Can you take this message?"

"At the end of my watch," he said. It would do.

"Thank you," I called back. I saw him nod, his eyes returning to the sea. I reined Suran south, and gave him a gentle kick. He broke into a canter, and then with further encouragement from me a gallop. I turned him east, along the track that ran up into the hills, climbing higher, until we reached the highest ridge. From here the land unrolled before me in all directions, and just to the east I could see the road, the road that ran from the Wall south to the Four-Ways Inn, before turning east to Casilla; the road I had ridden almost every mile of, save this most northern section.

What if I just kept riding? The idea shimmered in my mind like a sea-mirage, beckoning, but like those false visions of islands on the horizon, I knew it had no substance. I would be followed, caught, to stand trial not only for treason but also for desertion. I sat on my horse, feeling the wind in my hair, my eyes taking in the space and distance that had always been my deepest solace.

A flash of movement, high in the hazy sky, caught my attention. I searched the sky. There it was, again: a tiny speck, blinking in and out of the high clouds to the west, circling, until it suddenly dropped, straight down, plunging arrow-fast toward the sea. A *fuádain*, I realized, the wandering falcon, remembering the bird I had seen hunt from Donnalch's hand so few weeks earlier. But this one flew free.

Birel came for me the next morning. I had packed my bag in expectation, and given my thanks to Marta and Kyreth. Suran stood, saddled and bridled, at the gate. I sat on the porch of Marta's house with my mother, waiting. I had to keep our speech light, or I would break.

"Mother," I began, "I didn't realize you were such an honoured healer. But both Marta and Casyn say you are. Shouldn't I have known that?"

"Why would you?" she said simply. "And I don't know that I'm all that honoured. Tirvan has a few more books on healing and midwifery than some other villages, and I have spent time reading them. I have shared some of what

I have learned with other healers, by letters. That's all." She smiled. "And Marta is twenty years younger than I am, so she sees me as vastly more experienced. Although she knows things I don't, such as different methods to treat frost-burn."

"If there were somewhere you could go, to learn more, somewhere with more books, would you?"

"What do you mean?"

"Sorley—he was another student at the *Ti'ach*, the house of learning that I was at—told me there is one *Ti'ach* that specializes in healing. He said you could go there, for a season, if there was a peace. Would you, if you could?"

"Oh," she said. "I don't know. North of the Wall?" Her hands went to her hair.

"Yes," I said, "north of the Wall. The *Ti'acha* are unlike anything we have in the Empire: communities of men and women, dedicated to learning and teaching. I would have enjoyed my time at *Ti'ach na Perras*, I think, learning more history, and about peoples we didn't even know existed." I sighed. "But other events took over."

"Well," she said. "It's tempting, now Kira is qualified."

"And you might have things to teach them," I suggested. "Perras—he was the head of the *Ti'ach* where I was sent—was shocked to learn you knew of the Eastern Fever. He said he wished he could talk to you about it."

"But there would need to be a peace," she said.

"I think there will be," I answered. "Casyn told me that Lorcann—he will be the new *Teannasach* of Linrathe—will sign a treaty; we need to be allies, if the Marai are to be held back." And if the Emperor assuaged his anger with my punishment, and Cillian's, I thought.

I looked away, hiding my face from my mother, to see Birel riding towards the house. "It's time," I said, standing. Fear and relief battled inside me. I glanced up at the sky. "The weather will hold," I said, "for your sailing." My mother had gone to see Elga yesterday evening, after I had told her I would be leaving in the morning. They would sail on the afternoon's tide.

I let my mother hold me, but only briefly. She kissed me on the forehead. "Say hello to Kira, and everyone," I said. "I will write, when I know where I am posted." My mouth felt stiff, the words forced out, hoarse to my own ears. I thought I was trembling, but my hands on Suran's reins were steady. I swung up into the saddle.

"Farewell, my daughter," my mother said. I could hear the tears in her voice. Did she know, or suspect, more than she was saying? I raised a hand, willed a smile, and walked Suran forward to meet Birel.

"Ready, Guardswoman?" he asked.

"I am, Sergeant," I lied.

CHAPTER EIGHTEEN

WHEN WE WERE FREE OF THE VILLAGE, I moved up to ride beside Birel. "Where will I be taken, Sergeant?" I asked.

"First, to the General," he said.

"And then?" He did not answer, simply shaking his head. I realized it was unfair to ask him. "Where is Cillian?" I asked. "Do you know?"

"In the fort's prison," he said. "The northmen asked us to hold him."

Why? I did not ask. We rode to the gate-tower that faced Berge. On the flat ground bordering the fort, men were practicing swordplay. No one looked our way. The wooden gates swung open at Birel's command, moving noiselessly on their huge iron hinges. The street beyond was cobbled and ditched. Buildings lay on either side. I recognized them from the White Fort: barracks and stables, workshops and the baths, and in the centre, where the two major streets crossed, the headquarters. The shouts of officers, the ring of hammer on anvil, the smell of roasting meat from the kitchens; all were familiar.

Outside the headquarters Birel halted. We dismounted. A cadet appeared to take our horses. I followed Birel through a courtyard, where a cracked bowl as wide as I was tall sat in the centre, an incomplete border of blue tiles around its rim. I wondered what it was for. The walls of the courtyard were pillared and arched; every second arch was a window, some shuttered, some open. The centre archway on each wall held a door. Birel stopped. "Give me your bag," he said. I complied. He opened the door on the eastern wall, but did not cross the threshold. "General," he said. "Guardswoman Lena, as you requested." He gestured to me to enter.

Casyn sat at a beneath the window, writing. I blinked in the dimmer light of the room. He held up a hand, telling me to wait, as he finished what he wrote. I looked around. On the plastered walls, I could just make out a faint pattern in places, diamond shapes under the whitewash. I glanced down at the floor, remembering the pictures in the floor at the White Fort, but here the tiles were dull and worn. Casyn turned to me.

"Guardswoman," he said. "You are well?"

"I am, General," I said. "And I thank you for the horse. I have been riding daily, and can spend several hours in the saddle without discomfort."

"Good. Let me tell you what will happen now," he said bluntly. "I have been in correspondence with the Emperor. He wishes to oversee your trial himself, so we will be riding to the White Fort tomorrow, along with Cillian of Linrathe. Lorcann and our Emperor have chosen to hear your trials together: one trial, one consequence. A united voice."

"To send a message to the Marai, and to those who might support them," I said.

He nodded. "Exactly. And I must ensure that there is no difference in how you and Cillian are treated, now you are here at the Wall's End fort, so when our interview is done you will be taken to the prison, Guardswoman, for this night. And you will both ride shackled. We must be seen to be punitive." He frowned. "Is your mother gone?"

"She sails this afternoon," I said.

"Good. Have you anything to say to me, Guardswoman, before the sergeant escorts you to the prison? We will debrief on the ride, but is there anything you would wish others not to hear?" His voice was formal, brusque, but his eyes were not.

"Yes," I said, relieved I had this chance. I owed it to Cillian; he had saved my life. Perhaps I could save his. "General, you know I am good at seeing likenesses; it was how I recognized Garth." He nodded. "I think…" I hesitated, looking for a way to say this, "Is it possible that Cillian could be the Emperor's son?"

His eyes widened. He said nothing for some moments, thinking. "How old is he?"

He had not dismissed the idea. "Thirty-three."

"What do you know of his mother?"

"Only that she was very young; she lived just north of the Wall, and he has always been told his father was a soldier of our Empire. As far as I know, his mother died very soon after his birth."

"Do you know her name?"

I shook my head. "No."

"What did you see in Cillian, Lena, to make you think this?" he asked.

"The first time I saw him, I thought I knew him. Then I decided I was wrong, but every so often I would see a glimpse of something, a reminder—and then one day he was very angry, and he was exactly like the Emperor, on Midwinter's Day, after Colm was killed. And since then, I can't not see the likeness."

He leaned back in his chair, thinking. "Have you said this to anyone else?"

"Only Cillian himself," I answered.

"Cillian? Why?"

"Because he hates the Empire, General," I said, a flash of anger heating my words, "and I needed him on my side, on our side, to bring you word of the Marai, to not see us as another enemy."

"Well," he said, "I may wish you had not done so, but I follow your reasoning. But did Cillian?"

I shook my head. "I don't know. I fell ill too soon after the conversation to be sure. But he saw that an alliance with our Empire was better than being conquered by the Marai, although reluctantly, I believe."

"It is likely of little importance," Casyn said, "except that it might affect how he comports himself, at the trial. Do you have any influence with him?"

"Probably not," I said. "And what will it matter, General, if execution is to be the consequence, and the trial only a formality, a sham?"

His grave eyes studied me. "I did not say that, Lena," he said. "I said much depended on it. The Emperor has the right to determine another punishment, another consequence, but both he and Lorcann must agree."

"Banishment," I said.

"A possibility," he agreed. "Do you see, then, why it is important for Cillian to be co-operative, at the trial?"

I damped down the leap of hope that had arisen at Casyn's words. It was a chance, but a chance dependent on three men: one stranger, angry at the death of his brother; one little better than a stranger, angry at the world, and one the Emperor of a nation at war once again, who had to balance his new and fragile alliance with Linrathe against one life. But still....

"I do, General," I said. "I will do my best." I would do as Casyn requested, but this time it was for me, I thought. "I will be allowed to speak with him?"

"I will ensure it," he said. He stood. "Now, Guardswoman, I will have Sergeant Birel escort you to the prison." He went to the door. Birel entered promptly: he must have been just outside, I thought. How much had he heard?

Casyn returned to his desk to scribble a note. "Give this to Cormaic," he said to the sergeant. "We ride to the White Fort the day after tomorrow. Tell that to Cillian, please."

"Yes, sir," Birel replied.

"General," I acknowledged.

"Dismissed," he said, already turning to his papers. I followed Birel out through the courtyard and along a cobbled street, past barracks and workshops, to a small building adjoining the western wall of the fort. Built of stone blocks, it had been lime-washed once, but now only flakes of a whitish-grey remained; along with the lichens that grew on the bare stones, it gave the building a motley look. Small windows just below the roof were barred, and the door was guarded.

The guard saluted Birel. "Sergeant?"

"Place Guardswoman Lena in a cell adjoining the Linrathan's," Birel instructed. "They are to be allowed free conversation, and she is to have the same exercise daily as the man." He turned to me. "I will return the contents of your bag, Guardswoman, once I have searched it." I was led to my cell; a tiny room, big enough to hold a pallet on the floor, and a bucket, and nothing more. The door was an iron grate, allowing me no privacy. Cillian's cell was directly opposite. I had seen him stand as we came in, hands on the grate of his door.

"Lena," he said. "You are well?" He was pale, thin, his hair longer and unkempt.

"I am," I said. I walked into the cell, hearing the door locked behind me. "And you?"

"Well enough," he said.

"I am to tell you we ride for the White Fort the day after tomorrow," Birel said to Cillian, forestalling anything further he was about to say. Cillian only nodded. We watched the two men leave, hearing the outside door close and the key turn.

"We have leave to talk," I said to Cillian. "Talk freely, I mean. I have just come from the General Casyn."

"How kind of him," Cillian said, sinking down onto his pallet. "Having saved the Empire, and Linrathe, we are rewarded with prison cells, but are allowed to talk freely to each other. So very generous."

"Be reasonable..." I started to say. I stopped. Why was I defending the actions of our leaders? "You're right," I said, letting my banked anger flare. "It's minging unfair. Have you been locked up here the whole time I was sick?"

"Not quite," he said. "At first, I was given a decent room in one of the barracks, and consulted for hours on what I knew about the Marai, and their boats, and where Linrathe's forces might be, all reasonable questions, given the threat. I drew maps and estimated distances and was useful, Lena, useful to Linrathe and the Empire. But then word came back that the *Teannasach* was dead, and suddenly I was here, by the direction of Lorcann, to be tried for treason. Treason! After we saved them, you and me."

"Did you know they are trying us together, the Emperor and your new *Teannasach*, to show a united front to both our peoples? We are game pieces, Cillian, nothing more."

He looked up at that. "That's a different song you're singing," he said quietly.

"Ah, gods," I said, "I'm minging angry, Cillian. I feel like I've been lulled by reasonable words and gently-phrased requests ever since Casyn first came to Tirvan." I moved restlessly in the cell, wanting to pace, but there was not the space.

He laughed, a dry, mirthless sound. "Now you know why I have no love for the machinations of power, whether they are practiced by Emperors or *Teannasacha*."

"What do you know of Lorcann?"

He straightened on his pallet. "Older than Donnalch, by a year or two. Hotter-headed, quicker to anger, holds a grudge. That was why Donnalch was chosen *Teannasach* over him."

Not good. "Callan is calm, thoughtful, even reasonable—or so I used to think," I amended. "But if he is angered, then he is cold, ruthless even."

For all his bitterness, Cillian was clever. He smiled. "So, we must be careful not to anger either of them. That is what you are saying, isn't it, Lena? And 'we' really means 'me', does it not? But what is the point? The punishment for treason is death."

"Not necessarily," I said. "I read through the history of the Empire again. There are a couple of instances when Emperors banished those who had committed treason, or murder, rather than executing them. If Birel returns my books I will show you the passages."

"Emperors, maybe," he countered, "but in Linrathe's law the punishment is death. So perhaps you will be spared, but not I."

He had answered my question. Treason, I thought, probably meant death in all lands. But Garth should have died, for desertion, and yet the Empire, Casyn and Dern and ultimately the Emperor, had found another way for him to redeem his failure. Why not us?

Time passed. Coarse bread and a cup of water arrived, and with it my pack. I opened it, going through the contents. The books had been returned, and my blood-cloths, but my jar of salve for my scars, my tiny sewing kit, and my flint and tinder had been taken. I slid the history through the bars toward Cillian, telling him which pages to read. He read, squinting in the poor light, then slid the book back to me, shrugging. "So the Emperor has the right to commute a death sentence to exile," he said. "I don't think it matters."

I wanted to scream at him. Why was he giving up so easily? Because he was right, I thought. Lorcann would demand death, and regardless of what might be done under the Emperor's prerogative, Callan would stand with Lorcann.

A night and a day and another night passed. My dark thoughts of the first night did not linger; I woke the next morning believing once again that Casyn would find a way to convince the Emperor to pardon us, or at least commute our sentences to exile. I tried to talk to Cillian, but he, sullen and uncommunicative, spent most of his time sitting on his pallet, his knees drawn up, staring at the floor. If I spoke to him, he would answer, but he refused to be drawn into discussion of any possible defense. I gritted my teeth, holding back my frustration: for a man known for his skill in the analysis of strategy, he was not making any effort. As soon as what little light came in through the high, barred, windows faded, he curled himself under the single blanket and slept, or feigned sleep.

My own anger crawled through my gut and my mind, directed now inwardly, at my own choices. I lay awake in the dank cell, in the blackness, asking myself hard, brutal questions. Why had I gone along with everything asked of me, from the first day Casyn had addressed us in the meeting house at Tirvan? Just who had I been trying to please, or defy? I tracked my actions, my thoughts, back through the last two years, and beyond, but I found no answers.

A banging on my door awakened me. The cell was dark. I glanced up at the window. The sky was a dark grey, not yet dawn. "What is it?" I asked.

"Get up," the guard said. "You ride today." I heard Cillian mutter something from the opposite cell. I got up, used the bucket, straightened my clothes. I did not look at the door. If the guard watched me, there was nothing I could do about it, except crouch in such a position that only my thigh showed. I picked up my pack—I had used it as a pillow—and waited. My mouth tasted foul, but we had been given no water.

We were escorted out of the prison, one guard for each of us. Outside, two horses stood, tacked and ready: Suran and a dark horse, larger and heavier. "Mount," one of the guards said. I swung up into the saddle. My guard took my bag, pushing it into the saddlebag, before fastening a shackle to one ankle. He passed the attached chain under the belly of my horse, and shackled it to my other leg. I glanced at Cillian; he was chained in the same way. I expected our wrists to be next, but, surprisingly, it was not so. We sat on the horses. Sparrows chirped from under the eaves of the prison. The guards said nothing. I watched the sky pale, the stars growing dimmer, and then I heard the clop of hooves along the cobbled street. Casyn rode up, Siannon's roan coat gleaming in the faint light, Birel beside him.

"Guardswoman," Casyn greeted me. "Cillian na Perras, good morning. We have a long way to ride today; hence, the early start. We are to be at the White Fort the day after tomorrow, by mid-day if we can. We will stop to eat in an hour or so, but let us get underway." The western gates had been opened as he spoke. He rode forward.

"Follow the General," Birel said. "I will bring up the rear." We rode out of the fort. The street became a wider road, swinging south and then east around the wall of the fort. The eastern sky was a pale pink now. I glanced up at the tower at the southern gate, making out the silhouette of a soldier. At this early hour, only the guards on the night watch would see us leave. I wondered if Casyn had planned it that way.

Once past the fort, the road ran parallel to the Wall. The chains jangled quietly as we walked the horses, the weight of the shackles and the chains pulling down on my legs. Shorter stirrups would be more comfortable. I would ask for them to be adjusted, at our first stop.

Casyn slowed Siannon. "Ride beside me, Cillian," he said. "You too, Guardswoman." We did as he asked. "I have questions for you, Cillian na Perras," he said. "Sergeant, fall back, if you please."

"About what, General?" Cillian answered. "I have told you all I know, of the Marai and their ships and their numbers."

"This concerns you, not the Marai," Casyn answered equably. He waited, ensuring, I supposed, that Birel was out of hearing. "Tell me of your mother. Her name, and where she lived."

"Lena has told you her children's tale, then?" he answered. "That I am the Emperor's long-lost son, like a character in one of our *danta*, our story-songs? Based on a fleeting resemblance of dark hair and a grim mouth, or some such?"

"Not only that, although the resemblance is there," Casyn said. "Did you know, Cillian, that the Emperor is my brother? Or that we were in the same regiment for many years, so that he and I were stationed together on the Wall, some thirty-four years past?"

Cillian did not reply for a minute. "No," he said finally, his voice subdued. "I did not know that."

"And so, I am probably the only other man who knows of Callan's love for a young girl called Hafwen, whose family had a small holding perhaps an hour north of the wall, and who brought milk and meat to the fort for trade. That was allowed then, for there was, more or less, peace between Linrathe and the Empire. Callan was on guard duty, the first time Hafwen came with her father. A story that simple, and that old, Cillian. Was Hafwen your mother?"

I looked away from the pain on Cillian's face. "Yes," he said. "That was her name."

"He called her Wenna," Casyn said, his voice soft.

"He deserted her," Cillian said flatly.

"We were ordered south," Casyn said, "unexpectedly, and immediately.

There had been a massive storm on the Edanan Sea, with the loss of many ships and extensive damage to both the harbours at Casilla and the Eastern Fort. We rode out with only a few hours notice."

"He could have left word, a letter, something!"

"He did," Casyn said. "He wrote a note, to be left with the quartermaster."

"She never got it," Cillian said flatly. "Why should I believe he ever wrote it?"

"Because I intercepted it," Casyn said. "He was my brother, and he had already risked his life to see Hafwen, and mine, because I covered for him when he left his post. The note was tangible proof. I destroyed it."

"Fuck you," Cillian snarled, clapping his heels into his bay's ribs. The horse sprang forward, running full-out along the road. "Sergeant!" Casyn called. Birel immediately kicked his own horse into a gallop, following him. "Just keep him in sight," Casyn shouted.

"Does the Emperor know?" I asked Casyn after a moment.

He shook his head. "No. I will send him a letter, when we stop, to reach him tomorrow. He needs time to prepare himself."

"He has no other children," I said, half a question.

"No. A few months after we were sent to Casilla, he contracted the swelling complaint. You know it?"

"Of course," I said. "It's a child's illness."

"Yes," he said. "I had it, I remember, before my father came for me. But Callan must not have. He was eighteen, and in grown men there can be swelling here, too," he indicated his groin, "and those that have that sometimes cannot father children, afterwards."

"If he had known of Cillian's birth, what could he have done? You said he risked his life by his liaison with Hafwen, so how could he have acknowledged the child?"

"Ah," he said. "There is a difference between leaving your post to consort with a woman of the north, and at a later time acknowledging a child by the same woman. It was not the liaison itself, but the questions that would have been asked of the how and when, if our commander had discovered the relationship. By our laws, Callan was guilty of desertion, and I of abetting desertion. The penalty for that, as you know, is death."

"Dear gods," I said. "And you have just told Cillian this, knowing how he hates the Empire and the Emperor?"

"A gamble," Casyn said. "Only our reputations can be hurt now, mine and Callan's, and even then, I doubt it would be anything more than a nine-day's whisper."

We rode on. Peewits flew up from the flat land on either side of the road, circling, piping their mournful two notes. As we crested a small rise, I saw ahead of us a watch-tower, a small fort for two or three soldiers, and on the road before it, Cillian and Birel, still mounted. Two soldiers stood with them, one holding Cillian's horse's reins, one standing beside him, sword drawn.

"We'll stop here to eat," Casyn said. He trotted Siannon forward. The soldiers saluted him. "Stand down," I heard him say. "Sergeant, please remove the shackles, so that Guard Lena and Cillian na Perras may dismount."

My legs felt light without the iron shackles. Birel and one soldier led the horses off; the other remained with us, his hand on his sword's grip. Casyn motioned us in through the arched doors of the structure. "The latrine," he said, pointing to a wattled enclosure just inside the gate, "is just there." I glanced at him for permission, and at his nod went to relieve myself.

I emerged to find a soldier waiting for me. "In there," he said, pointing to another wooden hut built against the interior wall of the tiny fort. Inside, once my eyes adjusted to the dim light, I saw Casyn and Cillian seated at a table. Birel was busy at a small stove. I sat. Casyn was writing.

"Do you have anything you wish to say to the Emperor?" he said to Cillian. Cillian shook his head, not looking at Casyn. The general folded the paper. Birel brought over a small brazier. Casyn took his wax from his belt pouch, heated it, and sealed the letter, imprinting the wax with the carved stone in his ring. "This," he said to one of the soldiers, "must reach the Emperor at the White Fort with haste, but daylight riding only. Go now."

"Sir!" A quick salute, and the soldier was gone. Birel brought tea to the table. I heard the clatter of hoofs on the road, already galloping: he would ride at speed for an hour or so, switch horses, and keep going until he was too tired. The note would then be handed over to another rider.

I sipped the tea. From the wooden platter on the table I took a slice of dark bread and a piece of smoked fish, chewy and salt. We ate in silence. The fish made me thirsty. I drank a second mug of tea. Casyn got up and went out. I heard his footsteps on the wooden stairs that led to the watch-tower's platform, and the murmur of voices. I tried to think of what I could say to Cillian. He had eaten almost nothing. In the dark room, his eyes were hollow and black.

Birel finished clearing up. "I'll walk you to the latrine," he said to Cillian. Cillian pushed himself up and went out, followed by the sergeant. I stood too, and went out into the daylight, bending to wipe my greasy hands on a patch of damp grass. Cillian came out of the latrine; Birel went in. I saw Cillian glance at the gate.

"Don't," I said quietly.

He turned his head towards me. "I wasn't going to," he said. "I'm not that stupid."

"Riding off like that wasn't exactly bright," I said. "You're lucky Casyn is a reasonable man."

"You're still defending him," he observed.

"You're a minging idiot," I said. "You went running off as if you were trying to escape. The soldiers here could have killed you, should have, would have, probably, if Birel hadn't been right behind you."

He shook his head. "I wasn't trying to escape. I just needed...some distance. Some space."

"I know," Casyn said from behind us. "That is why I let you go. But not again, Cillian na Perras. Nor do you speak to me again as you did, or you will be riding on a leading rein with your hands bound and your mouth gagged. Do you understand?"

Cillian's mouth twisted. He looked at me, closed his eyes. "Yes, General," he said.

We walked and trotted along the road, not saying much. I watched the rise and fall of the land, and the birds, and the deer that bounded away, letting my mind wander back over the last two years, and beyond. Occasionally Casyn would relate a bit of history to do with the Wall's construction, or the road. At midday, we reached a larger fort, not as big as either the White Fort or Wall's End, but substantially larger than the small watch-towers. Here the horses were unsaddled and fed, and allowed to rest. By now, my legs and back ached, and I too was glad of the break.

Cillian was still quiet, but his face showed less strain. As we walked across to the kitchen, I noticed that the men here were not all Empire's soldiers; a group of Linrathan men crossed the open space. One, with a subtle gesture of hand and chin, pointed us out to his companions.

Birel escorted us to a small room at the back of the fort headquarters. Food and drink were brought. Surprising me, Birel did not stay with us. "The door is guarded," he told us, as he left.

I picked up a piece of bread. There was a small pot of a creamy substance: I prised a little bit out with the wooden knife that had been provided to taste it. Goose fat. The flocks would have been moving north a few weeks earlier, fat from their winter foraging, the hunting parties busy. I spread some on the bread, adding salt. Cillian looked away. "Eat something," I said, beginning to lose patience with his self-pity. "You need the energy."

He made an exasperated sound, but reached forward for the bread. "You saw my countrymen, pointing me out?" he said.

"Pointing us out," I replied, around a mouthful of food. "They could have just been surprised to see a woman at the fort. Most of the other Guards will have gone home to their villages."

He shrugged. "Maybe." He ate a piece of bread. "I thought you said the Emperor was reasonable? If he's anything like his brother, I don't think that's true."

"Why? Because he threatened to gag you, after you swore at him? He's our jailer. What did you think he would do? By the gods, Cillian, he let you ride away. How many men would have done that?"

"You're defending him again," Cillian pointed out.

"I'm not," I protested. "Well, maybe I am, but you're being unfair. I remember Donnalch threatening to send you back to the *Ti'ach* because you couldn't keep a civil tongue towards him, either. Is the problem our leaders, Cillian, or you?"

"And where in this fucking world has your politeness and compliance got you, Lena of the Empire?" Cillian snarled. "You're going to be sentenced to death, just like me. Why do you still believe our leaders are kind and reasonable men?"

Why indeed? "Because they have always treated me that way, I suppose."

"Even when they are trying you for treason? They do not care about us. Get that through your head." He pushed his chair back, standing to pace the tiny room.

"You are wrong, Cillian," I said. "Finn—he was a junior officer—told me they are trained to remember every soldier, and to live their lives to honour those who die, to give those deaths meaning." As I spoke, the reasons I had been trying to find became abruptly clear to me, the pattern obvious, like my sudden understanding of the map on Perras's wall. I already knew why I had given Casyn my trust; I had told my mother, just a couple of days before. Casyn had offered me a wider world, the adventure I sought, but one where I bore little responsibility beyond following orders. Because the times I had chosen my own path, when I had voted to learn to fight, and again when I had not ridden north when Casyn had first asked, both choices had lost me Maya.

Hating myself, for what I had not done, and for what I could not be, I had given my allegiance unquestioningly to Casyn and the Emperor, to their strength and knowledge and calm certainties, to their ability to shape the future. They had seemed, I realized, omnipotent. I went to where I would be welcomed and needed, where most of my choices were made for me, and where I might, just possibly, find a purpose to my life.

But, I thought, with piercing clarity, neither Casyn, nor even Callan, are the Empire: it is an idea, a political structure, and it does not care about me. Casyn may, does, but the machinations of Empire are not his to command, and they may not even truly be Callan's. The choice that will be made this time isn't about me as a person, but about the value of one Guard in the greater stratagems of war and peace. My purpose is to be something to be bargained, nothing more.

"They *are* decent men," I said. "You will never make me believe they are not, Cillian. But that does not make the rules of the Empire right, or just, or even some of their decisions the right ones, and," I said, taking a deep breath, "I do not think, any more, that I can trust them, as agents of the Empire, to show mercy to us. And that makes me angry, angry at them, and," I felt tears rising, "angry at myself, for letting myself hope that they would save me, and you."

Cillian sat down at the table. "Forgive yourself," he said, his dark, shuttered eyes holding mine. "Because you are no different than most others: you were told a story and you accepted it. Just like Donnalch let the *torpari* and fisher-folk of Linrathe believe he wanted to invade south to free the oppressed women of the Empire, just like your men believe that the legacy of the Eastern Empire is so sacred that there is no other life for them but the army, we are given reasons, reasons that sound plausible and rational and even unarguable, for why we are to do what our leaders wish. There was a time I tried to believe it all too, but that time is past."

"I think it may be for me, too," I whispered.

"Good," he said. "So what are we going to do?"

"What do you mean?" I asked. "What can we do? You're not suggesting we try to escape?"

He shook his head, impatience visible in every move. "Of course not. How are we going to defend ourselves, at the trial?"

"I tried to ask you that yesterday, and you wouldn't even think about it."

"I was not going to begin planning anything with you while you were still thinking your Emperor would just wave his hand and say, 'forgive them'," he answered. "I have no illusions about Lorcann. He'll have me beheaded as quickly as he can say 'guilty'. I need you to tell me what you know of the Emperor that might help us sway his judgment. How does he want others to see him? That's probably the most important question, but consider not only your own people, but ours. Tell me what you *know*, Lena, not what you feel."

What did I know? "I was told," I began, "that he does not see himself bound by tradition. I would agree with that. At the Midwinter proclamations, before the war with Linrathe began, he announced two changes: one to the military, one to how we—men and women—live our lives."

"Which were?"

"Cadets would have a choice, beyond soldier or medic: they could become builders, without the need to also learn the skills of warfare. And for us, there was to be a new Assembly, a new discussion of our existing Partition agreement, to validate it or to change it."

"Do you know what predicated these changes?" Cillian's voice was calm, his tone one of interest. He sounded, I thought, exactly like his father, asking me questions about my experiences on the road to the Winter Camp.

"The first one, the choice of becoming a builder, for the cadets, came from his own brother's experiences. Colm, the historian, was Callan's twin, so he knew that whether a man could be a good soldier, or not, had nothing to do with who his father was, or his mother, for that matter." I hesitated. "Do you know what is done to boys who cannot fight, in the Empire?"

"I do," he said. "They are castrated. It is unspeakable."

"Both Casyn and the Emperor agree with you," I said, noting the faint flash of surprise on his face. "That is why they wanted another, honorable path for such boys." I watched as he assimilated this new thought.

"And the Assembly?" he said after a minute.

"The rules of Partition had been broken once we agreed to fight. Callan did not believe we could just go back to those rules, once the need to fight was no longer there. A new Assembly was needed."

"This was his idea?"

"Yes," I said. "And not only his idea, but one I—and I imagine other women like me, on the road after the fighting was done—were charged with spreading, quietly and subtly, to other women, to make it appear that the desire for a new Assembly came from the women's villages."

"Now that is interesting," Cillian said. "Callan understands the importance of stories in shaping choices, it would seem. How can we use that?"

"Cillian," I asked. "What do you see, in your mind, when you are putting all these ideas together?"

"What do I see?" He looked at me, puzzled.

"Yes. All these facts, these ideas, what do they look like, inside your mind?"

He leaned back, his hands behind his head, eyes closed. "Like a map," he said, "with all the ideas connected by lines, or threads. Those that I can't connect are off to the side. If I bring one of those onto the map, it changes the connections and sometimes the positions of the others." He opened his eyes. "Does that make sense to you?"

I nodded. "Listen," I said. "Listen to this: 'He chooses his strategy and deployment based on this picture in his mind, a picture that changes with season and weather, or time of day, and yet he always knows what will happen.'" I quoted. "Someone said that to me about the Emperor once, Cillian. Your father's mind works like yours. Use that."

CHAPTER NINETEEN

CILLIAN HAD OPENED HIS MOUTH to answer me when the door swung open to admit Casyn. "Time to ride," he said. "Finish your food."

Five minutes later we were back up on our horses, the shackles reattached, clattering out of the fort. I glanced over at Cillian. His face was shuttered, distant: I guessed he was thinking out possible defenses. The sky had clouded over, and a strong wind gusted from the west, presaging rain. I had told my mother the weather would hold for her journey to Tirvan, I thought, but if the winds had been favourable, she could already be home. And this might be only local rain, the coast south of us still sunny and calm. I had seen weather change between one headland and another, when we had explored the coves and inlets for new fishing grounds.

I let my mind drift back to my life in Tirvan, remembering the scent of rain on the dust of the practice field as we learned to use the secca. That thought took me to a conversation with Dern, captain of *Skua,* over wine one night, when I had suggested that I had not followed Maya into exile due to cowardice. *Is that true?* he had asked. I had denied it, telling him that I had chosen to stay because the survival of Tirvan mattered more than one person. Did I tell him— and myself—the truth? At the time, I thought I had.

But what did it matter now? Whatever my true motives, I was here, facing the consequences of a choice I had made. How that choice followed on from a web of earlier decisions hardly mattered. It could not be changed. All I could do was to tell the Emperor what I believed: I had not considered the possible ramifications of my escape for Donnalch, nor for Darel, nor for the truce. I had been focused on bringing word of the imminent invasion to the Empire. I should have seen the probable consequence, at least for Donnalch. I had known Dagney was afraid for his life, that he was a captive, and that Fritjof had already had Ardan killed. But I had been afraid of the arranged marriage to Leik, and that fear had blinded me to any other consideration.

Anger surged through me again. I *should* have thought about it more, and because I hadn't, Donnalch was dead, and Darel. How would I ever face Turlo? What could I say to him? My horse tossed his head, uncertain of what my tightened hands and clenched knees asked. I forced myself to relax. "Shh, Suran, it's all right," I murmured to him.

Beside me, Cillian urged his horse up to beside Casyn. They spoke, but the gusty wind made it impossible for me to hear any words. I saw Cillian nod in response to something Casyn said, and then the next gust of wind brought the first drops of rain with it. In less than a minute the rain fell hard and cold, the wind whipping the drops so strongly they stung where they hit bare flesh. I brought Suran to a halt and turned to pull my riding cloak out of the saddlebags. I shrugged it on, pulling the hood over my head; in its deep pockets were leather gloves. Around me, the men did the same.

Suran's chestnut coat turned dark, and water dripped off his mane as we continued eastward. As we approached the next watch-tower, Birel trotted his horse up to beside Casyn. I saw Casyn shake his head. I guessed we would not stop. We had distance to cover, rain or no. Casyn raised our pace to a trot, warming both the horses and ourselves. We passed the watch-tower, situated at the top of a small rise, and continued on, catching up to a small group of carts moving supplies toward the next fort. The men saluted Casyn, staring at us.

The rain came in waves, never really stopping but giving us respite from the drenching every so often. In one of the breaks I turned to look at the sky behind us: it looked lighter toward the horizon. Perhaps the rain would stop soon, I thought. I straightened to see a horseman galloping toward us, a messenger, from the speed he was riding.

Casyn raised a hand for us to stop. The messenger drew his horse up, saluted Casyn, and handed him a sealed note. "From the Emperor, General," he said.

"Thank you," Casyn said. "Are you to take a reply?"

"No, sir."

"Ride with us to the next watch-tower; you can rest yourself and your horse there. We will stop briefly," Casyn ordered. He opened the note, scanning it quickly. He frowned, then refolded the note and slipped it into his saddlebag. "Forward," he said.

I glanced at Cillian, but his face showed me nothing. We rode on. The rain was definitely lighter now, the sky brighter. A curlew called. A stone-bird, flicking its wings, sang its sharp, tapping song from on top of a small bush. Suran snorted and rippled his skin. A pale and watery sun broke through the cloud; I pushed the hood back off my face to let the wind—a breeze now—blow through my hair. My back ached, and I needed a latrine. I hoped the next watch-tower wasn't too far.

I saw the beacon tower with its iron basket first, rising above a shallow dip in the land and the road. We trotted into the interior yard of the watch-tower; Casyn barely gave us time to relieve ourselves before ordering us into the small guardroom. The messenger had been given responsibility for the horses, instead of Birel.

The door closed firmly behind us, Birel lit a small lamp to give the room some light. "The Emperor tells me," Casyn said without preamble, "that Lorcann was displeased that we rode east without a Linrathan guard, even though he did not send one when he asked us to imprison you, Cillian. He has sent men to meet us. Once they reach us, I doubt any conversation between you will be tolerated. In addition, Lorcann demands, and the Emperor has acceded to this request, that we ride directly to the White Fort, not stopping until we reach it. At which time, your trial, Lena and Cillian, will begin, without time for discussion or counsel."

We were to arrive at the White Fort exhausted, cold and hungry, and go immediately to trial? What chance would we have, to defend ourselves? "That is unfair!" I said. "Why would the Emperor agree to such a request?"

"He will have his reasons," Cillian said.

"Yes," Casyn said sharply, "he will. And one of them may be that your *Teannasach* is now in his debt."

Cillian nodded. "Perhaps," he agreed. "And perhaps another is that tired and hungry, we will not have the energy or spirit to maintain any lies, any collusion."

"Were you planning on such?" Casyn asked.

"We are just going to tell the truth, General," Cillian said. "Calmly, if that concerns you. There is nothing else to do."

Casyn raised an eyebrow. "Does that truth include the subject of my questioning this morning?"

"If needed, yes," Cillian answered. "And it may be. I will not hide behind secrets at the expense of my—or Lena's—life."

"I would not expect you to," Casyn said. "I ask only so I can prepare the Emperor." He turned his head at sounds in the courtyard. "I think your escort has arrived," he said. "I hope for the best, for you both." He offered me his arm, in the soldier's gesture; I gripped it, wishing I could think of something to say. With a brief clasp of his hand on Cillian's shoulder, he opened the door, going out to speak to the men who had arrived.

I turned to Cillian. "I have a plan," he murmured. "I was going to tell you, but now you must trust me." Two men came into the hut, both middle aged, both wearing the tough woven cloth of Linrathe in its muted colours, but over it, leather vests and leggings, and swords on their hips.

"Cillian na Perras," one of them said. "We are sent by the *Teannasach* to guard you on your journey. Please come with us." With one last glance my way, Cillian did as they asked. Outside, we mounted, submitted to the shackles, and began to move away from the watch-tower, Cillian and the men of Linrathe riding ahead of Casyn, Birel and me.

The road was wide enough for us to ride three abreast. We trotted, but it was clear to me Suran was tired. "We cannot reach the White Fort tonight on these horses," I said.

"No," Casyn agreed. "At the next fort, we will switch horses, and again once or twice after that. I sent the messenger ahead to ask for replacement mounts to be ready. Be prepared for fast riding, Lena."

"Why did the Emperor agree to this?" I asked again.

Casyn shook his head. "I do not know," he said. "But I know very little of Lorcann, except what I saw of him during the truce negotiations, and even then Donnalch did most of the talking. Callan will have got to know him a bit better over these past weeks. He will have his reasons, but I do not know what they are."

"Cillian says he is hot-headed, quick to anger," I offered.

"That fits with what I saw," Casyn agreed. "Things were either right or wrong, and he was impatient, especially with detail. Quite different from the Emperor and Donnalch. I respected Donnalch, for all he was an enemy at the time."

"So did I," I said. "He was considerate, and thoughtful, and curious about different ways of thinking. And he knew how to inspire men to fight, even if it meant not always telling the complete truth, by drawing on what is dear to them to raise their anger. Did you know, General, that the common men of Linrathe thought they were invading us to free the women's villages from our unnatural lives, to let us be free to marry and live with our men and our children?" I did not try to hide the bitterness and anger that insinuated themselves into my voice as I spoke these last sentences. I no longer cared if Casyn knew how I felt.

"I did," he said.

"A common tactic, among military leaders, to tug at our heartstrings so that we will agree to their plans."

"One we use, yes. On occasion."

"As I know," I said, the anger spurting again at this calm admission. We rode a few paces without speaking. "General," I said, when I was sure I had control of my voice. "I find it hard to believe, now, that Donnalch made arrangements with Nevin and Vilnas to breach the Wall as his first course of action. Were there not approaches made for a peaceful alliance?"

"An alliance was not exactly what Donnalch wanted," Casyn replied. "He wanted free movement of people across the border, so that northmen, and women, could come and settle on our lands, but outside of Partition, and have access to the southern trade. In return, men and women of the Empire who wanted a different life would have been free to travel north of the Wall. It was too much, too sudden, even given the Emperor was already considering the need for a review of the Partition agreement, not to mention it was not exactly a fair exchange. Our lands, especially in the fertile south, would have been— are—very attractive to those who battle against long winters and thin and rocky soils in Linrathe."

"So," I said, puzzling it out, "had we had the new Assembly, and the vote had been to change our way of life, then he would have had something different to offer to Donnalch. A compromise, of sorts?"

"Perhaps," Casyn agreed. "That was the plan."

"Then why did Donnalch chose to invade when he did? Surely he could have waited to see the outcome of the new Assembly?"

"For one, he had no idea what Callan was planning. How could he? You know how the threat from Leste played into that idea; once we had asked the women's villages to fight, we had changed the agreement, and had grounds for a new Assembly. Had that not happened, it could have been years before the idea gained support."

"And the Emperor thought Donnalch would wait that long?"

"I think he might have, except—and I am guessing here, Lena, for none of this was ever said to us in any negotiation—that the ill-health and impending death of the Marai king made Donnalch act sooner."

"Yes," I said, "that fits something I heard at the *Ti'ach*." I thought back, remembering candles, and wine, and an evening-dark room. "That if Donnalch could negotiate a treaty of equals with the Emperor, then it would be time to challenge the terms of his treaty with the Marai, especially with a new king."

"Exactly so," Casyn said. "I am glad to have my guess confirmed. And if that treaty of equals with our Empire came after a show of force by Donnalch, all the better to demonstrate to the Marai that they were dealing with a strong opponent."

"Except Donnalch expected Åsmund to be king, not Fritjof, and he and Åsmund were childhood friends."

"Such friendships can mean little, when leaders sit down to negotiate," Callan said. "But Lorcann says they misjudged Fritjof's ambition: even among the Marai, to kill your own brother is nearly unheard of. He rules by threat and blood, and promises of great wealth."

None of this helped me, but it would give me something to think about, to quell the panic rising in my gut, the closer we got to the White Fort. I had one more question. "Did you really not know about the Marai?" I asked.

"Not really, no," Casyn answered. "We knew there was a king to whom Linrathe paid tribute for their northern borderlands, but beyond that, no. They had never been mentioned as a threat. The peace between them had gone on for so long, you see. Perhaps if Colm had lived, and kept up his correspondence with the scholars of Linrathe, or spent some time north of the Wall, we might have known."

The next fort lay just ahead of us. We rode through its western gate: horses awaited us. Soldiers helped transfer our saddlebags, and then we were riding again, fast now, galloping along the stones of the road.

It was not yet midnight when we rode through the gates of the White Fort. The sky danced with stars, the clouds and rain of earlier in the day blown further east. The sparks of light blurred as I looked up, exhaustion fogging my vision. I slumped in the saddle, waiting for my shackles to be removed so I could dismount.

I stumbled my way under guard to a latrine. Someone gave me a waterskin. I drank thirstily. We had had neither food nor drink since before the last fort, save for a few bites of dried apple and cheese, eaten as we rode.

I stretched, easing cramped muscles. Torches flickered on the wall outside the great wooden door that led into the antechamber of the hall. Behind those doors waited the Emperor, and the *Teannasach* of Linrathe, our judges. Birel appeared at my side. "Drink this," he said, "just a sip or two, not too much." I took the small flask, tipping a drop of the liquid onto my tongue, tasting smoke and fire. *Fuisce*, Donnalch had called it. I took a larger sip, and handed the flask back to Birel.

"Thank you," I said.

"Now, food," he said. "You're not facing a trial without food inside you, Guardswoman."

I shook my head. "I can't eat."

"You must," he said firmly. He handed me a slice of something. "Just nibble this," he instructed. I did as he asked. How could I refuse? The sweetness and spice of a dense, fruit-studded cake filled my mouth, the taste like that of the harvest cakes of Tirvan, baked rich and sweet to fuel the hard work of reaping. It almost made me smile.

"Where did you get this?" I asked.

"The Emperor has a liking for sweet things, when he can get them," he said. "I have friends in the kitchens."

"Did you give Cillian a piece, too?"

"His guards would not let me give it to him, nor the *fuisce*," he said, shaking his head. "Just water, they said."

He would be exhausted, I thought. I finished the cake. Birel gave me the flask of *fuisce* again; I swallowed a mouthful, feeling its warmth radiating through me. "Are you ready?" Birel said softly. I shrugged.

"As ever I will be," I answered. "Birel, thank you, for all you have done, now and in the past."

He saluted me; I returned the salute. Behind us, I heard the footsteps of Cillian and his guard. My heart pounded in my throat. I could barely swallow. Birel opened the door. The stone walls of the antechamber seemed to move in the gusting light of the torches. Boots pounded sharp and loud on the stone flags, echoing in the empty space. Birel knocked on the right-hand door of the pair that opened into the great hall; the sound reverberated. A detached, wandering part of my mind wondered what Cillian would make of the floor. My legs trembled.

The doors swung open to light and warmth, the two fireplaces and the wall torches blazing. Birel's hand was on my arm, lightly: I let him propel me forward, towards the long table where the Emperor and the *Teannasach* sat. Callan wore his dark grey robe and the pendant of silver; Lorcann his heather-hued cloak and golden torc. The clothes of power. I heard Cillian and his guard moving behind me. Callan's eyes followed him, watching him steadily as he came to stand beside me, but in the firelight I could read no expression on the Emperor's face, save perhaps a tightening in his jaw.

"Lena, Guardswoman of the Empire," the Emperor said, in his even, quiet voice, switching his gaze to me, "you stand before me tonight charged with treason, namely, the violation of the truce between the Empire and Linrathe, signed in this very hall. Specifically, you are charged with two crimes. One, the murder of a man of Sorham, a land subservient to Linrathe, during the theft of his boat, disregarding these words of the truce: 'no raid nor battle will be undertaken by either side during this time of truce, nor any action that leads to the death by violence of a man or woman of the opposing side'. Second, in escaping your captivity by Fritjof of the Marai, your actions led directly to the execution of Donnalch, *Teannasach* of Linrathe, also held captive by Fritjof, as retaliation for your escape. By the terms of the truce between the Empire and Linrathe, your life is doubly forfeit."

His eyes had been on me steadily as he spoke, only glancing at the paper in front of him once or twice. There seemed to be no opportunity for response. I felt sweat trickling down between my breasts, although I thought I was cold.

Lorcann cleared his throat, and began to speak.

"Cillian na Perras," he said, his voice rougher than Donnalch's had been, less musical, "you stand before me tonight charged with two crimes: one being the violation of the truce between Linrathe and the Southern Empire, signed in this very hall. In plotting with the Empire's hostage, the Guard Lena, to steal a boat, you committed a raid that led to the death of a man of Sorham, in direct violation of the words of the truce: 'no raid nor battle will be undertaken'. But that is the lesser of your crimes: the other is not a violation of the truce, but an act that led directly to the death of your *Teannasach*, namely, your flight from the court of King Fritjof of the Marai. For both crimes, the charge is treason, and your life is forfeit."

Beneath my feet, faces grinned and leered in the flickering firelight. I forced my mind to analyze what had just been said, the subtle differences between the Emperor's words and Lorcann's. 'Fritjof of the Marai', Callan had called him; 'King Fritjof' had been Lorcann's words. Did this matter?

"Guardswoman." Callan's voice broke into my thoughts. "What have you to say to these charges?"

"Emperor," I tried to say, but the word was a dry croak. Callan nodded to Birel. He walked forward to pour water from a jug, handing me the cup. I drank, a sip or two. Birel took the cup. "Emperor," I said. "The fisherman of Sorham tried to rape me; I killed him in self-defence. I acknowledge that I was trying to steal his boat, but only to bring word of the Marai invasion to you in time. I judged my responsibility to the Empire required that, and that responsibility was what I acted on. I did not think of the words of the truce, but if I had, I would not have considered my actions a raid or a battle."

"And the second charge?"

This was harder. "Again, Emperor," I said. "I knew Fritjof planned an invasion of the Empire; I believed you knew nothing of this threat or of these people. I acted as I did from concern for the Empire, and for our people, and," I added, glancing at Lorcann, "indeed, not only for the Empire, but for Linrathe, too."

"Acknowledged, Guardswoman," the Emperor said. I could smell the tang of my armpits. Was that all? I glanced at Cillian. He watched Callan, his face impassive.

"Cillian na Perras," Lorcann said. "What have you to say, to these charges?"

"I admit to the theft of the boat, *Teannasach*," Cillian said clearly, "but the murder of the fisherman was none of my doing. The Guardswoman had convinced me, and she was right, that we could travel faster in a boat than on foot or horseback. While the theft could be construed as a raid, it was in the greater good of Linrathe. And as to the second charge, Donnalch himself knew my plan, and approved it, knowing the risk to his life. Given that, *Teannasach*, there is no charge for me to answer."

Was this true? And if so, why had Cillian not told me? Lorcann leaned back in his chair, his eyes narrowed.

"Can anyone verify this tale," he asked, "other than the Guardswoman, of course?"

"Of course not," Cillian said, almost scornfully. "Donnalch would not have risked anyone else's life by telling them. And whom would he have told? Ardan was dead by then, and that left only the Lady Dagney and the Guardswoman. You know our laws: a *scáeli's* life is not to be risked, nor would the *Teannasach* have confided our plans to a hostage."

"Guardswoman?" Lorcann turned his eyes to me. "Did you know this?"

I shook my head. "No," I said. "I am hearing this for the first time."

"Tell me, then, how you discovered Cillian planned to escape."

I did not trust this man. But all I could do was tell the truth. "He told me," I said.

Lorcann shot his eyes to Cillian. "That is true," Cillian affirmed.

"Why?"

"Had I just disappeared, she—and the Lady Dagney—might have thought me dead, and attempted some rash action. Even though the *Teannasach* knew the truth, they would have little or no opportunity to speak to him privately. I thought it best the women knew."

"Then why did you let the Guardswoman join you? Surely then the Lady Dagney would have thought you both dead. Your logic is at fault," Lorcann said.

"Not at all, *Teannasach*," Cillian said, his voice icy. "Lady Dagney was housed in the women's hall; she would hear the gossip. The Marai women may not have been privy to what happened to me, but they would know that the Guardswoman had escaped. The *scáeli* would have worked out that we had gone together."

Lorcann grunted. "Perhaps," he acceded. "But still I do not understand why you brought her along at all."

"She proposed stealing a boat, saying it would be faster than foot or horseback. I could see she was right. She can sail; I cannot. Speed was of the essence, and so I brought her with me."

"To raid an innocent fisher family of their boat, and thereby their livelihood," Lorcann pointed out. "A crime against the truce, even before the murder."

"Would stealing a horse from a *torp* have been any better?" Cillian countered.

"Yes, man, it would have been," Lorcann said. "Firstly, one horse would not destroy a *torp*. It would be a poor *Harr* who had only one beast. Because you chose to allow the woman to go with you, you left a boy of twelve years an orphan, and with no boat for him to barter or trade for a place in another fishing family, so that he must throw himself on the charity of his *Harr*, or take to the roads in search of work."

"And secondly?" Cillian asked. His insouciance shocked me. Was he deliberately baiting Lorcann?

"D'you need to ask?" Lorcann scoffed. "There would have been no murder had you gone alone. Even had you raised the house while stealing the horse, I doubt more than a few blows and bruises would have resulted. The fisherman, himself a widower, found a woman under his hands as he wrestled with the person stealing his boat. What would you expect of him? He had the right to take what he wanted, under the circumstances. The murder is on the southern woman's head, but you are not innocent, man."

"You think that his right?" The words burst out of me. "Do women mean so little to you, *Teannasach*?" I spat the title. "Do you approve of how Fritjof treats the Marai women, then?"

The wall torches seemed to dim, leaving a circle of light around us, and darkness beyond. Lorcann glared at me. "Be silent, and be glad I am not your judge," he said. He turned back to Cillian.

"I believe you not, man," he said. "So, hear your doom. You are a man of Linrathe, and I am your *Teannasach*. I condemn you to death on these charges. At dawn, Cillian na Perras, your head will be on a spear, for the instruction of all."

The words echoed in the silence of the hall. Cillian's guard took him roughly by the upper arm, pulling him away. I looked from Lorcann to Callan, and back again.

"What," Cillian said, his voice almost conversational, "if I am not a man of Linrathe?"

CHAPTER TWENTY

I COULD HEAR MY HEART IN MY EARS. Cillian, head high, stared at the two leaders at the high table. Long moments passed.

"Tell me your mother's name, Cillian na Perras," the Emperor said, his voice pitched low.

"Hafwen," Cillian answered. "Her father was Hael, her mother, Mari. I was born just as winter changed to spring, thirty-three years ago."

"What is this?" Lorcann demanded. "He was a bastard child of a farm girl, it is true, but so are many others. He is still mine to rule and to judge."

"Not if a man of the Empire claims him as his child," Casyn said from beside me. "That agreement was made in Mathon's day, *Teannasach*, if you recall."

"Aye," Lorcann said angrily, "but it was about children, not grown men. Nor has such a claim been made in many years."

"That does not void the agreement," Casyn said.

"So? It is well known that Cillian na Perras's mother never named his father. He has no name to put forward, even if the soldier is still alive and willing to make the claim. You cannot pull yourself out of a well on a thread, man," he said, his eyes on Cillian, "and a thread is all you have. Accept your fate."

"You agree the father was a man of the Empire?" Casyn asked.

"Aye, that was always the story," Lorcann replied, "and I've no reason to believe it a lie. Had the father been a farm lad, there would have been a wedding, with the child born six months later. A nine-days whisper, but no shame to it."

"Then, *Teannasach*, were the father to claim Cillian na Perras, even now, do you agree he has that right? And that Cillian na Perras has the right to accept that claim, and be named a man of the Empire, not of Linrathe, by the agreement made between Mathon, Emperor of the South, and Iaco of Linrathe?" Callan spoke with authority, his voice that of the law-maker, the Emperor. Lorcann glowered.

"Aye, I suppose I do," he muttered.

Callan stood. He looked at his brother, a long gaze, before turning his eyes to Cillian. "Then, in the sight of this court, I, Callan, Emperor of the South, son of Col of the Sixth and Alle of Rigg, acknowledge this man, Cillian, to be my son, borne by Hafwen of Linrathe."

I heard a muffled sound from Cillian's guard, silenced by Lorcann's bark. "What? You claim him?"

"I do," Callan said. "He is my son, although I only learned of his birth yesterday. Do you dispute my right to do so, *Teannasach*?"

Lorcann shot his eyes to the Cillian's guard, and then to the door, and back again. Like a cornered fox. "No," he grunted finally. "If it suits you to be the one who executes him, rather than me, what do I care? It's all the same in the end."

The Emperor turned back to Cillian. "I ask you, Cillian of Linrathe," he said, "if you wish to acknowledge this claim and become Cillian of the Empire, accepting the responsibilities to the Empire that such an acknowledgement would bring."

"I do," Cillian said, his voice steady. "What words must I say?"

"That you acknowledge your mother by name, and me as your father, and that you will serve the Empire."

Cillian nodded. "I, Cillian, son of Hafwen of Linrathe, acknowledge Callan, Emperor of the South, as my father, and I pledge to serve the Empire, and," he added, "to accept the judgement of the Emperor as to my fate."

"I, Casyn, General of the Empire, witness this." Casyn touched my shoulder. I glanced at him. He nodded.

"I, Lena, Guardswoman of the Empire, witness this," I said, my voice barely above a whisper.

All eyes were on Lorcann. Callan gestured politely. "Would you prefer your soldier to witness?" Lorcann's lips clenched. He stood, slowly.

"I, Lorcann, *Teannasach* of Linrathe, witness this," he spat. "Let him go," he said to the guard. He turned to Callan. "He is yours, Emperor. I presume I am welcome to witness the sentencing?"

"You are, of course, *Teannasach*," Callan said. "Shall we sit, and continue the trial?" His eyes held Lorcann's. The northman's jaw twitched. With a bare nod, he sat.

When the scrape of the chairs had subsided, the Emperor spoke again. "Cillian," he said, "tell us what you saw happening between the Guardswoman and the fisherman."

"The Guardswoman fell as she approached the boat," he answered. "The fisherman was in pursuit. That was my fault. I broke a piece of wood underfoot, on the beach, and the sound roused the cot. When he reached her, they struggled, but he was forcing her against him, not pushing her away. That I could see, in the dark, but nothing more. Then he fell into the water. That is all I can say. The night was black."

"Thank you," Callan said. "Guardswoman."

I tried to speak, but my throat was as dry as salt fish. I coughed, and tried again. "Yes, Emperor?" I croaked.

"Cillian na Perras argues that the *Teannasach* of Linrathe approved his plan of escape, knowing it risked his own life. Did the *Teannasach* know of your plan to accompany him?"

"No, sir," I said. "Not that I am aware."

"Did anyone other than Cillian know?"

I shook my head. "No. The Lady Dagney asked, but I did not tell her, thinking it might be dangerous for her."

"Cillian, did you tell the *Teannasach* that the Guardswoman was accompanying you?"

"No, Emperor."

"Guardswoman, you knew your plans were dangerous, as you declined to let the Lady Dagney know them. But you did not think of the danger to the *Teannasach?*"

I hesitated. How to put this? "I knew the Lady Dagney thought his life in danger already," I said. "I did not think my escape would add to that danger."

Callan nodded. He looked at Cillian, and then at me, and then at Casyn, a long gaze.

"Guardswoman Lena, of Tirvan," he said. "Cillian of the Empire. I find you both guilty of the second charge, the violation of the truce between the Empire and Linrathe, an action which directly led to the death of the *Teannasach* of Linrathe. The charge is treason. The punishment is death."

I closed my eyes. Cillian's gamble had been for nothing. A trembling began deep inside me. I heard a chair scrape as someone stood. I swallowed, and opened my eyes. Callan was on his feet.

"I, Callan, Emperor of the South, sentence the Guardswoman Lena and the man Cillian to death, a sentence I commute to banishment, exile from the bounds of the Empire for all time, as is my right as Emperor. Lena of Tirvan, you are stripped of your rank in the Empire's army. Cillian of the Empire, Lena of Tirvan, you have three days to leave the boundaries of this land."

Banishment. I heard the word. Banishment. I was not going to die.

"Nae, Emperor, I cannot support that!" Lorcann cried. "The punishment for treason is death, and my brother's fate demands it. You cannot exile them instead!"

"I can," Callan said calmly. "It is within my right as Emperor, and there is precedence, as your brother would have known."

"You tricked me!" Lorcann shouted. "Guard, seize Cillian na Perras!"

Before the man could react, Cillian broke: running, he placed his hands flat on the table, vaulting it to stand beside the Emperor. Casyn pushed me roughly behind him, drawing his sword, shouting. A door flung open. Soldiers rushed into the room, swords drawn. Casyn raised a hand.

"*Teannasach,*" he said, "think again. Think of your own son, and that of your brother. We hold them hostage still, do not forget."

Lorcann looked around him. Outnumbered, Cillian's guard stood with weapons in their hands, but warily. Lorcann gestured to them, and they sheathed their swords. I sagged against Casyn, hearing my heart pounding in my ears. He took my weight with one arm, the other still holding his sword. Lorcann turned to the Emperor.

"Be uncertain of your peace, Callan of the Empire," he snarled. "I must weigh my choices: alliance with the man who killed my brother, or alliance with the man who forgave the instruments of his death. Which is the worse choice, I wonder?"

"I say again, remember your hostages, *Teannasach,*" Callan said softly. "But I too have lost a brother to treachery. I know how you feel."

"Do you?" Lorcann retorted. "And did you not kill both the murderer, and those who made the murder possible? And without trial, I believe?"

"For directly plotting treason, yes," Callan replied. "Not for the unintended consequence of an action to warn of impending invasion."

Lorcann stared at him. "And I say again, be uncertain of your peace. The King of the Marai has made me certain offers. I must consider them, even in light of your threats. Come," he ordered Cillian's guard. He stalked out of the hall, the torches guttering as the massive doors opened and closed.

Callan turned to the soldiers. "Escort them out to their horses," he said. "Be respectful of his position."

When the soldiers had gone, Callan took a deep breath. "Cillian," he said. "Be seated. You too, Lena. Casyn, will you call for food and drink?" I stumbled to a chair. "You must ride in the morning," he said. "There will be an escort, to the Durrains, for that is where you must go, of course."

The Durrains. The wall of mountains on the Empire's eastern edge. Beyond it, what? Once, there had been another Empire past those mountains, an Empire of learning and skill and a love of beauty, if the floor of the White Fort told me anything. The east, where no one in living memory had gone, except Fritjof of the Marai and his men. Who had not died of disease, and had returned to tell their tales.

Birel came in with food, more of the rich cake, cheese, wine. I accepted wine, and water. Cillian folded a piece of cake in half and ate it in three bites. I realized how exhausted he must be. Birel poured wine for the Emperor and Casyn, and then withdrew.

Cillian swallowed the last of his cake. He took a cup of wine, sipped, and then put it down. "Did you get what you needed, Emperor?" he asked.

A hint of smile played around Callan's lips. "I did," he said. "Lorcann, as I feared, is untrustworthy. He is still in communication with Fritjof, I would think. It is power he wants, not leadership. I will have to give thought as to what I can offer him, to keep him with me."

"Wait," I said. "This was planned? How?"

"Not planned," Cillian said, with a glance to Callan. "Played, hoping I saw the board rightly. But it was you who told me that the Emperor and I shared a trait, a gift, if you will, for tactics and outcomes. What would I need to know, I wondered, were I the Emperor in this situation?"

"If Lorcann could be trusted," I said, slowly, working it out. "So," I turned to Callan, "you let him judge Cillian first, and then you over-rode him, to discover his reaction."

"Exactly," the Emperor said.

"Once again, Emperor," I said, "we are pieces in your game."

"You could say that," Callan said. "But if so, it was one in which your life was a wager on the outcome, and Cillian was a willing player."

"Not willing, quite," Cillian said. "Compelled, for our lives, I would say."

Callan inclined his head, ceding the point. "Successfully," he noted.

"Yes," I said, all the fear and grief of the last days welling up. "And for that I am grateful. But my life has been a wager in your games for far too long now, Emperor. I thank you for saving it, and Cillian's, and as for mine I take it as fair payment for what you have asked of me, but no more. No more, Emperor. I welcome this exile, to be beyond your games." White-hot anger flared, goading me into these words. Did I mean them? Yes, I realized, I did. I had had enough.

"Lena," Casyn began.

"No!" I stopped him. "Casyn, no. I mean what I said. Cillian told me once he had no love for Empires; I understand him now. I am sorry if I disappoint you, but I am not a Guardswoman any more, and can speak my mind to you both. I have had enough of tactics, of intrigues and half-truths. I will be glad to leave."

"We have asked much of you, Lena," Callan said, a note of regret in his voice, "and you have served us well. But do not judge us too harshly. Even my actions, regardless of my reputed gift for strategy, may have unforeseen consequences, no matter how thorough the planning, and half-truths are sometimes all the truths we know." He gave me a smile, his eyes gentle, before turning to his son.

"Cillian," the Emperor said. "Before anything else, I have one thing to ask, and one to tell."

"Ask first," Cillian said.

"Did Donnalch truly approve your escape, knowing the risk to his life?"

A brief smile touched Cillian's lips. "I told him my plan. He said this, and nothing more: 'My brother must know that being *Teannasach* is about serving our people, not having them serve the *Teannasach*.' I took that to mean he knew he would die, and Lorcann would be the *Teannasach*."

"A fair interpretation," Callan said.

"And to tell me, Emperor?"

Callan's eyes were shadowed, the firelight accentuating the planes of his face. "I truly loved her, Cillian. But when I came back to the Wall, Wenna was dead, and no one told me of a child. Had I known, I would have acknowledged you, Cillian, with pride."

"Had you known," Cillian echoed. "But you did not: I was one of those unforeseen consequences, I suppose. I have lived my life half in exile, so perhaps, like Lena, I am ready to make it full exile, away from those who have judged me on my parentage, or lack of it. I too thank you for my life, twice, I suppose, both in the begetting and the saving." He raised his wine. "To the Emperor, then, for his benevolence."

"To the Emperor," Casyn repeated, standing. I too stood. "For my life, I thank you, Emperor," I said, as coldly as I could, surprised to feel the prick of tears. We drank the toast.

Callan stood, wearily. "Sleep, now," he said. "Birel will find you beds. Tomorrow you ride east."

"A moment," I said. "I have one more thing to do. Where is Turlo?"

"Not here," Casyn said. "He commands our troops still in Linrathe."

Regret and relief washed through me. "Is there paper?" I said. Casyn found me what I needed. I sat at the great table. 'I will remember Darel. He was brave and stalwart and full of fun,' I wrote. 'I will carry my guilt and sorrow for his death all my life.' Then I signed my name, folded the paper, and handed it to Callan. With a nod, he left the room, Cillian with him.

"Lena," Casyn began, his voice gentle.

"Casyn," I said, forestalling whatever he was about to say. "You told me, once, that you did not want to be a general, when you were my age. Will you tell me why?"

He laughed, a brief, mirthless bark. "Because I too hated the games, the shading of the truth, the stories we told and were told. But Callan was so good at it, at seeing how to make things happen—but he was impulsive, undisciplined: the affair with Wenna, the note he tried to leave, both were proof of that. I had to be by his side, advising him, to keep him safe. He is my brother. So, I did what I had to, although I prefer shoeing horses. I never thought he would rise so high." In the firelight, his face was weary, drawn with fatigue, and, perhaps, regret.

"Thank you," I said. He smiled.

"Sleep now, Lena," he said, "for a few hours. I will not see you again. My duty is to Callan."

I nodded. I felt no surprise, just the bleak realization of the inevitable, like waking on a November morning to see the first snowfall, knowing it presaged the hardship of winter. I had no tears left. My eyes were as dry as autumn leaves, and the taste of ashes was in my mouth.

†††††

The lower slopes of the Durrains were still in shadow, the sun not yet over the peaks. My pack lay on the grass, beside Cillian's, a bird bow and arrows strapped to it. Bedrolls hung below the packs, and two walking staffs leaned against a boulder.

"The track will take you up to some meadows," the soldier holding our horses said. "There's good hunting there, mountain hare and deer and grouse. There are game trails leading out of the meadows, but where they go?" He shrugged. "There are lots of stories. Some of them may be true. I guess you'll find out." He paused. "I envy you that."

I looked up at the path, bending out of sight among the boulders and the scrubby trees. Snow clung to the peaks, even now, halfway to summer. Cillian stood beside me, saying nothing. Part of me wished I was going alone; part of me knew that would be folly. I still did not know if I liked him, or could trust him. I was wary of his cynicism and his cold, tactical, thinking, but I had no choice. He was my companion in exile, at least until we crossed these mountains. If we crossed these mountains. He probably felt the same about me.

I turned back to the soldier. "Any advice, Galen?" I asked.

"Stay together. Stay dry. Take it slowly. The higher you go, the harder it is to climb. Let your body get used to it. You're not in any hurry; remember that."

I nodded. "You will send word?" I said.

"I will," he said. "I have your letter. And if the Emperor will allow me to ride as his messenger, I'll go, tell her how proud she should be of you."

Another half-truth. Better that way, I thought. Maybe half-truths were all we ever had, as Callan had suggested. I picked up the pack, shrugging it onto my shoulders, adjusting the straps. Beside me, Cillian did the same. I reached for my staff, settling my hand around its smooth surface, looping its leather strap around my wrist. I looked up at the path before me. A memory rose, a stone hall, morning light, words spoken: *What may still lie beyond the mountains and the seas.* Deep inside, I felt a frisson of anticipation, almost excitement.

"Lena," my father called. I turned.

"Go with the god," he said. "Both of you."

I nodded. I glanced at Cillian. He gestured me forward. I turned back to the path, away from the Empire, away from Linrathe, and began to climb.

THE CHARACTERS OF *EMPIRE'S HOSTAGE*

Characters who are a direct part of the story are in bold.
Characters who are mentioned by name but not directly a part of the story are in plain type.

Ardan – a man of Linrathe, Lieutenant to Donnalch
Åsmund – a prince of Varsland, brother to Fritjof
Bartol – the *Eirën* of Bartolstorp in Linrathe
Birel – Casyn's soldier-servant
Callan – the Emperor
Caro – a cook for the Empire's army
Casse – a retired Council-leader of Tirvan
Casyn – a General of the Empire, Callan's brother
Cillian – a man of Linrathe,
attached to the *Ti'ach na Perras*
Colm - Callan's twin and advisor
Cormiac – an officer of the Empire
Dagney – the Lady of the *Ti'ach na Perras*,
scáeli and teacher
Darel – a Cadet of the Empire, Turlo's son
Daria – a trader of Karst
Dern – the Captain of *Skua*
Dessa – a boatbuilder of Tirvan
Dian – a Guardswoman of the Empire, from Han
Donnalch – the *Teannasach* of Linrathe
Elga – a fisherwoman of Berge
Finn – a Lieutenant of the Empire
Fritjof – *Härskaran* of Varsland
Galen – Lena's father, a border scout
Garth – a Watch-Commander of the Empire,
Maya's brother
Gregor – a soldier of Linrathe
Gwen – a midwife and healer of Tirvan, Lena's mother
Halle – a Guardswoman of the Empire, from Karst
Herlief – *Härskaran* of Varsland, deceased;
father to Åsmund and Fritjof
Huld – a woman of Bartolstorp
Ianthe – a woman of Karst, Tice's sister
Isa – a cook at the *Ti'ach na Perras*
Jordis – a student at the *Ti'ach na Perras*
Kebhan – a boy of Linrathe, son to Lorcann
Kira - a woman of Tirvan, Lena's sister
Kyreth – an apprentice healer of Berge
Lara – a girl of Tirvan, Siane's daughter

Leik – a prince of Varsland, Fritjof's son
Lena – a Guardswoman of the Empire, from Tirvan
Lorcann – a man of Linrathe, brother to Donnalch
Marta – a midwife and healer of Berge
Maya – a woman of Casilla, once Lena's lover
Miach – a soldier of Linrathe
Niáll – a man of Linrathe, in Fritjof's service
Niav – a student at the *Ti'ach na Perras*
Pel – a Cadet of the Empire, Tali's son
Perras – the *Comiádh* of the *Ti'ach na Perras*
Piet – a fisherman of Linrathe
Rikter – a Cadet of the Empire
Risa – a shepherd at Berge
Rothny – *Fräskaran* of Varsland, Fritjof's wife
Ruar – a boy of Linrathe, Donnalch's son
Siane – a record-keeper of Tirvan, deceased
Sorley – a student at the *Ti'ach na Perras*
Tali – a woman of Tirvan, Garth and Maya's mother
Tice – a potter of Tirvan, deceased
Toli – a man of Bartolstorp
Torunn – *Konë* of Bartolstorp, wife to Bartol
Turlo – a General of the Empire
Valle – a child of Casilla, Tice and Garth's son

THE VOCABULARY OF *EMPIRE'S HOSTAGE*

The languages spoken in the *Empire's Legacy* trilogy are my inventions, but they are based on existing or historic languages. Pronunciations and grammar may not follow the conventions of those languages. Roughly, Casilan is based on Latin; Kurzemën is derived from a mix of Baltic languages, Linrathan primarily from Gaelic, both Scottish and Irish, and Marái'sta from Scandinavian languages.

Each word is followed by its pronunciation and then its meaning.

Abhaínne – *av-anne* – river
Af – *av* – with
Ag – *ag* – with
Allech'i – *a-leck-hee* – please
An – *an* – a
Arnek – *ar-neck* – arnica
Athir – *att-hurr* – father
Basi – *ba-shee* – pass
Be'atha – *bay-att-a* – food
Bluth – *blutt* – blood
Cailzie – *kall-yah* – capercaillie
Canri'ad – *kan-ree-ath* – lieutenant
Colúir – *col-oo-urr* – pigeon
Comiádh – *ko-mi-ath* – professor
Dalta(i) – *dal-ta(tay)* – student(s)
Danta – *dan-tha* – saga
Deir'anai – *day-urr-an-i–* (we will speak) later
Din – *deen* – your
Dhuarach – *thurr-arash* – dull, dulled
Dhur – *thurr* – dark
Eirën – *ay-er-en* – landholder (male)
En – *an* – an
Flodden –_vlodden – river
Fo – *vo* – from
Föla – *vo-la* – blood
Forla – *vor-lah* – sorry
Fräskaran – *vre-skar-an* – queen
Fuádain – *vwa-dai-een* – peregrine falcon
Fuisce – *vwi-schah* – whiskey
Geälis – *gi-ah-lish* – shining
Gistel – *gee-stel* – hostage
Glaéder – *glee-there* – welcome (literally, you gladden)
Hallah – *ha-lah* – hall
Handa – *han-tha*- direction, position

Harr – *harr* – landholder, nobleman
Härskaran – *herr-skar-an* – king
Ja – *yah* – yes
Konë – *koon-eh* –headwoman, wife of landholder
Ladhar – *lath-arr* – lute
Leannan – *lee-ann-an* – dearest
Lissande – *lish-and-eh* – shining
Liun – *linn* – heather
Lys – *lish* – light
Marái'sta – *mar-uh-ee-stah* – of the Marai
(referring to language)
Marren – *mah-ren* – south
Mathúyr – *mat-oo-ur* – musician
Mattai – *math-ay* – dull, dulled
Meas – *may-as* – thank you
Mer heirthra – *Mer hett-ra* – I am honoured
Merliún – *mer-lee-oon* – merlin
Min – *min* – mine
Motulva – *mooth-ul-fa* – arnica
Na – *na* – of, coming from
Na – *nah* – no
Scáeli – *schaa-lee* – bard
Secca – *sekka* – a throwing knife
Snámh'a – *shanv-ahh* – dipper (a type of wren)
Sostrae – *shost-ree* – sisters
Takkë – *tack-uh* – thank you
Tar'an – *tah-rann* – bread
Te – *tay* – to
Teannasach – *tee-na-shah* – chieftain
Ti'ach(a) – *tee-ach(ah)* – college(s)
Tien – *tinn* – a
Torp – *torp* – land held by an Eirën or Harr
Torpari – *tor-par-ee* – farmworkers, peasants
Tuki – *too-kee* – a prop for a falcon
Vaëre – *fah-ur-ay* – please
Vann – *fahn* – water
Yn – *un*– and

EMPIRE'S
EXILE

†††††

The swallows gather, summer passes,
The grapes hang dark and sweet;
Heavy are the vines,
Heavy is my heart,
Endless is the road beneath my feet.

The sun is setting, the moon is rising,
The night is long and sweet;
I am gone at dawn.
I am gone at day,
Endless is the road beneath my feet.

The cold is deeper, the winters longer,
Summer is short but sweet;
I will remember,
I'll not forget you,
Endless is the road beneath my feet.

Tice's song

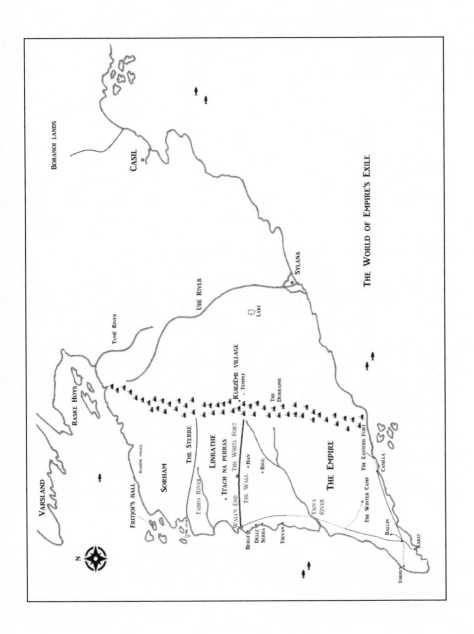

THE WORLD OF EMPIRE'S EXILE

PART I

You shall leave everything you love most dearly: this is the arrow that the bow of exile first lets fly.   Dante

CHAPTER ONE

I DID NOT TURN BACK TO LOOK AT THE LAND I was leaving, after Galen brought us to the path into the Durrains. I began to climb, always looking forward, and up. Anger fueled that climb, at first, cold fury at the sentence of exile. Perhaps I should have been grateful; I hadn't been executed, as I'd expected to be. My Emperor had given me a chance, small as it was.

"Take it slowly," Galen had said. He'd been further into the Durrains than anyone, but even he had no idea how high they were, or how wide. After a couple of hours of climbing, I needed to stop. I'd recovered from serious illness, including an infection in my lungs, not many weeks earlier. I hated showing weakness in front of Cillian, but if I were to have any chance of surviving in these mountains, I could not let pride override pragmatism.

We reached a small grassy meadow, scattered with boulders patched yellow and orange with lichen. I made my way to one of them, sitting down thankfully. I eased my pack off. Cillian had chosen a boulder a few paces away.

"Sorry," I said. "But I need a rest. I'm not as strong as I should be, after the illness."

"No matter," he answered. "Galen told us to take it slowly." He drank from his waterskin, sparingly. "Perhaps we should talk."

"About?"

"What we can expect from each other, as travelling companions," he said evenly. "I can build a fire, and pitch a tent, and use the stars to find my way, fairly well. I cannot use a bow, or butcher an animal. Or cook food, beyond a simple porridge and tea." His words were precise, with just enough difference in pronunciation to remind me our common tongue was not his native language.

"I can hunt," I replied, "and butcher what I kill. I can't cook much, either, but I can roast a rabbit over a fire. And I can navigate by the stars, too."

"I will be more dependent on you than you will be on me," he observed.

"That's not a good situation," I said. "You can't hunt at all?"

"No. Except to fly a falcon."

"I should teach you to use a bow, then," I decided. "If I am injured, or worse, dead, you need to be able to feed yourself." We had two small bows meant for birds and small animals, and a dozen arrows each. I hadn't realized that Cillian had no idea how to use his.

"That might be best," he agreed. He glanced up the mountain.

"Another few minutes," I said. He nodded.

"You should decide," he said, "as you are the one recovering." He drank another small mouthful of water. "One more thing, Lena. I would like this to be understood from the beginning. I am used to travelling on my own, rarely with a companion and never with a woman. I will respect your privacy, and you are in no danger from me."

"Nor are you from me," I said drily. I'd meant it to be amusing, but what flashed across his face looked like relief, to me. What had he thought I expected? "Seriously, Cillian, thank you," I said. "It is good to be clear, from the beginning. I have travelled alone with men, and even in the Empire there can be moments of awkwardness. Shall we go? When we stop at mid-day, I'll give you a lesson with the bow."

The climb grew steeper. At one particularly difficult spot, Cillian went ahead, reaching down to offer me a hand several times. I cursed my frailty silently: I should be good at this. The game trail levelled out, but he stayed ahead of me. He moved with grace, balancing easily on the rocks. Watching him, a memory tugged, but stayed hidden.

Only when we stopped to eat did I realize what that memory was. He'd crouched to open his pack, straightening after finding what he wanted in one fluid move.

"Cillian," I asked, "do you dance?"

"An unusual question to be asked on a mountainside," he observed. "But yes, I do. Why do you ask?"

I had flushed at his tone. "Our potter, Tice, was from Karst, where they dance from earliest childhood. You move like her, a bit."

"Do I? I did not learn from earliest childhood, but from about twelve. Dancing is a necessary ability for what I was ordained to become, by Perras's and the *Teannasach's* decree." Food in hand, he sat on the grass. I did the same, a comfortable distance away.

"What did you do, in Linrathe? Jordis said you were a student, but that can't be right, can it?"

"Why would you concern yourself with what I did? It is in the past."

"It may be," I answered, ignoring the rebuff, "but we're going to be travelling companions for the gods know how long. We probably should get to know each other, don't you think?"

"If you wish, although I do not see why it matters." He ran a hand through his hair, already unkempt. "Jordis was not incorrect. All *ti'achan*, even Perras and Dagney, are students for all our lives. But primarily I have been, or rather I was, for a dozen years now, a travelling teacher, to the estates of any *Harr* or *Eirën* who wished their nearly-grown sons, or sometimes daughters, to have a winter spent in learning. But that duty was almost an excuse for the second, which was to be a *toscaire*. An emissary, you would say. I brought news and ideas to the *Harr* or *Eirën*, and gathered their thoughts, and the news and rumours they had heard, and took them back to the *Ti'acha*, and our leaders."

"What sort of ideas?"

"Whether they supported Donnalch for *Teannasach*, for one, and then after he had been chosen, what their support for his plans were."

"Why didn't you fight?" I asked abruptly.

"Fighting is not required of all men in Linrathe," he said. "Those of us attached to a *Ti'ach* are exempt, and as a *toscaire* I had to be seen as impartial, or I would not be trusted with honest thoughts." There is something evasive in his answer, I thought, even though it sounds plausible.

"So, like our young officers, as a—an emissary—you were trained in protocols, in how to behave and act around all ranks of people?"

"Yes. Even to the halls of King Herlief, in Varsland."

"That training wasn't evident the first week or so I knew you." I hadn't planned to say that. "I'm sorry, Cillian," I said. "That was rude."

"As to that, an apology is due you, for the way I treated you when you first came to the *Ti'ach*, if not for later as well."

"Apology accepted," I said lightly. "But why? Will you tell me that?"

He shook his head. "Not at this moment. It is not something I would have spoken of, except to Perras or Dagney, and I lost that opportunity."

That had sounded honest. We might be together in exile, but that didn't mean we needed to be privy to each other's secrets, or innermost thoughts and feelings. I finished my cheese and oatcakes. "Shall we begin with the bow?"

Teaching Cillian to string the bow went smoothly. I demonstrated the hold, and how to position his hand to draw, and then I asked him to try. His arm pointed down too much. I reached up to adjust it, one hand under his shoulder blade, one on his arm. He flinched, moving away from me.

"You don't like to be touched?" I asked. I'd thought it had been only the idea of sleeping close to me on the boat we'd stolen that had disconcerted him.

"No," he answered. "I do not. But now I expect it, try again."

I kept my touch as light as possible, using fingertips only to position his arm and shoulder. His stance was off, too, I realized. "Cillian," I said. "I need to straighten your body. I'm going to touch you just above your hips. All right?" He nodded. I moved him. "Now, stand there and relax," I said. "You're far too tense."

I'd removed the heads from two arrows, and stood my pack on a boulder for a target. "When you're ready, look at the target, draw, and open the fingers on the string. Don't think, just do it."

I watched him will himself—there was no other word to describe it—into calmness, and shoot. The arrow fell short, but only by a tiny distance. "Try again." I said. I helped him position. This time he hit the pack. I had him shoot a dozen times. He'd done well, for the first time.

I told him so. He just nodded. "Better next time," he said. "Thank you, Lena."

We climbed on. I kept my bow strung; I'd seen several rabbits. The next one I saw fell to my bow. I gutted it quickly, and tied it to my pack. "When you can kill one, I'll teach you to do this, too," I told Cillian.

Mid-afternoon, we reached another wide meadow. "I suggest we camp,"

Cillian said. "We've come far enough for the first day." I assented, gladly. He went to gather firewood; I searched for water, finding a stream coming down off the mountainside. I filled waterskins, thinking about how to cook the rabbit. We had one pot, two drinking mugs, a spoon each, and our knives. I could stew it, or I could roast it. Stewing was easier.

Cillian proved as adept at building a fire as he said he was, and good with flint and tinder, too. By late afternoon the rabbit bubbled over coals. I'd stretched out on the sparse grass, staring at the sky, wondering if we needed tents tonight. No clouds marred the blue. A gyring speck caught my eye.

"Is that a *fuádain*?" I asked Cillian, pointing upward at the bird. He was sitting on the other side of the fire.

"Your pronunciation is appalling," he said drily, "but I think it is."

"I didn't exactly have much time for language lessons," I replied. His mockery had been light, and I couldn't find the energy to take offense. "How long have you spoken my language?"

"I began to learn when I was seven," he said. "So, yes, I have somewhat more experience. My comment was unfair."

Had he just apologised? Again? "I didn't take offense," I told him. "Seven? Is that usual?"

"Not usual, no," he said, reluctantly, I thought. "I was sent to the *Ti'ach* at seven; my grandfather thought it best."

"Then you've been there..." I did the sum in my head, "twenty-six years?"

"I lived there until I was eighteen," he corrected. "Since then, I have stayed occasionally, for differing lengths of time, but never more than a month or two."

"Then where is home? Was home, I suppose I should say."

He didn't reply. I sat up to check the rabbit. Another while, I decided. I didn't want it half-cooked. "It'll be ready in about half an hour," I told Cillian. He nodded.

"Home," he said. "I have been considering. I don't—didn't—have one."

"Nowhere you thought of as home? I haven't lived in Tirvan for three years, but I still think of it as home."

"No. I was welcome at any of the *Ti'acha*, and at many estates, but none of them were home."

"So exile isn't such a change, for you?"

"I am used to a greater level of physical comfort," he said, "but in some ways, you are correct."

That silenced me. At least he won't be homesick, I thought.

We continued to climb. Half-way through the next day, we reached a place where the game trail we followed began to descend. I could see where it went, along the shoulder of the mountain and onto the next, where it began to climb again. I glanced at the sun. The trail continued eastward, roughly.

We stopped to eat. Afterwards, I gave Cillian his archery lesson. I had to touch him again, to correct his stance; he turned too much to the left, a common error for a right-handed archer. He tolerated it, but I could see that it took effort.

He shot better. "Take a few steps back, and try again," I proposed. Again, he wasn't bad. I retrieved the arrows. "You are picking this up quickly," I told him. "I've taught before, and it usually takes someone longer than this. I—" I started to cough, deep, racking spasms. I bent over, hands on knees, trying to catch my breath. Cillian watched me, frowning. He handed me his waterskin.

"Should we camp?" he asked, as I drank.

"No," I said. "I'm all right. Let's keep going."

But by late afternoon I had to give in. The coughing fits were coming more frequently. At a sheltered spot, Cillian stopped walking. "We're camping here," he told me. I didn't argue. My heart pounded, and my head hurt.

"I haven't hunted," I said, after I'd rested for a while. He was gathering firewood.

"We have dried meat and cheese," he reminded me. "I think you should rest."

"I'll be fine."

"Lena." He put down the wood he carried. "Are you going to always be this stubborn? Or would it help you to know that I also need to rest? I am short of breath and I have a headache. Perhaps we have climbed too fast, forgetting what Galen said. What is our hurry, after all?"

He was, annoyingly, right. "None, I suppose," I said. "I have willow-bark; I can make enough tea for us both, if you wish."

"Not for me," he replied. He built the fire and lit it. I found my bag of remedies, putting a handful of shredded bark into water in the one pot and setting it at the edge of the fire. Cillian came over to me. "What medicine do you have?" he asked. "I should know, in case you are hurt, or ill."

"Not much," I said. "Willow-bark, anash, a salve. Some mint and ginger root. And a very small amount of poppy syrup, all Birel could get me."

"I don't know anash." I showed him the silvery-grey leaves, finely divided. "What is it used for?"

"A tea that helps with the pain I have when I bleed each month," I told him. "It's also supposed to be good for the Eastern Fever, whatever that is. And if it is drunk regularly, it prevents pregnancy."

Surprise showed on his face. "Reliably?"

"In my experience, yes. It isn't used in the north?"

"Not to my knowledge. There is mention of a similar plant in some ancient writings from Casil, but nothing known in Linrathe that I am aware of."

"The *Ti'ach* had ancient writings from Casil?" I had seen a map, but books?

"Copies, of course," he replied.

"In what language?"

"Casilan. The language of the inscription on Casilla's wall, you will recall."

Casil e imitaran ne. I did remember. "You can read Casilan?"

"Yes. Anyone taught at a *Ti'ach* can, to some extent. Some of us learn it more thoroughly."

"Can you speak it?"

"In theory. But as no one has heard it in many hundred years, how I was taught to pronounce the words may have little or no resemblance to how it should actually be spoken."

"If we reach Casil, you might find out," I said.

He actually smiled, a fleeting expression. "Unlikely. But a tantalizing suggestion."

We spent two days at the camp. By the end of the second day, walking was easier, and our headaches had gone. On the first full day, Cillian had wandered around the area, picking up pebbles. "What are you doing?" I had asked.

"Do you play *xache*?"

"Badly. Why?"

"I am looking for enough differently coloured pebbles to use as a *xache* set. We will have some long evenings to pass. I thought *xache* might help."

"I'm not very good," I said. I suspected Cillian played the game well. "Promise me you won't be sarcastic about my play."

"You can get better, if you will let me teach you. Consider it fair exchange for teaching me to use the bow." He paused. "I take promises very seriously, Lena. I will undertake to be gentle with you, about errors, but I would prefer to leave promises to larger matters. Is that acceptable?"

"Of course," I said. I'd used the word casually, but I was beginning to understand that almost nothing was casual with this man.

By the evening, he'd found what he needed. The board proved a problem. We finally drew a grid on bare soil with a twig, and used that. "*Xache*," Cillian said, "is a game of both tactics and strategy. Tactics are concerned with immediate actions, or those in the short term. Strategy looks at the longer goals, and at setting up the board for those goals, thinking ahead to what your moves will accomplish."

"Casyn told me it teaches leaders to think in terms of acceptable losses," I remembered.

"It does. Among other things. How would you start your game?"

I moved a piece; he moved one of his. I responded. "If you do that," he said, "I can take your piece in the next move. But if you had done this—" he showed me, "then you limit my moves. Do you see?" We tested moves; I explained my thinking, he evaluated and suggested.

"You teach well," I told him.

"And you are a good student; you see patterns. You could be a skilled player, if you choose."

I laughed. "You want me to learn so you have someone to play against," I teased.

He smiled, slightly. "There is some truth in that."

When we left the meadow, we moved more slowly. I'd stopped coughing after the first rest day, but I'd learned my lesson. We were deeper into the mountains now, but from the highest vantage points, all we could see were endless ridges and folds extending ahead of us, seemingly forever. "Did any of the maps show how wide the Durrains were?" I asked Cillian, as we stood looking eastward.

"Not that I remember." I'd asked him one or two similar questions, and I could recognize now the distant look in his eyes when he was thinking. He shook his head, looking frustrated. "I can't be sure," he said.

Over the days, I'd come to realize how self-disciplined he was, almost to the point of asceticism. He ate sparingly, less than I thought he should, and only relaxed when his self-imposed tasks, whether building our nightly fire or practicing with the bow, were completed. I guessed he had admitted to physical strain on the second day only to encourage me to rest.

But where failure on his part irritated him; failure on mine was met by quiet patience, and usually by a different approach to the problem. This was most obvious in our *xache* lessons, but he also told me stories in the evenings, usually of long-past battles, and asked me what I would have done, had I been a commander. A different sort of game. I realized he had imposed a definition on our relationship, at least while in camp: he was treating me as I guessed he had his students.

He squatted, pushing aside some broken rock to clear a path of earth. With the sharp edge of one stone, he sketched a map in the soil. "If the proportions of the map were correct," he said, "then the mountains here were shown as very wide." He sketched them in. "But that was only one map. Another one—it was older, and I have only seen it once or twice—had them perhaps half that width. So, truthfully, Lena, I don't know."

I looked eastward again. "These next peaks look higher," I observed. Snow lay on the peaks and slopes. I hoped we didn't need to go that high. We followed trails made by a goat-like creature, mostly. The goat-deer, as we'd christened them, dark, horned animals with pale faces, were too large for our bows; we ate mountain hare and a fat, squirrel-like creature that lived among the rocks, and the occasional grouse. Cillian could hunt the rock squirrels now; they moved slowly, and were not afraid of us, making them easy targets. I'd taught him how to gut and skin them, too, and he did it competently. If I did fall down a mountainside and die, he had a fair chance of surviving without me.

"Shall we keep going?" he said. We began to descend, Cillian in the lead. We clambered over some boulders, and he stopped. I came up beside him. Ahead of us lay an open area, steeply sloping and covered with flat rocks about the size of my hand, piled on top of each other like the stones of a shingle beach. The trail ran, faintly, across the slope.

"I don't like the look of that," I murmured.

"Neither do I," he replied. He looked up. Above us the rocky side of the mountain rose in jagged pinnacles. "But I don't see a lot of choice."

I looked down the slope. The rocks ended far below us at the edge of a valley. If we could get down there, I thought, we could walk along that edge—but then we'd have to climb back up. "What about going down?"

"Won't the rocks slide more if we go down them?"

"Yes," I said reluctantly. "They probably will."

I stepped forward. The rocks gave a little, slipping beneath my feet, but only slightly. I dug my heels and my stick in with every step. Slowly we moved further out onto the slope. "A bit like walking on a snowy hillside," Cillian said from behind me.

"Mmm," I agreed, concentrating on my footing. I kept my eyes on my feet and the trail, occasionally looking forward to gauge our progress. I stepped forward, and the rocks beneath my foot gave. I dug the walking stick in as my left leg slid down the slope. Shoving my heels down, I tried to keep my balance. Canted towards the hillside, my right knee almost touching the rocks, I came to a stop. Rocks bounced down the slope and into the valley below.

Cillian grabbed my right arm, and with his help I got myself upright again. I stood panting, waiting for my pounding heart to slow. "Thank you," I said after a minute.

"Ready?" he asked. We began to walk again. The rocks did not slide again, and after a few minutes I regained most of my confidence.

"Lena!" I turned to see Cillian, down on his side, sliding, the rocks beneath him flowing like water. I scanned the slope. Below him, to his right, a small tree held precariously to the rock.

"On your right!" I screamed. "A tree! Try to grab it!"

He looked, saw the tree, and twisted his body, reaching out. I saw him grab the tree. It bent almost parallel with the slope, exposing a root. Cillian got his other hand on the trunk, rocks bouncing and clattering around him. The tree held.

Cillian lay on his stomach, both arms over his head. He wriggled upwards slightly, then half-turned his body, digging one heel in, edging into a half-seated, half-prone position. Holding the tree with one hand, he used the other to help push himself up the slope until he was above the tree, his legs on either side of it. Then he looked up.

"Are you all right?" I shouted.

"My left ankle is hurt," he shouted back. "Possibly broken, but I don't believe so."

I swore. "I'm coming down," I shouted. I lined myself up with Cillian and the tree, then sat down, my knees bent. "Don't look up!" I called. A deep breath, and I pushed off with both hands.

A couple of seconds later I realized I should have put my gloves on: nicks and scrapes on my hands already stung. Ignoring that, I controlled my slide as best I could, conscious of Cillian, directly in my path. I splayed my body out as I slid towards him, hoping to slow my trajectory. "Behind you!" I warned him, and twisted to curl my body around his.

We both wrapped around the tree, shielding our heads as rocks bounced around us. I sat up first, hitching my way uphill to let Cillian get up. I could see him control a wince as he pushed himself back into a sitting position.

"Let me see," I said. I edged down below him. "I have to touch you," I warned him. I unlaced his boot, easing it off. My fingers explored his ankle. "Move it?" He did. "Not broken," I concluded. "But it will need rest. Stay here."

"Where would I go?"

I slid down the last part of the rockfall to the edge of the valley. There was no path, but we could walk along it. We needed to reach a spot where we could camp for several days, one close to water and preferably sheltered. "Cillian?" I called back to him. "I'm going to scout out a camp. Get your boot back on and lace it as tightly as you can, to keep the swelling down. If you can edge down to the bottom, where I am, do it. I won't be long, I hope."

I followed the valley edge. It began to slope downward, widening into a shallow bowl. A stream trickled along one side. This would do.

Cillian had managed to manoeuvre down the slope, when I returned. "Can you get up?" I asked.

"I lost my walking stick. I can't do it without one." I gave him mine. He pushed himself to his feet. I grasped his upper arm to steady him.

"Lean on me," I told him.

"I'll unbalance you."

"And if you fall? Who's being stubborn now?"

He grimaced, but he placed one hand on my shoulder. It took a long time to reach the place I had found, and his face was white and drawn by the time we did.

"Fire first, so I can make willow-bark tea," I told him. "Then I'll see to your ankle." I gathered enough wood to boil water. With the pot heating, I knelt beside him. He'd taken off his boot. I could see swelling, and the beginning of discolouration. From my pack, I took the cloth I used to dry myself after washing. I tore several strips from it, and found the salve. I began to rub it in, gently.

"Lena," Cillian said, "I would prefer to do that myself."

I handed him the pot. "Fine. But at least be practical, and let me bind the sprain."

He allowed it. I poured him tea, and left the pot close. "I am going to find more wood," I told him, "and something to eat. I'll pitch the tents when I return, if we think we need them."

I'd got used to sharing camp chores. The length of time it all took surprised me. But we ate grouse while the sky still held some light. The fire had burned to coals, but I would build it up again, before we slept.

"I trust," I said to Cillian, as I tended the fire, "you can manage to relieve yourself, without help?" I had cut a second walking stick for him.

"I trust so, too," he said, proving it a bit later by making his clearly painful way to privacy.

"No more tea," he said on returning.

"You need to drink, though," I replied. "Tea or water, but something. My mother always said it helped the body heal."

"You did not want to be a healer, Lena?" he asked. I looked up, surprised. It was the first personal question I could remember.

"No. I need to be outdoors, moving, doing something. Healers are too constrained, and there are always people demanding attention."

"As I am, right now. I apologize. I should have been more careful."

"It was an accident. I slipped, not long before," I pointed out. "Don't be so hard on yourself. You are only human."

"That," he said, with a quirk of his lips, "is not universally agreed. But I am trying."

"In both senses of the word," I said. Had he really just made a joke against himself?

"I am sure." He sounded serious.

"I was teasing, Cillian," I said. "I do actually like you, you know." I did, unexpectedly. He was odd, frequently stiff and distant, but his patience and constancy, and the respect he had earned from me for his self-discipline, were winning me over.

"I doubt I am worth liking," he said, "but thank you."

"You saved my life," I said sharply.

"That may be worth gratitude. Not necessarily liking."

"Why diminish yourself? Why shouldn't I like you?"

"You do not know me, Lena. What I have been, and done."

"You aren't giving me much chance to know you, are you?" I shoved another branch into the pyramid of wood I had built. My annoyance with him was increasing.

"No," he said. "I'm not." He sighed. "I am not an easy man to know, Lena. Nor to like, although you profess to. Personal conversation is discouraged, for *toscairen*. Reticence has become a habit, reticence, and cynicism, I am told. I am not proud of some of what I have done, both for Linrathe, and for myself, in the past, and that colours my outlook. But I am attempting to learn to move away from old habits, of thought and reaction. A fresh start, as it were, if one can do that at my age."

I sat back on my heels. "That's better," I said. "You've told me something honest." I glanced at the sky. "It's going to be cold tonight, I think. It's hard to believe it's summer, up here."

"I cannot take my turns with the fire. I'm sorry." He generally added wood at least once in the night; I did too, if it burned low when I woke.

"Don't worry. If you're cold, wake me."

Stars gleamed above me, thousands of them. I got up to add wood to the fire. I heard a sharp intake of breath, almost a gasp, from Cillian. "Are you all right?" I asked.

"Yes," he answered. "I stretched in my sleep, I think."

"I can make more tea."

"Don't bother. The pain is receding."

I went to him, placing my fingers on his ankle. Even through the wrapping, it felt hot. I moved my fingers up a little, checking to see if the inflammation had spread. "You're cold," I told him.

"A bit. But the fire is high again."

"I can sleep beside you. We've done it before." Reluctantly, on a small boat in the sea. It had kept me, and probably both of us, alive.

"I'll be all right."

"If you say so." I went back to my blankets. Why was he like this? Did he not trust himself, if I slept beside him? I realized I was making an assumption: I didn't even know if he was attracted to women. Or maybe he knew about Maya, and that made me repulsive to him. Stop thinking about it, I told myself. Go to sleep.

Four days passed. I hunted; we played *xache*, and I always lost, but it took more moves, now. Afterwards, we analyzed my play, Cillian showing me that I tended to risk too many pieces in my attempts to capture his queen. I might take that key piece, he pointed out, but lose the game.

On the first full day at this camp, I'd killed a kid of the goat-deer. Staying here for a few days, I could smoke the meat, and I had a use for the skin. "If I cut a square from the hide," I told Cillian, "and keep it weighted as it dries, it will shrink and go hard. If it works, we can draw a *xache* board on it."

He looked impressed. "A fine idea," he said. "Well done."

"Wait to see if it works," I told him.

We ate roasted kid, and a few early berries from a spreading ground plant. I recognized its small red fruit as edible. As I ate, I felt a familiar drag in my groin. I'd been expecting it: the moon had been full, a night or two earlier. "Do you want willow-bark?" I asked, digging into my pack.

"No. Just the salve. I dislike drugs, unless absolutely necessary."

"Just tea for me, then."

"Are you unwell?"

"No. Just my bleeding time. I think I told you I am in pain, the first couple of days." He nodded, apparently unperturbed. He is thirty-three, I thought, watching him rub salve into his ankle. He must have known enough women for this to be just part of life. I'd had to explain to Garth, but he'd been eighteen, and raised away from women.

As if he felt my eyes on him, Cillian looked up. "Some time ago," he said, "you asked me why I was so unpleasant to you, at the *Ti'ach*. You deserve an answer."

"Only if you want to tell me," I replied. Why now?

"I do," he said. "I told you I am not easy to know. But there was one man with whom I was comfortable, a son of one of the *Eirën*, but not by his wife. Alain was born to one of the *torpari* women, but he had been acknowledged and, unusually, accepted. We flew falcons together, and talked of ideas, and he did not care I had no father. The day you came to the *Ti'ach*," Cillian went on, "one of your escort brought me a letter, telling me Alain had died of wounds received weeks earlier, from a battle near the Wall."

"No one told me," I said.

"They didn't know," he said quietly. "I might have told Perras, or Dagney, I think, but with your arrival, it wasn't the right time. Perras was so excited about Colm's book. I never did tell them, in the end; nothing could be changed, after all."

I remembered something. "Is that why you...went away? Rode somewhere, I think?"

He gave me a questioning look. "Yes."

"It's what I would have done," I explained. "Or gone out on my boat, alone on the sea, if I'd been at home. I understand: an Empire's soldier was the last person you needed to see, just then."

"Nor did I want to ride north with Donnalch, as it was his war that had killed Alain. But it was what I had to do, although I made my dislike of it more than clear."

"Cillian," I said, caught in the intimacy of the moment, "I may transgress here—but was he more than a friend?"

"Not Alain, no." He didn't seem to mind the question. "I am not even sure I would have used the word friend, until I knew he was dead. It is not a relationship I think of as applying to me."

I could think of nothing to say. With another man, I might have offered an embrace. "I know what it is to lose a friend," I said finally. "I'm sorry, Cillian."

"That is kind of you, Lena," he replied. "Especially since it was I who was explaining my behaviour."

"At least you weren't responsible for his death."

He frowned, studying me. "Were you, for your friend's?"

"Yes. She was my cohort-second, at Tirvan. I ordered her back on patrol when she was upset about something, and she was killed. I should have known better."

"You see that as your fault?"

"My responsibility. Tice was angry at something that had changed her life, and during the invasion she had confronted the source of that anger. I think it blinded her to danger, and she didn't hear the man who killed her."

"Did she not also have a responsibility to control herself, to put anger aside to do her job?" He didn't sound judgmental, but rather the teacher again, offering a differing viewpoint.

"Yes," I admitted. "But what I should have known is that she couldn't, and therefore I should have ordered her off duty. That is where I failed."

"Anger can be very hard to let go," he said, softly. "The philosophy I attempt to adhere to, as explained in the *Contemplations* of Catilius, an Emperor of the East whose writings we know, says to be angry at something means you have forgotten that everything that happens is natural. But I could not believe that Alain's death was natural, and that it was my reaction to it that was at fault. We are here in part because my volition to act rationally failed. All we can do, Lena, is learn from our mistakes, and not let it happen again."

"Like *xache*? Life isn't that simple," I snapped. "My turn to apologize," I said immediately. "I'm irritable, because I'm in pain. When the tea works, I'll be human again."

I made tea again before bed, and the next morning.

"You are in pain every time?" Cillian asked, watching me.

"Every time, for a couple of days." He might as well know what to expect. "Except if I drink anash every day," I added, "and I don't have enough to do that for more than a few months. Nor was my mother sure it was safe to use for a long time."

"But you have, or you would not know its effects," he observed.

"Yes. We all did, in Tirvan, when the invasion drew close. Probably in other villages, too. A precaution, against what might happen."

"I see," he said. "Wise, under the circumstances."

"Yes," I said briefly. I didn't really want to discuss this. "Look, Cillian, I might as well be blunt." I said. "I will have to wash cloths, and myself, frequently, for a few days. I know from Jordis that this is very private, in Linrathe. I will be as discreet as I can be, and I apologize if you are made uncomfortable."

"I would just say tell me when you are going to bathe," he said, "but I am rather constrained, for now." Both of us preferred to be clean. We washed every couple of days, alerting each other beforehand for privacy.

"I will find a place out of your sight," I said.

"Did you know," he said, "that some ancient scholars thought women could control the weather, during their bleeding? And destroy insects in fields of grain, just by walking around the field?"

"Seriously?"

"It is what they wrote. Whether or not they actually believed it is another matter."

"I wish I'd known that, a time or two fishing. I wonder what I would have had to do, to control the squalls?"

"Strip off your clothes, I believe," Cillian said. "I remember you getting the boat under control in those gusts of winds. Would you have just stopped that frantic action, to undress?"

"Very practical advice," I said, laughing. Any discomfort I had felt discussing my bleeding with him, had disappeared. Probably his intent, I realized. "Did they really write that, or did you just make it up?"

"Oh, there's more," he said. "Cures for mad dogs, and diseases, and tarnishing metal. Very powerful, a woman is, at this time." I'd never seen more than a fleeting smile before. Now he looked truly amused.

"I thought these ancient writers were full of wisdom?"

"They can be. But in some cases, the writings are full of ridiculous ideas, as I have just described." He started to laugh. "As a boy, the people with no heads and eyes on their chests gave me nightmares."

I tried to imagine. "I can see why." Laughter changed him, relaxing his usually austere aspect. "Cillian," I said. "I've never seen you laugh before."

"I don't, often," he said. "Mostly with Alain. And there hasn't been much to laugh about, since. But this morning—you are very different than Linrathan women, Lena, open and unbothered by what is natural. I could not have said what I just told you to any other woman I have known; she would have been horrified that such things were written. But you were just amused."

"When you live with only women, most of the year," I said, oddly pleased, "of course it's just natural. But not all Empire's men are comfortable with the process, either."

"No? That surprises me."

"Should it? After all, they live apart from us from the time they're seven. I don't know how they learn about a woman's cycle. If it coincides with Festival, women just don't participate. I wouldn't be surprised if some men never know."

"I had not thought of that."

"I had to explain it, to Garth," I said. He looked at me questioningly. "Garth was at Tirvan, during the invasion." No need to go into the complex detail. "Afterwards, he and I rode south. I was taking word of Tice's death to her village, and he had an obligation to meet, in the same village. We were together for a couple of months."

"Not just as travelling companions, I think?" Cillian asked. Fair enough, I thought. I'd asked him about Alain.

"Not just."

"May I ask you something else?" His voice was hesitant.

"You can." I couldn't lament his lack of openness, and then be reticent myself.

"How old are you, Lena?"

Not what I had expected. "Are we past midsummer? We must be."

"Yes, by a few weeks now."

"Then I'm twenty," I answered.

"Two years adult?"

"Three, in the Empire, for women. Why?"

"I was just thinking about what I was doing, in those early years of adulthood. Travelling, teaching, learning." An odd inflection, on the last word. "Not so different than you, if you exclude fighting."

"A large exclusion," I said. "But I see your point. We have both—wandered."

"Good training, for what we are doing now."

"Mmm." I wanted to go back to an earlier part of the conversation. "Cillian, I think I may have given you the wrong idea."

"About?"

"Garth and me. We were lovers, yes, for a short while. And I cared for him. But it was his sister, Maya, who was my partner, on the boat, and in life. I loved her. I know that is—not accepted, in Linrathe, and if it bothers you, I won't talk about it again. But," I shrugged. "I thought you should know."

"Maya chose to leave Tirvan, rather than fight? Jordis told me," he added, at my look of surprise.

"Yes. Garth and I went to look for her, afterwards."

"Did you find her?"

"Yes. She wanted nothing to do with me, then and again later, because I'd fought."

"Why did you think your relationship would bother me?" He sounded genuinely curious, not asking a question to begin a teaching dialogue.

"Someone told me such relationships were not accepted, in Linrathe."

"At the torps, you are right. Is that where you were?" I nodded. "But at the *Ti'acha*, we take a wider view, understanding that men and women are not all the same in how they desire."

"More wisdom from the ancients?"

"In part, yes."

"And you, Cillian?" I asked suddenly. "Women? Men? Both?"

He was silent. "The answer to that is not simple," he said finally. "Women, once. Men—no, with one possible exception, unexplored. That broke a heart, I believe, which I regret. But neither, by choice, for some years."

"By choice?"

"Yes. The reasons for which I will not share, Lena. Not at this time, and likely never."

"Is that why you don't like to be touched?"

"Largely, yes."

"I'm glad you told me," I said. "It's easier, when I understand at least a little. I have no need to know more." I studied him. "But it's annoying, too."

"In what way?"

"I like you more every time we talk. And I am used to touching people I like, affectionately. Remembering not to will be hard. You will forgive me, if I transgress, sometimes?"

"I will forgive the occasional touch, if you do your best to not make it a habit," he said. "Has your pain gone?"

"It has. I should get water, and hunt, and then we can play *xache*."

CHAPTER TWO

WHEN CILLIAN'S ANKLE COULD STAND IT, we began to make our way east again. The days blended into each other. I lost track of how long we had been on the move. We each gained our share of cuts, bruises and blisters, suffered through bouts of digestive difficulties, and burned red in the summer sun. The constant diet of meat, supplemented by what berries we could find, and any plants I thought I recognized as edible, kept us going, but we'd both grown thinner.

We were easier with each other, after the days waiting for Cillian's ankle to heal. He smiled more, and told me more stories from the ancients, many of which made us both laugh. I honoured his request, and rarely touched him, but the occasional time I did, he didn't flinch.

A bank of heavy cloud rolled in late one afternoon. By the time we made camp, it was raining, and the rain continued over the next three days. On the third afternoon, the wind picked up, and the rain became icy, and driven.

"We need to find shelter," I said.

Cillian nodded. "A fire will be difficult, tonight," he said grimly, over the wind. A group of boulders provided a little protection. Cillian built a fire, but it smouldered and smoked, providing little heat. We would eat dried meat tonight: I couldn't have cooked, even if one of us had killed something.

"The wood is only going to get wetter," he said, piling more beside the stuttering fire.

"Put it in one tent," I suggested. "We should share the other tonight, Cillian. It's too cold to sleep apart."

He didn't argue. I helped move the wood into the one tent. Then we crawled into the small space of the other, throwing packs in ahead of us. I could just sit upright in the centre; Cillian, taller, could not.

Wind shook the oiled fabric, rain battering the outside. So far, the tent was dry, but it would leak at some point if the rain remained this hard. "We're drenched," I said. "We have to put on drier clothes." I had begun to shiver. I stripped off my wet tunic and breeches; my underclothes were almost as wet. Ignoring Cillian, I removed them as well, and found only slightly damp replacements in my pack.

He'd changed as well, but his hair still dripped water. "Dry your hair," I said, "or you'll just make everything wet again."

"Not easy, when you can't sit up," he said.

"Then I will." I found my drying cloth, and edged over to him. "I'll be quick," I said, rubbing the cloth over his hair. "That's better." We ate some strips of meat.

"Not enough room to play *xache*," Cillian observed.

"Talk to me," I said. "Not history, or battles, though. We've been travelling together for—how long?—and I still know very little about you. Or you me, for that matter. Not big things—we do know some of them, I suppose, but the little things."

"Fifty-eight days," Cillian said. "There isn't much to know about me, Lena."

"Of course there is," I said. "What's your favourite food, or drink? What's your best memory? The sort of things friends share, you know."

"I don't, actually," he reminded me. "But if you wish. What are the answers to those questions?"

"I will tell you, only if you give me an answer back. One for one."

"That is fair," he agreed.

"Fish, then, freshly caught, and cooked lightly, almost immediately."

"Lamb," he said, "in early summer."

"Mmmm. Yes." I said. "I'm surprised. You don't seem that interested in food, really."

"I appreciate good food. Or less good, when that is what there is, and I am hungry. But in either case, I prefer not to overeat."

"Drink is harder. Cider, and wine." I pulled the blanket around my shoulders and body. I wasn't getting warm.

"Wine, in moderation."

"See? This isn't so hard. Now, my best memory, that I'm willing to share, anyhow. The first time Maya and I took our new boat out, just the two of us, alone on the sea." He didn't reply.

"Cillian?"

"It is a very old memory," he said softly.

"This is a game," I said. "You don't need to tell me, if it's private."

"Perhaps I do," he answered. "I have my reasons. It is barely a memory, more a feeling of warmth and safety, and my grandmother singing to me, I think. At the farmhouse which was home, until I was seven."

I swallowed. I hadn't expected such raw honesty. "That's beautiful," I said. "And sad, at the same time." I shuddered.

His eyes narrowed. "You're shivering."

"Yes," I admitted. "I'm not getting warm." A hard spasm shook me, my teeth chattering. Cillian reached out, pulling me towards him in one move. "You hate this," I protested.

"I will hate it more if you die of cold," he said. "Lie down, facing me." He pulled the blankets around us both. "You should have said something." He began to rub my back. I shook, violently. He swore. "Closer," he said. I tucked my head into his shoulder. "Hands in my armpits," he instructed. "You are dangerously cold, Lena." I knew I was. All of us on the boats knew the risks of cold, especially wet cold. His hands rubbed my back, my thighs, my arms, encouraging blood flow, never letting my body move from his. Gradually, the shaking died to shivers, and stopped.

"I'm all right," I said eventually.

"You are not in immediate danger," he said, "but you are not all right. If you get cold again, before you are truly warm, you will die. Stay where you are." His arm held me tightly.

We lay listening to the rain. His hand moved rhythmically on my back, small circles. "I think you just saved my life again, Cillian," I whispered. "Thank you."

"Can you sleep now?"

"I think so."

"Turn over, then; you'll be more comfortable. But don't move away." I turned so my back was against him. He pulled me close. I could feel his breath on my neck, warm and reassuring. At some point, I slept.

His arm still held me close when I woke, warm, in the morning. His breathing told me he was still asleep, for which I was glad, because feeling his body against mine had evoked in me a stab of desire stronger than any I had felt in a long time. I fought the urge to turn to him, to offer what I knew he would not accept. I would only embarrass us both. I sighed, shifting slightly.

My movement woke him. He lay still for a moment, not letting me go. "Are you warm now?" he asked.

"Yes. Thank you again." I sat up, oddly reluctant to leave him. I crawled out of the tent, to a world washed clean and cold, the sky a brilliant blue. "It's a beautiful day," I called back. "We should let everything dry, before moving on."

Cillian rebuilt the fire with the marginally drier wood from the other tent, while I strung ropes to hang clothes. The temperature hovered near freezing. I made mint tea, just for something warm.

Neither of us seemed in much hurry to leave. There was an odd intimacy to the morning, as if our physical closeness last night had been more than it was. The tent dried slowly. Cillian went to gather more wood, taking his bow, and returned with a rock squirrel.

"We're not going anywhere quickly," I said. "Should I cook it now?"

"Yes. They are plentiful. I think you—and maybe both of us—should be eating more, Lena. You are very thin. I hadn't realized just how thin, until I was rubbing warmth into you last night."

I looked down at myself, and then at him, critically. "I see what you mean," I said. "You are thin, too. But I haven't felt hungry."

"Nonetheless."

"Right," I said. "So let's get this rock rat cooked."

We didn't leave that day. The sky stayed clear. "It will be very cold tonight again. We should share the tent, and the blankets," Cillian said, at the evening fire.

"Likely wise," I agreed. We played *xache* after eating, until my fingers began to drop the pieces.

"Tent," Cillian said. "You're getting cold."

I wasn't chilled, though, so under the blankets I didn't need his body heat too. I pillowed my head on my pack, yawning. "It's too early for me to be sleepy," I complained.

"Too little sleep, last night. Do you want to sleep, or talk?"

"Talk. Three more facts?"

"Why not?" His voice sounded amused.

"Something you love, something you hate, and...the name of your first love."

"You start."

"I love sailing," I said, "but really, it's the space, the emptiness out on the ocean. I felt the same, almost, riding across the grasslands."

"Freedom matters to you," he observed. "I too love solitude, time just to be quiet, to think."

"You know what I hate," I went on. "Being manipulated. Being used."

"We agree on that," he said. "Although I think I have been averse to it, much longer."

"You are somewhat older," I said.

"I have also done my share of using people. It makes it worse." He didn't elaborate.

"First love?" I queried, after a moment. "Maya, for me, from very young."

"I have no answer for that question," he said.

"You don't want to tell me?"

"There is nothing to tell. I have never been in love."

"Not even once?"

"No."

"Why do your answers keep making me sad?" I said crossly. "I would hug you if you didn't dislike it so much."

"You could try, if you like," he said, very quietly. "Last night was not unpleasant."

I bit my lip. What had that just cost him? I slid over, putting a hand on his chest and the other around him, carefully, lightly. I could feel the tension in him. I kept a distance between us, like dance partners. Slowly his hand came up, not to hold me as I expected, but to stroke my hair before settling on my back. He relaxed a little. I stayed very still. Could he feel how hard my heart was beating? His, under my hand, was equally fast. For the same reason? I fought the desire suffusing me. Nothing he wants, I told myself. Nothing he would respond to, from what he had said. Do not risk this fragile friendship.

"Well?" I murmured. "You haven't run away."

"No," he replied. "I haven't. Thank you."

"Well, good," I said. "It makes life a little less awkward, especially if we're sharing this tent."

I heard him chuckle. "I suppose it does," he said. He turned over. "Good night, Lena."

I moved away, a bit. I thought life had become a little more awkward, not less. But it was only physical desire born of proximity. Nothing more. I could cope.

A few days later we crested a high ridge. As usual, Cillian was in front, so he could give me a hand on steep or rocky places. He stopped. "Lena," he said, "come and see." I climbed up beside him. In a gap between two peaks, a glimpse of a flat plain could be seen.

"Oh!" I breathed.

"It's still a distance away," Cillian warned.

"But we can see it!" I said.

"A grassland," he observed. "Space and emptiness for you." He put his arm over my shoulders, touching me voluntarily for the first time without a pressing reason. I slipped an arm around his waist.

"Thank you, Cillian," I said.

"For what?"

"For remembering. For keeping me safe. For being you." I felt his sudden stillness, a breath not taken. "Cillian? Is something wrong?"

"No," he said softly. "Nothing wrong at all. Just that no one has said that particular thing to me, ever." His hand moved on my shoulder, a brief caress. I looked up at him. Something has just happened, I thought, but I don't know what.

"We have come a long way together," I said.

"Further than you know. You are a good friend, Lena."

"So are you."

"No. I am still learning. But you have helped me, forced me, almost, to keep a promise I made." He took my hand. In a gesture that seemed both practiced and completely honest, he raised it to his lips and kissed it. "Thank you."

I blinked back unexpected tears. "Will you explain, some day?"

"Perhaps. Some day. When I am sure I have succeeded."

A huge bird soared ahead of us, circling low over the ground before disappearing back into the valley. "That was no eagle," I said.

"No," he answered, "it wasn't. Or not one I've ever seen. That was bigger than a sea-eagle, even." We climbed up the last part of the ridge. Beneath us on the valley floor, directly below a rocky outcrop, a half-grown youngster of the goat-deer lay, still alive, jerking its head in a futile effort to avoid the bird's massive, hooked beak, aimed at its eyes.

I ran down the hill. As I approached, I swung my walking stick at the bird. It hopped back, but did not fly. "Keep it off the kid," I directed Cillian. I turned to the animal. It struggled to rise, but a bone protruding from a foreleg told the story: it must have fallen from the rocks above. The eye that had been exposed to the bird was gone. I knelt to slit the kid's throat, watching the light dim and die in its remaining eye. I stood, hauling the body up and propping it against a boulder to let it bleed out.

As I did so, my hand caught on something protruding from its side. I moved to examine it. It was the broken shaft of an arrow. My breath caught.

"Cillian," I said. "Look at this." I tugged on the shaft, and with a bit of effort the arrow came out: a roughly hammered metal head, set onto a whittled wooden shaft.

"People," he said. "Along the foothills, I wonder?"

"What did the maps show?"

"Many villages, perhaps even towns. But that was before the Eastern Fever, Lena. We have no idea what is left."

I nodded. "That arrow's been in the kid a few days at least; there's no fresh blood and the wound has festered." I had smelled the rot when I pulled the arrow out. "So maybe a hunting party out from a village, or maybe the kid wandered after it was hurt. Or maybe the village is just over the next hill."

"Or maybe it's not a village at all," he said.

"What do you mean?"

"There have been other exiles, over the years."

"I suppose," I answered slowly. My mind churned at the thought. I didn't want to meet people. I wanted to stay out under the sky, alone except for Cillian.

"In either case, there's not a lot we can do, except keep going, and pay attention," Cillian said. "Should we take some meat?"

"No. It could be tainted, from the poison in the wound. Leave it for the carrion-bird."

The enormous bird had settled on a rock a few paces away. Glancing up I saw several more of its kind, and a few ravens, circling. Very little would be left of the kid in a short time. I wondered, as we moved away, what the birds did in winter.

Every rustle and rolling pebble startled me that afternoon. Cillian too was watchful, but not with the same nervousness as I felt, or he hid it well. We camped that night along a middling stream. We'd stopped bothering with two tents, preferring the extra warmth two bodies in the small space provided, and the conversation before sleep. I slipped out to relieve myself in the middle of the night. The moon rose over the peaks, white and distant in the clear, cold night. I looked up at it, thinking about the passage of time. At home—at Tirvan, I corrected myself, the barley would be turning golden, but it would be another month before the autumn deer cull.

The next morning, a heavy frost rimed the bushes, and ice edged the quiet edges of the stream. Clouds had blown in overnight, and a cold breeze blew down the valley. I heated water, adding some fruit and leaves from the brambles, and set the left-over meat near the small fire to warm a bit. I had started to crave bread: a diet of meat and fat and fruit, when we could find it, did not satisfy me, after nearly three months.

Cillian appeared from down the valley. "The rocks are icy," he said. "Perhaps we should wait until the sun melts the ice this morning."

"What sun?" I replied. "Let's go up a bit higher, to keep our feet dry."

We packed up the camp, filled the waterskins, and climbed out of the shaded valley onto the ridge above us. A group of goat-deer bounded away, leaping from rock to rock. They stopped not too far away, facing their rumps into the wind, looking over their shoulders at us.

The wind at our backs had a cold bite. The day did not warm, nor the clouds lift; if anything, they grew heavier as we walked. A pair of ravens played on the gusts, croaking at each other, turning and spinning in the wind.

Rock squirrels were sparse today. My first two shots missed, the arrows blown off target, but my third provided the night's meal. We need to camp for a few days, I mused. When we had stopped mid-day, I had noted we had little dried meat left. Somewhere with plentiful game and a good supply of wood. I had no idea what we might find to eat out on the plain ahead of us.

I bent to gut the squirrel. What felt like a rain of pebbles hit me, hard and stinging even through the fabric of my tunic. White pellets the size of plum stones bounced off the rocks, already beginning to pile together. "Come," Cillian said urgently, his hand on my back. "We need to get out of this."

I followed him, the squirrel dangling from one hand, biting my lip against the barrage of hailstones. If anything, they were getting larger, and the sky darker. I covered my head with a hand, risking a sideways glance upward: huge charcoal clouds roiled above us.

We stumbled down the hillside, looking for rocks or trees or anything that would shelter us. My head ached from the constant tiny blows. A large boulder loomed ahead; Cillian tucked himself against it. I joined him. His arm went around me, pulling me against the rock, but it provided little shelter. Blood dripped from Cillian's cheek, and where I pressed against the rock I could feel bruises or worse. "We can't stay here," I shouted, my words almost lost to the wind and the noise of the hailstones. He nodded. I pulled my pack off, holding it over my head, and stepped away from the rock, keeping my face down. The force of the wind and the hail nearly had me on my knees. We could die here.

An arm caught mine. "Come!" a man's voice shouted. He half-dragged me down the slope and into a cave, not much more than a niche in the hillside. Cillian slid in beside us, another man with him. I collapsed, panting, onto the cave floor. The clamour of the hailstones echoed around us.

Eventually the hail slowed and stopped, to be replaced by heavy, pelting rain, cold when it splashed into the cave, but quieter. The man who had grabbed my arm looked down at me. "Exiles, yes?" he said.

He spoke my language, but haltingly, as if recalling long unused words. "Yes," I answered. "From your speech, I assume you are too?"

"I was," he said. "I am Fél, once an Empire's soldier. I killed another soldier in a brawl, some twenty years ago. I was lucky: the Emperor gave me exile, not death. But in all my years in these mountains, I have never met an exiled woman. What is your tale?"

"Too long for easy telling," I said. "I am Lena of Tirvan, but I also was a Guardswoman of the Empire, sworn to the Emperor's service. This is Cillian. We have been, until recently, at war with the North, and then a truce was declared. We broke that truce, and here we are."

"A Guardswoman!" Fél said. "Women are soldiers now?"

"Some," I said. The other man said something to Fél, in another language. Fél replied, in the same tongue.

"Ivor, here," Fél said, indicating the other man, "says it will rain for many hours. He suggests we light a fire and wait it out, a wise idea. Then, he said, glancing at Cillian and myself, "there will be time for a long tale."

The drumming of the rain persisted throughout the afternoon, a steady accompaniment to our voices. I spoke, telling Fél my tale, answering his questions about the Empire. "Callan, Emperor!" he said. "I remember him: he was a junior officer when I was a cadet. His father was in our regiment." He shook his head. "I would never have expected that!" He stopped me often, to relay a summary, I supposed, to Ivor.

When I reached my assignment as hostage to Linrathe, I paused. "This is where my tale joins Cillian's," I said. "Perhaps he should take over, for his story is not mine to tell."

"There is not much to say," Cillian said. He had sat quietly by the small fire Ivor had built, listening. "I was born to a girl of Linrathe, but it was known my father was a soldier of the Empire. Eventually, he learned of me, but not until I was a man grown. I chose fealty to the Empire over Linrathe, for reasons that will become clear, and exile was my reward."

"Exile, rather than death," I added. Cillian's guarded tale held a clear message: he did not want it known that his father was the Emperor. "As I said earlier, we broke the truce between the Empire and Linrathe, but only in what I saw—we saw—in our duty to our leaders. The far Northern people—for there is a land north of Linrathe, Fél, Varsland, where the Marai live—had planned an invasion, of both Linrathe and the Empire. We were their captives, and we escaped to warn our people. I killed a man, and because we fled the Marai's captivity, the *Teannasach* of Linrathe, Donnalch, who was also captive, was murdered by the Marai. Those deaths were our fault, it was ruled. Callan commuted our sentence to exile, and here we are."

"I see," Fél said. "But I do not quite understand why you chose fealty to the Emperor, Cillian."

"Because the new *Teannasach* would have executed me, for the death of his brother."

"And the Emperor had made it clear he would not?"

"No," Cillian admitted. "It was a gamble."

"You were lucky in your Emperor," Fél said, "as was I." He looked out the opening of the cave. "The rain slackens. We can go." He stood, stretching.

"Go where?" I asked.

"To my village," he replied. "When I crossed these mountains, twenty years ago, Ivor's people took me in. I am married to one of their women, and I have three children with her. I am Kurzemë, now."

When Fél had led us into the village—if a cluster of huts was a village—we had been fed, clothed, stared at by children and adults, questioned. Fél, acting as our translator, convinced the headwoman to give us an empty hut at the edge of the village: it was dilapidated and damp, its mud-and-wattle walls crumbling, but easy enough to repair. I suggested we simply pitch our tents inside it, out of the wind. The work of repairing the building seemed too much for a brief stay.

Fél had shaken his head when I proposed this. "There is nowhere for you to go, Lena," he had said. "Today's weather is just the start: snow will come in the next week, and then a hard and killing frost, turning the ground to iron. And then more snow. Autumn Festival will barely be over in the Empire when it is winter, here."

I had not known what to say. I had expected to travel for—how long? I hadn't thought about winter, not really, expecting that once we had left the mountains behind we would leave the cold behind too. I thought how stupid that was: even the grasslands south of Tirvan were fierce and inhospitable in the winter. But how should I have known to expect a winter that came so soon?

"But can we stay?" Cillian had asked. "Can your people support two more mouths over the winter?"

"You can hunt, can you not?" Fél had replied.

"Yes, for small game," Cillian answered. "Lena is experienced with larger animals."

Fél sat back on his heels beside the fire. "The women of the Kurzemë do not hunt: that is a man's job."

"But I will not be a woman of the Kurzemë," I said. "We need a place for the winter, not permanently."

"Where will you go, in the spring?"

"East, across the plain," I answered.

"Into the dead lands?" he asked. "We do not go far into them, only to a meeting place in the summer. There is little there to sustain life, and stories of huge bears on the plain."

I glanced at Cillian. "What lies beyond the mountains and the seas," I said softly.

"That story?" Fél said. He shrugged. "They are your lives. If you can hunt, you can stay. I will try to explain, to Grêt, the headwoman."

"Lena." He turned to me. "What skills have you, so I can be precise?"

"I fished, at Tirvan," I said. "I am good with the hunting bow and the bird bow, and I can wield a sword. And a knife, in warfare or defense."

"None of which are women's skills here," he replied. "Is there nothing you know that belongs to the skills of women, of hearth or healing?"

"A little of healing," I said. "My mother was a healer and a midwife, but I was not her apprentice. What I know is very slight. And all the things I can do are skills of women, in the Empire."

"Perhaps," Fél said. "But you are not in the Empire any longer, nor will you ever be again. That may sound harsh," he added, "but it is only truth, and a truth which you must accept. So you both must begin to learn the skills of a new life." He stood. "I will speak to Grêt." He turned to go, then hesitated, looking down at where we sat. "Are you together? Paired?"

"No," I said. "Travelling companions, friends, nothing more."

"Better that you let it be thought you are together," he said, "if you do not want the attentions of every unmarried man here. Or woman," he amended, looking at Cillian. "Grêt already assumed as much when she offered the hut: I suggest you do nothing to change that assumption."

The hut, built of woven willow branches between upright posts, packed with mud and hair, needed a lot of repair. Fél brought his wife, Kaisa, and between them they taught us how to weave the branches and add the mud. Cillian proved adept at the weaving, his long fingers interlacing and twisting the thin branches rapidly and precisely. I packed mud and wool.

Grêt, the headwoman, had made Fél bring me to her. She had listened in silence, then spoke to Fél for some time. I didn't think she sounded happy.

"Grêt says," Fél told me, "she has heard of women like you: you belong to the huntress. She's a goddess, here," he added. "You can keep your weapons and use them, but there will be a price. You will not mix with the other women, although you will guard them, sometimes. If you do a man's work, you must act like a man."

"Which means?"

"You will be expected to hunt, and guard the sheep, and guard the women if they go far from the village. There are wolves here, and bears and other dangerous creatures. You will not join in the women's rituals."

Grêt shot another question at Fél. "She is asking about Cillian. Why he would want a woman like you, who does not tend his hearth and bear him children."

"Tell her she must ask him." I wasn't going to try to invent a story for him.

He walked back to our hut with me. "You will need sleeping furs," he said. "We have extras; Kaisa will bring them to you. She will not shun you, but she will need to be careful, or the other women will shun her too. You are choosing a hard road for the winter, Lena."

Grêt may have said I would hunt with the men, but the men had other opinions. Especially Ivor, I learned: he refused to have me with him. Eryl, a man of Cillian's age who seemed to be in charge after the aging headman, Ludis, simply shrugged. "You can hunt with me, or Audo," Fél told me. "I am going to show Cillian our bow tomorrow; come with us, if you like."

I considered. Cillian's status here mattered, too. "No," I said. "Perhaps I better not. Is there something else I can do?"

"Audo always likes company when he checks his snares," Fél said. "He's slow, you realize. Up here." He tapped his head. "But you can go with him."

Two heavy furs lay inside our hut when I returned, dark, shiny fur. Bear? I dragged them over to the sleeping platform. No one slept alone here in the winter, Fél had said casually; children were sent to sleep with the elderly and unmarried youngsters shared beds with brothers and sisters or cousins. I was glad that Cillian and I were used now to sharing sleeping space. Even a few weeks earlier, he would have been uncomfortable.

For the first ten days I wondered if we'd made a mistake. The mild days suggested we could have kept moving. But overnight the weather changed: we woke to find snow up to our ankles, and more falling. After that, it was clear we had to stay.

Fél continued to act as translator and mentor, guiding us both through the expectations of the Kurzemë's daily life. He had taught Kaisa, his wife, some of our common language, so she too could speak to us, a bit. But, unsurprisingly, Cillian began to learn the language quickly, and when at night we discussed what we'd learned about the Kurzemë, he taught me new words, so that I too began to understand what was said and could ask and answer questions.

Cillian had adapted to the larger hunting bow with ease. For someone who hadn't touched a bow until only a few months earlier, he had become proficient rapidly, to my private chagrin: I thought he might be as good as I was, and I had taken years to be skilled. He joined the hunting parties regularly, for deer at this time of year. The carcasses were brought back to be butchered by the women, the meat being smoked for winter food. I could help with this, and did, to Grêt's grudging approval. I had no skill in working the hides, though, although my secca, sharper than the women's knives, proved useful in cutting the skins.

The grain harvest was another place I could contribute, joining in stooking and tying grain: scything was a skill I had never mastered. Nor could Cillian, to Ivor's derisive laughter, although I noticed he found reasons not to spend much time at the hard, back-breaking work. Even children gleaned grain from the cut fields, the older boys killing both the rabbits and rats that lived among the stalks with well-aimed stones thrown from leather slings. As at Tirvan, the autumn hunt and harvest were a time of communal labour, punctuated by evenings of food and merriment. It had a familiar feel that both reassured me and made me remember what I had lost.

Only one thing, or rather, one man, made me truly uncomfortable. I could handle being an outsider, not really accepted by either the women or the men. Ivor, however, was another matter.

The problem had begun with guarding the sheep. Eryl led the guard; Ludis was too crippled and infirm now. He had asked me to join the men near the sheep pens one afternoon: a wolf had been seen, unusual at this time of year. He strode up beside me, his broad, open face smiling. He carried two bows and two quivers of arrows.

"Grêt tells me you are to guard," he said. "I thought, maybe Lena needs a bow. I know you have one, but it is meant for birds, yes? So I brought one for you to use."

"Thank you, Eryl," I said. "That was thoughtful."

"You should shoot it a few times, get used to it," he suggested.

"I will," He was right: with an unfamiliar bow, I wouldn't be much use. Several other men and a couple of older boys had grouped themselves around something on the hillside. One of them, I saw with an inward shiver, was Ivor.

"Eryl, here," one called. I followed him over to where the men stood. Eryl crouched in the dusk, looking at the ground. "Wolf scat," he said, "fresh this morning. A young one, probably, pushed out of its pack." He turned to me. "Have you ever seen wolf scat, Lena?"

"No," I said, "I haven't. All the wolves had been cleared out of our part of the

Empire, although older women had stories of them raiding our sheep, too." I crouched beside him, ignoring the other men. This was information I needed, and Eryl was the best tracker in the village. "How do you know it's wolf scat, and not dog?" One of the boys made a derisive sound.

"Mostly from the little bones in it, and the amount of fur. And it comes to a point, see? Dogs shit more like people," he said, "or at least like people when there's lots of meat to eat." He turned his head back and forth. "The wind is off the mountains, so expect it to circle around, come at the sheep from below. I want good archers down that side. You, Ivor, and you two." He named two more men.

"Lena," he said, handing me a bow. "Show me what you know." There was no hesitation, no reluctance: this was a commander, assessing a recruit. I took the bow—it was of middling size, intermediate between my big hunting bow and a birdbow—found the grip, tested the spring in the wood. I felt the men watching me.

"What am I shooting at?"

"See the scar, on the trunk of that big oak?" I followed where he pointed. Ahead of me, uphill and a good distance away, a white patch gleamed in the sun. Not an easy shot, but not too difficult, either.

I nocked an arrow and drew, judging the pull. I released. The arrow hit the tree, but well below the scar. I heard a laugh. I shifted my stance slightly, thought about the wind, and shot again. This time the arrow hit the scar squarely, not dead centre, but close enough.

"Do it again," Eryl said. I did. "Can you hit a running animal?" he asked.

"I can," I replied. "I have hunted deer, with a larger bow. And birds and small game, of course, travelling over the mountains."

"Then I want you down where the wolf is likely to come." A sound of protest came from one of the men. Eryl turned. "I make the decisions, Karel," he said.

"Eryl," Ivor said, "the wolf will not come until dark. Shall we have a contest, to ensure your choices of the best archers are correct?" This was insolence, said to the hunt leader.

"You saw Lena shoot," Eryl said mildly.

"A contest anyway? To pass the time?" Ivor suggested.

"All right," Eryl said. "To pass the time. The same scar. Ivor, your idea, so you shoot first." I wondered at this: why had Eryl given in to Ivor?

Ivor took his stand, raising his bow. A left-handed archer, I noted: not common. He aimed and released. His arrow hit the top left of the scar. He frowned and shrugged. Karel took his place, hitting the scar a bit lower, still to the left.

All the men hit the scar, and not all on the left side. Eryl, who shot just before me, hit almost exactly in the centre. I had watched carefully, not just the men, but the movement of treetops and lower shrubs in the wind. There was, I judged, a gusty wind off the hillside, unpredictable, swirling above the ground.

My turn. I nocked, drew, and waited. I watched the shrubs near the oak, still holding on to a few red leaves, leaves that showed their silver undersides when

EMPIRE'S EXILE

the breeze blew. When all I could see was red, I let the arrow fly.

It lodged itself in the oak immediately beside Eryl's, to the laughter of one or two men and a string of invective from Ivor. Eryl turned on him.

"You wanted this contest," he growled. "Your shot was worst of all. I misjudged earlier when I told you where to guard. Go above the pens, instead."

I thought this was why Eryl had allowed the contest, but if I had been leading here, I would not have humiliated Ivor publicly. But the Kurzemë had their own customs, and Eryl outweighed Ivor by half.

We did not see the wolf that evening. Replacements came to relieve us some hours later. I walked back to our hut, the new bow in my hand: Eryl had told me to keep it. I heard footsteps behind me; turning, I saw Ivor and Karel on the path. I frowned. What were they doing here, at this end of the village? I stopped, dropping my hand close to my secca, always on my waist.

"Do you want something?" I asked.

"You are *devanī,* my mother says," Ivor said. Belonging to the goddess of the hunt, it meant.

"So they say."

"*Devanī* should share themselves with all men, for the good of the village and the hunt."

"*Devanī* choose where the huntress's blessings are bestowed," I said, thinking quickly. "A good hunter has no need of her intervention."

"Then you let Audo touch you?" Ivor sneered.

"Audo is not a hunter." Not a good answer.

"Two boys have their manhood ceremony soon. A *devanī* should lie with them to make them skilled hunters."

"You are not the *vēsturni,* Ivor," Cillian said from the path ahead of me. "You trespass in areas that do not concern you." He stepped closer, his bow in his hand.

"You tell me what does not concern me, stranger?" Ivor spat. Karel had said nothing.

"I tell you that I am the same as a *vēsturni,* in my own land, and that Aivar knows that. We speak of many things. Lena is *devanī,* yes, but she is also mine. Be careful, Ivor." Cillian was taller than Ivor, and older, and there was authority and warning in his voice. Ivor hesitated.

"Do you forget my father is headman? You too should be careful." He turned, stalking off into the night, Karel beside him.

"Thank you," I said. "I've made an enemy there. I outshot him in a contest this afternoon."

"Unwise," Cillian said mildly. We had begun to walk back to the hut.

"I know. I realized that afterwards. I will try to make it look like a lucky shot if I can."

"My apologies for claiming you as mine, Lena: I had no time to think of anything else."

I laughed. "I didn't mind. It's what we want the village to believe, isn't it?"

"I dislike implying I have control over you."

"You did it for my safety," I pointed out. "Why were you out, anyhow?

"I don't know, really. I'm not guarding tonight. But I was uneasy about you for some reason, so I came to meet you." We had reached the hut. Inside, the fire burned low, the pot of water we always left beside it steaming slightly. "Tea?" Cillian asked.

"Yes, but I can make it," I said. We drank a steeped mix of leaves and berries. I unstrung the new bow and coiled the bowstring, putting it on a shelf before pulling off my outdoor tunic. I changed boots for indoor slippers of deerskin; beside me, Cillian did the same. I ran a hand across his shoulder. "Thank you again."

I made the tea, and we sat by the hearth to drink it. The hut was cool, and would be cold soon, but there was enough warmth by the fire for a while. "Has Aivar said anything about what Ivor suggested?" I asked.

"No."

"Could you ask him? I don't want to ask Grêt. I'm not sure she'd tell me the truth."

"I can. But you wouldn't consider it?" He sounded shocked, I thought.

"Of course not! But if there is any such expectation, I'll need to make up a different ritual to replace it, one I can say is from my land. I could probably handle kissing each of the two boys instead." I sipped the tea. "There is an equivalent goddess in Linrathe, you said? Do you know anything about rituals?"

"Sorham, really, not Linrathe. I will have to think. She is not widely acknowledged, and there is little written about her. I can probably remember more about Casil's goddess, and the Kurzemë will not know the difference." He finished his tea. Standing, he offered me a hand up. "It's getting cold. We should go to bed."

We readied the hut and ourselves for the night. The hut would be cold, but not so cold that under the furs of the bed we needed to sleep closer to each other than the space demanded, for which I was glad: I still damped down desire, mostly successfully. I saw no sign that he was aware of my feelings. Given what he'd told me, I did not expect him to share them.

As the weeks passed and winter hardened its grip on the land, there was less for me to do. I guarded the women at the morning's trip to the river—a task necessitated by the loss of a woman to a bear, a few seasons back, I had discovered—and when they went out to gather firewood. I took my turn guarding the sheep, but the young wolf had not been seen again. Audo welcomed me on his daily checks of his snares, too; he was simple, and I often could not follow his rambling talk, but his snares were meticulously constructed and maintained. He usually gave me a rabbit or a squirrel, too.

Living with Cillian was easy, an adaptation of our routines on the long walk across the mountains. He built the morning fire while I did water watch and brought back our own full buckets; I did most of the cooking and most of the chores that were considered woman's work in the village, at least if they could be observed. Cillian had argued about that, but I had prevailed. "Wash dishes and clothes if you like," I had said, "but not publicly. Ask Fél about it, if you think I'm wrong."

I didn't know if he ever had, but he restricted such activities to the hut. I knew from Kaisa that Fél sometimes helped her with women's work, as well, particularly cooking, but he kept it quiet. He'd been a cook before his exile. The Kurzemë men had not known what to make of that, but his training with sword and spear had been enough for them to forgive it. But it had been a long time before they fully accepted him. Fél was not his real name, but a Kurzemë word meaning 'half': half-man, they had called him, instead of Oran, his real name. "Try to fit in, as well as you can," he'd told Cillian, early on. "I know you're not staying, but it will be easier for you both."

Cillian seemed content enough. Ludis, the aging headman, and Aivar, the *vēsturni*, were always happy to talk to him. New ears for their old tales, I assumed, but from what he told me, they also liked to hear what he could tell them, not the facts and history of Linrathe or the Empire, but the *danta*, with their magical beings and fierce beasts. In late autumn, he started to tell them to all the men, around their communal fire in the evenings. I was happy for him, but I missed our *xache* games and conversation, and there was no welcoming woman's fire for me.

But he did not join the men every evening, and even if he had, he would return to talk to me under the furs of our bed for a while before we slept. He probed their stories for mention of the Eastern Empire, but other than a few faint memories of a people they called 'the builders', they had no concept of an empire that had once ruled them. Eastward they never went, past the meeting place where all the villages congregated at midsummer. Beyond that, Ludis told Cillian, the plain went on endlessly, arid and almost devoid of life, inhospitable to travellers.

"I am curious about the meeting place, though," Cillian said. "Both Aivar and Ludis describe it as a ring of carved white stones. The track out to it is the obvious place to start our journey east, though, so I suppose we will see it, in good time."

"What happens at this midsummer meeting?" I asked. We'd finished eating, rabbit stew and oatcakes, a frequent meal. As on our journey over the mountains, Cillian ate sparingly, but he never complained about what food we had, to my relief. He also cooked the morning porridge while I was out on water watch, and probably better than I would have.

"I would say its real purpose is for young men and women to find a partner," he said. "Some trade, and family news. The *vēsturni* search for apprentices, too, I know that. Children suited to it are rare in these villages."

The *vēsturni* filled a role similar to the Linrathan *scáeli*: Aivar was the village's teacher and historian, keeper of the Kurzemë stories. He settled disputes, presided over marriages and death rites, and advised Ludis. As the Kurzemë had no written language, all the stories and songs had to be memorised and kept alive by frequent telling or singing.

"Aivar doesn't have an apprentice, does he?"

"No. He had one, but the boy—young man, really—drowned last year. A bad omen for the village, and possibly in more ways than one."

"What do you mean?"

"Aivar is not well. His lips often look blue and he coughs too much. They will look for a new apprentice this summer. Ludis tells me they might be able to convince another *vēsturni* to part with an older boy or even find someone fully trained, but there is a price for that. If Aivar dies without having trained a successor, the village will struggle with decisions and leadership."

"They need a council, like Tirvan." I suggested.

"Three leaders, rather than two? It would help. So would teaching the lessons embedded in the stories to more of their boys, but it isn't their way."

"And girls," I said. "Are you going to the fire tonight?"

"No. There is some decision to be made, a dispute to be settled, and Ivor complained loudly the last time I was present. Ludis knows not to expect me. So we can play *xache*."

"Why does Ivor hate us so much?"

"Precisely, Lena, he hates neither of us. He wants you, and is jealous of me." I wish there was a reason for that jealousy, I thought, watching his graceful, deft hands laying out the *xache* pieces.

"But he doesn't like me. He treats me like I am worthless."

"For some men, wanting has nothing to do with liking or valuing a woman. It is about power and possession, and Ivor perceives you as having power, and therefore he wants you," Cillian said. "But not to share that power, but to control it, or even end it." He finished arranging the pieces. "It is why I dislike ever suggesting I have any right to tell you what to do," he added, "but if Ivor thinks you are not mine, then I lose any power to protect you, in his mind. It is a dilemma."

"So you have power over Ivor because he thinks you control me?"

"And because I am older, and nearly a *vēsturni*, and he has some respect for that position. Speaking of which, I think I have devised a ritual for the two boys who will come of age at midwinter. One you can perform without insult to you, I hope."

"What is it?"

"Make them each an arrow fletched with feathers from a bird you have killed yourself. Present one to each of them at the midwinter fire. You may have to kiss the two boys, as you proposed, although I expect on the forehead would suffice."

"Cillian, that's brilliant! I could kiss you, for that suggestion."

He glanced up at me. "Best not," he said, but I noticed the tiniest hint of smile. "Are you ready to play?"

CHAPTER THREE

I WALKED ALONG THE RIVER THE NEXT MORNING, my bird bow in hand. The trail the hunters used to leave the village was hard-packed: no snow had fallen for a few days. Even so, the going was difficult.

A good distance along the path, a large black bird, red-capped, flew from one tree to another, clinging to the trunk. Perfect: woodpeckers had stiff tail feathers, ideal for fletching. I aimed and shot, and the bird fell.

I picked it up, turning to go back home. "A good shot," a voice said. Ivor. "But what do you want with a woodpecker, *devanī*?

"For a ritual, at midwinter," I said. "Do not delay me, Ivor."

"I go to hunt grouse," he said. He carried the wood-and-sinew *lümike* on his back, ready to slip his boots into when he reached deeper snow. "Give me your blessing, *devanī.*"

"Hunt well, Ivor," I said, hoping that would placate him.

"More than that, I think," he said. He took a step towards me, and grabbed my upper arm. "A kiss, at least."

I dropped the dead bird and slapped him hard across his face. He made a sound of pain and surprise, but he let me go. I had my secca out in a moment. "You dare insult me?" I said. "Touch me again, Ivor, and the huntress will guide this knife into your ribs." I picked up the woodpecker, the snow stained red where it had fallen, and pushed past him. My heart pounded. He laughed, a deep, horrible sound, but he did not follow me.

I plucked the wing and tail of the woodpecker, taking care not to damage the feathers, and found a place to hang them where they would be undisturbed. I had arrow shafts drying already: we needed to replenish our supply on a constant basis. I checked the ones I had; not ready, quite.

What to do with the body? I put my outdoor clothes back on, and walked over to Audo's hut. He sat at his fire, skinning rabbits. His dogs came to me, tails wagging: they knew me well, now. I patted them.

"Is this any use to you?" I held out the woodpecker's body.

"I can bait a snare with it, for fox or weasel," he said. "Thank you, Lena. You can have a rabbit, if you like."

"Thank you, Audo," I said. Rabbit stew again.

"Will you come with me tomorrow? I am checking the high snares." I knew he didn't like to climb the rocky slopes to the west of the village alone. I wondered, not for the first time, how old he was; his face was unlined, but his body was twisted around one hip. Perhaps he'd been born that way; perhaps it was an injury. He didn't remember.

"I will," I said. "In the morning." What would he do, next winter? What had he done, prior to my arrival?

Cillian's bow was missing, I noted when I returned to the hut. Maybe he was guarding the sheep; I couldn't remember what he'd told me. Or maybe he and Fél had gone hunting. I prepared the rabbit and fed the fire, standing the pot in the centre. With no warning at all, I suddenly remembered the feel of Ivor's hand on my arm, and the secca in my hand; then it blurred and blended with the fisherman in Sorham grabbing at my breast, his mouth on my neck, and the resistance of his flesh as I had stabbed him. I could see blood; the bird's blood in the snow becoming the man's blood on my knife. I stumbled out of the hut and vomited.

I used snow to rinse my mouth and face before going back inside. I forced myself to make tea, my hands shaking. What had just happened? I sat at the hearth, using one of the two furs we kept there as a shawl, wrapping it as tightly as I could around me, and sipped at the tea.

Cold air blew over me as the door opened. "What's wrong?" Cillian said sharply. "Did you get chilled?"

I shook my head. "No." I waited for him to remove his outdoor clothes. "I don't know exactly," I said. "I met Ivor, out on the trail. He grabbed my arm, and I slapped him. That's all. And then when I was cooking, I remembered, and then it wasn't Ivor but the fisherman, in the spring—and I could see blood." I started to cry. I stood up, letting the fur fall. "Will you hold me?" I asked.

"Are you sure you want to be touched?" he asked gently.

"By you, yes."

I leaned against his chest, still crying. I wrapped my arms around him, feeling his around me, lightly, and then more firmly. One hand began to stroke my hair. I felt completely safe, and comforted. My tears stopped. I wiped my face with one hand and stepped back. "Thank you," I murmured. "*Forla*, Cillian."

"It is fine, Lena," he said. He still held me, his hands light on my back. "I have never seen you cry before."

"I don't, very often. I didn't know I was going to." I had no desire at all to move away from the security of his arms, but I knew I was asking a great deal of him. "I'm all right now. You don't have to hold me any longer."

He didn't move for a minute. Then he let his hands drop. "I will talk to Aivar and Ludis," he said. "Ivor needs to be curbed."

"Won't that make things worse for both of us?"

"Not if I don't mention names. Is anyone else bothering you?"

I shrugged. "Karel makes comments, suggestions about what I do with Audo. No one else."

"Good. But two is enough: I will just say that some of the young men are mistreating you. I imagine they can work out who. Grêt may be tolerant of her youngest son, but I believe Ludis is less so."

A few weeks before midwinter, the day dawned to cloud and heavy rain, not snow. "There better be no bears today," I complained to Cillian as I dressed to go out. "My bowstring will stretch quickly, in this." I did my watch, water streaming down my hair, and lugged two full buckets back to the hut.

"Get changed," Cillian said, as soon as I was back. "The porridge will stay warm."

"Can we eat a little bit later? If I'm going to change, I might as well wash at the same time. And don't even think about going out," I said, seeing him glance at the door.

He settled at the hearth, his back to me. We'd worked out small matters of privacy in the first weeks. The hut had a latrine a few paces behind it, accessed though a second door, so that issue hadn't arisen. The Kurzemë valued cleanliness, and both men and women swam, separately, in the river until it became too cold to do so. From jokes Kaisa had made about washing Fél's back I knew bathing continued through the winter in the relative warmth of the huts. Cillian and I just left each other alone when either of us wanted to wash.

But that was not feasible today. I moved a bucket over to the far wall where a square of cobbles meant splashed water did not turn the floor to mud. Stripping off my sodden clothes, I washed in the cold water quickly. Heat from the fire hadn't warmed this part of the room. I dried equally quickly and dressed again, joining Cillian at the hearth.

"You're shivering," he observed.

"I'm fine," I said. "I'll be warm in a minute." He got up, returning with a drying cloth. Kneeling beside me, he began to rub my hair.

"Cillian," I protested, "I can do that."

"So can I," he said. I smiled, and let him. I relaxed into the gentle strokes on my hair, the fire warming me. "That should do," he said after a few minutes.

"Thank you." I turned my head to look at him. "That was kind, Cillian." Impulsively, I kissed his cheek, rough with stubble, a quick, light kiss. His eyes flickered.

"Sorry," I said. "Too much?" There were still boundaries.

He looked indecisive. "Perhaps not," he said. "I am not sure."

"Tell me when you are," I answered, lightly. "Breakfast now? I'm hungry."

We played *xache* by the fire, and I fletched arrows, teaching Cillian how to glue the feathers onto the shafts. The rain fell, steadily. "Tell me a story?" I asked Cillian.

"What would you like?"

"Wait," I said. "I'm stiff from sitting here too long." I stretched out on the fur, propping my head on one hand. He stayed sitting, cross-legged on the second fur. "Anything," I said.

He thought for a moment. "This is a poem by Halmar of Sorham, translated to your tongue."

War in winter sends sorrow soaring,
Hunger hurts, cold kills:
Ravens rejoice. Wolves wait;
Men moan, women wail:
Death in darkness, glory gone.

What manner of man chooses war
Over waiting, in winter
When wind can kill. Sunshine
For warfare; spear and sword
Flashing brightly, glory comes...

I listened to the words, and to his soft voice, becoming slowly aware I was, just then, oddly happy, and a moment later when his fingers began to stroke my hair again, even happier. Glancing up at him, I wasn't sure he even knew he touched me; his eyes were distant, remembering the words to the poem. I stayed still, until the poem was done and a cramp in my arm insisted I move. I sat up. His hand dropped away.

"Thank you," I said. "Does it have a name?"

"Just the first few words: *War in Winter.* It's a cautionary poem, meant to remind impetuous young men about the perils of winter wars. Donnalch didn't listen."

"No," I said. I didn't want to talk about that. "It was in Linrathan, originally? Why was it translated?"

"An exercise. I wanted to see if the verse form could be rendered in another language."

"You translated it? Cillian, is there no end to the things you can do?"

He laughed. "Yes. For example, I couldn't put it to music. I can pick out a simple tune on a *ladhar,* and nothing more."

"Did anyone else?"

He became serious. "Yes. As a gift to me. It was well-meant, and how does one refuse music, once it is written?"

"Why would you want to?"

"Because the boy who wrote it wanted more from me than I could give him at the time," he said softly.

"Oh," I said. "I remember you said something about that, once. I'm sorry. I shouldn't have asked."

"Lena, you don't have to apologize. You should know by now that if I do not want to answer a question, I will tell you. He has been on my mind, recently, that is all. He was from Sorham, and I wonder what Fritjof has done there."

"War in winter sends sorrow soaring?" It was clear to me why he had chosen this particular poem.

"Exactly. But we will never know, Lena."

"I suppose not," I said. I put my hand lightly on his. "I wish it could be different."

"As do I," he answered. "But while I may be able to change some things in my life, that is not one of them."

The rain stopped, the temperature dropping quickly, so that puddles froze to ice in half a day, and walking became treacherous. "Eryl says this will drive the *gemzē* down off the hills," Cillian told me. "We'll go out for them, in a day or two."

Audo's snares would all be frozen, I thought, and that proved to be the case. He and I took axes to the ice freezing them in place; one held a rabbit, coated and stiff, and one a weasel, gleaming white except for the black tail tip. Once the ice was shattered at each snare, we worked the knots until the snares slid fluidly again. It took us much of the day to do the eastern snare line. The western, on its rocky upland, would have to wait. I thought I might try, in a day or two, but the snares were beyond Audo's ability to reach.

Snow fell overnight, a heavy, wet fall that meant difficult walking, but covered the ice. Eryl took most of the men out after *gemzē*, soon after first light, leaving the oldest boys and the oldest men to guard the sheep. I went to free Audo's western snares.

I convinced his black dog and his brindle bitch to accompany me; they knew this routine well and would find the snares for me, I thought, if they were buried. They leapt and pushed through the snow, showing me where to go, waiting for me with lolling tongues. I had decided not to wear *lümike:* I found them awkward, and I had rocks to climb.

Half-way around the circuit the dogs began to whine, and then growl, hackles raised. I hadn't brought a bow, only my secca. What did they sense? A little further along, the brindle bitch began to bark, leaping up at an evergreen tree. I peered up into the dark foliage. About twice my height up, poised on a thick branch, a large cat crouched.

I'd never seen anything like it. It was more than twice the size of the wildcats of the Empire, and spotted, not striped, with a short tail and large ears tipped with tufts of fur. It stared down at me, golden eyes almost unblinking. Huge feet gripped the branch. Every muscle was tensed, ready to spring.

I called the dogs to me, ordering them down. They shivered and whined, but obeyed. The black dog, I noticed, stared ahead down the trail, not up at the cat. I followed its eyes. The carcass of a *gemzē* lay in the snow, half-eaten. The cat's kill. We must have disturbed it.

The snow around the *gemzē* was pocked with prints, one set leading to the tree where the cat crouched. I bent to examine them. The prints around the carcass had claw marks; the cat's did not. Wolves had taken the cat's kill from it before the dogs and I arrived.

When had the wolves been here? I wasn't a good enough tracker to tell, but the fact the cat had not left the tree told me it hadn't been that long ago. Going on would be dangerous. The snares would just have to wait. I turned, calling the dogs, and retraced my steps.

Eryl and most of the men were still out when I returned to the village. I found Ludis and told him what I'd seen. "How many wolves?" he asked.

"I couldn't tell," I told him. "More than one, though."

"They should not be this close to the village, this early in the winter," he fretted. "And taking a *lūši* kill, instead of hunting for themselves. Young wolves, I think, without the skill to hunt well."

I'd done what was required of me. I took the small animals from the snares to Audo, accepted a mountain hare as my share, and warned him of the wolves. "I will finish the high snares tomorrow," I told him, "if Cillian is free to come with me."

In the falling dusk, the hunting party returned. I went to help with the kills: this was something I could do. The men had brought back six *gemzē*, hanging from poles. Disembowelled and bled in the field, they would be hung tonight in the open, and butchered tomorrow, except for one. That one would be a feast for the hunters tonight.

Eryl came over to me as I was helping to skin the *gemzē*. "Wolves, you think?" he asked.

"Yes. Up on the ridge." I explained what I'd seen.

"A different hunt tomorrow, then," he said.

We both turned at shouting from where the other *gemzē* were being hung. "I want that hide!" Ivor berated Vesna. "Be careful with it." The carcass had slipped as Vesna had handled it, I assumed. As I watched, he slapped her hard across the face. Ivor's behaviour had changed towards me after Cillian's intervention, but not towards other women.

"Ivor!" Eryl strode over to him. Vesna bent back to her task, but I could hear Grêt scolding her. Supporting her son, as usual, I thought. I wondered if he would have acted so cruelly if Vesna had a husband to protect her.

I finished skinning the *gemzē*, leaving the butchering to others. I would help with the rest tomorrow; the snares could wait another day. The fire had already been lit; the hunters gathered around it, mugs of the thin beer brewed here in their hands. I didn't see Cillian. He'd probably gone to talk to Aivar.

"Come eat with Aetyl and me," Kaisa said from beside me "The men will all be at the fire until late."

I walked back to their hut with them. "Why does Ivor think he can act like he does?" I asked Kaisa. She shrugged.

"Because no one stops him. Grêt lets him do anything, and Ludis is old and has no control over him. Only Aivar could, once, but since he became ill, Ivor ignores him, too."

"The other men don't object?"

"Eryl does, and Fél, but not many of the others. They think he has power because he is the headman's son. But he will not be headman after; Eryl will. Maybe at midsummer he will find a wife and go to live at her village."

"Is that usual?"

"Sometimes women come to their husband's village, sometimes men go to their wife's. Either way. I think Ivor might go, because once Eryl is headman, he will have no status here."

I hope so, I thought. Not that I would be here, but for the sake of everyone else.

I was nearly asleep when I heard Cillian come in, the raucous laughter of men at the fire still audible, the beer flowing freely tonight. The men on sheep-guard would have just joined them, I thought. I wondered how sober the replacements would be. Cillian, I knew, would have made one mug of beer last and not accepted another, his self-discipline too ingrained.

He slipped into bed beside me. "Are you going wolf-hunting?" I asked sleepily.

"No. Eryl is only taking two other men. I am going to need to get warm, Lena." As it had grown colder we had begun to share body warmth again, always telling the other if it was needed. Pragmatism had eclipsed reserve in this.

I felt his hand on my back. "Gods, you are cold, Cillian."

"I stood talking to Fél too long, away from the fire."

"Well, get closer, then," I said, wriggling over to let him put his arms around me. I rubbed his hands. "Didn't you have your mittens on?"

"I did. It's just very cold tonight. And," he said, clear amusement in his voice, "my hands are not as cold as my feet." He placed one foot against my leg. Even through the thick socks we both wore I could feel the cold.

"Cillian!" I almost shrieked, before I started to laugh. What was happening? He was never playful. I wondered if he'd gone past his one drink limit tonight. "You're wicked. If you're going to come in this cold, I'll have to ask Audo for a dog." Audo, unmarried and on the fringes of village life, slept with his dogs for warmth.

"Please don't. I dislike fleas," Cillian said, drily.

"Are you, perhaps, slightly drunk?" I asked.

He laughed. "I don't think so. No, Lena, I am just happy tonight. I enjoyed today, the hunt; I find I like being good at something physical. And I enjoy Fél and Eryl's company. That's all."

We flew falcons together, and talked of ideas, and he did not care I had no father, he had said of Alain, weeks ago in the mountains. Here he was finding the same companionship, without the shadow of his parentage that had darkened his life in Linrathe. What if, come spring, he wants to stay? I thought suddenly. What would I do?

He raised one hand, pushing my hair back off my face. Very gently, he kissed my temple, his lips lingering briefly. "No, that's not all. I enjoy knowing I am coming home to you, too. Different sorts of friendship." The unexpected gesture took me completely by surprise. The beer must have been stronger than usual tonight, I told myself. For a moment, I wondered what would happen if I moved the hand I was warming to my bare skin. But no, I thought, that is not right. Even if he responded, it would not be right.

"Mmm," I murmured. "Just keep them straight. I doubt Eryl or Fél would appreciate being kissed."

He laughed. "Probably not. Although men do, in friendship, in Linrathe."

Well, I thought, that puts his kiss just now in a different light. "Are you warm yet?" I asked.

"Not enough to sleep, no. But the furs will be sufficient."

"Stay close," I said. "I may fall asleep, but you don't have to move." I liked feeling him beside me, his arms around me.

"Then I won't," he said softly.

Eryl and his companions did not find the wolves, unable to follow them into the high mountains. Two, Eryl reported, probably both young ones. He increased the guard on the sheep, both Cillian and I taking our turns. Neither of us were paired with Ivor or Karel, I noted. The snow continued to fall and the river ice thickened. Both wood and water collection took longer every day, and I was away from the hut for much of the shortening light.

I came home one afternoon to find Cillian teaching Fél the basics of *xache*. I watched them for a few minutes. "You play too, Cillian tells me," Fél said. "I always thought it was an officer's game."

"I learned from my aunt in Tirvan," I said. "Maybe she learned it from a lover; I never asked her. But I played very badly until Cillian taught me how to think about the game. Not that I'm a lot better now."

"You are better than you know," Cillian said. "Against most players, you would win much of the time." He spoke without arrogance, making a simple statement of fact.

"That would be a change," I said.

"You can play me when I know enough," Fél suggested. "Cillian, why don't you teach Eryl, too? I think he might like it."

"He might," Cillian agreed. "He has the right sort of mind. A good suggestion, Fél."

After that the men were often at our fire when their duties allowed. If there was food enough, Eryl sometimes stayed to eat with us. I grew to like him very much; he was thoughtful, with a leader's understanding of the people of the village. He was learning *xache* quickly; he was better than Fél at seeing the tactics involved, but it was Cillian's writing that truly intrigued him.

"You do not need to remember the stories? The marks on the bark tell them to you?" he asked. Cillian used birch bark to record the stories. I knew he found it unsatisfactory, but there was nothing else.

"Yes. Each mark makes a sound, and put together they make a word. Enough marks, and you have the words of the story."

"And anyone can learn this?"

"Almost anyone. I doubt Audo could. But most people, yes," Cillian assured him.

"Can you teach me?"

"I could." Cillian ran a hand through his hair. "But I would be teaching you to read the stories in Lena's language, which is also Fél's, not yours. I could teach you the sounds, but the words would not mean anything to you."

Eryl gave him a questioning look. "Lena's language? Not yours?"

"Not the language I spoke first, no. She and I were born in different lands across the mountains."

"How many languages can you speak?"

"Four, with yours," Cillian said. "Or perhaps five."

I did not know there were so many," Eryl said. "Fél can read these marks?

Then he could read the stories in his language and translate them to ours."

"He could."

"Aivar may die before midsummer," Eryl said bluntly. "Someone needs to keep the stories until we find a new *vēsturni*. Especially the ones that belong only to this village. If you write them, Fél can tell them to me, and the new *vēsturni*, and keep them from being lost. Will you do that?"

The fire for midwinter began to be built, in the centre of the village. Each woman brought logs and branches, and I was allowed to contribute to the pile. One or two pieces of wood each gathering; the fire needed to burn all night. At its very centre was a huge stump, turned so the trunk pointed down into the earth, supporting the roots. The men had dragged it there with ropes made of vines. It had been drying since the spring, I was told.

I hung tunics over the rope I had strung across the hut. They would take several days to dry, and smell of smoke when they were, but at least they would be clean. I had lifted the bucket to take it outside when Cillian opened the door. "Give that to me," he said. "I have boots on."

I let him take it, glad I didn't need to go out into the cold. Cillian returned, taking off his outdoor clothes, moving to the fire. I was drying my hands and arms.

He did not sit. I became conscious he was watching me. I looked over. "What is it?" I thought he looked troubled, or sad.

"I am sure now Aivar is dying," he said. "His chest hurts and his breathing is noisy, and his coughing worse."

"The cold will not help."

"No. I am saddened by it, Lena, even though it is as nature wills." He made a small movement towards me. I understood, and went to him.

"I'm sorry this makes you sad," I said, as I put my arms around him. He didn't reply, holding me tightly for a long minute. He relaxed his hold, but did not let me go.

"I am not sure why I am sad," he said. "Aivar has enjoyed his life, he tells me, and he is respected in the village and among the other *vēsturni*, according to Ludis. And he has children, both here and elsewhere." *Vēsturni* did not marry, but to bear a child to one was an honour, and their sons often became *vēsturni* in time.

"I didn't realize he had children here," I said.

"Yes. Eryl is his son."

"Eryl?"

"Can you see it?" I thought about Aivar and Eryl. Something about the eyes, maybe?

"Perhaps," I said. "Let me think about it, look at them again. Sometimes it takes a particular expression, for me to see the resemblance. With you it was anger."

"Which I so rarely let show."

"Nor Callan," I said. "And I happened to be there to see both."

"And here we are, because of that. Lives turn on small things." He sighed, and, surprising me, pulled me close again. "Lena, one reason Aivar's impending death saddens me is that he has lived alone almost all his days. As have I until this year. I have begun to value—" He checked himself. "No, that is unfair. I have valued for some time having you to share my life, day to day, and he only briefly had an apprentice. I am sorry for him, for what he has missed."

I didn't know what to say. I hugged him harder. "Be sad for Aivar," I murmured, "but be happy for yourself, that you have what he has not."

He kissed my hair, lightly, affectionately. I raised my head to kiss his cheek in the same way. Very slowly, he turned his head. Our lips brushed, the lightest of touches, and a second time, still just barely meeting. Desire flooded through me. I forced myself not to deepen the kiss.

"Lena," he said, "what *do* I have?"

"A friend," I whispered, "who would gladly be more."

"This is not unwelcome, then?"

"No. Not unwelcome at all."

"Even knowing I might not be able to go further?"

"Even so."

This time our kiss was not brief, although his lips remained gentle, undemanding. When it ended, he looked down at me, his eyes serious. "Now I need to think," he said. "As you should, too. I can do nothing lightly, Lena."

"I know that," I replied. "I wouldn't want you to."

When he came back in the dark of late afternoon, nothing more was said, and we did not touch. We played *xache* for a while after eating, but I found it hard to concentrate. Picking up the pieces to put them away, our fingers brushed.

"There are things we need to talk about," Cillian said softly. "Is this the right time?"

I nodded. "Yes."

He got up, put the game away, made us both tea, unhurried and deliberate. Before sitting again he added wood to the fire. I watched him, part of my mind appreciating the care with which he did all things; part of it acknowledging his physical grace, and the rest apprehensive about what was to be said.

Cross-legged, he sat on the fur, regarding me. "This will be a difficult conversation," he said, "and not one for which my training has prepared me. There are questions I need to ask, which you may not like."

"I won't know until you ask them," I pointed out.

"True. Then, to begin: what were you told about me, in Linrathe?"

"About you? I've told you what Sorley said. Jordis told me you were a student, and Dagney told me a bit. That's all."

"Nothing more?" he asked.

"No. Is there more?"

"There are things you should know, yes." He looked distinctly uncomfortable now. "My past encounters with women, save one, have been brief, and increasingly unsatisfying. In how they made me feel, you understand? All were initiated by the woman, not by me, and my motives in accepting were sometimes linked to my role as *toscaire*. There were whispers about me, in Linrathe, some of which were true. I am not proud of this, Lena. I traded my integrity cheaply, for too long. Catilius wrote *'never value anything as profitable to oneself which causes the loss of self-respect'*, but that is what I had done."

"Is this why you—abstained? The reasons you did not want to tell me, before?"

"Yes. Earlier, they did not concern you. Now they may."

"Are you telling me you have never been with a woman just for pleasure, or comfort, or because you like each other?"

"Pleasure, yes, when I was younger. Not the other reasons, no."

"And never in love." I didn't need the shake of his head to tell me the answer. "You said questions, Cillian?"

"Yes. This is the harder one to ask, because it will seem as if I doubt you, and that is not my motive. Will you believe me if I tell you I no longer know, if I ever did, how to judge why a woman would choose to—"

"To be your lover? You want to know why I would?" I studied him. He seemed so uncertain. Did he really not know?. "Not like this," I said. "I am not going to sit across from you and coolly list the reasons." I moved over to sit by him. "You can't hold me sitting like that," I said, "and I'm not telling you unless you do."

"Is that wise? Will we not be distracted?"

"Cillian, this is not a diplomatic negotiation. If I am going to tell someone why I would like to make love, I want to be touching them."

He unfolded himself and stretched out on the fur. I lay beside him, fitting myself along his body.

"That's better. Now listen." His hand rested on my stomach. I entangled my fingers with his. "Why would I be your lover? Because you make me laugh, and you make me think, and you are considerate and gentle and honest and kind. Because I like you, very much. Will that do to start?"

"Laugh and think?" he said. "I am honoured." I looked up him, catching the hovering smile before he sobered again. "Lena, this is no small decision for me. Can you tolerate one more question?"

"Yes. Although I may have one or two for you, too."

"That would only be fair." His other hand played in my hair. "I do not even know how to ask this. In my travels, the expectations were clear: a surreptitious night, or two, nothing more. But here, Lena, between us—?"

"For once it will be me who says the answer isn't simple." I paused, gathering my thoughts. "We have spoken of Maya, and Garth. I will need to tell you more, though, so you understand. Losing Maya devastated me, and when Garth came to Tirvan, it was almost as if she were there again. They were full brother and sister, and they looked very much alike. What Garth and I had together began as comfort, but by the end—we were together only a couple of months—I did care for him. I loved him, but companionably, not passionately, you understand? We would not have stayed together, even if that could happen in the Empire."

I reached for my tea and drank a little. "After some time, I went to Casilla, to share a house with a friend. She was raising her dead sister's child, who was also Garth's son. Somehow, Maya found us. She worshipped Garth when she was little, and she wanted to see him again. He should have come at Festival, to visit his son, except the war happened. I had not realized how much I still cared for her until she was there. Only she did not want me, because I had fought, and killed, and eventually she told me I had to leave. So I went to the Wall."

Cillian was listening quietly, but as I spoke he had eased himself a little closer, so that my head lay against his shoulder. He freed his fingers from mine gently and reached for the other fur, pulling it over us, making a warm space.

"Since then," I went on, "I have made love a few times. But never with the same woman more than once or twice, and never for anything beyond comfort, or pleasure. Which is what I offer you, Cillian: those two things, in affection and appreciation, and for as long as we decide together. I do not think I am capable of more, after losing Maya twice."

"Offered in affection," he murmured. "That is new to me."

"Not even—you said one encounter was longer?"

"Yes." Under the furs, his hand found mine again. "When I was much younger, I spent a winter in Sorham, in the north. The *Harr* there was older, and gone much of the time. I was there to teach his son from his first wife. His second wife was younger than he, and she invited me to her bed. I will not deny it was pleasurable, but it was clear it was all a game for her, a sport with an undercurrent, I suppose, of danger if the *Harr* ever discovered us. Outside of her bedchamber, she ignored me. By the time I left in the spring, she had stopped the invitations, and she did not even bother to say goodbye."

"That was cruel," I murmured.

He shrugged. "I was a diversion, nothing more. She was simply making that clear."

"I do have a question, now," I said. "If the north does not know anash, how is pregnancy prevented?"

"There are ways to share pleasure that do not risk conception," he answered. "The *Harr's* wife wanted amusement, but she and her husband were as pale as the northern people can be and a dark-haired child would have told a tale for all to hear. She was a skilled teacher, you could say. And as I am sworn not to repeat my father's mistake, Lena, I appreciated those lessons, if nothing else in the end."

The fire was burning down, the room cooling. I nestled closer. "There is something else you should know," I said. "This is not a sudden decision for me, Cillian. I would have welcomed this months ago, while we were still in the mountains."

"Truly?"

"Truly. But you had made it clear you had chosen another path, which I have honoured. Sometimes with difficulty."

"I didn't know."

"And if you had? Four months ago, you could barely tolerate being touched. I preferred you beside me as a friend to having you run away from me because I suggested we do more than share body warmth."

"Which I would have done. Perhaps not physically, but certainly in other ways. Your instincts were good, Lena."

"And now?"

"And now I am not running away, but neither am I running towards. Not yet. Do not be hurt by that, Lena."

"I'm not." I smiled. "Can I ask something else?"

"Of course."

"After your time in Sorham—and maybe even there—was the time from the first suggestion of interest to acting on that interest short? Like my experiences, on the Wall?"

"Yes. Often only a few hours, or less. Sorham, too. Why?"

"Because," I said, remembering Dern, "that means you have not known the pleasures of a prolonged courtship." I'd said no to him, in the end, but I still remembered how the possibility had made me feel.

He laughed, delightedly. "A prolonged courtship?"

"Why not? If you want. We have the time."

"I suppose we do."

I turned, so I was half facing him. "In the Empire, the first questions of courtship to be asked and answered are about our fathers' names."

"Who asks?"

"Usually the man, but not always. If you asked, and I was not interested, I would tell you that you did not need to know."

"And if you were interested?"

"I would tell you my father was Galen, of the sixth. To ensure we are not half-brother and sister, you understand."

"I do. So we have established that we are not, as we both know our fathers. What next?"

"Then we would spend time together. Go for a walk, perhaps."

"For three months?" Cillian suggested.

"A long walk. And at some point, we might hold hands."

"More than once, on steep places."

"And then embrace."

"As we are, now."

"The next step is to kiss, several times. After that, well, it varies."

"So perhaps I should kiss you again?"

"Perhaps you should." We were both laughing as our lips met. A good beginning, I thought.

The daylight shrunk even further, limiting the time for outdoor work. The sky held light for less than a third of the day, and the shadows of the mountains fell over the village in early afternoon, chilling the air further. Audo and I could not check his snare lines in one day, and we increasingly relied on preserved meat and fish.

No sign of wolves meant the sheep-guard had been relaxed, so neither Cillian nor I were needed very often. I found myself wondering about what he'd told me about his relationships with women, understanding in a limited way why such brief liaisons would repel his ascetic nature. Especially if the purpose was not to share pleasure, but to use the closeness—or the illusion of closeness—afterwards to persuade a daughter or sister or even wife of the *Harr* or *Eirën* to a point of view. It would be as if, I thought, Casyn had asked me to share word with other women of the Emperor's desire for a new assembly only in the privacy of a bed. I considered the idea with distaste.

Was this in part why Cillian had been so distant and cynical, when I first met him? Or had that cynicism been what allowed him to accept this as part of his work as a *toscaire* for many years? Did it matter? Whatever he had been, he had rejected these encounters long ago, and I couldn't remember the last cynical comment he had made. His humour was dry, and often pointed, but not cutting any longer. He is a very different man, I thought.

Our courtship was indeed slow, a kiss or two, some time each evening spent in each other's arms talking, or just watching the fire. I let him take the lead; I wanted no sense of expectation or pressure from me. But our kisses were deeper, and I had begun to think about drinking anash, guessing I would need it soon.

Fél still came to play *xache* in the dark of the afternoons, occasionally. Making tea one day, I handed Fél his mug, and then passed one to Cillian, who smiled up at me in thanks. Our fingers had touched as I gave him the drink. "Something has changed here," Fél said, watching us, his voice amused. "Not just travelling companions now, I think." He chuckled. "Was *xache* not what you had in mind for this afternoon, Cillian? Should we play another time? Ah, for a childless house, where love can happen at any time of day."

I hoped the low firelight disguised my flush. The Kurzemë were unrestrained in their discussion of physical love, although in mixed groups the comments were always light-hearted. "No matter, Fél," Cillian answered, "the evenings are long."

"That they are," Fél said, grinning. "But Aetyl does not sleep early, as she did when she was small. Enjoy the evenings while you can, before the babies arrive."

When he had gone, I turned to Cillian. "Did I embarrass you? I don't even know what I did, to make Fél comment."

"Why would you think you did anything? It was as likely me. Or both of us. And Fél is very perceptive; he had to be, to see the subtle clues about what he was doing wrong, or right, when he was first here." He came over to me. We kissed, briefly. "But his last observation, Lena?"

"Anash tea, remember?" I told him. "Don't worry."

"A new idea for me," he said. His expression was thoughtful. "A new experience."

"It's a pity you can't have the experience of drinking it," I replied. "It's horribly bitter."

He laughed. "Is it worse than the beer here?"

"Much."

"Poor you, then." He smiled down at me. "At Festival, when do you begin drinking it?"

"Two days before."

He took a deep breath. "Midwinter is in five days. I have a fancy, that a new year is an appropriate time to begin a new chapter of my life. For this courtship to become something more. Would that please you?"

"It would." I reached up to kiss him, a long kiss, and for the first time his hands began to explore. "Cillian," I murmured, "this is going to be a very long five days, if you do that."

Midwinter's eve, and the fire burned high. Food had been shared, and beer, and for once the sheep were unguarded, the fire and songs thought to be enough to dissuade the wolves. We sat with Fél and Kaisa and Aetyl, and beside me Audo and his three dogs. His brindle bitch, who had taken a liking to me, lay with her head on my feet.

Kaisa had instructed me in the expectations for tonight: come to the fire newly washed and in clean clothes, and bring something to give to the fire. The more precious, the better. The sun must be honoured, she said.

I had struggled to find something to bring. Audo sat with an ermine skin on his lap, his gift to the sun. My most precious possession was Colm's history of the Empire, and I certainly wasn't sacrificing that. Cillian had devised a solution for himself: a poem, written on a small piece of his carefully rationed paper. In the end, I gave an arrow, one of the small ones from the bird bow that had kept us fed on our journey across the mountains.

One by one, people rose to throw their offering to the fire, the men first. When they were finished, the women gave their gifts, and finally, me. Drumbeats had sounded throughout, and now the men began to sing. Audo, on one side of me, growled the words, not keeping time, but Cillian sang true. When did he learn the words? His singing voice was light, but clearly trained: Dagney's hand there, I thought.

Aivar rose as the song ended. Everyone quieted. The two boys who became men tonight stepped forward. They both looked tired and a little disoriented: I guessed they had fasted for at least a day. There had been rituals earlier for them, attended only by the village men.

In any other year they would now just be presented to the village as men, but I had something to do, first. Aivar, leaning on his stick, called my name. He and I had spoken a few days earlier about what I should do.

"This village has never had a *devanī*," he told me, "but others have. I remember what their *vēsturni* told me. A blessing from you is all I ask. Will you do that?"

I told him what Cillian and I had discussed. "Very good," he said.

I rose, the two arrows in my hand, walking to where the two boys waited. At a word from Aivar they both knelt. I kissed each boy on his forehead and placed an arrow in each waiting hand. "The huntress guides your hand," I told them as I did. Aivar had chosen those words.

"The *devanī* should give her blessing to us all for the new year," Ivor shouted, as I turned to leave. Other voices joined his. I thought I heard Grêt's among them. Aivar raised his hand.

"We..." He began to cough, a deep, racking cough. He tried again. "We do not ask for what we do not need," he rasped. "Our men hunt well. If we need the *devanī* to give luck to a hunt, she will give it at the time. Do not waste the gift."

Aivar's edicts could not be disputed. Ivor and his friends quieted. The drumbeats began again, and this time women began to sing, and a few to dance. More beer made the rounds, Cillian, as usual, refusing. In the northern sky, green lights flickered; shadows rose and fell in the firelight. Fél wrapped a fur around himself and Kaisa, holding her against him. "Keep Lena warm," he told Cillian, "or she'll have to cuddle Audo, or his dog." I glanced at Cillian. We had never touched in public.

"Then I better," he said. I moved close, tucking the fur around us, leaning into him. We listened to the drums.

Ivor walked by dressed only in a light tunic, spurning the cold. The empty mug in his hand told me what he searched for. He gave us a scornful look. "*Devanī*," he said. "Why waste yourself on this man?" One of Audo's dogs snarled. "Incapable *vēsturni* and idiots," Ivor spat. "I will show you what a real man is one day." He kept walking.

"Be careful of him, Lena," Fél warned.

"I am," I assured him. The drumbeats continued, faster; the dancing grew wilder. Under the fur, Cillian's hand began a gentle caress.

"Shall we go to our bed?" he murmured.

We rose. Fél looked up. "Sleep well," he said, "when you finally remember to sleep, that is." Kaisa laughed. "Can we send Aetyl to sleep with her cousins?" I heard him say to her, as we left.

In our hut the fire had burned to coals. Cillian added wood. "Do you need to make tea?"

"I did, earlier." My mouth was dry. I dropped the fur on the bed. We regarded each other across the space, in the light of the newly blazing fire. "It is a new year," I said softly. "Don't you have a fancy to fulfill?"

He crossed the room to me, beginning to smile; not his usual, quickly-gone smile, but one slow and genuine, lighting his whole face. My breath caught. He looks so much younger, I thought, and so beautiful. I saw tenderness in this smile, and vulnerability. He took me in his arms. I raised a hand to his face.

"This is something I haven't seen before," I murmured. "Why have you kept such a beautiful smile hidden?"

He turned his head to kiss my fingers. "My one legacy from my mother, I am told," he said. "As to why, it is just reticence, Lena, like much else about me, long habit." He bent to kiss me, a long, exploratory kiss. "Perhaps I will have more reason to let it show after tonight."

I didn't need to damp down desire now. My hands, low on his back, found his skin. I pulled him closer. Part of my mind noted the ridges of a scar under my fingers, but it wasn't important. Nothing was, except his lips on mine and his hands, under my tunic now, making me gasp.

"You are very sure?" he asked, his voice low and barely controlled. "Tell me now, if you are not."

"Yes." I fought to speak. "Are you?"

"I am." His mouth came down again, demanding now, insistent. How long has it been for him? I wondered, before I gave myself up to my need, and his. He hesitated once, just for a moment, and then there were only lips and hands and cresting pleasure, and unexpectedly, tears that were not mine.

He made neither apology nor explanation for the tears. Turning my head after the slower, gentler exploration that followed the urgency of our first lovemaking, I saw them glitter on his cheeks. I wiped them away with one finger, feeling an answering prickle behind my own eyes. He kissed my hair. "*Leannan,*" he murmured. "Accept the things to which fate binds you."

I didn't understand, but neither could I find words to reply. How could I have guessed, in a man so disciplined, so abstemious, the depth of his sensuality? Experience I had expected, given his age and what he had told me. I had assumed consideration. But tonight had been far beyond anything I had previously known. Cillian made love not just with exquisite skill, but with generosity, and reverence, and gratitude. The tears should have been mine.

CHAPTER FOUR

QUIET SOUNDS IN THE HUT WOKE ME. Cillian was at the fire, adding wood. I lay watching him, unable to keep a smile from my face. He had pulled on breeches but no shirt, and his feet were bare. He fed a last chunk to the flames and stood. Turning, he glanced my way. "Hello," I murmured.

He crossed the room to sit on the bed beside me, his face alight. I looked up at him. "Well," he said, one hand stroking hair back out of my eyes. "Good morning." He bent to kiss me, gently.

"I should get up," I said.

"Not this morning. I asked Eryl to do water watch for you."

"When?"

"Yesterday. In Casil, the goddess you are supposedly pledged to is the sister of their sun god. I told him that was true in our land too, and that you had rituals you must attend to, this morning."

"That was thoughtful." I freed an arm from the furs to touch him. "You're getting cold. Are you coming back to bed?"

"Would you like me to?"

I studied him. The tone had been light, but I sensed a real question had been asked.

"Yes," I said. "I would. Come and get warm and talk for a while."

He joined me under the furs. I turned to hold him, tracing a finger along his back. I felt the hard, ridged skin again. "Cillian," I murmured. "How did you get this scar?"

"Ah," he said. "That. I forget about it. It is not a good story, Lena, but it will have to be told sometime. I was six, I think. My grandfather had taken me to market with him, in the town closest to their farmstead. A group of boys tried to kill me: there is no other way to say it, no excuses that can be made. One had an old spear with a broken shaft, the gods know from where. He called me a traitor's bastard, and pushed me down and stabbed me."

"Oh, Cillian, how terrible."

"I don't remember much of it. I was very ill, close to death, I think, for weeks afterwards."

"Is that why you went to the *Ti'ach* so young?"

"I was sent for my safety. And for the safety of my grandparents; I learned much later that threats had been made against them too, if they did not rid themselves of me." I thought I heard, behind his calm voice, an undercurrent of pain.

"I'm sorry," I said. "I didn't mean to bring back bad memories."

"The memories are part of who I am, and you should know that," he replied. "And perhaps this is a good time for me to tell them to you, because right now, I may be happier than I have ever been."

"Dagney would be pleased," I said.

"Why?"

"She worried about you, she told me. She said she loved you."

"I did not know that she thought of me in that way." He considered. "Are you sure those were her words?"

"Completely."

"I wish I had realized. Another regret."

"All I am doing is making you sad again," I said, irritated with myself.

"Not sad. Meditative, perhaps." He shifted position to lie on his back. I moved so my head rested on his chest. He ran a gentle finger along the scar on my breast. "I am not the only one with scars," he observed.

My stomach growled. "Neither of us remembered to soak grain last night, did we?" I asked.

"No. We had other things to think about," he said.

"I can make oatcakes when I get up." I knew he wouldn't complain; accepting what came was part of the philosophy he tried to adhere to, as far as I understood. "Cillian? You spoke once of writings by an Emperor, a philosophy you try to live by, you said?"

"Catilius. He followed a way of life, of thought, that appeals to me: simply put, that nothing in life is either good or bad in itself. It is our reactions that make events appear positive or negative."

"So poor food isn't itself cause for complaint? You school yourself to accept it?"

"Perhaps it is a bit more complex than that, but yes."

It reminded me of something. "We cannot shape the circumstances to fit our lives, only our lives to fit the circumstances. What defines us, as men and women, is how we respond to those circumstances."

"Very elegantly put. Who said that?"

"Casyn."

"I knew they, or at least Callan, knew of Catilius's writings. Perhaps they are also followers of his thought."

"Perhaps. I wouldn't know."

We lay silent, his hand stroking my hair. When had I last lain like this, warm and content the morning after love, talking? When had he?

"Can I ask you something? But don't tell me, if you don't want to," I said. "How long had it been, for you?"

"Six years, and a bit more."

"A long time to sleep alone, and wake alone, and not be held," I murmured.

"I have never known anything else, until this year."

"No? Never what we are doing now, just lying together, talking, just— appreciating each other?"

"No. Just brief encounters, and a solitary bed afterwards, and nothing more than a glance or a hidden smile, the next day. You have been a revelation to me in many ways, *leannan*."

Leannan. Dear one, I thought it meant. Huld had called me that too, a casual word of affection, from her. But from Cillian, who did nothing casually, what did it mean? I listened to its nuances in my mind, turning it around. He *was* dear to me, and more so now. And I too was happier than I could remember being in a very long time.

But still I felt a tinge of unease. Had Cillian truly heard me when I had said all I could offer him was comfort and pleasure, and affection? I thought of the vulnerability I had seen in him yesterday. I could hurt him easily, without intent, and I did not want that to happen.

I remembered the tears on his cheeks. What we had shared last night had been a communion beyond my experience. And possibly his, too? *Right now, I may be happier than I have ever been*, he had said. This was not the time to raise doubts, to fracture his fragile happiness.

There wasn't much activity around the village, people sleeping late, many feeling the effects of too much beer. In the early afternoon we were playing *xache* idly by the fire. A whining at the door interrupted us. I opened it to find Audo's brindle bitch, injured and bleeding badly, looking up at me.

"Something's happened to Audo," I called to Cillian. We pulled on outdoor clothes and *lümike,* grabbing bows and quivers.

"I'll go for Eryl," Cillian said.

The dog floundered in the snow, one leg useless. "Stay," I told it. I could follow its trail, blood marking its route. I moved as quickly as I could, cursing the snow and my own clumsiness on *lümike.* The dog struggled behind me. The trail went east: Audo's lower snare line. A small blessing, possibly.

Cillian and Eryl caught up with me before too long. I surrendered the lead to Eryl, knowing his tracking skills were unsurpassed. The dog, far behind us, began to bark, and from ahead I heard an answering whine.

Audo lay by one of his snares, blood staining the snow. One dog was dead beside him, its throat torn; the other, still alive, but unable to rise, had crawled to him. It lay over his chest. Cillian bent to move it away as I dropped to my knees beside Audo. I felt for a heartbeat: faint, irregular, but there. "He's alive," I said. Most of the blood reddened the snow by one leg. His boot was missing and the bare foot was turning blue. I cut the leg of his breeches away. The leg was a mass of torn flesh, but it was not pumping blood.

"Wolf," Eryl told us, returning from a short distance away. "Only one. The dogs must have fought it off." He had the missing boot in his hand. I eased it back over Audo's foot; it was damaged, but better than nothing.

"How do we get him back to the village?" I asked. I checked the rest of his body; bites on one arm and both hands as well.

"I'll go," Eryl said. "We'll need a sled. Be vigilant: the wolf may not be far away." He began to run back towards the village.

"Give me your secca," Cillian said, sounding grim. "This dog is dying." I gave it to him, looking away as he held its head back to cut its throat. He dragged its body, and the other one, away from where I crouched by Audo.

"I should have been with him," I said.

"Lena, he has been doing this for years without you," Cillian reminded me.

"You cannot take responsibility for this." He held his bow, an arrow nocked, watching the hillside.

"I suppose," I said. I didn't go out with Audo every day. But usually it was because I had other responsibilities, not because I had chosen to spend a lazy, relaxed day with Cillian. We waited. I stayed by Audo. The wounded dog, arriving, curled up beside him. This dog would live, I thought. How would Audo stay warm at night without the other two? If he survived.

I could see Eryl returning, pulling a fur-heaped sled, Fél following him. Carefully, Eryl and Fél lifted Audo onto the sled, covering him with furs. Audo moaned briefly, lapsing back into unconsciousness. "Put the dog on too," Eryl directed.

At Audo's hut, Kaisa had the fire burning high and water heating. The men carried him to his bed, nothing more than a pallet covered by furs. We undressed him to bathe and bind the wounds.

Part way through, Audo woke, screaming, fighting our hands. "Keep him as calm as possible," I said. "I'll get the poppy syrup." Not bothering with *lümike*, I ran back to our hut to find my bag of remedies. Anash, too, I thought, against fever.

Back at Audo's hut, we held his jaw open. I poured a small amount of poppy into his mouth, massaging his throat to encourage him to swallow. We covered him with furs. When he had calmed, drifting back into sleep or unconsciousness, Kaisa finished bathing the wounds. "There is no more we can do," she said. "I will sit with him. Lena, you are covered in blood. Go and clean yourself and your clothes."

I looked down. She was right; blood stained my coat and leggings. "Your face, too," Cillian told me. I scooped up some water and washed my face, tasting the blood on my lips. Bile rose in my throat. I pushed down the nausea.

"It is too late tonight to begin a hunt for the animal," Eryl said. "Tomorrow, first light. Do you want to come, Cillian?"

"No. I will slow you down. I will guard the sheep."

"Or go with Lena to guard the women; they will need to go out for firewood tomorrow. Audo will need a fire by day as well as night for some time. I'd prefer two guards, with a wolf around that has tasted a person. Lena, you know his snares well: they will need to be taken down. Can you do that?"

"Eryl, if his snares are taken down, will you feed his dog?" The dogs, like Audo, ate primarily whatever he caught. The snares had helped feed us, too. "Or should I just keep the snare line going?"

He considered. "You can if you want. But again, not by yourself, unless we kill this wolf."

I glanced at Cillian. He shrugged. "Your decision, Lena. I will come with you, if you decide to do it."

"Then I will."

"Go," Kaisa said again. "Eryl, you will arrange with Grêt and Ludis for women to care for him, and for food and firewood?"

Cillian left with me. My stomach was still unsteady. At our hut, I stripped off the bloody clothes. "I'll clean them," Cillian said. "You sit. You are white, Lena."

"I hate the sight of human blood," I said. I took dried ginger root from my remedy bag, dropping it into a mug. Cillian built up the fire. As soon as the water had heated, I poured some on the ginger root. Even the smell helped the nausea. I sipped it slowly, feeling my stomach slowly settle.

But in the night, I woke, bile rising in my throat from a confused dream of blood and knives. I ran outside to vomit, heedless of what little I wore. I knelt in the snow, waiting to be sure the spasms were over. I felt a fur being draped over my shoulders, and a hand on my back. "Are you all right?" Cillian asked.

I nodded. "I think so."

"Should I make you tea, with the ginger root?"

"Would you? I'll come in, in a little while." By the time I did, the tea was waiting for me, and dry clothes, warming by the fire. I changed, and wrapped the fur around me again.

"What brought this on, Lena?" Cillian asked.

"A dream, of blood and killing," I answered. "It happens, occasionally." I drank a little of the tea. "I will tell you, but you might not like what you hear."

"I have watched you kill a man," he reminded me.

"True. That killing bothers me less. But when Leste invaded, my cohort—our job was to find the men who didn't surrender, who were hiding. We were trained to move silently, to use our knives, to be assassins. The first man I killed died badly. He was no more than a boy, and he tried to fight back, and I stabbed him, in the lungs, I realize now. He was choking on his own blood." I couldn't keep the tears back. "I couldn't stand seeing him like that, so I cut his throat. Like he was an animal, like you did Audo's dog today."

"Dear gods," Cillian said, moving to wrap his arms around me. "You should have told me this earlier."

"I know," I sobbed. "Before we became lovers. So you knew who I was. I'm sorry, Cillian."

"That is not what I meant," he said. "What you did was a mercy. I only meant I wished I had known, so I might have killed the dog out of your sight, and perhaps saved you this, tonight."

"Perhaps." I rested in his arms. "I think it might have been Audo's blood on my face, too. Tasting it."

"I can see that. Finish your tea, Lena, and then back to bed, before you get cold." Under the furs, I nestled against him, slowly getting warm, drifting into a dreamless, safe sleep.

††††††

As the days lengthened, the cold deepened. The snow stopped falling, clouds giving way to brilliant blue skies. We began to hear the wolves at night. The hunters reported finding the remnants of kills in the valley: a pack of ten or so, Eryl thought, from the tracks, not the pair of young ones.

Our routines did not alter, but gradually I noticed a change in Cillian. Aivar died at the dark of the moon, coughing blood, and after the ceremony for his death Cillian became quiet. I expected him to recover after a day or two, but he did not, although it took me a while to notice that he hadn't.

In these cold months, it was the practice of the Kurzemë to save fuel by families moving into one hut, crowded but warm. Firewood was hard to gather in the deep snow, and with Audo needing more than usual, the supplies dwindled. Fél and Kaisa invited us to share their hut, something I was reluctant to do. We compromised: during the day we ate with them and shared their fire, Eryl often joining us. Cillian and Fél were teaching him the stories. Only at night did we return to our own hut, accepting the good-natured teasing we received for this.

We had little private time together beyond the nighttime. Out on the snare lines, he was frequently silent; pensive, I thought, but I put it down to a need to counter the lack of solitude and quiet. The crowded conditions were beginning to frustrate me, and I was not unhappy he did not want to talk while we were out.

It was Kaisa, at an evening meal, who brought my attention to how little Cillian was eating. "One bowl of soup will not give you energy enough for the hunt," she scolded him.

"Kaisa, I am just not hungry tonight," he replied. "Please do not worry." But later, she took me aside.

"Is Cillian sick?" she asked bluntly. "He is not eating; have you not noticed?" I hadn't. I would pay attention, I assured her. Under the furs that night, I ran my hands along his ribs.

"Cillian, you are losing weight," I said. "Kaisa says you are not eating, and she is right, isn't she? And we haven't made love for days. What's wrong?"

He didn't answer immediately. I waited.

"I am just winter-weary, as it is called in Sorham," he said eventually. "Tired of confinement, I suppose."

"Is this worse than Sorham?" I asked.

"It shouldn't be," he said. He ran a hand down my arm, lightly. "In one way it is better than any winter of my life, *leannan*," he murmured. "But I admit to being discontent, Lena, without really knowing why."

"Oh, love, maybe you just need some time alone," I said. *Love?* Where had that come from? It was what I had called Maya. If he noticed the endearment, he didn't react. "I can ask Fél to accompany me to the snares." With the wolves still about, Eryl would not allow me to go alone.

"It might help," he admitted. "Solitude is something I am used to."

"And you have had almost none, for the last ten months," I pointed out. "Let me talk to Fél."

Fél was happy to accompany me. "Cillian misses Aivar," he told me, as we checked the snares. "They talked of things beyond me, the sort of thing officers learn about in the Empire. Philosophy, and such."

But even with Fél now helping with the snare line every few days, Cillian did not seem happier to me. Time alone was only making him more withdrawn. "I am beginning to worry about you," I told him, a couple of weeks later, as we returned from a nearly-silent check of the snares.

His eyes, shadowed, told me nothing. "Forgive me, Lena," he said quietly. "There is much on my mind."

"Would it help to tell me?"

"It is difficult to explain. I have spoken before of Catilius, and his *Contemplations.* You remember?'

"Yes."

"I have used his writings, which are about his own maturation into a philosophy to govern his life, as a guide to my own. I began this some years ago, and I believed that in exile I would find much in his thought to sustain me. But it is not the case."

"Why not? Or maybe I mean how is it not the case?"

"Ah," he said, sounding frustrated, "for several reasons. One is that I do not have his writings and so cannot see the thoughts in context, following their development. I am finding one or two contradictory, as I remember them, and that is part of it. But the fault is in me, I think, Lena. There is work to do here I should be glad to take on. Eryl wants me to develop a written Kurzemë language. It is an honourable and important task. But I do not want to do it."

"What do you want, then?"

"Things I cannot have. There is no use dwelling on them, Lena. I am angry with myself, for not being satisfied with what I have: my life, your companionship, friends here. You will have to be patient with me once again, I am afraid."

"I can be patient," I said, "as long as I know you are well."

How had he gone from being so happy just before midwinter, to these depths of discontent? All that had changed was that we had become lovers. Did the key to his unhappiness lie in that? I couldn't see how.

†††††

The weather had warmed just enough to allow us to move back to our own hut. I thought the relief from the demands of other people might improve Cillian's frame of mind, but I saw little evidence of it. My patience was beginning to fray as much through worry as frustration.

Perhaps, I thought, I am simply too pragmatic. Life had demands, and they needed to be met. I didn't necessarily like them, but I could adapt. I wasn't exactly leading the life I would prefer, either, but I hadn't given in to melancholy.

Eryl had come looking for Cillian earlier. They had gone off together, and I had gone to visit Audo. His leg had healed, mostly, although the muscles had shrunk and scarred and he could still barely walk. But he had been happy: the brindle bitch was clearly pregnant and there would be puppies soon. He would keep two, he told me. The rest, I knew, would be killed, unless someone wanted one.

Ludis, I mused, walking back to our hut, seemed content to leave almost all the leadership of the village to Eryl. After Aivar's death, Ludis had shrunk, withdrawn into himself. Grêt tried to speak for him, but it was clear the men saw Eryl as his successor.

"Lena!" Grêt called to me, just as I turned to enter our hut.

"Yes?"

"Tomorrow, we go to the meadow, to the trees, to begin to gather sap. You must guard us."

I nodded. "I will." No different from guarding them while gathering firewood, I thought.

Cillian did not return until dark. "Ready to eat?" I asked. I'd stopped asking if he was hungry.

"No. Can we talk, first?" He ran a hand through his hair, long now, long enough to tie back. He hadn't shaved in some time, I noted.

"Of course. Tea?" I offered. He nodded.

"What do we need to talk about?" I asked, once we both had tea and had settled by the fire.

"Eryl has asked me to stay. Until midsummer, at least, and the gathering of the villages, when they can find a new *vēsturni*."

"Do you want to?"

"What I want is not important. I should stay, if for no other reason to repay the hospitality and friendship he has given me."

I thought of the plain to the east, of its wide, empty space. Knowing it was there had sustained me this winter. But all Cillian was asking was to stay a further six weeks or so. I could do that. Anyhow, did I have a choice? I wasn't going without him. But his first statement bothered me.

"How can you say what you want isn't important? It is."

"*Do not indulge in dreaming of what you do not have, but look at the blessings you do, and remember how much you would want them, if they were not yours,*" he said, with the first hint of cynicism I had heard in months. "Good advice, would you not say, Lena?"

"Yes."

"And I agree. What I want is nothing but a dream of what I do not have, and as such should be ignored. But I seem to be unable to be rational. '*Let men see and know a man who lives as he was meant to live*', I was told, but understanding how I am meant to live is difficult for me, right now."

This is beyond me, I thought. "Is this what you used to talk to Aivar about?" I asked.

"Yes. He was not familiar with Catilius, of course, but he had his own philosophy, and could debate wisely."

"Which I cannot. I am sorry I am of so little help."

"Just listening helps me order my thoughts. I should stay, Lena, at least until midsummer."

"Then we stay."

"You do not have to stay too, you know."

I stared at him. "Don't be ridiculous," I said. "Of course I'm staying. Do you think I would abandon you?"

A muscle jumped under his eye. "I cannot ask this of you."

"You are not asking. I am offering." I was getting exasperated. "When we go, we go together. Agreed?"

"And if at midsummer, I decide to stay longer? Maybe forever?"

"Cillian, you can't."

"Why not?" He sounded serious.

"Because there is nothing here for you," I said. "No books, no real learning. You are wasted here, all your training and education. We need to keep moving, to find somewhere where...where you fit, better."

"What if there isn't anywhere? Would that not also be a waste of my training and education? Eryl wants me to create a written language for the Kurzemë, and teach it."

"But there are still no books for you, no thought, just a task. I can't believe that Linrathe is the only place in the world where learning is honoured," I said. "We just need to find another."

"Why 'we', Lena? Say Casil does still stand? What is there for you, who needs space and freedom?"

"Those are two different questions," I said slowly. "If I had stayed in Tirvan, if the last three years had never happened, in time I would have become a council leader, and dealt with the problems of a village, and lived my life not knowing there was anything more. But war came, and I met Colm, and then Perras and Dagney, and you, and now I do want to know more, to learn properly. At Casilla, if I needed space, I took my horse and rode out of the city. I imagine I can do something similar, wherever we go."

I hadn't answered his first question. I wasn't sure I knew the answer, except that when I tried to imagine the unknown future, I was no longer alone. I did not want to face the plain, or whatever lay beyond it, without him.

We had made love only rarely in the past weeks, but this night he turned to me under the furs, his lips on my neck questioning. I responded readily, wanting him, wanting the connection, the communion that still, for me, transcended simple pleasure. I thought the same was true for Cillian, too.

How, though? Surely the asceticism of his philosophy should not allow this? I wondered if it was part of his confusion, and why we made love less often now. I curled against him. His breathing told me he was still awake.

"Cillian? What is it that you want, that is only a dream?"

"What do I want? Books. Thought. You were right, Lena." He sighed. "And music, on a *ladhar*. My own language. Among other things."

"You are homesick."

"I suppose I am, in part. Aren't you?"

"I miss Tirvan, but I had already decided I wasn't going back, you know. But I miss familiar things, yes. I think it is worse for you, because there is so little of what is important to you here. And you are considering staying, Cillian? How could you be happy?"

"Is happiness what we strive for, Lena? Or is it to be useful, as I would be, bringing literacy to a people, which is what Eryl would like me to do?"

"I would like you to be happy again," I murmured. "You are not easy to live with, when you aren't."

"No," he said after a moment. "I do not suppose I am. If I am a burden to you, I apologize."

"A burden?" I said. "Cillian, do you still not understand? I—" I stopped, shocked at what I had almost said.

"Understand what, Lena?"

I found words, through the confusion in my mind. "You are my friend, my lover, my companion. Not a burden, ever, although a worry, sometimes."

"*Look at the blessings you do have,*" he quoted softly. "You are the best of them, *leannan.*"

"As you are, for me," I said, suddenly, fiercely, needing to. "I hope you know that."

"I have never thought of myself as a blessing," he said, faintly ironic.

"Nor would I have, once," I replied. "But I do now, as difficult and complicated as you are."

He turned so he could look down at me, in the dim light. He ran a finger along my cheek. "I am difficult and complicated, I know," he said softly, "and yet you still tell me I am a blessing? I am astonished." He kissed me, gently. "But also pleased. Should we sleep now? It is late."

I lay beside him, his hand on my thigh, feeling him slip easily into sleep. The familiar comfort should have allowed me to sleep too, but I could not. Over and over in my mind I heard the words I had so very nearly spoken: do you still not understand? I love you.

Stars gleamed on the eastern horizon as I stepped out of the door, water bucket in one hand, bow in the other. Yawning, I started down the path to the river. The ground squelched underfoot, soaking my deerskin boots. A wind blew off the mountains, a strangely warm wind. The day felt like sudden spring.

Voices in the half-light told me other women were about the task. I thought they sounded excited, this morning. Suddenly, I heard a deep creak, almost a groan, followed by snapping sounds, loud and explosive. Birds fell silent. The women cried out, a sound of exultation, running towards the river. I followed.

Another groan, a series of shatters, and then a splash, and another, and the unmistakable sound of water, running fast, and ice colliding and breaking. I reached the bank. The river, silent for so long under the winter's ice, ran free, pushing debris and chunks of ice up against the banks, carrying more as it churned its way eastward. The women fell to their knees at its brink, offering prayers, thanking their gods for another winter done. I did not kneel. My eyes moved along the river, and then behind us, and back to the river. Nothing moved.

Water collected, I returned to our hut, Cillian had built up the fire and was stirring the porridge, begun the night before. He glanced up at me, smiling. I smiled back, unable not to, and bent to kiss him.

"Will you talk to Eryl today?" I asked.

"You are still sure, this morning?"

"I am," I said. "We will stay till midsummer."

He nodded. "The river is running again. Did that make it easier to get water?"

"You recognized the sound?" I said. "I didn't know what it was, at first, until I saw what was happening."

"The river flowing free again at the end of winter was a time of celebration in Sorham, too," he told me. "I have been there when it happened, a time or two."

"The women were very pleased," I answered. Chopping the ice every morning—and often every afternoon, too—had been a huge and dangerous chore. We ate breakfast. Cillian, I noted, had a good appetite this morning. He saw me watching him.

"I am hungry, it seems," he said.

"One less worry," I told him. "What are you doing today?"

"I thought I might check the snares, the higher ones."

"Alone? I'm needed to guard the women this morning. Grêt said we were going to the meadow. The wind is very warm, and the snow will melt quickly today. I don't like the idea of you being up on those hills alone when the snow is unstable."

"Perhaps Fél will go with me. If he can't, I will check the lower line. So as not to worry you," he added drily, a smile playing on his lips.

"Thank you," I replied, as equally drily. A tap at the door made me look up. Kaisa peered in. "Lena," she said, "bring buckets."

Birch sap, boiled down, became a sweet syrup; we had not made it, in Tirvan, but occasionally some had come our way, with a soldier at spring festival. I'd never seen it harvested, or made, though. "I am coming." I said. Kaisa went on her way.

Outside, water dripped from icicles and snowbanks. The village women stood in the central clearing, talking and laughing. Children chased each other, throwing balls of the soft, clumping snow, excited. Clearly, this was a special day.

"Come," Grêt said, beckoning to us. As a group, we followed her out of the village, along the river, the rapidly-softening snow making walking difficult. We began to climb, which was even harder. I needed all the discipline I had learned on the Wall to keep focused on my task, and not on last night's epiphany. Ahead of us, a stand of birch trees spread out across a meadow, intermixed at the higher end with denser evergreens.

In the birch grove, we unloaded children and buckets. To my surprise, Grêt called me forward. She held out her hand. "Your knife," she said. "I will show you how to cut, and then you can do it. Your knife will cut deeper and better than ours, and make the work easier." I gave her the secca. This was not what I should be doing, but she was headwoman, and I would obey her, for the sake of peace. "Watch," she said, and made a deep slash in the tree, just at her waist height. From a bag hanging from her belt, she took a section of wood, carved to resemble half a hollow reed, pushing its sharp end firmly into the cut, then tapping it in with a mallet. Another woman stepped forward to place a bucket under the spigot. A drop of sap rolled down the conduit, splashing into the bucket.

"You see?" Grêt asked. I nodded. I made a slash in the next tree, stepping back to let Grêt examine it. "Deeper," she ordered. I cut again, getting the feel of the wood's resistance to the knife. Satisfied, Grêt pushed a spigot into the slash, and nodded to me to move on.

I worked my way up the slope, concentrating on the cuts. This is better than just guarding, I thought. It needs focus. The other women followed to place spigots and buckets. Halfway up I stopped to pull off my heavy outer tunic; I was hot from the work, and the sun warm. When I found Kaisa next to me, I asked her, in my own language, "what will you do with the sap?"

"Drink it, this first gathering," she said. "It is a—how you say?—it gives energy—after the winter."

"A tonic," I answered. "And then?"

She laughed. "Then we put the sap in pots near the fire, but not too near, and leave it there for one cycle of the moon, until it bubbles and foams. And then we have a big celebration!"

I nodded. There was no wine here, and only a thin, bitter beer. Whatever the birch sap fermented into, it would fuel a night or two of excess, I guessed. "Does Fél enjoy it?" I asked.

"He does now. Very much," she added with a sly glance. "Two of our babies begin from it, I think." She paused. "But he did not like it much at first, so maybe you won't either." She reached out a hand to my arm. "Those trees are not good," she said, indicating the birch intermixed with the evergreens. "Too thin, and the sun does not warm them to make the sap flow. We stop here."

I stretched, flexing my back, surveying the area. From the hillside I could see the river, running down and round a bend, and the treed slope of the other valley wall. A confined world, but larger than the crowded space of the village and the low-ceilinged, dark huts. I watched the flow of the river, free now after its winter's freeze, wondering where it went. Out to the plain, I supposed. Could it be followed? I bent to take a handful of snow, to clean the blade of my knife.

My eyes were on the secca—working the sticky sap off the blade without cutting myself needed care—when I heard a scream. I looked up. A child lay in the snow screaming in fright: approaching her was an animal unknown to me. The size of a large dog, heavily furred, it swayed towards her on stocky, muscular legs, a band of paler fur across its forehead. Its bared teeth and focused stare left no doubt of its intentions.

"*Jerv*," I heard Vesna moan. I straightened, slowly, my eyes on the beast, reaching for my bow. It stopped its approach, moving its stare to me, and then back to the child. She cowered, trying to curl herself into a ball. The *jerv* began to bound forward. Massive claws reached towards the child. No time for the bow, when my knife was in my hand.

The secca hit it just behind its front legs. It snarled and twisted, trying to bite at the embedded knife. Behind me I heard gasps and murmurs. Twisting and contorting, the animal shook the knife free, but blood pulsed from the wound, staining the snow bright red. It stopped its gyrations, panting a little, still looking at the screaming child, wavering. I let one arrow fly, and then a second. The *jerv* fell, convulsing. It twitched and lay still.

I walked forward to retrieve my arrows and my knife. I cut the animal's throat to ensure it was dead; blood drained but did not spurt. The little girl, in the arms of her mother, still wailed.

"Is the child hurt?" I asked.

"No," Grêt said. "Just frightened. We thank you. We will honour this in the village, tonight."

There was something I was supposed to say. What was it? I tried to remember. The hunters said it when they brought the kills home. Grêt waited. "I did only what I could," I said, the words coming back to me. She nodded.

We gathered up the children and the shed clothes and unused buckets, and walked back in a loose line to the village. The little one had stopped her sobbing and appeared to be asleep on her mother's shoulder. The other children walked quietly, subdued for now by fright. Kaisa made her way to my side.

"What was that creature?" I asked. "I've never seen anything like it."

"The *jerv*?" she replied. "They are cruel hunters. Be glad it was a female, and perhaps thin and weak from feeding her cubs. The males are twice as large, and vicious. Had you injured a male like that it would likely have turned on you." I shuddered, remembering the claws and teeth. "The men will look for the cubs. It will have a den dug in the snow somewhere near and there will be a trail to follow. The men will kill them all, with spears, and there will be more rabbits and deer for us next summer."

"What of its mate?" I asked. "Will it not attack the men?"

"If it is there, it might try, but it does not stay with the female and the cubs," she answered. "Like your men, Lena, in your land." She laughed. "I will say to Fél that I have tamed a *jerv*, because he stayed with me, and did not leave me to raise the babies without him."

We reached the outskirts of the village. The village's herd of sheep browsed on thin branches cut and thrown down for them, two men guarding them. Lambing had begun and the smell of blood attracted predators. Grêt called out as we approached the huts. Eryl and Ivor appeared. Briefly and succinctly, she told them what had happened. Ivor glanced my way, and back to Grêt, but he did not speak to me.

"You made sure it was dead?" Eryl asked.

"I cut its throat," I said. He nodded. I turned away, taking the buckets back to our hut. Behind me I could hear orders being given to the men, to collect weapons and begin the hunt for the cubs.

Inside the dark hut, I fed a few pieces of wood to the fire to heat water. Cillian had gone, perhaps readying for the cub hunt with the other men. I made tea, picked up my knife, and sat, looking out the open door. Throwing the secca at the *jerv* had been an act without conscious thought. I had been trained to kill men in that way in another life. I rubbed at the secca's blade and hilt with a skin, cleaning it of the *jerv's* blood and the last traces of sap, just enough of my mind on the job to keep me from cutting myself. The rest of my conscious thought grappled with last night's revelation.

Cillian. I tried to analyze my feelings with the objectivity I had learned from *xache*. I had gone from disliking him to a reluctant respect, and then to true liking coupled with strong physical attraction born of proximity and shared experience, and appreciation. And, I admitted, he is beautiful: handsome, graceful, deft—and what we share as lovers has been an epiphany itself. Was I mistaking all this for love?

No. Difficult and complicated as he was—and I had not been wrong, last night, to describe him that way—he had breached a wall in me I had believed impenetrable. Quietly, almost unnoticed, he had found a way into my heart. I did love him.

What did it change? On the surface of things, nothing. We were already paired, by fate and by choice. But there is still that slight distance in him, I thought, that untouchable core of reticence, something held back, except when we make love. I wondered, not for the first time, what that meant.

Should I tell him I love him? We were together, as companions and as lovers. I did not know what his philosophy said of love. Did I want to risk what I already had?

The men, Cillian among them, brought the bodies of the three *jerv* cubs back in mid-afternoon, and the fur and claws of the adult. The meat would be fed to the dogs. At the communal fire that night, I listened to words of praise and had three of the *jerv's* claws hung around my neck on a thong. The child I had saved was also honoured, a cub's claw tied around her neck. Drums pounded, the fire burned high, people chanted and danced and came to offer me drink and food and to touch the *jerv's* claws hanging on my breast, whispering '*devanī*'.

"You have brought us good fortune: this is a strong omen, on the day the ice was defeated," Grêt said, reluctantly, I thought. "There will be good hunting and a rich harvest this year." I guessed touching the *jerv's* claws was thought to bring luck, and let it happen as graciously as I could. But when Ivor's hand reached for my breast, not the claws, I slapped his hand away. He laughed.

"I have killed a *jerv*," he said. "I have my own claws. We are meant to be together, you and me."

"We are not. I am Cillian's." It was what Ivor would understand.

"The stranger? He is not a real man," he scoffed. "He does not give you children; all his potency is given to his words. I would give you a child after one or two nights."

"Go away," I said, letting my disgust colour my voice. He laughed again, trailed a finger along the claws, and sauntered away. I turned to see Grêt watching me.

"My son wants you," she said. "You would have much status, as his wife."

"Perhaps I would be the one who brought him status, or luck," I replied. I walked away, looking for Cillian. He was talking to Fél, near the fire. I stopped to watch him, testing my new certainty. *I love you.* The idea had settled over the day, beginning to feel familiar. Fél looked my way. He beckoned me over.

I went to them, hoping my new knowledge wasn't obvious on my face. But they had other things on their minds.

"Do you think our bird bow arrows can be used against geese?" Cillian asked.

"If you had to. Ducks, yes. Geese...you'd be better with a larger bow," I said. "Why?"

"There will be many geese on the waters, now, dawn and dusk," Fél said. "Time to hunt them. We leave this week, for three days."

"You are going?" I asked Cillian.

"Yes. Eryl and Fél have asked me to."

"I will find a larger bow for you," Fél told Cillian. "Lena, if you want, you can sleep with Kaisa and Aetyl, while Cillian is gone. If you don't want to be alone."

"Thank you, Fél," I said. "I may do that."

We walked back to the hut in the oddly warm night. "When are you leaving for the goose hunt?" I asked.

"The day after tomorrow, in the morning," he answered. "It is a long walk to where they gather at night, and we need to be there when they come in at dusk."

"Do you need to take food?"

"Fél said no." He looked up at the stars. "Do you realize these will be the first nights we have spent apart since we left the Empire, almost a year ago?"

"You'll be glad of the respite from me," I said, teasingly.

"Not at all. I have grown very used to having you near."

"Yes, well, don't put your arm around Ivor in the night," I said. He began to laugh.

"He will sleep as far away from me as he can, I think," he said. "Ivor does not like me."

"Ivor doesn't like anyone," I answered. "But he still wants me, so that means he dislikes you even more."

"Perhaps it is a good thing he will be with us."

"I can take care of myself," I assured him.

"I know you can," he said. "You deserved to be honoured tonight, Lena. Did it please you, to have your skills recognized?" He put an arm around my shoulders for a quick hug, an unusual gesture from him in public.

"Perhaps. Or maybe I'm just happy not to be worrying about you so much," I suggested. He laughed again.

"I have been a worry to you, I know. I am sorry, Lena. I have been confused, these past weeks; you know most of why. But I woke this morning with a clarity of thought that has been sadly lacking, and now I find myself calm again."

"I am glad," I said. "You have told Eryl we will stay?"

"Until midsummer, not beyond."

I was glad. Glad that he was happy again, glad that he had seen sense about staying. And glad we would be alone again together, in a few weeks.

We spent the next day checking the snares, and reorganizing Cillian's pack. We kept most of our belongings in our packs, as they could be hung from the rafters, limiting the damage mice and damp could do to our clothes and books and other items. Cillian did not want to take his books on the hunt, so we moved them to my pack, along with a few other small things.

The warm wind continued to blow; the snow was melting quickly. Already patches of mud showed on the south-facing slopes, and the village area was a morass of rivulets and wet, slushy snow. I washed some clothes, draping them over ropes outside, securing them with split willow pegs. Late in the afternoon, I heated more water to bathe.

Then I sat in the last of the afternoon sun to dry my hair, while Cillian bathed and trimmed his beard down to almost nothing. He stood in the door of the hut, shirtless, looking out at me. I smiled up at him. I had moved from shock to acceptance to joy in the last two days. I had thought myself incapable of love again, and whatever came of it, my secret bubbled inside me like a hot spring, warming all around it.

"Is your hair dry?" he asked.

"Mostly. Yours isn't, though. Come and sit in the sun."

He came to sit beside me. All around the village, men and women were finding reasons to be outside, in light tunics, or like Cillian, shirtless. He reached for my hand, twining his fingers around mine. "Eryl thinks we should go to the midsummer meeting with the village," he said, "and then start east from the meeting place."

"He is sure there will be a *vēsturni* who will join this village?"

"Yes. I think he even knows who, but he hasn't told me. Until then, I will continue to teach him the stories." He traced circles on my palm with one finger.

"You are being very distracting," I murmured.

"I intend to be." The slow smile I hadn't seen for weeks spread over his face. I didn't see vulnerability this time, just happiness. "Shall we go in?"

The banked fire glowed. We did not go to the bed but to the furs beside the fire. "I do prefer to see you," Cillian said. For the first time, we made love in the open, the warmth of the room just enough to allow it. Afterwards, Cillian spoke first, one hand stroking my bare skin, tracing a line from neck to hip. "*Thà mi beànnaicht,*" he whispered.

"Translate?" I murmured.

"I am blessed."

Much later, we made love again, quiet, gentle love, with sleep following quickly. The last thing I knew were his lips on my hair, and a barely audible whisper. "*Käresta,*" I thought he said, but I was too nearly asleep to ask what it meant. I liked the sound, though. I love you, I whispered back, silently.

With half the men gone to kill geese, I guarded the sheep every night. Lambing continued, and so guarding day and night was necessary. The warm wind no longer blew and the work was both cold and tedious, although the men who did the second shift had it worse in the bitterest part of the night.

On my first shift, I saw nothing more than a fox, darting in among the sheep to snatch at afterbirth. I couldn't get a clear shot at it, but one of the men did. Its presence had disturbed the sheep and they milled around, baa-ing, for some time. Even an hour later, they still seemed restless. Most of the village dogs had gone with the hunting party; only Audo's, and the two sheepdogs, remained.

At the end of my shift, I walked back tiredly to our hut. I didn't want to disturb Kaisa and Aetyl, and to be truthful I too was glad of some solitude. I would be warm enough, under the furs, alone. I fed a few logs to the fire, falling quickly into a heavy sleep.

Barking dogs woke me. I pulled on boots and outdoor clothes, found the bow, and ran up the hillside towards the sheep pens. An hour or so before dawn, I estimated, as I ran.

"What happened?" I said to the first man I reached.

"Wolf," he said. "Will you stay? I will try to track it, if you can."

He came back in the early light. "A pack," he told us. "We will need guards, all day and all night, double strength. And two guards on the women when they gather firewood, again. I will tell Ludis."

"I should have guarded the women getting water, this morning," I said.

"Go, then," he said. His name was Benis, I remembered. "They should have waited. They would have heard the dogs, too, and known something was amiss. Take one of the boys, as the second guard."

The snare lines went unchecked. I guarded the women getting water, and then getting firewood. I did another shift on the sheep in the afternoon, ate with Kaisa and Aetyl, and returned to the sheepfold after dark. Both sheep and dogs were uneasy, to my eyes.

Near the end of my shift the dogs exploded into a cacophony of barking, hackles raised. "Stay," Benis told me. "Some may circle around." I stared into the night, looking for movement. The moon was waxing; it lacked a few days to full, but it gave fair light. A shout from one of the men on the upper side of the sheepfold, and a grey shape slipped across my vision. I raised my bow, arrow nocked. Movement, again. I let the arrow fly. A yelp, and a snarl, and then another yelp, and silence.

My arrow had not killed the wolf; that honour belonged to one of the men. But mine had injured it, made it turn, perhaps, allowing the second arrow to find a fatal mark. The next morning, I examined the body. I'd never seen a wolf before. It was almost as long as I was tall, and I estimated its shoulder would have reached nearly to my hip. The dense, brindle fur felt soft under my hand. It was the teeth that made me shudder, remembering the damage to Audo's leg.

Any celebration of its killing would need to wait. The rest of the pack might move away with one of their number dead, or they might not, Benis told me. Once Eryl had returned, another organized hunt for the pack could happen, but right now there just weren't enough men.

The warm wind began to blow again that afternoon, making the first watch that night not as unpleasant. A heavy cloud bank hung over the mountains, but it appeared to be stationary; I hoped it did not presage more snow. The wind made listening difficult, and every movement of branch or shrub caught my eye. By the time my watch ended, I was tired, and my shoulders and neck ached with tension. I found myself longing for Tirvan's baths as I walked slowly back to our hut.

I heard movement behind me just a heartbeat before someone grabbed me, one hand over my mouth. "Mine now, *devani*," a voice said. Ivor. I twisted, knife in hand, but with his other hand he pushed my arm down, gripping my wrist. I brought a knee up, hard, missing his groin but unbalancing him, forcing him to take a slight step back, but his grip did not loosen. He began to wrench my knife hand around. He was very strong, and I was unpracticed and soft from the winter. My eyes flickered back and forth, searching. I tried to bite him. He laughed, pushing me down onto the cold ground. I dropped the knife. He was heavy, one leg between mine, shoving it up against me, his free hand working at the drawstring of his breeches. He freed his sex, hard against my leg, and with one hand pulled my leggings down my thighs. He thrust at me, pushing hard, forcing entry. I tried to gasp at the pain, but one hand—his left—held my arms. The other was across my mouth. *A left-handed archer.* I jerked my head, bit his hand. He let go of my arms to slap me over the face. I tasted blood. He brought his mouth down to lick it off, laughing. But my arms were free. I couldn't find the knife, though. I reached out. My fingers found the rock I had seen. I hit him and hit him and hit him, until blood matted his hair and he lay unconscious, or dead.

I pushed him off me and pulled myself to my knees. Moonlight showed me the knife; I picked it up, hands shaking so much I could barely sheath it. Make sure he's dead, my mind told me, but I could not. I pulled up my leggings, found my feet, and in a stumbling run reached the door of my hut.

I forced myself to stand still. No sounds came from outside. I took a deep breath, and another, leaning against the knife-scarred post. I had to keep moving. I found the water bucket, filled waterskins, washed myself. I took my bird bow and quiver from below the bed, gathered some food. Everything else was in my pack. I had to go.

CHAPTER FIVE

THE WAXING MOON RODE HIGH. I would have preferred a darker sky, but I had no choice. I moved less lightly than I liked, carrying my pack. A gusty breeze came down off the mountainside, carrying sound and scent away from the village: a blessing. I wanted to run, but I forced myself to keep to a rapid walk, using the foot roll that Tice had taught me, making my movement nearly silent. The path led along the river, past the pool where we swam and washed clothes, heading downhill. I reached the rapids, identified as much by sound as by the glint of splashing water in the starlight. I stopped. Beyond this, everything was new.

When would I be missed? At dawn, or soon after, I judged: earlier, if Ivor regained consciousness before then. If he was alive. Until daybreak, I would continue eastward on the path. Once there was enough light to see, I would climb back up into the hills, and hope to find a safe spot to hide. I would be pursued, I knew.

The rapids splashed and gurgled, obscuring sound. The moon had gone beyond the western mountains and the night was very dark. I needed to move more slowly now. I allowed myself a small sip of water, and continued on.

In the first glimmers of dawn I stopped again. Ahead of me I could hear the rush and roar of the waterfall, and to my left the cliffs mantled over me, blocking the eastern light. I put the pack down to find food, bread and one piece of cold meat. Chewing, I looked around me as the day brightened. The river ran wide but fast between shallow banks, edged with scrubby trees. Birds greeted each other and the sun, soft chips becoming morning song. I finished the food and stepped off the path to relieve myself, wincing when the urine stung.

Leaving the pack, I approached the riverbank. Holding firmly to a tree I allowed my feet to slip down the bank. I fell harder than I had planned onto my side, a foot dipping into the water. Pain flared in my hip. I dragged myself up and onto the path, biting my lip. I cut a ragged bit from the arm of my tunic and snagged it on an overhanging branch where I might have reached for balance. Did it look as if I fell in? Would anyone believe I had gone for water without putting my pack down first?

I turned to the cliffs, studying them, looking for a way up. The face in front of me was still dark, angled away from the rising sun, but the trail and the cliffs curved northward a short distance ahead. I shouldered the pack and moved forward, limping a little.

The hip pain eased as I walked. I followed the curve of the trail, and suddenly beneath me was a wide plain stretching out eastward towards the rising sun. On my right the river thundered over the edge of the scarp, spray glittering, soaking the path ahead where it began to snake down the steep drop; on my left, the cliff edge rose in broken columns skyward.

If my pursuers don't believe I fell trying to get water, I thought, then maybe they'll believe I slipped on the wet path and fell into the chasm. I looked up at the cliff face, away from the dazzle of the low sun. The blocks of rock, interspersed with channels of gravel and dotted with scrubby evergreens and grasses, looked impossible to climb. But slowly, as I moved a bit further along the path, I began to see a possible route.

For running men in daylight, I was no more than a couple of hours from the village. I could not take the time to search for a better way up. I balanced and tightened the pack on my back and turned to the cliff face, reaching up to find a handhold.

My left foot slipped once, and I when I tested the gravelly soil in the fissures it was unstable, as were the gnarled trees anchored in it. But of more concern was the lack of strength in my hands and arms. Without the demands of fishing or of the work at the Wall, where I had been as likely to be assigned to dig drains as to watch duty, I simply wasn't as strong. The wrist Ivor had wrenched ached. I needed, I realized, to be able to push myself up with my legs, like climbing a staircase, whenever possible.

I had to spend more time studying the choices, making less progress than I liked. I used my hands for balance, stepping from one small ledge to another, hugging the rock. I stopped to regain my breath, clinging to the cliff-face with one hand, looking upward at the choices ahead of me. On one higher ledge droppings from the *gemzē,* the goat-deer, lay scattered on the rock. We had followed *gemzē* paths before, crossing the Durrains: I should be able to follow this one.

Once I learned to find the signs, the choices the deer had made, I moved more quickly. The *gemzē* were more agile than I, and more than once I needed to use my arms to help me from one ledge to another, feeling the burn of muscle in my shoulders and ignoring the wrenched wrist. My legs began to ache. I stopped to rest, and suddenly I wondered if climbing back down the cliff was going to be possible. I almost looked down. Four ledges to go...then three...two more upward thrusts of my body and I was rolling onto the grass and gravel of the clifftop.

I heard the barking of dogs below me, still some distance away. I lay panting, aching from fingertip to toes. My hands stung in the cold air and my throat felt parched. I heard human voices below me now, as well as the dogs. I crawled behind a low bush, flattening myself against the ground.

In the still morning air I heard a voice. "Any sign, Karel?"

I did not hear a reply. If I moved my head slightly I could see the trail, not directly below me, but both the way I had come and the sinuous descent down the scarp. The men—or rather Karel and a boy—moved into my line of sight. Karel knelt, peering down the chasm. I saw him shake his head, straighten, look up. I didn't move. The sheepdogs milled about his feet. Karel moved towards the cliff face, disappearing from my view for a moment, then reappeared, looking upward.

"Just a *gemzē* trail," I heard him say, clearly. "She's gone into the river, as we thought. Nothing to do. We better get back."

I rested, waiting for my heart to stop pounding, considering my priorities. I needed to create a shelter, and when that was done, I needed to work out how I got off this clifftop. The first task was straightforward: I had a tent, and rope. I simply had to find a place to set it up. I scouted around the plateau, settling finally on the slope of a small depression rimmed with shrubs. Using a branch and my heels, I levelled out part of the slope; then I strung the rope between two stunted trees and hung the tent. A few rocks on the edges, the pack hung as high as I could manage, and my camp was done.

I glanced at the sun, nearly overhead now. I'd been awake for a day and a half. I should sleep, but I could feel that I would not. I walked back to the edge of the cliff to look out. Vast spaces—the ocean, the grasslands of the Empire—had always calmed me. I sat in the thin grass, and stared at the plain below me.

I traced the river, its course turning away far to the right to disappear behind the escarpment. To the north the mountains continued, blending into cloud and horizon. My eyes followed the trail, zigzagging down the bluff, then bending slightly to continue out into the plain. Eastward? I looked at shadows, tried to remember exactly where the sun had risen this morning. Eastward, or nearly so, I confirmed to myself.

I remembered the villages met at a ring of stones. I tried to find it, but I lost the trail in the contours of the plain. Scanning, I found several shapes, tiny at this distance and height, maybe boulders, maybe something else. One seemed pale, almost gleaming in the sun, but I couldn't make out what it was.

Exhaustion sank through me, weighing down my limbs, closing my eyes. I stretched out in the grass and fell asleep.

The croak of a raven woke me. The sky was the dark blue of evening; I guessed I had slept for six hours or so. I sat up, stiffly; stretching, I stood and found my way back to my camp. Nothing had disturbed it. I had hoped to hunt this afternoon, but my body had demanded sleep.

I lit a small fire, ate cold food, made tea. In the flicker of the fire I fashioned a couple of snares from sinew and set them where I had seen droppings earlier. Stars emerged, glittering against the black of the sky. I leaned back against the slope, looking north. There was the bear...and there the north star. I remembered looking up at these same stars from the bench outside the Four-Ways Inn, thinking how I could follow them home from anywhere. But I had travelled too far for that: the stars had not changed, but they could no longer take me home.

I tracked westward, looking for the hunter and his dogs, but the mountains obscured them. Far to the east, the hero raised his club. Had not the hero been exiled once? I tried to remember the story...something about murder, and a series of tasks set to bring him redemption. Cillian would know.

Cillian. I had avoided thinking about him. I wrapped my hands around the cooling tea. Where was he? The hunting party should have been back sometime yesterday. Surely, he would come after me? But Karel would have reported me drowned.

Did it matter, any longer? I shivered. Bleakness threatened to overwhelm me; no tears, just dry despair. I wanted his arms around me, the comfort and security of being held. Would he even want to do that, after what Ivor had done?

'Nothing in life is either good or bad in itself: it is only our reactions that make events appear positive or negative.' When had Cillian told me that? It was wrong. It denied the violence and cruelty of Ivor's attack. I focused on the words. Only our reactions. I stared up at the sky. What would his philosopher say? That I could not change what had happened, but I could choose my response.

I considered this. I could let Ivor's violence control me, crush me, which is what he had wanted. Or I could think of myself as wounded. Wounds healed, in time. Most of them.

I am wounded, I said firmly, to the scattered stars. I can heal.

In daylight, I scouted for water, and a way down, finding both together. Some distance from the camp, I found a stream, and in following it north and east, discovered it flowed down off the plateau in an eroded valley, not a simple descent, but feasible. I should go, I thought. If I get down off this plateau today, I can travel at night into the plain. But I did not. We had agreed to cross the plain together. But that was before, I reminded myself.

Midmorning, I knelt at the fire I had lit, roasting the small rabbit my snare had caught. The whine of a dog made me turn. Audo's brindle bitch ran to me, trying to lick my face. She barked. "Shhh," I told her. "What are you doing here?" Audo could not have come after me, with his bad leg.

"Lena!" Cillian's voice, calling. I closed my eyes in relief. The dog barked again.

"I'm here," I said, my voice a croak. "Here," I tried again, louder. I stood, letting the rabbit drop beside the fire. I heard running feet, and then he was beside me, reaching for me. I nearly fell into his arms, sagging against him, beginning to cry.

"Lena," he said, "*käresta*, I'm here."

"I was afraid you wouldn't come," I heard myself say.

"I'm here," he repeated. He kissed my hair. He let me cry, but when the tears slowed he spoke again. "You are shaking, Lena. You do know Ivor is dead?"

"I wasn't sure."

"Killed by wolves, or so the village believes," another voice said. I looked over. Eryl. "He was found with an arm missing, and one foot, and his head had been crushed in their jaws."

I shook my head, my face against Cillian's shoulder. "I killed him. He attacked me," I said. My voice was shaking as hard as my body. "He had me on the ground: he tried—he wanted to—he forced me. I had seen a rock. I reached for it, and I hit him over the head until he—stopped."

Cillian swore, savagely. His arms around me tightened. "Lena, *käresta*, I should have kept you safe." He was stroking my hair. I had stopped crying. He kissed my head again. "I hope he was alive, and awake, when the wolves came," he said, his voice low and angry and cold.

"I should have known," Eryl said. "I should have gone back, when he was missing that third night." Anger shaded his voice, too. "How could I have been so short-sighted? I wanted your company, Cillian, on the hunt, and did not think of the consequences of leaving Lena alone."

I turned in Cillian's arms. "And I wish I had not let myself become weak over the winter," I said sharply, "or he would not have taken the knife off me so easily, and it would have been in his ribs. I should have been able to protect myself."

"What do we do now?" Cillian asked. "We must go, Eryl. You do see that?"

"I do," Eryl said. "Karel reported you drowned. Lena, did you make it look that way?"

I nodded. "Yes. I didn't think it would fool anyone, though."

"Karel hoped you were dead, so he saw what he wanted. It was good thinking." He considered. "Give me the *jerv*'s teeth, Lena. I will stay out another day or two, and then return home. I will tell them I found your body far along the river, and brought the necklace back to prove it."

I handed him the necklace. "What about Cillian?" I asked.

"I will tell the village what I believe: that you fled from Ivor's attentions, and that you had wounded him before you fled. The wolves, smelling blood, took advantage of that. There will be little sympathy, except from Grêt and Karel, for an attack on a *devanī* and another man's woman, and, anyhow, you are dead. As for Cillian, his devotion to you has been obvious, and so he could not return to the village where you were dishonoured, and where Ivor's actions led to your death. His decision to go east into the plain will be derided as suicidal, but that is all. No one will follow you."

"Eryl, how can we thank you?" Cillian asked. "You are risking much to help us."

"Repayment, for what has come of my failure to judge what Ivor might do," Eryl said. "If I am to lead this village soon, I must not make such mistakes."

"Eryl," I said. "Can you let Fél and Kaisa know that I am not dead? I wish Audo could know, but that would be unwise, I realize."

"I will tell them." He stood looking at us. "Once you are off these hills, move only at night for a while," he said. "You do not want to be seen." He called the dog to him. "I wish you luck as you travel, and a safe home when travel ends, my friends." He turned to go.

"Wait," Cillian said. He walked over to Eryl, embracing him. "Thank you," I heard him say. "I have been honoured to call you a friend."

"Take care of Lena," Eryl said. He slapped his thigh, ordering the dog to heel, and walked back into the trees.

Cillian turned to me. "What can I do, Lena?"

"I don't know. Be patient with me, I suppose." I tried to smile.

"Of course." He looked very unsure. "You will tell me what you need from me, and if I upset you?"

"I'll try. I just don't know, Cillian. I have no experience, or even stories, to guide me through this."

He nodded. "I will listen if you want to talk, and hold you if that is what you need. I also have nothing to tell me what to do for you."

"Just don't quote your philosopher," I said. "I don't think I could stand being told that there was no evil in what happened."

"I wouldn't," he said grimly. "I am finding no guidance there, right now, at all."

We broke my small camp, working silently together as we had on so many mornings in the mountains, and then followed the stream down its valley, reaching the plain by mid-afternoon. The trail ran arrow-straight across the gently rolling ground. The grasses here grew sparsely, interspersed with low, silver-leaved plants I could not name. Cillian walked in near silence, angry with himself, I knew. I felt exposed: anyone looking down from the escarpment would see us easily. "I think we should sleep now, until dusk," I said.

The river curved southward, away from the trail. We walked along its bank, looking for a sheltered place, finding one under the hanging branches of a willow. The day was warm enough, and dry. Cillian dropped his pack and stretched out, the pack under his head. I did the same. We did not touch. I turned my head to look at him; he was watching me, his eyes troubled. He reached out a hand. I took it, feeling the strength in it. I rolled onto my side, and let the running river lull me to sleep, my hand still safe in his.

We ate cold food at dusk, not risking a fire, and waited for the moon to rise.

"How did you find me?" I asked. "You didn't climb the cliff?"

"No. We came across the top, from the high lands above the village. Lena, I should not have left you alone. I should have seen what Ivor might do." His words were bitter.

"How were you to know he would leave the hunting party early? Cillian, even your father could not see—does not see—all outcomes, famed as he is for doing so." I said, exasperation in my voice.

"I know," he said flatly. "I'm living proof of that."

"And no one knows that here but me, and only you care," I snapped. "Leave it behind, Cillian. I'm sorry I brought it up." I was in no mood to be kind. I was fighting self-pity, and he appeared to be giving in to it.

"Do you really not care that I'm Callan's son, Lena?" he asked. The question took me unawares.

"I don't know," I said slowly. "I don't think about it. It mattered in Linrathe, because it saved your life. But now? You're just—you." He looked over, at that. "Does it matter to you? Not that he's your father; of course that matters. But that he's the Emperor?"

He looked out into the night. "I have been defined by an absence, a void, all my life. I grew around that space, encompassed it within me like a tree with a hollow core. Now there is a shape, a name, in that space, and a bit more, but I cannot separate the man from the role, yet. Can you understand that?"

"A little, maybe," I said. "I knew who my father was by name, but in Tirvan, in the Empire, it didn't matter that that was all I knew. Some girls' fathers came to visit them, but mine, never, and I wasn't alone in that. I don't think I cared until I met Casyn, and then I had the merest glimmer of what it might be to have a father. Galen," I added, "didn't live up to Casyn, when I did meet him."

He laughed, but it was not a true laugh. "At least he didn't exile you."

"Well, in a way, he did," I pointed out: it had been Galen who Casyn had sent to accompany us to the Durrains, and tell us how to begin to cross them. "Callan saved your life, Cillian," I said again. "And mine."

"I know. But as my father, or my Emperor?"

The trail was wide enough for two people and smooth enough that we could walk quickly in the moonlight. The creak and buzz of night insects broke the silence sporadically, and once, far behind us, wolves howled. A pale owl drifted silently across the path.

The night wore on. The moon peaked, began its descent. We stopped for food and water. For the last hour, my groin had begun to ache, the familiar, dragging pain of my bleeding time. I moved away from the path, found my cloths at the bottom of my pack, tucked one in place. I still had some anash, but we could not risk a fire to make tea. I'd just have to put up with the pain.

The pain rose and fell as we walked, worse than usual. Sleeping on cold ground would be why, I thought, biting my lip. Nausea threatened. As the sky began to lighten, I saw a line of small bushes ahead of us: shelter, and perhaps some dead wood with which to build a small fire.

"We need to stop here," I said to Cillian.

Something in my voice alerted him. "What's wrong?"

"I need to make anash tea," I said. "It's my bleeding time, and I'm in a lot of pain, more than usual."

The bushes grew along a stream trickling out of rocks in a small gulley. At the stream's edge Cillian told me to sit. He gathered wood, building a small fire tightly against the edge of the rock, as hidden from view as it could be. I took anash leaves from my pack, broke them into water in the small cooking pot, and put it in the flames. Then I found a stone about the size of my fist and placed it in the fire.

I drank the tea as soon as I could, scalding though it was on my lips and tongue. The stone, hot from the fire, I wrapped in more of the blood cloths, holding it against my lower belly. I lay down, bringing my knees up, waiting in silent misery for the anash to work.

Ten minutes, fifteen. The pain began to ebb. Cillian knelt beside me and gently replaced the cooling stone with another. The small kindness brought tears to my eyes.

"Could you let me touch you?" he asked. "If so, would it help if I rub your back?"

"It might," I said. "You can try."

I lay on my side. He moved closer, reaching over me, his palm making firm circular movements on my lower back. It felt comforting, if nothing else. The pain faded. I fell asleep.

When I woke the sun told me it was mid-morning. I sat up. "Cillian?" I called, quietly.

"I'm here," he said, descending from the gulley's rim. "Are you feeling better?"

"Yes." The pain was a dull ache now, tolerable.

"I've been keeping watch," he said. "I didn't think we should both sleep. But I've seen nothing but hunting hawks and a fox."

"Good," I replied. "Do you want to sleep now?" I stretched. I was hungry.

"Soon. I want to show you something, first." He beckoned me over to where the stream emerged from the rocks. "Look at this carefully, Lena," he said. "See these blocks of stone?" Surrounding the spring were jumbled rocks, looking at first glance like fallen chunks, nothing more. But they were too regular and smooth, and in places two or three were still mortared together.

"The builders." The words came unbidden, a memory from something Cillian had told me months before.

"Yes. This might be the first evidence of the Eastern Empire, Lena. And look here." He crossed the gulley. "Look eastward, where the trail goes—it was easier to see when the sun was low, but if you look along the trail, can you see there are depressions, either side, quite far back from it?" He touched my shoulder to orient me. I flinched and he drew his hand back quickly.

I sighted along the trail where it ran out of the gulley and back out onto the plain. I could just make out what Cillian meant, slight dips in the land paralleling the trail. What did they remind me of? My mind flashed back to the Wall and the track we were building through the camp, cobbled, with ditches on each side. "Ditches," I said. "Ditches, on either side of a road."

"Yes," Cillian said. I glanced up at him. He was smiling, the teacher delighted with his student's observation.

"Cillian," I said, my throat suddenly tight, "right now, you look exactly like Colm when he was pleased I understood his teaching."

"Do I?"

"Yes. He was your father's twin, Cillian. And I think he would have been proud of you right now."

He shrugged. "I wouldn't know. But we should eat, Lena, and then I should sleep."

While he slept, I built another fire to make more tea. This time I made several pots, filling one waterskin with the liquid. I'd never drunk it cold and I had no idea if it would keep its potency this way, but I also had no idea when—or if—

I could build another fire after today. I fingered my supply of anash: only a few leaves remained. Not that it mattered, I thought, except I needed it for pain. Then I sat among the bushes on the gulley's western rim, keeping watch. I had my bow beside me. The water would attract animals, or birds, and some fresh food would be welcome. I scanned the plain, watching for signs of movement, but I saw nothing.

I grew stiff, and the ache in my groin was increasing. I drank some cold tea and got up to stretch my legs and back. Wandering along the gulley, a clump of bushes caught my eye, their silvery green leaves delicately divided. I broke one off, crushed it, brought it to my nose. Anash. Here?

But it made sense. If this was a rest stop, a water source on the long road west from Casil, then planting medicinal herbs would have been practical, prudent, even. Anash relieved pain and fever as well as preventing pregnancy: I remembered my mother telling me that its effectiveness in that way had been a chance discovery. And armies and travellers needed remedies against all manner of disease.

I picked a good supply of the leaves, spreading them out on a rock to dry a little. The tea had eased the ache. A high-pitched warbling whistle caught my attention; looking up, I saw a flock of birds approaching the gulley. I dropped down behind the bushes, moving slowly to my bow. The birds circled, calling, and landed at the water. Grouse-like, sand-and-black in colour, they bobbed and drank. I shot four, quickly.

The others scattered, calling shrilly. I picked up the dead ones. Cillian slept on. Back up on the gulley's rim I gutted and plucked the birds, found more firewood. Then I built up the fire again and woke Cillian.

The sun hung near the top of the mountains; dusk would come soon. When the fire had burned down enough, I made a lattice of green twigs and laid the flattened carcasses on it to grill.

"Lena!" Cillian hissed from his watch location. "Come here!"

Standing not far from the gulley, wary and alert, stood the biggest bird I had ever seen. Brown-backed and grey-headed, it stood the height of a small child on thick, pale legs. Long grey whisker-like feathers extended from its beak, sweeping back under its eyes. Nervously it spread its wings: even not fully extended, they were as wide as Cillian was tall. "That would feed a whole village," Cillian whispered. "Any idea what it is?" I had crouched beside him.

"No. It's magnificent, though."

"It wants water."

"We'll be gone soon," I said. I shifted slightly, and the bird, catching the movement, made a deep grunt and ran away in long strides. I laughed; I had expected it to fly, and the running struck me as incongruous.

"I am glad to hear you laugh," Cillian said softly.

"I..." I shook my head. "I don't know how to explain. There is one level on which I am all right. When I am there, I can laugh at this bird or talk to you about the road. I can function almost normally, I suppose. But on another level, deeper—I am hurt, Cillian, even if there is no wound." I felt tears welling.

510   EMPIRE'S EXILE

He put out a hand to me, tentatively. "Do you want to be held?" he asked.

"Do you want to?" I cried. "Do you want to touch me, now?"

"Lena, dear one," he said, "why would I not want to?" He held his arms out to me. I collapsed into them.

"Because I don't know if I can make love again," I sobbed. "He hurt me, Cillian. I'm frightened. I think he has spoiled what we had—and I don't want to lose you."

"I would be hard to lose, on this plain," he said. "Or anywhere else, Lena. We were friends before we were lovers, *leannan,* and we can be just friends again, for as long as you need."

Just friends wasn't what I wanted, but I couldn't find the words to explain. "Promise?" I said, like a little child. He didn't reply.

"Oh," I said, remembering. "I shouldn't have asked that. Not for a promise."

"It is not that," he answered, "I am not sure what it is you are asking."

I tried a smile. "Neither am I. Don't...go away from me, Cillian, even if I am difficult, and complicated, and a burden, right now."

"You are none of those things," he replied. "You are asking me for constancy, I think."

"I suppose I am." I had stopped crying.

He kissed my hair, very gently. "It was yours without asking," he said, "but if it helps you to hear it, then, yes, I promise."

"Thank you," I murmured. It did help; I suddenly felt a little less alone. "Come on," I said. "The little birds should be cooked."

The trail remained easy to follow. Other paths began to join ours from both directions. We grew close to the meeting place of the villages, I surmised. I hoped there was water there. Later, I stopped for no good reason, looking up at the sky. The hero lay ahead of us. We were still moving east.

"Cillian, do you know the story of the hero?" I asked, remembering. "That's him in the sky ahead of us."

"Yes. Don't you?"

"I was told it, but I've forgotten most of it," I admitted. "Tell me?"

"Darcail, he's called in our story," Cillian started. "Son of a god and a mortal woman, born with immense strength. But his father's wife, a goddess, was jealous of him, and drove him mad, and in his madness he killed his wife and daughters. The shame of this drove him into exile."

"And? Did he return from exile?"

"He did," Cillian said. "But only after doing a series of great deeds to redeem himself, including a descent into the underworld. But he prevailed, and when he died he was admitted to the realm of the gods for his valour, and so he stands there in the sky forever."

"Guiding us east," I said. "Is any of it true?"

"I doubt it," Cillian said after a moment, "if you mean was there ever a Darcail who did these things. I don't believe there are gods, or not ones that meddle with human lives. Dagney would tell you it is a story to instruct, to give hope that we can redeem ourselves no matter what we have done, if with great effort."

"Do you believe that?"

He did not reply. We walked towards the hero, fading in the first light of dawn. "I don't know," Cillian said suddenly, as if continuing a conversation. "I don't know about redemption, Lena, not for living people. Perhaps it is only for gods, and heroes from the past."

I finished the thought silently: perhaps it is only a story, like they are.

As the sun rose I saw a pale structure ahead of us gleaming in the sun. "What do you think that is?" I asked Cillian, but he just shook his head, frowning. As we came closer the indeterminate mass separated into a circle of broken pillars, pale and fluted. Two of the pillars stood taller than the others, with ornate carving at the top and a semicircle of stone connecting them.

"A circle of stones, Aivar told me," Cillian said, wonder in his voice. "I thought he meant a circle like the standing stones on the Raske Hoys, just boulders set in a ring, with a few carvings. But this!"

"It looks—sacred," I said; it evoked in me the same response as the floor at the White Fort, the sense of something ancient, great.

Cillian stared up at the pillars. "If the East could build this out here in this empty plain, what must Casil have been?"

We approached in awe. Closer, we could see the chips and breaks in the pillars, the pieces fallen to the ground, the broken remnants of flagstone in the centre. A firepit had been constructed in the middle, and the land cleared for a wide space around it. The *vēsturni* would meet here to exchange stories and news, while the people camped and feasted and made marriage agreements around them. But even broken and scarred, the temple—for it must have been—evoked wonder, and veneration.

We wandered among the stones for some time. I noted the whitewash of bird droppings on several of the pillars: hawks, or maybe falcons, using the height to survey the land. The base of some of the pillars were carved with what I thought were badly worn letters: Cillian, on seeing these, whistled and dropped his pack, searching it for paper. He began to copy the markings. I circled the temple. At the easternmost pillar I saw a small pile of objects at its base: crude beads, little carvings, a strange honey-coloured stone. Offerings.

Practical matters claimed my interest. I went in search of water, finding a stream some distance from the pillars: with one waterskin given to my tea, we had been running short. There were tracks, huge clawed footprints, in the dried mud at the edge. What were they? I would ask Cillian if he knew. Bear, maybe? They weren't fresh.

Today, I thought, we should sleep till noon, and then move again. We had food this morning, one bird to share between us. The other had been eaten when we stopped in the night. We needed to hunt again, and we could move faster in the day, as well.

Nearly an hour after we had stopped Cillian came over to where I sat by the stream. I had had little to do, and the pillars drew my eye, so once the small chores and necessities had been completed, I had simply sat and looked. He sunk to the ground beside me.

"Look," he said, opening his book. He had drawn the letters: **RCV**, and **NVI.**

"What do they say?" I asked.

"This is only a guess...but I think this one," he pointed to **RCV**, "is part of the name the East had for Darcail, or someone very like him. I don't know what the other letters mean. If I'm right, Lena, this was a temple to the hero."

"I didn't realize," I said in wonder, "that the story was that old."

"A thread connecting us to the past," Cillian said. "I wonder what the Kurzemë make of this place?"

"You would have learned, had we stayed until midsummer."

We ate, and then we slept out in the open: there was nothing to shelter us. We had talked before we slept, Cillian telling me a bit more about the hero's tale. I had lain on my side, listening, and at some point after I had laughed at some part of the story, he had reached out a hand to run his fingers along my hair, tentatively. His fingers were light, stroking gently, unthreatening. After a while I laid my head on his chest. It was daylight, which seemed to help. We had fallen asleep like that.

The dream began as it always did, with gouts of blood and a knife in my hand. In my sleep I fought the image, the boy choking on his own blood on the stable floor, the sound my knife had made as I cut his throat. I tried to move in the dream, to turn away, but I couldn't, and suddenly the dream shifted and Ivor lay on top of me again, his knee in my groin, hurting me, his hands reaching for his sex. I woke, hands flailing, shouting.

"Lena. Lena!" Cillian said, pushing himself away from my pounding hands. "What's wrong?"

I lay panting, trying to focus, to return to reality. "A dream," I said. My hands still flexed. Cillian reached for them, holding them loosely in his. I pulled away. "No. Don't." I could hear the note of panic in my voice.

"*Forla*," he whispered. I waited for my breathing to steady.

"Did I hurt you?" I asked.

"No. Would it help to tell me about it?"

The ache in my belly had not been just in the dream. "Can you give me my waterskin, with the tea?" I asked. I sat up, took several deep swallows, tried to breathe more calmly.

"Who were you attacking, before you woke? The boy at Tirvan?"

"No." He waited. "Ivor," I admitted. "The dream began in Tirvan...I tried to turn away from the boy, and I couldn't move, and then Ivor was on top of me again, hurting me..." I fought the tears, but they escaped, running down my cheeks.

He swore. "We had moved, in sleep, and I had an arm around you when you woke me. That's why you couldn't move. I am sorry, Lena."

Of course. I had awoken to that unconscious embrace almost every morning since we had become lovers. I tried to smile. "And my belly hurts, and that became part of my dream."

"Lena, I would never hurt you," he said. "But perhaps I should sleep away from you, for a while?"

"No!" I said, with an intensity that surprised me. But his words had felt like abandonment. "No," I said again, more calmly. "If you are willing to take the chance that I might hit you again, in a dream?"

"I am."

I wiped my cheeks. He reached out, touching my hand with his fingertips. I let him take it, linking his fingers between mine. He raised my hand to his lips. The gesture spoke of tenderness. "As long as you don't use the knife," he added drily.

Eastward from the temple the path simply disappeared. Nor could we find any trace of the ancient road in the soil of the plain. I kept us as straight easterly as I could using the sun: I would adjust our path as needed when the stars came out.

Afternoon became early evening. Not too far to the south a clump of bushes appeared on the horizon. I pointed it out to Cillian. "A water source," I said, "maybe on the road? If so, we haven't strayed far wrong." Like the first spring, the crumbling remnants of bricks lay in the small depression; at this one, though, the water was little more than a trickle, channeled into a rock bowl chiselled out countless years ago.

"If you set up camp, I'll look for the road," Cillian said. "It was easier to see, before, when the sun was low." He went to look.

I had begun to fill the waterskins when Cillian's voice, taut and low, called my name. I looked up. He was staring beyond me. Approaching me and the water, a huge brown bear walked steadily across the grass. I froze, crouched. At any moment it would see or smell me.

I forgot to tell Cillian about the footprints at the stream, I thought. The wind blew across the space between us, but it was a slight breeze, nothing more. "Stand up," Cillian said calmly. "Stand up, slowly, spread your arms. Don't run."

I forced myself up. The bear stopped, rose to its hind legs, its head moving back and forth. Cillian, behind me, kept talking. Very slowly he came to stand beside me, his large bow, nocked and half-drawn, in his hands.

"There are bears like this in Sorham and Varsland," he said, keeping his voice conversational. "I have met one or two in my travels. Do what I say and we should be unharmed. It may charge us. Do not run, Lena, your life depends on it. Trust me, käresta."

I stared at the bear. It is the size of a hill pony, I thought, feeling myself begin to tremble. I could see the long claws on its front feet. It sniffed the air, opening its mouth to growl, and ran at us.

"Stay still!" Cillian ordered. I fought the instinct to flee, fear coursing through me. I whimpered, trying not to cower. Beside me Cillian drew the bow, slowly. The bear galloped across the grass, closer, closer—and then it stopped, rearing up again, growling.

"You do not want us, bear," Cillian said. "You only want water. We will back away and let you have it." To me, he said, "slowly. Very slowly. I will keep talking." He did, addressing the bear, keeping his voice low and unthreatening. I stepped backwards, carefully, deliberately. One step, two, three.

The bear charged. I heard Cillian swear, sharply. I tried to turn, to—what? Take the bow from him? To run?—and tripped. I fell, covering my head with my hands, utterly terrified, sobbing with fear, waiting for those huge claws to rip into me. I could hear the bear's feet pounding the earth. I tried to push myself into the ground.

The pounding stopped. A strange sound, somewhere between a snarl and a whine, and then the thud of a heavy body hitting the ground and the thunk of an arrow, hitting flesh, and a second. Then Cillian, crouching beside me, his voice reassuring. "It's dead, Lena. We're safe."

I sat up. Very close—far too close—the body of the bear lay on the grass, two arrows in its neck and one in its eye. I hadn't heard the first shot at all. "Did you—the first arrow—in its eye?" I asked, almost incoherent.

"Yes." He held out his hand to help me up. I was shaking.

"Are you sure it's dead?" I asked.

"Not entirely. But it will be soon, if it isn't now." A huge pool of blood stained the ground beneath its throat.

Cillian's arm was around my shoulders. I leaned against his chest. "You just saved my life again. That's three times." His heartbeat was rapid and his breathing fast. He too must have been terrified, I realized. "That was a skilled shot," I said. "I doubt I could have done it."

"Nor could I have," he said, "without three days of hunting geese. But even so, luck was most of it." I looked over at the bear.

"Do you want a claw, the way I had the *jerv's* claws?"

"No. Leave it for the carrion-birds. We should get the waterskins filled, though, before it spoils the water." It had fallen close to the water's edge. We went about the task, although I kept one eye on the body. But it was clearly dead, now.

Later, after we had built a fire and eaten, and the first stars sparkled in the darkening sky, I put my arms around him. "I didn't say thank you," I said, "or tell you how courageous you were. Killing that bear was an act worthy of Darcail."

"No bears that I remember in his labours," he said, smiling.

"Worthy of, I said," I protested. "It was very brave," I added, seriously.

"Is an act brave when there is no choice except to do it or die?" he asked.

"No philosophy tonight," I said. "I wish..."

"Wish what, Lena?"

"I wish we could make love. I wish I could show you how I feel about what you did today, not try to find inadequate words." I could hear my own frustration.

"Telling me that is not inadequate," he replied. He kissed my hair. "Lie down with me and watch the stars come out." I stretched out beside him, his hand lightly on my hip. The sky darkened, only the western horizon still glowing, and the stars went from four or five to hundreds, and as the night deepened, to thousands upon thousands glittering above us. "Look north," Cillian said. "Do you see the lovers?" He pointed to them.

"What is their story?" I asked. I knew the names of the constellations, but nothing else.

"Perthèin rescued Dromédē from a monster about to devour her," he answered, a touch drily.

I laughed. "I had the wrong hero, then? I should have compared you to Perthèin?"

"I am no hero, Lena. What else could I have done today?"

"You didn't panic. You made a very difficult shot, and two more, quickly, and all of them accurate. That makes you a hero in my eyes."

"I had you to save, *leannan*."

"And yourself."

"That was less important," he said. He sounded completely serious.

"It would have been to me," I said fiercely. I wanted so much to be able to turn to him, but I could not. Not yet. But some day, I thought. *Courage comes in many forms,* Casyn had told me once. I had seen one of its faces today, for all Cillian dismissed what he had done. I will find my own courage to move beyond my hurt and revulsion, I vowed. Only then will I tell you I love you.

PART II

Love consists in this: that two solitudes protect and touch and greet each other.   Rilke

CHAPTER SIX

WE CONTINUED EASTWARD, FROM ONE WATER SOURCE to another, a day's walk apart. After the third day, I no longer needed to fill a waterskin with tea. We talked as we walked, he telling me stories from Linrathe, from Sorham, or about what he knew of the East; I telling him about the Empire. There was an unreality to this time, just the two of us alone in the seemingly endless grass. It felt sometimes like we had been always walking, and would go on forever.

At night we watched the sky, and Cillian told me more stories, the legends that belonged to the constellations. Occasionally as we sat or lay by the fire he would stroke my hair as he spoke. I found the caress comforting.

The fire was for heat and for protection against the animals that prowled the grassland, the large bow and quiver kept near. We slept side by side for warmth, and because I felt safer that way, and as long as it was my arm across his chest or my body nestled against his back, I could relax. He could hold me when I was awake, but in sleep the weight of his arm brought restlessness, and often dreams.

I awoke before him one morning, slipping away quietly to sit by the tiny pool a short distance from where we had slept. I liked the dawn birdsong and the movement of small animals to and from the water. I sat, letting my mind drift, watching the sun rise, the sky to the east turning from deep pink to a pale, clear blue. Another dry, hot day.

"Lena," Cillian said quietly, a courtesy he had adopted quickly once he realized I panicked if surprised, especially from behind. He handed me a mug of tea. I hadn't even heard him at the fire, I realized; perhaps the first time since the attack my senses had not been heightened. He sat beside me.

"Put your tea down," I said. I leaned over and kissed him, very lightly. He looked at me questioningly. I kissed him again. It felt comfortable. Unthreatening. Familiar.

"Another courtship?" he murmured.

"In a way. It might be very prolonged, though."

"We have all the time there is," he answered. "You decide, *leannan*." He put his arm around me, kissing my hair. I looked up at him. His eyes were very gentle. I leaned against his shoulder, wondering.

A few mornings later, I woke to find he had turned in the night to face me. One hand rested near my neck, and as I moved slightly it slipped down against my breast. The touch did not terrify me, but instead aroused a faint tug of desire, gone in an instant, but real. I stayed still, imagining. Considering.

We kept walking east. The land began to slope downward, almost imperceptibly and then definitely, and then below us in a fold lay a small lake, its waters rippling in the warm southern breeze that had sprung up during the afternoon. The sight of water! We had left the temple behind many days ago, and in that time had found only small seeps at each stopping place, enough to slowly fill waterskins and make tea, but not for bathing. Sweat and dust coated our skin and hair and clothes.

"Wait," Cillian said, a warning hand on my arm. "I know you want to go down there, *leannan*, but if there are people on these plains we should find them here. We need to watch for a while." We lay in the sparse grass, watching, for some time. Small trees rimmed one end of the lake, but I could see no paths leading through them. Other than a fox stopping for a drink and waterfowl feeding among the reeds at the lake's edge, nothing moved.

Even so, when we reached the shore, we made a thorough check for the remnants of campfires, for footprints, for any sign of human presence. Only when we had traversed the entire lake was Cillian satisfied.

"What first?" he asked. "Hunt or swim?"

"Hunt," I said reluctantly. "Otherwise we will likely scare off the birds." The ducks had seemed unperturbed by our presence, though. I wondered if they knew what people were, but caution said to harvest our supper while we could. A group of the brown birds dabbled, tails up, close to where we stood; quick work to shoot two. I gutted them, tied their feet together, and hung them over a branch. At the water's edge, I cleaned the knife and brought it back to where our packs lay.

"Done," I said. "Now let's get in that water." I stripped, letting my clothes fall: I would wash them later. Naked, I ran to the lake, splashing through the shallows. The ducks scattered. I could hear Cillian just behind me. When the water reached my thighs I dived, a shallow plunge forward, and submerged, glorying in the silky, cold caress of the water.

I scrubbed my body and hair with my hands, floated, swam, did it again, feeling my own skin. The sun sank lower. Maybe, I thought, we should stay here a day or two, wash clothes, rest. I rolled onto my back, spread my arms, let the water carry me, cleanse me.

"Fire," Cillian said, "and food." On the shore we pulled on a layer of clothes. Cillian gathered wood and built the fire, practiced and fast, while I skinned the ducks, breaking the bodies along the backbone to make them lay flat above the coals.

Our hands and faces were slick with fat after the meal. I went back to the lake to wash. The warmth of the day lingered; impulsively I pulled off my clothes and went back into the water. I heard Cillian laugh. I swam out a few strokes, flipped, and swam back to the shore.

"Were you an otter in another life?" he teased as I combed the water from my hair with my fingers.

"I like water," I said. "I told you about the baths at Tirvan."

He crouched to wash his hands and face, scrubbing his beard to remove the grease. I watched him, suddenly conscious of my nakedness, remembering the flash of desire earlier. Could I? "Get dressed," he said over his shoulder, his voice mild, "before you start to shiver."

I had to know. "I'd rather not," I said.

He straightened, turned. The breeze caught at his hair. "Lena?"

"Will you...could we make love?" I asked. "Or try to, at least?" He gave me a long, searching look.

"Are you ready?"

"I don't know," I answered. "But I want to try. Ivor treated me as if I were an animal to be hunted and taken. I want to feel...wanted for myself, again. Valued." There was another word, but I could not say it.

In the dying light I could not read the expression in his eyes. He smiled, slowly, holding out his hand.

We lay by the banked fire, near to sleep, watching the night sky darken from cobalt to black. A late duck quacked its way onto the water.

"Falling star," Cillian said. I found it, followed its arc until it disappeared.

"There is so much sky," I murmured.

"So much space for you," he answered. We lay silent again. Another star fell. "Lena, for you to trust me as you did tonight was a very great gift."

He had been infinitely gentle, infinitely patient, leaving all decisions to me. Tonight would be a memory of tenderness, and at the end unexpected passion: his body, encompassed under mine, the warm breeze on my skin, my name on his indrawn breath.

"How could I not trust you? You know what I need, so well, without me having to tell you. I needed gentleness tonight and that is what you gave me." He did not answer. "Cillian?" I said, softly.

"Lena," he said, his voice barely audible, "the violence that was done to you is unspeakable, and not something I can comprehend. But I do know something about being used, and the cold emptiness it brings. I thought you would turn away from me, after, but you asked me to stay. That was...unexpected."

"I felt safer," I murmured. That wasn't enough. I reached a hand to touch his face. "Sheltered." He turned his head to kiss my palm, his cheek against my skin.

"As best I can," he said roughly. "*Käresta*, you asked to be wanted, and valued. You must know you are."

"There was a third thing," I said slowly, "but I couldn't ask. Not until I tell you something."

"You can always ask, Lena."

"No," I said. "Not this. Not until you know."

"Then tell me."

"I was wrong when I told you all I could offer you was affection. So wrong." I hesitated, searching for courage. "Cillian, I love you."

He was very still. "Never did I think I would hear those words spoken to me," he said, his voice unsteady. "Lena, are you sure this is not just gratitude?"

"I am sure. I knew, before."

"The third thing, then, the one you could not ask, was it to be loved? But you are, *käresta*. Did you not realize? You are, with all my heart."

I woke sometime before dawn. I moved to look at him, just making out the planes of his face. He slept deeply. I lay watching, thinking, remembering other mornings: Maya, Garth.

It had been simple with Maya, two children growing into love, all Tirvan there to support us. Garth and I had been an interlude after war, the memory gentle. But I was no longer the girl, nor the woman, I had been. I carried so many scars, from violence recent and past, from war and loss, and his were as dark, and deeper. This night alone had not assuaged them, nor would many.

A bird trilled, the first sound of the new day. Cillian stirred. A thought came to me, a promise. He opened his eyes. I watched as he remembered, the flicker of wonder on his face, and his slow smile beginning. The bird still sang its morning benediction, welcoming the sun.

"Hello, my love," I said.

We stayed at the lake for three days, doing all the things that needed doing. I fashioned a fishhook, and we ate grilled fish as a change from birds, hanging more over smoky fires to cure. Near the southern edge of the lake I found what medicinal plants had survived and gone wild, picking mint, digging ginger root, and drying more anash leaves for tea.

I found myself checking where Cillian was every few minutes. I couldn't quite decide why, what the nature of the reassurance I sought was. Safety? A fear he would disappear, like otherworldly beings in children's stories? When he was close, I wanted to hold him, feel his arms around me, needing that shelter.

"Should you be," he had asked me that first morning, "the one to choose to make love, or not, for now?" But beyond that conversation, we spoke very little of what had changed between us. But he seemed to need the same reassurance as me: I would look up to find him watching me, and he found reasons to touch me as often as he could, undemanding touches, a hand trailed across my back, a kiss dropped on my hair in passing. When we swam, which was frequently, we played, chasing each other; I was a better swimmer than Cillian, but his height and length of arm often gave him an advantage. The games usually led to making love. At night we slept curved together, and I did not dream.

On the fourth morning the wind changed, switching round to the east, and the air was hazy. "We should be on the move," I said to Cillian, over breakfast.

"I suppose."

"We can't stay here forever," I said gently. "As much as we both might want to."

He grinned. "Only until the snow came." I laughed, but as much as he was joking, there was an undercurrent of truth to his words. We had little idea how far we had to go in the short summer of the plain.

We climbed out from the bowl of the lake and over the eastern range of hills to find the land falling away again, down to another endless stretch of grassland, this one even drier. On a flat area not big enough to be called a plateau, the ruins of buildings stood, surrounded by a wall.

"A camp?" Cillian asked.

"A fort," I corrected. "Look at the shape, the rounded corners on the wall, the layout of the buildings—it's just like the White Fort, or Wall's End. There were a lot of men here, once."

"It's well situated," Cillian said. "Water from the lake above us, piped down here somehow, I'm guessing; a long view over the plain below us."

"But they couldn't see what might be coming from the west," I pointed out.

"Probably guard posts up on the hills to the west of the lake," he suggested. He glanced back. "We were focused on the lake, looking for signs of people. I wonder what we missed."

"Well, we're not going back," I said. "If there were guard posts, I can tell you exactly what they would have looked like: I've spent enough time on one. I will draw you one, Comiádh, if you like." He laughed. We picked our way down to the ruined fort. The wind blew steadily, keening through gaps in the stone. Small wildflowers grew on the walls and lizards darted and froze among them, hunting insects. I looked around me. Buildings had crumbled, roofs and wooden stairs and doors gone into dust. I walked along the midline of the fort to where I thought the headquarters should be. A courtyard surrounded a large building. I stepped through the opening. In front of me was a line of arches, and in the centre of the courtyard lay the two halves of a huge bowl.

Cillian had followed me into the courtyard. "But I've seen this before," he said.

"At the Wall's End fort," I replied. "The headquarters there."

"All those years," he murmured, "and still loyalty to a plan, a way of thinking and building."

"If we go inside," I asked, "do you think the floor will be tile, and a diamond pattern on the walls?" He gestured me to go ahead. We stepped inside the space, open to wind and rain and animals. The floor was covered with a layer of sand, and the plaster had crumbled off the walls long ago.

I shivered, although the day was warm enough. "When do you think people were last here?" All those hands, all those lives, over how many years, given to building and maintaining this place, this symbol of Casil's order—and here it lay, empty and abandoned, under the relentless sun. Was this what we would find at Casil itself, if we found it?

"Five hundred years ago?" Cillian suggested. "I wonder if they thought, when they were building it, that it would stand long after their lives and their Empire's time were over?"

"Do people think like that?" I asked. "Beyond their own time?"

"Some, I think. Those who plan buildings and roads, write histories, make maps, I think they do." He had been walking around the walls of the room, examining the stones, as he spoke. "What do you write your history for, Lena? For whom?"

"For me," I replied. "I thought in doing so it would help me understand what was happening, make me think about how my life fit into—into the events of the day."

"Was that the only reason?"

"No," I admitted. "I started it after Colm gave me his history to read. I did think that maybe in a small way what I wrote might be useful to another historian, some day."

"So you were thinking beyond your own time," he pointed out.

"I suppose," I said. "But I can tell you, Cillian, that the soldiers actually building these walls and paths were not: they were thinking of their sore backs and nicked hands, and the sun or rain beating down on them, and when was the next meal break."

"The voice of experience," he said lightly. I frowned: the comment felt dismissive, somehow. But I pursued my thought.

"In what little I know," I argued, "the histories have all been written by men like Perras or Colm, or at the very least by generals and Emperors. Not by the men or women who build the walls or—or shoe horses, or fish. Isn't their point of view important too?"

"They would be," he said slowly. "Very few wrote, though, as you are doing. But I wonder if there is a way to find those voices, not perhaps in written histories but in song and story. It is an interesting idea, Lena, and one that could be important."

A yellowhammer sang its 'See-me see-me see-me please' from atop a wall. "We should go, *käresta*," Cillian said. "We likely have a long way to travel to find water."

There was no water, not the first night. Nor was there wood for a fire, but the dry, pelleted droppings of some deer-like creature littered the earth, and piled loosely, they burned well. We ate smoked fish, and I drank my tea, its bitterness enhanced by the dryness of my throat. The clear night turned cold and the dung fire gave off little heat; even close together, we shivered, sleeping restlessly.

Dust and wind became inevitabilities, and the heat of the sun grew. Our skin turned red, and then brown. We found water the next night, another enhanced seep, so we were still on the road. I thought about the immense, incomprehensible work of building a road through this almost-desert, feeding and finding water for men and animals. The fort below the lake must have been part of that supply; would we come across another, desolate and deserted, in a few more days?

Late on the fourth day Cillian stopped me with a silent hand on my arm. He tended to scan the horizon more distantly than I; other than for calculating direction, I was more alert to what was closer to us. I looked where he pointed. An enormous cloud of dust moved across the plain ahead of us, north to south. I tried to focus through the haze and my dry, stinging eyes, making out indistinct shapes. "People on horses?" I asked.

"Maybe. Let's watch." We crouched down. I found the waterskin, wet my mouth, passed it to Cillian. The dust cloud slowed, stopped. As the dust settled the shapes within coalesced into four-legged animals. No riders. No people. A herd of deer-like creatures milled around what I guessed was a water source.

I relaxed. The thought of meeting people frightened me, although I knew that we must eventually. Cillian watched the animals. "They are nothing I know," he said. "They have big curved heads and a single pair of horns, not branched antlers like deer."

"And they probably taste good," I said, "but even one would be too much, for us."

"In the plains behind us, except for that lone large bird, we saw nothing that would feed a settlement," Cillian answered. "These animals can."

We moved on, keeping an eye on the herd. It drifted south slowly. I guessed any grazing near the water was gone, and when we reached the spring, only thin grey soil surrounded it. The water itself bubbled up into a small pool, a bare layer of water over grey rock. It had been muddied by the animals, but I thought it would settle and clear.

Filling the waterskins took patience and time. When they were full, I scooped water onto my face and eyes, running my wet hands through my hair. Cillian knelt beside me, doing the same, working his fingers into his beard. I kissed his cheek, leaning my head against his for a moment. "*Käresta*," he murmured.

"What does that mean?"

"Just an endearment."

A scent, the briefest impression, caught my nostrils. I stood up, facing east, letting the wind push my already-dry hair off my face. A game-trail led off that way; animals came to this water from all around. Insects chirred, somewhere. I sniffed again.

"What?" Cillian asked.

I shook my head. "Probably nothing. But for a moment there, I thought I smelled woodsmoke and roasting meat."

He straightened, looking out into the dusk. "No fire that I can see. But we'll need to be alert tomorrow."

A few hours after sunrise, and already sweat dripped down my back and between my breasts. Overhead, a carrion-bird—the first we had seen for some days—made slow circles in the sky, gyring higher into the pale, clear blue. No clouds interfered with the sun. Beneath our feet the soil between the sparse, coarse grasses felt grittier, dry and dusty, chafing when it found its way into our boots.

On a slight rise in the plain, Cillian halted. "Look," he said, pointing. "Is that water?" I shaded my eyes with my hand. Light shimmered and gleamed along the eastern horizon.

"I'm not sure," I answered. "Maybe—but maybe not. It could just be heat haze." I followed the brightness north, then south. The shimmer of haze continued in both directions, but the wavering gleam did not. A lake? "I think it is water," I concluded.

"Probably where this trail goes," he replied. We'd chosen to follow the narrow, faint path since dawn for lack of any other guide. I had checked the sun frequently to ensure it was still heading east. We'd seen nothing of the animals that had made it, although from its width, the droppings, and the occasional mark in the soil, I felt certain they were the same deer-like creatures we had seen yesterday.

Cillian handed me the waterskin. I swallowed a mouthful, took another tiny sip, and gave it back to him. We resumed walking, not speaking: talking increased the need to drink and we needed to husband our water. The sun grew hotter every minute. Even if that is a lake, I thought, it is some miles off.

Swallows darted over the water, and as we approached a lanky heron launched itself slowly into the air, croaking. Gnats hovered in clouds over the small bushes at the edge. We stopped short of the bank, unsure of its stability, wary of what—or just possibly who—else might be here. Slowly we edged forward, keeping behind the bushes, crouching. Anyone fishing here, I told myself, would have seen us coming across the plain long ago. Tension rippled through me.

From the cover of the bushes I looked out across the water. I could make out a line of shrubs on the far shore. I looked east, then west. Nothing—no people, no animals—and no shoreline. I frowned, watching the water. A mat of grasses floated by, moving south. "Cillian," I said, "this isn't a lake. I think it's a river."

"A river? It's too wide."

"Watch that mat of grasses," I suggested, pointing. He found it, narrowing his eyes. I counted to ten, then twenty. "Well?"

"There's a current, certainly," he said. "But it could just be the outlet for the lake pulling those grasses southward."

"I can't see a shore, south or north," I pointed out, "just the far bank—and if this is a lake it's a remarkably straight one; that bank runs even with this one for as far as I can see." He gazed along the opposite bank, eyes tracing the bushes.

"You may be right," he said eventually. "How are we ever going to cross this?"

"Walk north," I offered, "and hope it narrows? It's flowing south, so it's only going to get wider in that direction. Do you remember anything from the maps?"

"Let me think," he murmured. His eyes became distant, trying to recall the picture the maps made, to overlay it on this land and this water. I waited, watching, listening.

"I think," he said finally, "that we are better to walk south: if this is the river I think it is, it will split into several channels further south when the land must become rockier, steeper. North of here the land is flat, and the river will still be wide."

"Does this river have a name?" I asked, but before Cillian could answer a loud trumpeting split the air. From upriver, several large greyish-brown birds, long-necked and long-legged, rose from the grasses. "Something disturbed them," I said. "Get down, among the bushes."

We crouched low, waiting. The birds circled, still calling, going higher, not looking to land. Whatever had flushed them was still out there. Suddenly a pair of ducks launched themselves past us, quacking noisily: the threat grew closer. Cillian crawled forward. I put out a hand, trying to stop him, fear rising in my throat. He ignored me, crouching at the river's edge, peering out from among the leaves. "Lena," he whispered, "come here. Look!"

I edged forward. Through the twigs and stems I could see the prow of a boat, curved and capped with a carven head, the sweep of oars carrying it forward. Cillian rocked back. "By the gods, Lena," he murmured. "That's a Marai ship."

CHAPTER SEVEN

MY SHOCKED EYES TOOK IN THE GLIDING SHAPE, the dozen oarsmen I could see, the people standing on board. One caught my attention: broad-shouldered but not tall, with a mane of red hair and a full, red beard. I stared. The man turned slightly, talking to his companion, a woman, and I had a clear look at his profile.

I scrambled to my feet, trying to run along the wooded riverbank. "Turlo!" I shouted, "Turlo!" Behind me I heard Cillian swear.

"What are you doing?"

I turned. "The man on board, the redhead—that's General Turlo. He's a friend, Cillian." I watched the boat slowing, the oarsmen reversing their sweep, bringing the ship into the bank.

"A friend?" He was studying the ship, eyes narrowed.

"The woman is the lady Irmgard," he said after a moment. "Åsmund's wife. What are they doing here?"

Fritjof's brother's wife, the one he had tried to force himself on. "We'll know in a minute," I replied. As the ship settled against the bank some distance ahead of us, Turlo vaulted over the side. I ran to him to be swept up in his bearhug, hearing his laughter and my name. I laughed too in between my tears, hugging him close, until a thought flashed across my mind.

"Oh, Turlo, let me go," I hiccupped. "I stink."

He laughed again and released me, looking over my shoulder to Cillian. He held out a hand. "Cillian, is it not?" he asked.

I saw Cillian take a deep breath. "General Turlo," he said, accepting the outstretched hand. "Well met."

"More than well met, *mo charaidh*. I am counted a good hunter, but not so good I can find two people in all this empty land. Fortune has smiled on us all today," Turlo answered, still grinning broadly. Behind him, other people were disembarking, approaching us. Hearing them, Turlo turned.

"Lady Irmgard," he said to the woman who stepped forward, "you'll accept two more on your ship?"

"Of course. This is the woman of whom you spoke?" she said in our language, her accent strong.

"Aye, that she is. You know Cillian, of course. What a wonder it is that our paths have crossed."

How did she know Cillian? He stepped forward, bowing. "*Ådla* Irmgard, you are gracious," he said.

"Cillian na Perras," she said. "Be welcome. It has been some years since we have traded thoughts."

"Thank you, my lady," he replied. As sunburned and windblown and filthy as I, yet the manners, the refinement, were impeccable, practiced. Trained as an emissary, he had told me once. A side of him I had never seen. "And this, my lady, is Lena, once a soldier of the Empire."

"Your deeds are known to me," she replied. "Be welcome, too."

"*Takkë*," I said, "my lady." She blinked in surprise at my use of her language, smiling in appreciation.

Another man had come up to us as we spoke. "Cillian, Lena," he said, a wide grin on his face. "I can't believe we found you!"

"Sorley? What are you doing here?" I asked. "What are you all doing here?"

"We'll tell you," Turlo interrupted, "but for all our sakes, lassie, the pair of you need water, and not just to drink. And then food, I think, and stories to be told as we travel."

Clean, fed, and with cups of a thin beer to drink, we sat on the deck. The ship had pushed out from the bank and we were moving steadily south along the broad river. Turlo insisted we tell our story first.

"Very little to tell," Cillian said, when I suggested he start. "It took us about three months or a bit more to cross the Durrains. The weather was vicious at the end; we were caught in a hailstorm that might have killed us, but we were found, luckily, by two men from the nearest village. One of them was a man of the Empire, exiled twenty years ago."

"What was his name?" Turlo asked.

"Oran," I said.

"Oran of the sixth?"

"I don't know," I said. "He never said. He's known as Fél, now."

"I'm glad to know he's alive," Turlo mused. "Killed a man in a stupid fight: the soldier had stolen a piece of meat from the kitchens, a particularly good piece that Oran had put aside for something. They had words, the soldier threw a punch, and Oran hit him with the iron frying-pan he happened to be holding. Cracked his skull."

I burst out laughing. "I'm sorry," I said. "What a thing to be exiled for."

"Aye," Turlo said regretfully, "and he was a very good cook. But the law is the law. What can you tell us about the people who took you in?"

"They call themselves the Kurzemë, a loose federation of villages, maybe twenty in all, scattered along river valleys on the eastern side of the Durrains," Cillian answered. "The language has some similarities with *Marái'sta*. Illiterate, skilled hunters, basic metalwork, political structure is a headman, a headwoman, and a *vësturni*. This last is difficult to explain, but essentially he is the wise man of the village who keeps their history and traditions. Once a year they meet collectively at a location on the plain for talks, marriages, trade."

Turlo chuckled. "I see I shall have to have you write my reports for me," he said. "Is that written down, by the bye?"

"Of course," Cillian said, "With more detail. Yours to read whenever you would like, General."

"Go on," Turlo said.

"Lena, your turn," Cillian said. He was leaving it up to me to tell the reasons we left, or not. Not seemed the better choice. I would be as concise as Cillian, or as close as I could manage.

"When spring came," I began, "we resumed our journey. There is a dry grassland between the Durrains and this river, but there are also the remnants of a road, and stopping places where springs have been channelled or pooled. And the ruins of a temple, and at about half-way, the ruins of a fort."

"A road?"

"The barest trace," Cillian said. "But a temple, yes, a circle of carved pillars, once roofed, dedicated to a hero, a quasi-god of the East."

"And the fort, Turlo," I said, "had the same plan, down to the same courtyard and the same big bowl in it, as Wall's End."

"How Perras would like to know this!" Sorley said.

"And where did this road go?" Turlo asked.

"To where we met you at the river, I believe," Cillian said. "We lost all trace of it in the last part of our journey, but it had run directly east, and Lena kept us on that bearing the whole time."

"Well done, both of you," Turlo said. "Does this river have a name?" he asked, turning to Cillian.

"*Ubë*, if I remember correctly."

"I have little doubt of that," Turlo answered, a touch drily. "Can you tell us anything else about it? We have been navigating on what some of the lady Irmgard's men remember hearing from Fritjof's crew when they first returned, and Sorley's faint memories of a map or two."

Cillian explained what he remembered, the three channels, suggesting rockier, broken land. "Rough waters, then," Turlo said. "How much further south?"

"If the maps were accurate—let me think." We waited. "It took us fifteen days to cross the grasslands, but three were rest days, so twelve—I would say a four-day sail, maybe five, from where we met."

"I will let the steersman know," Turlo said, turning to Irmgard. "With your permission, my lady?"

"Of course," she said. "I have told you before, command him as you need." She had remained quiet until now, clearly listening. I had glanced her way on and off, covertly studying her. Fair-haired like most northern women, I guessed her to be Cillian's age or a bit younger. Clearly the ship was hers. But other than her oarsmen and two women attendants, she was alone.

I remembered something. "Sorley," I said, "when we met, you said, 'I can't believe we found you'. Were you looking for us?"

"Not directly," Turlo answered, "and certainly not here. But we are bound for Casil, if there is a Casil, and we thought you might be too. It was there I would have searched for you."

"Why? We are exiled." A thought struck me. "Surely you are not, too?"

"No, lassie, we are not, or not in the way you mean. I would have looked for you, because exiled or no, you are dear to me and I wanted to know you were safe, if I could."

"As I wished to know you were, Cillian," Sorley said. "And Lena, of course," he added, with a slight bow of his head to me, "but it is you that Dagney and

Perras and all the *Ti'ach* would most want word of, if we return."

"I would not want to be a worry to them," Cillian said, faintly ironic. Sorley shook his head slightly.

"You haven't changed at all," he said, smiling. "You were always a worry to them, you fool."

Cillian was taken aback by that. I could see it on his face, briefly, until he recovered his composure. "Was I now?" he said. "I will write a most abject letter of apology, then, and send it with you."

Old defenses. Sorley just shook his head again and said nothing.

"General," Cillian said, turning to Turlo, "what did you intend to convey by 'not exiled in the way you mean'?"

"Ah," Turlo said, "now we come to it. This is not good news, not at all, so prepare yourselves."

It would not be, I thought, for Turlo to be here. A cold fear began to gather inside me.

"There are three parts to it, so it will take some time." Turlo continued. "Lady Irmgard, would you like to begin?"

"Mine may be the simplest," she said. Her voice, although accented, was clear, a woman used to authority. "You were both at Fritjof's hall," she gestured towards us, "so I need not tell that tale again. He had me imprisoned, with my women, a bit north of there. But not all there were as loyal as he thought, so by certain bribes I got a message to what remained of my husband's men, and they brought this little ship to rescue me, while Fritjof was—looking elsewhere, fighting to the south. I did not feel safe, anywhere in Varsland, and it was my steersman, Geiri, who suggested we sail east, saying Fritjof would never seek me there. So we began, and then my tale joins that of the lord Sorley and the General."

She fell silent. Her fear of Fritjof must be strong, I thought, to risk a voyage into unknown lands.

"Mine is also simple," Sorley said. "My father supported Fritjof. Our family, a very long time ago, came from Varsland, and it seems that in his heart he thinks of himself as Marai. I had left the *Ti'ach*—it was almost time for me to go, anyhow—because I felt I would be needed at home to help defend our people. I met one of our *torpari* on the road, fleeing south with a bag on his back and only a stick as protection. I turned around and went back to Linrathe, and then from *Ti'ach* to *Ti'ach*, with messages." He paused, swallowed, struggle clear on his open face. "This is hard for me to say to myself, and worse to a countryman. Cillian, Linrathe has fallen."

I shivered, from the news and from the piercing fear of how Cillian would react. His face was still. I put a hand on his arm, willing him to not give the reflexive, brittle response I was afraid of. He took a deep breath, and I saw I had misjudged: the stillness had been focus, not shield.

"Lorcann. He did support Fritjof, then?" Cold enveloped me. Had we gambled and won our personal stake, only for the next roll of the dice to lead to this?

Turlo spoke, his voice firm. "The Emperor's choice, his, and only his. He knew the risks, better than anyone. This is not your grief to carry, either of you."

"How can it not be?" Cillian said bitterly. "Would he have decided as he did, had I been just a random man of Linrathe? Lorcann would have been satisfied with my life; he could have exiled Lena, and let me die, and we—you—would have peace. You know that was the right thing to do, General. You gave your son to this cause; why should not the Emperor have done the same?"

"Darel was a soldier," Turlo said, his voice rough, "and soldiers die. It is our truth. And that was not your fault either," he said, looking at me. "Linrathan men killed my son, in confusion and anger, and I hold neither of you responsible." He cleared his throat, falling silent.

I wiped tears from my face. I wanted to put my arms around Cillian, to feel him hold me, sharing this terrible grief, but this was not the place. I felt the weight of the silence. No, I thought. No.

"There is more, isn't there?" I asked in a small voice. "Turlo, why are you here, and not at Callan's side?"

I had once thought Turlo irrepressible. The delight of our unexpected meeting must have pushed aside care for a few hours, but now I saw the anguish he had hidden. "Not the Empire too?" I whispered.

"No," he said, "not quite, or not when I left. But the Marai had far more ships and men than we could know, and with the men of Sorham, and some of Linrathe, with them...when I left, our troops—our people—were being beaten back from the coast.

"When you, Cillian, were at the Wall's End fort, you told us that Fritjof had claimed to have sailed east to another land and come home safely. We—The Emperor and Casyn and myself—talked about that off and on, and one night, when the situation had begun to look desperate, Callan gave me my orders: go east. Maybe the Eastern Empire lives on, he said, and maybe, just maybe, they would come to our aid. I argued, as you can guess, but Callan *is* the Emperor, and it was an order."

"And it had to be you," Cillian said, "because you can pass as a northerner, and the route I told you about was east from the Raske Firth."

"Aye," Turlo said. "So I travelled up along the Durrains, and sometimes in them, with Galen, for part of the time, until I sent him back. In northern Linrathe I ran into Sorley. We soon sorted out we were on the same side, and he chose to come with me." There was more to that, I thought, but it could be told later.

"And where the Tumë drains into the *Firth av Raske*, they met me and my ship," Irmgard said. "Travellers from three lands, with one goal, meeting like that? The gods decreed it. And now we have Cillian na Perras, who can guide us? The gods, again. We will make this voyage safely."

My mind flicked back over what Turlo had said, thinking. Pushed back from the coast. "Callan will retreat to the Eastern Fort, if all else is lost?" I asked.

"Yes," Turlo said bleakly. He tried for a smile. "Quick, as always, Lena." But I barely heard him. *Pushed back from the coast.*

"Turlo, what about the villages? What has happened to Tirvan?" A hand on my back. I ignored it. "Tell me!"

"Oh, lassie," he said. "I do not know for certain, not for Tirvan. But I know what happened at Berge, and it was bad, lassie, very bad. I cannot give you hope."

I moaned. Words and images pounded my brain: Ivor on me, thrusting his sex between my legs, and then Kira, and Lara. The sound of swords. The smell of blood. My mother. I should have been there. I wailed, curling in on myself, dropping onto the deck, rocking, keening my loss and anger and guilt. I should have been there.

There were voices, hands, but hands hurt. I pushed them away.

"No, Turlo," Cillian said. "She has been injured. It needs to be me."

He knelt beside me, picked me up, his arms around me wrapping me as tightly as a swaddled babe. He rocked me, whispered words I did not take in, and gradually I calmed. I still sobbed, but slowly the sobs subsided. Tears flowed, but the racking frenzy had ended. Cillian took my face in his hands to wipe the tears away, his hands as gentle as I had ever known them. "Oh, *käresta*," he said. "I would have saved you this if I could. I am so sorry, Lena, so very sorry."

I leaned against him, the whirling images dwindling. Anger began to rise. I could handle anger: it could be sheathed like a knife, and brought out again when it was needed. I took a deep breath, and another. "Cillian," I whispered.

"I'm here."

"I know. I need...to be angry right now, so I can deal with this. Not at you, never at you, even if it seems like it. Do you understand?"

Compassion, and something more, in his eyes. "Completely." He kissed my forehead, resting his head against mine for a moment. "Do what you need to, *käresta*."

I stood, looking at the others. Sorley gazed at Cillian, an odd look on his face. But it was Turlo and Irmgard whose attention I needed.

"Lady Irmgard," I said, my throat sore from weeping. "This is your ship, so I need your permission for what I am about to ask." She bowed her head in assent. I turned to Turlo. "General, I am out of training. Is there a sword I can use?"

"Aye," Turlo said after a minute. "A sword will help. But not today, Lena." He was holding a small flask in his hand. "Drink a bit of this," he said. "You need it."

I took the flask, tasting the fire of *fuisce*. I swallowed a mouthful, raw on my throat, and a second. It did help, in that I could contain and corral the anger raging in me. Turlo was looking over to where Sorley and Cillian stood talking, just too far away to hear the words over the sweep of the oars.

Sorley said something to Cillian, who looked away, and then back. Sorley reached out a hand to grasp Cillian's shoulder. Cillian spoke, looking grim. What has happened to the Ti'acha, if Linrathe is in the hands of the Marai? What is Sorley telling him? I had given no thought to this in my own overwhelming grief.

Cillian looked over to me. His face softened for the briefest second before his expression changed again, to mastered pain.

"You do care for him? This is not one-sided? For it is certain he cares for you." Turlo said quietly. "I am sorry to pry, but I must know, because it will affect how you both react if we are in danger."

I could access anger. Beyond that was despair. Was everything else I knew gone?

Cillian, still watching me, concern in his eyes. Not everything.

"I love him, Turlo."

"I am glad, lassie," he said. "A thing to be treasured in such a dark world." He held out the flask. "Give your *kärestan* the *fuisce*. He needs it, too."

"Kärestan?"

"I forget you do not know the language. *Käresta* for you, *kärestan* for him. 'Beloved', either way. Not a word any man of the north uses lightly, and," he glanced at Cillian, "certainly not this one, from what I have been told."

Beloved. *Just an endearment.* Another day, it would have made me smile.

At sunset the ship moored against the riverbank. Irmgard and her two women slept on board, it transpired, with guards from the crew. The rest of us slept, or stood watch, along the bank.

Irmgard sent Sorley to offer me a place with them. I thanked him, asked him to tell her no. I helped gather wood and prepare food, falling back with remarkable ease into the routine of making camp with competent, experienced soldiers.

I had taken Cillian the *fuisce*. Sorley had excused himself, leaving us alone. Cillian had uncapped the flask, taken the drink. "Thank the general for me," he said. "I needed that."

"Is it bad? In Linrathe, I mean?"

"Bad enough. Not as bad as your home may be," he added quickly, "because Linrathe is nominally an ally. The *Ti'acha* are somewhat safe. Fritjof doesn't seem to understand what they are for, and someone quick-witted has led them to believe they are houses of holy men and women. He has some concept of that, so he is, for now, leaving the older inhabitants alone. But the younger men, from *Ti'acha* or *torp*, have been conscripted, and as for the girls..." He shook his head.

I frowned, confused. "Why is Lorcann permitting this?"

"No one has told you? Lorcann is a prisoner, or dead, probably the last. He went to Fritjof, and once the agreements were in place, and Marai men among the Linrathan, Fritjof betrayed him."

I no longer cared about time or place. I put my arms around him. "This is not your fault," I said fiercely.

"Is it not?" he replied, his voice as bleak as a winter moor. "I cannot find another way to see it."

"Then it is mine, too."

"No, Lena, it is not."

"The Emperor made his choices, knowing this was a possible outcome." I echoed Turlo's argument.

"He did. But I also saw this outcome, or most of it, and I chose to ignore it. What it would mean, for the people. I put other things first."

"Your life, you mean." I was growing angry.

"Yes. And what is one life, Lena, against all these others?"

"To me, everything. Or had you forgotten?"

"I had not, nor will I, ever." He kissed my head. "Lena, *käresta*, leave me for a while. You have anger to sustain you; you are using it even now. I need to find something to do the same for me."

I left him, going to help with what I could on the ship and then in making camp. I was chopping at a large piece of tree when Sorley came over to give me a hand.

"Whose neck are you imagining?" he asked. I glanced up. He wasn't smiling.

"Fritjof's," I said briefly. "Who is it for you?"

"Lorcann."

We worked in harmony and silence until the wood was in pieces. Carrying it over to the fire, I asked, "Sorley, how did you come to be here? There is more to the story than you told."

"There is," he agreed, stacking wood. "I was acting as a messenger, from *Ti'ach* to *Ti'ach*, as I said. They are centres, for information and supplies and sometimes shelter, if possible, for those of Linrathe who stand against Fritjof. There are quite of few of us, quite a few.

"It was Perras who sent me north, to look for allies among Åsmund's men. I speak the language, and I know the land. I left from the *Ti'ach na Iorlath*, so I could use the mountains as protection. I must have been only a day or so ahead of the general, and one day I was caught by Galen, the general's scout."

"My father," I told him.

"I did not know that!"

"Why would you? I only met him last year, myself. The Empire is a different place than Linrathe, Sorley."

He nodded his agreement. "Anyhow, he had me in bowshot range without me ever hearing him approach, and then disarmed and tied up in about a minute. It wasn't hard to convince him I wasn't Marai—most can't speak your language—but it took a bit more to persuade the general I was an ally. Your name helped. The rest you know."

We carried more wood. "Do you know what happened to Jordis and Niav?" I finally asked.

"No. Only that they were taken away."

"But Perras and Dagney are unharmed?"

"They were when I left. Perras had a bad cough and I know Dagney was worried for him, but the same could be said of many of the last winters."

But those were winters with food and fuel and wine. With a huge army to feed, Fritjof would not leave much for the people. I didn't need to say this. Sorley came from a farming estate; he would know.

"Is there a leader, for the people of Linrathe who oppose Fritjof?"

"No one man. Natural leaders have emerged, but they rally around Ruar's name. Donnalch's son."

"Is he still hostage?"

"He and Kebhan, yes, somewhere in the Empire."

I remembered them, Ruar a boy of twelve or so; his cousin two or three years older, sharing the platform with us when the treaty proclamation had been made. Kebhan would be old enough to fight. Whose side would he be on, were he free to choose?

We finished our work. Sorley dusted his hands off on his breeches. "Can I ask you something now, Lena?"

"Of course," I said.

"Then tell me, if you will. What *have* you done with Cillian?"

Gods, how I needed that laughter. "Oh, Sorley," I said, wiping my eyes, "thank you for that."

He was still chuckling, although the laughter hadn't stripped the sadness from his eyes. "You are most welcome. But there was a serious side to that question, in truth. Although I suppose it is none of my business."

"You can probably guess most of it."

"And the pieces I cannot are truly not for me, or for anyone else but the two of you. But I will say this, Lena: I would have wagered my entire inheritance against the possibility of what I saw him reveal earlier today. I wish—"

"Go on," I said.

He smiled again. "I wish Perras and Dagney could know. Especially Dagney."

"So do I. I know how much she cares for him."

"We all do, you know," he said gently. "Although he frequently makes it difficult. Most of the time, actually," he amended with a quick smile.

"When it was just the two of us and the world was far away, it was remarkably easy, " I said. "But you heard him, Sorley; he is blaming himself for Lorcann's deceit and Linrathe's loss." I looked at the frank, concerned face of the man beside me. "I'm sorry, Sorley. I should not burden you with my private worries."

"But no one else here has known Cillian as long as I have," he said, "and whether he would acknowledge it or not I count him a friend. A dear friend. If there is anything I can do to help, tell me."

After the meal, Sorley went on board the ship and came back with a small *ladhar*. He tuned it and began to play, a gentle tune at first, and then faster ones: drinking songs, I guessed. The oarsman sang lustily. But at some point he changed the tuning a bit, and what he played then were long, slow, sad ballads. He sang the words sometimes, and sometimes just let the music carry the feeling.

Cillian had not appeared. Turlo had come to sit beside me. There was grey in his beard and hair now, I noticed. He didn't ask where Cillian was, for which I was glad.

"The lad's a master on the instrument," he said, "although it would be good to hear music from our land."

I remembered a night at the *Ti'ach*. "He knows one song, at least the tune. I don't know what it's called. The one that begins 'The swallows gather, summer passes?'"

"I know it. Will you sing it with me if he plays it?"

I didn't want to. But it was Turlo asking. I said yes.

Turlo went to speak to Sorley. I watched him explain. Sorley nodded, adjusting the tuning again. He played the first few notes. Turlo came back and held out a hand to bring me to my feet.

I let Turlo's deep voice and the *ladhar* lead.

The swallows gather, summer passes,
The grapes hang dark and sweet;

On the third line, I joined in.

Heavy are the vines,
Heavy is my heart,
Endless is the road beneath my feet.

The sun is setting, the moon is rising,
The night is long and sweet;
I am gone at dawn,
I am gone with day,
Endless is the road beneath my feet.

The cold is deeper, the winters longer,
Summer is short but sweet,
I will remember,
I'll not forget you,
Endless is the road beneath my feet.

The last notes died away. Turlo put an arm around my shoulder. "A sad song, that," he said. He looked up at the sky. "It's not Midsummer yet," he said, "but I wish there were someone to play the *Breccaith* tonight, for all our losses."

I found Cillian sitting by the riverbank. I slipped down beside him. "You missed the music," I said.

"I heard it from here." He put a hand on my shoulder briefly. "I have something to tell you, Lena. You are not going to like it."

A tiny tremor of apprehension ran up my spine. "What?"

"Do you remember asking me about Darcail?"

"The hero? Yes."

"You asked me if I believed we can redeem ourselves, as Darcail did?" He did not look at me, but at the dark ribbon of water in front of us.

"You said you didn't believe in redemption," I reminded him.

"I said I did not know. I still do not. But regardless of what I said, all those days and weeks ago, I find there is only one possible response for me to what has happened in Linrathe."

"What are you saying, Cillian?" The tremor had become a wave.

"I need to try to atone for this terrible thing I put in motion, Lena. I will see this ship safely to the sea, if I can. And then, *käresta*, exile or not, I must go home."

The wave crested, froze, and shattered into a thousand shards of cold anger. "You think you can be a hero?" I derided, "are you a minging idiot? What do you think will happen, Cillian? Even if you could get back on your own, you'd be dead a day later."

"A chance I will have to take, then."

"It would be a waste," I said, as coldly as I could.

"So was Alain's death," he said bleakly. "We argued, you know," he added. "I told him he was a fool, for fighting. As you are saying to me now. We parted badly."

I scrambled to my feet. "And you going off to die will change that? Irmgard offered me a bed on the ship. I think I'll accept it, after all."

He didn't reply. I stalked off, shaking. I couldn't go to the ship like this. I walked upriver, away from the fire and the snoring oarsmen. My legs felt suddenly weak. I dropped to the ground.

I sat a long time, looking out over the river, thinking of what had almost certainly happened at Tirvan, to my sister and my mother and the women I had grown up with, and what my own response had been. Then, memories. The night in Tirvan, when I let Maya go. Sending Tice back on patrol. An afternoon at the winter camp, when Casyn asked me if I would ride north to defend the Empire. An oath sworn. And a private vow made one morning.

I walked back along the riverbank. Cillian was stretched out on the grass, not sleeping, his eyes reflecting starlight as I went to him. I lay down beside him. "You are not going home," I said. "Not until we have taught you some things, and not without me."

CHAPTER EIGHT

HE HAD SIMPLY HELD ME AS WE BOTH WAITED for the night to pass. Neither of us really slept: what my mind conjured at Tirvan, and likely his for Linrathe, did not allow it. Nor did we talk. Near dawn I slipped into a doze, but sounds of the ship being readied woke me soon after. I lay, weary and dispirited, not wanting to face the day. Cillian sat up.

I tried to smile for him. "Hello, my love."

"Lena," he said. He bent to kiss me, briefly. "I have not changed my mind."

"Neither have I." I made myself sit up. "We need to talk to Turlo, though. I asked him for a sword, yesterday; I am out of practice. We need one for you, now, to begin to learn."

"You would make a swordsman of me now?" He was trying for lightness this morning, but it was taking effort.

"Learn to use a sword as quickly as you did the bow, and I'll worry less."

"You will not," he said, serious again. "There was truth in what you said to me last night. But how can I not go back?"

"I understand, Cillian," I said. "I wasn't really angry, just afraid. But I have to go with you."

On board, after we had eaten, Turlo called me over. He handed me a sword. "I thought this looked the right size."

I tried a stroke or two, one guard. My muscles remembered, but the unfamiliar moves would take their toll.

"Thank you, Turlo. But now I have another request. Can you find one for Cillian, too?"

"Cillian? Why?"

"I want him to learn."

Turlo gave me a long, assessing look. "Having a sword in your hand to channel your anger makes sense for you, Lena, as it would—it has—for me. It does not for him. What are you planning, lassie?"

"My planning, General, not Lena's," Cillian said from beside us.

"Aye? And what are you planning, man?"

"To go back to Linrathe once I have helped get this ship to the sea. I owe it to them."

"And I suppose you are going with him?" Turlo turned to me, as angry as I had ever seen him.

"You know I am," I said, meeting his eyes, defying the quickly kindled fury in them.

"Aye. You would, of course. But I will not allow it, for either of you."

"General," Cillian said, "you cannot stop us. We are not yours to command."

Turlo's anger vanished. He chuckled, mercurial as ever. "Ah, man, that is where you are wrong. Come, sit, and let me enlighten you."

He motioned us to the back of the ship. "Sorley," he called, "bring me my satchel, will you? Then come; I may need you, when these two learn what I have to say. Leave the sword, Lena."

I followed him to the stern, confused. Cillian was frowning, and his eyes had that distant look they held when he was analyzing a situation. We found places to sit.

"Comfortable?" Turlo said. "Thank you, Sorley." Sorley settled down beside Cillian. "Now, Lena of Tirvan, Cillian of the Empire, you will listen to what I have to say. But before I start, you might read these, first."

I took the folded paper. The seal was the Emperor's; I had seen it before. I glanced at Cillian. He had not taken his, but his eyes were on Turlo. "Of the Empire?" he repeated softly. "General, tell me he has not?" He laughed, an almost desperate sound.

"He has. Are you surprised? Or are you, the gods forfend, suggesting you do not want to be pardoned?" Turlo asked.

"Pardoned?" I said, or tried to.

"Read it, Guardswoman, but yes, it is a pardon. For you both, although this man of yours doesn't seem to want it. Your man, and mine now, of course. I am your commanding officer, Cillian, because like all men of the Empire, you are, perforce, a soldier."

I wasn't taking this in. "Turlo, what are you talking about?" Pardoned?

He laughed. "D'you both need a mouthful of *fuisce* again? I hadn't planned to spring it on you quite this way, but you forced my hand. It's simple, lassie. Callan has pardoned you both, and by the laws of the Empire you are again bound by the oaths you swore."

"No!" I said. "Wait, Turlo. Do we have any choice in this?"

He looked genuinely surprised. "I don't know, Lena. Pardons are rarely given, and I doubt ever refused."

Oars dipped and fell, and water lapped against the riverbanks. I could hear my own breathing. "Recalled to my oath, you say?" Cillian asked, quietly.

"Aye."

He was, uncharacteristically, struggling for words. "I am," he said finally, "doing my utmost best to keep a private vow, or rather two, ones I do not wish to share. But I cannot meaningfully honour those, yet forswear my public oath. I pledged to serve the Empire, and to accept the judgement of the Emperor as to my fate." He paused, his eyes travelling to me. "Lena, *käresta*, forgive me. I will accept the pardon, and honour the oath I swore."

My heart had begun to pound, listening. I too had made a private vow, and to keep it I had to be by his side. So I had to accept this pardon and be again a soldier of the Empire. Is this what I want? I needed more time to think about it, and there was none. I would do as my heart told me, I thought, fiercely. "There is nothing to forgive," I said, as clearly as I could. "It is only a longer road home. I am still coming with you."

Turlo cleared his throat. "Well," he said, "I am glad that is your decision, both of you, because I was under strict orders to bring you both back."

"Do I swear the oath again?" Cillian asked.

"No. The first swearing holds. Lena's, I witnessed, and I am assured by both the Emperor and his brother that yours was made properly and freely, Cillian." I looked up then, hearing a change in Turlo's voice. He was grinning; Cillian's expression was wry.

"I might argue I was under some duress," he said.

"Aye, you can argue that, if and when there is ever a proper tribunal in which do it."

"Why should the laws of the Empire hold sway on a Marai ship on a river in unclaimed lands?" Was that *amusement* in his voice?

"Unclaimed?" Turlo countered, and I could see he was enjoying this. "I disagree. We have met no one the whole length of this river, nor did you on the grasslands it borders, am I right?"

"You are."

"Then do these lands not still belong to the Eastern Empire?"

"If there is an Eastern Empire, the argument could be made."

"And? Continue the line of reasoning, if you will."

"I had no idea," Sorley said to me under his breath, "your officers were so well versed in dialectics."

"And since the Empire to which I am sworn names itself as subject to the Eastern Empire if it stands, and as heir to it if it does not, then in either case the laws of the Empire are the laws of this land."

"Very good," Turlo said, a broad grin on his face.

"Unless," Cillian added, "the Eastern Empire does still stand, and no longer claims these lands, or, has laws that overrule those of its client Empire. But until we reach Casil to learn if either of these scenarios is true, then my previous statement holds." He was, amazingly, laughing.

"I concede that point," Turlo said. "You'd be wasted as a swordsman, *mo charaidh*. But you'll take instruction with a blade, nonetheless. As for your rank, let me give that some thought."

"General," Cillian said, his voice suddenly serious again.

"Aye?"

"Thank you. You—and the Emperor, of course—have shown me a way to respond to what has happened in Linrathe, and the Empire, honourably. Not by an act of folly, as my first impulse was."

"Do you think we have not all felt that way?" Turlo answered, his voice as serious as Cillian's. "To be here, seeking help on the thinnest thread of legend, rather than fighting for our homes, not knowing what is being lost or won, while we are gone? And if we do go back, only to discover all was lost in our absence, will we not all carry to our deaths the wish that we had stayed, to fight and fall with our brethren?" He fell silent. "I would have been concerned had you not wanted to go back," he added, after a moment, "very concerned. I am glad to know I did not need to be."

A call from the steersman claimed Turlo's attention. I had sat down again, needing to, suddenly, and was staring at the unopened paper in my hand. Too much had happened—again—in a day. I needed time and space to think, but my mind spun with exhaustion.

Cillian held out a hand. I took it, letting him pull me to my feet. He kept his fingers intertwined with mine. "I am sorry about last night," he said. "I should have thought more, and spoken less quickly."

"I would say it was the opposite."

He frowned. "What do you mean?"

"Had you actually talked it out with me, but even better with Turlo or Sorley, you would have heard their side of the argument before this morning and saved us all a lot of heartache." I was, I realized, truly irritated with him. Or I was just too tired and sad to be gentle, and maybe the time for that had passed. Soldiers could not be gentle, very often.

"I suppose. I am not good...have not been good at that sort of conversation. I can only say again: I am sorry, *käresta*."

"Dagney didn't get that far in the lessons, Cillian. How about speaking to me in my own language?"

"Lena," he began, but I cut him off.

"Leave it," I said. "I'm out of sorts. Too much has happened. My turn to ask to be left alone."

When he had left I walked to where the sides of the ship came together in a V. I leaned at the stern, looking down at the water, at the waves the ship's passage made rippling behind. Did I want to be a Guardswoman again? I remembered my words to Callan, at the White Fort, after our trial: 'I welcome this banishment, to be beyond your games.'

But it was all beyond games now; it was hard, bloody, despairing work, with little chance of success. I wondered suddenly what this ship was called. It should be 'Arrow', I thought, because that it what it was: an arrow let fly from a desperate bow, sent into darkness, hoping beyond reason that it would find its target.

And that the target would receive it.

I sat with my back against the boards of the hull, letting the sweep of the oars and the increasing warmth of the sun lull me into sleep. I had nothing to do: sword practice would have to wait until the first rest break. Irmgard had fled with the barest minimum of men, and so the oarsmen had no one—except Turlo and Sorley, and now Cillian and me—to spell them off. A break was needed every two or three hours. Motion and exhaustion collaborated, and I slept.

I woke when the ship stopped. The oarsmen disembarked to eat and stretch out on the grass, or to walk to relieve cramped legs. I fetched my sword and went looking for someone to practice with.

I wasn't about to challenge an unknown Marai man, and as I doubted Irmgard and her women were either interested or competent, I was only looking for Turlo or Sorley. I found Sorley. "How are you with a sword? I asked.

"Adequate. Do you want to practice?"

While he was gone, fetching his sword, I tried my blade again. It felt heavier. Or had my arms just lost the strength gained from years of fishing?

Either way, I could only strike and parry with Sorley for half an hour before my shoulder muscles began to burn. No chance, yet, to work off any of the seething anger. "Enough," I said, after he had forced my blade down yet again.

He grinned. "I can see you know what you're doing. You're just out of practice."

We had attracted spectators. Several of the Marai men had come to watch. One said something to Sorley as we walked back to the ship. It didn't sound complimentary.

"You don't want to know," Sorley said, when I gave him a questioning look.

"Probably not," I agreed. "Where are Turlo and Cillian?"

"They walked downriver," Sorley answered. "Said to stop for them when we met them."

On the water again, I remembered my pardon. I should read it, I thought.

"Do you want to see what a pardon from my Emperor looks like?" I asked Sorley. I broke the seal. Folded inside the parchment was a smaller piece of paper. I read the parchment first. Clearly an official document, it was in precise, formal characters, listing my name and rank, the date my sentence had been handed down, and the date of its rescindment.

I handed it to Sorley. "Brief, but I suppose it says all it needs to." While he scanned it, I unfolded the paper. It was in Callan's own hand.

Guardswoman, if this reaches you, you know the war goes badly. In rescinding your exile, I recall you to duty. When last we spoke, you welcomed exile. If this remains true, then may the soldier's god forgive me. Callan, I.

I swore. Sorley looked up, but a shout from the riverbank claimed our attention. Turlo and Cillian ran towards us. "Horsemen!" Turlo bellowed, pointing. On the far bank, a group of riders, bows drawn, galloped towards us. The oarsmen dropped the oars, leaping to unhook the shields from the side, accepting swords or axes as they were distributed. Shields raised to make a barrier against the coming rain of arrows, weapons in the other hand, poised and ready in a very few minutes. Practiced fighting men.

The horses pounded along the bank. Sword or bow? I had used a bow since girlhood. I ducked behind the line of men, keeping low, running for my bow.

I didn't make it: I didn't have to. One of Irmgard's women pushed it towards me, along with a quiver. "*Takkë!*" I said, reaching for an arrow to nock. Not mine, I noted: these arrows were tipped with metal. Someone had been thinking.

I heard the hail of arrows hitting the shield wall, a grunt of pain as one found flesh, the incomprehensible commands of the strangers' leader. More arrows fell. Who was the leader? I crawled forward.

A flight of arrows whipped across the river, towards the horsemen. Who?—

and then I realized: Irmgard and her women. I had misjudged, once again.

"The dark-haired man on the horse with the red tassels on its reins," I said to Sorley. "Get the men to cover me."

I focused on the leader and let a bit of my sheathed anger free to block out anything else. From behind the shields I aimed and drew. The shields parted to let the arrow fly; a moment later, again, for the second arrow. The first hit the man in the thigh; the second the horse, in the neck. Neither shot should have killed, not from my small bow. But horse and man fell, one screaming in rage, one in pain, and the force of the fall drove the arrow deep into the man's thigh.

Blood gouted, a crimson, pumping flood. "He's dead," Sorley said. The horseman milled, shouted, let fly a few more arrows. One dismounted, cleanly dispatching the injured horse, and then remaining beside his dying leader.

I felt the ship moving, being pushed across the river. Men vaulted over the side, shields up, swords or axes raised, Marai battle cries on their lips. They were going for the horses, I realized, slashing at legs and bellies, stabbing upward to disembowel. Without their horses, our attackers stood no chance. The four left died quickly.

The oarsmen returned, laughing. They vaulted back onto the ship, put their weapons and shields away, and pushed the ship back to the other bank where Turlo and Cillian waited.

"Well done, Lena," Turlo said, clapping me on the shoulder after climbing aboard. "Thank Irmgard," I managed. "I just aimed the arrows." The smell of blood and guts and excrement threatened to overwhelm me. I turned away, willing myself not to vomit. I walked away quickly to retch over the side of the ship. Five men, now, the little voice in my mind said.

"Leave her," I heard Turlo say. "Killing takes some soldiers this way."

I stayed by the rail longer than I needed to, staring away from the carnage. Footsteps made me turn; I still disliked being approached from behind. One of Irmgard's women offered me water. "*Takkë,*" I said, taking the waterskin. I rinsed my mouth, spat, swallowed several mouthfuls, handed it back. "*Takkë,*" I said again. She shook her head.

"*Na.*" She pointed at herself, then at me. "*Takkë.*"

I smiled as best I could and mimed shooting an arrow, pointing at her and nodding. She gave me a delighted smile back, half-curtseyed, and went back to Irmgard.

"Lena," Cillian said from a distance behind me. "Are you all right?" I shrugged. "They would have killed us without compunction," he pointed out.

"I know," I said, irritation flaring. "I've done this before. It doesn't necessarily make it easier."

"Is there anything I can do?"

"No. Yes. Stop being so understanding all the time." I buried my face in my hands. I felt him lean on the rail beside me. "Cillian," I said, "please go away."

He went. I made my way to the V of the stern and curled up against it. I could hear raised voices near the prow: Turlo and Geiri. The ship didn't move. I wanted to be back in the grasslands. I wanted the only thing I killed to be grouse. I wanted not to be a soldier.

But I had to be. I had a vow to keep and a terrible anger inside me that had to be answered. My mother and sister and all the women who had raised me and nurtured me and loved me were desecrated and dead, or enslaved. All the fears that had driven us to change our way of life two years previously when Leste had threatened us with invasion had come true. I had fought then without compunction. I would do it again.

I walked the twenty paces or so to the prow where the others were deep in conversation. Men were taking down the sail. I wondered why. "Lena," Turlo said. "Welcome. We are discussing what to do."

"What do we know?" I asked.

"Very little. So, at this point, reconnaissance is needed. I am going scouting tonight, and until then we will move slowly south with the four of us on lookout."

"Seven," Irmgard said firmly. "There are seven of us. You have more planning to do. Let me and Hana and Rind watch first while you talk."

"Aye," Turlo said after a moment's consideration. "That would be helpful. Lena, will you instruct the women?" Turlo had taught me, and the other Guards, how to keep watch on the Wall. I remembered him telling us to look for what wasn't there, as well as what was. I hoped I could make these women understand.

We moved a little way distant. "I will translate," Irmgard said. "Hana and Rind do not speak your language."

"And I have only one or two words of yours," I admitted. "So, keeping watch: you are looking for movement, of course, but that is not all." Over the next ten minutes I explained about watching the behaviour of birds and animals, of movement in grasses or trees that was against the wind, of looking in all directions, including behind us. "Try to use all your senses: listen for unexpected or out-of-place sounds, sniff the air."

Rind—the woman who had brought me water—said something, and Irmgard smiled. "Rind says the horsemen will stink, and not just of their horses, so maybe we will smell them."

"Maybe," I agreed. I told them where to position themselves on the ship. Then I returned to the discussion.

"I'm just wondering how many people we need to do this.," Sorley was saying. "The more of us there are, the more chance of detection."

"Aye," Turlo said. "We'll need at least ten or twelve, I would think: four to deal with the horses, perhaps, and the rest for the village. Again, I'll know more after tonight."

"Can I come with you?" I asked. I felt, rather than saw, Cillian's start of protest.

"No," Turlo said. He held up a hand to stop me from speaking. "I have been doing this for over thirty years and I prefer to scout alone. I need you here heading the watches; you are the most experienced at that. That's an order, Guard," he added, smiling.

"General," I acknowledged, unwillingly.

"Do you have anything to contribute to our planning?"

"Don't assume the women won't, or can't, fight," I said, remembering my own expectations about the Marai women earlier. Turlo chuckled.

"You would think we would remember that, given our strategy against Leste," he said. "Good to remind us all, though."

But a horrifying thought had followed. "Turlo," I said, "there will be children."

"Yes," he said slowly. "Yes, there will be children."

No one spoke. Sorley looked shocked. Cillian's face was remote. "It would make us little better than Fritjof," I said.

"Find us an alternative," Turlo said simply.

"Bribe them?" Cillian said. "Offer tribute, whatever we can gather now, with promises of more when we return?"

"It is a huge risk," Turlo argued.

"What if we capture their horses," I asked, "and demand safe passage in return? If they value them as highly as you suggest they might, would that work?"

"Maybe," Turlo said thoughtfully. He glanced at the sun, dipping westward. "I need to sleep a little. Wake me at dusk, if you will." He had, I knew, the soldier's knack of sleeping anywhere, at any time. He'd be snoring in five minutes.

Sorley stood. "I need to clear my mind," he said. "I'll be at the stern."

Neither Cillian nor I spoke for some moments. "I cannot kill children," I said finally.

"Nor can I," he answered. "I have learned to kill animals, but I am still not sure I can kill a man." He held out his hand. I took it, entwining my fingers in his. I had something I needed to say.

"Earlier," I said, "I'm sorry. *Forla, kärestan.*"

A smile flickered. "Your pronunciation is appalling," he murmured. "Who told you?"

"Turlo. Not intentionally. I don't know why I thought it mattered so much."

"For all the reasons it matters to me that you have just used my cradle tongue. Thank you, my love."

I put my arms around him, needing his touch, his solidity, against the horror of what we were confronting. He wrapped his arms around me, resting his head on my hair. I turned my cheek into his chest, closing my eyes, gathering strength. When I opened them again, I saw Sorley, at the stern, looking at us. Even over the twenty or so paces I could see that it was Cillian he held in his gaze, and I could see, too, the longing on his face.

CHAPTER NINE

I CLOSED MY EYES AGAIN, TURNING MY HEAD AWAY. But I must have tensed. "What is it?" Cillian murmured. I felt him move his head. "Sorley," he said after a moment. "I had hoped that was done with."

"He was the boy you spoke of, who wrote music for you?"

"Yes. This is not the place to talk of it, Lena. Wait until we have some privacy."

"Lena!" Irmgard, calling me. She was pointing downriver. "Something moving." I went to look. The bushes at the far riverbank, some distance ahead, were indeed moving. I held up a hand to Geiri, who snapped a command at the oarsmen. The ship slowed. I watched, intent. A large head pushed out of the bushes, bent to drink. Deer. I relaxed.

I spent the next hours on watch. After the first hour we began to move again, slowly. I gave Sorley and Cillian the same brief lesson on attention, and told the women to rest. I knew from the Wall it was difficult to concentrate for too long: our shifts there had been four hours, for trained and experienced Guards.

Turlo woke in the late afternoon. Movement in the sky behind us, the way we had come, had just caught my eye; when I saw he was awake I called him over.

"What is it, lassie?" he asked, immediately alert.

"Carrion-birds." I pointed. "Where we killed the horses." And the men.

He swore under his breath. "If their fellows have missed them, those birds will arouse suspicion."

"Or perhaps they will think the birds are attracted by the remains of butchered deer?"

"Aye, maybe. But that too will make them wonder why the hunters don't return, maybe not tonight, but tomorrow. We will have to act tonight if possible."

He gave quick commands as dusk fell. No fires. No music or singing, nothing that could be heard across the plain. Weapons to hand. No one to go further than ten paces from the ship. "Lena," he said. "You are next in rank to me; you are in command here until I return. Lady Irmgard, your men will follow Lena's commands." It wasn't a question.

"Certainly," she said, and after a quick exchange with Geiri, he too nodded.

"*Ja*," he said. "*Ja*."

A few slices of cold meat, a swallow or two of water, and Turlo was ready to go. "Listen for the wood-owl," he said, and then as the ship came close to the left-hand bank he slipped over the side and was gone.

It is hard to wait, in silence, in the dark, and remain alert. We had no idea how far Turlo had to go, or when to expect him. The moon—only three days past new—would not rise until dawn. I sat, and then I paced, and sat again, away from Cillian. I couldn't let him distract me. Some of the men played a betting game with their fingers, in complex patterns I couldn't understand, and in complete silence. I thanked whatever gods there might be for trained men.

When it was very late, I went to stand against the side, trying to see out onto the dark plain. A slight breeze blew from the west. Cillian came to stand beside me, and then Sorley.

"Z-wit!" I sagged in relief. Turlo came out of the dark and the men reached for him. He landed easily on the deck. "Water?"

He drank deeply. "Now," he said, wiping his mouth. "Good news. There is no village, or none that I can find. There is another party of hunters, about two hours east of here. We will need to deal with them before dawn. The carrion-birds Lena saw earlier will be back in the morning and attract attention."

"How many should go, and who?" Sorley asked.

"Six should do it. There are five men again. Sorley, can you butcher an animal?"

"Yes," he said. "Pigs and sheep, many times."

"Horses?"

"If I must."

"Good. Will you come?"

"I will," he answered.

"Ask Geiri for his best four men," Turlo directed.

It took less than ten minutes for them to be ready, and gone into the night.

"We should sleep," Cillian said, a few minutes later. I shook my head.

"I can't, not yet. Maybe in a while. Can we talk?"

"About?"

"Sorley, first?"

He looked troubled. "There is no reason we cannot leave the ship now?" he confirmed. "Then let's walk," he said. "This will take some time, and Irmgard—although I believe she is asleep—can understand us." We climbed over to the riverbank. The night was very dark.

"It began some years ago," Cillian said, when we were far enough away. He pitched his voice low, regardless. "Sorley came to the Ti'ach as a young man of eighteen, as many of the landholder's sons do, to learn from Dagney and for some exposure to wider thought before returning to take up their duties to their people. I was at the Ti'ach that year, after a time away, and Perras asked me to oversee some of his work.

"Had I wished to be something more than simply his teacher, Sorley would have welcomed it. I did nothing to encourage him; in fact, after a discussion with Perras, I was suddenly needed at a different Ti'ach."

"Poor Sorley." A night bird called, twice, and was silent.

"I thought it was an infatuation, nothing more."

"And if you had realized it wasn't?"

"No." He shook his head. "Not," he said, at my questioning look, "because he is a man. I will admit to an attraction. But I had nothing to give him, and by that time I knew myself well enough to understand that." He paused. "I had, just that year, decided that celibacy was preferable. I was determined to keep to that."

"Maybe he had something to give you."

"Lena, he was a boy of eighteen from remote Sorham, wholly incapable of dealing with me. I would have torn his heart out."

"And I am from a fishing village, and only three years older," I pointed out.

"You are much older than he was, in so many ways, Lena. You understand that the world is not always kind, and you have loved before. Nor am I the same man, quite, that I was then."

"I think his heart may be torn, regardless," I murmured.

"It may be," he agreed, "but I have done my best to not be culpable, except by just existing. You seem perhaps overly sympathetic to Sorley."

"I am."

"Why?"

I turned the thought around. "How would you feel, if I did not love you?"

"As if I had been exiled from life itself again," he said without hesitation.

Oh, Cillian. Had I truly thought you cold and distant, once? It took me a second to respond. "Sorley might say the same."

"I cannot believe he can feel that way, without encouragement, without anything between us except proximity." I heard frustration in his voice.

"But he does," I said gently. "To still show it after six years and much separation? He must. And now you and he are together again, on a small boat, and he knows something he didn't before."

"Which is?" The river flowed on beside us, glittering under the stars.

"He sees us together. Don't you see how much worse that makes it for him?"

He exhaled. "Yes," he said after some time. "But, Lena, what can I do?"

"I don't know," I said honestly. "But Turlo needs to be apprised."

"Why?"

The question surprised me. "For the same reason he asked me what was between the two of us. Because it affects how we react when the other is in danger."

"Of course. A foolish question."

"Cillian," I said sharply. "This is not your fault, nor mine, but neither is it Sorley's. I think we only have two obvious choices: to ignore the situation, or to confront it. In either case Turlo needs to be told. I am guessing that this is not the first time he'll have had to deal with something like this."

"No," Cillian said tiredly. "I will talk to Sorley. A conversation that I expect to be as difficult as any I have had as a man."

"You have survived them all," I said, lightly.

"Yes," he replied. "But a friendship—or what I thought was a friendship—that I have so recently come to value may not." He turned, looking back at the ship. "But I will need to do this alone."

"Of course," I said. "Tell him what you just told me, Cillian. But be kind. Don't mock, either Sorley or yourself."

"Myself? You would deny me even that protection?" The reflexive response.

A revealing choice of words, I thought.

"I would, on this," I said slowly. "Cillian, if you had not got past that defence with me, I might not be here with you now. You know that. Doesn't Sorley deserve the same honesty?"

"I will try, Lena. That's all I can promise." There was a trace of impatience in his voice. We kept walking. "Whatever else is on your mind, Lena, it will have to wait," Cillian said after a few paces. "I am beyond tired, and there are things weighing heavily on me."

"You should have told me that."

"Well, Sorley was one of them, and you have helped me see what I must do there." I could hear the fatigue now. I searched for words.

"If I can help with the others, you will ask?"

"Of course, *käresta*. He stopped. "Do we have to sleep on the ship? I would like some space."

"We don't have to," I said. "The night is warm enough."

Cillian, I think, was asleep in five minutes. I lay beside him, watching his steady breathing. *As if I had been exiled from life itself again*, he had said. But none of us could see our fates, and I was a sworn soldier, with a bloody, desperate war awaiting me.

Why did anyone choose to love, to accept this terrible, heart-breaking responsibility to another?

Later, before dawn, his voice, whispering my name, woke me. I lay still for a moment, letting my first startled reaction calm. "Yes?" I said sleepily. His hand roved down my body, his touch and his clear need quickly evoking a response from me. I rolled over. His hands and lips were more insistent than I had ever known, and underneath my undeniable arousal was a tiny quiver of fear. I buried my face in his shoulder, breathing in his scent, focusing on the sensations his hands were creating. He swung himself over me. "Keep your weight off me," I whispered.

"I will," he said, and then his mouth came down on mine and we lost ourselves in the rhythm and demands of love. Release, for both of us, came quickly, and he collapsed over me, breathing hard. But the feel of his body on mine did not overwhelm me. It just felt—natural.

Except, as I realized after a minute, he was falling asleep again. "Cillian," I said, "you're heavy."

"Mmm?" he murmured, and then, "oh, gods." He pushed himself off me. "*Käresta, forla, forla*. Are you all right?"

"I am," I said, unable to keep from smiling. "I am more than all right. Go back to sleep, my love."

He rolled on his side. I curled beside him. Wounds do heal, I thought, as sleep claimed me.

But a wound healed on the surface may still be open, underneath. In the dream that came soon after, it was Ivor's weight on me that I struggled against, fear coursing through me. I woke wet with sweat, my heart pounding. I lay still, trying to calm myself. Tears puddled in my eyes and overflowed. Would I ever be free of the memory, or would it always be there, insinuating itself between Cillian and me, blighting what we shared? If his touch began to elicit this reaction, how could I cope? I made myself turn, move closer to him. I lay breathing in his scent, a tang of sweat overlaying the essential smell of his skin, comforting, safe.

I was still awake at first light when I heard sounds from the plain. My thoughts had gone down another path, perhaps even bleaker. I scrambled up. Cillian stirred. "Turlo?" he asked, sleepily.

I knelt to kiss him. "Hello, my love. Yes."

Relief lightened my mood. As they came closer I could see Sorley, leading a horse laden with something. The oarsmen walked slowly, but other than one with a rough bandage around his arm, they appeared unharmed. Turlo brought up the rear, visibly tired.

It had all gone smoothly, he reported, revived by a tankard of the sour beer. There had been, as he had judged, five more men. The horsemen had hunted successfully earlier in the day and several gutted and bled carcasses lay in the camp. "My only misjudgment," Turlo admitted, "was the number of horses. I should have realized they would have pack ponies. But Sorley handled that."

"I did what I had to. Some I killed, and some I let run from the smell of blood, and this one I kept in case it was needed to ride back to the ship for help," Sorley said quietly. "I'll let it loose now."

Oarsmen gathered wood to roast the two butchered deer brought back from the camp. The other plunder from the raid was bows, larger, stronger bows, and the long arrows to go with them.

The fires burned down enough to begin to roast the meat. Rind cleaned the injured oarsman's arm and bound it again: he had taken an arrow, shallowly. Still, it meant one of us—or Geiri—would have to take his place rowing, for a few days.

"We'll eat, and then sleep, and move on again in five or six hours," Turlo directed, as the smell began to remind me we had eaten only scant, cold food last night. I swore under my breath, remembering: no fires had meant no hot water. I had forgotten the anash. It shouldn't matter—but neither should I take the chance.

I went back to the ship to find my pack and my supply of dried leaves. As I dug for the small bag, my fingers found the parchment of my pardon. I wondered, suddenly, if Cillian had read his, and if Callan had sent him a private note too. Was that one of things on his mind? So many things crowding us, now.

I made the tea at the edge of one of the fires. Turlo sat on a log, alone: I took my tea over to sit with him.

"Lena," Turlo greeted me. "I did not ask; were there any problems yesterday?"

"None," I answered. "The Marai women did well on watch, and the men are more than competent, as I'm sure you know."

"Aye," he said. "I am glad it was a hunting camp we raided, not a village, Lena, for your sake."

"No children," I said. "Yes, so am I."

"No children," he mused. "But one boy, perhaps thirteen."

Almost the same age as Darel. "Oh," I breathed.

"I made sure he died cleanly and quickly," Turlo said. "It was all I could do. He would have been a man by their measure, or he would not have been there."

"Like Darel," I said. "Turlo, I—"

"Callan gave me your note," he said roughly. "It was kind, lassie. I kept it."

"Turlo," I asked suddenly, "what happens to soldiers who cannot kill?"

He turned a questioning look on me. His eyes, as blue as the sea, had lost some of their brightness this past year. "It depends," he replied. "In peace, we find them another role, for a while or forever. There is always a need for men to work with the horses, or cook, or teach cadets. Even in war, if the killing has brought them to a state where they are dangerous to their comrades, we will relieve them if we can. But there are times when they must honour their oaths, when every man is needed." He cocked his head. "Are you asking for yourself, lassie? I saw that killing takes you hard, yesterday."

"I have killed five times," I said, "and it gets harder, I think, not easier."

"That is not a bad thing." He paused. "Five, Lena? I know of four: the two at Tirvan, the fisherman, and yesterday."

How like Turlo to remember. "The fifth was a Kurzemë man."

"You killed one of the people who took you in? Why?"

I hadn't even said the words to Cillian, not fully. I shook my head.

"Oh, lassie," he said. "I think I can guess. But you killed him, after?"

"Yes."

He put his hand over mine. "I am so sorry." We sat silent for some time, his fingers stroking my hand gently. "Cillian must know?" he asked finally.

"Yes. I am—all right. We are all right, together." I felt myself blushing.

"You are brave, Lena," he said, "and there are depths to Cillian I should not be surprised by, if blood tells." My lip trembled at his words. "Lassie, what is it?"

"I am so afraid I will lose him, because he says he does not think he can kill, and I have, and will." I bit back a sob.

"Which is how you lost your Maya," Turlo said slowly. I nodded. "Lena, all I can tell you is what I tell any of my young soldiers, when one is a swordsman and the other on the horselines, or a medic, and they come to me with this dilemma. It is something that must be worked out between the two of you. But remember this: Cillian was ready to go back, untrained and alone, and he could not have imagined that doing such would not involve killing, at least in self-defence, and that is all you have ever done."

Turlo's calm logic soothed me. "I should not have bothered you with this, and especially not right now, when you are tired." I said.

"Of course you should. It is part of my job. But you do need to talk to Cillian,

Lena, and," he added, "you need to tell me the outcome, mind, once you are sure."

"I will. I understand why you need to know."

"Aye. Just as I did need to know what happened to you at the Kurzemë village," he said gently. "It matters."

I supposed it did. I nodded.

"This is new between you and your man, lassie?" he asked. An unexpected question.

"We have been lovers since midwinter. But truly loving each other? Since the spring."

"I might wish we had not found you until Casil, then, to have given you more time. I am no expert on love, Lena, although I was true to my Arey for all her life. But you are barely together, and now you have had to hear hard, hard news, and been asked to make difficult decisions, all in a space of a day or two. It is a very great deal to ask of a love as new as yours." He sighed. "But life is rarely how we would order it. Are you all right now, Lena?"

"I am. Thank you."

He grinned, his eyes suddenly bright. "I hope you work it out, lassie, because when two of my young soldiers cannot reconcile, I can always reassign one to another company. What I could do with the two of you, on a small ship, I have no idea."

I ate my share of venison before finding a flattish place on the grass to sleep. I'd been awake all night again. Sorley was also sleeping, so there was no one to practice swordplay with, and I didn't think I had the energy, anyhow.

When I woke, Cillian sat on the grass beside me. "How long have you been there?" I asked.

"An hour, maybe. I wasn't going to wake you."

"You didn't." I sat up, yawning. "Did you eat?" I took a second look at him. He had cut his beard off and shaved. His jaw was pale now, compared to the rest of his face. "When did you shave?"

"Before I came over to sit by you. Lena, did you read your pardon?"

"Yes, and the note Callan wrote, as well. Did you?"

"Yes." He lay back, hands behind his head, staring at the sky. "I had a note from Callan too. That's why I went walking, to think about its implications."

"I guessed that. Mine gave me pause, too."

"Tell me?"

"It isn't much. Just that he asked the soldier's god for forgiveness if I would have preferred to stay exiled over being recalled to duty. I can't decide if he's sincere, or trying for sympathy. Playing games, again." The bitterness that had crept into my voice surprised me.

"I believe it is sincere. The days for game-playing are past at home, Lena," he said quietly.

"Why are you so sure?"

Cillian sat up again. "That will take some time to tell. Do you want to listen?"

"Of course."

He took his note from Callan from a pocket. "Read this first, then I'll explain."

Cillian, if this reaches you, you know the war goes badly. In rescinding your exile, I recall you to duty in the Empire, as your oath to me allows. You know more of the Marai than any other man I can trust. We need that knowledge, if we are to have any chance to prevail. I require you by my side, to advise me. Callan, **P, I**

"What do the letters after his name mean?" I had meant to ask Sorley earlier. "Mine was signed in the same way, but only with the **'I'**."

"The **'I'** is the first letter of the Casilan word for Emperor. It is how all Emperors indicate their rank, back to ancient days."

"And the **'P'**, on yours?"

"Casilan, again. An abbreviation for 'father'. Which is what gave me pause, as you put it. Because the order and size of the letters tells me—and he would have known I would understand—that he is writing first as my father, and only secondly as the Emperor."

"He said he would be proud to acknowledge you," I said slowly, remembering.

"And I him, it seems." A wry smile, quickly gone. "Lena, what this note raised for me are questions of loyalty, and where my allegiances lie. About private vows and public ones. But for you to understand those questions at all—and I am not sure I do, completely—I must tell you about the last night at the White Fort."

"Tell me, then." I shifted, to sit cross-legged, facing him.

"You and Casyn stayed behind in the hall while I went with Callan, remember?"

I thought back. "Yes. I had a note to write, to Turlo."

"The Emperor took me to a smaller room where a fire burned, chairs near it. There was more wine, and food, and maps and scrolls spread out on tables. It must have been his private chamber. He said 'Cillian, this will be the only hour I am likely to ever have with my son. Will you do me the honour of speaking with me, for that time?'

"It would have been discourteous of me to refuse; he had, after all, just saved our lives. So I sat, and accepted wine, and at first we talked of the Marai, and how he might induce Lorcann to remain loyal, and then a bit more widely, about the Eastern Empire. I could do this; it was little different than a hundred other conversations I have had, over wine, late at night, with an *Eirën* or a *Harr* or even with the *Teannasach*. Then Casyn came in—you had gone to bed?"

"Yes. Birel came for me."

"With Casyn there, we spoke a bit about the trial itself, but in a detached manner, another discussion of tactics. But by now it was very late, I was very tired, and I had had quite a bit of wine. All things I had been well-taught to avoid in any sort of diplomatic talks—and that was how I was thinking of the conversation. Casyn made some jest at the expense of Callan and I reacted, openly, without restraint, I suppose you could say. I saw my father go rigid, and I am not exaggerating, Lena. It took Callan a minute to speak, but when he did, he told me, 'You have your mother's smile'. He said it was the first thing he noticed about her, smiling up at him at the gate, asking for permission to bring cheese in to trade.

"I couldn't frame a response to that—it was so unexpected—so I said nothing. The room was very quiet for a while. Callan hadn't taken his eyes off me. Finally, he spoke again. 'I look at you, Cillian,' he said, 'and I see the two people I loved most in this life: Wenna, and my dead twin. I wish you could have known Colm; you would have had so much in common.'

"'I have read his letters to Perras of the *Ti'ach*,' I remember saying. 'A fine mind.'

"'And so much more', he answered. 'I would wish that he had had your choices, Cillian, for the price he paid to be a man of scholarship rather than of arms was too high, far too high. But had you known him, you might have learned something else from him.'

"I remember Casyn said something to him, very quietly. Callan stood then; I could see the agitation in him. I started to stand too, but Casyn indicated for me to stay seated, so I did. 'I will speak,' Callan said. 'Surely a man has the right to give his only son advice once in his life? I had less than a day to gather intelligence about this man who might be my son, and then only these last few hours to judge for myself. There was a common thread in what I was told: a brilliant, incisive, analytic mind, but a cold, cynical, isolated man.'"

"And you said?" I could imagine Callan saying this, in his calm manner.

"'A fair description', I believe."

"No." I shook my head decisively. "Even then, Cillian, I would not have agreed. Not quite."

"That was what Casyn said."

"I'm not surprised. Go on?"

"Callan said, 'I agree with my brother, I think. But to me that description is far too close to the heart of you, and that is why I wish you could have known Colm. I cannot know what your losses have been, and your pain, although I wish I might, but they cannot be what Colm lost: his manhood, any chance of physical love, any chance of children. But he was never bitter, never angry, and he cared about people, all sorts of people, as Lena may have told you. I do not know what you will find in exile, Cillian, but if I could have one wish for the life that I have saved this night, it would be this: that you find your humanity. For your beautiful, laughing, mother's sake, and for your own. *Let men see and know a man who lives as he was meant to live.*'"

Cillian's voice had changed, telling me these last words. Earlier, it had been the precise recitation from a memory trained to recall. These words he would have remembered, training or not, I thought.

He exhaled, a long sigh. "What does one say to that? Perras and Dagney had said similar things to me in the past, and even Alain, once, but," he paused, "but somehow, it did matter that the man now speaking the advice was my father, and was both invoking my mother's name, and quoting Catilius. And that he had saved my life."

"What did you say?" I asked softly.

"Nothing. Those were almost the last words my father said to me. He held out his arms; I allowed the embrace. I hope I returned it. And then he left the room."

He ran a hand through his hair. "And that brings me to my dilemma. Because I made a promise to myself, in my mother's name and his, that I would do this; I would get past the justifications I had made to myself for being that cold, cynical, isolated man I was reputed to be, and find, as he asked, my humanity. Because of course," he added, "I should be able to do that, with my—what was it?—brilliant, incisive, analytic mind."

"I would say you have succeeded." He would always mock, I thought, although now it was usually turned on himself.

"Perhaps. A bit. Enough to see something I may not have before."

"Which is?"

"I owe my father a debt, I believe. I owe my Emperor allegiance, as uncomfortable a concept that is to me. The man has asked me, in both guises, to come to his side, which is why I believe the need is real. But by accepting the pardon, and therefore acknowledging that I will do as he has both asked and commanded, I am breaking, I think, my second private vow."

"You *think* you are breaking it?"

"It concerns you, as you may have guessed, *käresta*. Will you tell me something? Would you have accepted the pardon, with all its implications, if I had turned it down? Would you still prefer exile, Lena?"

After sleep the answer was clear. "I wish with all my heart that we were still wandering free and unencumbered on the grasslands, or camping by the lake," I said. "But Casyn told me once that how we respond to the circumstances of our lives is what shapes us, as men and women, and I must respond to what has happened at home. The only meaningful way to do so is to accept the pardon and become a soldier again." I paused, ordering my thoughts. "But I did not want to. Cillian, I lay awake all last night struggling with the same dilemma. In honouring my oath to the Empire, I too may break a private vow, one I made to you."

He reached out a hand to me. I took it, entangling just his fingertips in mine. "Tell me one thing," he asked. "Can your vow be kept only if we are together, as mine requires?" I nodded, not trusting words. He hesitated, his voice diffident, suddenly. "I will tell you, if you want."

"No," I answered. "Don't tell me. I'd rather not, either—unless you truly want to know?"

"No. Not now. If there is a future past war and grief, when circumstances are less likely to force us to break them, perhaps then."

"If there is a future past war and grief, Cillian, and we are alive to see it, I will speak any vow you wish, private or public," I said fiercely. His fingers tightened on mine, but when he spoke, it was lightly.

"Be careful of what you offer, Lena; I may hold you to that, someday."

"You might not want to, Cillian. War asks terrible things of us, and you may not—want me, afterwards." I had not planned for this conversation, now, but here it was.

"Because you have killed, you mean?" He was too perceptive, sometimes.

"I loved Maya, Cillian, and she left me because she would not kill, or even fight, and I would. I know the idea revolts you, too, and there is already blood on my hands, and there will be more. If that makes me repulsive to you as well…" I trailed off. What would I do, if it did?

"It will not," he said firmly. "This was one of the things on my mind; I will not pretend otherwise. It would be different if you killed without compunction, or the gods forbid, for pleasure, but I saw what the act does to you, yesterday, and that death was barely your doing. And—" He looked away, and then back. "I should not have said I did not think I could kill. I would have killed Ivor, had I known, and had I had the chance. I am clear on that, in my own mind."

"His is the one killing that does not haunt me," I admitted.

"Nor should it." He grinned suddenly, shifting the mood. "I suppose I *had* better learn how to use a sword, had I not?"

I laughed. "Yes. But learn from Turlo; I am not capable of the finer points of swordplay. I spent more time falling over it than using it, at the beginning. You need a more competent instructor."

"Something you are not good at?" he replied. "I confess myself surprised."

CHAPTER TEN

I CAUGHT UP TO TURLO AS WE BOARDED THE SHIP. "All is well," I told him. He acknowledged my words with a quick smile.

"I am glad, lassie. Cillian," he called, "come over here. Time for you to start learning the sword."

There was nothing for me to do. Geiri had not let any of us take over the injured oarsman's place. "He says we are all too weak, and we will throw off the rhythm," Sorley explained. "Either he will row, or we will go more slowly, with ten pairs." My short sleep hadn't really revived me: fatigue felt as if it had seeped into my bones. What I really wanted was to be alone, to sort through the last few days, to give way to the terrible grief that lay heavily inside me. But there was no chance of that.

I listened to Turlo, instructing Cillian on grip and stance. My thoughts drifted back to Casyn, teaching the same things to us on the field at Tirvan. But I couldn't think about Tirvan, not here, not now. I swallowed, and focused again on Turlo's words: it wouldn't hurt me to hear this again, I thought.

Sorley sat down beside me. "Did you want to practice, when we stop?"

"Yes, of course. Did you still want to build a target?"

I considered. "Yes. We should practice with the new bows, so we will need one."

"We'll need to cut withies on the bank, then, to weave a frame. I can't think of anything else to use."

We watched again in silence. The space at the stern was too small for real practice, but Turlo was having Cillian try the positions of the basic guards. I tried to watch with the dispassionate eye I had used to judge my cohort's knife skills. Cillian had been agile enough in the mountains, and he had an inherent grace that had served him in learning the bow, but nothing that he had done in the past had prepared him for the sword. I had had strong arms and shoulders, from fishing, and I had struggled. As he was doing, now. I wondered how he would react when the oarsmen, inevitably, laughed.

I glanced at Sorley, and immediately away again. I wanted to say something to him, to try to ease what I saw on his face, but this was not for me to acknowledge. "Let's look at those hunting bows," I suggested.

His face cleared. "A good idea," he said. We found the bows, piled against the side. I didn't recognize the wood of the staves, striped with varying hues of golden-brown. They were beautiful, and well-made, but nicked and rough to the touch in places. Sorely went off, returning with a pot of grease and some pieces of woollen cloth. We began to rub the grease into the wood, feeling it become smooth under our fingers.

I was testing the flexibility of one bow, and its ease of stringing, when Turlo and Cillian joined us. Cillian, flushed with exertion, was breathing quickly. I grinned at him. "You're going to be sore," I warned.

"So Turlo tells me," he said wryly.

"One those bows is yours, lassie," Turlo said. "Choose for yourself, and the arrows you need."

I continued evaluating the bows for size and suppleness, finally choosing one with a darker streak through the wood: I liked it, and it was quickly recognizable. Sorting through the arrows, I took six, but in my judgement most needed fletching again: the feathers were ragged. Easy enough to find new ones, on a river where ducks were plentiful. I would see what I could shoot at the next mooring.

"Who are the other bows meant for?" I asked.

"Whoever can shoot them; myself and Sorley, if needed." Turlo replied.

"Cillian, too," I added.

He turned to Cillian. "You can shoot?"

"A bit."

"A bit?" I said. "Turlo, he shot a running bear in the eye. He is very good."

"That," Turlo said, "does not surprise me in the slightest."

"May I teach Irmgard and her women?" I asked. "They are competent with the small bow, so it shouldn't take much teaching."

"Why not? If the women agree."

We moored again in mid-afternoon and disembarked: Cillian and Turlo to work on some basic strokes, and I to shoot ducks. I wanted the longest, strongest flight feathers, and from a grown bird I could hope for four or five per wing. Three ducks would give me the feathers I needed.

It was quick work. The common green-headed duck of the river seemed to have little fear of people, and they tended to keep close to the sides. I left the carcasses and my bird bow on board—I could work on fletching as we travelled—and went to see if Sorley needed help.

He wasn't gathering withies, as I had assumed, but watching Turlo and Cillian, along with some of the oarsmen. Our swords lay on the grass beside him. Turlo was demonstrating a strike, transitioning with it from Eagle's Guard into the Horn Guard. He moved smoothly, economically, but he lacked the pure grace of Casyn with a sword. I wondered if Callan handled a sword like his brother. I thought it likely he did.

"Our turn," Sorley said. I picked up my sword and followed him out onto the field. I took a quick look at the sky, at the sun's position and the lack of clouds. Then I let my mind go back to Tirvan, and the feelings I had been suppressing.

"Call the guards and strikes," Turlo told us. I positioned my sword in Snake's Guard, called it, and began to swing.

I saw Sorley's eyes widen slightly after the first few moves. His jaw tightened, and his moves became more precise, focused. We circled and swung, thrust and parried, calling the positions. I hit hard, channelling my grief and anger, and he took the hits and gave them back. He understood, I think, and we became opponents each could rage against.

I couldn't keep it up, though; I simply wasn't strong enough, and the intensity with which I was handling the sword was wearing me out. Belatedly I realized this wasn't what Turlo had wanted, nor what Cillian needed to see. I signalled to Sorley and dropped my sword point to the ground.

"Well, lassie, at least you called the moves," Turlo said drily.

"I'm sorry, Turlo," I panted. "That wasn't much of a training demonstration."

"No," he agreed. "But you needed it. Both of you," he added, with a glance at Sorley. He turned to Cillian. "What did you see?"

"Near the end I could guess what the next guard would be, and the next strike, from the position of the blade. But only for the last three or four."

"That's more than most can see at their first lesson. Good. Maybe next time they'll take it a bit slower to let you see more." He turned to me. "Best swordplay I've ever seen from you, Guard."

I was still out of breath. I shook my head. "Wore me out too quickly."

"Aye, well, you're out of practice," Turlo said. "It'll come. Fight with your head and not your heart next time."

He was right, of course; the rage itself was exhausting. I took a few deep breaths, pushing the anger back down. "Sorry, Sorley, I should have warned you."

"I worked it out," he answered. He grinned. "I haven't had a fight like that since my brother took me on after I claimed the best pup from our bitch's litter."

"All brawn and no grace?" Turlo asked.

"I never said I could dance with a sword," I answered.

"And I," Cillian said, "am a far better dancer than a swordsman."

"Do not let the Marai men hear that," Turlo warned, grinning. "You're going to be the butt of their jokes for a while, *mo charaidh*, as it is."

"I expected that," Cillian said ruefully.

"Aye, well, don't react, play along with them if you can. A wager of some sort would help, if you've got anything to wager."

We had coins, a purseful each, given to us at the White Fort, before we left. Some complicated payment, we were told, but I thought the money more likely a gift, from the Emperor, or Casyn. But it was Sorley who provided the solution.

"These are Marai men, Cillian," he said. "Bet them a story told at the fires at night. They'll be happy with that, and if they start to see you as a *scáeli*," he shrugged, "well, they'll stop expecting as much from you, and not give you such a hard time."

"A fine idea," Turlo said.

"Yes, it is," Cillian answered. "Although I am hurt by Sorley's lack of confidence in my ability to learn the sword. Will you play your *ladhar* for me, *mo charaidh*, while I tell of sea monsters and giants?"

"You know I will," Sorley answered. "And remind you of the words if need be. *Danta* were never your strong point, now were they?"

"Undermining me at every turn," Cillian complained. Suddenly, a wave of happiness washed through me; despite everything, for this moment, being here with these three men was a source of joy.

We walked back to the ship. One of the oarsman shouted something at Cillian; he called back in *Maráí'sta*, the conversation continuing as we boarded. Another man made a comment and I saw Cillian tense just a little, his fingers flexing, before he answered, apparently cheerfully. Beside me, Sorley inhaled. I looked at him questioningly. "That last was ribald," he said. "You don't want to know."

Geiri snapped a command and we began to move. I had arrows to fletch. Sorley went to the pile of withies, sorting through them. Cillian stayed with Turlo, talking.

By the time we moored again, I had fletched my arrows. "Help me build a frame?" Sorley asked, so while Turlo took Cillian off for another sword practice with a group of oarsmen as spectators, I helped him lash withies together to make a butt, stuffing it with reeds.

I retrieved the new bow and the arrows. Pacing off a reasonable distance, I nocked the arrow, aimed, and let it fly. The draw on the bow was a little lighter than I had expected for the weight of the arrow and the first shot dropped too soon. I made the necessary adjustments and shot again, hitting the target close enough to the centre to be pleased.

"Sorley?" I offered, once I'd shot all six arrows. I'd brought back a bow for him, too, but my arrows were the only ones properly fletched right now. "The draw's a bit light," I told him as he moved into position. Like mine, his first shot wavered, but the others were on target.

Another shouted conversation in *Maráí'sta* told me sword practice was over. "I better tune the *ladhar*," Sorley said. "We'll be using it tonight." I wondered what the wager had been.

Cillian came over to us, along with a few of the oarsmen, clearly wanting to see this lesson too. "Let me shoot again," I said to Sorley, and without looking at the Marai I shot three arrows, quickly, into the target. Then I handed the bow to Cillian. "The arrows are bit heavier than I would judge the bow's force is meant for," I told him. "So you will have to draw it back a bit further than you think, and aim a little high, so the arrow can fall." He nodded, stepping into position. His first shot was respectable, the arrow falling more than it should but still striking the edge of the target. "Better than my first shot," I told him. "Can you adjust for that?"

"I think so." He shot again, this time hitting the middle third of the target. The next shot was even better.

"Well done," I said. I remembered something from our training at Tirvan. "A contest?" I suggested. "Two arrows each, nearest to the centre?"

"What are we competing for?" Cillian asked. "I have already lost one wager." "Just—glory," I said.

The oarsmen caught on quickly, and to their shouts we shot our six arrows. Sorley won, but none of the shots were terrible. A call from the Marai made Sorley and Cillian exchange a glance. "They want us to do it again," Sorley said. "There are bets laid."

Another round, and this time my arrow lay closest to the centre, with one of Cillian's a hairsbreadth's away. The oarsmen cheered. "One more time?" I guessed. "Let's back up, just a bit."

I shot first, as the winner of the last round, then Sorley, then Cillian. My first shot was on target but not close to the centre, Sorley's a bit better. Cillian's was wide, hitting the butt, but the height was good. "Watch your stance," I told him as we prepared to shoot again. My second shot hit centred but too high. Sorley's came in beside mine, and Cillian's just below us both. Not the dead centre, but good enough. I grinned in delight, hearing groans from the losing oarsmen.

"You see the flight of the arrow in your head, and the adjustments are like strings between your mind and your hands, am I right?" Turlo's wry question startled me. I hadn't realized he was watching.

Cillian closed his eyes, thinking. "Yes," he said after a moment. "That's right."

"Your father's words." Turlo snorted. "Only man I know who can best me with a bow."

"Not the sword?" I asked.

"No. Casyn is the swordsman. Callan is good with it, but he's a master with the bow. Well, we'll make you competent with a sword, Cillian, but there's no point in wasting talent. Choose one of the bows as your own."

As promised, Cillian told a long story in *Marái'sta* at the fire that night. Sorley played his *ladhar*, sometimes singing a few verses that I assumed belonged in the story. I watched Cillian for a while, seeing yet another facet to him. He'd done this with the Kurzemë, too, but I had not been welcomed to watch, there.

He has used this exile, I thought, not just lived through it. He has been shouldering tasks, like Darcail, working towards becoming something more than he was. What have I done? I've just been who I was before. Maybe a bit stronger. A bit more determined? I didn't know.

Turlo shifted beside me. "Walk with me, lassie?" he asked. "The music's good, but listening to a long story in a language I don't know is going to put me to sleep." We walked away from the fire, to where we would not disturb the story.

"We'll sail later tomorrow," he told me. "Cillian asked for an hour to talk to Sorley, away from us all."

"I knew he planned to."

"Aye." He glanced back at the fire. "The lad's hiding it well tonight, in front of the Marai."

"You saw it, before Cillian spoke to you?"

"Aye. Officers learn to see these things."

"Casyn told me once you were a born leader," I said impulsively. "That you understood men instinctively."

"Did he now?" He shrugged. "Perhaps. Your Cillian is a brave man, having that conversation with the lad."

"It's gone on too long, and now with us together—"

"He told me," Turlo said. "How old is Cillian, Lena?"

"Thirty-three—no, thirty-four," I replied. "Why?"

"I knew Callan at that age," he mused. "All three of them, actually; I am only a handful of years younger. I would not have predicted, then, that Callan would be Emperor."

"Fél—Oran—said much the same," I remembered. "Why not? He seems, to me at least, to have all the qualities an Emperor should have."

"Aye, he does now. Not then. He was late maturing, Callan, impulsive and ill-disciplined. Unpredictable. Not like his son, I would say."

I turned to look towards the fire. "I don't know, Turlo. When I met Cillian, last year—he seemed to me younger than his age, and there was a degree of ill-discipline, I would say, and moodiness. Although he was mourning a friend, so perhaps I am being unfair."

"You would know," Turlo said. "May I say something to you, lassie, that I have no right to say, except that you are dear to me?"

"Of course, Turlo."

"Casyn is my friend, and what I say now may sound disloyal. But he would forgive me, for the reasons I have. I watched him give up what he wanted from his life, to protect and guide his brother."

"He told me that."

"He *told* you?" I heard the genuine surprise in Turlo's voice.

"Yes. He'd said to me once that he hadn't wanted, at my age, to be a general. At the White Fort, after the trial, I asked him why. He told me what you just have. He said he never thought Callan would rise so high."

"Well, now." Turlo seemed lost for words. "So he would not mind this conversation at all. Lena, lassie, I see the same potential in Cillian that emerged in Callan when he passed thirty-five. He is meant to be a leader, an influential man. I would hope, *mo stóir*[6], that you do not do what Casyn did."

I frowned, puzzled. "What do you mean, Turlo?"

"Give up what you want from life, to make his dreams yours, because he needs you," he said bluntly. "Because you are meant to be a leader, too."

"Turlo," I said, "we could all be dead tomorrow, or next week, or in six months. Do any of us have dreams, beyond winning an impossible war?"

"I doubt it," he said. "But you have never spoken of what might be, if we were to win?"

"Never," I said. Not quite true, but that was not for Turlo's ears. "How could we? We were exiles, until a few days ago. If we had reached Casil, and found a way to build a life, whose dreams would we have been following?"

"Then I apologize for what I have said."

"No, Turlo." I smiled at him. "No need. Let me tell you something. When I was healing, in Berge, before the trial, I had realized I could not go back to Tirvan. I

---

[6] My dear

couldn't see a place for me there, without Maya. Or maybe that was part of it, and the other part was it was too small a life now I had ridden the length of the Empire, seen Casilla, served on the Wall. I'm not sure." I was thinking this out as I spoke, but it had the ring of truth to me. "And then I liked it at the *Ti'ach*. I liked the chance to learn, to try to understand our history. If there is any future, beyond war, then I think it will be something I cannot see now. Except that, the gods willing," I said, quietly, "Cillian will be there."

"Aye," Turlo said. "I hope that is true, for you both." He brightened. "I should know better than to worry about you, lassie. But keep my words close, if you will."

Blood and violence and pain ripped through my dreams that night. I awoke sweating, my heart pounding, but from the silence around me I must not have screamed. I rose to my feet as quietly as possible, moving to the edge of the river. Cillian did not stir.

I sat down on the grass, shivering a little as the night breeze dried the sweat on my body. The scar on my breast ached. I tried to sort through the images, looking for a reason I had dreamed tonight. Tirvan, of course, my unconscious mind churning through what I could not bring myself to picture awake. Ivor. Berge.

Why Berge? I had spoken of it briefly, to Turlo, earlier. Turlo...Berge. Words floated in: *Arey, her name is, from Berge*...when he told Donnalch who Darel's mother was. *I know what happened at Berge, and it was very bad*, and, *I was true to my Arey for all her life.*

Oh, Turlo. Darel, and then your love? How do you keep going?

So much pain, for us all. I wanted arms around me, but Cillian had a difficult task ahead of him in a few hours. I could deal with this. The thoughts and images intruded at random times, day or night, and usually I just pushed them down, feeding them to the snake of anger that lay coiled within. But now I let them flow. I saw the Marai ships, and their men, arriving at Tirvan; I saw the swords and axes in their hands and what they did with them, and the faces of the women desperately fighting back, and losing. And I saw—and felt—what else the men did.

I didn't cry. I am past tears, now, I thought. I lay back on the grass and let the images come, and when they stopped, I was as exhausted as if I had wielded the sword for an hour. But I had moved into a different place in my mind, from the flames of rage and grief to one of cold acceptance, and a colder wish for revenge.

Cillian woke at dawn. I had gone back to lie beside him, and surprisingly had fallen back into a dreamless sleep. His quiet movements roused me.

"Hello, my love," I murmured.

"*Käresta.* I tried not to wake you. *Forla.*"

"It's all right." I watched him flexing his shoulders. "You're sore, this morning."

"No matter; it will pass." He leaned over to kiss me. "I am going to walk. I need to think about what I am going to say to Sorley."

"Tell him what you told me."

"I will. I just need to think about how." He stood, stretching, and walked off up-river. I watched him for a minute, not envying him his morning task and how Sorley would react. And how we would all cope, afterwards, on a small ship. Would it have been better to just keep ignoring the situation?

I didn't know, and Turlo hadn't suggested it as a better course, so the outcome would just be something more for us to deal with. Another sorrow to shoulder. Because it was a sorrow, even among all the larger ones.

After some time I walked a little way up-river to where a small, treed island created a sheltered side channel, to bathe. Mostly I bathed, or swam, at night when darkness gave me privacy, but I was lethargic this morning and the water would help. I had washed and was turning for the ship when Cillian called my name.

He caught up with me. "Otter," he said, smiling, trailing a finger through my wet hair.

How did I deserve this, amidst so much sorrow and loss? "You've worked out what to say?" I asked.

"I think so. Walk back with me."

I thought about telling him what I had realized about Turlo's losses last night, then decided no. Later. At the ship, Sorley leaned on the rail, casually talking to Geiri.

"*Mo charaidh, siollë liovha?[7]*" Cillian called up to him.

"*De'mhin[8],*" Sorley replied.

"*Meas.*" I listened as they walked away. Cillian's voice, conversing in his native tongue, was different: less precise, less measured, more expressive. He cannot speak to me that way, I thought, and for a second, I felt bereft, and jealous of Sorley. But only for a moment, until I mentally shook myself into pragmatism and went to shoot more ducks.

Cillian came back to the ship alone. I went out to meet him. He looked tired, and resigned. I didn't ask, just walked with him until he was ready to talk.

"Sorley asked to be left to walk; he'll catch up with us at the first mooring," he said. The ship moved slowly enough.

"Was it bad?"

"Hard, rather than bad. For both of us. I think he understands, though."

"Are you all right?"

"Yes. I need something to drink, but otherwise, yes. You do not mind if I don't tell you much more?" he asked gently.

---

[7] My friend, walk with me?

[8] Certainly.

"Of course not."

"He did want me to tell you something. He said, 'Tell Lena I'm glad it's her.'"

"Oh," I said. "Will he talk to me, do you think?"

"Give him a bit of time, but yes. Can I ask why?"

"I thought it might help him to hear something." I stopped, confused. "Cillian, I've never said this to you, and now I'm thinking of telling Sorley."

"You're blushing, Lena," he said, a thread of amusement in his voice. "What is it?"

I searched for the words. "If you had asked me even half a year ago to envision myself partnered with someone, well, it wouldn't have been a man."

He looked down at me, his smile spreading slowly across his face. "I don't think I know what to say to that," he murmured.

I spread my hands helplessly. "I chose freely. You know I love you."

"I know, *käresta*. And I know you loved Maya. It might help Sorley to hear that, if you are comfortable telling him."

"I'll see," I answered. I needed to think about it.

We set off again. I fletched arrows; then, at the first mooring, we set up the butt again. I was matching shots with Cillian, with Turlo watching us, when Sorley appeared. He looked tired and I thought his eyes were red-rimmed. "Go find food, lad," Turlo said, "and a mug of beer. You look like you need it. In fact, I'll come with you. I could use a draught as well."

Geiri whistled, indicating the break was over. On board I went back to fletching but I soon ran out of feathers, so the rest of the arrows had to wait. Sorley dozed in the stern. Cillian was talking to Geiri, probably about where the river went, and Turlo was talking to Irmgard. I had, for the moment, no one to talk to and nothing to do.

We all needed space from each other, and time to think, because I watched the land pass for most of that sailing time alone. The ship was quiet except for the oars and the occasional exchange among the rowers. I looked around once: Turlo was sitting against the side near the bow, snoring. Cillian stood near him, gazing out over the river. I thought he looked pensive. I let him be.

At the second mooring Sorley offered to match swords with me, and we gave Cillian a measured demonstration. Sorley didn't want to practice archery, though, and nor did the women, so I watched Cillian's lesson. He had improved a little; his moves were smoother, but still uncertain. The oarsmen had already won another story earlier, so fewer of them came to heckle. It added to the odd feeling—not quite peaceful, but quiet, almost meditative—of the day.

After the evening meal, Sorley played a few songs, and then Cillian joined him to tell the *danta* he had chosen for the night. They spoke, and I saw Sorley nod, changing the tuning on his *ladhar*. Whatever the story was, it raised cheers and laughter from the Marai, and while I couldn't understand the words, just watching Cillian tell it, the gestures with hands and arms, the change in tone and volume, had me transfixed.

When he was done, and after he had made it clear to the oarsmen he was finished for the night, he came to sit beside me, carrying a mug of the thin, sour beer. "What *danta* was that?" I asked, after he'd eased his thirst. "They certainly enjoyed it." Sorley had started to play a rollicking tune and the Marai were shouting along.

"One of the favourites. There's a dragon, and a hoard of gold, and a hero to beat the dragon and win the treasure. It's almost a children's tale, but all the Marai and half of Sorham love hearing it."

"Why do you say it, instead of singing it? You can sing."

"Tradition." He took another swallow of beer. "Sorley could sing it, because he is playing. Because I am not, I speak it."

"Odd," I said.

"Probably a test for the *scáeli*. It's easy to remember the words to a song. Saying the *danta* is harder."

"Did Sorley have to prompt you on it?"

"Not this one. It was partly why I chose it. I wasn't sure he wanted to talk to me, really."

Sorley played several drinking songs, toe-tapping, undemanding, spirit-lifting music. It was growing late when he stopped; playing a few chords with one hand, he gestured Geiri over. They spoke for a minute, then Geiri turned to say something to the oarsmen. They quieted.

Sorley adjusted the tuning on the ladhar and played a few notes. "Oh, Sorley," Cillian whispered beside me.

"What is it?"

"This song," he murmured. *"An dithës braithréan[9]."* It's a lament, a song of farewell between two brothers separated by war." He took my hand. "He is singing this to me, Lena."

Sorley continued to play the tune, slowly, the notes dropping like tears into the night. "On midsummer's night," he said, pitching his voice to carry, "if I understand correctly, the soldiers of the Empire play a song for their lost. I do not know the song, and it is not midsummer, but tonight I offer this for all we have loved, and all we have lost."

Another soft, mournful descent of notes faded into the dark, and with the next, Sorley began to sing. Nothing disturbed the music: drinking cups were lowered, conversation ended. His voice, deep and slightly rough, told his anguish and grief to the night, to the stars, to all the world. A lament, I knew, for what he could not have, but also a gift to us, a song for our losses, too. It was not the *Breccaith*, but it served. When the last notes drifted out over the river, I was openly weeping, and the firelight glittered on the tears in Cillian's eyes.

---

[9] The Two Brothers

CHAPTER ELEVEN

WE WERE READYING TO SAIL NEXT MORNING when Geiri stopped, his hand up, a sudden broad grin on his face. He said something, but I didn't need a translation. The wind had changed. It blew now from the south, and it carried with it the faintest smell of the sea.

I closed my eyes against the wave of homesickness that swept through me, a fierce wanting of my boat and the salt spray and returning home at sunset with a full hold, into Tirvan's sheltered harbour. As Maya and I had done, bringing *Dovekie* home to hear Tali's casual announcement of an unscheduled council meeting, that last evening before the world had changed forever.

But if we could smell the sea, it was not that far away. Geiri and Cillian were already deep in conversation, Cillian using a spread hand to indicate to Geiri which channel he believed the ship should take. If the maps are accurate, I thought. It didn't occur to me to doubt Cillian's memory.

Turlo beckoned me over. "You and Sorley, bows to ready on each side." I found my bow and quiver and positioned myself on the right side, near the front of the ship. On either bank, the grasslands were giving way to a rockier landscape.

An hour later the first channel of the delta angled away to our left. We continued on our course, mooring after another hour to rest the oarsmen. Geiri cut the break short, ordering the men back to work. They complied without obvious complaint: like me, they wanted to get to the sea.

The river widened a bit, descending over a series of stepped drops, taking all Geiri's and the oarsmen's skill to keep us straight. And perhaps, I thought, as we jostled towards one drop, upright. A command from Geiri, and two oarsmen slipped overboard to fight their way to each bank with ropes to help guide the ship through. Geiri growled something at Cillian; he was clearly unhappy with this route.

The land flattened again, becoming marshy, flowing among reeds with the occasional island of willow trees. Insects began to whine and bite. The reeds on either side meant we could see little beyond the water. It felt enclosed, and it made me nervous. Occasionally birds flew up, in twos and threes, large ones I didn't recognize. I slapped a biting insect, cursing.

The sun moved to its zenith and began to descend. The wind had died, and the insects were worse.

"Turlo!" Sorley called. "A boat, ahead!" I saw it a second later. The curve of the river had given Sorley a better view. Geiri snapped a command and we slowed and stopped.

The boat approached. One man, dark haired and bearded, stood at the prow, and behind him half-a-dozen archers. Whose bows were bigger and arrows longer than ours, I noted. So had Turlo. He signalled us to lower ours.

Their oarsmen brought the boat alongside. We eyed each other. The dark-haired man asked something. To Turlo's shaken head, he repeated the question in a different language, and then another, I thought, and then another. At the last question, I saw Cillian's eyes narrow. He held up a hand and replied in a language I didn't know, but sounded—almost—familiar, as if there were elements in it I should recognize.

The man looked puzzled, but after a moment his face cleared, and he replied. Cillian answered, evoking the same momentary confusion. Several more exchanges occurred, the dark-haired man looking amused, then disbelieving, and then startled, and in the last thing Cillian said I thought I caught Callan's name, and the word Casil.

Sorley had come to stand beside me. "What language is that?" I whispered, slapping at the biting insects.

"Casilan. I can't follow most of what they've said; I can read it, fairly well, but I never really learned to speak it. No one has actually spoken it in Linrathe—or the Empire, I suppose—for hundreds of years, except at the *Ti'acha.*"

The archaic version of your tongue, I remembered Perras telling me.

I studied the boat. High-prowed and almost equally high at the stern, it was broader than our ship and not as long. Stable on the sea, I thought. A pair of eyes were painted on the bow. I let my eyes travel to the archers. Well-kept bows, the wood oiled and the nocked arrows straight and smooth, with metal heads. The men held them nearly at full draw easily, and their quivers were full. A knife hung in a curved sheath at each archer's waist. Trained men.

"*Westani!*" I heard the dark-haired man call, and then something I did not understand, but his gestures made it clear: follow him. The archers lowered their bows, and the rowers began to manoeuvre the boat around. Cillian took a deep breath, exhaling slowly. I thought he looked bemused.

"Well done, *mo charaidh,*" Turlo said. "Now, will you translate?"

"If I understood everything," Cillian said, "and I am not entirely sure I did, the man's name is Mihae and he is the leader in the town he is guiding us to, which is called Sylana, I think. I told him we are from the Western Empire—which he did not believe, at first, and may still not—sent by the Emperor Callan to Casil. I did not tell him why. And as he did not question that at all, I think we can conclude that after all these years, Casil still stands as an important city in the east."

The significance of this took a moment to sink in. Casil, whose people had built the temple in the plain, and the nearly vanished road across that plain. The Eastern Empire of memory and legend. A place to ask for sanctuary for Irmgard and succour for the West. The thread of hope had just become a little stronger.

"That any of us can speak to this man at all is a marvel," Turlo said.

"It is—disconcerting," Cillian answered, "to know that I have just made myself understood in a language learned only to access ancient texts. Although," and he glanced my way, the tiniest hint of amusement on his face, "my pronunciation was appalling, it would appear. But I can improve that, no doubt."

"Aye, well, you'd best, as you are going to have to do all the speaking for us. Here and at Casil," Turlo said. "You need that rank now, too. Captain will do, but your appointment is adjutant, to me, so of the third. Understood?"

"Sir," Cillian said, without a hint of irony.

Turlo turned to me. "Guard, you are clear on the ranks here?"

"General," I replied.

Turlo grinned. "But only when necessary. I think we can all relax again."

"What did he call, at the end?" I asked. "*Westani*, it sounded like?"

"It was," Cillian said. "People of the west."

As we followed, I told Turlo my observations, of the boat and the archers, the others listening. "How did they know we were coming?" Sorley asked.

Turlo gestured to me. "The birds," I said. "I think someone saw the flights of birds we frightened. Either that, or there was someone out in the reeds in a small boat, but I think it was the birds."

"Aye," Turlo said. "I agree with Lena. Now, Cillian, what impressions do you have of our safety?"

"I don't know," he replied. "I am sorry, General, but for me to speak Casilan is not like speaking *Maráì'sta*, or even your language, which is now almost as familiar to me as my own. I must see the words in my mind, to read them, almost, and that took all my concentration, that and translating what I heard in the same way. I could not do that and listen for inflection and watch his face and hands, as I normally would."

"I did," Irmgard said, unexpectedly. "I have experience of this, with my husband. I think he will not kill us, but his eyes were not always looking at you, Cillian; they saw the swords and axes too, but his hands did not clench. He looked at me and my women with interest, too. We are not a threat, I think. He will want tribute to let us pass."

"And surety for our weapons," Turlo added. "Lady Irmgard, do you remember anything more from Fritjof or his men?"

"Fritjof did not speak of such things to me," she said, her hatred of him evident in the way she said his name. "But Geiri told me the men talked of trade, yes. *Râv* and *alfban*..." She turned to Cillian. "I do not know how to say these words."

"Amber and ivory."

"Yes, these, for food and metalwork and a fine cloth. It is what we brought, as much as we could. To buy me safety in Casil, I thought."

"We may need to use some of it here," Turlo warned. "To buy us safe passage."

"If we must," she replied. She turned back to Cillian. "Did he speak of me?"

"He said this, *Ádla*, if I understood it correctly: 'You have brought women. Good'." His voice, I noticed, was measured, unembarrassed, giving a simple translation. "I took that to mean that we would not want...access to the town's women, but I am not sure. I apologize, *Ádla*, but I could not think fast enough to find a way to clarify his meaning."

"You do not need to apologize," she said. "He made no mention of Lena?"

"I think," Turlo interjected, "that he may not have realized Lena is a woman, if he did not look too closely."

I could see Turlo's point. Rind had cut my hair for me, tsking over the task, but I had insisted. It was cropped so that it did not blow in my eyes, as I liked it. I wore a loose tunic which disguised my small breasts, and breeches, and I had held a bow. At a quick glance, I could be a young man. I would wager, though, that one of the archers would convey my sex to Mihae as they sailed: they had studied Sorley and me, as we had them.

A thought occurred. "Lady Irmgard," I asked, "do you know if Fritjof's men sailed beyond this place?"

She asked Geiri. He shook his head.

"Geiri thinks not. They spoke of coming to a sea, and trading, and returning home."

"Then," I said slowly, "if Fritjof brought back new ideas on how to treat women, then these are the people he must have learned those ways from."

"Can we use that?" Cillian said. "Will Mihae negotiate more honestly if he believes we are civilised, by his lights?"

I bit back my first response. This is not about you, I reminded myself. This is about all our lives, and more: we need to reach Casil.

"Perhaps," Turlo said.

"But," I said, trying to keep my voice calm, "unless Fritjof made this part up to suit himself, the leader of the people can...claim any woman he wants, and she cannot refuse. We cannot accede to that."

"No!" Irmgard exclaimed. "Or what have I fled from?"

Turlo and Cillian exchanged a look. "Then," Cillian said, "I suggest this. That you are being sent to Casil as an offered bride, in hope of forging a new relationship. One that will bring traffic and trade to this place, as ships move between our lands and Casil. You and your women must arrive inviolate."

"That might work," Turlo said. "Although will he then feel obligated to offer us women?"

"We say no, if he does," Cillian said. "Sorley, make sure the oarsmen understand that."

"What about Lena?" Sorley asked.

Cillian looked at him, and then me. "I doubt they are so uncivilised as to demand another man's wife," he answered. "If you can tolerate the deception, Lena?" Irmgard made a sound of protest, but did not speak.

"If we said she was not just your wife, but my daughter?" Turlo asked. "Both a soldier, and a soldier's daughter, taught her skills with bow and sword by a doting and unwise father? Would that help shelter her?"

"Shelter her," Cillian repeated, a nuance to his voice I didn't understand. "Yes. Another layer of status. I like that, Turlo. Lena, can you accept this?"

"Say what you need to," I replied. "It is all a story, after all."

The reeds gave way to open fields, diked and drained, and then to a town spread out along the left bank and the shore. Ahead of us was open sea. Gulls screamed and soared, congregating around the fishing boats returning to the harbour. The houses were stone and wood, well-built, and both canals and paved paths provided access.

The oarsmen brought the ship into the harbour wall, blocks of stone cut and laid to prevent erosion. I wondered where the stone came from, both for this and the houses. The boat was tied, bow and stern, against the jetty.

Mihae waited for us where a paved path abutted the harbour wall. He was, I realized, eyeing me closely. Abruptly he spoke to Cillian, who replied calmly, gesturing to himself and Turlo. They spoke for a few minutes. Mihae, laughing, added a few last words. Cillian exhaled. "He had thought you a boy, Lena, but he has accepted what I have told him: you are Turlo's daughter, a solder in our army, and also my bedmate. He said he had heard of such women, and made a few predictable comments, which I will not translate. "

"Now what happens?" Sorley asked.

"We—Turlo and you and I, not the women—wash, and make ourselves as presentable as possible, and then we go to eat, to be observed and studied and talked about, as Western barbarians, no doubt." Cillian said. "At some point, Mihae will broach the idea of a fee to be allowed to leave. I will need to know exactly what Irmgard is willing to give up, before we start."

"They will do all this tonight?" I asked.

"Of course," Cillian said. "We are weary, and out of place, and therefore vulnerable. The wine will be offered freely, too: be cautious, *mo charaidheán*[10], drink sparingly, and water it well if you can."

Mihae himself came, only a short while later. Two women were with him, which I thought odd. He called something up to Cillian, who frowned, and then responded with what sounded like a question. The conversation went back and forth, neither man sounding happy. I watched Mihae, seeing the change in his stance, the anger building in his body. I glanced at Turlo: he had seen it too. Quietly he reached for his sword, moving to stand beside Cillian. As I did, my hand on my secca.

Cillian said something, very firmly, an undercurrent of anger—real or feigned, I wasn't sure—in his voice now too. Mihae made a gesture of unwilling capitulation, and spat something. He gestured: come. Cillian held up a hand, saying something now in a conciliatory tone.

"He wanted Irmgard and her women," he told us. "Fritjof apparently told him he would send women, pale women, Mihae said, and he thought we had brought them. He has no concept that we and Fritjof are not from the same people, in part because of this ship, I suppose. I cannot let him know Fritjof is an enemy, or they may not let us pass at all. "

"Aye," Turlo said, "I can see that."

"He has accepted, I hope, the story I have told him about Casil, but he will

---

[10] My friends

demand more tribute instead. I must speak to Irmgard, before we go. Sorley, tell Geiri to have the oarsmen on watch, with weapons to hand. I do not entirely trust Mihae."

Mihae waited impatiently as Cillian spoke rapidly to Irmgard. He shouted something, after a minute or two. Cillian called something back, and then turned, smiling, apologetic. Practiced deference, I thought, watching him, insincere but convincing. It made me just slightly uncomfortable, seeing him do this, so apparently easily.

The men went off toward the centre of the town. The women Mihae had brought stayed, sitting cross-legged on the jetty, beside the ship. Why? Perhaps Mihae did not trust the men of the town to leave us unmolested, and the women's presence was to tell any man that we were not to be approached. I wasn't convinced by my own argument, though.

"Lady Irmgard," I said, a minute or two later, "I am worried." I explained about the women, below. "If we need guarding," I said, "is the ship safe?"

"You think like a soldier," she said. "I think like a woman who has had some experience of this. The women below are not guarding us from men; they are ensuring we do not leave this ship. Only they are allowed to be here with us, but there will be men not far away."

I had not thought of that, and I told her so. "Your life has been different," she said, shrugging. "I would not have thought of it either, not so long ago."

I thought about how to frame the question I had. Just ask, I told myself. "Lady Irmgard, why did you react when Cillian suggested I pretend to be his wife? It is only a subterfuge."

"Is it?" she asked. "Cillian na Perras is a man entitled to respect, honour, even, in his own land."

"But we are not in his land, Lady," I persisted, "and he is Cillian of the Empire, now."

"And son to the Emperor, I understand? And so, a man of status?"

"No," I said, a glimmer of comprehension appearing. "Emperors are elected. There may be expectations for their sons, but no predetermined status."

She raised an eyebrow, clearly doubting me. "Ask Turlo, if you do not believe me," I offered. "And since status matters to you, you should know that my mother and my aunt are headwomen of my village." Were, I thought, and pushed the idea away. I wondered why I was defending myself to her. It was not as if she could convey her doubts to anyone beyond our ship. But I did not want to make an enemy of her, and I did not want trouble with the Marai men.

"Would you be his wife, if you could?" she asked suddenly.

"In the Empire," I said slowly, "we do not think in those terms. Men and women may pair, even for a lifetime," I added, thinking of Turlo and his Arey, "but there is no formal agreement made. And they do not live together."

"Not even in old age, should they both reach it?"

"No," I answered slowly. "Not even then." Why not? I wondered suddenly. Why not then? I had never thought of love extending to the end of life, but why would it not? I had made an unspoken promise to Cillian, and the nature of the promise meant we had to be together, until one of us died. And in the Empire I had left—and we were sworn to—that was not allowed.

"It seems a cruel way to live," Irmgard observed.

"Perhaps," I said. "It was all I knew."

"We—Åsmund and I—held Cillian na Perras in high regard, the few times he came to King Herlief's hall, for his learning and his insight. And his wit," she added. "A man with distances in him, to be sure, but good, amusing company."

"Fritjof treated him like a clerk," I said.

"Fritjof!" She spat the name. "He cared nothing for civilised speech; he preferred drinking with his men. I cannot remember if he ever spoke to Cillian, or if he was even at the King's hall, when Cillian was there." She calmed herself. "Of you, I thought, a soldier, a fisherwoman, yes?" I nodded. "What can she give him? And what does she want from him, other than to raise her status? She has no learning, no depth of thought: all she can offer is pleasure, which does not last."

It was an apology of sorts. "Status was the last thing on my mind, Lady Irmgard," I said. "It is just not how we think, in the Empire."

"I can see that. And I see too that you are happy together. You remind me of Åsmund and myself." She smiled, sadly.

"May I ask you something?" I said, impulsively.

"Go ahead."

"Had you no children, Lady Irmgard?"

A flash of pain crossed her face. "Two," she answered. "Two sons. Fritjof took them. Seven and eight, they are, my two boys." There were tears in her eyes. "They are lost to me, and were before I fled."

"I am sorry," I said. "I should not have asked."

"There is a price for all our choices," she answered, head high, the princess again. "We leave something, or someone, behind, each time we choose."

Very late, I heard the men return. I waited. After a while, Cillian came to our sleeping place on the deck. He leaned against the rail, bending to take off his boots. "What happened?" I whispered.

"Lena," he murmured, his voice hoarse. "I thought you'd be asleep." He lay down beside me. "Too much depends on my imperfect ability with a language I never expected to speak, let alone negotiate in," he answered. "Being able to read ancient philosophers does not have much application here."

"You should sleep," I observed. He sounded discouraged, and worn out.

He shook his head. "I can't, not yet."

"Turn over, onto your stomach." He did as I asked, too weary to argue. Gently, I straddled his back, reaching forward to begin to massage the muscles of his shoulders and neck. I could feel the knots of tension under my hands. Cillian groaned as I dug my fingers in, and then sighed, a minute or two later. The tension was beginning to ease. I kept massaging, but with less pressure, hearing his breathing beginning to slow. Only when I was sure he was sleeping did I stop stroking his back. I slipped off him to pull the blanket up, and slid in beside him to be there when he woke.

Shouts from the guard woke us before dawn. We scrambled to our feet, reaching for weapons, gathering with Sorley and Turlo mid-deck. But there was no need. Marai oarsmen pursued three boys along the jetty, other men stood alert at each end of the ship, scanning for movement. I studied the harbour. I could see nothing that appeared threatening.

A man ran towards us from the town. I tightened my hold on my secca. "It's Mihae," Cillian said. "Wait." He stepped forward to meet the headman.

This hadn't been a serious attack. It hadn't been a distraction, either, to pull our men and attention away from the ship. Then, why? Only one possibility made sense: they had wanted us disturbed, woken far too soon. Cillian and Turlo had not slept until the early hours of the morning. Tired negotiators made mistakes. I said as much to Turlo.

"Aye," he said, "I expect you are right."

We watched Cillian and Mihae talking, Mihae's face and hands indicating apology, regret. Cillian, stern and unsmiling, listened. Eventually he nodded, spoke, then turned to return to the ship.

"Mihae claims just an irresponsible band of boys, out for fun. One of them has a sword wound on his leg, for his enjoyment."

"Do you believe him?" Sorley asked.

"No," he said, "it was a ploy, I have no doubt. To complicate the negotiations. He'll expect us to ask for reparation for the attack, since he had placed the ship under his protection and failed, while they will ask for payment for the wounded boy."

"Which they are not entitled to, as he attacked," Turlo said. "But we will call the matter even, in the end, I expect."

"Why are today's negotiations more difficult?" I asked. "What is different from last night?"

"Of course, the women do not know," Turlo answered. "Forgive me, Lady Irmgard. It was too late last night to disturb you. I had meant to tell you over breakfast."

"No matter," Irmgard said. "But you will tell me now, please."

"After much discussion," Turlo said, "Mihae agreed to twenty-five percent of the amber and ivory we carry as his fee to allow us to leave."

"You agreed to this?" she asked. I thought she looked upset.

"No," Cillian answered. "I made it clear you had to approve."

"This is more than I want to give," she said. "I will need my treasure, in Casil."

"We will not get to Casil," Cillian said bluntly, "if you do not agree. Even with the oarsmen, *Ádla*, we would be easily overpowered. Perhaps this morning's feint was also to remind us of that."

"I have no choice, then?" she murmured.

"Not truly," Cillian said. "If it matters, *Ádla*, his first price was half."

Sorley said something to her then, in *Marái'sta*. She looked uncertain for a moment, and then she nodded. "I accept," she said. "Come speak with me, *laerth*, while I decide what to give?" He followed Irmgard to her part of the ship. I turned to Turlo.

"Do you have any idea of how long today's negotiations will take?" I asked.

"No, lassie, I don't. Much depends on the complexity of Mihae's demands, and our—Cillian's—ability to detect and respond to that complexity." He shook his head. "Do not take this badly, lassie, but I am glad he was not negotiating our truce with Linrathe at Donnalch's side. We might not have done so well, had he been."

"What is still to be decided?"

"An agreement of tariffs, for when ships begin to trade between our lands and Casil. It was what he offered in exchange for a reduction in the amount of treasure. "

"But—" I began.

"But trade is not our goal, the ships will never come, and we have no authority to do so?" Turlo supplied. "All correct, lassie. But we cannot let Mihae know that, or what our real mission is, and so we must go through these talks treating them seriously, paying attention to each detail as assiduously as we would if trade were our intent."

"Hampered," we heard Cillian say, as he joined us, "by a negotiator whose knowledge of trade agreements is nil, and is unsure of the precise terms and subtleties of the language."

"Do not undervalue yourself," Turlo said, sharply.

"Sorley," Cillian said. "You must tell me the words I need. You know more about negotiating prices and tariffs than any of the rest of us. Come." They walked to the rail, Cillian already focused on Sorley's explanations. I felt drained, from the rapid awakening, and the rush of energy needed, and then not needed. I went back to our sleeping area to sit. Maybe I could sleep again, but I doubted it. I closed my eyes, drifting.

"Lena," Cillian, said, softly. I must have drowsed. I opened my eyes. He knelt beside me. "Before I forget. *Meas*, Lena, for last night."

"For what? What did I do, Cillian?"

"Ah, *käresta*," he replied. "Something no one has done for a very long time, not since my childhood, I believe. You saw what I needed, and you gave it to me, without question."

Now was not the time to tell him of the dream by the riverbank. "Cillian, of course I did. Is that not what you have been doing for me, since the spring? It is what you do for someone you love."

"I am still learning that," he said softly. He smiled. "*Thà mi gràh agäthe*, Lena," he said.

"Are you going to translate that?" I asked.

"I could leave you guessing," he mused. "I had better go."

"Cillian," I said. "Turlo says your negotiations have been brilliant. You can do this."

"Perhaps," he replied. He was standing now. "About that translation..."

"Yes?"

"Nothing you do not know. Just I love you."

CHAPTER TWELVE

I DID KNOW. BUT HE HAD NEVER USED those exact words before, and it mattered, somehow. Which, after I had blinked away the tears, took my thoughts down some unexpected paths. I found my journal, and my pen and ink, and after I heard the men leave, I sat on the deck to write.

I tried to sort out the inchoate ideas forming in my mind. About language, and meaning, and if all concepts were universal, and could be translated. About the gap between intent and comprehension, between what was meant and what was understood, and the assumptions and shared experience encompassed—or not—in any exchange.

I had stopped to flex my aching fingers when Sorley arrived back at the ship. "Lena," he greeted me. "You are wanted, so I have been sent for you."

"What for?" I asked.

"I am not sure. The negotiations are done, over the trade terms: Cillian was splendid today, firm and precise. I think he is growing comfortable speaking Casilan. Now it is all being written down. I will be needed then, to check the rates and terms, but until then, my job is to fetch you. But we have some time."

I stood up, glancing over the rail of the ship. The tide was out. Birds probed in the exposed mud, and shellfish clung to rocks and pilings. It was all so familiar, and so foreign. Beyond the harbour, I could see water, deep blue, stretching out to the horizon. Sorley followed my gaze.

"Does it remind you of home?"

"A bit. A lot, in some ways." I looked at the man beside me. "Sorley," I asked, impulsively. "Why don't you hate me?"

He flushed. "I can't," he said, not looking at me. "Cillian loves you. How could I hate anyone he loves? Anyhow, I like you, liked you before, at the *Ti'ach*, I mean. I told him to tell you I was glad it was you. Didn't he?"

"He did," I answered. "Thank you, for that. I didn't look for this, you know, Sorley. It took me by surprise, because I would have expected that were I ever to give my heart so completely to anyone, it would have been to a woman." I stopped. "I am not sure what I am trying to say."

"That love comes where it will, and not where we may want it to?" he offered.

"Yes. Exactly that."

"What a pair you are," he said, trying for levity. "Both surprised by each other." He must have seen my puzzlement, because he added, "Cillian said something similar, about being taken unawares."

His hand rested on the rail. I put mine over it, squeezing lightly. He turned his hand to grip mine. "He needs friends, Sorley," I said quietly. "Friends who can talk to him of ancient poets and Linrathe's history, and in his own language, and teach him about tariffs...and play *xache* with him. I can do none of those things, except play *xache.*"

"Has Irmgard been saying things to you? I told her yesterday she was wrong."

"We talked, yes. But Sorley..." I hesitated. Should I be asking of this of him, to listen to my fears?

"Go on," he said.

"She is not entirely wrong, is she? I watch him now, and I see a man accomplished beyond my understanding, learned and...honoured for that learning, Irmgard said. Welcomed for his insight, and his wit. I hear him called brilliant, incisive, and I see what he has done here, these past two days. I can fish, and shoot a bow, and throw a knife. There is a discrepancy there, don't you think?" I had not meant to say so much, but once I gave voice to my concerns, I couldn't stop.

Sorley shook his head firmly. "You underestimate yourself," he said. "You have far more to offer than those things. But, even if that were true, Cillian has made a promise to himself about you, and he never breaks his promises. Not since childhood, after what Donnalch said about him."

"Wait," I said. "Sorley, I'm not sure what you're talking about."

"He has not told you this?" he asked, looking contrite.

"No."

"Perhaps I should not, then." He watched a gull chasing another. "Or perhaps this is fair. I will not tell you anything that you would not have heard, had you stayed at the *Ti'ach* longer. Because when Cillian had made a promise to himself, he always told Perras, and eventually others; I think it helped him to keep them, at first, and then became habit, or part of the ritual. Is that reasonable, Lena?"

"I think so." I thought, too, that he needed to talk about Cillian, and that I should let him.

"So as I understand it, when Cillian was eight or so, and Donnalch...thirteen, I suppose, the talk over supper one night was of a statement one of the ancient philosophers had made. I never remember their names," he added, "just what they wrote. Whoever it was had said 'All there is to know of a man's character is laid down in his first seven years.' Apparently, Donnalch said that he believed this to be true, and it was why he would never fully trust Cillian, because his mother had been a traitor to Linrathe, and if his grandparents had raised their daughter to be such, then they must have raised Cillian the same way."

"But that is so cruel," I gasped. "Donnalch? He seemed so...fair."

"And he was, in almost everything. But I don't think he ever, quite, changed his mind about Cillian. Who took it badly, as you would expect a boy of that age to do. Perras," he paused. "It's odd: I always think of Perras as an old man, but he'd have been about the same age Cillian is now, newly *Comiádh*, then. Anyhow, Perras told him that he would have to work hard to counteract that belief, because Donnalch would not be the only person who thought that way, as wrong as it was, and he—Cillian—would have to be a man of impeccable trust, and always, always, keep his word. And as far as I know, he has."

"How could he swear an oath to the Empire, then?" I couldn't make sense of this.

"He had never sworn one to Linrathe, or, to be precise, to Donnalch. Either he would not, or Donnalch would not accept it. I don't know which."

I thought back to what Cillian had said, in our first real conversation in the Durrains. *As a toscaire I had to be seen as impartial,* he'd told me. We'd been talking about why he hadn't fought. I'd thought the answer incomplete, at the time.

"But the outcome of this is, Lena, he will not break his promise to himself, about you."

"He told you, then?"

"Yes. I think, as I said, telling someone is part of the ritual." He smiled, a little sadly. "I am aware, Lena, of the trust he put in me, with that."

"More than trust," I said, silently thanking Cillian for the generosity, for making Sorley know he was valued.

"You know he has not told me what it is?" I asked suddenly. Sorley looked surprised, and then puzzled. "I asked him not to," I clarified. "I have also made a promise, concerning him, but it seemed like tempting fate, to exchange them in a time of war and uncertainty, when so many things might cause us to break them against our will."

Sorley nodded. "I can see that." He was quiet again. "Would it...suit you, Lena, to have me hold that promise too?"

It seemed right, somehow. "Would you do that, for me? For us?"

"How can I not?" he said, softly.

"Then yes, so you can tell him, if I die in this war without it spoken."

"Tell me, then,"

"He said to me once that he had never known anything except waking alone," I said. I saw the brief flash of hurt in Sorley's eyes. "My vow is very simple. I promised that, if it were in my power, he would never do so again." Could I keep that promise, if this wound would not heal? Would he want me beside him?

He smiled. "They fit, yours and his. But I should say no more. He will keep his vow, Lena, as I know you will keep yours." He hesitated. "I do not hate you, Lena, you must see that?" I nodded. "Nor am I jealous. Envious, rather, but also happy, that he found the love he needed to leave behind his vow of celibacy, even though he would not, for me."

I had encouraged Sorley to talk about Cillian, because I thought he needed to. And because I wanted to hear it, I acknowledged. But now my mind roiled. The love he needed? But at midwinter, I had been clear with him about what I offered, and he had made no mention of love to me. Would he have, though? I tried to put it out of my mind. I had to focus. I had a role to play in front of Mihae in a minute or two, one that might be important for us all. I could not let my private concerns interfere with that.

I put my hand on the hilt of my secca as we walked towards the central hall, hoping its feel would focus me on what I had to do. It helped, a bit. By the time we entered the hall, I was calmer.

I saw Cillian's eyes narrow just slightly when he saw the secca, and then the tiny nod of approval, or understanding. Only he and Turlo and Mihae sat at a long table, vellum and pens in front of them, the kidskin covered with writing.

Mihae gave me an assessing look. I made myself return the gaze, evaluating him as well. I was a soldier, I reminded myself. His hair, not quite as dark as Cillian's, fell nearly to his shoulders, and his eyes were green. The beard was neatly trimmed, and when I glanced at his hands I saw the fingernails were clean, and clipped. A civilised man, making the best arrangement he could with these unexpected foreigners. What did he want from me?

"Sorley," Turlo said. "Will you read over this agreement and ensure the figures and terms are correct? Cillian wrote this, from his notes; it will be copied later, and I will ask you to read the copy, too, at the time."

"Of course," Sorley said, taking the vellum and moving to the best-lit part of the room.

"Lena." Turlo turned to me. "Mihae has a request. It is a request from him, and not an order from me, mind. Sylana trades with Casil, although their boats will not go that way again for some weeks. He has offered us a map, and a talk with an experienced captain, but for a price."

"Which is?" I asked. Both would be of great value to us, but how did I come into this?

"His men are dismissive of the idea that women can be soldiers. He would like a demonstration of your skills, so that they might be more prepared for what women can do, were they ever to encounter them, in battle."

"Which skills?"

"Bow and knife, if you would."

Was there a trap in this? I glanced at Cillian. He was listening, his eyes a little distant. I could see the shadow of fatigue under them.

"Is there more to this than appears?" I asked bluntly, of both Turlo and Cillian.

"Not that I can see," Cillian said. "General?"

"Nor I. Although we should ask exactly how these skills are to be shown. A map is not worth it, if he wants Lena to engage in bow or knife combat, with their men."

"Ask him, too, if I will be allowed my own knife, and my own bow."

Cillian asked. Mihae smiled, nodded, shook his head, talked.

"For the knife, just thrown at a target. For the bow, they will make some goats run, and you are to shoot one while they are moving. Nothing more, he says. And your weapons, in both cases."

"Do you want me to do this?"

"The information would be extremely useful," Turlo answered.

"Then I will."

Turlo walked me back to the ship for my bow and arrows. "If we can conclude things reasonably soon," he told me, "we can sail on the evening tide."

"How far, to Casil?"

"Not sure, lassie. A couple of weeks? We'll know more later, if the trader captain is honest, and the map accurate."

"You've been gone a long time already," I said. I didn't need to say more.

"Aye," Turlo said. "A worry. This is a very faint hope, as I'm sure you know, Lena."

"I know," I said. "An arrow, I thought, one arrow, shot into darkness, hoping to find its target."

"A poet, are you now?" he said, with a faint grin. "Although the analogy is apt, lassie." He grew serious. "I am your general speaking, for a minute," he said. "Something you need to understand. You are deserving of promotion, and I dislike leaving you as a Guard while Cillian now has an officer's rank. But, it is necessary, and you should know why. This is a rule that has, we believe, come down to us from Casil, and so it must be kept in case it is still in force, there. Relationships between officers and men are acceptable; between two officers, no. So were I to give you the promotion you deserve, you would not—might not—be allowed to be with him. And I would not do that to either of you."

"General, it is your adjutant you need by your side, to translate and analyze and negotiate," I said, "not me."

"Not entirely true," he answered. "Your thoughts are often useful. You are very much like your father in some ways, Lena, and he would never accept promotion. Although I often found ways to bring him into discussions, so I can with you, too." We walked a bit further. "I also want you by my adjutant's side," he said, "because I can see how what I am requiring him to do is burdening him. But I have no choice, and I must use my two soldiers as I best can, for the Empire."

"Ask Sorley, too," I said. "I know he is not yours to command, but—may I speak freely, General?"

"You may."

"It seems a small thing, but I think it matters. Cillian is different, somehow, when he speaks his native tongue. I think he finds some relief in not having to always speak another language, maybe especially now. I know you are nearly fluent, but you are his commanding officer...Sorley is a friend. Could you encourage Sorley to talk to him?"

"Can Sorley do this, given what lies between them?" Turlo asked.

"I am still speaking freely?"

"Yes,"

"Then, yes, I believe he can. I think he will, if you couch it terms of lessening the burden on Cillian. He is not going to stop loving him, but is it not better to channel that love into something useful for them both? Especially since there is no escape for Sorley, here, or on the ship?"

"Aye," Turlo said thoughtfully. "And that quality of thinking, both caring and pragmatic, is why you should not be just a Guard. I will speak with the lad."

On a clear area outside the hall a target had been raised. Men thronged the perimeter of the field, talking and laughing. Cillian came over to me.

"He wants five throws. It seems too simple, but I can't get him to tell me anything more."

I shrugged. "We'll find out, I suppose."

Mihae indicated where he wanted me to stand. I nodded. Then I faced the target, standing very still, judging wind and the flatness of the ground. I took my secca from my boot sheath, said a silent prayer to a goddess I didn't believe in, and threw.

Right on target. A young man ran over, pulled the secca from the butt, and brought it to me. I smiled at him, positioned myself, and threw again. And a third time. This time, when the secca was returned to me, Mihae asked something.

"Can you throw, kneeling?" Cillian translated.

I could. But I hadn't practiced that since Tirvan, two years before. I sank to one knee, estimating, trying to let my muscles and my mind remember. A slightly different shoulder movement, a slightly different knife position.

The secca hit the target off centre, but within the marked ring. Comments and shouts from the men. I hadn't heard them, on the previous throws. I stood up.

"Can you change hands?"

"No." I shook my head, turning to Mihae. "No."

I had one more throw. I stepped into position. I heard a footstep behind me, and suddenly I was back in the dream. My fingers clenched on the secca, and I began to crouch and turn.

Cillian said something, sharply. The footsteps grew closer. Mihae's voice, too close to me. More footsteps, fast, coming at me. I swiveled on my rear foot, dropping my knife arm to bring the secca up low, lunging forward at the man behind me. He sidestepped, with a dancer's grace, my knife brushing a sleeve. My body's momentum moved me forward. I used the force to spin again, bringing my knife up this time, but he was ready for me. He caught my knife arm, held it up, using his other arm to pull me tight against his body. I couldn't move. I struggled, fear and anger coursing through me, kicking and twisting. "Lena," Cillian said. "Lena, it's me. I'm here. It's all right. You're safe." The words, repeated and repeated, finally broke through. I sagged against him. He loosened his hold slightly. "Can I let you go?"

"Yes," I said. He released me. "Did I hurt you?" I asked.

"No. A few bruises, maybe, and a graze, if that. I haven't looked." He glanced at the sleeve of his tunic. "It's nothing."

I turned to glare at Mihae. He held up his hands as if to indicate he had meant no disrespect. "He wanted you to throw blindfolded," Cillian said. "He was going to tie a scarf around your eyes."

I gave Mihae a long look, as disdainful as I could make it, and then without more than a glance at the target, I turned and threw, in one fluid motion. The secca hit just left of centre. I stalked over to retrieve the knife, my head high, hoping the trembling I could feel was not visible.

"That was the fifth throw. No more," I said, hearing Cillian's quiet translation. Mihae relayed the words to the crowd, which gave back mutters and one or two shouted comments, or questions. I ignored them, and Cillian disdained telling me what they'd said.

Turlo waited for me, when I came back with the knife. "That's enough," he said. "You're not using the bow, after that."

"Turlo," I said. "I am. Don't ask me not to."

"I'm not asking. I am ordering you, Guard."

"No," I said, keeping my voice low. "You may try me for insubordination if you wish, but I am not, remember, doing this under orders. You were very specific about that. I am doing to gain us information we need. You are, in your own words, burdening Cillian beyond exhaustion to get us away from here. Do not stop me from using my skills to help us once we are free to leave."

His eyes went to Cillian. "Don't," I said again. "This is not his choice, nor am I his to control."

He exhaled. "Against my better judgment," he said. "Do what you need to, Lena."

We followed Mihae, and the crowd followed us, through the town to a field at the edge. Eight or nine goats grazed on the rough pasture. My anger was gone, replaced by cold, clear purpose. The shot would be slightly downhill, and the breeze here felt stronger, straight off the water. The light was good, though, the sun still nearly overhead. There was enough breeze that the sea was choppy, eliminating most reflected glare. I judged all this as we approached. I'd shot deer, at Tirvan, under similar conditions. But not with this bow.

I thought about the bow's weak draw, and the heavy arrow, and where I needed to stand. The goats grazed placidly. They would send a dog out among them to get them to run. I would shoot when they neared the wattle fence closest to me. I raised the bow, nocked an arrow, sighted.

"Mihae says," Cillian told me, "he'd like the brown-and-white doe, but any will be acceptable." I found the goat in question; she did stand out, which would help. I nodded.

"I'm ready," I said. I was ready, until they sent five children out to chase the goats.

Little children, five or six years old. None of us had thought to ask how the goats would be made to run. I let the bow drop slightly. "Don't do it," Cillian said.

"We need the map, and the instructions," I answered. I was still cold, and very clear. "The test is not killing the goat. The test is whether I will do it, with the children there. Wait. Look for the pattern. I will need you to tell me when to shoot." I didn't bother to look to see if he agreed.

I forced myself to concentrate, watching the goats, watching the children. Mihae said something; Cillian growled an answer. I kept watching. The children were chasing the animals, but they weren't getting in among them, but staying at the edge of the herd. If I shot low, aiming the arrow's drop for the very edge of the fence, there would be almost no danger to a child.

I raised the bow again. Someone watching gasped. Part of my mind wondered if one of the children was his. I wasn't going to try for the brown-and-white doe; I was just going to shoot into the mass of animals when they crowded against the fence, and hope I killed one. "You see?" I murmured to Cillian.

"Yes."

"Tell me when they are rounding the corner again. I want them all along the close fence."

I drew the bow, holding the draw, focusing on the shot, not the animals. "Soon," Cillian warned, and "Now." The goats massed along the fence, and the arrow flew.

One of the children must have seen it, because he or she screamed. The goats scattered, but one lay kicking. Not the doe, but a smaller, brown animal, with the arrow just behind its front leg. I handed Cillian the bow, and walked down to cut the animal's throat, in front of all the men.

I wiped the blood off my knife and my hands and walked back to where Mihae stood. "You owe us a map, and your captain must tell us the truth," I spat. My tone would not need translation. I gathered the bow, and the quiver, feeling the energy drain from me. "I must stay," Cillian said. "Sorley will walk you to the ship, and fetch Geiri."

"Can I not walk back by myself, now?" I said.

"Perhaps," he answered. "Or perhaps not, not safely. I would prefer to not worry about you, Lena." It was mildly said, but the rebuke was there. He had other things to concentrate on, for all of us, and my pride should not interfere with that. Nor, it seemed, would the fact that I had tried to kill him, earlier.

Sorley gave me a worried look, but he said nothing. He escorted me to the ship. I sat, drained of energy. Sorley went to speak to Geiri. I needed food, I knew. After a while I got up, found what remained of the bread and soft cheese from breakfast, and made myself eat. The deck was hot in the afternoon sun. I stretched out in our sleeping place.

I didn't sleep. I didn't think much about what I had done, or why. I just drifted, letting images float by, suspended in some place out of time. After what felt like a long while, I heard voices. Mihae, and a woman's voice, and then Cillian's. They had come for the fee.

I heard Cillian's footsteps on the deck. He came over to our space. He placed a rolled kidskin in his pack, then knelt beside me. "I only have a minute," he said. "Are you all right, *käresta*?"

"Just tired," I said. I sat up. "Cillian, what can I say?"

"There is nothing to say," he said. "You were threatened. You reacted. That's all."

"I tried to kill you!" Why was he always so calm, so reasonable? I answered my own question. Because he is trained to analyze, and to be dispassionate in his conclusions.

"No, Lena, you did not. Mihae threatened you, in your mind. I stepped between you, because murdering our host seemed to me to be a waste of all our negotiations, somehow."

"Why do you do that?" I demanded. "Always deflect, like that?"

"Years of practice," he said, almost lightly. "Years of avoiding how I feel, I suppose." He took my hand, his long fingers curving around mine. "We should talk about what happened today. But right now, Lena, I am weary, and there is one more thing to do that cannot be put off. Will you come to see the fee paid? Or, rather, to see the beauty of what Irmgard is giving up?"

"Do you want me be there?"

"Always. But I also think you should be, to be respectful of Mihae. We do hope to come back this way, before long."

The ivory and amber given, we were free to go. We had two hours until the tide. Turlo turned to Cillian. "I suggest you sleep, until just before we sail, but I have one last thing to ask of you. Will you walk with me along the jetty?"

I went to pick up my journal, to record the day's events. I heard my name; the breeze blew towards the ship, carrying the words. "Can you be impartial and tell me if she is fit to fight?" Turlo asked. "I am aware of what has happened to my Guard. But unpredictability is dangerous."

"I have not the experience to make that judgment," Cillian answered. "But I can tell you with certainty that the same thing will happen again, if Lena is startled from behind, and feels threatened."

"Aye," Turlo said. "Even you?"

"I try not to approach her that way, or if I must, to say something to her as I do."

He always called my name, if he came up to me from behind. I stayed still, listening.

"You are sure you are not injured?"

"A scratch where the secca brushed me, and there will be a bruise on my left ankle."

"Aye, well, I've had worse over the years from pulling apart fighting cadets," Turlo said, with a laugh. "Your first wounds of war. But may I stop being your general, and presume to be your friend?"

"No presumption, Turlo."

"Then may I say that I am concerned, a bit, for you both? This will be a hard balance, now you outrank her, and while that may seem of little consequence now it will not be, if things go as we hope. Officers of the Empire know that they may have to send their sons to almost-certain death, and that is difficult enough. Could you send her into desperate battle, Cillian?"

"No," Cillian said. "I doubt I can."

"That is why I asked as a friend," Turlo said. "So I will tell you both, later, that Lena is under my direct command, bypassing you. Not a usual arrangement, but nothing is usual, any more." He paused. "May I ask one more thing?"

"Of course."

"I am not sure this is even a question, and you do not need to answer, mind. But Lena is very dear to me. You are much older than she is, Cillian."

"I am," Cillian answered. "I am not unaware of this, Turlo. Would such a difference in years be of consequence, in the Empire?"

"No. Not quite, although it approaches what we consider unsuitable," Turlo said. "Ah, what does it matter anyhow?" he added. "Just take care of her, *mo charaidh*."

"I will," Cillian said. "I am sworn to. *Ar fosidh di, mo chaol iômhlán.*"

"To shelter her, all your life?"

"Yes. As best I can."

"It was more than I could do, for my Arey," Turlo said, so quietly I barely heard the words.

"I am sorry, Turlo. I have some idea, now, of what pain you must feel."

"Aye," Turlo replied. "And I hope you never feel it. You need to sleep. I'll send for you, when it's time to sail."

I turned away. Shelter me. My own words to him, about how he made me feel, turned into a promise. Sorley had said our vows fit. I saw why. My thoughts returned to earlier in the day, to my thoughts about language, about words spoken and words understood, and the gap that could exist between those two things. He had been, was, would always be sanctuary and refuge for me. Not protection: that was not possible, in the world as it was, or in any world. He understood that, I thought. As best I can. It was all any of us could do.

PART III

...a towering pride in his sensibility, and an endearing disposition to be a hero.
                                                                    Fry

CHAPTER THIRTEEN

I THOUGHT I WAS A GOOD SAILOR, but those first days on a Marai ship taught me otherwise. Even well-ballasted with rocks, the ship lacked the stability I was used to on *Dovekie*, and until we had become used to the sway, everyone but the Marai men—and even one or two of them—was seasick and wretched. I cannot imagine what the voyage would have been like in bad weather. But the sun shone, and the wind blew steadily from the west, the rectangular sail billowing out and sending us forward. By the third day out, I had found my sea-legs and my stomach had stopped writhing.

Turlo looked pale and drawn, but his spirits were high this morning. Cillian and Sorley were less cheerful, being careful with the food provided for breakfast. As the morning went on and breakfast stayed down, Sorley especially began to recover. Mid-morning, he approached Cillian, who was sitting, arms around his knees, doing nothing. Recovering, I thought; three days of seasickness on top of his efforts at Sylana had left him drained. Sorley crouched beside him. *"Imirdh xache liovha, mo charaidh?[11]"* he said.

"Xache?" Cillian replied, clearly puzzled.

"Thá[12]. Faich[13]." He opened the skin bag he carried, to take out intricately carved game pieces. They must be part of Irmgard's treasure. How did he convince her to let him use them? Cillian took one, turning it in his fingers. *"Hálainn[14],"* he murmured.

"Thá," Sorley agreed. From beneath his arm he took a rolled kidskin, spreading it out on the deck to reveal inked black squares alternating with plain ones. Suddenly, Cillian grinned. "Lena," he called, "come here, would you?" He gave me the game piece. "Hold it behind your back, in one hand. You choose," he said to Sorley.

"Left," Sorley said. I held out the game piece.

"I will go first," Sorley elected. "It is the only advantage I will have, no doubt."

---

[11] Play xache with me, my friend?

[12] Yes

[13] See

[14] Beautiful

Cillian would be all right, I decided. I had been too sick myself these last days to give him the attention I thought I should have. Not that there was much I could do. I had ginger root, dug at the lake, and I had made a tea with it for us all, but if it was effective, the results didn't last for long. I couldn't keep the anash down, either, but I didn't think it mattered: I had been drinking it regularly the last time we made love, and there would be no other time now until Casil, at least.

I made my way to the stern, where Turlo stood. "Feeling better?" I asked him.

"Aye. But I know why I didn't choose the ships when I was twelve."

"I did, and it didn't help. Every boat is different. We should be fine now, unless we hit bad weather," I told him.

"Then let's hope we don't," he replied with feeling. I glanced back at where the two men played *xache*.

"Thank you for that," I said, indicating the game with a movement of my head.

"I will give them today to recover and enjoy some leisure, but tomorrow we need to begin planning." Turlo said.

"What do we need to do?"

"Several things. Mostly falling on Cillian, again, I'm afraid. We will need letters, to be sent to whomever makes such decisions about allowing us to see the Empress. I want to keep the lady Irmgard's petition separate from ours."

We knew more, now, from the trader who had given the map and his advice. Casil had an Empress, Eudekia, ruling as regent for her baby son after her husband had died last year. They were at war, he said, a long-standing conflict with an eastern neighbour that didn't seem to affect trade, but treaty negotiations had begun before the Emperor's death, and he thought they probably were at peace now. When Cillian had relayed that, the first evening on the ship before seasickness had taken hold of us, we had exchanged dubious glances. Surely there was more reason to think Casil would have been defeated, under those circumstances? But Cillian had asked and the trader captain had been unworried: when he'd been there last, only a few weeks earlier with the spring trade of furs, the talk of the port had been no different than many previous visits.

Turlo glanced to the prow where Irmgard and her women lay on furs. They had been equally seasick. "So, Cillian will need to write that letter, and then another, detailing who we are and what we are asking."

"Sorley can write in Casilan, as well," I pointed out.

"Aye, I know. But not with the skill in diplomacy Cillian can."

"That can't be all."

"No. What are we asking for? What can we offer them, in return? What do we do if they say yes to Irmgard and no to us? If she wishes to keep her ship and her oarsmen, we have no way to return home, except overland. And many other questions that will arise from those discussions."

"I see," I said. "We are making some large assumptions about Casil, aren't we?" I added. "That their idea of Empire is the same as ours; that they will remember us, or believe us, and care."

"Aye. All of those."

"Callan was truly desperate, wasn't he? To send you, one of his best generals, and a friend, on such an impossible quest?"

"He was, lassie. You have to be prepared that we will go home to a land lost and a people defeated, if we get home." He sighed. "But that must not influence our planning. And another thing to do, for my adjutant: I want him to teach us some basic Casilan."

Laughter from Sorley, followed by a stream of Linrathan. "He lost in six moves," Turlo said. "He is berating himself for ever thinking he could play."

"Cillian plays exceedingly well," I said.

"Of course he does," Turlo said. "It is a game of strategy and tactics, determining what the effects of each move could be not just in the immediate but several turns ahead. Callan has no equal at it, although I'm not sure who I'd wager on, if he and Cillian were playing." He considered. "Probably Callan, at that: he has the years of experience."

"Lena," Sorley called, "come and play Cillian, so I can see someone else be humiliated."

The game had, of course, attracted spectators. I remembered Dern telling me once that soldiers bet on anything; it appeared the Marai did, too. "You play him," I suggested to Turlo.

"Aye, maybe I will. Not that I'll win."

Nor did he, although I could see he gave Cillian a better battle than I would have, by far. Then, reluctantly, I played Sorley, with Cillian and Turlo watching. Sorley beat me, but only after a fair fight. He bagged the pieces, carefully. "I better give these back to Irmgard; she will allow us to use them, but she wants them under her care, otherwise."

Both Turlo and Cillian looked better for the time spent playing; more colour in their faces, and brighter eyes. Cillian stood up, stretching. "I might even be hungry," he said, sounding surprised.

"Just eat lightly," I warned. "A little food, every few hours."

"General," Irmgard called, from the bow. He went to her, then beckoned us over. She was sitting up, looking pale, but like the rest us recovered from the worst of the sea-sickness. "I have something for each of you," she announced. "To show my gratitude, in what you did to make us free of that town."

"General," she said, handing Turlo a silver armband decorated with animal heads. "For you." He took it, surprising me by bowing.

"Lady Irmgard," he said, "thank you." He slipped it on; it fit his arm well.

Sorley's gift was a thinner armband, and mine was an amber pendant with an insect embedded in the stone. "*Takkë*, Lady Irmgard," I said, "*Takkë*. It is beautiful."

She turned to Cillian. "Cillian na Perras," she said. "I would have a private word with you, if you will?"

"*Ádla*Irmgard, of course," he answered. We had been dismissed. From the stern, I tried not to watch them. Cillian rejoined us after a few minutes.

"What did she give you?"

"An apology, and this." He showed me a small ivory pot, carved with a running, intertwined ribbon. "It's an ink pot, or can be used as one."

"It's lovely. What did she need to apologize for?" He didn't answer, but with a movement of his head beckoned me away from the others.

"For her assumptions about me, and also about you."

"I see," I said. "Even in Varsland?"

"If it served my purpose, yes," he said. "I will not be dishonest about this, Lena."

For a moment it felt as if I did not know him. A thought struck me. "Not—?"

He laughed, gently. "No. Not Irmgard, of course, and not these serving women, either. That would have been difficult. And it was many years ago, *käresta*. I am not that man, any longer."

For the next week we sailed eastward, a steady wind keeping us on course. Every few days we anchored at spots shown on the map to take on fresh water, and sometimes fishing boats from scattered villages hailed us, or followed us for a while, but without aggression.

When the ship was under sail, we could practice on deck with a sword in a limited way. There wasn't room for two people to take each other on, but the guards and strikes still could be rehearsed. I felt the motions getting easier as my muscles regained strength, and this was true for all of us, I thought. With Geiri's approval, I tried line fishing, as much for something to do rather than trying to provide fresh food. I did catch some fish, but I was glad we weren't relying on me to feed us.

Turlo kept Cillian busy. Writing on the deck of a ship wasn't easy, as I knew from my journal, and writing formal letters, where the appearance of the letter mattered as well as what it said, was a challenge. I heard him curse more than once and sigh, before carefully scraping the vellum to erase an error caused by a lurch in the ship, or a slip of the pen.

But mostly, we talked. Sometimes just the four of us, sometimes with Irmgard. Every possible outcome at Casil was analyzed, debated, argued. Irmgard was in tears when Cillian and Turlo made her understand that the fiction Cillian had proposed at Sylana, a negotiated marriage, might be the best protection for her in Casil. "Not right away, and not to the first man who offers," Turlo said. "But your resources will not last forever, and you will be vulnerable, my lady. You must consider it."

"I will have Geiri, and his men, to protect me," she argued.

"How long can you pay them?" Cillian asked gently. "And house you and your women, and the men, and feed you all? *Ådla*, I know you mourn Åsmund, and I know you loved him. But you must think of what will be best for you."

She wiped her tears. "How strange still, to hear you speak of love, *laerth*. There was a time you would have only acknowledged that I mourned. Would you give Lena the same advice?"

"To do what is best for her, for her survival, yes," Cillian said. "But Lena's skills are not yours, *Ádla*, and it might be her ability with bow and sword, or with fishing, for all I know, that would give her other choices. Not ones you have."

She smiled, sadly. "I will think about this. I would not be Fritjof's plaything, I who have been Åsmund's wife. But perhaps, in time, a good man, of sufficient rank. I will need to think more." With a word to Rind and Hana, she withdrew to the bow.

"Geiri does not plan to stay," Sorley said quietly.

"No?" Turlo asked.

"No. He hates Fritjof passionately. Åsmund was his lord, and he wants his chance to avenge him. There are several of the men who feel the same."

"Aye, well, they'll be welcome," Turlo said. "But the lady Irmgard will not be pleased."

So Geiri harbours the cold, still blade of vengeance in him too. Aloud, I said, "fewer mouths to feed, though."

If he felt as I did, he would not be swayed, I was certain. The talk turned to how many soldiers and ships and weapons Casil might send. This was pure speculation, and Turlo stopped it quickly. "We must be precise in what we ask," he said. "What is it we need most?"

"Ships," Sorley said, "to meet the Marai at sea."

"Archers," I added. "The Marai do not use bows, and we can kill men before they leave the ships, or from a distance if they are on land."

"Both good ideas," Turlo said.

"I'll make notes." Cillian began to get up, to fetch pen and paper, but Sorley stopped him.

"You do enough," he said. "I can write this, as it's only for us."

"Thank you." Sorley gave him a quick grin and went off for the equipment. Cillian needing him at Sylana, to instruct him on tariffs and check the figures, had benefited Sorley, I thought. He was finding ways to be with him that were—what? Bearable, I supposed.

Other than the occasional game of *xache*, and music and stories of an evening, every day passed in much the same way. I thought the lack of privacy to relieve ourselves would disconcert Irmgard and her women, but they took it in stride, balancing on the edge of the ship as needed. I, like the men, stripped and swam every couple of days, preferring the salt on my skin and in my hair over not feeling clean. Sometimes, the other women joined me, although Geiri kept the Marai men's eyes away from Irmgard. When my bleeding time began, a week or so after we sailed, I swam daily, and sometimes twice a day. But its onset made me realize how much had happened in one brief month.

A few days later, a day dawned with little wind. As the sea-anchor was hauled up, Geiri ordered the men back to rowing. The sea lay smooth until after the sun had reached its zenith, and the glare off the water hurt my eyes. And not just mine. One of the oarsmen—Rafn—began to complain, I learned through Sorley, of headache.

I used some of my willow-bark to make a drink for the man. But by mid-afternoon he was worse, aching all over. The wind had risen and we were travelling under sail again. More willow-bark did nothing. As evening fell, he began to shake.

"Fever," Sorley said. I touched the man's skin. It was clammy. A hint of fear appeared in my mind.

"Cillian," I called. He came over. "What do you remember about the Eastern Fever?"

He crouched beside me. "Very little. What do you want to know?"

"Symptoms, I suppose. Treatment. Anything."

"You would need someone from the *Ti'ach na Iorlath* for that. Are you not jumping to conclusions? This could be any summer fever, from bad food, perhaps?"

"He hasn't been sick, or had loose bowels. Look at him, Cillian."

The man's teeth chattered as he shook. Geiri put furs over him. Sorley had gone to speak to the Marai women. "They have no ideas," he said when he returned.

"Anash will not hurt him," I said, wondering if that were true. "And it is the only remedy I know with any connection to the Eastern Fever." I thought about my supply; there was enough.

I made the tea as strongly as I thought I could and still have it palatable. I wondered if Rafn would drink it, and if he would keep it down. It was horribly bitter, but I had grown used to it over time.

By the time I brought it to him, Rafn had thrown off the furs, sweating profusely. "Help him sit up," I told Geiri. I held the cup to his lips. "Tell him this tastes terrible, but he must drink it." Sorley relayed the message. Rafn took a sip, and spat it out. "Na!" I said, and held the cup up again. This time he swallowed the tea, grimacing, and over the next few minutes we got most of it down him. He fell into a restless sleep.

At dinner, fish stew made from the dried supplies, and a rough biscuit, one of the other men pushed his bowl away. Geiri questioned him, sharply. "His head hurts, and he does not want food," Sorley told me. The stewpot had been cleaned and filled again with water. It steamed over the firebowl. I tested it with a finger: hot enough. I put handfuls of anash into the pot, stirred it, and left it to settle and steep. I'd used nearly half my supply, I noted.

Geiri took the cup of anash over the man, who shook his head. They argued, and in the end the man drank it down. But a few minutes later he stumbled to the side and vomited. He sank down against the side, and I could see he was shivering.

By morning we had three sick men: Rafn, Detlef, who had fallen sick at dinner, and Ulv. Detlef concerned me the most: he simply could not keep the anash down, hot or cold. The other two alternated between chills and fever, the violent shivering giving way to profuse sweating. Rafn hallucinated, thrashing under his furs, sometimes taking two men to hold him down. Ulv lay quieter, occasionally moaning. But each bout of shaking left Detlef weaker, and even

Geiri could not get him to drink anything.

In the night, I had remembered what Dagney had told me about the ring game, and the red rash of the Eastern Fever. Whatever this was, then, it wasn't that, but the anash appeared to help, so I kept giving it to them. Rind and Hana and Sorley helped, cooling the men with cloths dipped in water when their fevers ran high and piling on furs when they shivered.

"If anyone else falls ill, I do not have enough anash," I told Turlo and Cillian on the third day after Rafn had complained of headache.

"No one else is showing symptoms," Cillian said.

"No. And we haven't kept them separate at all. Maybe no one else will. Maybe something gave them this fever, but not anyone else. I wish I could talk to my mother." The words brought sudden tears to my eyes. I did want my mother, and not just because I needed her healer's wisdom. I wanted against all odds to know she was safe, to see her hands retying her hair as she thought out a problem, to hear her calm, reasoning voice. I began to cry. "I don't know what I'm doing."

His arms went around me immediately. "Shhh, käresta," his voice murmured. "You're tired."

"Aye," Turlo said. "Step down, Guard. The others know what to do. You're resting until we eat tonight."

He was right. I would be of no use if I too fell ill, or was simply confused by tiredness. I stepped back from Cillian's embrace. "General," I said, acknowledging the order. Suddenly I wanted the feel of water. "May I swim first, before I rest?"

"Aye," he replied. "Adjutant, keep an eye on her in the water. But I want you back working on these plans before too long, mind."

I stripped, realizing as I did that I had not changed shirt or breeches for several days, and slipped over the side into the warmth of the sea. Cillian was right behind me. I submerged, running my hands through my hair, before turning over and floating, the waves rocking me. Cillian swam over to me.

"As if you need anyone to keep an eye on you in the water," he said.

"Turlo was being kind, giving us a little time together," I replied. I had my eyes closed against the sun.

"I know. Would you tell me about your mother, Lena?"

I had not told him much about her, avoiding it because he had grown up without his. I had spoken more of *Dovekie* and fishing, and council meetings, than I had of my family. "Her name was Gwen," I answered.

"Is," Cillian said quietly. "Until you know with certainty, she is not lost. You are holding on to your end of the thread. Just as she will have been doing for you."

"Is," I repeated. "She is healer and midwife to Tirvan, along with my sister Kira. Kira has a different father," I added. "She—my mother—is a council leader, along with her sister Sara."

"Do you look like her?"

"My mother? No. She's rounder, and a little shorter than me, compact. Our hair is close in colour, although hers is darker, but she wears hers up on her head, and it was half-grey, the last time I saw her, in Berge. And her eyes are blue. I look more like Galen, if you remember."

"I suppose you do," Cillian said, treading water beside me. "In build, and his eyes were hazel, too, weren't they?"

"Yes."

"Your childhood was happy, *käresta*, I can tell, with your mother, and sister."

"And aunts and cousins, and all the women." I smiled, remembering, feeling the grief not far below. "Thank you, my love. I think I will sleep now."

We swam back to the ship. As we dried, Cillian made a quiet sound of contemplation. I looked at him questioningly. "Gwen," he said. "My mother was Hafwen, or Wenna, as my father called her. Just a coincidence, but still... Go and sleep now, Lena."

Detlef died that evening, convulsing and screaming before slipping into unconsciousness and then death. With little ceremony, ballast rocks and one axe were placed inside his tunic, his belt tightened around his wasted frame to hold them in place, and his body given to the sea. The other two men still cycled through bouts of shivering and sweating, but they were no worse, and no one else had fallen ill.

My supply of anash grew very low. I was guessing as to the smallest amount I could drink each evening. I would, I decided, give up my own daily tea if I had to: we weren't going to make love on the ship, and even if there was opportunity once we reached Casil, well, we could find other ways to be together, as Cillian had pointed out once. And maybe, I thought, I can get more anash, once we're there.

But it did not prove necessary. Rafn and Ulv began to improve the next day, their fevers abating. They were as weak as newborn rabbits, but they were going to live. After another day, I reduced the anash to morning and night doses, with willow-bark as needed in between. Had the tea made a difference? I had no way to know.

CHAPTER FOURTEEN

FIVE DAYS LATER, IN THE LONG RAYS of early evening light, we came to Casil.

For the three days previous, we had sailed past villages that straggled up the coastal cliffs as the land rose steadily. The shouted conversations with fishing boats had increased, and we made a few trades for fresh fish, and any information about rocks or shoals the fishermen could give us. This morning had dawned clear, as all the days did, but with a fair breeze. To the north the land rose even higher, and from our anchored position in the sea we could see a tall tower at the top.

"Geiri says that's the headland marked on the map, and once we pass it we turn north," Sorley reported.

"If we are allowed to," Turlo said. "If we can see the tower, they can see us. Expect to be challenged." Sorley repeated the words to Geiri in *Maráis'sta*. Geiri grunted acknowledgment and spoke to his men.

"We are clear on our stories?" Turlo asked. We had debated this yesterday, not for the first time. There was no issue regarding Irmgard: Cillian would relay her true story. But for the four of us, what was best, once Irmgard's status had been settled and we were free to present our own petition? At the heart of the question had been Cillian, and to a lesser extent, me. Turlo would be presented as exactly what he was: a senior officer, sent in the Emperor's name to request help from Casil. Sorley was a noble from Linrathe, speaking for the people resisting Fritjof there. But was Cillian simply Turlo's adjutant, or was he the Emperor's son?

"Present me as your adjutant," Cillian had argued, "until we know more about how Emperors are chosen here. We believe it to be an inherited position, or why else would the Empress be regent for her son? But she could be clinging to power, or being propped up by powerful men as a figurehead. We can always reveal the other later, if it is necessary."

"I suppose you are right," Turlo had said in the end. "We should hold that fact in reserve. Now what about Lena?

"I am going to make you an officer, lassie," Turlo decided. "I know the difficulties, but as an officer you will, I hope, be allowed whatever privileges may be offered; as a simple soldier, I am afraid you will be separated from us."

Put like that, I saw no option. "I suppose." I would at least be close to Cillian, this way. "All right," I said.

"Cohort-leader, again, then," Turlo said. I had been offered this, on the Wall as well, but I'd had had enough of making decisions then and turned it down. I nodded.

"Done," Turlo announced. "Cillian, explain yourself as a translator, negotiator, whatever words you need to use, and Lena as a junior officer, brought along as part of her training."

Sorley exhaled loudly. "I don't like this," he said. "Why are we misleading people we hope to be our allies?" I didn't entirely disagree with him. Something about these conversations bothered me.

"Not misleading," Cillian said, "just revealing as little as possible, couching our roles in simple terms to begin with. If this Empire has indeed gone on unbroken in the five hundred years since we were last in contact, these will be people skilled in the arts of diplomacy and negotiation, far more than any of us. They will expect us either to be unschooled in those arts, our request for help simple, or, they will assume at least some subtlety from us. It is like playing *xache* with a new opponent. It is never wise to give away your strategy in the first few moves."

"But our request for help is simple," Sorley argued.

"Is it?" Turlo and Cillian exchanged a look. "Sorley, we have spoken of this before. Do you think, *mo charaidh*, that they will give us assistance simply because the West has kept faith with them for all these years?" Cillian asked. "They will want something in return, if they agree."

"What? What can we give them, in return?"

"At the very least, tribute. At the most, our independence. You must accept that we may be exchanging Marai overlords for those of the East, a known horror for an unknown, possibly. What we hope is that the East has retained those aspects of our own societies that we consider civilised."

"But our own two countries don't agree on that," I said.

"They do not," Cillian agreed. "Which is why much of Sorham and Linrathe sided with Fritjof. If Åsmund were on the throne of Varsland, and he had approached the *Teannasach* with an eye to a different treaty between Varsland and Linrathe, one that emphasised our commonalities, Linrathe would have moved towards Varsland, not the Empire. Do you not agree, Sorley?"

"I suppose so," Sorley said.

"Nor would the Empire have seen Linrathe as a natural ally," Turlo said. "All this will likely have to be revealed in any discussion of support from Casil. But slowly and carefully."

"I am going to have to decide what Linrathe would give up for help from Casil, am I not?" Sorley asked.

"Either you or me, Sorley, and I have no right to do so now, nor ever did," Cillian answered. "You are noble, and can at least claim some authority."

"How does leadership in Linrathe work?" I asked. "Donnalch was chosen *Teannasach*, was he not?"

"The *Teannasach* always comes from one family," Cillian replied, "although not always the oldest in the direct line, and sometimes not even from the direct line, if there are no male heirs, or there are doubts about competency. Lorcann's son could be the next *Teannasach*, in theory, if Ruar were deemed unsuitable."

"But as both are still boys, who would be—regent? Is that the right word?"

Cillian frowned. "A good question, and not one I can answer. Donnalch and Lorcann had one uncle: if he is still alive, it would most likely be him. If he is dead—" He shook his head. "It is too tangled to work out, from this distance, not knowing who lives or is dead."

"But is there a council of advisors to the *Teannasach*?"

"Yes. They meet twice a year. But they advise, not direct, the *Teannasach*. Why are you asking this, Lena?"

"I am trying to understand what authority Sorley might have."

"About the same as you have, to speak for the Empire's villages," Turlo said, "if I understand this correctly."

"Which is none," I pointed out.

"Which is not something we had considered, at all," Turlo replied. "Cillian, is this something else to hold in reserve?"

"It might be," Cillian said. "I will need to think about that, how and when it might be useful."

A wave of anger engulfed me at his words. "Can you hear yourself?" I said. "You are playing games, just as Callan did, using Sorley and me as pieces to gain an end. How can you?" I had wanted to escape this, this callous interplay of power and politics. As had he, I had thought.

"Because I must. We must. Because this is not about power, but about the lives of men and women we care about," he replied, gently. "And I am using myself, too, and Turlo, and Irmgard, in a way. I promise you both that I—we—will do our best to have you choose as freely as any of us can. You saw, just now, that the idea of you representing the women's villages of the Empire was new, for both Turlo and me, and Sorley has known his role for some time."

"I have," Sorley said. "It just wasn't real, until now, and perhaps I had not realized all the ramifications. I suppose none of us can, until we know what Casil might ask of us. Cillian, did you mean these words? That you promise to let us choose as freely as we can?"

"I did."

"Then that is all I need to hear. I trust you to do what is needed, and counsel me in what is best for Linrathe."

My quick anger had subsided, leaving discontent in its wake. But what had I thought would happen in Casil? Of course there would be long, detailed, subtle negotiations. We hadn't got out of Sylana without them, and all we'd wanted to do was pass through. And Cillian had made a promise. "Forgive me," I said. "I too trust you both, to do what is needed." I caught Cillian's eye. *"Forla,"* I murmured. He smiled, slightly, acknowledging the private apology.

"True authority or not, you must think about what the women's villages might want, and what they might give," Turlo said, "for you are the only person who can speak for them."

"I understand," I replied. I didn't want to do this. But nor did Sorley want to make decisions for Linrathe. I watched Cillian run a hand through his hair and along the back of his neck, stretching to relieve tension. Turlo looked grim. None of us wanted what we had been brought to. Not just we four, but Irmgard and her women, and even Geiri and his men. I had to accept that. I was twenty-one, four years an adult. It was time I acted like it.

The crew adjusted the sail, and Geiri leaned hard on the steerboard at the right of the ship. The sun had passed its zenith a couple of hours earlier. We began to curve around the headland. Almost immediately, three ships began to approach. We slowed.

One ship came up beside us on each side. The third stayed behind. We waited, weaponless, hands at our sides, except for the men needed to work sails and ropes. Irmgard stood at the bow, Rind and Hana with her. I hope we looked unthreatening. The left-hand ship came in very close, the rowers positioning the long oars to allow it. A man—short haired, shaven, dressed in tunic and cloak, sword at his side—called out.

Calmly, Cillian replied. His Casilan sounded, to me, much more fluent and much more confident. He held up the rolled vellum. The two ships manoeuvred even closer until it could be passed, tied to an oar, from one to the other.

The man on the Casilani ship read it, frowning. He looked up, his eyes raking our ship, focusing on Irmgard and then on Turlo and Cillian. He glanced down at the letter again. "*Séquer!*" he called, and then something to his men. They began to row.

"Follow him," Cillian translated. "We have passed the first test."

"What did the letter say?" I asked.

"It is Irmgard's petition for sanctuary," Cillian answered. "It outlined her reasons for fleeing, and that we—her escort—are from the Western Empire, sent by the Emperor to protect her. Sorley, I am afraid your role was not explained; I thought it would complicate the petition too greatly."

"You know best," Sorley replied.

"The hope was that the Empress will look kindly on another royal woman's petition for sanctuary, and the mention of the Western Empire will catch her interest. I imagine that archaic written Casilan may also be a curiosity, and perhaps a validation."

It took several hours to cross the wide bay. The Casilani ships maintained a steady pace, not too fast, spaced around us. I watched their ships: higher than ours and half again as long, wider beamed for stability, and with a different sail arrangement. Warships, I thought.

"Look!" Cillian said. I turned from my study of the ships to look. Ahead of us stood a tall tower tipped with flame, and on either side wide jetties curved out to nearly meet the tower, creating a huge, sheltered basin. Behind that, lit with gold by the westering sun, tall buildings of stone lined the harbour.

"*Casil, your powers are these: to make the peace and ensure the rule of law, to show mercy to the conquered and overcome the proud,*" Cillian said. Sorley joined him on the last phrases, confirming my thought that Cillian was quoting someone.

"What's that from?" I asked.

"A long, long poem, a *danta* of sorts, I suppose, about the legendary founding of Casil," Sorley said. "I don't think I remember any more of it but that line. Donnalch liked to quote it."

"I remember learning that as a cadet," Turlo said. "I didn't know it was from a long poem, though."

"It's strange," Sorley said, "that the Empire, which sees itself as an heir to Casil, has lost the learning that Linrathe had kept, although we were never subject to the East."

"Aye," Turlo agreed. "Perhaps our focus was too narrow, concerning ourselves with war and defense only. But those choices were made generations ago."

With every choice, we leave someone or something behind, Irmgard had said not very long ago. The idea echoed in my mind. What choices would be made, by us or for us, here in this ancient city?

The ship drew up against the quay, following pointed directions and shouts. The commander of the ship to whom Cillian had given the letter disembarked from his own docked ship to come over to us. He and Cillian spoke for several minutes, apparently amicably. Then the man nodded and walked away, not back to his ship, but up the quay towards the buildings.

"We are to stay here. We will be guarded, and curious on-lookers kept away. There are latrines in the building over there," he pointed, "and we will be escorted as needed. Rufin—he is a commander of the watch on the headland— will take the letter to the appropriate authority, he says. He also says he doubts anyone will see us tonight, but if they wish to see us tomorrow, expect to be taken to baths where we can be made respectable before we are allowed in the presence of any official." Cillian grinned. "We probably do need that, wouldn't you say?"

We were windblown, salt-encrusted, and in the case of the men, unshaven. If Casil had baths, I liked it already.

I was tugging a comb through my hair the next morning when Rufin reappeared, another man and a woman beside him. He beckoned Cillian up to the quay where they spoke for some time, the other man occasionally adding something, the woman quiet.

Rufin clapped Cillian on the shoulder, said something, looked over to us watching on the ship, and saluted. Then he strode off down the quay. Cillian turned back to us.

"Well," he said. "Geiri and the oarsmen are to stay here, for now. They will be housed shortly. We are to be taken to the baths and then to a house that has been assigned to us. The Empress—or at least an official—is being generous. We will be given not just the house, but servants to look after us, and clothes appropriate to Casil, I am told."

"Servants to spy on us, no doubt," Turlo growled.

"Of course," Cillian said. "It is the rest of it I wonder about: who is the Empress attempting to impress with this show of munificence? I doubt it is just us."

"Does it matter?" I asked, longing for the baths.

"I suppose not, not at this moment," he answered. "The woman's name is

Prisca; she is aware you speak no Casilan beyond a few words. Follow her. We go with Sergius, here."

Irmgard and her women disembarked, and we followed Prisca along the quay and past buildings of stone and brick, rising several storeys, taller than anything I had seen in Casilla. At a gate, we were joined by two soldiers, who flanked us through a narrow passage to a waterway. A boat awaited us, broad and flat, propelled by a man with a long pole.

The boat moved along the narrow waterway, quickly joining a river flowing between grassy banks. Buildings lined each side: built of stone, with tiled roofs, they abutted each other in long rows and blocks. We passed beneath a bridge, arching over the river, enormously high brick walls extending from either side. Those make Casilla's walls look like a sheep enclosure, I thought, and then we rounded a curve in the river.

Above the lower buildings, a huge structure, its front a series of arches between three towers, rose. Long walls extended back, three storeys showing a blank face to the river, but set with arches on the ground floor, and with towers at set distances. And above it—could it be that tall, or was it on a hill?—a vast building, shining almost white in the sun, built with graceful curves and arches and columns, dominating the view. We passed under another bridge, and the boatman poled us up to a low jetty.

I glanced at Cillian. Rapt, he studied the buildings. Turning to one of the guards, he asked something. The man grunted an acknowledgement. "The palace," Cillian told us.

"What is the long, walled building below it?" Sorley asked. "I feel I should know."

"The *Arénas Ingenírus,* I think." The guard nodded, pointing. He asked Cillian a question, his eyes widening at the answer.

What still may lie beyond the mountains and the sea. Callan's words, at the White Fort. The reality of what we had found here was beyond anything he could have imagined. The city went on and on beyond the palace. I turned to look at Turlo. He sat beside Irmgard, staring up at the buildings. Overwhelmed, I thought. As was I.

We climbed up onto the jetty. People passed, some staring, most ignoring us. They wore, for the most part, knee-length tunics of varying quality; some men had weapons on their belts, and cloaks over one shoulder. Women's tunics varied in length, but were longer; to my eye, I thought the better quality the material, the longer the tunic, denoting social status, I assumed.

The steward, Sergius, made a clear hand gesture: follow him. He walked beside the building Cillian had called the *Arénas.* How had he known that? We passed through cobbled streets lined with brick buildings, accessed through tall archways. I glimpsed gardens and fountains through the arches, and people sitting on benches, talking, eating. The street opened out into a wide, grassed area, thronged with more people, and at one end of the green space, a square building, steam rising from a central chimney.

Our escorts stopped. "There are different areas for men and women," Cillian told us. "Follow Prisca. We will meet you later, I presume." Prisca turned through an archway, stepping into a portico and then through a wide door into a cool, broad room. An old woman sat behind a counter, piles of cloths behind her, and a deep bowl of soap cakes beside her.

We were handed strips of cloth, and a piece of soap each, before we again followed Prisca into another large room. Benches and pegs lined the walls, clothes hanging from a few of the pegs. I began to undress, hanging my clothes on the pegs and leaving my secca in its boot sheath. I didn't like doing that, but I didn't know what else to do with it. After a brief hesitation, Irmgard and the other two women also undressed. Naked, we entered another room, this one heated, and steamy. Several women, wearing only a cloth around their hips, waited for us. Attendants, I guessed. Prisca gestured me forward to stand on a grated section of the floor, taking my towels from me. One of the women stepped forward and began to ladle water from a bucket over me. I sighed at the feel of warm water and began to soap myself.

Irmgard and her women, understanding what was to be done now, positioned themselves, and for the next ten minutes we luxuriated in the process of becoming clean. My attendant took my soap from me and washed my back and hair, skilled fingers kneading my shoulder muscles as well. When we were all thoroughly clean, and rinsed, we were ushered into the baths proper.

I slipped into the pool of hot water and closed my eyes. How long since I had lain in a proper bath? I wondered idly if these were fed by hot springs, or the water heated by fire. Prisca had not come with us, and no one else entered the room. Were other women being kept from the pool because we were here? I thought it probable, and was glad.

We soaked for a very long time. Irmgard asked the occasional question about the baths, but mostly we just lay in the water, staring up at the ceiling, watching the water's reflection ripple on the figures of gods and goddesses painted there. On the walls shimmered pictures and designs picked out in tiny tiles, like the floor of the White Fort: fruit and animals and entwined patterns. I wondered when the baths had been built.

Eventually, my thoughts became clearer. As welcome as these baths were, and as magnificent as the city appeared to be, we were here for a reason. Several reasons, beginning with the women beside me. I thought about Irmgard and Hana and Rind, staying here in this new land, among people whose language they did not speak and whose customs they did not know. Casil was civilised: would that make a difference, or would they feel as exiled as I had with the Kurzemë? It was so far from her home. Such bravery, to come such a distance.

Prisca stepped into the room almost silently. "*Séquer, gratifi,*" she said, beckoning. Yet another room, and another pool, this one cold. I took a breath, and slid in, waited a minute, and got out. Surprising me, Irmgard and Hana and Rind did the same. Irmgard must have seen my face, because as she got out, she said, "In my land, we get very hot, in a small room with heated rocks, and then we jump in the water, or roll in the snow. This is much the same."

We were led to a room where narrow tables stood. We were to lie on these, Prisca indicated, on our stomachs. An attendant approached each of us, and began to comb out our hair. Mine took no time at all, and then I felt an unguent, smelling of lavender, being applied to my back, and firm hands begin to rub it in. I lay still. These hands, a woman's, did not threaten me, even when they moved to my lower body and my thighs. She worked down my legs, clicking her tongue at the condition of my feet, callused and rough after our long walk across the plain. Withdrawing for a moment, she returned with a rough stone, and began to rub it across the calluses. I drifted, letting her do as she liked, enjoying the sensation of being cossetted. Beside me, I heard Irmgard sigh.

My feet took some time. Finally my attendant finished with them, and by a tap and a small tug on my arm made me understand she wanted me to roll over. I did, and she continued applying the balm. Her hands, on my hips and belly, induced a tiny flicker of something close to arousal. Just a physical response, I assured myself. As she reached my breasts, she stopped, tilting her head questioningly, holding out the jar of ointment. I nodded, and scooped out a bit, massaging it into my breasts. Then she took over again, finishing my upper chest and arms. I thought she was done, but she shook her head, and opening another small pot, applied a different cream to my face and lips.

I felt thoroughly indulged. I sat up, glancing over at the Marai women. Irmgard, on the table beside me, was on her back, and as I watched her attendant offered her the unguent for her breasts. Irmgard shook her head, indicating to the woman to go ahead. The stab of desire that shot through me as I watched the attendant rubbing the cream into Irmgard's breasts shocked me. I looked away, confused and dismayed.

I should not be feeling this, I told myself. I slid off the table. Prisca, seeing my movement, brought me a pile of clothes, light in colour and fabric. There were thin undergarments, and then a slightly thicker tunic with short, loose arms that fell below my knees, and it all fit almost perfectly. The mundane act of dressing grounded me. My response means nothing, I argued in my head, just old memories. I turned to Prisca. I didn't know how to ask her for my knife.

But I needn't have worried. She held it out to me. "*Gratiás,*" I said, hoping I remembered the word correctly. I had no sheath for it. But again, Prisca had thought this out. She produced a thin belt, with a sheath, and after I had put it on, she bloused the tunic over it, nodding.

We again followed Prisca out into the street. Dressed as we now were, we attracted no attention. One soldier stepped away from the wall of the bathhouse to escort us through another maze of cobbled streets. The screams of the gulls drew fainter. We passed more huge buildings, and what felt like hundreds of people, stopping finally outside a house on a wide, clean street. The building, all three storeys of it, was plastered in a pale coating, and roofed in reddish-brown tiles. Wide windows behind narrow balconies stood shuttered against the afternoon sun. We stepped through a portico and into a cool, tiled hall.

Stairs ran up from this hall to a higher floor, and then a third. On the highest floor, bedrooms opened off a common area, and doors at one end opened onto the flat roof of the floor below. Prisca threw bedroom doors open, clearly inviting us to choose. I shook my head, and pointed at the floor below. She frowned.

I pointed to my secca, and then again to the floor below, and then stood at something that approximated how the guards had stood, waiting for us. Prisca looked puzzled, but she shrugged, opening her hands wide in acquiescence or incomprehension. Below us, I heard the men's voices, and feet on the stairs. I went down to join them.

All three looked as if their ministrations had been as good as ours. Turlo's hair and beard had been neatly trimmed, shorter than I had ever seen either. Both Cillian and Sorley had been shaved, and their hair cut. A spicy scent rose from their skin. They were dressed in clothes like mine, the tunics shorter and with shorter sleeves, but of the same light fabric.

"Weren't those baths wonderful!" Sorley said.

"Very," I said. "Cillian, can you tell Sergius, or Prisca, that I am not sleeping on the top floor with the women? I tried to make her understand, but I'm not sure she did."

"Of course," he said, and conveyed the message to Sergius, who had been opening the doors, much as Prisca had. Sergius replied with a question and a lengthy conversation followed.

Cillian held up a hand to Sergius, turning to us. "Sergius's first question was to ask we all slept alone, which allowed me to ask about customs here. Even knowing he will be relaying everything he learns back to the palace, we are going to need to trust him, within reason. He tells me that since the Emperor Adricius, whose *quincalum*—the word means 'freely-chosen partner', not a slave or a servant—was an officer, the prohibition on relationships between officers was rescinded. So, General, unless you object, I will tell him that we only require three rooms."

"I have no objection," Turlo said.

"Lena?" Cillian asked.

"Of course," I said.

He spoke to Sergius, who nodded, impassive, and opened the door of one bedroom, offering it to Cillian with an outstretched hand. We stepped inside. The room was large and the bed wide. Shuttered windows opened to the sky; the building beside us much shorter than ours. At the far end the room, a door opened into a smaller room, housing a washing area, and a latrine.

"I think," Cillian said, after Sergius had left us, "we may have robbed Turlo of the best bedroom."

"Turlo," I said, "is quite likely to sleep on the floor, even in the best bedroom."

Cillian laughed. "He does seem able to sleep anywhere, at any time," he said. He sat on the bed, and then lay back. "I, on the other hand, am looking forward to a bed again, and this one is very comfortable." He grinned at me. "As perhaps we will find out, tonight?" he said, dropping his voice.

"It would be a shame to waste the bath," I murmured. "But, that reminds me, Cillian. I am nearly out of anash. I can show Prisca what I have and try to ask her for more. Do you know the Casilan word for it?"

"No," he said. "I will ask her, if you like. The conversation may make her uncomfortable, though; it is not men's business, I would think."

"I'm sorry if it will embarrass you."

"Not me. Prisca." He sat up. "Those baths were nearly hedonistic," he said.

"Hedonistic?" It wasn't a word I knew.

"Purely for pleasure, self-indulgent."

"You do look very—groomed," I said, sitting beside him. "And you smell delightful."

"Groomed is a good description," he agreed. "I felt a bit like a horse being prepared for parading." He leaned over. "You smell like lavender."

A discreet knock at the half-open door interrupted us. "*Pranderum*," Sergius announced.

"Food," Cillian translated.

Food was a flat bread, and a black, tangy, stoned fruit I didn't know, and figs, which were familiar to Turlo and me, along with cheese and a thinly sliced dried sausage. Sergius had laid the food out on a sideboard, along with a flask of a pale wine and a jug of water. We collected food and wine, finding places to sit around the room. The food was fresh, and delicious. Irmgard and her women did not join us, and from the platters being carried upstairs, I concluded they were eating separately, and somewhat differently, from us.

"They are treating her as the princess she is," Sorley said, when I commented. "We are only her escort." He rose and fetched the flask of wine, offering it to us in turn. I refused, but Cillian held up his glass and Sorley took it, his fingers just brushing Cillian's. I wasn't sure if it had been purposeful, but Cillian simply smiled up at him, not ignoring the touch, I thought, and not minding it, either.

"When do you think they will call Irmgard to the palace?" Sorley asked.

"I don't know," Cillian said. "They may send someone here first, to talk to her. But I don't think they will wait too long; it would seem inconsistent to give her this house and staff, and then ignore her. But we will have to remain here until we know what is happening."

"Aye, well," Turlo said, "we are all due some rest and relaxation."

"How did you know the name of that building? *Arénas* something?" I asked Cillian.

"*Arénas Ingenírus*," Cillian supplied. "The great field of games, approximately. I read about it. I remembered it was below the palace, so it wasn't a difficult conclusion."

"What sort of games?"

"Horse racing, and men testing their skills against each other in weaponry and strength and speed."

"Do you know the names of other buildings?" There were so many...and so old, if Cillian had read of them.

"A few. It is strange, to see them standing, while before I never knew if they were real, or exaggerated, or completely legendary. It makes me hope that the library is real."

"The one Perras told us about?" Sorley asked. "With not just the writings from Casil but from Heræcria, as well?"

"Yes."

"What is Heræcria?" I asked, puzzled.

"A much older city further east, whose writings and thought influenced Casil, and by extension, your Empire, and what is taught and learned at the *Ti'acha*," Cillian answered.

"How much older?"

"Another five hundred years, more or less. You are looking a bit astounded, Lena, if I may say so." He grinned.

"I am," I said. "I had no idea. And there are books from this city?"

"Perhaps. If the library is real, and if it is still there. I will find out, at the proper time."

"Can you read the ones from Heræcria?"

"About as well as you could read the ones in Casilan, *käresta*," he admitted. "A word here and there. I would still like to see them, though."

"I would like to see their practice grounds and barracks, and know how their soldiers are trained," Turlo said. I wondered if it was a rebuke: we were talking about books, when we were here to ask for military help.

"Sorley," Cillian said mildly, "you are going to have to remember your Casilan quickly. I cannot translate for Turlo in the barracks and Irmgard in the palace at the same time."

And was that a reminder to Turlo to put first things first?

"Aye," Turlo said. "The Lady Irmgard may have to make do with you, if you are willing, Sorley. I will need my adjutant." I frowned, slightly. There was some tension here.

"I'll do my best," Sorley said. "Cillian, do you want to play *xache*?"

"Why not?" Sorley went in search of the pieces and the kidskin; Irmgard's box of treasure had been brought from the ship, I learned. Cillian went to find Sergius, who appeared carrying a table. He placed it in a well-lit area of the room, moved stools to either side, and left, after a look to Cillian, who thanked him.

Turlo moved to watch them play, and after a minute or two I fetched my journal and began to write. Over the course of the afternoon, I played Sorley, and then Turlo, and finally Cillian.

"In Linrathe, who was good enough to give you a challenge?" I asked, after losing.

"Perras," he answered. "Donnalch, although he rarely agreed to play me, and Alain was almost good enough. And," he smiled, remembering, "Dagney is very good. As is your father, Sorley," he acknowledged.

"I remember you playing him one evening," Sorley said, "before I came to the

Ti'ach. I might have been sixteen?"

Cillian ran a hand through his hair. "Early spring," he said. "I stayed three days.

"Yes."

"I gave you and your brother a *xache* lesson the next day, and then we flew hawks for mountain hare in the afternoon, did we not?"

"You remember," Sorley said, looking pleased.

"Yes," he said. "And then you played for us that evening, and there was dancing." Something flickered in his eyes, vanished. "Would you play for us now?"

"If Rind will lend me the *ladhar*," Sorley said. "I'll go ask."

I had watched Cillian's face during the conversation with Sorley. A moment of constraint there, I thought. What had he remembered? But he had recovered, quickly, appearing comfortable with Sorley, and generous, I decided, offering him friendship and affection. If I were Sorley, could I learn to accept that as enough? Had Maya treated me this way, I might have stayed in Casilla.

Sorley came back with the *ladhar*. "The lady Irmgard asks if you would go to speak with her, Cillian. After the music will do, she says."

"I'll go now," Cillian decided. "She has questions, no doubt, and she should not be kept waiting."

Sorley tuned the *ladhar* and began to play a tune. He did not sing, just played the light, almost plaintive notes quietly. I sat cross-legged on my stool, listening. The song was not sad, quite; melancholy would be a better word. I closed my eyes, wanting to think about all that had happened in the last day. I was in Casil, city of legend, a city I hadn't really believed was real, and was magnificent beyond what I could have imagined. I remembered the look in Cillian's eyes, and Turlo's too, as we had sailed in, past the lighthouse and the wharves. What had they seen? Turlo, I thought, saw the Empire unconquered, the belief and hope proven true. And Cillian? A centre of learning, of poetry and thought and art, a place where his agile mind could be tested and refined. The place I had hoped we would find for him.

I heard Cillian come back down the stairs, but I didn't move, or open my eyes for a minute. When I did, he was standing at the sideboard, turned slightly away from me. He was pouring wine, a glass goblet in one hand, the jug in the other, his head bent towards his task, dark hair falling over his forehead. The sleeves of his tunic were rolled up above his wrists, the pale fabric contrasting with his tanned skin. How I love you, I thought. I will not let my bad dreams come between us.

He turned to see me looking at him. Smiling, he offered me the wine. I shook my head. Sorley still played, a soft melody. Very far away, distant from wine and music and the symbolic battles of *xache*, a war raged in my land, in all our lands. It would be easy to forget that in this city, to lose ourselves in its comforts and civility.

Sergius came in, quietly. In his hand was a rolled scroll. He handed it to Cillian. Turlo sat up; Sorley stopped playing. Cillian read the letter.

"We—Turlo and Irmgard and I, as the translator—are summoned to the palace, later tonight, for an audience with the Empress. After the evening meal. An escort will be sent."

He spoke to the waiting Sergius, who inclined his head before leaving. "We will need the appropriate clothes, which Sergius will see to," he told Turlo. "We should prepare Irmgard; will you come with me, General?"

Sorley spoke, after they had left. "So, it begins," he said.

CHAPTER FIFTEEN

DINNER THAT NIGHT WAS SERVED ON THE FLAT ROOF of the first level, the sun dipping towards the sea. Sergius served us, and then left us to ourselves. We ate more of the warm bread, with a rich, tangy oil to dip it in, crisp greens, and chicken roasted with honey and spices. There was more wine, but both Cillian and Turlo watered it well and drank sparingly.

Prisca came in with a plate of pastries and a mug of tea for me. I sniffed it: anash. "*Gratiás,*" I told Prisca. The pastries were sticky, soaked through with honey, but Prisca had returned once again with small bowls of water, and cloths, and either through tact or usual practice, she took my hand, dipped my fingers in the bowl, and wiped them, showing us all what to do. I smiled at her, and picked up my tea, preparing myself for its bitterness, especially after the pastry. But she had put honey in it, too, thankfully.

Cillian pushed his stool back. "We should dress," he said. "Lena, join me?"

I carried the mug of tea into the bedroom, closing the door behind me. The clothes Sergius had chosen for him lay folded on the bed. "Talk to me while I get ready," he said, already stripping off his tunic.

"When did you find time to ask Prisca about the anash?" I asked.

"Before we played *xache*, when I went downstairs to find Sergius," he replied. "She did not seem bothered by the conversation. It's called *benedis*, here, by the way."

"Thank you. Running out now we have some privacy again would have been inconvenient."

He laughed. "But not unsurmountable, you know."

"I know." The tea I'd been making for some days had been very weak; I was glad to be drinking a stronger brew tonight. Cillian had gone to wash. I finished the tea, waiting.

He came out drying his face. "This is not how I hoped to spend tonight, *käresta,*" he said. "At least let me hold you." I went into his arms. As I ran my hands up his back, I could feel the tension.

"Are you worrying about this audience?" I asked.

"A bit," he admitted. "More than a bit."

"Sorley said you were magnificent, at Sylana."

"Sylana is not Casil, and Sorley is not an unbiased judge," he answered, but he seemed to relax a little.

"You have met an Emperor before," I reminded him. "And his blood runs in your veins. Remember that, when you face this Empress."

"That might just help," he said after a minute. He kissed my hair, and then, in a lighter tone, added, "I thought it didn't matter to you that I was Callan's son?"

"It doesn't, and you know it," I answered. "But it's useful, sometimes. Now you had better finish dressing. Turlo will be getting impatient. I'll go and placate him."

I went out to the sitting room. Turlo paced before the windows, dressed in what our steward had deemed appropriate for a general: a fawn-brown tunic and a short, darker cloak, banded with a deep green and fastened with a pin of copper inlaid with green stones. I wondered if Sergius had chosen the cloak and brooch with Turlo's hair in mind. "Turlo," I said. "You look uncommonly handsome."

"Aye," he acknowledged. "It is all necessary to give the right impression to the Empress, I suppose. Is Cillian ready?"

"Nearly," I replied. "He is just dressing."

As I spoke the door to our room opened, and Cillian stepped out. Turlo and I turned. "By the god!" I heard Turlo say. My breath caught. Sergius had selected clothes in shades of grey, the tunic pale. The cloak was a darker grey; its band was white, and the pin silver. Cillian looked polished, and beautiful. He also looked almost exactly like his father.

"Was this your doing, Turlo?" Cillian asked quietly.

"How could it be? I cannot speak the language. It is coincidence only, *mo charaidh*."

I stared at Cillian, remembering. Callan, dressed in his grey robe edged with white, his silver pendant of rank shining in the torchlight, sentencing us at the White Fort. The resemblance was strong. But it was more than the clothes, I realized, and more, even, than the physical likeness of facial bones and hair and height. Regardless of his private doubts, Cillian exuded a quiet confidence. *He is meant to be a leader, an influential man,* Turlo had said to me, not so very long ago. I shivered, suddenly, an inchoate foreboding suddenly threatening. There will be women here, I thought, who share his love of learning and thought, who could provide a challenge for him at *xache*, and speak to him in Casilan.

"I expect Sergius chose these clothes to make me unobtrusive, then," Cillian said.

"Not the word I would use," Turlo said under his breath.

Sorley, hearing voices, came out from his room. He stopped, looking from Turlo to Cillian. "Well," he said, in exactly the right tone, "don't you two clean up well?" Oh, Sorley, perfect, I thought, as both Turlo and Cillian began to laugh. Footsteps on the stairs from the third floor made us all turn. Irmgard descended, followed by Rind.

The men stopped laughing. She wore a dress of pure white, except for the hem and the ends of the sleeves, where a narrow band of purple edged the white, and her cloak was also white, with the same narrow purple edging, but fringed in gold. Her hair was dressed high, and she wore golden earrings. She was a princess, and dressed to acknowledge it.

"*Ádla*," Cillian greeted her. "These are the clothes provided for you?"

"They are," she answered.

"You understand the importance of this? That your rank has been recognized?"

"Yes," she said, "I do. I remember Åsmund telling me this, once. This is good, yes?"

"Very good," Cillian answered. She smiled, looking from Cillian to Turlo.

"The steward has chosen well for you both, too," she observed. "You are most suitable to accompany me."

"Glad to hear it, lady Irmgard," Turlo said. A clatter of boots on the stairs, and Sergius led two soldiers into the room.

"Our escort," Cillian said. He glanced at me, smiled, and walked behind Turlo and Irmgard, down the stairs. Sorley and I watched them go.

"What did I walk in on?" Sorley asked. "There was a bit of tension, I thought."

"You wouldn't know, of course," I said. "It was Cillian. By some chance, Sergius chose clothes for him in the colours Callan wears when he is—formally being the Emperor, I suppose. Dressed in them, Cillian looks so much like him. It took both Turlo and me by surprise."

"He has changed, more than I could have thought possible," Sorley said quietly.

"More than I can know," I said. "Turlo says he is very much like his father at the same age." I hesitated. "Sorley, did you feel some strain between them, earlier? When Cillian said you would need to translate?"

"Yes. But I wouldn't worry about it. My guess is Turlo is feeling out of place, whereas Cillian seems very much at home, wouldn't you say? Do you want to play *xache*?"

"No," I answered, after a moment's consideration. "Forgive me, Sorley, but I am tired. I think I will try to sleep."

"No matter," he answered. "I will go and talk to Rind and Hana. Sleep well, Lena."

"Before you go," I said, "could you ask Sergius for wine for our room? Cillian may well want some, when he returns."

"I can," he said, grinning. "Wine and beer are among the words I didn't forget. I'll have him place some in Turlo's room, too."

"Thank you, Sorley." He went downstairs, and I sat again, waiting for Sergius. He appeared quickly, carrying a tray with a flask of wine and two glasses. In the bedroom, he placed them on the low table. "*Gratiás,*" I offered, receiving a nod in return. He slipped quietly out.

An oil lamp burned, giving just enough light to see by. I lay on the bed. I wanted to sleep, but my mind churned with images and feelings: the streets and buildings and crowds of the city; the luxury of the baths, the comfort of this house. I wondered what face of Casil I would have seen, had Cillian and I made it here on our own. Would that have even been possible?

Not even worth thinking about, I told myself. But if we had, my mind persisted, he would still be mine, not this sophisticated, refined man I do not know. Very much at home, Sorley had just said. I turned, restlessly. Stop it, I told myself. He is still Cillian, still wanting my reassurance, my touch, tonight. What is really bothering me?

I had briefly yearned for a different touch, earlier today. The desire had felt like betrayal.

I got up, poured myself wine. Then I wrapped a robe I found hanging on the door around me and went out into the sitting room again. I stood, listening: no sounds from the upper floor. I crossed the room and tapped on Sorley's door.

"Lena," he said, opening the door, obviously surprised. "Is something wrong?"

"Yes. No. Sorley, can we talk?"

"Of course. Out in the sitting room, I think, just in case one of the servants comes in?"

The wine from earlier still sat on the sideboard. Sorley poured a glass. We settled on the couch. "What is it?" he said gently.

"Do you know what happened to me, in the Kurzemë village?" I asked.

"Not really."

"Ivor, the headwoman's son, raped me," I said. I had finally said the words. He closed his eyes. "I thought perhaps."

"I killed him, though," I added.

"Good for you," he said softly. "But you are all right, now?"

"Yes and no. Sorley, are you sure you can hear this?"

"Go on."

"Cillian was away when...when it happened, and when I told him, and afterwards...he was so gentle with me. He has helped me heal, as much as I have, but Sorley, that healing is only for him. With him. But today, at the baths..."

"Yes?"

"Were you massaged?"

"Yes."

"As were we. Were your attendants male or female?"

"Male. I assume yours were women?"

"Yes. Sorley, you know I have loved women. Today, the touch...aroused me, a little."

He sipped his wine. "If I am honest, it did the same for me. Why is this bothering you, Lena?"

"Is it not a betrayal?" I asked.

"Ah," he said. He was silent, considering. "No," he said finally, "I do not think it is. I think you are forgetting that you both have past experiences and that neither of you are strangers to desire. Regardless of what Cillian may have chosen, six years past, he was a man of twenty-eight when he made that choice. I doubt he is immune to—to the right stimulus, either. Why should you be different?"

"I suppose," I said.

"The betrayal would come if you acted on the desire," Sorley added. "In that way, Lena—among many others—I am glad you two are together, because it frees me from that feeling of disloyalty. I do not have Cillian's strength of will, and a life of celibacy has not been possible, for me."

"Oh, Sorley," I murmured.

"It is all right, Lena," he said. "It is odd, but I feel as if I belong to myself again, after all these years. I still love him, but differently." He put a hand on mine. "Listen to me talking about myself, when it was your concerns I was meant to listen to."

"But you did," I answered. He had, although his words had both calmed a fear, and fed another.

"There is something else, too," he said. "In the Empire, Lena, what if your life had been different, and you had stayed in Tirvan with Maya, and you had chosen to have a child? Would you not have been in the opposite situation, feeling desire for a man, then?"

"That would be from necessity," I argued.

"But not without its pleasures, surely?"

"Well," I said, "I hope not. I cannot speak for all women, though."

"All women do not matter here."

I had refused Dern, regardless of physical attraction, because I would have been disloyal to Maya. But I had never denied his ability to arouse me, not then. Why was today's reaction any different?

"Thank you, Sorley," I said. "You are right, of course. I needed another view, and," I tried a grin, "I didn't think I could talk to Turlo about this. I hope you didn't mind."

"Not at all. I wanted an opportunity to tell you how things were changing for me, anyhow." He smiled. "But tonight, in those formal clothes—he is beautiful, isn't he?"

"He is," I agreed. I leaned over and kissed Sorley on the cheek. "I am so glad you are here with us." He put an arm around my shoulders.

"Thank you for trusting me," he answered. "Ah, Lena," he added, "we are a bit like two planets orbiting the same sun, are we not? Maybe we need each other, to reflect just enough of his brilliance so that neither of us are consumed."

Later, just as I was falling asleep, I considered Sorley's last words to me. There was a different truth in them, but I couldn't reach it, not now. He is such a good friend, I thought, and then I slept.

I woke when Cillian came in. It felt very late. The oil lamp still burned, though, giving just enough light so that the room was not black.

"Cillian," I whispered, sitting up. "There is wine, if you want some."

"Käresta," he said quietly. "Sergius told me. Thank you for thinking of that. It will be welcome." I heard him pour a glass. He brought another lamp over to the bedside, to light it from the flame of the one burning. Setting it down, he bent to kiss me, gently.

"What happened at the palace?" I asked.

"Quite a lot. I think we have an agreement about Irmgard, but the details must wait until tomorrow, käresta. I am very tired." He laughed, softly. "We seemed destined not to enjoy comfortable beds when we have them."

"It is only one night," I protested. I wasn't sure I minded. I was determined to talk to him before we made love again. "Do you want me to massage your shoulders?"

"The walk back through the streets, under the stars, was oddly peaceful," he answered. "I am more relaxed than I thought I would be, so, no. I would rather just hold you." He drained his wine. I watched him undress. He slipped under the bedcover, and I nestled against him, feeling his lips on my hair. "Wake me at noon," he murmured.

I opened our bedroom door quietly. Cillian still slept. I went to the window to release the shutters, letting the midday light stream in. I heard him stir.

"Hello, my love," I said.

"Lena," he said, still half-asleep. "I woke a little while ago. But you weren't here, so I went back to sleep, it seems."

"I'm here now. Are you hungry?"

He grinned, stretching. "Yes, but not for food. Come back to bed?"

"It's the middle of the day," I protested, hesitant. We hadn't talked. But I could feel my body's immediate response to his suggestion.

"Did that stop us at the lake? There is a lock on the door," he added.

"And Sorley and Turlo have gone to the ship," I said. I slid the bolt shut and went to the window.

"Leave the shutters open. I do prefer to see you, you know," he reminded me, reaching for me as I came to the bed. He slid his hands down my body. I closed my eyes, absorbing the sensation. "Lena," he murmured. "The light is for us both. Look at me."

I opened my eyes. His exploring fingers made me gasp, but I kept my eyes open and let my hands begin their own voyage. Watching his face reflect his body's responses, I began to understand why he wanted to make love in the light, how intimacy and trust deepened when we allowed ourselves this honesty. No shadow of violence marred that sunlit afternoon; it was a time of laughter, of discovery and sharing, and when I finally lay against him, spent and languid, something had changed for me, I thought, a deeper healing begun.

I nestled closer, kissing his chest. "*Kärestan.*"

"Either your pronunciation has improved, or I have grown used to how you say that," he said. "It was what my grandmother called me, you know."

"I didn't. I'm glad you told me," I said. "Did you see her again, after you were sent to the *Ti'ach*? When Casyn came to Tirvan, the first time, he talked about having to leave at seven, and about the comfort and love he missed. But he also spoke about returning as a man."

"After I learned that the Empire's boys were taken to be cadets at seven," he said, "I used to play at that, pretend my father had come for me. But no, I did not see either of them again. It would have been dangerous for my grandparents. They died, very close together, when I was thirteen or fourteen."

He was telling me this calmly, almost detachedly, but there was an undercurrent of pain in his voice. "You would have felt so alone then," I said.

"I did," he concurred. "I assumed that would be my lot, until you. *I planned to live with my bed unshared, but love tricked me.*" He kissed me, lightly.

"That's not Catilius," I said.

"An ancient poet, from Heræcria. We should dress and go out, Lena. There is a city to see. I am free until this evening."

"Yes." We should. A city of beauty and learning, outside our door. I did not want to end the intimacy of this time, but I wanted to see Casil almost as much as Cillian did. I sat up.

Washing before we dressed, I ran a finger up his back, slightly damp with sweat. "Do you want me to wash your back?" I asked. He handed me the cloth, and I soaped and rinsed, wiping the wet cloth across the scar and down his left hip to catch a stray drop of water.

"Go any lower and I won't want to go out," Cillian warned.

I laughed. "You managed six years of abstinence and now you're insatiable after three weeks?"

"I had no idea what I was missing," he said. I put my arms around him, resting my head on his back, not caring it was damp.

"Loving someone does make a difference," I agreed.

"Yes," he said. "It does. But not only that."

"What, then?"

"I had promised myself I would not repeat my father's mistake, you remember? There is only one way for a man to truly ensure a child will not be conceived," he said evenly. He turned so he could look at me. "Did I not say you were a revelation to me, *käresta*?"

"Oh. Really?" I thought back, remembering the slight hesitation the first time we had made love. "Oh, Cillian," I started to laugh. "I'm not laughing at you, my love," I said. "I'm just so surprised."

"I thought you might be," he admitted, but he was smiling. I kissed him.

"Can I ask something?" This seemed like a good time.

"Of course."

"The vow you made to yourself, about celibacy? What were the terms for ending it?"

"What has Sorley said now?" he asked.

I felt myself flushing. "That you had found the love you needed to end it. But we did not love each other at midwinter."

"You did not love me, to be accurate," he said calmly.

"Cillian? Are you telling me you loved me then?"

"I believed I did, yes. And the vow depended only on me finding a partner whom I loved. I did not expect the feeling to be returned; that would have been too much to ask."

"Why didn't you tell me?"

"*Käresta*, you had just told me only a few days earlier that you could offer me only pleasure, in affection." He took a breath. "I did tell you, actually, only in a way I knew you could not understand."

I thought back. I couldn't remember anything. "How?"

"Do you remember me saying *'Accept the things to which fate binds you'*?" I nodded. "The next part of that quote is *'and love whom fate brings to you'*."

I rested my head on his chest. "Oh, Cillian. I wish I'd known. Is that what was wrong, much of the winter?"

"Yes. I thought I would be content with what you had offered, but I wasn't. I wanted more, against all my philosophy and expectations. And then you told me I was difficult and complicated, but also a blessing, and I began to wonder if you cared for me more than I knew."

"More than I knew," I admitted. "Until that evening."

"Truly?"

"Truly. I almost told you I loved you, and the thought shocked me almost as much as I think it would have you."

He laughed. "What a pair we are, Lena."

"Sorley said that, too,"

"And he was right." He let me go to begin dressing, in the light clothes of the previous day. I dressed, too, thinking about what he had just told me, and something he had said earlier. I walked back into the bedroom. Cillian sat at the window, looking out.

"*Believed* you loved me?" I asked.

"I would have sworn it, at the time," he said, turning, "but, *käresta*, if that was love, what do I call what I feel now?" He wasn't smiling, and what I saw on his face was close to anguish.

There was so much need in him, and underlying it, fear. He is so newly come to love, and so aware that our time together may be brief, I thought. The last time he had let me see this, it had frightened me, but what I felt now was calm, a simple acceptance. "Love grows, when it is returned," I said.

He smiled at that, and with the smile his face cleared. "My wise Lena," he said. "What would you like to see, in Casil?"

"Can we find the market, or shops?" I asked, relieved at his change of mood.

"Of course," Cillian said. "What do you need?"

"A new journal. Mine is nearly full." I retrieved my purse of coins from my pack. After a moment's reflection, Cillian did the same.

Sergius met us downstairs. Cillian said a few words to him, and a soldier appeared. We were to be escorted, or guarded, I discovered. I glanced at the man curiously; I'd never seen someone with skin so dark. Sergius asked a question, and said something more. Cillian nodded, turning to me. "Give the guard your purse, Lena. Sergius tells me it is safer; cut-purses do not target soldiers."

I saw the sense in that, although it took me a minute to work out what a cut-purse was. I handed the man the leather bag, and he slipped it and Cillian's into a pouch on his belt. Then we went out to see Casil.

The guard—Druisius, Cillian told me—led us along the street of houses. In the distance I could see a tall, circular building, enormous to my eyes, its first three floors a series of tall arches, divided by pillars. "What is that?" I asked.

"The *Prægrandeum*," Cillian answered. "Another place for games, and spectacles." Druisius turned. "*Vérum!*[15]" he said. "*Quomo sicare?*[16]"

Cillian answered. Druisius became friendlier, and more voluble. He led us past the huge building. Underfoot, the ground had been paved. Trees along the edges provided some shade, but heat and light radiated off the stones. I could feel sweat on my neck, and under my arms.

We followed the curve of the arena, and then ahead of us stood a statue taller than I could easily comprehend. At least half the height of the building it flanked, looking to my untutored eyes like a perfect replica of a man, the bronze figure wore a rayed headdress, and held a sword. I stopped walking, staring upward. How had anyone made that? I glanced at Cillian, seeing the awe I felt mirrored on his face.

"*Prægrandus Sûl*," Druisius told us.

"The Giant of the Sun," Cillian translated. Around us, people walked past, servants on errands, groups of men or women in twos and threes, strolling slowly in the heat, talking. No one looked at the statue. Did you just get used to something like that?

Beyond the statue a tall fountain bubbled and splashed. Druisius led us over, gesturing to the metal cups chained to its rim. He showed us how to hold the cup where the water sprang out from the central pillar, letting it overflow the cup for a minute before drinking. The water was cool and vaguely metallic.

I looked around, trying to comprehend the city. All of this had been here, while in the West we had been forgotten, abandoned. *Why?* Whatever the Eastern Fever had been, Casil had recovered. But they had never bothered to find out what had happened to the lands they had once ruled: not just my Empire, I thought, but that vast plain we had crossed. That had all been theirs, once, too.

Would our presence here raise those questions? I looked up at the statue again. Was that how Casil had seen itself, a giant towering over the world? If the Empress, and her advisors, once reminded of her client Empire, decided they wanted it again, how could we stop them? The enormity of the task facing Turlo and Cillian astonished me.

Mostly Cillian, I acknowledged. Turlo might have the power to say yes or no, but it would be Cillian who would choose the words, make the arguments, try to sway Casil's subtle and sophisticated leaders to his view. A responsibility and a burden I could not imagine, and yet one he appeared to be shouldering without complaint. How could I add my own private concerns to that burden?

Druisius gestured us forward. A long, rectangular, colonnaded building lay ahead of us. We walked up the wide stairs and into its cool interior. Mosaics lined the walls, and our footsteps echoed on the tile floor. Two statues of seated women, back to back, stood near one end. Druisius, his voice ebullient, gave

---

[15] Correct

[16] How do you know that?

Cillian a long explanation.

"This is a temple," Cillian told me, "dedicated to Casil, but also to a goddess of love. Druisius tells me it is the largest temple in Casil."

"I can't imagine how they built all this," I said. A thought struck me. "Are they building anything new, Cillian? Or living among past glories?"

"An interesting question," he replied. "Everything we have seen has been in good repair, so there is no lack of money and skill, it would appear. But it would be worth knowing, because it would tell us something about how they view themselves, and their place in the world."

The contrast between the temperature in the temple, and the heat outside oppressed me. Cillian had asked something of Druisius, and they were deep in conversation. I walked beside them, wishing for shade, past more tall buildings and an arched monument covered in inscriptions and carvings to a long, enclosed, paved area. At one end of this rectangular enclosure, a huge statue of a horseman stood; at the other, a tall, carved column, flanked by two buildings.

"The Forum of Ulpius," Cillian told me. "The column is carved with representations of some of his victories, and the two buildings are the libraries, one with books from Heræcria and the other with books from Casil. Druisius tells me they will be closed now, but we can look in on them."

The libraries were open to the air, but a metal screen closed off access. The grey floor, striped with a golden stone, shone even in the dim light. Each wall had columns, not white like most I had seen, but of a creamy hue flecked with purple, framing wall recesses. Tables and stools lined the floor.

"Where are the books?" I asked.

"Those wall recesses have cupboards, and the books are in there, to protect them," Cillian answered.

"This Emperor valued them, to build a library so beautiful," I said.

"He did," Cillian agreed. I looked over at him, seeing both wonder and longing on his face. "To spend even part of day here would be a thing beyond belief."

"Could you?"

He shook his head. "I don't know. Perhaps. But even to have seen it, to know it stands and the books are here—that is enough."

Watching him, seeing his pleasure at the idea and reality of this library, a memory from earlier in the afternoon arose in my mind, of seeing a different sort of pleasure taking hold of him. A wave of desire followed the image, startling me in its intensity. I couldn't keep from smiling.

Druisius spoke to Cillian, who listened, nodded, and turned to me. "Druisius says it is hot, and if we want to find a *taberna* for a drink before they are too crowded, we should do that now."

I assented, gladly, and we followed our guard along a passage and out into a large market. A long, curved building housed many shops, and on the paved area in front of the permanent shops, dozens of market stalls overflowed with food and fabric, sandals and pots, and a hundred other things. Conflicting odours floated in the air: fish, meat, sweat, perfumes. People jostled and chattered, but they made way for Druisius in his uniform, and therefore for us.

Druisius indicated a shop in the curved building. Inside, books bound in leather or fabric lined one set of shelves; others held individual sheets of paper, rolls of vellum, and scrolls. While Druisius spoke to the shopkeeper, I looked at the books until I found one I thought was a good size for my pack. I pointed it out.

Druisius leaned on the counter, speaking sharply. The shopkeeper replied with what sounded like a protest. Markets everywhere, I thought, remembering haggling in Casilla over the price of a belt. I was glad to let Druisius do the bargaining, here.

He finally agreed on a price, and we paid the proprietor. He looked at the coins suspiciously, bit them, then pulled out a small set of scales and weighed them. Satisfied, he handed over my book, and a small pot of ink powder. Druisius took them, accepting that it was his job to carry the articles. The ink-pot went into a pocket, and the book rested easily in his big hand.

Then he grinned, mimed drinking, and with a sideways cock of his head led us to a *taberna*. We passed several that looked almost identical to my eye, but he was our guard, and our guide. He shouted something to the serving girl as we passed through the dark room and out into a courtyard, where several tables stood among a few trees and a fountain. Sparrows chirped and pecked among the tables, and the trees cooled the space just a bit. One table was empty.

Wine and water appeared, and a dish of the small, black, tangy fruit. Cillian poured wine, leaving space for water, and offered a glass to Druisius, who shook his head, saying something that sounded like a reproval. Cillian smiled.

"Druisius is appalled by my manners. I should have offered you the wine first. My apologies, Lena," he said, giving me the glass.

"Tell him I say he deserved the first one for being such a good guide and bargainer," I answered. I watered the wine while Cillian spoke. Druisius laughed and inclined his head to me. He took the second glass of wine.

I was glad to be sitting down. My mind felt stuffed full of sights and sounds— and there were so many people! Cillian and Druisius were talking again. I drank my wine and ate one or two pieces of fruit, listening to the fountain and the sparrows chirping, thinking about what had happened at the library. Did it mean other memories were receding?

Cillian turned to me. "What else would you like to see?"

"As if I would know," I said. I thought a moment. "Can we go up on the city wall?" I wanted space, and quiet.

He raised an eyebrow at the request but relayed it to Druisius, who frowned and then nodded, spreading his hands. I took that as a 'maybe', an opinion confirmed by Cillian a moment later. "He says it will depend on who is on the gate."

We finished the drinks, paid, and walked with Druisius across the market square, turning into a wide street which curved westward, ending at the city wall. I stared up at the looming structure, trying to imagine the work involved in building it, even in making the bricks it contained. Druisius chatted with the guard, who, after a minute, stepped aside to allow us to climb the internal stairs.

I was out of breath by the time we reached the top. I stepped out behind Druisius onto a wide walkway, broken by guard towers every thirty paces or so. We could see the city below us, the *Prægrandeum* easy to find, and once I had found that, I could retrace our steps. Further away, another circular building caught my eye. "What is that?" I asked, pointing.

"A temple," Cillian answered, after listening to Druisius.

"Temples and arenas," I said. "Why do they need so many?" I turned away from the city, to look down over the river. The breeze came from that direction and I wanted to feel it in my face. From up here, I could see along the river to the harbour where Irmgard's ship lay at anchor. I wondered where Geiri and his men were housed, and if they were comfortable. Looking this way, I could see fields and trees, and people working in orchards.

Cillian came to stand beside me. "Such a contrast," he said, "from inside the city to outside." He put his hand on my back, and I leaned against him. Druisius said something, warning in his tone.

Cillian stepped away from me. "*Gratiás,*" he said to Druisius. "Apparently it is not proper for you to touch me in public. Only a *scrapta,* a loose woman, would do that."

"A loose woman?"

"A woman who sells her body for men's pleasure."

I blinked. "Do women do that?" I asked.

"Yes. And men, too. Both for other men, and for women." The distaste in his last words made me flinch. He had turned away from me, looking out across the fields and orchards.

I didn't know what to say, or do, not up here on the wall with Druisius nearby. "Cillian," I said softly. A brief shake of his head told me to leave it alone. I looked down, closer to the wall. Below us, in a walled, dusty area, a group of mounted archers were practicing, shooting arrows at a target. I frowned, studying them. "Cillian," I said, "are those archers below us women, do you think?"

He looked down. "I would say so." A quick question to Druisius followed. "Yes, they are: part of the army. Women can be archers, mounted or not, he tells me."

I watched them, part of me longing to be down there with them. I could practically feel the bow in my hands. The drills were orderly, each woman riding forward at a signal from the instructor. The target hung loose, and someone made it swing as the rider approached, so the arrow had to find a moving object. The horses must be responding to knees and voice, I thought, not the reins. How hard would it be to learn to do that?

"We should go, Druisius says, before we are noticed," Cillian told me. "He doesn't want to get his fellow guard in trouble."

We spoke very little on the walk home. As we entered the house, I could hear a *ladhar* being played. By now, I could separate Sorley's style from Rind's, and this was Sorley playing. Druisius, handing me my purchases, stopped to listen. He asked a question. Cillian gestured him upstairs. He followed us. Sorley looked up as we came in, smiling his pleasure at seeing us.

"This is Druisius, Sorley," Cillian said. "He has been an excellent guide this afternoon. He heard you playing and wanted to see the instrument." Sorley held the *ladhar* up. Druisius took it, running his fingers along the strings, a practiced motion.

We left the musicians talking. My feet hurt from walking on the cobbled and paved streets in thin sandals. In our bedroom I dropped down onto one of the stools, massaging a foot.

"Wine?" Cillian asked.

"Yes, please." He poured a glass, leaving it to me to choose how much to water it. His own in hand, he sat on the other stool. He raised his glass to me.

"To Casil."

"What did you think? It must be strange, to see these buildings you have read about."

"Like finding the landscape of a dream is real," he answered.

"That's a lovely image," I said. Should I ask him about what he'd said, up on the wall? No, I decided. He had indicated I should leave the subject alone; it was his to raise, not mine.

"Well," he said, "I am supposed to be good with words, am I not?" A trace of cynicism etched his voice. I frowned. Twice now today, these echoes of old defenses. He smiled, ruefully. "And I am not sure why I said that. A thought, but not one relevant to this, or any, conversation between us."

"Are you concerned about tonight's audience?" I asked. It would explain his mood.

"Yes. Not for Irmgard; that is a good agreement, and while they may ask for a small change here or there to remind us they have the upper hand, I am not expecting any difficulties. But once that is done, Lena, then it is time to begin our real business here. And that I am concerned about."

"I was thinking about this earlier, about what you had to do, when we were looking at the statue of the sun giant," I said. "Casil ruled the world, once, and may think it still does—and we are only a little forgotten piece of that world. And you must try to convince them they should help us."

"Exactly so."

"What can I do to help you, Cillian? This is such a huge burden you must carry."

"I—we—will need your thoughts, on what the women of the Empire would see as acceptable to give up," he answered. "At some point."

"I know that," I answered. "I meant for you, not for the negotiations. What can I do for you, my love?"

He considered. "Is it fair to say I don't know? I have never attempted anything this large before, and I have never had anyone to care about my needs, either."

"There are two sides to that," I said slowly. "With a task so difficult to do ahead of you, I don't want to be part of—of the weight on your mind."

"That is not what you are, at all," he replied. "You lighten the weight, *käresta*; you don't add to it. You, and increasingly, Sorley, in a different way. He is becoming to me what Alain was, but now I can admit to needing a friend."

"I am so glad." I was. "You will tell me what I can do, what else it is you need, in the next days?"

"As best I can, yes. But you may need to be patient with me, again."

I am not going to tell him about the dream by the riverbank, I decided. He had far more important things to occupy his mind. I would deal with it on my own.

CHAPTER SIXTEEN

"IRMGARD SEEMS PLEASED WITH THE AGREEMENT YOU REACHED," Sorley said, over dinner.

"I don't actually know the details," I said. "What will happen to her?"

Cillian had just taken a bite of food. He gestured to Sorley to go on with the explanation. "She will stay here, in this house, with most expenses covered, I gather. For eight months, she will attend the Empress, be introduced to men the Empress deems suitable, and allowed to choose whom she will marry. If she can't decide in those months, then at the end of the time she agrees to let the Empress choose for her. Is that right, Cillian?"

"Yes. She understands that the marriage, however it happens, may take her away from Casil. It will depend on the nature of the alliance the Empress wishes to strengthen."

It sounded cold to me, but if Irmgard was satisfied, that was all that mattered. "What happens to Rind and Hana?"

"Appropriate marriages," Cillian said.

"Do they get a choice?"

"Not really. But that is no different than in Varsland, except there Irmgard would have chosen for them. It is not outside their expectations, Lena."

I wasn't sure that made me more comfortable. "What was the original offer?"

"Four months, not eight, and some details around the oarsmen. We argued that it was unfair to ask Irmgard to choose among potential husbands before she had some proficiency with the language, and the oarsmen that chose to stay needed some guarantee of work. She is being provided with a language tutor and will be allowed to keep three of her men as personal guards, although she will need to pay them. The rest will be given work on the ships or at the harbour, if they wish."

"We argued?" Turlo said. "You did."

"In consultation," Cillian said mildly. "Is that not my role?"

"Aye, it is. One the Empress is taken with, it appears."

Cillian did not reply. We finished the meal, talking of the city and its sights. Prisca brought me my tea and a bowl of dried fruit, dark brown in colour. I tried a piece: it was chewy and sweet, and when I bit into it, the interior was a golden yellow. I took a second piece.

"Do we need to go over what is to be said tonight?" Cillian asked Turlo.

"Aye, we should. And review the letter of petition, perhaps?"

Cillian nodded. "I will change, then come to your room." He stood. "Stay here and enjoy the evening, Lena."

Sorley waited until both men had left. "What's wrong with Cillian?"

"He's nervous."

"And he doesn't want you with him?"

I laughed, gently. "Sorley, he needs solitude sometimes. As do I. There's nothing wrong."

"You know him so well." I thought I heard a hint of wistfulness in his voice.

"In some ways. What did Druisius think of the *ladhar*?"

He accepted the change of subject. "He plays a similar instrument called a *cithar*. He says he'll bring it when he's not on duty and show me, let me play it. I'm looking forward to that."

"Rind is letting you play the *ladhar* a lot."

He shrugged. "She says she's too busy for it right now, and I can use it until we leave. Lena, I talked to them today, and both she and Hana are perfectly happy with the arrangements. I know it's not how things are done in the Empire, or Linrathe, but you don't need to worry for them."

"I won't, then." It really wasn't my concern.

I heard Cillian's footsteps at the door. He came back out onto the roof, dressed in his court clothes, carrying a rolled vellum scroll. "Expect me to be late," he said to me.

I stood to go to him, holding him lightly so as not to mar his finery. He pulled me into a tighter embrace, not caring about his clothes. He kissed my hair, and then my lips. "Wake me, if I'm asleep," I murmured.

"Perhaps," he said, letting me go. Sorley had also stood, and for a moment the two men simply looked at each other, until Cillian spoke. "Wish me good fortune, *mo charaidh*, for all our sakes."

"Always," Sorley said. Cillian smiled.

"*Meas*, Sorley," he said. "It matters."

We watched him walk across the sitting room to Turlo's door. "Shall we stay out here?" Sorley asked. The evening was cooling, and a light breeze made being outside even more appealing. I agreed. There had been a thread of discord between Turlo and Cillian again, and I didn't want to overhear an argument.

The sun went down. Fireflies began to appear, flashing brief sparks against the growing dark. I heard the guards on the stairs. Sergius came up. Seeing us on the roof, he came out, then after a word from Sorley, went to Turlo's door to knock. The men came out, Irmgard came down with Hana, and were escorted away by the guards. Silence fell.

"Sorley," I said, "I never told you how it ended, with Maya. May I?"

"If you like." He was being polite, I knew.

"I had gone to live in Casilla, with a woman called Ianthe, and the child she was raising, Valle. Just sharing the house, you understand? Valle was the son of Maya's brother, Garth, and Ianthe's sister Tice, from Karst village. It's a long story; maybe I'll tell you, someday. I had found work on the fishing boats, that spring, and I was happy enough.

"In early summer, Maya arrived, unexpectedly. She and Garth had been unusually close as children, and she still idolised him. She was determined to help bring up his son. She moved in, and after a while, she and Ianthe became lovers." I hadn't admitted that to anyone else, not even Cillian.

He looked away. He understood now why I was telling him this.

"And I think that would have bee—all right. I could have stayed. Garth and I had been close, and I liked being with his son. Without the war, I would have seen Garth at Festival when he came to see Valle. I always thought that was at least half the reason Maya had come, so she could see her brother again. But she became distant. Unwelcoming. In the summer, she asked me to leave. So I did."

"Did you still love her?"

"Yes," I admitted. "I hadn't thought I did, but living with her again—yes. I still think about her, and hope she is alive, and happy."

"You would have stayed, if she had welcomed you?"

"I think so. Sorley, you heard Cillian, just now. It is not just me who is glad you are here."

He smiled. "I'm beginning to believe that. We are growing more comfortable with each other." He picked up his *ladhar*. "Music?" he offered. I nodded, then remembered something.

"Can you ask Prisca for several more oil lamps for our bedroom?"

"Of course. But why?"

As much as I had come to appreciate Sorley, this was private. "When Cillian comes in, late, sometimes he likes to make notes," I said. "The one lamp doesn't really give enough light."

He appeared to accept that. I waited for him, watching the stars appearing. He came back with the *ladhar*, and shortly afterwards Prisca carried a tray of lamps into our room, coming out with one for our table. Sorley tuned the *ladhar* and began to play, gentle melodies. I listened. Tiredness began to seep in, making my eyelids heavy. I didn't want to sleep, yet, though.

A quiet tap at the door, and Druisius stepped out onto the roof. He held a stringed instrument, larger than the *ladhar*. Sorley stopped playing to greet him, beckoning him over. Druisius smiled at me, pulling out a chair to sit by Sorley, showing him the *cithar*. He offered it to Sorley, who took it, fitting a hand onto the neck. Druisius reached out to adjust his hold, moving Sorley's fingers slightly. Their eyes met.

"Sorley," I said softly as I stood. "I'm tired. I'm going to bed now. Thank you for the music. Enjoy the night."

Prisca had left six lamps on the low table by the window, beside the one she had lighted. I moved three to each of the small tables either side of the bed. Movement had woken me up, a bit. I retrieved my journal and began to write about the day. I couldn't find the right words to describe how Casil had made me feel, though, so I gave up. I might as well sleep, I thought. I would wake when Cillian came in, regardless of how quiet he tried to be.

I was wrong about that, though. When I did wake, I was alone in the bed, but I had the sense of someone else in the room.

"Cillian?"

"I'm here," he said quietly. "Did I wake you?"

"No." I sat up. I had shortened the wick on one lamp before I had gone to bed.

I could see his silhouette in its faint glow, nothing more. "Have you been back long?"

"A while. I needed some wine, and to think, before I tried to sleep."

"What happened at the palace?"

"For Irmgard, what we expected. The Empress made a few changes regarding the oarsmen, but nothing that mattered. So that is done."

"Then what is wrong? Did she refuse our petition?"

"Not exactly. She promises she will consider it, but she is asking us to do something first. Something not inconsiderable." He sounds tired, and discouraged, I thought.

"What?"

Casil, he told me, had been at war with several countries to the east and north of it on and off for centuries, but more recently for the past fifteen years. Allegiances shifted and allies came and went, but after the battle in which the Emperor had been killed, eight months previously, peace talks had begun. Good progress had been made until eight weeks ago, when both sides had reached an impasse. The Empress had asked Cillian and Turlo to resolve it. Fresh eyes and minds might see a solution, she had said. Only then would she consider assistance to the West.

"But—" I didn't know what to say first. "That could take weeks. Months. You don't know the lands, or what has been offered and refused, or the history. And will your authority to do this be recognized?"

"Our authority is given by the Empress. We have been given two days to review the history and the existing treaty proposals, so in a very few hours I need to begin reading, and instructing Turlo in what I read. And yes, this could take weeks, or months."

"But will she not expect a treaty advantageous to Casil?"

"To some extent, yes. But Eudekia is not just a figurehead Empress, Lena. Her grasp of history and politics is keen. When she made this proposal tonight, she spoke of the Emperor Adricius, who was Ulpius's successor and Emperor through the devastation of the Eastern Fever. Remind me to tell you about that, some day," he added. "When the worst of the plague was over, Adricius realized he could not maintain the Empire as it had been; he chose to abandon lands and consolidate his strength in Casil and lands close to it. The Empress referenced this tonight, indicating that she was willing to do the same for peace, and to ensure she had an Empire to leave to her son."

Cillian's voice had changed as he spoke. He sounds interested, I thought. Intrigued.

"Do you want to do this?" I asked.

"I must. *We* must: Turlo will be fully involved. I am no general. But consider this, Lena: it will let me see how the Empress and her advisors think, what they consider appropriate to include in a treaty, how they bargain. All to our advantage when the negotiations for support begin."

And what if you cannot bring the two sides to peace? I wondered. What happens then?

"I should try to sleep," Cillian said, "although I am not sure I will. And more wine will only slow my mind in the morning."

I leaned over to adjust the wick on the lamp. "There are other ways to help you relax."

Morning light woke me. "Hello, my love," I said sleepily.

"Lena," he greeted me. "I have been thinking. I will need you and Sorley, to make notes. It will be faster than me trying to read and write, and Turlo will need notes to refer to. Perhaps you and Sorley can divide the day between you, and do that for me?"

"Of course," I said. I remembered something. "Wait until breakfast to ask Sorley."

"Why?" Cillian asked, as he got out of bed.

"He may not be alone."

"Ah," he said. "Druisius?"

"Yes."

"Good," he said, after a moment. "He seems a decent man." He went to wash and dress. I moved the lamps back to the low table; Prisca would not concern herself if I left them where they were, but I was uncomfortable in allowing her too much insight. Everything, I knew, was being relayed to the palace. I wondered briefly if that was Druisius's role too, then rejected the idea: Sorley and I were not important. I hoped I was right: Sorley deserved something real, and uncomplicated by intrigue.

Turlo was decidedly out of sorts at breakfast. "How are we supposed to make a treaty for a war we know nothing about?" he growled.

"We will know more, in a day or two," Cillian replied. "It is a puzzle to be solved, Turlo, and one we can find the answer to."

"I hope you are right," Turlo said.

Sorley came to breakfast alone, but in a buoyant mood. "Of course I'll help," he said, when Cillian told him the plan. We finished eating. Sergius came to tell Cillian our escort had arrived, and a few minutes later we walked through the morning streets to the palace.

The building was truly enormous. We were shown to a medium-sized room, with several tables and stools. On one table, a map had been unrolled and weighted down; on another, a pile of scrolls and vellum sheets awaited attention. Two men, both grey-haired, stood at another door.

Cillian spoke to them at length, at one point gesturing Turlo forward. Finally he turned to us. "These two men are Atulf, from the Boranoi, who speaks for Casil's opponents, and Quintus, who has negotiated for Casil. Their role is only to answer questions. We should begin with the map, so we all understand the borders and the disputed lands."

In the end, Sorley and I both stayed. There was enough to do for us both: scribing, finding names and places on the maps, sorting through documents and keeping them organized. Sorley proved the better organizer, and I was the faster writer.

Cillian read a document, or part of it, and then told me what to write in summary. Sometimes he would take the paper from me to add a few words, or occasionally a sketch, or the answers to questions posed to Quintus or Atulf. I handed summaries to Turlo, and every so often Cillian would stop reading to have a quiet discussion with him, usually leading to more questions for the two previous negotiators.

My hand ached by late morning, but I ignored it, concentrating on keeping my writing legible. Food and drink arrived and we stopped long enough to eat. But the pile of documents remained high, and as the afternoon wore away, I wondered if we could get through them in the time allotted.

In the late afternoon, Cillian put down the vellum he was reading, rubbing his eyes. "Enough," he said. "Turlo, I suggest we talk again, after a meal, to ensure we agree in our understanding of what we learned today."

"Aye," Turlo said. "Is there a copy of the map we can take to the house?"

"I'll draw one," Sorley offered. I helped tie scrolls and order the sheets of vellum. I had long ago stopped trying to understand what I had been writing, how it all connected. Certain names had repeated, but who had conquered what, and when, and for whom, was nothing but a jumble in my mind.

"Thank you," Cillian said to Sorley and me as we walked home. "The task would have been impossible today, without you."

"Aye," Turlo said. "And it nearly is with you both helping, and would be, without your ability to find what is important among all those words, Cillian. I see a pattern emerging, I believe."

"And from that pattern, the shape of a solution, I think," Cillian said. "But I can't be sure, until I have read the rest of the documents."

In our room, he dropped onto the bed, stretching out. "Do you still have willow-bark?" he asked.

"Yes, I think so." I went to my pack to check.

"Would you mix me a draught? My head is pounding." I wasn't surprised; the writing on some of the scrolls had been small and faded.

"Wine or water?" I asked.

"Wine, but water it well. Today's work is not done."

I gave him the drink, and went to relieve myself and wash my face and hands. Ink stained my fingers, impervious to soap and water. "Let me rub your back," I suggested, when I came back to the bedroom.

"No," he said. "Your hands will be aching. I have done that much writing in the past."

"They are," I agreed, "but not as much as your neck and shoulders. Or I can ask Sergius to fetch a bath attendant?"

He rolled onto his chest. "Not too long, or I will fall asleep," he warned.

"Would that be a bad thing? We have some time before dinner." I began to knead his shoulders.

"I do not like napping. I wake up with my thoughts confused. Talk to me, instead."

Strange, I thought, how I can know exactly what that scar on his back feels like, and yet not know he doesn't like to nap.

"Do you really see a solution?"

"Potentially. The largest issue is the eastern trade route and who controls it. But I need to know more." He stopped. "Did you hear footsteps outside the door?"

"Sergius, maybe?"

"Maybe. We should not speak of this here. Tonight, when I talk with Turlo again, can you and Sorley stay in the sitting room? Music, if Sorley has the energy, would be even better."

"But the servants don't speak our language." His shoulders felt looser, under my hands.

"We will mention names of cities, the river—I would prefer to be cautious."

"What about Sorley and Druisius?"

Cillian swore. "You are sure they are lovers?"

"If not now, soon. Could he be a spy?"

"It is possible. I hope not. One of us needs to ask Sorley not to talk to him about what we are doing." He sighed. "Awkward, coming from me."

I saw his point. "I'll do it."

"*Meas, käresta.*" He flexed his neck. "That's better. Lena, would you mind leaving me alone until dinner? I need some silence."

I bent to kiss the back of his neck. "I'll go and talk to Sorley. I'll come back when it's time to eat."

I left him to find Sorley, who was sitting outside, a glass of wine in his hand. A good idea, I thought, and went to the sideboard first, to pour myself one. Then I joined him in the cooling evening air.

"Where's Cillian?"

"Resting," I answered. "And letting willow-bark soothe a headache. He has a request for us." I explained to Sorley about ensuring the servants couldn't overhear tonight.

"I can play, certainly."

"There's something else," I said. "We can't talk about what we are doing to anyone. That must include Druisius, Sorley."

He flushed. "He's not a spy for the palace."

"I—we—don't think he is. Cillian is being very cautious. Everything we are trying to do here depends on this treaty, Sorley."

"You're right. Druisius and I—we talk about music, and instruments, and songs, mostly."

"I like him. He's kind; he stopped me for behaving incorrectly, while we were out yesterday. Women don't touch men in public here, I have learned."

"He is kind," Sorley said. "And a good musician."

Turlo came out from his room. Seeing us on the roof, he joined us. "One glass of wine won't cloud my head," he decided, pouring one, and adding a little water. He sat at the table. I told him what Cillian had asked us to do, and why. "Aye, better to be wary," he agreed. "Although—what were their names?

Quintus and Atulf?—know what Cillian asked questions about."

"They do, but not what he was really interested in," Sorley said. "I was paying attention; I didn't always have as much to do as Lena. He asked questions about every document, even if he didn't really want to know details. And he wrote the answers down, every time. But he'll know what was important, and what was diversion."

"I cannot match him for subtlety," Turlo said. "I expect that is what the Empress saw, to ask us to do this."

"I thought that was due to how he negotiated for Irmgard," Sorley said.

"Aye, in part. But they had long conversations, Cillian and the Empress, both nights, after the negotiations were done. She called him back, and Irmgard and I had to wait some time. With wine and other comforts, so not a hardship. I suppose she was judging if he could handle this task."

Why hadn't he told me that? A memory nagged at me: 'little different than a hundred other conversations I have had, over wine, late at night, with an *Eirën* or a *Harr* or even with the *Teannasach*.' That was why; it was just part of the work of diplomacy, not worth mentioning.

Prisca came out with plates and bowls, to ready the table for dinner. We moved to the low wall at the edge of the roof, looking out over the city, glowing golden in the setting sun. Voices floated up from the street, and the sounds of wheels and harness and the clop of hooves. Familiar, and yet foreign.

"I had better fetch Cillian," I said, seeing Prisca with a basket of bread. He was sitting by the window, looking out. "Dinner is almost ready. Is your headache gone?"

"It is," he replied. "Thank you, *käresta*, for taking care of me."

"I was pleased you asked," I replied. "Was it so very hard?"

He smiled. "Not very. But not what I am accustomed to, either."

"I spoke to Sorley," I told him. "He will play tonight, and he understands about Druisius."

"Good," Cillian said, standing. "Shall we eat?"

Over dinner, I talked about seeing the women practicing archery from horseback yesterday. "I would like to learn how to do that," I said.

"The women from Han can shoot arrows from horseback," Turlo told me, "and their horses are broken to it, although it's not something we do, except to hunt, occasionally."

"It could be useful, against a Marai force on the ground," I pointed out. "Or even to shoot at a close ship, and be able to retreat quickly."

"Aye, it could," Turlo said thoughtfully.

"Why do you not learn, then?" Cillian said. "After tomorrow, Turlo and I, and Sorley if he is willing, will be busy with the negotiations. I would like you there, Sorley," he added, turning to him, "because you read Casilan, and understand it. Another pair of ears and eyes will be useful, and they will not deny me a scribe."

"I would be honoured," Sorley said. "Perhaps Druisius could arrange for

Lena to learn from the archers?"

"A very good idea," Cillian said. "Will you ask him, Sorley? If this is what you want, Lena?"

"Yes," I said. I did want it. I wanted the simplicity and the demand of a bow, and a horse, and a target towards which I could channel that cold sliver of revenge that lay deep inside. I had been ignoring it, letting it be quiescent, patient, but it wasn't gone.

"I'll talk to him, then," Sorley said. "Beginning tomorrow, or as soon after as possible?" I nodded.

After we ate, Cillian and Turlo exchanged a long, resigned look, and took themselves to Turlo's room to talk. Sorley fetched the *ladhar*, and we sat in the living room, Sorley playing desultorily. Sergius came in and out, filling wine flasks and oil lamps. He approached Turlo's door.

"Should I stop him?" Sorley murmured.

"No. It would arouse his suspicions. He'll knock, and they'll stop talking."

"And hide the map, I hope."

Coming back from Turlo's room, Sergius said something to Sorley. Sorley smiled, shook his head, replying in a mild voice. He waited until Sergius had gone downstairs before translating. "He suggested the night was fine, and we might want to sit outside. I declined. I think Cillian was right."

"Good to know," I said.

Druisius arrived shortly afterwards, his *cithar* in his hand. "I should stay," I said to Sorley. "Sorry."

"It's all right," he assured me. "We're just going to make music. And you should be here when I ask him about the archers, anyway. I'll do that, right now."

As far as I could follow, Druisius asked a lot of questions, but all ones Sorley could answer. Finally Sorley turned to me. "He says he will ask tomorrow. I have assured him you ride well and that you shoot a bow very well, but that you have never done the two together, and that is what you want to learn."

"Thank you, Sorley," I said. "*Gratiás, Druisius.*"

Druisius grinned. The men began to play, slowly, copying notes and chords, the two instruments blending pleasingly. The music was not familiar. This must be a tune from Casil, I thought, listening to the unusual melody, its notes not following the patterns I knew. Sorley's face was intense, concentrating on the new demands on his fingers and his mind, but as he grew more confident, he began to smile. The music merged and swirled, something new being created, and, I thought, watching the glances between Sorley and Druisius, something else being fed. I wished I could leave them alone. I wouldn't have wanted anyone else around, those first days with Cillian.

CHAPTER SEVENTEEN

THE SECOND DAY OF READING AND NOTES and discussion passed much as the first, except that it was much later when we finished. We would all need willow-bark, I thought, as we walked through the early evening streets to the house, but Cillian seemed quietly satisfied. He closeted himself with Turlo again after we ate, but this time I decided Sorley and Druisius, playing music again in the sitting room, were enough to dissuade Sergius. I took my aching head to bed.

At breakfast the men were quiet, Cillian's eyes distant, as if he were rehearsing arguments or analyzing potential opposition. As we finished eating, Sorley turned to me. "Druisius will take you to the archers this morning, if you still want, Lena. He spoke to their captain yesterday, and she is happy to give you some training."

"I'd like that," I said. "Thank you, Sorley."

In our room I hugged Cillian, feeling both the strength and the tension in him. Sergius had, with his usual efficiency, provided the appropriate clothes, not as elegant as the court dress, but of finer quality than his everyday tunics. "I will see you tonight," I said.

"Maybe," he replied. "I have no sense yet for what the hours of negotiation will be, or the requirements of us in the evenings. I expect today, and perhaps tomorrow, we will hear from Quintus and Atulf; they were not allowed to present their views these last two days. Then the real work of forging an agreement will begin."

"Surely you will be allowed your evenings?" I asked.

"Some, yes, I expect," he told me. "But think of Fritjof's hall, Lena. We were all expected to be present at dinner, and entertainment, and it will be little different here, I think. The disputes of the day will be smoothed over by the formality of diplomatic dinners, with the Empress present at least for a few minutes, to remind us all she is paying close attention."

"When do you have time to discuss your responses, to plan the next move?"

"Late at night, or early mornings, or not at all. Sometimes, the response must be made in the moment, and this is in part why I need Sorley. His Casilan has improved, and I want him to be translating for Turlo as the words are spoken. Otherwise, I could find myself needing to make a counterproposal without Turlo's understanding, or agreement."

"But with the authority, yes? From the Empress?"

"Yes. But—and this is another form of diplomacy, Lena—the next negotiations are for what Casil will demand from the Empire and Linrathe in exchange for their support, and then the authority must lie clearly in Turlo's hands. I must maintain at least the illusion of his primacy during these first talks, or have his position weakened in the ones that truly matter to us."

"You are doing this while all I will be doing is riding horses and shooting arrows."

"Skills that could prove decisive in a battle," he pointed out. "I can, I hope, persuade the Empress to send support, and perhaps give some useful thoughts on how to best deploy that support, but battles are won or lost through the skills and courage of soldiers on the field. But," he bent to kiss me, "those are thoughts for another day, *käresta*. Now I must go and listen to old grievances, and offer a new solution."

I wished I spoke Casilan and could go with him to watch the negotiations. To watch him do this work, to try to comprehend it. And not only, I realized, because I would understand Cillian better, although that was part of it, but because I would learn from it, as I had learned to think about each move in *xache*, and its implications.

When Cillian had gone, I found the sheath for my secca and strapped it on my belt, blousing the tunic over it to disguise it. I wondered how I would ride in these clothes. Perhaps the archers would lend me whatever they wore for today, and Prisca could get me the equivalent.

I heard a tap on the door. Druisius waited for me, grinning a greeting. He gestured me forward, and we went out into the still-cool morning, along narrow streets shaded from the sun, heading for the city walls. I thought he was more alert, his eyes always moving. My skin prickled. As we turned from one street to another, I saw three men ahead of us. One, slightly in the lead, turned, perhaps hearing our footsteps. He began shouting and the men started pushing each other. I saw the glint of a blade. Druisius said something, running towards the men, his short sword in his hand. One turned to challenge him, feinting with the knife. The other two scattered, but one ran directly towards me.

The brawl had been a diversion, a ploy. My hand went to my waist. They will not expect me to have a blade, I thought. I saw no weapon in the man's hand: his plan was just to overpower me, drag me into one of these buildings while Druisius was occupied. Where had the second man gone? I turned as if to run, shielding my right hand from view, pulling the secca from its sheath. Druisius shouted, one word, over and over. As the man reached for me, I half-crouched, pivoted, and stabbed my knife into his abdomen.

Too high. I felt it deflect off his ribs, tearing through skin and flesh. But he screamed in pain and doubled over. I ran towards Druisius. His man was on the ground, his leg bleeding from a sword wound. I heard footsteps behind me, and spun, secca out. Two guards approached at a run, one stopping to apprehend the man I had wounded. The second shot questions at Druisius, who answered in short, angry bursts.

It all took a long time to sort out. The guards took my secca, examined it, asked questions I couldn't understand. Druisius intervened. Eventually, they gave me my knife back and took the two attackers away.

"Druisius," I said. I had been thinking, while the guards talked. He looked at me. "Cillian," I said, and touched my mouth, shaking my head. He frowned. I shook my head again. He did not need to be bothered by this.

"Sorley?" he asked. I pointed to myself, and then my mouth, and repeated 'Sorley'. I would tell him. He nodded. Then he pointed homeward, and then towards the wall, and gave me a questioning look. Where did I want to go?

If I went back to the house, I would only brood on what had happened. Better to be doing something. I pointed towards the wall.

We passed through a gate and out into a broad training ground, with stables at one end. No one was on the field. "Junia!" Druisius called. A dark-haired, muscled woman, half a head taller than me, came out from one end of the stables. She glanced at me, asking Druisius a question. I heard my name in the answer.

"Lena," she said, turning to me. I smiled. She gestured me towards the building. I followed her into a tack and equipment room smelling of leather and oils. She gave me an assessing look, then took a pair of leggings from a shelf, holding them out to me.

I put them on under my tunic. We walked along the row of stalls until the second last, where a bay horse stood, browsing on hay. Junia pointed to the horse, and then to me, and then to the tack room. The first test, I realized.

I pointed to myself, said 'Lena,' and then pointed at the horse. Junia smiled. "Roseus," she told me.

I walked into the stall, saying his name, letting him get used to my voice and my smell. I patted his neck and held my hand out to let him smell me. A gelding, I noticed with relief. He wore a rope head-collar. I took hold of it and led him out of the stall.

He stood easily to be tacked up. Junia pointed out a saddle and a sheepskin to go under it, and watched as I swung both up onto Roseus's back. The saddle was heavier than I was used to, and higher at the front and back. More importantly, there were no stirrups. I tightened the girth, bridled the horse, and went back to tighten the girth again. Junia nodded.

I led the gelding to a mounting block and swung up into the saddle. The higher pommel and cantle made up for the lack of stirrups in a way, but I wasn't quite sure what to do with my feet. But I had ridden Tirvan's hill ponies bareback as a girl. I settled myself in the saddle and reined Roseus out onto the field.

He was well trained. I took him through his paces, learning that he changed direction with either rein or leg signals—that made sense, I thought, for a horse carrying an archer whose hands would be occupied—and had an easy trot and a comfortable canter. After a few rounds of the training area, I reined him in in front of Junia.

"*Bêne,*" she said. I dismounted and tied the horse where Junia indicated. We went back into the equipment room, and from a rack on the wall, she handed me a bow.

Compact and deeply curved, it reminded me of the bows we had taken from the plains riders. But I had never seen one constructed like this. It had three layers, I realized as I examined it: a central layer of wood, between horn on the inside and what looked to me like sinew along the outer curve. As I compressed it to fasten the bowstring, I felt its resilience: the draw would take more strength.

I saw from Junia's pursed lips and nod that I had surprised her, probably by stringing the bow on the first attempt. She took a quiver of arrows from the wall and we went back outside. Targets stood against one end of the field. She showed me where to stand and gestured me to shoot.

I tested the draw of the bow first, slightly startled by the initial strength needed. On horseback, with no stirrups to brace against, this would be a challenge, I thought. I nocked an arrow, and shot, repeating the action several times. All the arrows except the first hit well inside the target.

"*Bêne sagiteri*[17]," Junia said. At her gesture I unstrung the bow. She took it from me, pointing to the horse. I untied him and mounted again. She grinned and reached up to tie the reins together, dropping them on his neck. She folded her arms, nodding slowly, telling me to ride without reins and without hands.

After several tries, I worked out how to tell Roseus to move forward rather than turn, and then how to change gaits. His easy trot was less easy, without hands, and at a canter I slid to one side, righting myself with a lurch of my body. Oddly, this did not seem to bother the horse. I realized I had no idea how to make him stop. I tried a calming noise, coupled with firm pressure from both legs. To my surprise, it worked.

Junia stepped forward and took the reins. I slid off the saddle, feeling the pull in my inner thighs. She grinned again, touched my shoulder, and looked over at Druisius, who had watched the whole session sitting in the shade. He got up. We were done, I assumed.

Druisius and Junia spoke for a few minutes, then, with a sideways movement of his head, Druisius indicated we were to leave. "*Gratiás,* Junia," I said, and turned to pat the gelding. "*Bêne* Roseus. *Gratiás,*" I said to him, making Junia laugh.

At the house I washed the smell of horse and sweat away, and heavily watered a glass of wine. With nothing to distract me I could not keep my thoughts from what had happened on the way to the training ground. What had the men wanted? Had I made trouble for myself, stabbing my attacker? Druisius would testify that I had only been defending myself. Reliving it, I could feel my heartbeat pounding in my chest. I added more wine to my glass and went out to sit on the roof.

Prisca brought my solitary meal. I ate, wondering what to do with myself. After a while, I fetched my journal. Carefully, I drew a picture of the bow, labelling the parts, and making a few notes. I wrote down some words for which I needed translations. Then I went upstairs, and, with apologies for disturbing her lesson in Casilan, asked Irmgard to borrow the *xache* pieces.

---

[17] Good archery

I thought about possible battles and how horse archers could be used for much of the afternoon, lining pieces up and moving them around, making notes and drawings. I thought about hills and valleys, marshes and woodland and city streets. Only in late afternoon did I return the game pieces to Irmgard.

Sorley came in not long after. He looked tired. Turlo and Cillian, he reported, were to dine at the palace tonight. Sergius would take their court clothes over to the private baths. A glass of wine in hand, he dropped onto one of the benches in the sitting room.

"What happened today?" I asked.

"Atulf told his side of the story. The man is voluble. Cillian asked a lot of questions. I wrote down the answers so Turlo could understand, and that was all. Did you go to train?"

"Yes, but something happened on the way. Is Druisius around? He should be here when I tell you."

Sorley fetched Druisius, and between us we told Sorley about the attack. After a long conversation between the men, Sorley turned to me. "Druisius says they have determined it was a random kidnapping attempt; you were with a guard, so worth a ransom. It happens here. He says it was his fault; he should have taken you a different route, and will tomorrow. And he says your knife skills are impressive."

"I misjudged and the knife hit a rib; otherwise the man could well be dead," I said. "But perhaps that might have caused problems. Sorley, we cannot tell Cillian, or Turlo; they have too much else to concern themselves with. Will you ensure Druisius understands that, and the other guards, and Sergius and Prisca?"

"I will," he said slowly, "but, Lena, are you really not going to tell Cillian?"

"Not now," I prevaricated. "After the talks are done. I am not hurt and the men are dealt with. Had I been targeted because of who I am, to influence these negotiations, then he—and Turlo—would need to know. But Druisius says it was random."

Sorley looked doubtful. "But we cannot silence all the guards, and Cillian may hear it at the palace. What do I say if he asks me about it?"

I hadn't thought of that. "If he asks you, then tell him, but also tell him it was my choice to say nothing." I couldn't ask Sorley to lie for me. He nodded.

"That's fair." Druisius said something. "Right," Sorley replied. "Druisius says to tell you Junia sent a message: she is beginning to train a few new recruits in the afternoons. You are welcome to join them."

The days settled into a pattern. Most nights Cillian and Turlo came home very late. I didn't try to wait up for Cillian; tired and often sore from the archery training, I went to bed at my usual hour, waking when Cillian came home, usually just for a few murmured words. Far too early in the mornings, he was awake again, reading notes or talking to Turlo before returning to the palace.

In the early afternoons, Druisius escorted me by a longer route on wider streets to the training ground. There were two other women training with me.

We rode bareback for some days, learning to guide the horses with only legs and voice, and then we rode with an unstrung bow, discovering how handling it affected our seat and balance.

The day we began to ride with a strung bow, practicing drawing it as we rode, I fell off Roseus several times. Instinctively I wanted to raise my body to draw, and when I did, I lost grip and balance. After the second time, Junia called me over to her. I reined the horse close.

She mimed drawing the bow, and when I did she put one hand on my belly, pushing backwards, forcing me to drop onto Roseus's back. I understood immediately. I nodded, and she let me go. I urged Roseus into a canter again, and, concentrating on keeping a deep seat, drew the bow. I stayed on the horse.

The feel of Junia's hand low on my belly remained with me as I groomed Roseus after the training. Don't let it bother you, I told myself. What had Sorley called it? The right stimulus. I untied the gelding, leading him back to his stall. As I closed the door, Junia put her hand on my arm.

"*Baineas*?" she asked. "*Lavi*?"

Sorley was doing his best over our dinners together to teach me some basic Casilan. I sorted through the words I had learned. Junia was asking me if I wanted to go the baths. After three falls off Roseus, it sounded like a very good idea.

"*Itá*[18]," I said. She grinned, calling over to Druisius. He shrugged, and took his place behind us as we walked. Junia led us back through a gate and into the city to a smaller bathhouse than the one Prisca had taken me to. A statue of the huntress goddess, bow in hand and dogs at her feet, stood outside it. One hand of the statue rested on a dog's head, and as we passed Junia reached out to touch it. The stone gleamed from countless fingers. I followed Junia's example, feeling as if it were appropriate, somehow.

Inside we gathered our towels, were rinsed off by the attendants, and settled into the hot pool. Junia's body was muscled and lean, her shoulders wide. Several scars snaked over her arms and one thigh. I wished I could ask her about actually fighting, about how the mounted archers were deployed, and when.

I closed my eyes, letting the hot water pull the ache from my back. For some time, I soaked in the heat, enjoying the feel of the water, until I felt Junia's fingers trail down my arm. Desire stirred. I did not open my eyes. I took a deep breath. The fingers asked again. I opened my eyes and looked at her, at the question in her eyes. *Every choice leaves something behind.*

Very slowly, I shook my head. She cocked hers. Are you sure? she was asking me. Again, I shook my head. "*Habea quincalum*[19]," I tried. She looked surprised.

---

[18] yes

[19] I have a (male) partner

"*Quincalum?*" she asked. "*Non quincala[20]?*"

"*Quincalum,*" I repeated. She gave me a wry smile, and shrugged. I smiled back, trying to indicate I wasn't offended by her interest.

She didn't appear to take my refusal badly. After the cold pool and the massage, we dressed companionably and went out to find Druisius. They chatted as we walked. At the junction of two streets Junia left us, calling '*crasti*'. I'd have to ask Sorley what that meant.

"*Gratiás,* Druisius," I said, as we reached the door of the house. What does he really think of his assignment, I wondered, escorting me around the city, spending much of his time just waiting? But he was always cheerful. As usual, he grinned, and went off towards the kitchen. As I entered the sitting room, I glanced out to the roof, looking for Sorley. Cillian and Turlo sat at the table, wine glasses in front of them, talking. I went to join them, giving Cillian a quick kiss. "I wasn't expecting you," I told them as I sat down.

"We made the first proposal this afternoon," Cillian told me. "Quintus and Atulf are deliberating with their advisors. Tomorrow they will make their objections and modifications, and we will begin the trades and compromises." A trace of cynicism coloured his voice.

"It is all taking too long," Turlo complained.

"The treaty must be seen to be fair and balanced, and well-considered." Cillian answered. I didn't think this was the first time they'd had this discussion, somehow. "Three or four more days will do it, I believe."

"Aye," Turlo said, sounding doubtful.

"You," Cillian said, turning to me, "have been at the baths." He would have smelt the lavender on my skin when I kissed him, I realized.

"I fell off my horse three times today," I told him. "The baths help with the aches."

"The lessons are going well?"

"Yes. It's more difficult than I thought it would be, but I'm learning."

Turlo stood. "You two have seen little enough of each other," he said, "and Cillian and I perhaps too much. A nap will be welcome. I will see you at dinner."

I smiled up at him, appreciating his courtesy. Cillian waited until he had gone. "We have quite a while before dinner," he observed softly. "Turlo has gone to his bed. Might we follow his example?"

Later, his fingers circled the bruises on my hip, already purple from this afternoon's falls. "They look painful," he said.

"They're tender," I answered. "Nothing more. I shouldn't fall any more. Junia—she's the captain of the archers—showed me what I was doing wrong."

"Sorley tells me she was impressed by your skill with the bow. Or so Druisius told him."

"It's a much better bow. I want to buy one; they are made of three layers,

---

[20] Not a female partner?

and somehow that makes the arrows fly further than a bow of the same size made just from wood. I don't understand why, though."

"I wouldn't know," Cillian said. "Does Junia?"

"I can't talk to her to find out."

"If she can read—and I assume she can, if she is a captain—then I can write the question out, she can write down the answer, and I, or Sorley, can translate it for you."

"Don't you have enough to do?" I asked. "What does '*crasti*' mean, by the way?"

"It's a casual way to say, 'I will see you tomorrow'."

"That makes sense," I said. I didn't want to think about Junia any more. "Can we talk about the negotiations?"

"Broadly. What did you want to know?"

"Why is Turlo out of sorts?"

His caressing hand stopped. "He wants to complete them, so we can begin our own talks with the Empress. But I believe Quintus may be involved in those, too, and I—we—cannot afford to antagonize him. So we must be thorough, and responsive to his concerns. Which takes time."

I heard frustration in his voice. "I'm sorry, Cillian," I said. "I didn't mean to spoil the afternoon."

"You have not," he answered. "None of it is ever far from my thoughts. There are several major issues: the northern border, ownership of some islands, and the trade route east. I believe the proposal we have made regarding the trade route will stand; the bargaining will be over the exact location of the border, and the division of the islands."

"Who will get the trade route?"

"Neither Casil nor the Boranoi, or both, depending on how you look at it. I have proposed this: that Casil takes the west bank of the river, and the Boranoi the east; each builds docks and warehouses, and all taxes and tariffs are set jointly and equally, by a committee comprised of equal numbers from each side."

I considered this. "What if they can't agree?"

"Then the proposal goes to the Empress and to the Boranoi king, and together they decide. Neither side wants war again, so it is in everyone's best interest to reach a compromise."

"It's brilliant," I said. "None of the committee members will want to earn the displeasure of his leader, and so they will all be reasonable."

"My belief is those appointed to the committee will not want to give up the bribes and underhand payments they will collect from the traders, and that will be why they do nothing to jeopardize their positions," Cillian said drily. "Either way, I believe the proposal will stand."

"Cynical man," I said lightly. He smiled, but the smile did not reach his eyes. "Cillian, what's wrong?"

"Nothing, *käresta*. I am just preoccupied." He was telling me to leave the subject alone. Perhaps he just didn't want me reminding him of what he spent almost every hour on; he had needed to relax, and I had not respected that.

I reached up to kiss him. "And I am not helping. What can I do, my love?"

"Not very much. You will need to be patient with me, as I told you." His hand resumed its light movement on my hip. "What have you been doing, when you aren't training?"

I told him about borrowing the *xache* pieces and planning mock battles. "Turlo is right," he said. "You are thinking like a leader, you know." He stretched and sighed. "We should get up, *käresta*; it must be nearly dinnertime."

At dinner, Cillian encouraged Sorley to talk about the instrument he was learning, the *cithar*. "It's different than the *ladhar*, but more in the tuning and the length of the neck than anything else," Sorley explained. "And the music is mostly in a different key, and uses quarter tones, so the notes slide into each other. I can't really explain beyond that. You're not musicians."

"My ability to pick out a simple melodic line on the *ladhar* to accompany a *danta* does not qualify me to be called a musician?" Cillian asked with a straight face.

"You know it doesn't." Sorley grinned. "You truly disappointed Dagney, you know, by refusing to learn anything more."

"Yes," Cillian said. "I do know. Not the only way I disappointed her, I expect, and a regret. Who would like to go walking with me, after dinner? I would like to be out of a building for a while."

"You are not expecting the Empress to ask for you, for your usual evening discussion of the day?" Turlo said. I thought I heard an odd emphasis on 'discussion', and a touch of acerbity in his comment. I glanced at Cillian, but his face showed me nothing.

"I hope not," he said briefly. "Lena?"

"Of course," I said.

"Sorley? Druisius will have to accompany us, I suppose, so you should come along."

"I'll be glad to."

"I cannot convince you, Turlo?"

"No. City streets are not to my liking. Perhaps I will go to the harbour, though." This is happening too often, I thought, Turlo left on his own, while the three of us are together. But I couldn't change it, if Turlo refused to come with us. And the three men are together all day, and he and Cillian late into the nights. They probably have had enough of each other's company.

We had no real destination that evening, happy to walk for the sake of walking. But eventually we found ourselves at the market. Despite the setting sun, traders still shouted and people still haggled, looking for end-of-day bargains. A man carrying a basket of vegetables brushed against me. Cillian put a hand on my back, guiding me out of the way.

"Lena!" I heard the voice behind me. I turned to see Junia, grinning.

"Junia," I said, smiling. "My trainer," I explained to Cillian. He spoke to her in Casilan. She was regarding him with clear curiosity; she would have seen the touch, I realized. Well, now she knew I had told her the truth. Cillian asked a question, and she began to explain something. He stopped her.

"A drink at the *taberna*?" he suggested to us. "Lena wants to know how the bow she is using is constructed, and why, and Junia will explain. But better over wine than standing here in the market, don't you think?"

The *taberna* was less crowded than I thought it would be at the end of the day, and the serving girl, seeing us, went out to the courtyard, and with sharp words evicted a group of youths from a table. Sorley grinned. "She says they have sat for hours over one small flask of wine, so they don't deserve the table," he said.

"We should buy them another flask," Cillian said. He spoke to the girl. She smiled, and nodded, calling to the young men.

"I hope you told her to water it first," Sorley said, sitting down. The server brought us wine and a bowl of crispy roasted peas. Cillian poured the wine. Junia took a sip and began to talk again. Cillian listened intently, nodding.

"Junia says the three layers work together. When you draw the bow, the sinew on the outside stretches and the horn on the inside squeezes together, and when you release, the horn springs open and pushes the wood. At the same time, the sinew shrinks back to its original size, pulling on the wood. Together, they make more force in the bow, so the arrow goes further than if the bow was just wood."

I tried to envision the behaviour of the materials in the bow when I drew. It made sense, I thought. "*Gratiás*, Junia," I said. To Cillian, I added, "ask her if I can buy one to take home with us."

"She will have to ask her superiors," he relayed back to me.

Druisius looked up. "Cillian," he said, pointing. Another guard had entered the courtyard. He came over to us, handing Cillian a note.

He read it, quickly, and swore under his breath. "I am summoned," he said. "*Käresta*, forgive me. I had hoped for one evening together." He stood, looking down at me, a rueful expression on his face. I smiled and shrugged.

"Empresses cannot be ignored," I murmured. He turned to go, then stopped. Turning back to me, he held out his hand. Puzzled, I gave him mine. He raised it to his lips. "Neither should you be.*"* he said, and left. Junia, I noted, watched him go.

What had that been about? Kissing my hand was acceptable, but also a very public gesture. For whom? Junia? The second guard? I didn't know.

We sat over the wine for a while longer. Junia excused herself after she had finished her glass. Once she had gone, Sorley turned to me. "Junia seemed excessively interested in Cillian."

"Yes," I said. No one could understand us, so there was no point in not speaking. "She—expressed an interest in me, earlier today at the baths. I told her no, I was partnered. With a man, which surprised her. I suppose she was curious about him."

"Probably," Sorley agreed. We sat in silence for a while, until he and Druisius began talking. I didn't mind not understanding. I watched the first stars appearing. Bats flitted over the courtyard, hunting insects.

"We should go, before it is too dark," Sorley suggested. Druisius left coins on the table. As we walked home, Sorley asked, "was it hard, saying no to Junia?"

"No. I belong with Cillian, Sorley. Anything else is just a stimulus, as you said."

We began to shoot arrows at stationary targets, first from a standstill, then from a walk. Over the next few days we progressed to trotting and cantering, and firing both facing forward, and turned in the saddle. I missed the target several times at the canter, but slowly my mind and body began to make the necessary judgments, and suddenly I could put it all together and my arrows flew home.

I barely saw Cillian, and when I did he was increasingly preoccupied. I tried not to ask about the negotiations. Turlo said very little and I thought I sensed tension between them. Sorley concurred. "I don't know what, though," he said. "Turlo doesn't wait for him any longer in the evenings, though, Druisius tells me. The Empress wants a summary, every night, and Cillian is often with her for some long time."

Junia had remained friendly, not taking my rejection to heart. The next afternoon I arrived at the training ground to find we would be shooting at a swinging target, rigged to spin and move when a rope was pulled. The target, made of stuffed cloth, had the shape of a man.

Not surprisingly, we all missed the first few times, even from a trot. The next pass, I tried not to think, letting muscles and instinct tell me when to shoot. I hit the target in its shoulder. When my next turn came, I signalled Roseus to canter and as we came within shooting distance I let the arrow fly. It lodged firmly in the figure's thigh.

For a moment I truly believed I saw blood. Bile burned my throat. I brought Roseus to a halt and swallowed. It's a stuffed dummy, I told myself. I reached into my mind, past the revulsion, finding the ice of revenge. Then I urged my horse back to speed and shot again, and this time I felt only satisfaction at the arrow in the target's chest.

Junia gave me a long assessing look before nodding her approval. When we finished, and the horses were groomed and stabled, she suggested the baths again, this time including the other two women. As I began to undress in the changing room a spot of blood on my leggings caught my eye. The moon had been full, a few nights earlier. I was due to bleed.

I showed Junia, briefly, shaking my head. The baths would be forbidden to me during this time, I was sure. She gave me a wry smile, confirming my thought. I dressed again and went out to find Druisius, hoping he had stayed; he could have well gone off for a drink, as normally I would have been some time at the baths. But he was hunkered down in the shade. He looked surprised to see me, but gave a little shrug and walked back with me to the house.

I found my blood cloths, pinned one in place, rinsed the leggings. Daily use of anash meant no cramps, thank goodness. But I was lethargic, as usual. I stretched out on the bed and let myself drift into sleep.

Blood drenched the dream: mine, a boy's, Ivor's. I thought it filled my nose and mouth and I gasped for air, forcing myself to breathe, to wake. My heart pounded. Sweat dampened my neck and hair. I lay still, orienting myself, trying to think. This was not the first time the dreams had come during my bleeding time. Was there a connection? Or had it just been the act of shooting arrows at a life-like dummy today?

I got up and washed away the sweat. I had just pulled on a clean tunic when Cillian came in. "Hello, my love," I said. "I wasn't expecting you."

"Lena," he said. He wasn't smiling. "Will you sit? I wish to talk to you." He sounds very formal, I thought.

"Wine?" I offered. He shook his head.

"No. Not for me."

"What's wrong?" I didn't sit.

"You were attacked in the street, quite a few days ago, I understand," he said evenly. "Why didn't you tell me?"

"Because you have more important things to concern yourself with," I said. "Druisius and I took care of it, I wasn't hurt, so why worry you? How did you hear of it?"

"One of the guards told me. The men involved were sentenced today, and he thought I would want to know the outcome."

"Which was?"

"To become quarry slaves. Lena, why did you not trust me with this?"

"Trusting you has nothing to do with it," I answered. "Distracting you from your work does. Even now, should you not be at the palace?"

"Not for a short while. I would have preferred to know. You were in danger."

"Briefly." I was getting annoyed. "I am a soldier, Cillian. This kidnap attempt was minor compared to what I will face in the war. Are you going to expect me to tell you about every sword thrust or axe swing that misses, in every battle? And if I did, how well would you keep your mind on analyzing tactics with the Emperor?"

"Perhaps you should have told me, so I could assess if it were random or part of an attempt to influence the negotiations," he said, in a precise, cold voice.

"Is that a real possibility?"

"Yes. There have been other—actions."

"Well, perhaps if you had told me that, instead of barely speaking to me this last week, I would have told you that Druisius considered that but the guards determined it was a random attack," I snapped. "Why did you not trust me with that, Cillian?"

He took a deep breath. Very deliberately, he poured two glasses of wine, adding water before he handed one to me. I said nothing. The last question had been mine, and I wanted an answer. I took a mouthful of wine.

"At least in this I can still speak the truth," he said eventually, his voice quiet, "it is not that I do not trust you. Lena, these negotiations are difficult and the ones to come will be even more so. Perhaps I see conspiracies where there are none, and why tell you of my worries if they are unfounded?"

"Because they are your worries, and perhaps you need someone to listen to them?" I suggested, my brief flare of anger done.

"Or speaking them makes them worse, by making them real," he answered. "I must get back. I am sorry, Lena, for my anger. But if anything else happens, please tell me."

"I will," I said. He left without finishing his wine and without kissing me. I took several deep breaths. He had asked for patience, the last time we had really talked. I would have to try to practice it.

Sorley and I had eaten a light supper, neither of us very hungry. The house felt confining; I wanted space and solitude, and I wasn't going to get it. At least out here on the roof I could see the sky.

I heard feet on the stairs. We turned to see Turlo approaching. He sank onto a bench at the table. "It's done," he announced. "Both sides have accepted the treaty." He reached for wine. "Now we can begin what we came to do." He sounded tired, and not particularly happy.

"You must be relieved," I said. "Is Cillian still at the palace?"

"Aye. Expect him to be late. He is with the Empress, and perhaps her advisors." He drank his wine. "But we must talk, now. Lord Sorley, you must decide finally what you are prepared to give up, in exchange for Casil's help." His use of Sorley's title told me this was not a conversation between friends.

"Will you tell me what you think, General?" Sorley replied. "And, let me say this. I will not decide tonight, and not before talking to Cillian. It is—was—his land too. I need his thoughts."

"Fair enough," Turlo said. "But we can at least review possibilities. A map would help."

I fetched paper and a pen. Sorley sketched a rough map of Linrathe and Sorham, and the coastal islands. "The islands are a problem," Turlo told us. "I have learned that, these last days. Too many places to hide, in and around islands, so they can serve as a place to conceal boats and men. Dividing up islands among powers does not breed trust."

"But we cannot give the Marai the islands, or they will always be on our borders," Sorley argued.

"They will always be on your borders, regardless," Turlo said. He traced a finger along the line of the Sterre. "North of here, in Sorham—it is a very wild land, at least by the Durrains."

"And throughout," Sorely agreed. "The coastal lands can be tamer in some places, but mostly it is a high and difficult land, with farming in the valleys and sheep on the hills."

"Where are your lands, Sorley?" I asked. He pointed to a coastal area, very far north.

"They were here," he said. He looked down at the map again. His face, always expressive, held a dawning realization, and immense pain. "We cannot take Sorham back, can we?"

"I do not think so," Turlo said. "Not now. At best we can hold Linrathe, but nothing north of the Sterre. We will ask for fifteen hundred men and a dozen ships. They will offer fewer, and we will settle for that in the end. How many fewer, I cannot judge. Cillian thinks perhaps half that, or a bit more. But say eight ships and eight hundred men. Enough, if the Empire has not fallen, and we still have some of our own ships and men, to drive the Marai back. But not enough to scour these islands and coast and the hidden valleys and fastnesses of Sorham, endlessly."

"I do see that. Especially when the sympathies of many lie with the Marai," Sorley said, his voice bleak. "Better to use men to fortify the Sterre."

"Aye," Turlo said. "But talk to Cillian. He may have other thoughts."

"But Linrathe?" I asked. "You still believe it can be retaken?"

"I do," Turlo replied. "It is smaller, and its coast is easier to defend. And its people are fighting back; they do not welcome the Marai, not most of them. But even that, mind, will come at a price."

"What price?"

"The same one our Empire will pay, Cohort-Leader," Turlo said. "Casil has lost lands in gaining peace with the Boranoi. The Empress will face criticism for agreeing to that. But less so, if she can point out that in exchange, she is reclaiming a long-lost portion of the Eastern Empire. Our centuries of independence are over."

Cillian had alluded to this, weeks ago while we were still on the ship. "But Linrathe never belonged to the Eastern Empire," I said.

"It did not," Turlo agreed. "But that will change. Exactly how will be part of the negotiations, no doubt, and largely up to you, my lord Sorley. You are all the voice of Linrathe we have."

"No," Sorley said, in clear anguish. "Cillian must help me decide."

"Help, yes," I said, as gently as I could. "But, Sorley—did you swear allegiance to Donnalch?"

"Yes."

"He did not," I reminded him. "Not sworn to your last legitimate leader, and with an oath given to the Empire? Cillian cannot be Linrathe's voice. Just as Turlo is reminding me that I am going to have to agree to the end of the Partition agreement, as the only woman of the Empire present, you must make these decisions for Linrathe. We did know this would come, Sorley."

"Yes, I know." Tears shone in his eyes. "There isn't any choice, is there?"

"Not that I can see," I said. "Perhaps in some of the details. Cillian said he would let us choose as freely as we could, remember?"

Sorley nodded. I put my hand on his, to comfort him a little. "How will this work, Turlo?" I asked. "Will Sorley and I have to be present for the negotiations, so we can make what choices we can?"

"I believe so," he answered.

"I should send word to Junia to not expect me, then," I said.

After a while Sorley went downstairs, to find Druisius, I thought. Turlo regarded me in silence for some minutes. "You seem very calm, lassie," he said eventually.

"Resigned," I said. "From what I have seen of Casil, better to be ruled by them than the Marai, though."

"Aye," he said. "If we must be ruled by anyone. Ending the Partition agreement will only be part of it."

"I know," I said. "And did not Callan want that, anyhow?"

"He wanted a new sort of agreement. One made by our own men and women."

"Turlo, he must have known that if Casil came to our aid, there would be a price."

"I suppose he did." He looked troubled. "Did you learn what you needed to, about archery from horseback?"

"Enough," I said. "I have questions for you, but they will wait for the voyage home."

"Once we are home, Lena, I will recommend that your role is to train and command a squadron of mounted archers. Will that suit you?"

"Yes. Thank you for that, General." I wondered if he had realized the same thing I had: in the press of warfare, I was a liability on foot, as likely to attack a fellow soldier who came too close to me from behind as I was an enemy. On a horse, I felt safer.

Sorley came back without Druisius. He picked up the map again, studying it, looking for alternatives, I supposed. Suddenly I was very tired. Too much had happened today.

"I think I'll go to bed," I said. In our room, I changed into my light sleeping shift. Replacing my blood cloth, I was surprised to see only a few spots staining it. Unusual, for me. Maybe the anash? I tried to remember if my mother had ever said anything about that. I couldn't recall her doing so, but a fragment of conversation came back to me. She had been instructing Kira, my sister and her apprentice. 'Bleeding can be affected by illness, or emotional turmoil,' she had said. 'The bleeding may come at odd times, or be lighter than usual, or sometimes heavier. Women often experience this just after their sons leave. It is not a cause for worry, unless the changes continue.' Emotional turmoil sounded right to me. I wouldn't worry, then.

CHAPTER EIGHTEEN

MOVEMENT IN THE ROOM WOKE ME. The first grey light of dawn barely let me see Cillian searching through his pack by the window. I watched him for a minute without speaking.

"Hello, my love," I said. He looked up.

"Lena. I am sorry to have woken you." His voice was impersonal, making only a polite apology.

"No matter. Is there anything I can help with?"

"I have found what I came for."

"Do the talks begin today?" I asked. "And will Sorley and I be needed?"

"They will begin today, this afternoon, to be precise. I doubt you or Sorley will be needed at first, so if there are things you should do, with the mounted archers or elsewhere, then please do them today."

I nodded. I would go to thank Junia in person, then. "Have you seen Sorley?" I asked.

"No. It was very late when I got back."

"He wants to talk to you, about Sorham and Linrathe. He wants your advice."

"This morning, then." He stood. "I have notes to write and there is only enough light outside. You might try to sleep again."

He closed the door quietly. I lay still, willing myself not to let frustration make me cry. He had not spoken to me in such a detached way since the first week of our exile in the mountains. I glanced at his side of the bed. I could see no evidence he had slept there. Where, then? Or had he not slept at all?

When the sunlight was brighter, I got up. Out on the rooftop, only Turlo sat at the table. "Good morning," I greeted him.

"Lassie," he said. "Sorley and Cillian have gone walking, to talk. Help me solve a problem."

Prisca brought fruit juice and more bread. "What is it?" I asked Turlo.

"It seems the Empress, or more likely her senior advisors, have raised a barrier. When Cillian was negotiating for Casil, that was all well and good: he had been appointed to the role by her and that gave him the authority. But now she is challenging his right to negotiate for the Empire. An Empress does not negotiate except with an equal, or an almost-equal, it seems."

"With an Emperor's son, perhaps?" I said.

"Aye."

"Then where is the problem? I thought we had decided to hold back that part of Cillian's identity unless it was needed. Now it is."

"He wants our approval to reveal it. Yours and mine, as citizens of the Empire."

"He has mine," I said. "Do you have reservations, Turlo?"

"Aye, one or two. Mostly that he is supposed to be my adjutant, or my advisor, and I believe the Empress will see our roles reversed: he as the chief negotiator, me to advise him. But Callan's authority rests in me, and it must be my name on the agreement."

"Did not he send a letter with you, making you his representative?"

"No, lassie, he didn't. None of us in the Empire can write in Casilan. I did not know anyone could, until Cillian."

"I see," I said. "Turlo, is there another way? If not, I think you will just have to be pragmatic and let Cillian take the lead. If she will believe he is the Emperor's son. How does he prove that?"

"The seal on your pardons, and your private letters. Callan's ring has been passed down from Emperor to Emperor: the impression it makes is faint now, but if you look closely, you can see the eagle. It is the same eagle as on Casil's flag. Cillian believes that will be enough to convince her, that and the way Callan signed his private note, apparently."

"As his father first, and then as the Emperor," I said. It must have been his letter he was looking for, earlier.

"Did he now?" Turlo looked surprised. "That should be enough, then."

I did not see Sorley until much later that day, after I had returned from the training field. He had not come back to the house in the morning while I was there.

"Did you stay with Cillian all the morning?" I asked.

"No. I went to see Geiri. I needed some different company. Cillian and I talked for an hour, no more."

"Was he helpful?"

"He was very analytical. Cool. He told me exactly what he thought would happen, given several choices of where we might try to stop the Marai."

"And?"

He sighed. "Sorham made its choice, I suppose. Or at least its landholders did, most of them. Including my father. But our *torpari* didn't make that choice, and I think the closer estates are to the Sterre, the more likely that their *Härren* did not welcome the Marai. I wish I knew what my brother thought. I wish I knew why my father preferred Varsland over Linrathe. But none of it matters. We cannot take Sorham back. I see that now."

"I am sorry, Sorley," I said.

"I can live with that, almost," he said. "But, Lena, how can I be the one to say 'if Casil supports us, and we win, Linrathe gives up her independence and becomes subservient to the Eastern Empire?' I have no authority to give away Ruar's inheritance."

"Ruar is not of age," I said. "Who should speak for him?"

"A man of the *Teannasach's* line."

"What did Cillian say?"

"That he would argue my position, but it might come down to no choice. Would I be willing to forfeit Linrathe as well?"

"Oh, Sorley. Did he have no advice other than that?"

"No. He was very remote, Lena."

"He is like that with me, too, Sorley. The work seems to demand it."

"Another price to be paid? I will make that decision, Lena; I will give away Linrathe's independence if I must. Even though it might make me a traitor in Ruar's eyes, and be my death sentence."

"Sorley, no! It is unfair of Cillian to make you bear that burden alone."

"Nonetheless, he is. And as you pointed out yesterday, he cannot be Linrathe's voice. But no one in Linrathe, except Lorcann and his followers, wanted a Marai king, so I suppose the *Teannasach's* line has betrayed its people and lost its authority. So it might as well be me. I am doing this for Perras and Dagney, and Jordis and Niav, and the *Ti'ach.* As close a place I have to call home, now."

Could not Cillian be at least a little sympathetic? He must still care about the *Ti'ach*, and Linrathe. Anger kindled by Sorley's words burned slowly inside me. I tried to think rationally. Cillian had said he would let us choose as freely as we could. Did that mean all he could do was show us the alternatives, and their likely outcomes, and let us decide?

How Cillian functioned on the little sleep he was getting I could not comprehend. Sorley, called to the palace on both of the next two days, came home for a late dinner and did not go out again. He looked worried. Questioned, he shook his head. "I am not sure they are going to support us," he said.

Cillian, who ate at the palace, came to bed in the early hours of the morning, and breakfasted early. I continued being patient, greeting him as usual if I woke when he came in, or in the morning, if I saw him. I was not needed at the palace. After the first day of waiting, I had gone back to the training field each afternoon.

Four days into the negotiations I heard him dress and go out just as the sun rose. I got up, pulled my robe over my sleeping shift, and followed him. He was at the roof table, as usual.

"Hello, my love," I said. He looked up from the paper in his hand.

"Lena. You are up early."

"I thought we might talk, for a few minutes. Cillian, you look terrible." He did. Fatigue purpled the skin beneath his eyes, contrasting with the pallor of his cheeks. His face looked thinner. "You are not getting enough sleep."

"It does not matter," he answered. "I can sleep when the agreement is signed." Prisca came out with bread and cheese and fruit, placing them in front of Cillian. She pointed to the food, and then to me. I shook my head. I didn't want food this early.

Cillian made no move to eat. "Are you making progress?" I asked.

"Yes." He broke off a piece of bread. "We settled what to do about Linrathe last night. It took longer, as we could make no firm promises, only proposals. Today we begin talking about the Empire."

"And Sorham?"

He shook his head. "It belongs to the Marai now." He said it straightforwardly, his voice devoid of emotion, but a small muscle jumped in his cheek as he spoke.

"Are you going to need me, now you are talking about the Empire?"

"Not today. But Sergius should always know where to find you, in case that changes." He pushed the food away. I put my hand on his. He did not move to clasp it, or entwine his fingers with mine.

"Cillian," I said, and then again, when he did not look at me. "There is something wrong. Tell me."

"It is just that I am using everything I have to offer to keep the Empress looking favourably at our petition," he answered. "There is significant opposition." He pushed his stool back. "I will be at the palace, if you would be so kind as to let Turlo know."

His words unsettled me. I felt vaguely nauseated. I ate a piece of bread, which helped, a bit. What had he been telling me? Just that all his energy and thought was going to these talks, I told myself.

I dressed, and when I heard Turlo and Sorley in the sitting room, I went back to the rooftop table. "Cillian has gone to the palace," I told Turlo. "You are talking about the Empire, today?"

"Aye, we are." Turlo answered. "In a day or two, lassie, we will have given our independence away. Callan will be the last Emperor of the West, in his own right."

"What will he be, if anything?" I asked.

"Cillian has unearthed a title: *Princip*. Leader. We will see what the Empress thinks of it. Although," he added, "if it comes from him, she's likely to approve."

"He says there is opposition."

"Aye. Quintus. Cillian is fighting it in a way I would not have thought possible."

He didn't elaborate. Sorley put a hand on mine, and when I looked at him, shook his head. "Later," he mouthed.

Turlo finished eating and left to dress for the palace. "I am sorry about Sorham," I said to Sorley. "Cillian told me, this morning."

He spread his hands. "There was no choice. Did he tell you anything else?"

"Not about Linrathe. What was Turlo alluding to, Sorley?"

He looked away. "Cillian and the Empress—they are very close, Lena. He is very attentive, and she treats him with an intimacy that suggests—other intimacies, I suppose. He is with her until extremely late, every night."

"He wouldn't," I said automatically. But—*I am using everything I have to offer.* "Sorley," I asked, "what does Druisius say about the opposition?"

"Soldier's speculation. But if he has it right there is quite strong opposition to sending boats and men so far away, with the peace with the Boranoi so newly established. What are you thinking, Lena?"

"It will just be the tools of diplomacy," I said briefly. "Excuse me, Sorley. I am not feeling well."

I made it to the latrine before I vomited. I rinsed my mouth and lay on the bed, thinking. Would he go that far, to ensure Casil's support? Would he do this to us? My thoughts circled and twisted. He had not touched me in days. I thought about his sudden self-disgust, up on the city walls, and his unexpected public kiss of my hand at the *taberna*. His cryptic comment: *at least in this I can still speak the truth.* I gave up trying to think. I needed to move. I changed my clothes, found Druisius, and went to the training ground.

Junia did not mind that I was early. I found work to do, with the horses and the tack, and in the afternoon my arrows flew with an accuracy that reflected my cold concentration. I went to the baths with her and the other recruits, and even stopped at a *taberna* with them for a drink. Druisius had to wait outside: it was a *taberna* for the female soldiers only, it transpired. A statue of the hunting goddess stood in the centre of its small courtyard, and when I left I gave her hand a rub.

Still, physical activity and several glasses of unwatered wine were not enough to make me sleep that night, so I knew Cillian had not come home—or at least to bed—at all. At dawn I gave up, and got up. I felt unwell after no sleep and too much wine, but several glasses of water helped with that. An idea had begun to coalesce, but it was too soon to examine it closely.

"Stay close today," Turlo told me at breakfast. "We may need you. Both of you, if things go well."

I sent word to Junia that I would not come today. Sorley and I played *xache*, and he played the *ladhar*. I thought he was working on a new tune, something that sounded like a blend of his music and Casil's. I wished I had something equivalent to occupy my mind.

The summons came just after midday. Prisca, always efficient, had ordered two new tunics for me, suitable to wear in the presence of the Empress. I chose one at random, barely noting its finer fabric and intricate embroidery, and pinned on the matching shawl. In the sitting room, Sorley waited for me, Druisius with him. Downstairs, a second guard joined us, to my surprise. Druisius not taking any chances, I wondered, or did our destination require more outward show?

We were delivered to a side door of the palace, to be led down wide corridors to a fair-sized room furnished with tables and benches, and two couches. Paper and vellum lay on one of the tables, along with a pen, and a flask of wine and a jug of water sat on a sideboard. "We wait here," Sorley told me.

I paced, and sat, and paced some more. Sorley simply sat. "I wish we had a *xache* set," I told him, at one point. But finally the door opened and Turlo came in. He went directly to the wine, pouring himself a small amount.

"It is done," he said. "Cillian has insisted you both sign, as well, so it is clear there is agreement from us all. Ten ships, a thousand men, supplies. Enough to turn the tide, if it has not overrun our lands by the time we get there. And one task for you, Lena, to confirm the route you took across the plains, on an old map."

"What did we give up?" I asked.

"In the Empire? What we thought: Callan becomes *Princip*, subservient to the Empress. Casil's laws take precedence; the Partition agreement is ended. Some reorganization of the army. Settlement of Casilani people on our lands. Tribute, after a few years."

"And Linrathe?" Sorley asked.

"Not so different," Turlo said. "Except that Ruar, should he make it to his majority, remains *Teannasach*, but as a client ruler of Casil. A bit more freedom to keep your own laws, but with tribute to be paid as well."

Enormous sadness and enormous relief battled inside me. I went to Sorley, embracing him wordlessly, and then turned to Turlo. "Lassie," he said, enfolding me in his arms, "we have done the best we can. I hope the price is not too high, for you."

"For us all, surely?" I replied.

"Aye," he said. "For us all. Now," he said, becoming brisk, "let me tell you the protocol." He explained how we were to behave. Then we went to sign the treaty.

We followed Turlo through the wide door into the next room. He stopped a few paces in, and both Sorley and I dropped to one knee. The Empress sat at the end of a long table, littered with scrolls, a large map taking up a portion of the space. Her hair was the deep red of copper, and simply twisted and pinned on the back of her head. She wore a long tunic of a deep bluish-green, trimmed with gold, and her shawl reversed the colours. No jewels, except for earrings of gold set with a green stone. I did not think her beautiful, but her face showed intelligence, and good humour, and she was younger than I had expected.

Cillian sat on her left-hand side. She turned to him as we entered, asking him a question. Her hand touched his forearm. He smiled, answering her, seeming completely at ease. Somehow he looked less tired here. Her eyes came back to us and she made a small gesture with her hand, the meaning clear. We stood, and with a graceful move she turned in her chair, extending a hand. Sorley moved forward, knelt again, and kissed it. Then she looked at me. She did not ask me to move, but turned again to Cillian. They spoke, quietly, for a few moments. She studied me again, and then beckoned me forward.

Turlo had explained that I was not of sufficient rank to be offered her hand to kiss. I knelt in front of her, waiting.

The Empress spoke. "Stand," Cillian said quietly. A large sheet of vellum, with close writing, lay on the table in front of the Empress. Two signatures— Turlo's and Cillian's—had already been added. Cillian's, I noted, had the words '*filus Imperium de Westani*' appended. I thought I could translate that without help.

There was very little ceremony to the signing. I added my name, and Sorley his. Cillian dictated some words for Sorley to add, explaining who he was, and his loyalty to Linrathe. Only then did the Empress sign, below all our names. We had our agreement.

"One last small task, for you, Lena," Cillian said, his voice unemotional. "If you would look at this map?" He indicated the far end of the table. The map that lay there reminded me of the one Perras had shown me in his study at the *Ti'ach*. But on this one, the line of the road that ran from the Durrains to the river was clear. The Temple of the Hero was marked, and so was the fort below the lake. I traced my finger along the road.

"This is the road," I confirmed. My finger stopped at the lake. I had to do this, now. I turned, to look directly into Cillian's shadowed eyes. Remember what you told me there, I sent to him silently. *It is an empty place,"* I said.

I saw the almost imperceptible nod. "It is," he said quietly. "A place I would not go again, if there were a choice. But that waits on my Empress's pleasure."

My Empress. I swallowed. "Lord Sorley, Cohort-Leader, you are done here," Cillian said. "The guards will escort you home."

I did not cry. I lay on our bed, dry-eyed, and thought. About a conversation on the plain, just before we had reached the temple, and another, the night we had learned what Lorcann had done. When Sorley knocked on the door, much later, I thought I was calm.

"What is he doing?" Sorley asked, as soon as he was in the room. "I heard what he said to you."

"Being a hero," I said. "Being Darcail, I think."

"I don't understand." He sat down. "What do you mean?"

"What do you remember about Darcail? There must be a *danta*."

"He had a series of labours to complete, to find redemption for an evil deed. Which he did successfully, and ended up a god, or nearly a god."

"Right. Cillian and I talked about him, a time or two on our journey. Do you remember the last labour?"

"To do something in the underworld, and return safely. I don't remember what."

"It doesn't matter. Only that it takes him to the underworld."

"And how does in intend to return safely?"

"I don't know. I don't even know if Cillian realizes what he's doing. Sorley, do you know why he chose celibacy, when he did?"

"More or less."

"Do you know how his previous choices made him feel?"

"Empty and cold, he said. Is that why you said what you did, this afternoon, about an empty place?"

"Yes. Sorley, that lake is where he told me he loved me, and I him. It is not an empty place for us. You heard his response. He knew what I was asking him."

"He has offered himself to the Empress, hasn't he?" Sorley said. "Regardless of the cost, to him or to you?"

"I doubt he has made a direct offer. Rather, I believe he has made it clear he will not refuse her advances. Which she appears to be making, very publicly, whether just for pleasure, or for politics, I am not sure."

"He must be desperate to ensure this treaty."

"Yes," I agreed. "This will destroy everything he has worked to become this last year. He will break so many promises to himself, and one of those was made in his mother's name. All because he believes himself responsible for Lorcann siding with Fritjof, and what happened to Linrathe, and, like Darcail, he is looking for redemption."

"But how can he break his vow to you, Lena?"

"He isn't," I said. I had worked this out, too. "Or at least, not one of them. He vowed to shelter me. If he can obtain Casil's promise to help the Empire, is he not providing me with the best shelter he can, in saving my land?"

Sorley swore. "So what do we do?"

"If he comes home tonight," I said, "I have a plan. But he didn't, last night."

"He slept with the guards," Sorley said. "Druisius told me. He said he didn't want to disturb you."

"Tell Druisius to lock the door tonight, then. Or make sure there is no spare bed. Whatever he can, to make Cillian come to our room. Now we need to speak to Prisca, and you and I have some work to do."

Dawn was only a short time off when Cillian came in. I had been dozing, not truly asleep. I moved to sit cross-legged on the bed. He stood in the dark room, not speaking.

"Hello, my love," I said.

"Lena." He could barely speak. Good, I thought. I wanted him off-balance, vulnerable.

"Have you come from her bed?" I inquired, as calmly as I could.

"No."

"Not yet?"

He sat down on a bench. "Not yet."

"But the offer has been made?"

"Alluded to, indirectly, by her. It is only a matter of time."

"Cillian, why have you done this?"

"Her advisors wanted no part of our petition. They told her we do not matter; there was nothing we can offer to make the gift of troops and ships worthwhile. Quintus tried to bribe me, with citizenship and property; I still believe they may have threatened you. None of those worked. I expected an attempt on my life, which did not happen, probably because the Empress was inclined towards me, after the peace I brokered with the Boranoi, and they would not dare to hurt me if I were in her favour. Far enough in her favour. I did say I would use myself in these talks, to save the Empire, and Linrathe. Which I have done." There was no expression in his voice at all.

"An Empress and an Emperor's son," I said, as lightly as I could. "And now an Emperor's heir, am I right?"

"By Casil's laws, yes."

"She is intelligent, I can see that," I said. "There was a *xache* board in the room; does she play?" He made a sound of assent. "And she is well read?"

"Yes. She even reads Heræcrian."

"A worthy partner, then. I see only one problem, or perhaps two."

"Which are?"

"She does not love you. She cares only that you are Callan's son."

"You are right. But she may come to care for more than that, in time."

His response to my next words was crucial. "And you do not love her. Will that change too, in time?"

"No," he said hoarsely. "Lena, do not ask me this, please." I heard the catch as he spoke my name, the crack in the carefully constructed wall holding back feeling. I had had a long time, waiting for him to come home, to practice the words Sorley had taught me, one of them chosen so precisely. I thought I had the pronunciation correct.

"Do you really think I am going to let you do this?" I said. "*Thá mi gràh agàthe,* Cillian. *Ná mi tréigtha, kärestan. Ná mi tréigtha, do thóille.*" I love you, Cillian. Do not abandon me, beloved. Do not abandon me, please.

I heard a long, shuddering breath, and another, as he fought for a control he could not reach. He covered his face with his hands, turning away from me. I slid off the bed and went to him, kneeling in front of him, wrapping my arms around him. My words of love and fear, in his own language, had done what I had hoped they would. I held him until his sobs began to diminish. Then I reached for the flask of wine I had asked Prisca for, earlier in the evening. There was just enough light through the shutters to see, now. Carefully, I poured one glass, and gave it to him. "Drink this, my love," I said. "You need to sleep."

Prisca knew how to measure a dose of poppy. Cillian slept for four hours, which is what I had requested. He woke slowly, blinking in the filtered light of the room. I sat on my half of the bed, Sorley by the window.

"Lena," he said, a bit groggily. "What did you give me?"

"Poppy in the wine," I told him. "You needed to sleep."

"I do not like being drugged."

"I remember. But this was medicinal," I told him. "I learned a few things from my mother, and that was one of them." He went to the latrine. I heard water splashing, and when he came back his face and hair were damp. He looked from me to Sorley. His lips quirked, just slightly. The drug was still affecting him, I realized.

"Both of you? Is this a conspiracy?" That had taken effort, I thought, but better than anger, or sullenness.

"It is," I told him. There was a knock at the door. Sorley took the tray of food from Prisca. She had sent the usual breakfast offerings, fresh flat bread, soft cheese, and figs. "Eat something," I told Cillian. "And drink water, a lot of it."

"What are our choices?" Sorley said, after we had eaten.

"Our choices?" Cillian asked. "Surely mine."

"Ours," I said firmly. "You are not alone, Cillian, in this, or anything, any longer. It is time you realized that, fully."

"Get used to it," Sorley added, bluntly.

"I came up with one idea," I said, keeping my voice light, "but it doesn't work. At first, I thought we should find a priest from that temple popular with newlyweds, and have him marry us. But then I decided the Empress probably would find a way to have any marriage dissolved, so I discarded that idea. And then I thought that perhaps we should just talk to her. All of us. No diplomacy, just the truth. Including something I think you have forgotten, Cillian."

"You cannot stay, unless you were planning to commit treason against your Emperor. He ordered you home."

He frowned. "When?"

"What does your letter say?"

I watched him thinking. Comprehension took longer than I expected. "*I require you by my side,*" he said finally. "That is an order, I suppose. But Eudekia could still command a betrothal, or even a marriage, before I went back. Callan is not truly Emperor, now."

"Isn't he, until he also signs the agreement?" I asked. "But regardless, why would the Empress of the East want a man who did not love her, and had broken almost every promise he had made, as her consort? What sort of prize would he be? And how would she ever trust him?"

"You would tell her that?"

"I would," Sorley said. "I will. Do not doubt me on that, Cillian. I will. Even if you tell me not to, if I can find a way."

"I believe you," he replied. "And you, Lena? Why would you still want me, now? I broke a promise to you."

"You did. You promised to be constant, and you have not been. But in breaking that promise, you had a chance to save the land and people that you love, and keep me safe. Is that not true?"

"I thought it was."

"Then I can forgive you. I made much the same choice, once." I did not take my eyes from his. "You need to forgive yourself, too. Will it help to remember that it is not some mythical hero whom I love, but you, difficult and complicated and flawed as you are?"

"And I," Sorley added, quietly. "Shall I leave you now?"

"When are you due back at the palace?" I asked Cillian.

"Two hours after mid-day."

"Then, no. We have some thinking to do, and you need to visit the baths, my love. Wine and poppy and strong emotion have left you less than fragrant this morning. You would offend the Empress. Although perhaps that might not be a bad thing."

The men were ready to leave for the baths. I would meet them outside the palace; my job, in the time before that, was to ensure Turlo did not know what we were doing. We had decided—or Sorley and I had—that he had no part in this.

"Sorley," Cillian said, "would you give me a few minutes with Lena?"

When the door had closed behind Sorley, he looked at me. His dark eyes were clear again, and gentle. "Lena," he asked, "who chose the one word you used, earlier?"

"I did. Sorley just taught me how to say it."

"I thought so. I doubt any other would have had the same effect." A hint of a smile played on his lips. "You planned that very carefully, did you not? Waiting until I was past exhaustion to ask what you knew would undermine my defenses, and then...taking a battering ram to them. Almost cruel, one could say."

"Possibly."

"How did you know?"

"I worked it out, from things you have said, and not said. You were seven, Cillian, and not an Empire's boy, prepared since he could talk for leaving, and waiting eagerly for it. You were barely over a physical attack that nearly killed you, and then suddenly taken away from everything and everyone you loved. If you did not, in your deepest self, fear abandonment, there would be something wrong with you." Fear it, and somehow also think it both your fault, and your due, I thought.

"There has been something wrong, these last days."

"Only a misplaced desire for atonement, my love. Your last task in this war awaits you at home, not here. Your father made that clear."

"*Käresta*, I do not deserve you." He still had not touched me, I realized. I thought he might not, until this was done.

"Yes," I said, "yes, you do. Me, and Sorley, and Alain, and Perras and Dagney—and others, too. Go to the baths, Cillian. Sweat out the remnants of the poppy. You need a very clear head this afternoon."

But in the end, neither Cillian nor I stood in front of the Empress to plead with her to let him go. Sorley did it all. Turlo, I discovered, had gone to the harbour. So I went to the palace alone, except for an escort. But in the anteroom where we met, Sorley had changed the plans.

"I have requested an audience, for myself," he told us. "I will thank her for her generosity towards Linrathe, but then I have other things to say to her."

"I should be there," Cillian argued. He looked far better; still tired, but his skin was less pale, probably from the heat and the lotions of the baths.

"No," Sorley said. "Your presence might inhibit what I have to say. I am insisting, for once, Cillian."

"And me?" I asked.

"Again, no," Sorley replied. "I thought this over, at the baths. I have only been in the Empress's presence a few times, but I do not think she likes other women very much. Certainly not one whom she would construe as a rival."

He was with her a long time. Cillian and I sat, not speaking very much. Footsteps sounded occasionally in the hall, but from the adjoining room I could hear nothing at all. Finally the door between the rooms opened.

"The Empress requests your presence, Cillian," he said. Cillian stood, adjusting his cloak. He glanced at me before walking steadily into the next room. Sorley closed the door.

"Well?" I asked.

"She has a very fine mind," he said. "And a great deal of compassion, but she demands the truth. She will not be easy on him, but I believe she will let him go." He went to the wine on the sideboard and poured a glass. "Lena?" I shook my head. Not yet. He watered it, and drank it down. "I found myself telling her things I did not expect to. Not all were mine to tell, truly, so I hope both you and Cillian will forgive me."

"I forgive you anything, if it means she relinquishes any claim on him."

"I also pointed out what you did, this morning: knowing he had broken so many vows, how could she ever trust him? She seemed to take that seriously. I hope I am right, Lena. In another life, you know, they would be well suited."

"Yes," I said. "I think I do know that." In another life, I would still be with Maya.

The door opened. Cillian came in. Closing it, he leaned against it. He looked at the two of us somberly. I held my breath. "That was worse than the worst tongue-lashing Dagney ever gave me as a child," he said. "And all the same technique: sorrow at my behaviour, regret that I had hurt people, a flash of anger, ending with a penance and forgiveness." His slow smile began to light his face. "And then she told me she has decided to marry the Boranoi heir, because he is better situated to help her take back the grasslands west of the river. In a year or two, she said. When her people have forgiven the peace treaty, and have seen the benefits of the trade arrangement. Sorley, whatever you said to her, *meas, mo chariadh gràhadh, meas.*"

He crossed the room to embrace him. I had seen the quick start of tears in Sorley's eyes, and I thought I knew why. My friend, whom I love, Cillian had said. I felt tears pricking behind my own eyes, at the thought.

He turned to me. "I have a penance to do." Slowly, he dropped to both knees in front of me. "*Käresta,*" he said, "do you forgive me?"

"Is this what the Empress asked of you? To ask my forgiveness, on your knees?" I wasn't doing a good job of holding back my laughter.

"Yes." He too was trying to not laugh. "In her world, *käresta*, for an Emperor's son to diminish himself in such a way to a mere soldier would be penance indeed."

"But I have never cared whose son you are," I pointed out. "Get up, Cillian. I forgave you last night. Sorley can report you did your prescribed penance. I may think of my own, later." I stepped into his arms. We held each other, tightly, for a long moment, until I moved back, just a bit, turning to look at Sorley. He was watching us, smiling. I held out my hand. "Come here," I said. "Cillian needs you too, you know. We both do."

We walked slowly home. We were all drained, from too little sleep, from worry, from the relief of fear. At the house, we collapsed onto the benches of the sitting room. Sorley looked longingly at the sideboard. There was no wine; Sergius had not expected us back yet. "I don't have enough energy to get up and order any," Sorley said.

Druisius had followed Sorley's eyes. He said something, then ran downstairs, coming back a few minutes later with his *cithar*, Sergius, and wine. At a word from Druisius, Sergius served us all—something he never did—and then, after a small bow to Cillian, left us. Druisius smiled a little wryly and addressed Cillian, sounding apologetic.

"He says," Cillian told me, "that the household was told days ago what my rank is, and he will be reporting Sergius's lack of respect. I told him not to; I preferred it this way. But that we appreciated the wine." He laughed. "And does Druisius know who you are, my lord Sorley, if we are playing games with rank?"

"A landless farmer with a courtesy title of no real meaning, you mean?" Sorley asked. Wine and fatigue and relief were bringing us to the edge of uncontrolled hilarity.

"Listen, both of you. Neither of your lovers care a whit for your ranks and titles, or lack of them," I said. "I am sure I can speak for Druisius on that." Sorley looked surprised, for a moment, at my words: his relationship with Druisius had never been quite so openly acknowledged, even between us.

"Let me find out," Cillian said, grinning wickedly. He spoke to Druisius, who looked shocked, then turned to Sorley, asking a question.

"Cillian," Sorley moaned. He spoke rapidly to Druisius, who continued to look doubtful. I should intervene, I thought.

"Druisius," I said, to get his attention. He looked at me. "Remind him," I said to Cillian, "that I am only a soldier too."

He did. Druisius gave me a long considering look. Then he grinned, and nodded. He said something to Sorley, and picked up his *cithar*, beginning to play softly.

"Troublemaker," I said to Cillian. He shook his head, slightly.

"I have my reasons," he murmured.

Turlo came in, not long after. He stopped at the top of the stairs, taking us in. Sorley, unable to not make music, had fetched the *ladhar*, and he and Druisius were harmonizing on a Casilani tune. I had moved from my bench to sit on the floor at Cillian's feet, leaning against his legs. His hand played in my hair.

I looked over at Turlo. He smiled, tentatively. "Lassie," he said, sounding relieved. He had been worrying for me, I knew. I smiled back at him.

"Come and enjoy the music, Turlo," I said. "And have some wine. The quality has improved, now Sergius has been reminded of Cillian's rank."

Turlo's eyes narrowed. He poured wine, and sat on the bench closest to us.

"I have a small update for you," Cillian said softly. "But it must not be made public, at all. There will be a betrothal announced, at a later date, between a certain high lady of our acquaintance, and the heir to the lands to the north."

Cillian, I thought, you are incorrigible. He had crafted what he had said to keep Turlo in suspense until the last word. Turlo's face went from a frown to a broad grin. He gave a bark of laughter. "Excellent news!" he said. He schooled his face into sternness. "I will have words for you, Adjutant, when we are alone."

"Don't bother," I said. "He's been scolded enough. Let's just celebrate, Turlo."

We requested an early meal, something light, and the sky was not yet dark when we went to bed. Neither of us had slept more than a few hours in days, even including Cillian's drugged sleep last night, and when I had stood up after eating, I had swayed with fatigue.

I slipped under the coverlet, fighting to keep my eyes open. Cillian lay down beside me. I turned to him. He touched my face. "I would very much like to make love," he murmured, "but I just can't."

"Good," I said, "because neither can I. Sleep well, and long, my love. I'll be here in the morning."

Of all the nights for me to dream of violence, this was not one when I would have expected it. But perhaps, I thought later, I knew we were going home now, that the war could no longer be ignored. The images were all from Tirvan, of blood and death on both sides, and on my hands. I woke trembling. Cillian's arm lay over me, for his reassurance as much as mine, I understood now. I lay still, thinking with the clarity that sometimes comes in the darkest hours of the night.

I might never be free of this, I thought, not truly. Violence done, by me and to me, has left its scars. There may always be fear, and revulsion, and more savagery lies ahead. But with him, I am sheltered, and safe, and I can cope.

But I sheltered him, too, I knew. I had touched on the truth, that first night at the lake: the darkness within us both was more than one night, or many, would assuage. I could only guess at what he must have felt, at seven: terrified, but also culpable. He had built his defenses against loss, constructing a demanding code of behaviour distancing himself from connection and love. How old had he been, when he first heard the hero's legend?

In each other we had found healing, but neither of us were whole. If time, and the gods I did not believe in allowed, perhaps, but that grace was unlikely to be given in a time of war. I did not know where need ended and love began, for either of us, and I did not think it mattered.

I turned towards him. The moon was well past full, but the night was clear. Enough light shone through the shutters that I could just see his face, untroubled now in sleep. I touched his cheek with one fingertip. "*Käresta*," he murmured, not waking, and reached out, pulling me closer. I settled against his chest, and closed my eyes.

We woke late, and it was even later before we left our room. Prisca was bringing the mid-day meal. Sorley grinned at us. He looked relaxed, and refreshed, and I suspected part of his morning had been spent much as ours had been.

"Turlo has gone to begin calculating supplies needed, or some such," he told us. "I was to tell you that he expects nothing from either of you, today. Or me, for some reason."

"Very good," Cillian said. "There are some things I would like to do today. A question for you first, *mo bhráithar.* Would having Druisius accompany us home please you?"

Sorley's eyes widened. He flushed. "But, how could he?"

"There is a line in the treaty that allows us to hand-pick a few of the men— or women—to join us. It was meant to ensure we had the best commanders, up to a certain rank. For example, I could request Junia, so that she can train mounted archers, in the Empire. I cannot request Quintus, even if I wanted him."

"Druisius is bored as a palace guard," Sorley said. "I will have to ask him. To answer your question, yes, it would please me. But only if he wants it too, and only after I ensure he truly understands where my greatest loyalties lie."

"Let me know." He turned to me. "Shall I request Junia?"

He has grown used to authority, I thought. Turlo might have something to say about who should come. "I don't know," I temporised. "Turlo asked me to take on that role, once we are home." I tried to think clearly. "She would have to accept being second to me. But her knowledge would be invaluable." Did I really want here there?

Sorley's foot touched mine, under the table. I glanced at him. He gave me a questioning look. "What is it?" Cillian asked.

"Junia made her interest in me known," I said. "I made it very clear I did not return that interest. It does not seem to have worried her. If Turlo agrees, I think we should request her to come." She would be valuable. The needs of our army must take precedence over any private concern I had, in this.

Cillian smiled. "So we have all caught someone's attention here in Casil, have we?" he said. "I wonder if Turlo has?" he mused. "There is attraction in the new, it is said."

"Cillian," I said, "speculating on your superior officer's private life is not done. Stop it, now."

He laughed. "Shall we go to the market after we eat? There is something I want to buy."

"And I," I said. I had thought of it, waiting at the palace.

Heat bounced off the pavement and the buildings. Not long after mid-day, there was little shade to be had. I glanced up at the Giant of the Sun as we passed: I, at least, had not yet grown used to it. Only servants and soldiers were out: the more leisured classes would be resting, or sitting in treed courtyards, out of the sun.

At the market, the vendors sat under woven canopies, some fanning themselves. "Now," Cillian said, "I need Druisius's help with my purchase. Lena, can Sorley help with yours? We can meet at the *taberna* afterwards."

"Well," Sorley said, after Cillian had clapped Druisius on the back and strode off with him, "that was—directive."

"Mmm," I agreed. "It may be a good thing he will be reporting directly to Callan, once we are home."

"What is it you want to buy?"

"A *xache* set, so we have one for the ship. We still have your kidskin to use as a board, don't we?"

"Yes. What a good idea. I hadn't thought about not having Irmgard's to use."

We found the *xache* pieces, carved from wood, in one of the small permanent shops. The pieces lacked detail, but they had a simple beauty, and would serve. Sorley bargained with some skill, and my purse lacked only half its coins when he was done.

The *taberna* was busy, as usual, but the serving girl, recognizing us, found us a table. She brought wine, and water, and a dish of roasted beans, and two more glasses when Sorley asked. I poured water only; I was thirsty. The trees shaded us, just a little.

I saw Cillian come in, alone. He crossed the courtyard towards us. "Druisius is just finishing up the bargaining," he told us. "He'll be here shortly."

"What did you buy?" I asked.

"Be patient," he said. "You will see. Did you get what you wanted?"

I showed him. "For the ship."

"A good thought. We will all appreciate it. *Meas,* Lena." He poured wine, holding up the flask. "There is a toast I would like to make. Will you join me?" I added water to mine. He raised his glass. "To you, *käresta,* and you, Sorley, *mo charaidh gràhadh,*" he said. "I am blessed beyond understanding in the two of you. Thank you for what you did." He hesitated. "Catilius wrote, *Accept the things to which fate binds you, and love whom fate brings to you, but do so with all your heart.* Fate brought you both to me, and I love you both, with all my heart."

Sorley blinked. "You will make me cry," he murmured. And me, I thought.

"Not my intent," Cillian said. "But I will help you make music." Druisius came towards us, a *cithar* in his hand. "This is for you."

Sorley turned. Druisius handed him the *cithar,* grinning broadly. "*Sede*[21]," Cillian said to Druisius, pouring him wine. Druisius sat, his eyes on Sorley, gauging his reaction. Sorley drew his fingers across the strings, listening to the resonance.

"It's lovely," he said. "But Cillian, you can't give me this."

"I can and I have," Cillian replied. "I trust Druisius has chosen well? If you like, you can think of it as a present for us all, so that we will have music on the long journey home. But as you are the only one who can play it, I am giving it to you."

"Now I will cry," Sorley said, but he was grinning. "*Bêne, amané*[22]," he said quietly to Druisius, before turning again to us. "I wish there was something I could give you in return."

---

[21] sit

[22] Well done, lover

"Maybe there is," I said on impulse. "Not exactly for us, though. Don't you think there should be a *danta* about Irmgard, and you and Turlo, and I suppose Cillian and me, and what we have done? And who better to write it than you?"

PART IV

How can man die better than facing fearful odds for the ashes of his fathers and the temples of his gods?   Macauley

CHAPTER NINETEEN

WE SAILED OUT OF CASIL ON A MORNING TIDE, the four of us—five, now—together on the first ship, Rufin in command. He had asked to come, we had learned. On the mast, under the eagle of the Eastern Empire, golden on its red field, flew the standard of my Empire, the White Horse and the Wall on a green background. It had been made in Casil, after the agreement had been signed.

I suppose we should have been looking forward, but we all watched Casil recede, the white buildings shining in the morning sun. Our last days had been crammed full of tasks, Turlo and Sorley in long consultations with commanders and quartermasters, determining men, equipment, and supplies. I had done whatever they asked, which mostly had been a combination of being a messenger and checking manifests, work both boring and precise. I had taken special care with the two dozen bows of wood and horn we had been given. Junia would travel on the same ship that carried them, to ensure their safety.

Turlo had argued with Cillian about Druisius, but not about Junia. "I would have asked for her, too," he said. "But Druisius is only another soldier."

"He is not," Cillian had said firmly. "He matters to Sorley, and that should matter to you, Turlo. And," he pointed out, "it relieves a certain tension among us. I will leave all the other appointments to you, General, but I ask your indulgence in inviting Druisius to join us."

"Aye," Turlo had said reluctantly. "I see your point. Druisius may come, if he wants. Now, Adjutant, you are excused duty until I tell you. I cannot spare the cohort-leader, but you need some rest and relaxation."

"I can rest on the ship," Cillian argued.

"That was an order, Adjutant. Lassie, talk some sense into him," he growled, and left us alone.

We regarded each other over the rooftop table. Cillian still looked tired, the faintest hint of purple under his eyes. He was quieter, too, with a contemplative stillness that was new.

"Do as Turlo has told you," I said. "You need to rest."

"I am weary," he admitted. "These have been difficult weeks."

"There have been so many demands on you. Translator, scholar, negotiator."

"Yes."

"Adjutant, friend, lover."

He smiled. "The last is not a demand."

"Perhaps not," I said. "But, Cillian, when was the last time you did not have to consider anyone but yourself? When was the last time you were alone?"

"For more than a few minutes? Somewhere on the river."

"For a few days, do what you want. Turlo and Sorley and I can oversee the preparations to leave. Borrow a horse and ride out of the city. Ask for access to the library; you know you want to see it. You have earned time to yourself."

"I would prefer to spend time with you, *käresta*."

"I have work to do. *Kärestan*, we have scarcely been apart for over a year, excepting this last couple of weeks. Do you realize that? I remember you telling me you love solitude, time just to be quiet, to think, and you have had next to none. There is a long voyage on a crowded ship ahead of us, so take what you need, and what you deserve, while you can." I smiled. "You would regret not spending time in the library, you know."

He reached to entangle his long fingers in mine. "You are right," he agreed. "To have been in Casil, and not at least seen the library properly—I would lament it, later."

"Just don't get so engrossed you forget to come home," I said. "Your days are your own, but I lay claim to your evenings."

He had done as Turlo had ordered, coming home to tell us of the marvels of the library, and the conversations he had with men he met there. That the writings of Casil and Heræcria were known in the forgotten West amazed them, and he had been offered copies of some books unknown to him, to take back. In exchange, he had offered to translate a history of Linrathe, and Colm's history of the Empire, and send them back to Casil. "A task for the ship," he had explained. The fatigue faded from his face, and the tension from his body, over those few days.

I was still unaccountably tired: not exhausted, but lethargic, and the fear and stress of the last weeks had made my stomach sour. Prisca, after consultation, made me teas with mint and ginger, which helped, and I ate fewer of the acidic black fruits. I had developed something close to an aversion to the anash, but I could not stop drinking it until we sailed. I might feel sluggish over my work, but in the privacy of our room, lassitude disappeared. We had come too close to losing each other, and while we did not speak of why, the need to affirm our love ran high in us both.

And then we had said our farewells and boarded the ship. The voyage, we had been told, would take about a month. The first few days we did very little: Turlo looked green, and while Cillian and Sorley did better than on the Marai ship, they were careful with food and drink, as was I. Druisius, completely unaffected, laughed at us, but gently, and kept an eye on Sorley.

Druisius had become part of our lives easily. Always good-tempered, he and Sorley played for us almost every evening, and he accepted any task he was given. He began to learn our common tongue, and with Cillian's grinning encouragement called Sorley 'my lord' much of the time. Sorley took his revenge by referring to Cillian as '*filus Imperium*'. It was all gentle fun, and even Turlo just shook his head and let the men tease each other.

The lessons in swordplay began again once we were all accustomed to the movement of the ship. Casil's soldiers used a shorter sword, and Druisius proved adept at both using and teaching it, in conjunction with their large shield. Most mornings, we practiced on a cleared space at the stern of the ship, behind the rowers. Rufin, the captain, came to watch occasionally, and once offered to spar with Druisius, to the delight of his off-duty men.

I wondered what the villages we passed thought, seeing the ten ships and the handful of supply boats moving steadily west. Larger and with a deeper draught than the Marai ship, the Casilani ships dropped their sea-anchors and sent smaller boats for water, when necessary, and Rufin told us the men had strict orders not to disclose the purpose of the voyage. But the headman of Sylana knew, of course, and as we approached the town, I wondered what might be said of our purported trade agreement with them.

As we drew closer to the settlement, and the marshes beyond, I thought again of the three Marai men who had fallen ill. The Empress had sent a physician to serve her troops; he was on board a different ship, but I assumed we might stop longer at Sylana. Through Cillian, I asked Rufin if it was possible to speak with him. He agreed to arrange it.

Sorley offered to interpret, while Cillian went with Rufin and Turlo to meet Mihae. I had no desire to return to the town at all, preferring to stay on board, comfortable in my tunic and leggings. A small boat ferried the physician to our ship and he climbed nimbly up on board.

Gnaius, short and compact, with a trace of grey in his hair and neat beard, settled on the deck across from me. Through Sorley, he asked how he could be of help.

"Ask him what he knows about the Eastern Fever, what the symptoms are. Is there always a rash? You saw what happened with the Marai who fell ill. I'd like to know if it might have been the fever."

They spoke at length. Sorley turned to me at one point. "He'd like to see the drug you gave them." I found my pack in our sleeping area on the deck and pulled out the small package of anash. I handed it to Gnaius. He rubbed a pinch between his fingers, smelled it, and finally tasted a tiny amount. He nodded, and spoke to Sorley again.

"He says no, it was almost certainly not the fever, but this was still the right thing to give them. How did you calculate the dose?"

"I guessed," I said bluntly. "Tell him a handful in this much water for the tea," I estimated with my hands, "and then a small cup, four times a day."

Gnaius smiled. "You guessed well," Sorley told me. "He would have made it weaker and more frequent, to reduce the chance of them vomiting it back up, but as they lived, you did no harm."

Two of them had lived, at least. Could I have saved Detlef? I would never know. "What was it?" I asked.

"A disease of the marshes, he says. It has killed many people, in the past. So the marshes were drained, near Casil, and other places, and the illness stays away, mostly."

"*Gratiás,* Gnaius," I said. We had passed through marshes, on the river above Sylana. It had been hot, and the air close. Why had some men fallen ill, and not others? "And the Eastern Fever?"

"Arises every few years, but not as badly as the writings say it once was. Only children die now, and only some: most who have it survive. But many generations back, it killed many, many people." Gnaius indicated the anash. "He says that is the right treatment for it, too."

The physician asked a question. "He'd like to know about medicine in our lands. I can tell him about the *Ti'ach na Iorlath,* and how our healers are trained, but how is it done, in the Empire?"

"I can't answer for the army," I said, "except to say they train medics. In the villages, it is an apprenticeship, as for all our work."

Another question. "Do your women's healers do surgery?"

"No," I said. "They set broken bones, treat ailments with herbs and teas, and perhaps excise a festering thorn, but not surgery. Unless pulling a rotting tooth is surgery."

Gnaius laughed politely at that. "*Gratiás,*" he said, rising. He and Sorley walked back to where he would disembark, still talking. I put my anash back in my pack. I would need it against the pain of my bleeding time, in a few days.

Rufin and Cillian and Turlo returned from Sylana, looking relaxed. "Rufin believes there is little in the agreement we signed earlier that will be a problem," Cillian told me. "Mihae sent his greetings to you, by the way."

"How nice of him," I said drily. I told Cillian what Gnaius had told me. "I might have saved Detlef, had I known to dilute the anash."

"You did your best," Cillian said gently.

"I know," I said. "But I was diluting the tea for myself. Why didn't I think of it for him?"

"Geiri couldn't get him to drink even water," Cillian reminded me. He stretched, flexing his arms above his head, and I heard a seam on his tunic tear. His shoulder and back muscles had grown, from the daily training with the swords. He swore.

"Change to another tunic and I'll fix it," I said.

"I can do it. Fifteen years of solitary travel did teach me a few useful skills."

"I'm glad to hear it," I said. "But I need to do something with my own, for the same reason. Putting a few stitches into yours will only take a minute or two." Mine were too tight as well, pulling uncomfortably across my breasts, making them sore. I'd need to let them out a bit at the seams.

I sat in the shade of some barrels to do the repairs. Cillian went to play *xache* with Sorley, who now could give him a decent game, although he still lost most of the time. I'd finished with Cillian's tunic, and one of mine, when Turlo came to sit beside me.

"Lassie," he said. "I've been putting off this talk, but seeing your man being a diplomat again today reminded me. Will you tell me what happened, in Casil?"

I bit off a thread. "With the Empress, you mean?"

"Aye. Was it all an act?"

"No, if by an act you mean he had no intention of going through with it. You should be asking Cillian this, Turlo, not me."

"I should, aye. But I believe I owe you an apology for my part in it, and the two things go together."

"Why would you apologize, Turlo?"

"Because I did not tell you what I saw, and what I feared, with the success of the negotiations hanging on it."

"Is not your first duty to the Empire, Turlo, and not to individual soldiers under your command?"

"Aye. Still, lassie..."

I relented. "You did warn me, if a little obliquely. I accept the apology, although I think it unnecessary."

"Would he truly have married her?"

"Had Sorley and I not intervened? Yes, had she required it. We reminded him of where his true duty lay, to Callan, and then Sorley convinced the Empress to drop her claim on him. You will have to ask Sorley what he said to her: he did it alone."

Turlo raised an eyebrow. "Alone? Sorley? Perhaps I underestimate the young lord."

"Perhaps you do," I said with a smile. "Perhaps we all have, in the past."

"And that was all, lassie? Convincing him of his duty to Callan?"

"No," I said, on the edge of fond exasperation, "no, Turlo, it was not all, but some things are between myself and Cillian, and not your cohort-leader and adjutant. Are they not?"

He coloured, slightly. "They are, lassie," he said. "But your general cares about his cohort-leader. Forgive my prying. I can see that all is well between you."

"It is." I paused. "Now it is my turn to pry, Turlo. Is this hard for you, being with Cillian and me, and now Sorley and Druisius?"

"Now that latter did surprise me," Turlo said. "I had thought it a brief thing, but I was wrong. Is it hard? No, lassie. You are all young, or nearly so. I had my years with Arey. I wish I could hope you will have as long."

"A thousand men and ten ships," I reminded him. "Our chances are much better, now."

"Possibly," he said. "If the White Horse still flies above the Eastern Fort, I will believe that. Two more weeks, and we will know."

Turlo's question had stirred my own curiosity. The next morning, while Cillian sparred with Turlo, I beckoned Sorley over. We leaned against the side of the ship, letting the breeze dry the sweat from our swordplay. We were in new territory for us now, beyond the mouth of the river we had travelled down to Sylana, moving west on the sea.

"Sorley," I began, "what did you say to the Empress? Will you tell me?"

"Ah," he replied. "I wondered if either of you would ask. Yes, I'll tell you. But if Cillian asks you, tell him he must come to me directly. Is that fair?"

"It is."

He looked at the water. "I told her a story, about a boy from a remote estate, and a young envoy who came to stay a night or two and was graciously interested in the boy's pursuits. And what that led to, a year or two later." He gave me a rueful smile. "All that was mine to tell. But then I told her why he turned me away, both to prevent me from being hurt and to keep his own promise to himself. And how long he had kept that promise, and why he had finally let it go. I told her what he had been like before you, and what he would be like without you. I asked if she could live with only the likeness of a man, knowing that below the polished surface was emptiness and despair." He swallowed. "And a few other things, but I think they were mostly irrelevant."

"Oh, Sorley," I breathed. "What courage that took. Courage and love."

"The courage came from the love. For you both, you know."

I put my hand on his. "Do you remember," I said slowly, "telling me that you and I needed each other, to ensure that neither of us were consumed by Cillian's brilliance?"

"Yes."

"There was another truth there. Brilliance is only one side of him."

"I know that, now. It cannot be easy for you, Lena."

"I have my own darkness, Sorley, because of what Ivor did to me, and for other reasons, and somehow he and I—balance the dark places in each other. I doubt I am easy for him, either. But I have watched how he has let himself admit how much he cares for you, needs you, too, and I am afraid for you. That you will not live the life you might have, that you should, because you will put his needs first." I was echoing Turlo's words to me, I realized.

"What life should I be leading, with Sorham sacrificed? I could argue that all you have said is true for you too, but you would never leave him. Why would I, given the choice?" He turned his hand to clasp mine, giving it a squeeze. "I have heard the man I have loved for many years tell me he loves me too. Not in the way I would have chosen, once, but it is enough. I have marvelled at your generosity in finding a way to include me, and I hope you will continue to. I am making this choice freely, Lena."

How could I deny him this? "Sorley, you can stay with us forever, as far as I am concerned. And not just because Cillian loves you, and needs you, but because I do too. But will Druisius be content, to be—on the periphery?"

"Druisius came only in part for me. He wants the adventure, too."

"Does that bother you?"

"No. How can it? I was honest with him from the start. I care for him; we enjoy each other, and the music is a big part of what we share. But Cillian will always come first, Cillian and you, and he knows it."

The first of the thunderstorms hit late that afternoon. Rufin, experienced in reading sky and winds, had the sail down and the sea-anchor dropped before the worst began. We huddled under whatever cover we could find, the rain lashing us. Around us the other ships rode out the storm, their sea-anchors keeping them from turning broadside to the waves to be swamped and sunk. I admired the skill of these ship captains: these were not easy waters to navigate. The winds fluctuated, over the course of the day, as land and sea temperatures changed, often growing stronger towards evening. Rufin kept us well out from shore, away from the dangers of shoals and submerged rocks. We had been lucky on the Marai ship, I realized: further east, and earlier in the summer, the waters had been calmer. The little vessel, designed for rivers and coastal sailing, could not have survived this voyage.

The storm lasted less than an hour, the skies clearing rapidly. We had all been writing, before the winds had rocked the ship too much to allow us to continue: I in my journal, Cillian working on his translations, and Sorley matching words to a tune. He had taken my *danta* suggestion seriously, and occasionally asked one of us for a rhyme, or a suggestion of a better word. He would write the story he knew first, he told us, and then ask us to help him with ours. I thought about that, sometimes, what I would include, and what I would leave out.

The storms became a frequent occurrence: not daily, but frequently enough that Turlo fretted about the delay they caused. Rufin shrugged. He would not risk ships and men by trying to sail, or even row, while the storms raged. Nor should he, Turlo admitted. We grew inured to drenchings, and drying out, bedraggled, in the wind and sun. At least it was warm. I'd had enough experience of cold rain on *Dovekie* to be grateful for that.

Even with the delays from bad weather, I thought we made good progress. Rufin had a map, copied from an ancient one in the library, and occasionally he showed us where we were. But he refused to be certain about how much longer we would be at sea. It depended, he told us, on the storms and the wind.

†††††

I eased myself out from under Cillian's encircling arm, making my way to the stern as quietly as I could. The moon, closer to new than full, had risen. I stared up at it, knowing its waxing and waning were immutable, its rhythms fixed.

I had been due to bleed over a week ago. I thought back over the last weeks, the signs that I had ignored, believing them to be easily explicable: the mild nausea, the lethargy, the tightness of my tunics over my tender breasts. Even the light spotting, last month. I was a midwife's daughter. I may have chosen the boats, but I could not escape knowing the signs of pregnancy.

I must have diluted the anash too much, when I was treating the sick oarsmen. I put my hand low on my belly, thinking, remembering a sunlit room and an afternoon of love. You must have been conceived then, I thought.

I glanced back to where Cillian slept. My mother's counsel, to so many young women, ran through my mind. Do not send word until the third month has come and gone, she had told them. Too many first pregnancies end, because your body is not quite prepared for what it must do. I would heed her advice and wait until another full moon had waned.

Suddenly, another memory rose. *I promised myself I would not repeat my father's mistake.* Its implications disturbed me. Surely, he had meant only that he would not leave a child fatherless, as he had been? But we had spoken only of how to prevent pregnancy, not of its possibility. If I raised the subject now, would it not make him wonder? And what would I do, if he did not want a child?

In the world I had grown up in, I would have chosen when to bear a child, chosen a man I liked to father it, and brought it up, for seven years or longer, with Maya's help, and that of the village. But that world was gone, and regardless, my bond with Cillian was outside its practices, and perhaps its understanding.

I glanced at the moon again, calculating. Three weeks to the next full moon, and a week after that, for surety. We should be home, and in the midst of war, most likely. I could be dead, by then. Another reason not to tell Cillian yet.

In Casil, I remembered, the goddess of the hunt was also the goddess of the moon. I don't believe in you, I told her, but please show me what to do.

†††††

Sorley called me to the prow of the ship in mid-morning. "Look," he said, pointing. "Is that cloud, or are those mountains?"

I stared westward. Grey-blue humps, blurring into the sky, lined the horizon. I traced them along the land to the sea. "I'm not sure," I said, "but I think they are mountains."

"Rufin?" Sorley called. The captain came over. Sorley repeated his question.

"*Montibera,*" Rufin said, and added something more.

"Mountains," Sorley confirmed. "He says we will reach them tomorrow, and to be prepared for rough sailing, as we do. Lena, those are the Durrains. We are nearly home."

I glanced northward, where the wide plain Cillian and I had crossed lay, and in the foothills of the mountains, the Kurzemë village. I didn't want to think about that, at all. But an uncomfortable thought had been plaguing me for some days. What would I have done, if Ivor had left me pregnant?

I had teased out the reasons for this over the last few nights. My own unsought pregnancy had turned my mind towards the women of Tirvan and the Empire, who might be carrying children conceived in violence. Might have given birth to such children, I realized. Reflexively, I moved my hand towards my belly. You were conceived in love, little one, I thought. For that, I will be forever grateful.

"You are preoccupied, *käresta,*" Cillian had said to me, a few days earlier. "What is it?"

I had wondered if he would have noticed, either that I had not bled, or that I had not brewed anash against the pain. With privacy, he almost certainly would have: even before we were lovers, he had been aware of my cycle, living together in close proximity as we were. But he hadn't appeared to. Thankfully, the mild nausea had passed, and while I had vomited more than once in rough seas, I was far from alone in that.

"I am just apprehensive, I suppose," I had answered, "about what awaits us, at home."

"As am I," he had told me, touching my hand. We were circumspect about affection, sensitive to the different customs of the Casilani, but Sorley's teasing insistence on calling Cillian 'son of the Emperor' had had an unexpected benefit. The Casilani crew treated him with great respect, and me as well, as his *quincala*. I let my fingers brush his palm.

The changes I had noticed in the days before we sailed had not disappeared. He was still quick to smile, and to respond in kind to Sorley's banter, but there was a new gravity to him. Like Casyn, I thought, or Colm. We had all changed, though, I mused: Turlo's once irrepressible good nature subdued; Sorley now a man of quiet determination. And I? I had found strength I did not know I had, to fight back against what threatened me, and for what I loved.

At the stern, Cillian and Turlo finished their swordplay, watched as usual by some of the crew, and Druisius. Like soldiers everywhere, they wagered on the outcome, but now the wagers for and against Cillian were nearly equal. He would never have Casyn's lethal grace with a sword, but he was competent, and occasionally he did make a series of strikes and guards look like the steps of a dance. Had he begun younger, I thought, he might have been very, very good.

We beckoned them forward, showing them the mountains ahead. Turlo took a deep breath. "In a day, or two at the most, we will know," he said. "I pray to any god listening that we are in time."

Rufin had been right to warn us. The winds blowing down off the mountains roiled the waters and slowed progress to nearly nothing. The sails came down, and the rowers changed shifts every hour. At nightfall, Rufin ordered the sea-anchor dropped, and extra men to the watches, in case of high seas. We slept fitfully, the ship rocking wildly.

But sometime in the early hours, the wind dropped, and by mid-day we were among the islands where the Durrains met the sea. Rufin took us through them carefully, many eyes looking for danger along the passage marked on his map, the rowers keeping to a slow, steady rhythm. Turlo paced, his face set and white. With each westward sweep of the oars, I felt the tension in me building. My eyes did not leave the distant shore.

Then we were past the last island and there, standing high on a headland above the tidal marshes, stood the Eastern Fort. Turlo's eyes strained to see the flag, snapping in the strong off-shore breeze. A gust caught it, blowing it out parallel to the shore. The White Horse of the Empire shone against its green field.

Turlo gave a bark of laughter, and then a strangled sob. Tears ran down my cheeks unabated, as I turned to hug him, and then Sorley, and Cillian. Everything we had done had been worth the cost. We were in time.

Rufin brought the ship as close as he judged safe, and anchored. We had been seen: men ran to the jetties that rose above the tidal creeks, shouting. Oarsmen lowered a small boat, and the four of us were rowed, so slowly, it seemed, to disembark on the quay where the Emperor waited for us.

Callan's hair was almost entirely grey now, and his face haggard. His eyes moved from Turlo to Sorley, and then to Cillian and me, almost expressionless, a contained hope fighting for release. "General," he said to Turlo, "report."

"Ten ships," Turlo said, "and a thousand men. Swordsmen and archers, Emperor. Will they suffice?"

Hope broke free of discipline, a smile beginning on his lined face. "They should," he said. "They will, the god willing. Welcome home, Turlo." They embraced, a long, intense hold. Tears pricked my eyes.

Turlo stood back. "Emperor," he said, "may I present the Lord Sorley of Linrathe, who joined me in that land, and whose knowledge of the northern lands and the Marai language were invaluable. He was also central to the Linrathan resistance, and his knowledge of that too may serve us well."

"Lord Sorley," Callan said. "You are most welcome, and you have my thanks for the service you have given. Linrathe still fights back, from what I am told."

"Emperor," Sorley replied. "If there is no true *Teannasach*, my skills and my sword are yours, if you will accept them."

"Ruar is not of age, and no other of the *Teannasach's* line has risen to leadership," Callan said. "I will be glad of your sword, Lord Sorley."

He looked at me then, and then, longer, at Cillian. His eyes returned to me. "Lena," he said.

"Cohort-Leader, Emperor," Turlo said. Callan nodded.

"Cohort-Leader," he repeated. "Welcome home."

"Thank you, Emperor. Thank you for my pardon," I said. "You have no reason to beg forgiveness of your god, on my behalf." I had tried to school my face to immobility, a soldier reporting to her superior, but I couldn't. I grinned as I said the words.

"Thank you for that courtesy, in remembering to tell me," he said, a hint of dryness in his tone. He turned to Cillian. Their eyes met. Mine went from one to the other, seeing the likeness, seeing the question on Callan's face, and the waiting stillness on Cillian's.

"My Adjutant, Captain of the Third," Turlo said quietly. "Without whom, Emperor, we would have failed. Make no mistake about that. That we reached Casil, that we brought back these ships and men: this is all due to Cillian. Who has skills in diplomacy that surpass yours, and who just happens to speak Casilan, and read it, too." Turlo's voice had changed, to amused asperity. "And he will beat you at *xache*, and rival you with a bow. In the name of the god, Callan, my friend, welcome your son home."

"No," Cillian interrupted. "Not yet. Forgive me, Emperor, but I have one thing to say, first. You had a wish for me, you may remember. A wish that, because you made it in my mother's name, I tried to fulfil. *Let men see and know a man who lives as he was meant to live."*

"I remember," Callan said. "I am pleased to hear you tried. Did you succeed?"

"Ask these three," Cillian said. "My respected superior officer; my dear friend, and the woman I love." Callan's eyes widened, at that. "If I have not, then I will accept only a welcome from my Emperor. But if I have fulfilled that wish, then I will be honoured to be welcomed by my father, as well."

"Do they know what that wish was?"

"Lena does. The others, no. You should be aware that I have known the lord Sorley for many years. He is possibly the best judge."

Callan raised an eyebrow. "Lord Sorley," he said. "I expressed a wish to Cillian, the night I exiled him. I had gathered some intelligence about him which, concisely put, described him as a cold and cynical man, a description he did not disagree with. I told him I hoped that in his exile he would find his humanity. Would you report to me on that?"

"Was that the impetus? I wondered," Sorley said. "But to report, Emperor. That description was almost fair, and a year ago I too might have agreed. No longer. Cillian is annoyingly good at more things than are reasonable, and yet modest about most. He has a tendency towards self-sacrifice that needs watching, and a generosity of spirit unlike any I have known. He also has a biting sense of humour, and loves Lena beyond life itself, I believe. Is that sufficient, Emperor?"

Callan began to grin. "I think so. Turlo, do you have anything to add?"

"Not I. Nor to dispute, mind."

"Lena?"

"I am afraid my judgement is skewed, Emperor, as I love him." Callan nodded, slowly. I glanced up at Cillian. He was looking at his father, and as I watched, he began to smile, slowly, radiantly. A gift, I realized, to Callan, a memory. The girl who connected them was embodied in that smile; both had lost her, but only one of them had known her. Cillian could hear the stories now, and I thought Callan would tell them, if time and war allowed. I desperately hoped it did, for their sake, and for the child I carried, who was the thread that joined the future to the past.

CHAPTER TWENTY

SORLEY OFFERED TO STAY AT THE JETTY, to help sort out men and equipment. There would just be space, within the walls of the fort, for the tents the Casilani troops had brought. Between Sorley and Druisius, who understood more of our language than he spoke, they would help the officers assigned to this task get them settled and organized.

"Lena!" one of those officers called, as I walked along the jetty towards the fort buildings. I looked over to see Finn. I waved, grinning. I'd liked him, the weeks I'd spent at the Winter Camp.

Doors in the outer wall opened for us, and I followed my Emperor to his headquarters. The pattern of this fort, like Wall's End, followed the same template as the deserted fort beneath the lake, although years of use had added buildings and expanded the original rectangular shape.

Inside, Callan told us to sit. "There is to be no formality, today," he insisted. "But food is short, so if you have eaten, I will not offer more. Wine is also in short supply, but we brew a beer that is palatable, after a fashion. Will that suit?" A cadet had followed us into the room, and at a word from Callan, went to fetch a jug of beer and mugs. He came back carrying the tray carefully.

Mugs distributed, and the cadet dismissed, Callan waved us to stools. He remained standing. "For an hour," he said, "no talk of war, until Casyn joins us. I have sent word. He will be overjoyed to see you, as I am. Later we will find you rooms; there are other women here, Lena, and no doubt space can be made in their barracks for you."

"Callan," Turlo said, "a favour, if you would?"

"Of course," Callan said. "How could I say no to you, just now? What is it you want?"

"This is irregular, but allow these two to remain together, if you can. I have my reasons for asking."

"It is irregular," Callan said slowly, "and they are both officers."

"A law long abandoned in Casil," Turlo told him.

"Turlo," I said, "I—we—appreciate your kindness, but I am prepared to sleep with the other women. We knew this would be likely." We had talked about it, in the last few days, neither of us liking the idea, but accepting it might be necessary.

"Barracks space will be assigned, and a private room found for Cillian," Callan decided. "I know that beds assigned are not always beds slept in, and as Lena is under your command, Turlo, you are responsible for her discipline. Cillian I am claiming as adjutant and advisor to me, effective immediately. I do not police my officers' private lives. Will that suffice?"

"Aye, it will," Turlo agreed.

"General, if I may?" I asked.

"Lena?"

"May I share a tent with Junia, from Casil? That would save rearranging beds in the barracks, and Junia will be understanding if I am...very late returning." I would ask Sorley to speak to her.

"A sensible solution, lassie," Turlo said. "I approve."

"And do you, Cillian?" the Emperor asked.

"I would prefer no subterfuge, but I understand the need," he answered. "And I appreciate the consideration. We are unused to being apart." I saw the smile playing on his lips. "Which could be argued to be at least partially your responsibility, I suppose."

Callan looked startled for a moment, before beginning to laugh. "I suppose it could, at that. An outcome that I did not expect, but, may I say, pleases me. Now, tell me of Casil."

We spoke of the city, and the Empress, and what we had done there, for some time, drinking the thin beer. Callan barked with laughter when Turlo told him of Cillian's solution to the impasse between Casil and the Boranoi. By tacit consent, no one mentioned his desperate courting of the Empress, in the last days of our negotiations, although I wondered if Turlo would tell him, privately.

Turlo began to speak of the agreement itself. The Emperor held up his hand. "Wait," he said. "Casyn should hear this too."

"The agreement concerns Linrathe, too," Cillian pointed out. "Should not the *Teannasach's* heir be present as well? And if so, then Sorley too, as he signed for Linrathe."

"Ruar is only a boy," Turlo protested.

"Perhaps. But when Donnalch was his age, his father was including him in meetings and talks, as an apprenticeship, you might say. Were not Ruar and Kebhan present for some of the negotiations at the White Fort?"

"They were," Callan agreed. "Should Kebhan hear the agreement's terms, too? His father was the last *Teannasach*, as misguided as he may have been. Kebhan swears he is loyal to Ruar, and Linrathe."

"That depends on what message you want to send," Cillian answered. "Does the leader of the Western Empire wish to make a clear declaration for Donnalch's direct line as the legitimate rulers of Linrathe, or be cautious, acknowledging that either boy has a claim, and the authority lies in the house, not the individual?"

"And which do you think I should do?"

Cillian shook his head. "I cannot speak for Linrathe, Callan. I have no right, nor ever did. I was always the neutral envoy, unsworn to Donnalch and his house. You must ask Sorley."

"*Kärestan*," I interrupted, purposely using the Linrathan word, "you may not allow yourself political views. But you are not neutral about the land of your birth. Can you not give the Emperor a private opinion?"

I am speaking out of turn in front of my Emperor, once again, I thought. I glanced at Callan, to gauge his displeasure at my intrusion. I need not have worried. He had not heard what I had said, past the first word.

"*Kärestan*," he whispered. "I have not heard that word for thirty-five years."

No one spoke.

"Callan," his son said into the silence. "I know now you did not leave her by choice. Only your oath to the Empire had a greater claim. I understand, finally." He hesitated. "And I have some understanding, too, of the price you have paid, all these years."

"Do you?"

"A small part. But may we leave that conversation for another time? It is better suited to a late night, and wine, if there is any to be had."

"Aye," Turlo said roughly. "There is wine; we brought it from Casil. Along with grain and oil. And when the supply ships are unloaded, they return to Casil, and they must take the agreement, with your signature, Callan, back to the Empress. We have a day, or two, no more."

"You are right," Callan said, focusing on Turlo. "I will consider your advice, Cillian, and consult my brother as well. But unless he has strong objections, I believe I will make the declaration in favour of Ruar." He strode to the door, opening it. "Cadet! Go to the docks and find the Lord Sorley, and escort him here." He began to close the door, then stopped. "Ah," he said, "Casyn. Excellent timing. Come in and greet the travellers."

Casyn's first embrace was for Turlo, but his second was for me. "Lena," he said, "I am so pleased to see you safe and returned to us." I couldn't speak. I hugged him tightly, smiling through tears.

He turned to Cillian, who was standing, quietly waiting. "And you, Cillian," Casyn said. "Welcome home. We need you."

"I am glad to be here," Cillian said, gravely. Casyn continued to look at him.

"It is uncanny," he said finally. "Like looking back into the past."

"Aye," Turlo said. "And it was worse when he wore grey and white, his court clothes in Casil. But your father's line always left a strong stamp."

"I would be pleased to hear of this, one day," Cillian said drily. "But have we not more important things to discuss, just now?"

Will you look like these men, little one? I said to the baby in my womb. This is your grandfather and his brother.

"Yes, we do," Turlo said. He took a rolled vellum from his pack. The copies of the agreement—one to be signed and sent back, one for Callan to keep—had been delivered to us just before we sailed, the Empress's signature in place. He spread it out on a table, weighing down the edges.

A discreet tap at the door announced Sorley's arrival. He was introduced to Casyn, and given a drink, before Callan posed the question of Linrathe's heir to him.

"I think," Sorley said after consideration, "that we should go over the agreement first, so that we are sure of our positions, and the reasons for the concessions made to Casil. Even if there are disagreements, it would be better for us to be clear on those, than argue in front of the boy."

"But you believe Ruar is the rightful heir?"

"I do," Sorley said firmly. "When I left Linrathe, it was his name that was spoken as a rallying point. Kebhan would be forever tainted by his father's treachery."

"You are likely right," Callan said. "Casyn, your thoughts?"

"I agree with Lord Sorley," he answered. "What does Cillian think?"

"I had not answered," Cillian said. "But I will tell you now, as your advisor, I too agree with Sorley."

"Then shall we go through the agreement?" Callan asked. "Although I see you must translate it."

"This is the one you must sign," Cillian said, "but there is a copy in our language, in Turlo's keeping. I made it on the ship. Sorley has confirmed the translation is accurate."

"As best I could," Sorley clarified. "I am not fluent in Casilan. But the major points are correct."

It took well over an hour to go through the agreement. I sat quietly, knowing I had little part in this, watching the men. The Emperor and Casyn, pragmatic and seasoned, showed little emotion, although both the primacy of the Eastern Empire's laws, and the change in Callan's title, evoked response. Turlo and Cillian answered questions and rebutted arguments calmly. Only once did the Emperor turn to me.

"You signed this, Lena, on behalf of the Empire's women?"

"I did, Emperor. The end of the Partition agreement was under consideration already, I felt, and while this is more sudden, and not of our doing, the result is the same."

He nodded. "And almost an unnecessary part of the agreement, as our laws give way to Casil's." He picked up a pen. "This will be my last act as Emperor of the West, then, to sign this agreement. *Princip* will take some getting used to."

"Wait, please," Cillian said. "There is one aspect of this you may not have considered, and as it directly affects me, I would like us to be clear on its implications."

"Explain."

"By the East's laws, *Princip* will be a hereditary position. I am your heir, Callan, and I have no wish at all to lead the Empire one day. No wish, and no military skills to do so. The Marai will remain a threat, in our lifetimes. I ask that we add a clause removing me from the inheritance in favour of your brother. If Casyn will accept that, of course." I heard Turlo's sound of protest.

The Emperor put the pen down. "That is a very great thing to ask," he said, "and I will need to consider it carefully. But for you to be thrust into a role you neither want nor have been trained for is also large. I do see that. Casyn and I are close in age, though, and even outside of war, we could die within a year or two of each other. His children are daughters. Who would succeed, then?"

"Casil has an Empress," Cillian pointed out. "Cannot the Western Empire have a *Principe*? Even as regent for her son, if there is one?"

"What of your own children?" Callan asked. "Should you give away their rights to succeed?"

I tried not to react. It is a theoretical question, I told myself. I sat very still. Cillian, I saw, was taken aback by the query. He gave a low laugh. "Not something I had considered," he admitted. His eyes met mine. "Perhaps," he said, "there are some conversations that need to occur, before this can be resolved. Casyn, are your daughters here?"

"One is. One is on the Wall. But Talyn is the oldest, and the one I could see as regent, at least. She was not a soldier, until this last year, but Han breeds and trains the Empire's warhorses and her knowledge of weapons and tactics is considerable. Would you consider a joint regency, Cillian, for either her child, or yours?"

"Perhaps. There are other considerations. I was born and brought up in Linrathe. And I am a pardoned exile. Would not both those be reasons to pass me over, even if I wished to succeed?"

"Possibly," Callan said. "But your children, I am assuming, would also be Lena's, and she is a woman of the Empire."

"And also a pardoned exile," I said.

Callan shook his head. "History can be rewritten. It would not be hard to spread the story that the exile was never real, but a way to send you East without raising suspicions." Half-truths, I thought, once again.

"I suggest we leave this until we have had a chance for some private speech." Casyn said.

"The supply ships will not leave tomorrow," Sorley told us. "That gives you a day, or a bit more."

"Then we leave it," Callan decided. "But we need a decision in the morning. And we bring Ruar into the discussion only after that."

We moved to the large table, a map spread out on it. Small figures, like *xache* pieces painted different colours, stood on the surface. Along the coast, and inland for nearly half the distance between the coast and the mountains, the figures were blue. East of a rough line running from Casilla to the Wall, and along the Wall itself, green figures representing the Empire spread across the map.

"We hold Casilla, as you see," the Emperor said, "and all lands inland from about here." He traced the irregular line. "Of the women's villages, only Han and Rigg are known to be safe, but their women are scattered too, serving on the Wall or here. I am sorry, Lena," he added, glancing my way. "Most of the retired officers and men have returned to duty; Jedd, for one, advises me, and rides patrols, for all he is past eighty. We hold the Wall, with help from Linrathe's loyalists, and last I heard that included the Wall's End Fort, although the price we paid to do that was very high." Berge, I thought. He let the Marai take Berge, to save Wall's End.

"My thoughts, with these reinforcements from the East, are to use the men and boats in two ways: to send the ships along and around the coast, pushing the Marai ahead of them. Casil's ships are larger and stronger than the Marai's, and the decks higher, which gives them an advantage in combat. The Marai fight with sword and axe, and are vulnerable to archers.

"At the same time, I send troops overland, towards the Taiva, to push the Marai occupying the land back to the river. If we can engage them in battle here," he pointed to a spot a distance up from the mouth of the river, "where the land rises to the north, we have a good chance of destroying many ships and men, if we choose our time. There are shoals at the mouth of the Taiva, but the Marai ships are light and can pass over them at high tide. But if we fight to an ebbtide, we can prevent them from moving out again, I believe."

"Is there a place upriver, not too far, where reinforcements could wait?" Sorley asked. I saw the spark of realization in Cillian's eyes.

"The Battle of the Tabha," he said. He turned to the Emperor and Casyn. "It was the battle between Linrathe and the Marai, many years ago, that resulted in the long peace between them, fought on a river in Linrathe. The Marai should have prevailed, because they had reinforcements hidden not far away, but the river flooded, men on both sides died, and the truce was called. It is an interesting idea, Sorley."

"Will not the Marai know this too?" the Emperor asked.

"They will. They have a song about it, as does Linrathe. But Fritjof thinks of songs as entertainment, not instruction, or believes himself to be above their instruction. Geiri might know more." He explained who Geiri was.

"Send the cadet to find him," Callan said to the room. I stepped away to obey the order.

"Do we have enough troops, even with the Casilani, to keep some in reserve?" Casyn was asking when I returned.

"Perhaps," Turlo said. "How many horses do we have? Han-trained horses, mind."

"Many," Callan said. "I cannot give you an exact count. Why?"

"If mounted archers headed that reserve force, even a few dozen would be able to wreak much havoc in a short time. The Marai would not expect them at all, and were a mounted force able to cause fear and confusion, it would give a momentary advantage."

"There is a piece of high ground overlooking the river, on the south side," Callan said. His eyes held the same distance as Cillian's did, when he was thinking. "It is where I plan to direct the battle. Behind it is a coombe opening onto the river, completely hidden from sight. As the tide ebbs, horses could be ridden along the sands. But we do not have mounted archers."

"Aye," Turlo said. "But we can. I will tell you in a moment, Callan. But first, what about the island in the middle?"

"Fritjof will direct the battle from his ship," Callan said. "We know that, by now. But he will use that island for his first attack, across the causeway, almost certainly."

"A shield wall, then, at the causeway's end?" Cillian asked.

"Or can we take it first, with men who can pass for Marai, to confuse?" Turlo suggested.

"I can pass as Marai," Sorley said.

"We could take the island first, but I think it would be certain death for the men we sent; Fritjof's men would massacre them. Better the shield wall," the Emperor said. "I have another task for you, Lord Sorley. Key to this plan is engaging the Marai who hold the coast between the Wall and the Taiva. That engagement must come from the troops on the Wall, who will need to leave the Wall and move south. Many of the troops on the Wall are Linrathan, and they will be reluctant, I think, to stop their harrying of the Marai within Linrathe. I need you to ride north, along the Durrains, to Linrathe, and convince them to support this plan. And to do that, I believe, you will need to take Ruar with you."

"That is a long and dangerous journey, for one man and a boy," Casyn objected. "Five or six days, at the quickest, with extra horses and travelling every hour of daylight and some of dark. Does Ruar need to go?"

"He does, I believe," Cillian said slowly. "My countrymen will need their *Teannasach's* son, to be convinced. We—they, I should say—are sworn to the man, not the country. Sorley, you would agree?"

"I would. May I take one guard as well, Emperor? Ruar will be better protected by two than by me alone."

"Yes," Callan replied. "Choose whom you will. Now, Turlo, explain to me about these mounted archers."

"They are used in the East," he said, "and they are a women's cohort. Lena spent much time learning the techniques, while we were there, and one of their officers returned with us. If we have enough women from Han and Rigg, or others—men or women—who are good archers and good riders, I believe that between Lena and Junia and your daughter, Casyn, we can create the force we need."

"Their bows are different from ours, Emperor," I said. "Smaller, but stronger. We have two dozen."

Callan nodded. "Do it," he said. "Yours to organize, Cohort-Leader." He scribbled a note. "This will give you the authority to requisition horses and troops, and anything else you need. Begin tomorrow." He thought for a moment. "Your daughter's rank, Casyn, is also Cohort-Leader, is it not?"

"It is."

"Lieutenant, then, Lena. You have no objection, Turlo?" He shook his head.

"Thank you, sir," I said, as required. I supposed the promotion had been necessary.

The cadet returned with Geiri. The steersman took three steps into the room and dropped to a knee. Cillian spoke to him. Geiri shook his head, remaining as he was.

"He wants to offer you fealty, Emperor," Cillian said. "As do the men with him."

The Emperor crossed the room, taking Geiri's hands in his. "Tell him I accept," he said. Cillian translated. Geiri kissed the Emperor's hand. "Now tell him," Callan said, "he is not to kneel to me again." He helped Geiri to his feet, the man's face reflecting his surprise.

"Irmgard told him what the Empress expected in Casil," Sorley told me. "I didn't think to let him know the protocols were less formal here."

Cillian and Geiri spoke for several minutes. I heard Fritjof's name, more than once. "He says," Cillian relayed, "that Fritjof is a coward at heart. He boasts, and reminds men of past glories, but he uses fear and punishment to make them do what he wants, once he has convinced them to join him. He kills his own with impunity, for the smallest transgression, but not consistently. It depends on his mood. Sometimes he rewards handsomely, too. He believes himself above any laws, and does what he wants."

"That fits with what we have seen," the Emperor said. "And it explains why he never leaves his ship. He sends his men out, but directs the fighting from a distance. His son commands on the field."

"Leik?" I asked.

"Yes. What do you know of him, Lieutenant?"

"Fritjof had promised me to him," I said. "I met him only once. Cruel, is my assessment."

"Again, that fits. Do you have any particular grudge against him, Lieutenant?"

"No. He spoke to me the one time, at a banquet. That was all." Although he had been a large part of why I had fled Fritjof's hall, I reflected, beginning the sequence of events that had led us—all of us—here. But I would not seek him out on the field in revenge.

No opportunity for private speech came until late. Sorley had arranged the fiction of where I slept with Junia, while I had had a quick word with Birel. He had greeted me with a quiet "Good to see you again, Lieutenant," as he showed us to the room assigned to Cillian. It was not large, but Birel had managed to find us a bed big enough for us both. How he had known of the need, and of my promotion, remained, as always, a mystery.

"Birel," I had said to him, "the Lord Sorley will also need a larger bed, although he will only be with us for a night or two. Can you arrange that?"

"Of course, Lieutenant," had been his only reply. Druisius was a low-ranked soldier; if Sorley chose to have him share his bed, no one would comment. I was glad Druisius would be riding north, too.

Finally, we were alone. One lamp only burned; I could not ask Birel for more, with the shortages. I would cope, I told myself. I closed the door, and turned to Cillian.

"I know we have to talk," I said, "but I have not held you for over a month, not properly. That first, please?" I went into his arms.

"*Käresta*," he said, bending his head to kiss me, a kiss that quickly deepened, threatening to end all chance of talking. Reluctantly, I pulled away.

"Soon," I murmured.

"What we have to talk about might be better considered after love," he said, his voice thick. His desire fed mine, pushing other thoughts away.

"Mmm," I murmured. "You may be right, at that." Perhaps it would. I raised my mouth to his, feeling his hands travelling on my body. He broke away, suddenly.

"There is only one lamp. Will you be all right?"

"I should be. We know what to do, by now."

"Now," I said, curled against him, one finger tracing circles on his chest, "we need to stay awake long enough to talk."

"Yes." He put his hand over mine. "You are distracting me," he said gently, "and I should have my mind on what we need to discuss, not—other things."

"Sorry. Where do we start, Cillian? Callan's question took you completely by surprise, I could see that."

"It did. I have been thinking about why. I suppose it is because I have always thought of fathering a child as something to be avoided, not something I might welcome."

"And would you?" I asked. "Would you welcome it?"

"The idea terrifies me," he said simply. "I accepted the possibility once we were together. But I have no idea how to be a father, for obvious reasons."

"You had no idea how to love me, either," I pointed out, trying to stay calm.

"True. But you are an adult, Lena, able to tell me what you need, and when I misstep. A child cannot do that, or by the time they can, it is too late."

"What do you remember of the years with your grandparents? Not details, necessarily, but how you felt."

He considered. "Snatches of scenes, around the farmyard, riding on the cart. But how I felt, before the attack? Safe. Sheltered."

"Then you do know what a child needs, kärestan."

"It cannot be that simple."

"No," I agreed, "but it is a large part of it. Enough to begin with, I believe."

"And what about you, käresta? Would you welcome a child?"

A question too late in the asking. "Not just to be Princip," I said. "Not just for the Empire. But for us, yes."

"Truly?" His fingers smoothed my hair, rhythmically. "I will need some time to get used to the idea. It is too new for me to respond to quickly. But that is not what we must decide for tomorrow." He propped himself up on one elbow, looking down at me. "Should a theoretical child of ours be heir to the Western Empire, or not?"

But this was not a theoretical child. Should I tell him? But he had just said he needed time to adjust to the idea of fatherhood, and my chances of miscarriage were still high. And war waited.

"How do we make that choice, for a child?" I asked. "If we say yes, we bind her to an enormous responsibility, and one she may not want any more than you do. What about her freedom?"

"We are not necessarily binding her, or him, if the succession for Princip follows the rules of succession of the Eastern Empire. They are not so different from the way the Teannasach is determined: the best candidate from a house. So Casyn's daughters, or their children, would always be contenders. It is what allows me to ask to be overlooked. The question is this: do we ask that our children also be removed from consideration?"

"So if we had several children—not necessarily the oldest, or any of them?"

"Correct."

"There is something you should know," I said. "Casyn does not want to be *Princip*, either. He told me years ago that he had not wanted to be a general, and last year, at the White Fort, I asked him about it. He told me he had done it all for Callan, to keep his impulsive, ill-disciplined brother safe. And then Turlo told me much the same not very long ago. You are asking a very great deal indeed of Casyn."

"Impulsive and ill-disciplined? Callan?"

"Apparently. Until he passed thirty-five, Turlo told me."

"So I am ahead of him by a year?" Cillian murmured. "Lena, are you telling me I should not refuse the succession?"

"I think you need to talk to Casyn before that decision is made, and perhaps even his daughter, the three of you together. I cannot see how this can be an individual decision."

He lay silent. "I did not look for this, when I gave Callan my oath," he said finally. His fingers flexed against my hair.

"How could you have?

"Am I being unfair, *käresta*?"

"No. You had some good arguments, yesterday, about why you should be passed over, and I think they are meaningful. You are being cautious, and perhaps a little impulsive. You do still tend towards making decisions without proper consultation, do you not?"

He smiled, ruefully. "I suppose I do. Perhaps I cannot claim a year's lead on my father, after all, in a race towards maturity. I will talk to Casyn. But we have still not decided what to do about our speculative children and the succession."

"If it is not binding, on the oldest or any," I said, "then would we not be limiting their choices, if we say no?" He thought for some time. I waited.

"We will be honest with them, Lena, about the—weight of such a position, and the sacrifices?" Will, I noted. Not would. Cillian was never imprecise. I felt one tension fade, just a bit.

"We will."

"We may all be dead in a month, and none of this will matter. What do I tell the Emperor tomorrow?"

Little one, I thought, is this the right decision? Perhaps I will tell you of this conversation, some day, and ask.

His eyes were very dark in the flickering light of the lamp, and troubled. I wanted so much to take his hand, to place it on my belly, to tell him. But the time was not right. "*Kärestan*, I have always told you I did not care that you were the Emperor's son." I said. "And that is still true, in that it has nothing to do with loving you. But it seems we cannot escape its consequences. I do not think we have the right to refuse the succession for our children."

CHAPTER TWENTY-ONE

WORK BEGAN IN EARNEST, THE NEXT MORNING. I met my captain, who told me I had his full permission to do whatever the Emperor required. That done, and Callan's note in hand, I went in search of the stables and paddocks, picking up Junia on the way. She grinned at me, walking beside me through the rows of tents, looking around much as I had in Casil. I wondered what she thought.

At the stables, a tall, dark-haired woman groomed a mare, clearly, even to my inexpert eyes, a Han-bred horse. She turned at our approach. "Lieutenant," she said. "I am Cohort-Leader Talyn. How can I help?"

She had Casyn's eyes, and something of his gravity. A strong stamp, Turlo had said. "Cohort-Leader," I said. "How did you know who I was?"

"I had seen neither of you before and you fit Casyn's description," she said. "And this is?"

"Junia, from Casil. Junia, Talyn. She does not speak our language," I explained, "but she is an excellent trainer. She has taught me everything I know. Did Casyn explain what we are to do?"

"He did. We know something of archery from horseback; the horses are accustomed to it, as part of their training, but it is rarely done. I am curious about it."

A shout, from along the stable block, and then a woman was running towards me, calling my name. "Grainne!" I threw my arms around her, hugging her close. I had not seen her since Tirvan, three years previously.

"Oh, Lena, it is so good to see you," she said, tears running down her cheeks. "Do you have word of anyone else?"

"I just arrived yesterday," I said.

"With the ships? You went East, with General Turlo?"

"Yes."

"Guard," Talyn said, "you are allowed the reunion, but be aware this is our new lieutenant."

"Are you? Oh! I am sorry."

"Don't be," I said. "I am so glad to see you, Grainne. Who else is here?"

"Rasa, and Dian. Dian is Cohort-Second. Most women from the grassland villages went to the Wall. I don't know where anyone from Tirvan is. Maybe the Wall, or Casilla. Or—" She stopped talking. "You do know what has happened, Len—Lieutenant?"

"Yes. We have work to do, Guard." Grainne, I remembered, had always been prone to emotion. "Cohort-Leader, we brought twenty-four bows of a type new to me, and perhaps to you. Are there three women who can go with Junia to the ship, to bring them back here?"

"Certainly. Grainne, fetch Rasa, and another, please."

"Junia," I said. She had gone to the mare, and was bending to examine its feet and hocks. She straightened. I mimed drawing a bow, and pointed at the ships.

She nodded. As we waited for Grainne to return, she indicated the mare.

"*Bêne*," she said.

"*Itá*," I agreed. "Yes. Good horse. *Bêne ecus*."

"Good horse," she echoed. Grainne returned, with two other women, one smiling broadly.

"Lieutenant," she greeted me. I offered her the formal soldier's embrace, and then tightened my hold. "Rasa," I said. "I am so glad you are safe, and Dian too."

"As safe as any of us are," she said. I stepped back. Talyn introduced the third woman, from Rigg, before they went to fetch the bows.

"Dian is leading a patrol," she told me. "Cadets, mostly. She won't be back for a couple of hours. I have been alerted that I will be needed this morning, or possibly later, for a discussion with the Emperor, so my time is yours until then. Where should we start?"

We walked and talked, looking at horses and equipment. The women came back with the bows. Talyn sent the three horseguards back to work, and she and I and Junia examined them, looking for damage. Two needed the sinew regluing, but the rest were unharmed.

I strung one, and handed it to Talyn. "Its draw weight is greater than you will expect," I told her. She raised it, drawing expertly. Her face reflected astonishment.

"That is surprising," she said. "With the right arrows, this will be lethal. You can shoot this?"

"Fairly well," I said.

"Show us?"

I agreed. "But Junia after me," I said. "You say the horses are trained to this: leg and voice commands, then? Run through them with me?"

A few commands from Talyn, and two butts appeared in the training field, one at each end. A compact Han gelding was led out. Junia's eyes widened at the stirrups. "Let me put him through his paces," I said, and rode out onto the field. A few circuits, the last with no reins, and I was ready to shoot.

I thought it had probably been a while since the gelding had heard arrows fly past his neck, so I shot the first one from a gentle trot. I felt the tiny sideways flick he made, and patted him reassuringly. We trotted to the other end, and I shot again, and this time he was steady. I urged him to a canter. After four more shots, I pulled him up. As I had thought, the stirrups made it much easier.

Junia had watched closely, studying the commands to the horse. She mounted, settling into the saddle, fitting her feet into the stirrups. She was taller than me. Rasa stepped forward, and adjusted the stirrups. Junia looked uncertain, but she rode out into the field, trying the gelding's gaits. I noted how she stood in the stirrups, testing the idea. Comfortable, she rode back for the bow.

After the first shot, every arrow hit almost at the centre, and from a greater distance and speed than I had attempted. Junia shot both from standing in the stirrups, and with her feet kicked free of them and her seat low. I had never seen her shoot before, or ride, but watching her was like watching Casyn with a sword, lethal grace in every fluid move. I shared that thought with Talyn.

"I was thinking exactly that," she said. "If she can teach us this, we have a new weapon against the Marai."

In late morning, Dian and her patrol returned. We had become good friends on the ride from Casilla to the Wall, two years earlier, and we hugged for a long time. "Oh, Dian," I said, "I am so sorry. I had to leave Clio to the Marai, last year. I had no choice."

"Couldn't be helped," she said. "It was a brave thing you did, Lena, you and the Linrathan man. Who turned out to be the Emperor's son? It's like a midwinter's tale, the brave deeds, and then exile, and then returned to your rightful place. Places? He's here too, isn't he?"

"Cillian, his name is," I said. "Yes, he is."

"And you found Casil, and brought us ships and men," she said. "Definitely a midwinter's tale come to life. Except that in a story, you and Cillian would have sworn undying love."

I began to laugh. She gave me an assessing look. "Oh, Lena, really?" she said, joining in the laughter for a moment before sobering. "I hope your tale has a happy ending, then."

We rode again, so Dian could see the possibilities. "Junia rides differently," she observed, as we watched.

"Casilani saddles don't have stirrups," I told her, "and the shape is different. But she's adapting quickly to the stirrups, using them to advantage." I turned to include Talyn in the conversation. "Junia was a captain, in Casil, which I believe was equivalent to cohort-leader here, so we need to acknowledge her rank as well as her expertise. I'd like to appoint her as instructor, and give her the same authority as Dian, but only on the training field. Any objections?"

"She speaks only her own language?"

"Yes. But she taught me regardless. And I think she'll pick up words quickly."

"It's your decision, Lieutenant," Talyn said. "But I have no objection. How will you let her know?"

I considered. We had two Casilan speakers, and one would be riding north shortly. Even if I considered Druisius's limited ability to translate, he would be leaving with Sorley. A thousand men to integrate with the Empire's troops, and one translator? Who would also have a myriad of other duties? He will have planned for this, I thought.

Junia dismounted, leading the gelding over to us, grinning. "Lena," she said, and mimed shooting, and then a moving object. "*Itá*," I said. "In Casil," I told the other two women, "we shot at a moving target, a human form made of cloth and stuffed, hanging in such a way it could be made to swing and twist."

"A *pavo*," Talyn said. "We use them, but not for archery. But there isn't one here."

"*Pavo*," Junia said. "*Itá*. Yes." We looked at her in astonishment.

"The same word?" Dian asked.

"Our language developed from Casilan," I said. "So perhaps it's not surprising we have kept some words."

"Well," Dian said. "I think we can build a pavo, at least a crude one. With your permission, Lieutenant, Cohort-Leader, I'll assign some guards to that task, this afternoon."

I nodded. "I will be with the Emperor for part of the day," Talyn told her, "so you will need to take charge while I am away. Unless the lieutenant is remaining here?"

"For a while," I told her.

"Who's this?" Dian asked. I followed her eyes. Sorley and a boy of twelve or thirteen walked towards us. Ruar, I realized. He'd grown a bit, in the last year.

"The Lord Sorley, from Linrathe," I told her. "He travelled with us. And Ruar, the Linrathan hostage, and heir, but I assume you know him?"

"Yes. He rides patrol with us, as did Kebhan, until he joined the archers this year."

"Lena," Sorley said. "I'm glad you're here. I'm looking for Cohort-Leader Talyn?"

"That's me," Talyn said. "How can I help, Lord Sorley?"

He handed her a note. "Ruar and I, and one other, ride north today, to the Wall. We need horses for fast travel; we must be there as quickly as is possible."

Talyn's practiced eye studied Sorley, assessing his weight. "Who is the other?" she said. He gave her a name.

"Not Druisius?" I said, surprised.

"No," he said briefly. "I need a guide, and Druisius is needed here, to translate the best he can."

"I see," I said, unhappy for him. "Sorley, can you translate for me, while you're here? Tell Junia our ranks, and that she is to be instructor here; her rank is Cohort-Second, the same as Dian's, but her authority right now is only on the training field. And that we are building a pavo."

He relayed all this to Junia. She grinned, and nodded. "*Gratiás,*" she said.

"Cohort-Leader, I was also to tell you the Emperor requests your presence in a short while, and that you are to eat with them," Sorley said. Talyn gave a brief nod. He turned to me. "Lena, can we talk privately?"

"Cadet Ruar, go with the cohort-seconds to choose horses," Talyn said. "Lieutenant," she said to me, and left us. We waited until they were beyond hearing distance.

"You are leaving soon?" I asked.

"As soon as the horses and equipment are ready. I came to say goodbye."

"I'm sorry Druisius isn't going with you. It doesn't seem fair."

"He understands. Lena, because I am leaving...and because I may never see either of you again, Cillian told me what you discussed last night. Both about the succession, and about how he feels, about being a father, someday. I told him that any man who can teach as patiently as he can should not worry. I hope I did not overstep."

"You can't, Sorley. Thank you. He will miss you; we both will." That sounded inadequate. "I don't want to think about not seeing you again. Please come safely home. We need you, and we love you."

"That's what Cillian said. I will do my best, Lena." I put my arms around him. "You should tell him your promise, Lena, in case I am killed. I told him that, too," he murmured.

"Perhaps I should. I know his; he didn't tell me, but he told Turlo, and I overheard."

"That's cheating," he said, trying to laugh. I kissed his cheek.

"Sorley," I said. "About Cillian being a father someday—it's sooner than he knows. I'm pregnant."

"What? Are you sure? You haven't told him?"

"No. I am not yet past three months, and our practice in the women's villages is to keep quiet until then. I am only telling you because you are leaving." And because you may die, or I might.

"I am honoured you told me," he said. His face became serious. A muscle jumped, under his eye. "Lena, if the worst happens, but I am alive—do I tell him?"

"I would say no. If you can accept that. If I die, and he knows that our child died with me, he will tell you, if no one else. If he doesn't know, why add to his grief? But it will have to be your decision, if you are the one left by his side."

"If the gods demand a life, I hope it is mine," he said. "Lena, please be safe."

"I will try." He hugged me tightly. Tears dampened his cheeks when he stepped back. I brushed them away, trying to smile, and kissed him gently on his mouth.

"Both of you," he murmured. "I am a fortunate man. Goodbye, Lena."

"Go with the god, Sorley."

We spent the afternoon choosing horses and discussing training schedules. Junia repaired the two damaged bows as we talked, and strung and tested each of the twenty-four. As we did an inventory of arrows and equipment, a shelf of cloth strips caught my eye.

"I will need breast bands," I said. "Are there enough to me to take two or three?"

"Certainly," Dian said. "But I'm surprised you need them."

"I find with my body turned more in the saddle," I improvised, "the bowstring brushes my breast."

"Good to know," she answered. "Others may find the same." I took three, pushing them into my breeches pockets. Even when I had hugged Dian, and Sorley, I had inwardly winced at the tenderness of my breasts. Last night, my body's responses after a month of abstinence had masked any discomfort, but I would have to think of something to tell Cillian. I hoped the bands would help.

In late afternoon, Talyn returned. Cillian accompanied her. I began to introduce him to Dian, and then stopped. "I don't know your rank now," I told him.

"Major," he said easily. "Adjutant and Advisor to the Emperor, Cohort-Second. I remember your name. You were at Tirvan in the battle against Leste, were you not, and then later rode north with the lieutenant?"

"Yes," Dian said. "Good of you to remember, sir." How easily he was slipping into the protocols and expectations here, I thought.

He spoke to Junia in Casilan, smiling at her response. "Junia asks me to tell you your horses are excellent, and she is impressed by your soldiers. But her bows are better."

We laughed. "They are," Dian said. "Lieutenant, a word?" We walked away from the others. "I am out of line, I know," she said, grinning, "but your prince is a very handsome man, Lena. I am envious."

"He is not a prince," I said, laughing.

"He would be in the midwinter's tale," she said. "Surely the Emperor's son is close enough?"

"Thank you for your thoughts," I said aloud. My back was to Talyn and Cillian, so they couldn't see the grin. "I agree with your assessment. But, Dian," I added, quietly, "our relationship cannot be public. We are both officers. You know, and Talyn, and Junia, but I would prefer if the guards I command did not, nor others. If rumours become a problem I will address it."

She nodded. "Understood, Lieutenant."

Cillian and I walked back to the headquarters together, observing the appropriate protocols between a junior officer and her superior. Insignia of rank had not yet been found for us, so we escaped the salutes we would otherwise have been required to respond to, but we still needed to behave as expected. Nor could we talk of what had been decided: too many ears, around the camp.

"Tell me?" I said, as soon as the door to our room closed behind us.

"Talyn is an intelligent woman," Cillian said. "Thoughtful. She and I have agreed to be co-regents, if necessary, until one of our children—ours, or hers, or her sister's—is determined to be an appropriate and willing successor."

"Are you happy with that, Cillian? It is not too much?"

"It is a compromise, and one that may never happen. Casyn has agreed to be the heir. The co-regency would only be necessary if he dies before one of our children is ready to inherit."

"He took that on?"

"He said he had to, for the Empire. But that if he was still alive in ten years, and if Talyn's son, who is eight, I gather, and a cadet—was willing and suitable, he would retire in favour of the boy."

"I hope for his sake that happens. He deserves it. He and our council leader Gille—they had a few weeks together, the summer he came to Tirvan, and he looked content, just shoeing horses and teaching us to fight."

"I am glad the decision was out of my hands. Callan agreed I could not be the direct heir, for the reasons I gave yesterday."

"And Ruar's reaction to the agreement?"

"Remarkably mature. He was more interested in what it meant for movement of his people between our two lands, and whose laws took precedence, than in the change to being a client ruler. The *Teannasach* serving his people. Donnalch taught him well."

"And now he's going home, to rally his people, or at least those on the Wall."

"He was pleased by that. Although he may change his opinion, after a day or two in the saddle."

"Why didn't Druisius go?"

"Sorley needed a guide, and we need Druisius here, with Sorley gone. They both understood." He ran a hand through his hair. "I didn't like it, but it was the right thing to do."

"He said you told him the same thing I did: we need him, we love him, and to come home."

"Yes. We had a few minutes alone. It is difficult, now, to imagine life without him." He paused, looking diffident. "Did you kiss him goodbye?"

"Of course."

"So did I." Men did, in Linrathe, I remembered.

"That's what he meant!" I said. "I kissed him, on the lips, and he half-smiled and said, 'both of you'. I'm glad you did, Cillian. It will be a good memory for him." Cillian looked slightly relieved. "You didn't think I'd mind, did you?"

"Not really. But I still thought I should tell you."

"You didn't need to. Speaking of kissing—?" He laughed, and put his arms around me. Against his chest, my breasts twinged, reminding me of the excuses I needed to make.

"Are you eating with Callan tonight?" I asked, a moment later.

"Yes. Probably most nights. I'm sorry, Lena."

"Don't be. I'll eat with the other junior officers. There are friends here for me to catch up with."

"Good." He had turned to look at some papers on the table. "And then Callan has asked me for an hour, when the day's work is done each night, to talk. I don't want to say no, *käresta*, but it might limit our private time."

"And we will be an army on the move, very soon," I said. "But take that time to be with your father, while you can. You can always wake me up." He looked up from the map in his hand.

"I suppose I can," he said, smiling. "Another bed not to waste, for the few days we have it?"

"Exactly. But, Cillian," I said, as casually as I could, "archery from horseback is different from on foot. The bowstring brushes my breasts and makes them sore. I'm trying to learn to shoot both right-and-left handed," I added. Not a bad idea, I thought. Perhaps I'll try it. "I'm going to wear a breast band, to reduce the contact, but—"

"Be gentle?" he said.

"Yes."

"I don't remember this being a problem in Casil."

"It's the stirrups. They change the position of my body." They did, actually. None of what I had told him was untrue.

"I'll remember. But tell me, if I misjudge."

Later, I asked Birel for directions to the junior officers' commons. Entering the room, I saw Finn, talking to another man I didn't recognize.

"Lena!" he said, as I approached. "What a thing you have done, you and General Turlo and the others." He offered his arm, in the soldier's greeting. "We have hope again."

"Finn." I was truly pleased to see him; he had been a good friend, at the Winter Camp. I glanced at his insignia. "Captain now, I see."

"I'm still alive," he said grimly. "And you?"

"Lieutenant. I will be commanding a horseguards division."

"I have been remiss with introductions." The other man, another captain, greeted me cordially. "Lena is from Tirvan," Finn told him, "and as you must have heard, was with General Turlo in Casil. There is a story there to be told!"

"There is," I said, "but you know I can't tell it." There would be an agreed version, and until I knew what I could speak of, and what I couldn't, I would be circumspect. "I was with the Emperor, yesterday, and so while I know in general where we stand, I have few details. Could we talk about that, instead?"

"I'll leave you to catch up," the other captain said. Finn found us a quiet corner, and the steward brought two mugs of beer.

"Where to start?" Finn said.

"I don't want to make you relive it," I said. "Why don't I just ask a few questions, and you tell me what you can?"

"A good idea."

"Gulian and Galdor?" They had been at the Winter Camp with me, too.

"Galdor is dead; he was killed early on, in the first raids. Gulian was on Leste, as he hoped, and then he was sent to the Wall, so I don't know. Josan is dead too."

"I'm sorry." Two of them, at least, had been Finn's friends. I drank a bit of the beer.

"Midsummer, the *Breccaith*," he said, "was terrible. So many gone. Did you remember it, wherever you were?"

"After a fashion," I answered, remembering Sorley's haunting, heartbreaking song. "A different tune, but the same intent, a lament for those lost."

"It's the intent that matters," Finn said. "The general would have wanted it."

"For Darel? Yes. And I, for Darel, and Tirvan, and others as well."

"That news must have been hard, Lena. I wish we had been able to keep the villages safe."

"I wish I had been here," I admitted. "But we cannot change what is done. Where are the youngest boys, Finn? I haven't seen them here."

"Casilla. Our hold on it is secure; the walls are strong, and the harbours guarded by two of our ships. The oldest men, from the retirement farms, supervise them, teach what they can, keep them busy. Is there someone you were wondering about?"

"My cousin, Pel. But don't concern yourself with it."

"I could ask. But, Lena, in a few days I will be riding to Casilla, to supervise the unloading and distribution of some of the food brought from the East. It is not just the cadets at Casilla: many of the women who escaped the Marai are there. Tirvan is very far north, and so it is more likely they would have tried to reach the Wall, but perhaps there will be someone at Casilla. You could come with me, and see who you could find."

"The Marai did not enter the city?"

"No."

Maya would still be safe, then. And Valle. "Could I go?"

"I will speak to your captain. Your cohort-leader is more than competent; they should be able to do without you for a day."

"One last question, Finn, and then I will tell you a little about the East. Do you have any word of a ship called *Skua*?"

"*Skua*. Dern's ship?" I nodded. "They went north, early in the fighting. I have heard nothing since, but there is little reason I would. Communication between the Wall and here is difficult. The generals should know, though. Do you still have Casyn's confidence?"

"To some extent, I suppose. I will ask him, if I can. Thank you, Finn. Now, what would you like to know about the East?"

I told him about Casil, about its buildings and statues and libraries, and its wide streets and markets. I described the Empress, and the house we had stayed in, and the baths. He didn't ask about the support they had granted, or what we had given in return. Only the dregs of the beer remained in our mugs when he asked one more question.

"And this man who is the Emperor's son? What's he like?"

Inwardly I sighed. The questions would be inevitable. Would our relationship become an open secret among the officers? "Cillian," I answered. "Very much like the Emperor at the same age, Turlo says, and not just in appearance. Educated beyond anything I know of in the Empire, trained in diplomacy, analytic. Very disciplined." I added.

"He must have been an asset, then, in whatever negotiations had to be made?"

I shrugged. "You know I can't talk about that, Finn."

"I know," he said. "Didn't hurt to ask. Shall we eat?"

I made my way back to our room, wondering as I did how long it would be before my comings and goings from the senior officer's quarters were noticed. Birel, of course, would say nothing, and order his staff to stay quiet, but rumours would begin, regardless. I wondered if I really cared.

Cillian had not yet returned. I made a few notes about the next day's training before I readied myself for bed, taking advantage of the privacy to look at my breasts. I couldn't see any changes, except that I thought they were slightly larger. Would he notice? If so, I'd have to think of something to explain it. I left the oil lamp burning, very low.

I had fallen asleep almost immediately. Cillian woke me, coming in. It didn't feel late. He bent to kiss me, his lips soft, a greeting, not a question. "Did you find your friends?" he asked, as he undressed.

"One. Others are posted elsewhere, or dead."

"I'm sorry."

"I expected it. Cillian, will you tell me what the Emperor is allowing the senior officers to know, about the agreement, and the East? I am asked, and I need to know what I can say. In the morning, or another time."

"In the morning. They were only told tonight, so no one else will know until tomorrow." He slipped into bed beside me, pulling me close. He kissed my hair. "Callan and I talked, over wine, tonight. He asked me to forgive him, Lena. He said he should have realized a child was a possibility, and asked more questions, but his grief at my mother's death overwhelmed him."

"Did you forgive him?"

"Yes. I had some time ago. I told him I understood how he had felt, the blankness, the surface actions taking over from a deadened mind, when he knew she was gone. That I had experienced the same, and you were still alive, just lost to me by my own actions, I thought."

"What did he say?"

"He asked me to explain. I told him, clarifying that it was my last move in a game going badly, a sacrifice to ensure victory. But that even so, had I not thought it was my best chance under the circumstances to keep you safe, I would not have done it. And that he needed to understand that, if he was to judge my advice to him in the next days and weeks."

"I had guessed you were trying to protect me," I murmured. "Sorley asked me how you could leave me. It was what I told him. How did Callan react?"

"He just nodded, and then he started to tell me about my mother. Just a little: what she looked like, how tall she was. I have no memories, of course, and what I was told by my grandparents has been lost, if they told me anything."

"Generous of him."

"Yes. *Käresta*, I would like just to feel you beside me tonight, before I sleep."

I turned, nestling beside him, my back against his chest. His encircling arm dropped lower than usual, remembering to avoid my breasts, I realized. His hand rested on my belly. Can you feel your father's hand, little one? I asked silently, knowing it was a fancy. But the thought made me smile, nonetheless.

CHAPTER TWENTY-TWO

TRUE TO HIS WORD, FINN ARRANGED FOR ME to accompany him to Casilla. The supply ship had moved along to coast to the city's harbour the day before; Finn's job, and nominally mine, was to supervise the unloading.

Four soldiers rode with us, to supplement the older men resident in Casilla. Fields stretched out on either side of the road, planted to grain or vegetables, or grazed. The Marai had not come this far east, so these lands, mostly belonging to retirement villas but some to Casilla, still produced food. Elsewhere in the Empire, Finn told me, land lay barren, last year's crops rotting, animals slaughtered by the Marai.

A cool breeze blew off the sea, but the day would be hot. I had left Casilla on a day much like this one, two years ago, after Maya had told me she no longer wanted me to live with them. The city itself would be hotter than the countryside, the stone of its buildings and streets capturing the heat, trapping it. Knowing this, I had worn only a light tunic and breeches, my secca belted to my waist, and my lieutenant's insignia pinned to my shoulder. I also carried a bow, one of the new design, and a quiver. That had been Talyn's idea. "You'll be in the saddle for quite a while," she'd said. "It will give you an idea of what they are like, to carry."

We had left very early, just after sunrise, so it was not yet mid-morning when we reached the eastern gate of the city. "Do you know Casilla?" Finn had asked, as we approached.

"Yes. I lived here for half a year, or a bit more, before I rode to the Wall."

"Then I don't need to give you directions. We'll be at the harbour until mid-afternoon, at least. Join us when you are ready, but you shouldn't ride back alone. If you need to leave the horse, use the army's stables on the men's side; otherwise, there will be difficulty about payment, you understand?"

"I'll go there first," I said. "I'll be better on foot; some of the streets are narrow, as you must know."

At the gate, Finn spoke to the guards for a minute before we passed through. "It's quiet," he told me. "The supply ship is waiting for us. The patrols that ride west and north have seen no Marai, on land or sea, and the scouts report movement northward. They'll have seen the Eastern ships arrive, no doubt."

We rode through the streets, busier than I remembered. But Finn had said that many women had sought refuge here, behind Casilla's walls. I had thought it such a fine city, but the gate inscription was right: this was not Casil. Who had had the words chiselled onto the city wall? *Casil e imitaran ne,* they said: it had been Cillian, I remembered, the first night I had met him at the *Ti'ach,* who had confirmed their true meaning. I hadn't liked him at all, then.

I had told him, last night, where I was going today, and why. We had been drifting into sleep, when I realized I hadn't let him know my plans: we saw each other only briefly, as little as we had in the last weeks in Casil, early mornings and very late. There were advantages, I had reflected: he wasn't around to notice I wasn't making anash tea, and in the dim light of the room he was unlikely to notice any changes in my body. Touching me as gently as I had requested, his hands and lips had also not discerned a difference, or nothing he had mentioned.

I smiled at the juxtaposition of the two thoughts: the memory of last night's lovemaking, and how I had disliked him, at the *Ti'ach*. *Choice is better than chance*, the Karstian proverb said, but it was chance that had brought us together. Or had it been? Was it not a result of choices we had made? And why was I thinking of this, today?

Because I was going to find Maya, whom I had loved once, and lost, as a consequence of choice. Cillian had listened to my plans, without comment. Only when I had finished explaining did he speak. "I will not stay to talk to Callan privately, tomorrow night," he'd said. "Unless you would prefer to be with your friends?"

"I will need to let Grainne know what I find," I said, "but that can wait. We were never close friends. But Cillian, don't give up that time for me. I'll be all right."

We reached the army stables. I unsaddled the gelding I rode, and led him into a stall. A cadet, perhaps ten or eleven, appeared. "I'll take care of him, Lieutenant," he said, "water, and a bit of hay, and a rubdown."

"Where can I put my bow?" He told me. "Do not let anyone touch it," I warned.

Out in the street, I stood a moment, getting my bearings. I was on the army's part of the city, divided by the Partition agreement into the woman's town, the army's harbour, and the market, common to both. How long will it take, I wondered, for those barriers to fall, once the new laws are known?

I began to walk, through the market and along a wide street, and then into narrower ones. I had walked this route every day, to and from the fishing harbour, the months I had spent in Casil. I could do it without thought. Everyone looked so thin, I noted; not starving, but the privations of the last year had left their mark. How far would the food we brought go?

I turned a corner. I had arrived at the Street of Weavers. I walked along the narrow, cobbled street, stopping at a green door. There had been pots of flowers, outside the door, the summer I left. Not now. I knocked.

Maya stood in the doorway, her face slowly changing to shock. She's thin, I thought. "Lena," she whispered. Her eyes flicked to the insignia on my shoulder. "Still a soldier, I see."

"Yes. I am in Casilla to help oversee a shipment of grain being unloaded at the harbour. I came to see if you were all right."

"We are," she said. "Grain, you said? For us, or for the men?"

"Both. Grain and oil. The distribution will begin tomorrow. Is Valle here?"

"No. Ianthe takes him out, in the mornings when it is still cool. They are probably at the harbour. He is fine; he is growing. Lena, what is going to happen? Will the Marai come?"

"Not if we can help it," I said. "I can't tell you more, but there is hope."

"Hope? And what will there be, even if the Marai are defeated? Everything is gone, Lena. You do know that?" Her voice wavered. "No one kept us safe."

"No," I said. "No one did; no one could. The enemy was larger than we knew. What there will be, if we prevail, will be something different, something new. Different choices, for you and Valle."

"I don't want something new," she said. She never had.

"I know. But we cannot go back. I only came to see how you were, Maya. I am needed at the harbour. Give Ianthe and Valle my greetings."

"Wait," she said. "Lena, I am—glad—to know you are alive. I wonder, sometimes. Do you know where Garth is?"

I shook my head. "No. His boat went north, months ago. If I learn, I will send word, if I can. You know Pel is here, in Casilla?"

"Yes. I went to enquire, once. He is fine, they said, but they wouldn't let me see him. It would disrupt him, the officer told me. I suppose he was right."

"Probably."

"Your sister is here, too."

"What? Kira? Where?" Hope leapt. "Anyone else?"

She shook her head. "I don't know. I didn't speak to Kira; I didn't want to know about Tirvan. I just saw her, on the street, a couple of months ago."

"Where?" I asked again.

"Try the Street of Healers."

"Maya, thank you." I turned to go, then turned back. "Maya, everything will change. We can't stop it. I wish I had time to tell you where I have been, and the things I have seen and learned."

"It's all still an adventure to you, isn't it?" she asked, her voice tired. "I hope you find Kira. Goodbye, Lena." She shut the door.

I tried not to run on my way to the Street of Healers. I turned into the lane, my eyes scanning the people I saw: it was busy here, women, some with children, come for consultations. I stopped a woman. "Kira, from Tirvan," I said. "Do you know where I can find her?"

She pointed. "There." A tall building, the door propped open.

"Thank you," I called. I went in. My eyes took a minute to adjust to the darker interior. Several women sat with others, talking. They looked up as I came in. "Kira?" I asked.

"In the stillroom," one said. "Back there."

I pushed through a curtain. My sister's back was to me: she stood at a table preparing herbs. "Kira," I said.

She turned. "Lena!" She stood still for a moment, then rushed forward. "Oh, Lena," she cried, throwing her arms around me. Her sobs racked her body. I held her as closely as I could. She was, I estimated, at least six months pregnant.

When we had both stopped crying, she led me to a bench. "Sit," she said. "I'll make tea." While she did, I watched her. Too thin, behind the pregnancy. She was so like our mother, economical with her movements, finding the practical thing to do. She handed me the mug, and sat across from me.

"I thought you were exiled," she said. "I thought I would never see you again."

"I was pardoned," I told her. "How are you here, Kira?"

"The Marai man who took me came south," she said. "I escaped. Casilla was the closest safe place."

"Kira—"

She shrugged. "I was lucky, I suppose. One man, not many, as some had to—serve." Horror washed through me. What was my experience, to theirs? Or Kira's? Once, and I had killed him. I shuddered.

"The child is his?"

"Of course. I will do my best to love it. There are many of us, in the same situation."

I groped for something to say. "Kira," I said. "I was forced too. But only once. I can only begin to imagine what you have experienced."

"You were lucky, then." She shook her head. "No. I shouldn't have said that. Once is still too many times, Lena. Lucky is not the right word. I'm sorry."

I gestured wordlessly. She looked at me, her eyes narrowing slightly. "Three months ago, Lena?"

She was a midwife. "No," I said. "In the spring."

"But you are pregnant."

"Yes. Almost three months, as you deduced." I tried to smile. "Mother trained you well."

I saw the pain on her face at my mention of our mother. "Then—?"

I put the palm of my hand on my belly. "I am lucky," I said. "She was conceived in love, Kira."

Her face changed. "So soon after you were raped?" I nodded. She studied me. "You are so strong, Lena. You always were. Did he know what happened to you?"

"Yes. He helped me heal, and he helps keep the darkness, the dreams, at bay. As I said, I am lucky."

She smiled. "You are still together, then? Does he know about the child?"

"Yes, and not yet. Mother always said not to tell, until three months had passed. Just after the next full moon."

She nodded. "My advice too."

"Kira, a question?" I told her about diluting the anash. She shrugged.

"Most likely," she said. "But you said you made it in batches, and kept it? It may lose its potency. We were always told to brew it fresh. Does it matter?"

"Not really. Although I should explain to Cillian why it didn't work."

"Cillian. That's a northern name." She furrowed her brow. "Why is it familiar?"

"He's Linrathan. Or was."

"The Linrathan man who was exiled with you?"

"Yes. How did you know?"

"A messenger came. Your father, Galen. He told us. Mother said she was glad he was with you. He'd saved your life once, she said. She thought you would take care of each other, in exile."

"We did. I wish Mother could have known," I said, acknowledging the truth neither of us had touched on. I blinked at tears.

"It was truly terrible, Lena," she said. "They came at dawn. We had almost no warning. Everything we had learned about fighting...we tried, but there were too many. They killed all the older women, and the littlest children. They took the older children to a ship, and then the rest of us..." She took a deep breath. "Some of us were claimed by one man, as I said. Others were...shared. Even girls of eleven and twelve."

"I wish I had been there," I said, trying to push away the pictures in my mind. But I shouldn't, I thought. This is what happened to Kira, to Tirvan. I should not shut it out.

"No!" she said fiercely. "I am so glad you were not. You could have done nothing to change what happened. At least one of us is untouched by that violence."

"Grainne, too," I said. "She is safe, and at the Eastern Fort. And Maya is here, in Casilla."

She nodded. "I knew Maya was here. I am glad to hear about Grainne. She is a soldier, then?"

"Yes. Under my command, it turns out. I lead a horseguard cohort." I hesitated. I should not speak, but this was my sister. "You can tell no one this, and especially not the details," I told her. "We brought reinforcements, Kira, from a distant land. A thousand men, and ten ships. The Emperor is planning their deployment as we speak. We can take our land back, and we will, soon."

She smiled, at that, before a frown crossed her face. "You will be fighting, then? In danger?"

"Yes," I said simply. "It is what I must do, Kira. I must respond to what the Marai have done, to you, to Mother, to everyone." I put my hand on my belly again. "What would I tell her, if I did not?"

We talked, and cried, and talked again, into the afternoon. "I must go," I told her finally. "I won't be able to come again. I will try to send word, after, if I can."

She hugged me. "Can I be a healer for a moment, and not just your sister? What we have talked about today...you will dream, or react badly to unexpected things, because of it. We have each other, here, to help us through it, and understand why. Will you—will Cillian understand, and help you?"

"I tried to kill him once," I said wryly, "because someone approached me from behind. He stepped between that man and me, and I went for him, with my knife. He understands. I told you, Kira, he helps keep the darkness at bay, and that darkness is not just from the rape."

"He sounds remarkable. I wish I could meet him."

"Maybe you will, someday. Will you go home, Kira, if we win back our land?"

"Maybe. I don't know. Will you?"

I shook my head. "I don't think so. I don't know where I'll—we'll—go, but I don't think it will be Tirvan."

We held each other for one long, last minute. "You are the strong one, Kira," I told her. "You're dealing with everything alone."

"I'm not alone," she said. "Not when so many women share my experience. Think of us when you fight, Lena."

I would. The vengeance that had lay quiescent woke again, setting my jaw and clenching my fists as I walked back to the stables. My hands trembled. I took several deep breaths, trying to calm myself.

Finn and the soldiers were just saddling up when I arrived. He glanced at my face. "Bad news?" he asked quietly. I shook my head.

"Not really." I saddled the gelding, retrieved my bow and quiver, and swung up into the saddle. We didn't talk until we were on the road leading back to the Eastern Fort.

"Did the unloading go well?" I asked.

"Yes. The food will be welcome. Who did you find, Lena?"

"A friend, and my sister. Thank you, Finn, for arranging for me to come."

"Were they well?"

"Well enough," I didn't want to talk about the truth, with Finn. We rode in silence. Insects buzzed in the heat. A few people worked in the fields, hoeing weeds. The soldiers behind us talked desultorily, occasionally laughing, relaxing after a day's work. We approached a belt of trees. Shade would be welcome, even for the few minutes it would take to pass through.

We were almost at the far side of the trees when shouts from the soldiers made us wheel our horses around. Six men, swords out, slashing at the horses. Dark haired, part of my mind noted. Not Marai. A horse screamed. Two down, their bellies ripped and bleeding. Two soldiers on foot, parrying blows with their short swords. "Dismount!" Finn shouted.

I pulled the gelding up, dropping the reins, reaching for my bow. I nocked the arrow, drew, waited. The horse stood, obedient. I let the arrow fly. It took the man in the back, driving deep through his leather tunic. He screamed, and fell. I had another arrow nocked, and another man fell to it a moment later. I could not get a clean line on the others, the fighting too close. Finn rode into the melee, his longer sword slashing down. One man broke and ran. I kneed my gelding into a canter, past the fighting, and my arrow took the runner high in the shoulder.

I turned the horse, looking back. It was over. The attackers were dead, or mortally wounded. Finn knelt by a downed horse, opening a vein in its neck. I rode over, dismounted. One of our soldiers lay on the ground, another beside him. His leg bled badly. Not bright red and pumping, though, I noted. I pulled my light tunic free of its belt, reaching beneath it to loosen the cloth band binding my breasts. I handed it to his friend, who wrapped it around the wound, competently and quickly.

Finn stood from beside the second horse. "Retrieve arrows and their weapons," he told one of the soldiers. "Begin with that one," he pointed to the man who had run, "and make sure he's dead. Can you ride?" he asked the man with the leg wound.

"Yes, Captain."

"Who is least hurt?"

"Me, I think," one of the soldiers said. "The lieutenant's arrow took care of the man I was fighting."

"Take the best horse, and ride back to the fort at speed," Finn told him. "Report the attack, and have them send carts for the dead horses." We couldn't waste the meat, I realized.

The soldier sent to retrieve weapons returned. "He's dead," he said. He pulled the other two arrows from the bodies, wiping the heads on his tunic before giving them to me. The smell of blood threatened to overwhelm me, suddenly. I swallowed, hard.

The worst-wounded man was helped up into the saddle of the largest horse, his friend behind him. The last man went up behind Finn. We began to ride, slowly, back towards the Eastern Fort.

"Lestians?" I asked Finn.

"Yes," he said, grimly. "Deserters, most likely. They were probably scouting for the Marai. None have been reported for some weeks, though. I was complacent, I fear. We were lucky you were with us, with the bow."

"It was a good test of the weapon," I said. I had killed three men this afternoon, I thought. I saw the blood on the road again. I was going to vomit. "I need to relieve myself," I said to Finn. "I'll catch up." I did not want the soldiers to see my reaction.

He nodded, and rode ahead. I slid off my horse, falling onto my knees at the side of the road. I retched, violently, spasms shaking my body, tears coursing down my cheeks. I could still smell the blood.

I sat for a minute, wiping my lips. Standing, I took my waterskin from the saddle, rinsed my mouth, took a drink. When I was sure I wouldn't vomit again, I remounted, kicking the gelding into a trot to catch up with the men. I was still shaking, slightly, but I could master that.

"You'd better report to your captain," Finn told me, as we rode into the fort. "Tell him I am taking full responsibility." I took my gelding to the stables, unstrung and stored the bow, and washed my face before I went in search of the man. He listened, impassively.

"Your new bow proved useful," was all he said. "An unexpected test in the field. I will speak further with Finn." Dismissed, I thought about what to do. It was late afternoon. I would wait until tomorrow, to speak to Talyn and Dian. I felt soiled, sticky, as if I had been spattered by blood, even though my tunic was stained only by dust and sweat.

I went to our room. I'd found several doors that led into the corridors of the building, and I alternated using them as much as possible. This time, though, I took the most direct route. I closed the door, stripping off my clothes. I poured water into the bowl, and washed, breathing steadily, staying deliberate, and calm.

Then I dressed again, and went to the commons. Finn came in, a bit later.

"Good thinking on that leg wound," he told me. "The medics say he'll be fine. No one else had more than shallow cuts." He signalled for beer. "I took a bit of a reprimand, but it was deserved." The steward brought the beer. He took a deep draught. "You're good with that bow, Lena. I gave you full credit, in my report."

I told him about the construction of the weapon, glad of the diversion, and how I'd learned to use it, in Casil. We ate bread and cheese, and after eating a dice game began. I played until a glance outside showed me the sun had set, and the first stars had appeared in the darkening sky. Cillian had said he would not stay to talk to the Emperor tonight: I had told him not to come home early. Which would he do? If I went back, and he wasn't there—I didn't want to be alone, right now. He wouldn't look for me, I knew. But nor could I go looking for him.

I stayed for another few throws. Then I walked back through the dusk. Cillian wasn't in our room. I paced, thinking. *Are you going to expect me to tell you about every sword thrust or axe swing?* I had asked him, after the attack in Casil. I had told my captain the bare details, and Finn and I had analyzed the fight, on the ride back. That wasn't what I needed Cillian for. I had shot those arrows with cold precision, with focused vengeance, for my sister and all those like her, for the horror she had described to me today. A response. Now I wanted my refuge from violence, arms around me, hands stroking my hair. A refuge denied to most, I told myself. Why should I be any different?

I was on the bed, curled in on myself, when he came in. It wasn't late. He looked at me, and swore. "What happened? Why didn't you send Birel for me?"

"It wasn't fair to," I said. He sat on the bed beside me.

"Tell me."

"I found Maya," I said, "and my sister. Maya is fine. She hasn't changed."

"And your sister?"

"She's alive. Fine, I suppose. She told me what happened. They killed all the older women. My mother is dead. Then they raped all the girls, and the younger women, and took them as—as slaves." I began to cry. "Kira escaped," I gasped. "But she's pregnant."

He lay beside me, stroking my hair. "*Käresta*," he murmured, making no move to touch me other than with his gentle, undemanding fingers. I shuddered.

"How can I let you comfort me?" I said. "Who comforts them?" I turned to let him hold me, to bury my face against his body, to be sheltered. For now. I wasn't strong enough to do anything else.

Much later, when the tears had run out, he left me for a few minutes, returning with wine. "I thought it was in short supply," I said, trying to smile.

"It is. But you need it." He handed me the cup. "*Fuisce* would be better, but Birel has gone to bed."

I drank some of the wine. "Kira told me that knowing...hearing her tell me, would make me dream, or react. I will make sure my secca is nowhere near the bed." A weak joke, I knew.

"Probably best," Cillian said gravely.

"She said she would try to love the child," I told him. "I keep thinking—what if Ivor—? I don't think I could want a child who came from violence."

"It didn't happen, *käresta*," he said. "You were saved that."

"But what if I hadn't been?"

"The child would be innocent," he said gently. "Perhaps that is what Kira has realized?"

Perhaps it was. He was right, of course, and he had his own reasons for knowing it. "Can you sleep now?" he asked.

"Maybe."

I didn't think I would, but exhaustion defeated distress. I slept, dreamless, until dawn. Cillian was already awake, lying quietly beside me. "Lena," he greeted me.

"Hello, my love."

"How are you?"

I considered the question. The images had receded, just enough. "I am— better. I'll be all right." Early mornings were our private time together. "But I don't think I can make love this morning."

"I had assumed that," he said. "You decide when, *käresta*." He hadn't touched me, I realized. Letting me be in control. I put a hand on his chest.

"You could hold me, though." I turned towards him, finding the spot on his shoulder where my head seemed to fit. I put an arm across him. He stroked my back, gently.

"There are other things that happened yesterday that I should tell you." I said, after a while.

"Can I ask something, first?"

"Of course. What is it?" His voice had sounded just slightly uncertain.

"Maya. You said she hadn't changed. Lena, she has first claim on your heart. Do you want—"

I cut him off. "Cillian, how can you even ask me that? What claim she had is long over. When I said she hadn't changed, I meant she was still unhappy. She just wants everything to be as it was. You are foolish, sometimes, you know," I added.

"Maybe I am, at that." He kissed my hair. "What do you need to tell me?"

"We were attacked, on the way back." I told him what had happened.

"Deserters," he said, analytic now. "The Emperor will have been told, but we will need to think about them more closely. If they were scouting for the Marai, they will have seen at least the supply ship."

"They are all dead. But when they don't return, the Marai will realize that, and send more scouts, so they will learn soon enough what support the East sent."

"Which means we need to increase the patrols."

"But, Cillian, if they were just scouts, why did they attack us?"

"I don't know," he said thoughtfully. "I would have said they wanted the horses, to return to the Marai more rapidly with their news, but you said they killed the animals?"

"Only two. By forcing two soldiers to fight on foot, did they think the other two would dismount as well? They only had short swords, remember. Not all the deserters needed a horse, if the purpose was to get the news back to the Marai as quickly as possible. One or two would have done."

"One man grabs a horse, while the others fight? Possibly."

"Which means the mounted patrols are in more danger now, does it not? If the Marai scouts get close enough to see the encampment, or the ships, they will again want to return as quickly as possible."

"And the patrols are mostly younger cadets, with one or two horseguards with them." He swore. "It would mean reassigning men to that task. Even with long swords, the cadets cannot be expected to fight off Marai, and it is worse if the scouts are Lestian deserters. They have had training in our fighting techniques."

This was, I reflected, a very odd conversation to be having, in the warmth of our bed. Odd, too, to be discussing warfare with Cillian, as equals, or nearly so.

"What has happened to the Lestian soldiers?" I asked. "Surely they could not be trusted? Most, if not all, were taken into the army unwilling."

"Some swore fealty, a second time, and are still among the troops," he said. "Some deserted, in the confusion of the early days. Those who would not swear were killed."

"That was harsh."

"Yes. But what choice was there? Men could not be spared to guard prisoners. My concern is that Callan accepted oaths after the first men who refused were killed. Those oaths were made under threat, and I wonder how much they can be trusted. But he says those men are scattered among the squadrons, purposefully, and are being watched, and that we need the numbers." He stretched. "We should be getting up, I suppose. My concern about the Lestian oaths is between us only, *käresta*. Is there anything else I should know?"

"Yes," I said, "reporting to a senior officer in bed is not usual army practice, Major. You are new to this, so you might be unsure on protocol."

"I will neglect to tell the Emperor and his other advisors exactly where we had this conversation," he said gravely.

"Good." I raised my head to kiss him. "As officially I am not even here, it might be difficult to explain."

As we dressed, Cillian turned to me suddenly. "*Käresta*, forgive me. I should have asked before. How were you, after the ambush? You killed three men."

I shrugged. "The usual reaction. I don't seem to have much control over it. I hid it from the men," I added. "Not good for morale, for them to see an officer vomiting after fighting."

"True."

"What are you doing today?" I asked. I didn't want to dwell on yesterday's attack.

"Working with the Casilani officers and ours on the words for basic commands, as usual. Then, tactics, possible deployments. Turlo is working on a detailed map of the land on either side of the Taiva, with help from various officers and men, and of the route Callan thinks the army should take."

"Is Druisius proving useful?"

"Immensely. He's learning the language rapidly. He worries about Sorley, though."

"So do I. I wish there was some way to know."

"If, when we reach the Taiva, there is no Marai force waiting for us to the north, then he—they—will have done what they were sent to do. We are unlikely to know before. But I share the worry, Lena. For Sorley and for Ruar."

We kissed, one last time, before I pinned my officer's insignia to my shoulder. We had agreed that while we wore our badges of rank each day, there would be no physical contact, even in the privacy of our room. A clear demarcation of private and public, although our conversation this morning had strayed over that line.

"I'll see you tonight," I said. I closed the door quietly behind me, choosing a different route out of the building than I had used the day before. Were we fooling anyone? Probably not. But no rumours had reached my ears, either.

The day passed routinely. Junia came back from her lesson in commands, and she and I drilled the chosen archers on the butts. We moved the best onto the pavo, later. Dian came back from patrol; Junia went to work with the bowyers—they were making another dozen bows in the Eastern style—and I took a patrol out. I carried a bow. After yesterday, I thought it prudent. I'd ordered Dian and Talyn to do the same.

We rode a large circuit, north and west of the fort, me and three cadets, all under fourteen. They'd been trained well, their eyes constantly in motion, their minds on the job, listening, watching. Nothing moved. There was no game to startle: it had all been hunted, and even the smaller birds were trapped by the men. We had scouts out, as well, I knew, individual men who could move through the landscape virtually unseen. I guessed they saw us. We did not see them.

Riding back in, I considered what a Marai scout might see. We should overlap the patrols, I thought. Right now, there was a break: Talyn would start out just as I returned, and take a different route, but the perimeter was unguarded for a short time. Ideally, we needed one, or even two, full patrols added. I would speak to my captain.

I found him later, in the commons. He listened to my idea, nodding. "Given yesterday's incident, I agree," he said. "I'll find six more cadets to assign. Who will lead?"

"Two of the horseguards," I said. "Rasa, and there's a woman from Torrey who's calm and competent. I'll send each out with a patrol tomorrow, and the next day we can start the new schedule. I've told the patrol leaders to carry bows, as well."

"Good thinking. You're valuable, Lieutenant," he said. "Having the confidence of the Emperor's new adjutant is likely useful, too."

I swore to myself. Had it started? "Captain?"

He smiled, slightly. "Don't worry, Lieutenant. The connection is not widely known. But as you are my lieutenant, it was felt I should know. Just remember that anything reported to him should also be reported to me."

"Sir," I said. That had been a very mild reprimand, but a reprimand, nonetheless. "We did discuss possible danger to the patrols if the Marai scouts were after horses. That was why I ordered the leaders to carry bows, sir."

"If there is any sign of an increased threat, then add another horseguard, with a bow, to each patrol," he said. "I will tell you if the scouts report anything. Is that all, Lieutenant?"

"Yes, sir."

"Good. There is a dice game waiting for me."

Dismissed, I asked for food, and found a spot to sit. Finn wasn't around. I ate quickly. I could join a game, but I wasn't in the mood. I left the commons, walking down towards the harbour. A gate in the fort's wall stood open, a cobbled path leading down to the jetties. I followed it for a bit, and then I sat on the side of the dike, looking out over the marshes. The tide was rising, water flowing into the creeks, changing the mudflats to a network of waterways. A few small boats bobbed at their moorings. Beyond the marsh, the Casilani ships rode at anchor, along with two of our smaller ships.

I sat a long time, watching the land change to sea, and the gulls over the water. No one bothered me. Space and silence and solitude: I knew why I needed them, this evening. Cillian had casually dismissed the killing of the men of Leste who refused to swear fealty. Pieces to be sacrificed to a greater goal. And I did not disagree. What had we become, in the face of war?

Chapter Twenty-Three

"Another beer?" Talyn asked, signalling the steward. I still had half a mug. I indicated not. She had ridden the last patrol, and the heat today had been stifling, so I wasn't surprised she was thirsty.

"The dun filly is ready," she told me. We'd been discussing which of the horses in training could move into regular use.

"She reminds me of my Clio," I said.

"Full sister. That's why. Do you want her?"

I considered. I liked the chestnut gelding I rode regularly, and we were used to each other. But I should have a second horse. Before I could speak, though, a cadet appeared at my side.

"Lieutenant," he said, saluting. "A note."

I took the paper. The wax seal held no imprint. 'I am free this evening,' the note read. 'Would you join me?'

I thanked the cadet, dismissing him. "Sorry, Talyn," I said. "I've been summoned."

"Give my cousin my greetings," she said quietly. "Most of us don't smile at notes from a superior requesting our presence," she added, at my look of surprise.

"Good night, Talyn," I said, grinning. I stepped out into the evening. The western sky still held some light, streaks of pink and purple painting the horizon. A light breeze moved the air now, providing some relief from the heat. I took the most direct route to the headquarters, the note in my hand providing a reason.

In our room, Cillian sat studying a map. He put it down when I came in. "Why aren't you with the Emperor?" I asked, crossing the room to kiss him. We had barely seen each other in days.

"I declined wine and conversation, tonight. We move out in the morning." I had expected this, any day. We were ready, but it did not stop the frisson of fear that ran up my spine. "This will be our last night together until the battle is over, and I am needed very early tomorrow."

We had not made love since I had gone to Casilla. By the time the images had faded enough for me to be ready, the demands on our time had increased. Brief embraces had been all we had shared.

"Callan sent us wine," he added.

"Tell him thank you, tomorrow," I murmured.

"And I begged a second lamp, from Birel."

He hadn't moved, looking up at me, a hint of smile on his lips. I bent to kiss him again, a long kiss, this time. "It was hot today," I said. "I need to wash. You could pour us wine, while I do."

Both lamps still burned. We were wasting oil. I reached over to snuff one, and lower the wick on the other. The room held the heat of the day, although the sky beyond the one small window shone with stars. Cillian lay sprawled over his half of the bed, letting the air dry the sweat on his body. I stretched out, reaching for his hand, to entangle fingers.

I turned my head so I could see him. He was looking at me, his eyes even darker than usual in the low light. All the unspoken knowledge of what war might bring had fuelled an urgency and a passion tonight beyond anything we had shared before, greater even than the sunlit afternoon in Casil. Neither of us were ready for words yet.

A tiny breeze stirred the air. Cillian got up, filled the wine glasses, handed me one. I sat up, my back against the wall. He sat beside me. We still hadn't spoken. He touched his glass to mine. "Drink, and then sleep, *käresta*," he said softly. "We have told each other everything we need to, have we not?"

Not everything. I could almost tell him, now. But if I did, it would change tonight, and the memories of it, this last night we might ever have together. Not even our child should intrude, I thought.

"We have, *kärestan*," I answered. "Wake me in the morning, before you leave."

I swung up into the saddle, adjusting the bow on my back after I had settled. My cohorts would ride flank guard during the days of the march. The foot-soldiers, both the archers and men armed with the short sword, a shield, and one light spear, had already set out, followed by more heavily-armed Empire's men. Behind them were the commanders: the Emperor, Casyn and Turlo, their bodyguard and messengers, as well as Gnaius, the physician, and the Emperor's adjutant.

I was to ride guard at the rear, or the front, alternating the cohorts if I chose, but I was not to flank the commanders. I understood the directive. Similar orders would have been given wherever relationships were known.

I had seen Druisius, briefly. He marched in the first line of Casil's troops. His position would allow him to act as a translator, if necessary, although by now the system of horn signals, shouted commands, and drumbeats was understood by the Eastern officers. The men would do as they were told. He had waved, grinning, and then made a face of apology and saluted me. I had returned the salute, hiding a laugh.

We travelled as lightly as possible, with only packhorses in the baggage train, animals that would double as reserve mounts if needed. Each of us carried enough food for two weeks, flour and cured meat, cheese. The pack animals carried medical supplies, extra weapons, the commanders' tents.

The carts began to move. I gave my cohort its last instructions, and moved my gelding to ride beside the rearguard: cadets and older men, mostly, along with the medics and cooks. Ahead of and beyond the army, mounted scouts who had left at earliest light searched out threats: Marai troops, Lestian deserters. I wished, sometimes, I had been chosen for that role. Working alone would have suited me.

Tedium was the best description of much of the march. I alternated where my cohort rode, but after a day or two it didn't seem to matter. Staying alert for many hours at a stretch when nothing threatened was a skill I had, but still I found it wearisome.

We skirted Casilla on the road; beyond it, we turned northward on a track, beaten earth, wide enough for half-a-dozen horses to ride abreast. I thought, from what I could remember of the map I had once had, it went to the Winter Camp, now in the hands of the Marai. If they hadn't deserted it. The Casilani ships had sailed a few days before the army marched, flying their bright banners of the East, archers and swordsmen on board. Their job, to threaten the coastal Marai, driving them north to the Taiva, should have alerted the invaders to the renewed strength of our army, if the Marai scouts hadn't already done that. The hope was the Winter Camp would lie empty.

The rain began on the fourth day, a steady, light rain that seeped into everything. We halted, long enough to check the oiled wrappings on food and weapons and to find cloaks. I took mine off after an hour: I could be wet from rain, or wet from sweat. The track grew muddy from foot passage and hooves, pocked and slick. Cresting a rise, my gelding slipped, flailing for footing, his back quarters not finding purchase. I kicked my feet free of the stirrups and jumped off, leading him to the edge of the track. He found his feet, and followed, favouring one hind leg.

I ran a hand down his legs. Nothing serious, I decided, just a strain. I swore. I was ahead of the packhorses and extra mounts. I waited, and when they reached us, I found the dun filly and swapped over the tack. He would only need to walk, now. The filly sidled and mouthed the bit: she needed a firm hand. I checked her misbehaviour, guiding her onto the track.

She settled down, remembering her training. I relaxed, too much. Trotting to regain my position, the filly shied violently at a stump. I hit the ground, hard.

The filly immediately dropped her head to graze. I lay still, testing limbs. I wasn't hurt. *I* wasn't. Little one, I thought, panic in my interior voice, are you all right? I sat up, and then stood, gingerly. This was why I had kept quiet.

My back hurt, but it was the pain of impact, not cramping. I walked the filly for some minutes, listening to my body. Nothing happened. I mounted again, walking the horse, praying silently. Huntress, I asked, keep her safe. Let her live.

We made camp, on sodden, muddy ground. I still felt all right, but I tried to move carefully, setting up my tent and helping with camp chores. I put my cloak on again, thinking obscurely that keeping warm might help.

"Are you all right, Lena?" Talyn asked me. The evening's fire hissed in the continuing rain. I had winced, shifting position. One hip hurt.

"The filly threw me," I admitted. "I'm sore, stiff, but nothing serious. My fault, for forgetting how green she really is."

"Walk a bit in the morning before you ride," she said. Good advice. As early as I felt I could, I went to bed. The tent was damp, I was damp. The night passed unpleasantly. As soon as light filtered through the tent, I got up. Other than the hip, and a general stiffness, nothing hurt. I found a private place and explored with my fingers. No trace of blood. Perhaps the prayers had worked, I thought. Or perhaps I was just lucky.

We packed away wet gear and began the day's march. Mid-morning, the sun came out, and along with it, the Marai.

A scout gave us just enough warning. The message passed along the lines: thirty men, or thereabouts. Well-armed. Casyn wheeled his horse away from the Emperor, giving orders, moving men up, dropping the lightly-armed foot-soldiers back. Archers nocked arrows, their bows half-drawn. I took my cohort left; Talyn, right. I had claimed my gelding back this morning, a small mercy: I didn't need to be dealing with a green horse, right now. We halted, flanking the men on foot, staying back, bows ready.

The land rose slightly before us, giving the advantage to the Marai. Except that thirty against hundreds was madness, a wild act of defiance. They charged down the slope, shouting, swords and axes out, shields up. A third fell to the archers before they reached the front line. Metal clashed against metal; men shouted, screamed. Swords stabbed, axes hewed. Our troops pushed forward, shields making a tight wall, advancing relentlessly. One of the Marai broke, running, and another. I snapped a command, and drew my bow. I watched one fall, my arrow between his shoulders.

Then, silence, except for a moan, quickly ended. I looked over. The Marai lay dead, or dying. Three of our men were down, the medics running to them. Casyn rode forward. "No prisoners," he ordered. "Take their weapons."

"I'll get the arrows," I said to Rasa. I rode over to the two we had shot, pulling the arrows free. I had to twist them, tearing flesh, to do so. They came out with a wet, sucking sound. I didn't even try not to vomit.

I rinsed my mouth with water from my flask, spat, and then rinsed the arrowheads. Rasa had ridden up to me; I handed one to her. "Horrible, isn't it," she said. I nodded.

"I always spew," I said. "I can't seem to help it. Just a reaction." Better she heard me acknowledge what happened, than try to hide it, I'd decided.

A shadow made me look up. A raven soared above us. How did they get here so quickly? Could they smell blood? I didn't want to see what they would do to the dead men. I turned my horse, riding back towards the rear. As I passed the command group, I glanced over. Cillian watched me from his black gelding. I saluted, the only acknowledgement I could give him, and kept riding.

As we approached the Winter Camp, I grew increasingly nervous. I tried to analyze why, my gut telling me it was something about the place itself, not the chance the Marai still held it. I let my memories of it float in my mind as my eyes moved constantly on the hillsides. Hillsides: that was it. The Winter Camp occupied a natural bowl among hills, sheltered from wind and some of the worst winter weather, but vulnerable to attack. I had wondered, in the time I had spent there, if it needed to be patrolled constantly when invasion threatened. I would know, later today.

A scout returned, reporting to the Emperor. We continued on, no commands or messages passing up the line. I guessed the scout had found the camp deserted, a guess that proved correct in the late afternoon. We followed the track through a low pass in the hills, to the fields below.

The camp area wasn't flat, but instead sloped upward to the south. The Emperor's tent, and those of his commanders, were pitched on the highest point of the slope, and others, more or less by rank, below. Horse-lines were set up near a stand of trees, exactly where they had been three winters past. The camp came together quickly. Fires were lit and food began to be cooked.

My captain found me. "Horse patrols until dark," he told me. Unsurprised, I organized the cohort, explaining as best I could remember where the path was, just under the ridgeline. I would ride with them: I was the only one who knew anything of this place. I ate, standing, then went to claim the dun filly. I had ridden the gelding all day; he deserved his rest.

After the first circuit of the hillsides, I split the eight of us into two groups of three, sending them in opposite directions, plus two of us to watch from the highest places. I thought this gave us the best chance of seeing movement. I took the northern side, watching from a pinnacle that gave a good view of the land to the north and west.

Movement caught my eye. I watched, my bow ready. Two men came into view below me, but they were just walking, casually talking. I recognized the clothes of the Empire. What were these two doing away from the camp?

I rode down to them. An older cadet, and a soldier. I didn't know either of them.

"Names?" I asked, confronting them. The older man muttered his name.

"You don't remember me, Lieutenant?" the cadet asked. The question bordered on insolence, but his voice, with its northern intonations, told me who this was.

"Kebhan," I said. He'd matured. I hadn't recognized Lorcann's son. "You know you can't be out here. Back to the camp," I told them. "Stay within its bounds. I could have shot you."

I escorted them back up the hillside. As we reached the perimeter track, one of the patrols met us. Dian reined her horse in. "Why were Kebhan and that soldier out of the camp?" she asked.

"Looking for a private place, perhaps?" I said.

She frowned. "Doesn't fit what I've heard of Kebhan, but, what do I know? Nothing to report, Lieutenant," she added. She kicked her horse into a trot to catch up with her companions. I sat my filly, watching the hillsides, thinking.

At dusk, we rode down off the hills. Guards would be set, but not on horseback. We'd done our job. I rode to the camp, found the archers' captain. I told her what I'd seen.

She nodded. "Thank you, Lieutenant. I'll deal with them."

I took the filly back to the horselines. A cadet offered to take care of her, but I turned him down. I wanted her to get to know me a bit more. After unsaddling,

I began to curry her, speaking to her quietly as I did.

"Lieutenant."

I remembered to straighten, salute. "Adjutant."

The cadet appeared, saluted. "Sir? Do you want your horse?"

"No," Cillian said. "Thank you, Cadet." Dismissed, the boy went back to his work, but I knew he could hear anything we said. "You and your cohort did well against the Marai, Lieutenant."

"The shot was longer than I had previously attempted," I said. "So was the other horseguard's, sir. The bows are the key."

"We learned much in Casil," he answered.

"And since," I replied.

"I would like a demonstration, Lieutenant, when we have dealt with the Marai." His voice gave away nothing.

"Of course, sir," I replied.

"I will look forward to it. You are—valued, Lieutenant." The memory hung between us, his words at the lake. *Wanted, valued, loved.*

"Thank you, sir." I could think of no way to give him the same message. He stepped a little closer.

"The filly is Han bred?"

"She is." The horse's body stood between us and the cadet. He put out a hand, stroked the filly's neck. The brush of his fingers against mine could have been accidental. "I prefer," I added, "not to leave her to others, if time allows. It is a weakness of mine, sir, to want to be with what I care about."

"A strength, I think, not a weakness, Lieutenant," he said. "One that is appreciated by your senior officer." He stepped back. "Good night, Lieutenant. Sleep well."

"Good night, sir." I didn't watch him leave. I finished grooming the horse, smiling to myself.

The track that led north from the Winter Camp ran through the grasslands, sere and dry at the end of summer. This land had been held by the Marai, but we saw no sign of them. Between the advance of a large army, and the harrying ships on the coast, we were driving them north.

I wondered, riding at the flanks of the army, scanning the plain, if Sorley and Ruar had reached the Wall, if they were even now fighting the Marai there. I had sought out Druisius, at a brief halt yesterday.

"You are well?" I had asked.

"Yes. Cillian, he ask me too. Good man. No news, Sorley."

"No," I had said. "Nor is there likely to be." He had nodded, accepting.

Dust rose in clouds around us, settling on our clothes and hair, drying lips and throats. Frequent streams cut the grasslands, so water was not a problem, luckily. I ordered our horses' eyes and nostrils bathed at every halt. At camp each night, we shook dust out of blankets, and felt grit on our teeth when we ate.

On a morning of brilliant sunshine, the track we followed met the road.

Three years ago, I had said farewell to Casyn and Turlo here. The Emperor called a halt. The message spread: replenish food if necessary, and be prepared to move rapidly. We would leave the pack animals here. The Taiva lay a day's march ahead.

††††††

Across the Taiva, campfires burned on the shore and the higher land, mirroring ours. I walked among my cohort, speaking words of reassurance I wasn't sure I believed. The Emperor and his commanders were doing the same, out among the soldiers; I would speak only to my own mounted archers. Grainne, and Rasa with her—I would not separate them, tonight—I had sent to the horselines, hoping the care of the animals would help keep Grainne's mind off tomorrow. The others were calm enough, or hiding their fear well.

The guard I was speaking to suddenly jumped to her feet. I turned, to see the Emperor standing beside us. "Sir," I said.

"Sit," he directed the guard. "Please. You need your rest. Lieutenant, a word?"

I followed the Emperor away from the fire, beyond hearing distance of the soldiers.

"Lieutenant," he said. "Lena. I expect obedience, for what I am going to tell you now."

"Sir?"

"Tomorrow, I have chosen to deploy most of the mounted archers on the field. But you will be in the coombe, with five of your best guardswomen. You, and they, are to remain in reserve, unless you hear a signal: five rapid drumbeats. Otherwise, you do not engage. Understood?"

"Yes, sir," I said. "May I ask why, Emperor?"

"Think of what you did in Tirvan, Lieutenant. The same role here, except the weapon differs."

"Sir." We were to be assassins again, my riders and myself. "And the targets?"

"Any man who still commands. You will know. If the day goes well, you may not be needed."

"Emperor?"

"Lieutenant?"

I had to ask. "Was this your adjutant's idea?"

"No. My brother's. Cillian knows nothing of it. Nor will you tell him, Lieutenant."

"Sir." The moon had not yet risen. I could barely see his face, but I thought he had told me the truth.

"I trust your discretion, Lena," he said, his voice gentler. "There will be deaths tomorrow, too many, but yours need not be among them. I will not order you out of the battle entirely. You may be required. But I will not rob my son of you, if it can be prevented." He paused. "Nor you of him. We are all in peril, tomorrow, myself and Cillian included. I swear to you that if I can keep him safe, I will."

"Thank you, sir." They should not be in real danger, I thought, on their rise of land.

"Get some sleep, Lieutenant." He turned to go.

Prudence warred against generosity in my heart. "Callan," I said, using his name purposely. He stopped, turning back.

"Lena?"

"Can I trust your discretion, if I tell you something Cillian cannot know? For his safety, to keep him focused on the battle, tomorrow, not for any other reason."

"If that is the true reason, yes. What is it you are keeping from him but not from me?"

What impulse had led me to this? I took a breath. "I am carrying our child."

Silence, for a long moment. "You cannot know what joy that brings me," my Emperor said, his voice rough. "But I should order you off the field, under the circumstances."

"And tell Cillian what, as the reason? Emperor, hear me out. This child is his, but it is also mine, and I must respond to what has happened, to my mother and sister and too many women in Tirvan and elsewhere. I need to be able to tell my child what that response was, not that I stood on the sidelines. She may be your heir, Callan, and she will need to understand duty, will she not?"

"She will," he said slowly. "But you will fight only if you must. My earlier orders stand. Your captain will inform your cohort-leader, so it is clear the order comes from above."

"Thank you, Emperor." It had been the right thing, to tell him.

"I will pray for your safety," he answered. "I will send Cillian to you for an hour, in a little while."

He found me sitting with Talyn, by her fire. She looked up as he approached. "Adjutant," she said. "Cousin. Shall I leave you?"

He shook his head. "Thank you, Talyn, but no. We will walk, I think. Lena?"

I stood. "I will see you soon, Talyn." We walked beyond the fires, along the river's edge. Sand shifted under our feet. Above us, a million stars glittered. We reached a place where the river had cut into the sand, a series of stepped banks held in place by coarse grasses.

"Shall we sit?" We settled onto the sand. "Unpin your insignia," he reminded me. He did the same. We were free of rank, our private selves. He wrapped his arms around me.

"Hello, my love," I said.

"*Käresta*," he replied. "Callan gave me an hour."

"It was kind of him."

"Lena, if I say the word 'home', what do you see? Don't tell me, yet."

Home. He was looking forward, beyond tomorrow's horrors. A way to find hope tonight. I closed my eyes, hearing the soft sound of the river, the gusty breeze in the grasses. My mind found Tirvan, and rejected it. Not Casilla, either. Unbidden, the image of a stone hall, nestled in its valley, appeared in my mind.

Was I just reaching for what I thought Cillian wanted? Perhaps, in part. But I remembered Dagney's kindness, and Perras's deep interest. I smiled to myself. A sense of peace, of safety, pervaded the memory.

"Not what I expected," I murmured.

"Hold on to it. But hear me out, before you tell me."

"Of course."

"I have travelled for all my adult life, *käresta*, as you know," he began. "I did not mind—I had no reason to stay in one place—and as this last year brought me you, I count myself fortunate. But sixteen years is quite a while to be always moving, and I am weary of it. I would like to stop travelling, Lena, when this war is over. To find a home. To belong. But it is not just myself I must consider, and perhaps not just you, either."

He doesn't know, I reminded myself. "Sorley."

"Yes. His home is gone, Lena. I would like to tell him he always has one with us, if you agree. He may have other plans, of course, but I want to say this to him."

"He won't have other plans," I said. "And of course I agree. Cillian, I know what he thinks of as the closest place he has to a home, now."

"Which is?"

"The one place we all share, *kärestan*," I said. "The place we met. Home is the *Ti'ach*, is it not?"

"Is it?" he asked. "You would do that for me?"

"Not just for you. For me, as well, to learn, and for Sorley, too." And for you, little one, I thought, to give you books and music and language, and to prepare you to be heir to the Empire, if that is your fate.

"And Tirvan?"

"Tirvan is gone, and what will be rebuilt will not be the same. There is nothing there for me. But can you go back, Cillian? You are a citizen of this Empire, and potentially regent to its heir."

"I can. In the afternoon we came to the decision about the succession, I raised the question. Neither my father nor Casyn objected, in part because they see merit in sending the potential heirs—Talyn's children, right now—to the *Ti'acha* for a while, to learn Casilan and be educated in their writings and thought. Such a plan would be simpler, if I—we—were there. Ruar too had no objection: he looks for closer ties between our lands, not barriers."

I leaned against him. A conversation with Dagney echoed in my mind. 'There is shame for a woman to bear a child outside of a formal partnership, even if the father acknowledges it,' she had told me. I cared nothing for implied shame for myself, but Cillian could not allow his child to endure what he had. I may have to marry your father, little one. After all, I did offer, once. Tomorrow night, I will tell him of you, and we will decide.

"Linrathe, then," I said. "The *Ti'ach*. But you must teach me Linrathan." His arms tightened around me. I looked up at him. The moon had risen. I could just see his face.

"Will you sleep tonight?" I asked.

"Unlikely."

"If you do—I am with you when you wake, my love. Always. You are not alone. I promised."

"Such a gift," he said softly. He kissed my hair, his lips lingering. "This past year, even when you were simply sleeping on the other side of a campfire, or beside me without touching, even then I felt—secure, I suppose, more so than I remember feeling since I left my grandparents' care. Just knowing you were there, and would be, every morning. I promised to try to make you feel the same way. Sheltered, you told me."

"You have," I said. "You have been my refuge, Cillian, my sanctuary, and you always will be." A gust of wind rattled the grasses. If he replied, I did not hear the words. I raised my head for one last, long kiss, and then he stood, holding out his hand.

"Time does not stop," he said, "for all we wish it might."

Near the fires, I freed my fingers from his. He touched my face. "*Thà mi air a bheth beànnaichte.* I have been blessed, *kâresta,*" he whispered, before he left me.

†††††

We moved into position in the darkness before dawn, leading our horses to the small, hidden coombe over the hilltop. The setting moon, waning just past half, gave little light. I'd given my cohort lessons in moving quietly, but it was difficult to muffle the sound of six horses. Movement in both camps would disguise our travel, I hoped, and in the sea-fog that had come in overnight, the direction of sound would be hard to determine.

On the field bordering the river, I could hear men taking their positions, and on the river itself, more sounds of weapons, and movement, and voices floating over the water. I settled the guards in the bowl of the coombe as the first light began to grow in the east. The fog was low, and would disperse with the sun. "Five rapid drumbeats," I reminded them. "We do not move until then. Expect it late in the battle." I did not plan to wait blind, though. Crossing the hillside to reach the coombe, I had noted a place where I thought I could be hidden, but still watch the field. I would be safe, not violating the Emperor's orders.

I'd analysed my archers constantly during the march, thinking about who should serve on the field, and who with me. Over the days, I made my choices: Junia, Glynn from Torrey, two others. I had wanted Rasa, and Dian, but I knew their skills would be needed in the battle. I'd discussed all this with Talyn, before I decided. She had concurred, especially about Junia. "She's the best of us," she'd said.

"Glynn," I said quietly. "I will watch, from further up the hill. You oversee here. Understood?" To the group, I said, "try to relax. Eat a little. Stay quiet." Heads nodded. I left my gelding with them, and made my way back up to the rocky outcrop I had noted. I settled between the boulders. In the rising sun, I could see the field, and below me, to the right, the high sweep of land from which the Emperor would direct the battle: the Emperor, his runners and signallers, and Cillian, there to translate, analyze, advise. *I require you by my side*, his father had written. *You know more of the Marai than any other man I can trust.*

Tendrils of fog lay between the river and the land, and along the shore of the sea. Between its patches, I could see Marai ships at the mouth of the river, and upstream, to an island in its middle. I counted twenty ships. Eight hundred men, then, unless they had hidden troops on land, or more ships out on the sea, beyond the headland. We had more, I believed; twelve hundred men and women on the field below us, and more on the Casilani ships that lay waiting, out of sight. The advantage was with us, then. My mind ranged back to the early days of our exile, the evening spent in *xache* and the analysis of old battles. Numbers always mattered, Cillian had told me, if the troops could be trusted.

I scanned the field. Flat land, on the south bank, for a hundred paces, perhaps more, and then rising slowly. Closer to the mouth, the meadowland changed to saltmarsh, channelled and muddy, treacherous underfoot. On the north bank, the land rose more rapidly, only a narrow strip of mud between the river's channel and the scarp at low tide. I could see why the Emperor had chosen this place for the battle: the landscape favoured us.

I watched our troops move into position; ranked swordsmen and archers arranging themselves on the meadow, my mounted cohort behind them. So many. They looked formidable, to me. I found Turlo, red beard bright under his helmet in the rising sun, across from the island, commanding the right half of the army from a bay horse; Casyn, on a chestnut, had the left, closer to the river mouth and the marsh. Both men held their troops back from the river, a strip of land perhaps five paces wide left open.

The day brightened. I let my eyes travel back to the Marai ships. Men stood on their decks, shields and swords or axes in hand. They stood easily, not revealing fear, confident. The tide ebbed rapidly; already I could see banks of sand and mud near the river's mouth, divided by deep channels of water. The Marai had no escape, I realized, until the tide rose again. Desperate men fight harder, I remembered Cillian telling me, a year ago or more, citing an ancient battle at a narrow pass. Geiri had said Fritjof used fear and punishment to make his men obey. Did that mean they were apprehensive about this fight? If so, they were not showing it.

On the island, many Marai waited, weapons ready. 'Fritjof will use that island for his first attack, across the causeway,' Callan had said. Leik commanded on the field. He must be among those men. I searched, not able to pick him out from among the mass of pale-haired Marai. One horse, tacked but blanketed, stood restlessly, its head swinging. It must be Leik's, I thought. One ship, the dragonhead on the prow brightly painted, its sail moving in the light breeze, lay beside the island. Fritjof's.

I glanced down, to the high ground below me. Only the signallers and runners, and the Casilani physician, Gnaius, stood there now. My eyes returned to the field, searching for Cillian, and the Emperor. From the rear of the lines, the standard-bearer, the flag of the Empire blowing behind him, rode forward. Beside him, on an almost-white horse, Callan galloped to the front of the army. The Emperor wore his grey robes, his silver pendant catching the sun, reflecting daggers of light. His head was bare. He reined his horse to a stop directly across from Fritjof's ship. Just behind him, wearing the unrelieved black of the Emperor's Advisor, rode Cillian. I tried to continue my analysis of the field, but fear had begun to insinuate itself behind my self-control.

"Fritjof, king of the Marai," the Emperor called. "You are outnumbered. Will you cede, and give me your word you will return north to your own lands?" Cillian repeated the words in *Marái'sta*, his voice, pitched to carry, reaching the men on the island and the ships. A clatter of weapons against shields answered him.

Fritjof climbed onto the side of his ship, raising his hand for quiet. He held a spear. He shouted something; his men rattled weapons against shields, longer this time. Fritjof waited. I thought the man beside him was Niáll, who had kidnapped Dagney and me for Fritjof, last spring. He would be Fritjof's translator. When the Marai quietened, Niáll shouted, "King Fritjof says give him gold, and he might. Gold and armour and weapons now, and the same, every year."

"All you will have from me is spear tips and sword blades," Callan replied. "You can see our strength. The tide ebbs. Your ships can leave here now, or not at all. Choose, Fritjof."

Cillian translated. Fritjof laughed. He raised the spear and threw it. From the island, men began to pour across the river. The causeway, I remembered, seeing the water coming barely to the ankles of the running men. Callan wheeled his horse around, galloping along the bank, Cillian and the standard-bearer just behind him, the flag streaming, passing where the causeway met the land, making for the command location on the hillside below me. Clods flew from the horses' hooves. Men converged at the end of the causeway, shields raised, forming a wall, blocking the Marai warriors. Metal clashed against metal. Shouts and cries rent the air. Marai men began to fall, the tidal waters ebbing past their bodies. I forced myself to watch, to analyze, to keep my eyes from Cillian on the hill below me.

What was Fritjof doing? These men had no chance of breaking through our shield wall. This was a distraction, I realized. My eyes scanned the ships. Men leapt overside, into what was now shallow water. I glanced down: Callan spoke rapidly to his signallers, commanding, his eyes on the field. Trumpet blasts and drums relayed directions. Cillian stood beside his father, watching Casyn's troops, I thought, and the more distant Marai ships. He had always taken the long view, on our travels.

A volley of arrows from behind our swordsmen, and Marai fell into the water, blocking and tripping their compatriots, screaming in pain. I couldn't make sense of the massed movements, couldn't see the patterns. The mounted cohort, Talyn at its head, raced along the bank, arrows aimed at the ships and the men still pouring overside. More men fell, but some gained the bank.

Swords rang. My cohort reached the causeway, shot again, circled and rode back towards the saltmarsh. I looked north: no movement on the high ground above the river. No hidden Marai troops joining the battle, yet. At the causeway, the water had dropped. The Marai abandoned the flagstones, spreading out along the bank. The shield wall held, but men battled men, axes and swords swinging. I saw Finn, wielding a sword with lethal accuracy, and Casyn, riding along the bank, his swordblade a blur.

Closer to the mouth of the river, the fighting was fiercer, Marai reaching the land in numbers. Our men were falling now. I saw blood, and bone, and heard screams of pain. I thought I could smell blood, knew it to be a fancy. My stomach heaved. I tried to look away, but I couldn't. Sunlight bounced off sword blades and shield bosses. *Sunshine for warfare.* But the sun was easterly, and the Marai to our northwest. The flashes of reflected light worked in their favour, not ours.

Rapid movement at the causeway: a white horse galloping from the island, its rider dressed in grey. As Callan was. The rider pushed the horse up the bank, through the massed men, shouting 'Retreat' in our language. What? Who? My breath caught. Men, hearing the shouted command, hesitated, swords checked just for a moment. Trumpets rang out from the hill below me, and drumbeats. The white horse galloped among our army, its rider still shouting his command to retreat. Its green saddle cloth bore the symbols of the Empire. Men turned, both back to the river and away from it, confounding each other, creating chaos. Casyn and Turlo screamed commands to the confused men, over the repeated drumbeats. Fear and frustration gnawed at me. I narrowed my eyes, watching the white horse and its rider. Leik?

The Marai began to push our men back. The white horse swung around. The rider shouted in *Marái'sta,* rallying his men. An arrow flew by his head; swords swung at the horse. He galloped on, unharmed. More Marai leapt and ran from the ships closer to the south bank, men held in reserve until now. The response came quickly, the mounted cohort galloping along the bank, shooting rapidly at the advancing men. From further back, arrows arched from the bowmen. Blood soaked into the sand of the riverbed—and then at a shouted command from Leik, Marai axemen turned, to throw their weapons at the horses' legs. As Geiri's men had, at the steppe riders. I should have remembered that. I heard the animals' screams, and that of women, as they began to fall. I saw Grainne go down. Grief and anger coursed through me, and a desire to be out there, with my bow and my knife, killing.

Sickened, I watched; my eyes drawn from the carnage to the Emperor, and back out to the field. The Emperor and Cillian spoke rapidly, hands moving, new signals ringing out. Even from a distance above them, I could see the tension in Cillian's shoulders, the severe set of his jaw, a hand running through his hair, revealing his uncertainty. The Emperor looked equally grim. Neither had foreseen this strategy.

Suddenly a troop in the left flank turned, moving away from the river. What now? A second troop began to follow them. From below, rapid drums, and the troops slowed, some stopping. I heard a more distant drum roll.

Comprehension dawned: the Marai knew our signals. We had been betrayed. Fritjof was using our own codes to confuse our troops. Trumpets rang from the hill; drums beat harder, louder. I watched the Emperor shouting instructions, sending runners, signalling for his horse. The Marai pushed forward, taking advantage of broken formations, gaps in the defense. Fritjof, on his ship's thwart, laughed.

I saw Cillian look out at the field. I followed his gaze, to Leik, on the white horse.

I turned to run down the hill. I threw myself up onto my horse. "The man on the white horse," I snapped. "*Ecus alban.*" We galloped out from the coombe, along the sands. I heard a shout from the river: we had been seen. I nocked an arrow at the gallop. I heard Junia call behind me. She urged her horse past mine, leaning left, standing in the stirrups. No, I thought, too soon, Junia. Wait. I screamed the last word. I couldn't remember the Casilan translation. Junia, ignoring me, drew, held the shot, still galloping. She released. Leik had just shouted something, standing high in the saddle, pointing towards the hillside. Junia's arrow flew, unerringly, the strength of the triple-layered bow behind it. Too far, I thought, too far. Leik turned to urge his horse forward. The arrow hit him squarely in the chest. He fell, grasping air, tumbling backwards off the horse.

Controlling my horse with my knees, I turned to the river. I had an arrow ready. I kept the horse galloping. A sword blade swept by me, but I felt nothing. The horse did not falter. Behind me, among the troops, I heard a commotion, but I had my target. Fritjof stood on the side of his ship. He had been laughing, calling encouragement and derision, until Leik fell. He threw his head back, laughter changing to howled anger, and grief. Vengeance lay cold inside me, focusing me, slowing time. I aimed. I could do this. Huntress, guide my hand, I prayed, and let my arrow fly.

I pulled the horse up. The arrow flew across the water, across the mud, too slowly, I thought. Fritjof still shouted his rage to the sky, one fist upraised. I watched the arc of the arrow. It began to descend. I pulled another from the quiver, nocked it, aimed, waiting for the sword blow from behind, or the fall of my horse to an axe. I am so sorry, little one... I raised the bow, released.

The first arrow sliced through Fritjof's throat. His raised hand dropped, clenched at his neck. Blood spurted. He gurgled, spewing blood, toppling into the shallow water below his ship.

Joy bubbled, for vengeance gained. I heard shouting. Screams of rage and defiance from ahead of me; from behind me, what sounded like grief, or despair. Different voices. Casyn's voice, thundering above the sounds of battle: "Turlo! To the Emperor!" Joy curdled into fear. I turned in the saddle. Turlo galloped towards the high ground, to where the Emperor and Cillian stood. Or should stand. I couldn't see them. My eyes searched the hillside. Where? Where are you, Cillian? I scanned the field, cold dread rising. Had they left the hillside? I hunted for Callan's white horse, and the black gelding. My eyes went back to the hill, and this time I could see.

I turned my horse, urging it forward, pushing through the soldiers, shoving our men and Marai alike aside. Hands grasped at me; I slashed at them with reins and fists. I couldn't see. I kicked the horse again. A shout, from somewhere: my name. The hill stood before me, men bending over bodies. My horse slid to a stop. "No!" I cried, kicking it. It sidled sideways, snorting. Someone held its head. I fell off the saddle, starting to run.

Arms grabbed me. I twisted, reaching for my secca. The hold tightened. "No, lassie," Turlo said. "Stay here. Stay here." I sobbed. I fought him, but he was too strong. I sagged. Tears blinded me. "I can't see." Turlo freed one hand. I wiped my eyes, but the tears didn't stop. Bodies lay scattered on the hilltop. Why couldn't I find Cillian?

"Kebhan," Turlo growled. "Traitor. Him and some of the Leste men, among the archers. They're dead, lassie."

Who did he mean? Where was Cillian? Gnaius knelt beside a body, grey cloaked. Arrows across his back, deeply embedded. I wiped my eyes again. Gnaius's hands probed. He looked up, shook his head. "Callan," Turlo whispered, "Oh, Callan. No." He sobbed, a deep, rough sound.

Men bent to lift the Emperor, and now I could see the body beneath. Arrows pierced his left side and thigh, over the scar left by the last attempt to kill him. My vision darkened, red and white sparks blurring together. *If I can keep him safe, I will.* Callan's words. Anger surged through me. But you didn't, I thought. You didn't. Blood pounded in my ears. Gnaius had knelt again. His hands moved on Cillian's body. I tried to see what he did. The darkness grew. There was a chasm behind it, a void.

"He didn't know," I cried. "He didn't know."

"Lassie, he did. He knew you loved him. How could he not?" Turlo said, through his tears.

Gnaius raised his head. The world shifted, spun. The red roaring dark split open, and I fell.

EPILOGUE

THE LAST STUDENT DRAWS HER BOW and lets the arrow fly, hitting the edge of the target. "Enough, for today," I tell my three pupils. I supervise the unstringing, and the gathering of arrows, and send them back to the *Ti'ach* for drinks. From the far end of the field, I can hear the clang of swords. I turn to watch Sorley and Druisius, with their students, practicing one-on-one. The boy is good, graceful, giving Sorley a challenge; the girl, only a beginner.

We have peace, for now. The Marai have withdrawn north. The Wall is deserted, except for the fort at the sea; the gates stand open, allowing the free movement that was Donnalch's dream. The soldiers—from the Empire and from Linrathe—are at the Sterre. Sorham belongs to the Marai, still.

I take the targets off the butts, and then I too walk back to the hall, although my day is far from done. I am tired; I sat up late last night writing my conclusions for the task Dagney set me, an analysis of certain *danta,* so late that I overslept this morning, a thing I hate to do. But we are all busy, here at the *Ti'ach,* and everywhere, in Linrathe and the Empire. We are rebuilding our lands, our villages and torps, and at the *Ti'acha,* new students have arrived. Kira keeps me informed about Tirvan, and their lives there by letter, but my life is here, at this long stone hall nestled in its sheltered valley.

Casyn visited just last week. He comes to see Ruar, for where else would the boy be but here, at the *Ti'ach* his father loved, under the tutelage and guidance of the *Comiádh* and Dagney? Much of their talk is of the Marai. Casyn believes this peace will not last; that sooner or later, the enemy will return. The tribute we pay to keep them north of the Sterre will, someday, not be enough. The threat seems distant, illusory. Our lives here are concerned with teaching and learning, music and story. Nonetheless, we teach the weapons of war now, too.

The battle which won us this dearly-bought peace was nearly four years ago. My daughter is three, born six months after I put an arrow into Fritjof's neck. She is strong and curious and brave, with her father's dark eyes and his slow, radiant smile, and had I not known I was carrying her, there was a time I might have wished for death. I named her Gwenna, for both her lost grandmothers. She is with Isa, in the kitchen, being kept busy while I teach.

As I enter the hall I hear the door to the *Comiádh's* study close: Ruar, finished his lesson in Casilan. He, or perhaps we, will visit Casil, one day. I smile at him, going to the kitchen to collect Gwenna. Dagney is still teaching: the notes of a *ladhar,* inexpertly played, drift out from her rooms. Isa gives me tea for the *Comiádh*; his leg was paining him earlier, she tells me, and I should save him the trouble of coming for it.

It is time for Gwenna's lesson: she is learning her letters. We walk through the darkening hall, tap on the door, open it. Gwenna runs ahead, climbing up eagerly onto a stool by the table. The *Comiádh* turns from the fire. He is thinner:

the toll of his long illness, thankfully past. "Here you are, little one," he says. She giggles.

His eyes find mine. We have not yet met today, because I overslept, because we are occupied with students, with motherhood, with life. And so there are words that must be said, a private ritual begun to birdsong in the breaking light of dawn, by a lake on an endless plain.

"Hello, my love," I say.

THE CHARACTERS OF *EMPIRE'S EXILE*

Characters who are a direct part of the story are in **bold**. Characters who are mentioned by name but not directly a part of the story are in plain type.

Aethyl – a girl of the Kurzemë, Fel and Kaisa's daughter
Aivar – the *vēsturni* of the Kurzemë
Alain – a man of Linrathe
Arey – a woman of Berge, Turlo's lover, Darel's mother
Åsmund – a prince of Varsland, brother to Fritjof, deceased
Atulf – a diplomat of the Boranoi
Audo – a man of the Kurzemë
Benis – a man of the Kurzemë
Birel – Casyn's soldier-servant
Callan – the Emperor of the West
Casyn – a General of the Empire, Callan's brother
Cillian – a man of Linrathe, Callan's son
Colm - Callan's twin and advisor, deceased
Dagney – a woman of Sorham, the Lady of the *Ti'ach na Perras*, *scáeli* and teacher
Darel – a Cadet of the Empire, Turlo's son, deceased
Dern – an officer of the Empire, Captain of *Skua*
Detlef – an oarsman of Varsland, loyal to Irmgard
Dian – a Guardswoman of the Empire
Donnalch – a *Teannasach* of Linrathe, deceased
Druisius – a palace guard of Casil
Eryl – a man of the Kurzemë, hunt leader
Eudekia – the Empress of Casil and the East
Fél (Oran) – a soldier of the Empire, exiled, now a man of the Kurzemë, Kaisa's husband
Finn – a Captain of the Empire
Fritjof – *Härskaran* of the Marai of Varsland
Galen – Lena's father, a border scout
Galdor – an officer of the Empire
Garth – a Watch-Commander of the Empire, Maya's brother
Geiri – a steersman of Varsland, loyal to Irmgard
Gille – a woman of Tirvan, briefly Casyn's lover
Glynn – a Guardswoman of the Empire
Gnaius – a physician of Casil
Grainne – a Guardswoman of the Empire
Grêt – the headwoman of the Kurzemë
Gulian – an officer of the Empire
Gwen – a midwife and healer of Tirvan, Lena's mother
Hafwen (Wenna) – a girl of Linrathe, Cillian's mother, deceased
Hana – a woman of Varsland, waiting woman to Irmgard

Herlief – *Härskaran* of Varsland, deceased; father to Åsmund and Fritjof
Ianthe – a woman of Karst, Tice's sister
Irmgard – a princess of Varsland, Åsmund's wife
Isa – a woman of Linrathe, housekeeper at the *Ti'ach na Perras*
Ivor – a man of the Kurzemë, son to Lumis and Grêt
Jedd – a retired General of the Empire
Jordis – a girl of Linrathe, student at the *Ti'ach na Perras*
Josan – an officer of the Empire
Junia – a woman of Casil, Captain of the horse archers
Kaisa – a woman of the Kurzemë, Fél's wife
Karel – a man of the Kurzemë
Kebhan – a boy of Linrathe, son to Lorcann
Kira – a woman of Tirvan, Lena's sister
Lara – a girl of Tirvan
Leik – a man of Varsland, Fritjof's son
Lorcann – the *Teannasach* of Linrathe
Lumis – the headman of the Kurzeme
Maya – a woman of Casilla, once Lena's partner
Mihel – the headman of Sylana
Niáll – a man of Linrathe, in Fritjof's service
Niav – a girl of Linrathe, Isa's niece
Pel – a boy of Tirvan, Lena's cousin
Perras – a man of Linrathe, the *Comiádh* of the *Ti'ach na Perras*
Prisca – a woman of Casil, housekeeper
Quintus – a man of Casil, advisor to Eudekia
Rasa – a Guardswoman of the Empire
Ravn – an oarsman of Varsland, loyal to Irmgard
Rind – a woman of Varsland, waiting-woman to Irmgard
Ruar – a boy of Linrathe, Donnalch's son
Rufin – a Captain of the Guard in Casil
Sara – woman of Tirvan, Lena's aunt
Sergius – a man of Casil, steward
Sorley – a nobleman of Sorham, loyal to Linrathe
Tali – a woman of Tirvan, Pel and Maya and Garth's mother
Talyn – a woman of the Empire, Casyn's daughter
Tice – a woman of Tirvan, Valle's mother, deceased
Turlo – a General of the Empire
Ulv – an oarsman of Varsland, loyal to Irmgard
Valle – a boy of the Empire, Tice and Garth's son
Vesna – a woman of the Kurzemë

THE VOCABULARY OF *EMPIRE'S EXILE*

The languages spoken in the *Empire's Legacy* trilogy are my inventions, but they are based on existing or historic languages. Pronunciations and grammar may not follow the conventions of those languages. Roughly, Casilan is based on Latin; Kurzemën is derived from a mix of Baltic languages, Linrathan primarily from Gaelic, both Scottish and Irish, and Marái'sta from Scandinavian languages.

Each word is followed by its pronunciation and then its meaning.

Ádla – *ehd-la* – princess
alban – *all-bann* – white
alfban – *alf-bann* – ivory (walrus)
amané – *ah-man-eh* – lover(male)
an dithës braithréan – *ann dith-ess bray-trey-an* – the two brothers
anash – *ah-nash* – herb used against fever and conception
ar fosidh di, mo chaol iômhlán – *ar vo-sith dee, mo kol ee-oh-vlan* – to shelter her all my days
Arénas Ingenírus – *a-ren-ass in-gen-i-rus* – the arena of games
bêne – *ben-eh* – good
benedis – *ben-ed-is* – contraceptive herb (anash)
Breccaith – *breck-ath* – lament
Casil e imitaran ne – *Cas-ill eh imi-tar-an nay* – Casil is not equalled here
cithar – *kith-ar* – stringed instrument, zither
Comiádh – *ko-mi-ath* – professor
crasti – *krast-ee* – (see you) tomorrow
danta – *dan-tha* – saga
de'mhin – *di-vin* – certainly
devanī – *di-van-eh* – acolyte of the goddess of the hunt
do thóille – *doe tho-ill* – please (literally, with prayer)
ecus – *eck-uss* – horse
Eirën – *ay-er-en* –landholder, lord (male)
faich – *vach* – see
forla – *vor-lah* – sorry
fuádain – *vwa-dai-een* – peregrine falcon
fuisce – *vwi-schah* – whiskey
gemzē – *gem-zee (hard g)* – chamois (antelope)
gratiás – *gra-tee-ass* – thank you
gratifi – *grat-if-ee* –please
habea – *hab-ee-a* – I have
hálainn – *ha-lay-inn* – beautiful
Harr/Härren – harr/hurren – landholder(s), lord(s)
imirdh xache liovha – *im-irth zachee leefa* – play xache with me

itá – *ee-tah* – yes
ja – *ya* – yes
jerv – *jerff* – wolverine
käresta/kärestan – *ka-resta/kares-tan* – beloved
Kurzemën – *kur-zem-un* – of the Kurzemë
ladhar – *lath-arr* – lute
laerth – *lay-erth* – scholar
leannan/mo leannan – *lee-ann-an* – dearest/my dearest
lūši – *loo-shee* – lynx
lümike – *loom-ick-eh* – snowshoes
manto – *man-to* – wait
Marái'sta – *mar-uh-ee-stah* – of the Marai (referring to language)
meas – *may-as* – thank you
mi – *me* – I
mo bhráithar – *mo vra-ith-arr* – my brother
mo charaidh – *mo kar-aith* – my friend
mo charaidh gràhadh – *mo kar-aith gra-hath* – my beloved friend
mo charaidheán – *mo kar-ad-ee-an* – my friends
mo stoír – *mo sto-er* – my dear
ná mi tréigtha – nah me traig-the – do not abandon me
non – *non* – not (a)
pavo – *pah-vo* – quintain
Prægrandeum – *pre-grand-ee-um* – stadium
Prægrandus Sûl - *pre-grand-us sol* – Giant of the sun
quincala/quincalum – *kin-call-ah/kin-call-um* – freely-chosen partner
râv – *ravv* - amber
sagiteri – *sadg-eh-ter-ee* – archer
scáeli – *schaa-lee* – bard
scrapta – *scrap-tah* – prostitute
secca – *sekk-ah* – throwing knife
sede – *seh-day* – sit
séquer – *say-ker* – follow
siollë liovha – *sholleh leefa* – walk with me
taberna – *ta-bayr-na* – tavern
takkë – *tack-uh* – thank you
Teannasach – *tee-na-shah* – chieftain
thá – *thah* – yes (literally, 'is')
thà – *ta* – am
thà mi gràh agäthe – *ta me grah ag-ut-eh* – I love you
thà mi air a bheth beànnaichte – *ta mi ar a vet be-an-nach-tay* – I have been blessed
thà mi beànnaicht – *ta mi be-an-nacht* – I am blessed
ti'ach(a) – **tee-ach(ah)** – college(s)
ti'achan – *tee-ach-an* – member of a college
torp – *torp* – land held by an Eirën or Harr

torpari – *tor-par-ee* – farmworkers, peasants
toscaire/toscairen – *tos-care/tos-car-en* – envoy/envoys
vérum – *vay-rum* – correct
vēsturni – *ves-tur-nee* – historian
Westani – *wes-tan-ee* – people of the West
xache – *za-chee* – game similar to chess

AUTHOR'S NOTE

Thanks are due to far more people than I can include. To my parents, both now deceased: my father, Harry Thorpe, for inculcating both a love of history and a love of fantasy—he introduced me to *The Lord of the Rings* when I was perhaps eleven, and my mother, Enid Thorpe, for telling the town librarian in no uncertain terms that I was to be allowed to read anything I wanted, not only children's books, also when I was eleven. To my late brother, Christopher Thorpe, for introducing me to the works of Guy Gavriel Kay, my greatest influence, and my sister, Katie Thorpe, for reading early drafts and making always-useful suggestions.

To Jeremy Luke Hill and the Vocamus Writers' Community in Guelph, thank you for being the support and cheerleading writers need. To my fellow members of the Arboretum Press Collective, for reading, suggesting, editing, reviewing and listening—this wouldn't have happened without you. To the Minett family, who own The Bookshelf, Guelph's superb independent bookstore, thank you for the space to write on Monday mornings, for hosting book launches, for carrying my book—you've made more than one dream of mine come true through your welcoming of local authors and independent presses.

My beta and sensitivity readers, too many to name, have provided valuable input and insight, and corrected some mistakes before the books went to press, so very appreciated.

Finally, and always, there is Brian. Critique partner, plot analyser, endless listener, the bear's greatest advocate...*Meas, kärestan.*

Guelph, November 2019

Made in the USA
Las Vegas, NV
11 August 2021

27993224R00423